Avatars of the Pantheon
Book 2
Four Girls Find Their Way

Jackson Owens

Dedication

I would like to thank my loving wife Christina for putting up with me during the process of writing this book, and for being a supportive beta reader. My friend Will for being my second beta reader and providing quality feedback on the story and the book. I would like to thank the avatars who would not let me take the easy route on their stories and refused to leave me alone until I had their voice down pact. To the chaos that sparks big creation, the force of change that molded impromptu scenes into the larger narrative like they were always part of the plan, the war of good ideas that lead to turbulent battles until the best ideas stand tall the only survivors and the unity that keeps everything weaved together. And finally, I want to thank you the reader, I hope you have the same thrill reading this story that I had writing it.

Contents

Chapter 1

Journal Entry: April 19th, 1910

We are now on the second day of our three-day passage to Laminae, where we are to deliver the intelligence left by Brother Albert to Apex Tabitha Sanderlin via Brother Theodore. In response to my request, The Order has provided Stormfang with one of their newer mana-leeching boats—a sleek and versatile craft from the boathouse. As compensation for the first leg of the journey, The Order has agreed to resupply the ship with provisions and operational essentials.

The avatars have, curiously enough, acclimated themselves to the crew almost seamlessly, perhaps an aftereffect of their prior voyage to Order Island. Miss Griffin has elected to work among the deckhands, her presence marked by a tireless energy that seems to invigorate the sailors. Miss Nozaki, on the other hand, has taken command of the galley with such efficiency and authority that she might as well have been hired by the captain. Miss Fournier has become an apprentice of sorts to "Sparks," the engineer responsible for maintaining and enhancing the Stormfang's complex systems. Meanwhile, Miss Salazar, already a longstanding member of the crew, has resumed her duties as operations officer, with her brand of controlled chaos that speaks to both her loyalty to the vessel and her expertise in command.

As for myself, I have been assigned a state room, marked by an odd little drawing of an island on the door. During waking hours, I will rotate between the avatars as a note-taker, assisting them with their tasks and interactions. This arrangement has already led to some friction.

A matter of greater concern is our impending meeting with Apex Sanderlin's representative. Due to our precarious position regarding the Aurorium Clan and the circumstances surrounding Miss Griffin, the Apex herself has chosen not to appear in person. She has, however, issued a specific directive: under no circumstances is Miss Griffin to be seen during the meeting. The reasons for this caution are unspoken, though I suspect they are tied to the delicate politics within the Aurorium and the investigative skill of the Aurorium clan's membership.

[-----⊞-----]

Sophie stood in the Stormfang's exercise room, curling a weighted bar attached to the floor by taut cables. The machine was set to a middle difficulty level, not too easy, not too hard. Working the deck was strenuous enough, and she didn't want to overexert herself. This was her third of five sets, part of a routine designed by Eclipse

Baker. With her back to the door and her gaze fixed out the circular porthole at the endless ocean, she let herself sink into the rhythm of the exercise.

The door creaked open behind her. Footsteps entered the room, but Sophie didn't turn. She focused on finishing her last few reps. Somehow, she knew it was one of the other avatars. How, she wasn't quite sure.

The voice confirmed it: "That looks like a good workout."

Sophie returned the bar to its resting hooks and turned to face Regina, the shorter girl with silver hair and an earnest smile.

"Thanks," Sophie replied, catching her breath. "I'm working the deck today, so I'm keeping it light."

"Can you show me how to be strong like you?" Regina asked, stepping closer.

Sophie blinked. "What?"

"You're really strong," Regina clarified. "I bet you could've beaten that murder woman, Hema, easily. I think... if I'm going to get my family back, I'll need to be strong like you."

Sophie's expression softened. "Oh, I see... So, you want me to help you train?"

"Yeah," Regina nodded enthusiastically. "And fight too."

"You want me to teach you how to fight?" Sophie asked, raising an eyebrow.

"Yeah!" Regina repeated, her determination palpable. "I'm a fast learner. I'll work hard, I promise."

Sophie paused, unsure how to respond. "Why don't you ask Annabelle to teach you?" she finally suggested, because she noticed how close Annabelle and Regina were.

Regina hesitated, searching for the right words. "Well... To be honest, I think you're a better fighter than she is. I mean, I'm sure she can fight... just maybe not as well as you."

For a moment, Sophie was silent—then she burst into laughter, covering her face with one hand. Regina shifted awkwardly, feeling self-conscious. Embarrassed, she took a step back. "Never mind," she mumbled, looking at the deck and her shoes, wondering: *What am I going to do if I don't train with Sophie?*

"No, no!" Sophie said between laughs, stifling them to a grin. "I'll help you train...I just have one request."

Regina's smile returned. "What is it?" she asks while wondering what special Aurorium thing Sophie would ask her to do.

Sophie glanced left and right as if conspiring, then leaned in with a mischievous smirk. "Work it into a conversation sometime that you think I could beat Annabelle in a fight. You'd be doing me a huge favor."

Regina beamed. "Okay … I'll try!"

Sophie gave her a grin Regina had never seen before, full of playful confidence. "But you have to say it while I'm around," Sophie added with a wink. Then she shifted back to business. "Alright, let's start with strength training. Step up to the bar and lift it as many times as you can. Let's see what you've got."

Regina steps up to the bar, gripping it firmly. With a deep breath, she pulls it to her hips, the cables stretching taut. After a moment of hesitation, she curls the bar, muscles straining as she fights to lift it to her chest. Her face contorts with effort, but she finally manages to bring it all the way up. Quickly, she lowers the bar back to her hips and turns to Sophie with a wide grin.

"That's good, right?" she asks, hopeful.

Sophie blinks in disbelief. *Did Regina really only manage **one curl**?* Still, not wanting to discourage her, she nods and says, "That's a good start. Here, let me get a set in, and we'll adjust the difficulty a bit."

Taking the bar from Regina, Sophie positions herself and begins her set with effortless control. The bar rises and falls into a steady rhythm, each motion smooth and deliberate. Regina watches with intense focus, eyes set on Sophie's movements. Sophie's violet hair catches the sunlight filtering through the porthole, and Regina marvels at how easy she makes it look, like opening the pages of a book.

Sophie's so strong... I'll work until I can do it like that, Regina resolves silently.

After twelve reps, Sophie lowers the bar to the floor, then crouches to turn the dial twice, reducing the resistance. She steps back and waves Regina forward. "Alright, your turn. Let's see how many you can do now."

Regina nods, determined. She grips the bar, pulls it to hip level, and exhales slowly. Summoning all her strength, she curls the bar again. This time, it's much easier. She mimics Sophie's technique, lowering the bar slowly and lifting it quickly and steadily. As she pushes through the set, each rep becomes more difficult than the last. By the time she hits seven, her arms start to tremble.

Sophie watches closely, silently encouraging her. "Come on... you've got this," she mutters under her breath as Regina struggles through reps eight and nine.

With a deep breath and a fierce grit of her teeth, Regina forces out a tenth curl before letting the bar drop with a loud clang. Panting, she turns to Sophie and asks, "How was that?"

"Good," Sophie replies, smiling at the girl's determination. "Really good work." She nods approvingly and adjusts the machine back to her preferred difficulty.

As Sophie begins her final set, she catches Regina's gaze locked on her. She realizes Regina is studying her every move. *Is she... admiring me?* Sophie wonders with a grin. She puts on a bit of a show, curling the bar with perfect form, pausing for a second at the top of each lift before lowering it in a controlled descent.

Regina's silver eyes remain fixed on her, absorbing every detail, posture, technique, breathing. She mentally records it all, preparing for her next set. Sophie feels a surge of pride as Regina's admiration fuels her performance. Finishing her tenth rep, she lowers the bar to the ground with a flourish and announces, "Your turn."

"Okay!" Regina exclaims, her enthusiasm renewed. She grabs the bar and starts her set. The first five reps feel easy, allowing her to focus on mimicking Sophie's technique. But as she reaches the sixth, a burning sensation creeps into her arms. With each subsequent curl, the fire spreads, making the movement increasingly difficult. Still, she pushes through, clenching her jaw as she completes her tenth rep.

Dropping the bar just as Sophie had done, Regina wipes sweat from her brow and grins. "How was that?"

"Great!" Sophie says with genuine praise. "Your form is almost perfect." She gives Regina a hearty slap on the back.

"Thanks," Regina replies, trying not to wince. Sophie probably hadn't meant to hit so hard. She rubs the spot for a moment but quickly shakes it off. "Your turn," she offers.

"Nope, I'm good," Sophie says with a chuckle. "But you should do one more set in a minute to finish off your arms. I'm heading over to the pull ropes." She gestures to a set of ropes nearby, threaded through channels in the wall and ending in cloth-wrapped metal rings designed for pulling exercises.

As Sophie adjusts the setup, Regina remembers something from their last voyage. "Hey, Sophie," she starts, "I have a question about your bullets."

Sophie glances back, puzzled. "My bullets? What about them?"

"The symbols carved on your bullets... they look like rune magic," Regina says, curiosity lighting her silver eyes. "Can you teach me some of them?"

Sophie pauses, her expression softening. "That's from my dad's magic," she replies quietly. "He only taught me one rune before he died."

Her gaze grows distant, memories pulling her back to those early days. She remembers her father's steady hands guiding hers as he showed her the 'burning bullet' spell, emphasizing every stroke of the fire rune until she could draw it perfectly. It was after her promotion to Sentinel that their training sessions intensified. Almost every day, her father taught her how to shoot, his pistol becoming hers in time. He was patient, proud, and determined to make her a capable Aurorium Sentinel.

But then he was gone.

After his death, her mother took over her training, throwing herself into Sophie's development with fierce determination. She was thrilled that Sophie had inherited their family's magic. Under her mother's guidance, Sophie learned Kiroku-Mbili, a powerful blend of movement and melee techniques. Those training sessions had been grueling but precious. They shared a closeness during those hours that Sophie would cherish forever.

Sophie's mind drifts to her brother, Benjamin. He would get envious when Sophie and their mom trained together after school. He used to sulk in the corner, pouting as he watched the "Griffin girls put in their work." She'd tease him about it, laughing at his exaggerated scowls. But those moments were gone now, just echoes of a life that felt worlds away.

With a sharp breath, Sophie shakes her head, clearing away the memories before they can overwhelm her. She steps to the machine, adjusting the difficulty dial with a steady hand. Grabbing the cloth-wrapped rings, she takes a few steps back and begins rowing, pulling the rings in a controlled motion that works her back and arms. The physical exertion grounds her, pushing aside the painful weight of the past.

"Work now, cry later," she silently repeats one of her mother's refrains to herself, her muscles tightening as she pulls again, finding strength in the rhythm of the exercise.

[----- ⚓ -----]

Annabelle stood on the Stormfang's observation deck located at the aft of the ship, her focus on the churning wake trailing behind the ship. Slowly, she raised a hand, coaxing the water upward. The sea obeyed, forming a spout that rose about ten feet before crashing back into the waves.

She brought her hands together in front of her chest, inhaling deeply through her nose as she gathered more mana. With another sweeping motion, she summoned a second spout. This one stretched taller but remained too thin to hold its shape. Annabelle frowned. *It's gotta be wide enough for a man to stretch his arms out*, she reminded herself, Smitty's rule for her training echoing in her mind. If the spout was too narrow, it didn't count.

"Ten waves and ten spouts every day," she muttered to herself, mimicking Smitty's gruff voice with a smirk.

4

The waves were done. Just two more spouts, and her self-training for the day would be complete. Annabelle centered herself again, hands pressed together as she controlled her breathing. The next spout rose steadily, broader this time, but it barely reached eight feet before faltering. Her mana reserves were running low.

Just one more...

She inhaled through her nose, exhaled through her mouth, and tried again. This time, the spout shot up to an impressive height: six meters; but the column was too thin. It wavered, collapsing under its own weight before fully forming. Frustration boiled over as Annabelle cursed under her breath and stomped her foot on the deck.

Rubbing her face with both hands, she leaned heavily on the railing, her body sagging with exhaustion.

"I think I can help you," came a calm voice from behind.

Annabelle glanced over her shoulder and saw Lisa sitting at the serving table, two bowls securely locked into the table's holders. The green-haired avatar smiled at her, casually sipping from a cup of tea.

Annabelle raised an eyebrow. "What'll it cost me?" she asked, suspicion lacing her voice.

"Nothing," Lisa replied, setting her cup into its holder before rising gracefully from her seat. She walked toward Annabelle, with a warm and genuine smile. "I just want to help."

Annabelle huffed softly, turning her gaze back to the sea. "Nothin's ever free, Princess."

"I am not asking for anything," Lisa said, leaning on the railing beside her. A few strands of her long green hair fell across her face, catching the light like threads of emerald. "We are supposed to be working together, right?"

"I guess," Annabelle muttered. She didn't trust offers of help without strings attached, but she also knew she was hitting a wall. Lisa's experience could give her the edge she needed. "Alright, what am I doing wrong?"

"When I create a water column with my Earthbloom magic, I have to balance both power and form," Lisa explained patiently. "I weave a spell circle to maintain that shape throughout the cast. I think when you use your spell, you're pouring all your energy into power but leaving technique to chance."

Annabelle frowned, still confused. "I don't get it."

"Here, let me show you," Lisa said, standing upright and motioning Annabelle to follow.

Reluctantly, Annabelle straightened, stepping back up to the railing. She eyed Lisa warily, unsure what this *green girlie* had planned. "Okay," she said, holding her hands out in front of her, palms up.

Lisa smiled encouragingly, her voice steady and supportive. "Alright, now watch carefully."

"When I draw a spell circle, I have to channel mana while shaping it correctly," Lisa began, holding her hands out. "If I don't, the circle can fail or, worse, backfire, causing *mana backlash*."

"But me magic don't use spell circles," Annabelle replied, scratching her head under her bandanna. "How's that supposed to help me?"

"Your pirate magic." Lisa continued.

"Maelstrom Mastery." Annabelle corrected firmly.

"Sorry, Maelstrom Mastery," Lisa said with a nod. "It's a direct influence system. That means instead of using a circle to shape the magic, you send your mana straight out to control the sea and create the effect you want."

Annabelle crossed her arms and tilted her head. "Alright, what's yer point, Princess?"

Lisa smiled patiently. "The point is there are two key things any mage has to balance when casting: channeling and shaping. From what I can tell…" she gestured toward the turbulent water where Annabelle's last spout had collapsed, "… you are over-channeling. You're pushing out too much mana without shaping it properly, which is why each spout you make comes out different."

Annabelle frowned. "But I made the spout," she muttered defensively.

"Sure, but look at this," Lisa said. She raised her hand and conjured a large, exaggerated green spell circle without any runes. Its edges shimmered softly as she began to channel mana. "This is a basic spell circle."

"Okay," Annabelle responded, watching with mild curiosity.

"Now, if I channel too much mana without shaping it to match…" Lisa demonstrated by carelessly pushing more energy into the circle. The green glow shifted erratically, flashing through silver, blue, red, and orange as the circle's shape twisted, deforming into a bloated oval. It jerked and swelled, eventually contorting into a chaotic scribble-like star. "See what happens when I don't control the shape?"

Annabelle's eyes widened slightly, a spark of understanding lighting in them. "I think I get it," she said, her gaze fixed on the unstable spell. She marveled at how the shape and colors shifted randomly, almost like a fish flopping out of water. "You're saying I'm pushin' me mana—"

"Channeling," Lisa corrected with a gentle smile.

"Right. I'm channelin' me mana too hard, and I need to…" Annabelle paused, searching her memory for the right words. "…shape it better to get the spell I want."

Lisa dispelled the mangled circle and nodded. "Exactly. Try channeling less mana and focus on shaping—like you did when Smithy taught you."

Annabelle shot her a glance. "Smitty," she repeated with emphasis. "Not Smithy."

"Okay, Smitty."

Annabelle closed her eyes and took a deep breath, centering herself. She visualized the water as a sleeve around her hand, then imagined her other hand smoothing the top of the column like a cloth over a table. Slowly, she pushed out half the mana she usually would. A spout began to rise, stronger and more stable than before. It looked like a pillar of stone as it climbed higher and higher. When it finally reached its peak, the water burst outward in a spray before crashing back into the sea.

"How was that?" Lisa asked, watching intently but unsure how it was supposed to look.

"The spout wasn't tall enough," Annabelle admitted, catching her breath. "I got tired and lost control at the end. This mana shapin' is hard."

Lisa chuckled softly. "I understand. When I was in training, my mistress made me practice mana shaping for hours every day. My fingers would sting so bad every day."

Annabelle flexed her hands, feeling the ache from shaping her spell. She wondered how many more spells she'd need to cast to make her fingers sting like that. "Sounds like yer magic learnin' was real tough," she said, a rare note of sympathy in her voice.

"It was," Lisa agreed, a little surprised by Annabelle's empathy. "Earthbloom magic demands precise control. My mistress was strict she'd smack my knuckles with a ruler if my circles weren't perfect."

Annabelle thought of Smitty and realized, with some amusement, that his training methods *ain't so bad after all*. As the memory of her duty schedule flashed in her mind, she straightened and walked over to the table where two bowls of oatmeal and cups of juice were secured in the holders.

"What's all this, then?" Annabelle asked, eyeing the setup.

"I brought you a bowl of oatmeal," Lisa said as she walked over to the table. "I wanted to eat breakfast here. Jeffie told me you were practicing your magic, so I thought I would bring you some oatmeal and juice."

Annabelle narrowed her eyes suspiciously. "Okay, Princess. What do you want?"

"What?" Lisa blinked, confused. "I do not want anything," she reassured her.

"Come on, Princess," Annabelle pressed, her tone sharp. "Why can't you just tell me what you want?"

"I swear, I do not want anything," Lisa insisted, baffled. "Why is that so hard to believe?"

"Because yer not this nice," Annabelle replied bluntly. "You lot from the Sacred Acres live by them rules of skullduggery, *screw them before they screw you*. Ain't that right?"

Lisa frowned, offended. "What? That is not true. I just wanted to do something nice for you!"

"Sure ye did," Annabelle said, her voice flat. "So, what's the real story? I'm sure the food's good, but I'd like to know what the price is first." She smiled slyly. "I could owe you, if that's what you want."

Lisa sighed and shook her head. "Look, I know we got off on the wrong foot. I was hoping we could sit down, talk, maybe get to know each other better. That's all."

Annabelle pulled out her pocket watch and checked the time, 7:30 a.m. With a shrug, she sat down at the table. "Alright. I can give ye half an hour."

She took a bite of the oatmeal and immediately froze, eyes widening as the flavors hit her. Fruity sweetness blended with warm molasses, all carried by the comforting richness of oats. "Oi, this is so good," she said reflexively.

Lisa smiled, pleased. "I'm glad you like it." She took a bite of her own oatmeal, savoring the peaceful moment.

"So, Princess, what do you want to talk about?" Annabelle asked between bites of what she mentally dubbed *happiness in a bowl*.

"I am not sure." Lisa replied thoughtfully. "Where do you go to school?"

"I don't go to school," Annabelle said with a shrug. "Did all me learnin' at sea." She gestured to herself with her thumb.

Lisa blinked, caught between surprise and curiosity. "Wait... you have never been to school?"

"Nope." Annabelle answered casually, taking another bite.

"But I've seen you do math," Lisa pointed out, puzzled.

"Aye."

"And you understand complex concepts, like societal structures," Lisa continued, trying to piece it together.

"Aye," Annabelle said, her annoyance beginning to build. "Told ye, Princess. Did all me learnin' on the sea."

Lisa bit her lip, sensing the tension. "Okay... so where do you think I go to school?"

Annabelle raised an eyebrow. "No idea, where?"

"I attend the Valorcrest Academy in Laminae," Lisa said proudly.

"Oh so, ye go to school with Regina?" Annabelle asked, genuinely curious.

"She does not attend the academy," Lisa explained with a slight air of superiority. "Only the upper echelon from the Seven Kingdoms goes to Valorcrest. She probably attends a Kingdom School."

"There's the real Princess," Annabelle teased with a smirk.

Lisa frowned. "Why do you keep calling me *Princess* anyway?"

"Because it suits ye so well," Annabelle said with a mischievous grin.

Lisa straightened in her seat, momentarily flattered. "Thank you." But something did not add up. "Wait... then why do you call Regina by her name?"

"'Cause I like her," Annabelle said with a grin, enjoying the moment as she watched Lisa put the pieces together.

Lisa's eyes widened as realization struck. "Wait, **you are making fun of me!**"

"Nooo," Annabelle drawled, dragging out the word. "Why would I do that?"

Lisa crossed her arms, exasperated. "I swear, I am just trying to be nice to you."

Annabelle raised an eyebrow and, in her proper voice, imitated her green-haired fellow avatar: "*I'm better than everyone, and Regina could never go to my special school.*" She switched back to her own voice. "Never mind that she learned *yer magic in a week* while juggling two or three others."

Annabelle drained the juice from her cup, setting it down with a clink. "Even the Copper doesn't look down her nose at the rest of us. But you? Born on a bed of crop crowns, you can't help but lord your parents' money over everyone."

Lisa bristled at the insult but decided not to engage. Taking a calming breath, she said, "I am sorry. I did not mean to look down on anyone."

Annabelle studied Lisa's face, seeing the sincerity in her eyes. Her tone softened as she reached out and gave Lisa's hand a gentle squeeze. "It's okay, Lisa. The oatmeal and juice were really good though, Thanks."

Lisa, determined to make things right, asked quietly, "What can I do to fix things between us?"

Annabelle's eyes widened. "What's that now?"

"I want to prove I am not looking down on you," Lisa said. "How do I do that?"

Annabelle's devilish grin spread across her face. Without missing a beat, she leaned in. "Help me pull a prank on the Copper."

Lisa blinked. "What? No way. I am not doing that."

"Oh, yer no fun," Annabelle teased. "And here ye say ye want to be me friend."

"Why would I help you prank Sophie?" Lisa countered, frowning. "She has been through so much, that is just mean."

"Aye, she's been through more than most," Annabelle admitted, leaning forward slightly. "But how would you feel if everyone treated you like an outsider just 'cause you lost all yer peoples?"

Lisa paused, taken aback by the question. She hadn't considered Sophie's situation from that angle. "I had not considered that," she confessed softly. "But I still do not think a prank will help her feel better."

"Ah, ye just gotta trust me, Princess. I know these tings," Annabelle said with a wide grin. "This is how us privateers bond on a ship. Ye've noticed how close the crew is, haven't ye?"

Lisa wanted to steer the conversation in a different direction. "I am just trying to understand, how exactly do you learn mathematics from the sea?" she asked.

Annabelle chuckled. "Aye, missy, think about it. A privateer crews a ship to make coin, right?" She leaned back, crossing her arms. "If ye crew a ship, ye get a percentage of the ship's takings. Most ships pay around 5 percent for cake runs and up to 20 percent for the hard stuff. If ye can't figure yer share, someone'll take advantage of ye faster than a storm at sea."

Lisa tilted her head, intrigued. "Okay, but what about governments and history? How did you learn about that?"

"Well," Annabelle said with a mischievous grin, "I did spend some time ashore learnin' that from a school mom. Felt so wrong not bein' on a ship, though, all that land, no ocean breeze. Drove a lass crazy." She paused, then turned the question back to Lisa. "How 'bout you, Princess? You go to yer fancy academy all yer life?"

"No," Lisa replied, shaking her head. "I only started attending Valorcrest for secondary school." She drained the last of her juice, placing the cup down thoughtfully. "I didn't go to primary school at all."

Annabelle raised an eyebrow. "Didn't go to primary school? What'd ya do instead?"

Lisa sighed and explained, "The kingdom places a high priority on training Earthbloom mages, So when I showed an affinity for it, I was enrolled in special training with Mistress Hestra and also taught by Sister Brunhilda."

"So, ye spent yer time learnin' magic and doin' school with yer school mom?" Annabelle asked, her curiosity piqued. "Sounds boring."

"Not exactly," Lisa replied with a small smile. "At first, yes. I spent long hours with the mistress, learning to properly cast Earthbloom spells. It is a lot more complicated than one would think." She paused, remembering the harsh early days of training. "But once I got it right, I was required to serve the Church of the Harvest. My job was to use my magic to spread the goddess' blessings over the crops."

Annabelle tilted her head. "Yer goddess is named *Harvest*?"

Lisa chuckled. "No. She did not like it when I called her that, either. Her name is Unity. Who's your goddess?"

"Chaos!" Annabelle declared proudly, beaming. "And she's a pirate just like me. Her ship was ... amazin'!"

Lisa nodded slowly. "That... makes total sense," she said, unable to suppress a grin.

Annabelle gave her a sly look. "Is yer goddess a princess like you?"

Lisa shook her head, strands of green hair swaying with the motion. "No, I do not think so. She's just... a goddess. Her garden was so vast and lush. I imagine she worked incredibly hard to cultivate it."

Annabelle glanced at her watch and sighed. "Sorry, Princess, I gotta go. My shift's about to start." She stood and grabbed her jacket from the back of her chair.

Lisa hesitated, then spoke up. "One thing, how do I get you to call me by my name instead of *Princess*?"

Annabelle's grin widened mischievously. "Help me prank the Copper," she said with a playful wink before turning to leave.

[-----✝-----]

Marcus sat alone in the galley, eating a bowl of oatmeal with a cup of coffee on the side. His pistol, strapped to his leg beneath his pants, pressed awkwardly against his thigh, forcing him to shift in his seat to get comfortable. He sighed quietly and took another bite.

An older man approached the table, Sparks, as Annabelle Salazar had called him. "Mind if I sit here, sir?" Sparks asked, gesturing to one of the empty chairs.

"Of course," Marcus replied, motioning to the seat across from him. "And please, you don't have to call me sir. Brother Marcus is just fine."

"Thank you, Si...Brother Marcus," Sparks returned as he sat, setting down his own bowl of oatmeal and coffee. Without further ceremony, he dug into his meal with gusto.

Marcus studied the man as they ate. Sparks was clearly older than the other privateers on the Stormfang, though he gave off an oddly youthful air. Unlike the rest of the crew, who wore tight-fitting clothes and bandanas, Sparks wore a pair of overalls covered in pockets of various colors, each seemingly added at random over the years. His shirt sleeves had more pockets sewn in, and his short, uneven hair lacked the customary bandana. *Sparks is an odd one, no doubt.*

Out of curiosity, Marcus asked, "Mr. Sparks, how long have you been a privateer?"

Sparks paused mid-bite and glanced upward thoughtfully, as if searching for an answer in the air. "What year is it again? 1910, right?"

Marcus nodded.

"Fifteen years, then," Sparks answered. "I've crewed on seven ships: the Crazy Horse, Belle Dame Marée, Moonlight Siren, Nordhund Jua Kundi, Ronin Corsaire, and now the Stormfang."

"That's quite a list," Marcus remarked. "Have you always been... sorry, I don't know your title on the ship."

Sparks looked up, as though the question had never occurred to him. "Title, huh? Guess you could call me the ship's tinkering engineer." He paused to consider further, then continued, "And nay, I wasn't always an engineer. Like most I started as a deck mate on my first few ships, but that's a lotta hard work fer not much coin. Things changed when I crewed the Moonlight Siren. The fix it man got himself arrested in Umbrathorn, something about photographs of a royal princess and some missing jewels." He waved his hand dismissively. "Captain Segal asked me to fill in until he found a replacement. That's where I met Kidd and Belle."

He took another bite of oatmeal, followed by a sip of coffee. "After that, I stuck to working in ship repairs. Eventually, I came aboard the Stormfang. Now I mostly tinker, coming up with new ways to make things on the ship work better."

Marcus nodded, picturing Sparks' journey. "Sounds like you've lived quite a storied life among the privateer vessels."

"Arrr," Sparks replied with a half-hearted shrug, finishing his oatmeal and turning his full attention to his coffee. After a moment of silence, he glanced at Marcus curiously. "I gotta ask... are ye really the girlies' butler?"

Marcus blinked, caught off guard by the question. He mulled over the comparison, thinking about his duties as the avatars' guide. After a moment, he smiled and said, "I've never thought about it that way. I suppose it's not too far off. Though, I'm not sure they can fire me like a regular butler."

Sparks chuckled. "Aye, but you can't exactly quit neither. Didn't the last fella in your position die? Butlers don't usually have to die for their employers."

Marcus winced slightly at the reminder. He hadn't been prepared for that observation. "Fair point," he admitted. "Maybe I'm more of an extra butler than a traditional one."

"Arrr," Sparks said with a grin. "Look at us, sittin' here at breakfast, making up new titles."

Marcus chuckled as Sparks took a large gulp of coffee, their conversation settling into a companionable silence.

Marcus smiled, satisfied with the conversation, and took a sip of his coffee. "If you don't mind me asking," he began, "what are you and Miss Fournier working on today?"

"The green missy wants an oven installed," Sparks replied. "So, the silver missy and I are figuring out how to do it without, ye know, burnin' up the ship." He said with a smirk and took another gulp of coffee.

Marcus raised an eyebrow, thinking aloud. "Now that I think of it, I've never been on a privateer ship that offered baked goods. Probably because they didn't have ovens to handle that kind of thing."

"Aye," Sparks agreed with a grin. "Far as I know, this'll be the first time a privateer ship's got a functional, long-term oven."

"I am guessing you like being the first to do things?" Marcus asked with a knowing look, sipping his now lukewarm coffee.

"Nay," Sparks corrected with a wry smile. "I like bein' the first to do things right." His tone carried a hint of smugness, as if he took pride in surpassing those with less skill.

Marcus nodded in acknowledgment. If Sparks could keep up with Miss Fournier's brilliance, then he was likely worth his weight in coin.

"If ye excuse me, Si...Brother Marcus, I've got work to gets done," Sparks said, standing and collecting his empty bowl and coffee cup.

"Nice talking to you," Marcus replied with a friendly nod and smile.

Sparks returned the gesture and made his way to the counter, depositing his dishes and utensils into designated cutouts. Marcus watched him go, then glanced down at his coffee, just one gulp left. This was the best coffee he'd had outside of Order Island, and he silently appreciated whatever Miss Nozaki had changed in the recipe.

Thinking ahead to his day, Marcus mentally reviewed the avatars' rotation schedule: Regina, Sophie, Lisa, and Annabelle. Since his last task the previous evening had been with Miss Griffin, his morning would begin with Miss Nozaki in the galley. He looked forward to seeing what the day had in store.

"Oi, servant!" Annabelle's voice rang out, breaking his thoughts. She stood in the doorway of the galley seating area, grinning mischievously. "Are ye ready to do some work?"

Marcus exhaled softly. "Miss Salazar," he replied, "it's Miss Nozaki's turn." He checked his watch, 7:20 a.m. "In ten minutes, as you all agreed."

"Nay," Annabelle shot back. "It's me turn."

"Excuse me," Lisa's calm voice called out from behind the counter. "It is my turn, Annabelle," she stated firmly.

Annabelle scoffed. "Ye just had a turn. He don't even cook," she protested, pointing at Marcus.

Lisa didn't respond with words. Instead, she leveled a cold, disapproving stare at Annabelle.

"Fine," Annabelle muttered, throwing up her hands. "and ye say you wanna be me friend," she added dismissively before turning to Marcus. "I'll see ye on the bridge at 8:30... on the dot." With that, she strode out of the galley seating area.

Relieved, Marcus let out a quiet breath and finished his coffee, now cold. He gathered his bowl and cup, depositing them in the cutouts for dishes and cutlery. Then, looking over the counter, he asked, "Miss Nozaki, what are we doing this morning?"

"I was talking with Jeffie," Lisa began, "and we decided on chicken stew for lunch today. Since we made fried chicken and boiled vegetables for dinner yesterday, we'll use the leftover chicken pieces for the stew."

She motioned to herself and Jeffie. "While we organize the chicken, we need you to go into the storeroom and get a count of all the vegetables. Make sure to note whether they're whole or partial pieces."

Marcus opened his mouth to respond, but Lisa preempted him. "That's all I have for you this morning. If that's too much, I can always let Annabelle take my time."

Marcus paused slightly at the thought of whatever task Annabelle might assign him. He quickly replied, "That will be fine, Miss Lisa. Do you have a pad of paper I can use?"

"I have one right here," Lisa said with a smile. She reached under the counter and produced a sturdy wooden clipboard, papers secured by a gray metal peg. Handing it over to Marcus, she added, "Thank you," preemptively acknowledging his help.

Marcus accepted the clipboard with a polite nod and headed to the pantry's cold storage room. The space was long, likely running the entire length of the galley, with shelves lining both walls. A machine at the far end blew air over a block of ice, keeping the room chilled. Where the ice came from was anyone's guess, probably another one of Mr. Sparks' ingenious contraptions. Marcus made a mental note to ask Miss Fournier how the cooling system worked. If it could be refined, the Order might want to study it.

The room was divided into three sections. The front held boxes labeled "Beef" and "Chicken," presumably the same ones Lisa and Jeffie would soon retrieve for today's meal. The second and most extensive section was dedicated to fruits and vegetables, well-stocked thanks to a recent resupply from The Order. Marcus noticed several boxes marked with a large "U." Curious, he pulled one down and opened it to find it half-filled with tomatoes. He quickly deduced that "U" stood for "*used*" likely due to a system influenced by Lisa's previous experience working in the governor's mansion kitchens in Verdantia. This simplifies his task, he only needs to inventory these "U" boxes.

Pulling a pencil from his shirt pocket, Marcus got to work. After roughly twenty minutes, Jeffie entered the cold pantry to collect the "U" chicken boxes. With his task complete, Marcus returned to the galley and handed the clipboard to Lisa, who was diligently cutting chicken meat from the bone.

"As requested, an inventory of the leftover vegetables," Marcus reported, placing the cold clipboard on the counter near Lisa.

"Thank you," she said without looking up, focused on slicing as much meat off the bones as possible.

"How much time do I have left?" she asked after a moment.

Marcus glanced at his watch and replied, "Approximately fifteen minutes until Miss Salazar's time."

Lisa turned to look at him and noticed he was shivering, blowing into his hands for warmth. Feeling generous, she said, "How about you take a break and have another cup of coffee to warm up?"

"If you change your mind, I'll be in the galley seating area until your time is up," Marcus assured her. He poured himself another cup of coffee from a pot secured to the stove with a locking system and a spigot for easy access.

After taking a brief break to enjoy the warm drink, Marcus made his way up to the bridge. He spotted Annabelle and Sophie working near the main mast. Annabelle was pulling on a thick rope that held the mainsail in place. Harmon tied the rope to a metal loop attached to the mast. Once the knot was secure, both girls released the rope and stepped back.

"Good work, for a shore-lover," Annabelle teased with a grin, giving Sophie a playful shove.

Sophie rolled her eyes and shoved her back. "Yeah, whatever," she said with a smile.

Marcus crossed the deck and announced, "Miss Salazar, it is now your turn."

Annabelle's face lit up with enthusiasm. "Aye!" she exclaimed. "Let's go, Brother Marcus. There's much fer ye to do."

With a grin of her own, she led the way, her energy infectious as Marcus followed across the deck.

Annabelle strode past Marcus, who followed her as they made their way to the captain's operations room behind the ship's helm. Inside, Captain Lowe sat behind a sturdy desk, absorbed in reading a report, likely from the night crew, or perhaps Sparks' daily plan.

"Morning, Cap'n," Annabelle called out cheerfully.

The captain raised a hand in acknowledgment but didn't look up from his papers.

Annabelle turned to a tall cabinet on the right side of the room. As soon as she opened it, a chaotic mess of maps, charts, and various objects tumbled out onto the floor. Marcus raised an eyebrow as a boot and what appeared to be a plate from the galley rolled free among the maps.

"This here's the map cabinet," Annabelle explained, waving a hand at the pile of clutter. "I've been meanin' to organize it for a while. So, yer gonna sort it out, make it nice and tidy so we can actually use these here maps."

Marcus stared at the heap of papers and random junk. "Looks simple enough," he said dryly, nudging the boot aside with his foot. "But how exactly does organizing maps help you with being the avatar?"

Annabelle paused and assumed an air of excessive dignity, speaking in her proper voice. "Brother Marcus, I simply cannot focus on the priorities the Goddess of Chaos entrusted to me while such crucial tasks remain undone," she declared, placing a hand dramatically over her heart.

"It does sound quite taxing," Marcus replied, his sarcasm carefully masked beneath a polite tone, sure she could think of something worse for him to do.

"Aye, ye understand me plight," Annabelle said with her proper voice. "And when yer done, I'll have more tings fer ye to do." She headed toward the door, adding, "I'll be in the powder mags. See you later." before closing the door behind her.

Marcus let out a quiet sigh and turned to Captain Lowe. "Captain, do you mind if I use this table?" he asked, referring to the large worktable nearby.

"Go for it, mate," the captain replied without looking up.

With permission granted, Marcus set to work. He began by emptying the cabinet altogether, pulling out an assortment of maps, tools, and other random items stuffed on the shelves. It quickly became clear that the disorganization was caused by the crew using the cabinet as a dumping ground for anything they didn't want sliding around the room.

Once the non-map items were removed, the maps fit easily on the shelves. Marcus sorted them by region and purpose, navigational charts, storm tracking maps, and trade route diagrams, before moving on to the random objects.

By the time he was halfway through his task, Captain Lowe left the room, leaving Marcus alone with his thoughts. As he worked, his mind wandered to the recent events in Granmark and Laminae. The conspiracy's actions were troubling. It was clear they had targeted both Miss Sophie and Miss Annabelle, either for capture or assassination. But what about Lisa? No direct actions had been taken against her. And Regina? She had only come to Granmark because Brother Albert had summoned her there.

Marcus considered the assault on Aurorium Granmark further. The conspiracy seemed intent on eliminating Sophie Griffin. *Why? What about Sophie was so crucial or dangerous to their plans?* It was a question he resolved to investigate during his next rotation with Miss Griffin.

His thoughts returned to the task at hand. He surveyed the scattered items on the table: ten plates, several pieces of silverware, two cups, a wrench, two flathead screwdrivers, a study guide for Maelstrom Mastery, two boxes of nails, a spool of half-used wire, a hairbrush, four fountain pens, and three tubes that lit up when shaken. Marcus shook one experimentally and watched as it glowed with a soft light.

He deduced that the officers likely used the map cabinet to store loose items from around the ship. It was easier than putting things back in their proper places. He sorted the objects by category, dishes with dishes, tools with tools, so he could quickly return them to their respective locations. Just as he was finishing the organization, Captain Lowe returned to the room.

"Oi, was all of this in me map locker?" Captain Kidd asked, stepping into the room and surveying the chaotic collection of items on the table.

"It was," Marcus confirmed. "I assume the officers were using the cabinet as temporary storage."

"Nay," Captain Kidd corrected with a shake of his head. "All of this is Belle's doing." He walked over to the door and called out, "Belle! Get in here!"

From somewhere outside, Marcus heard Mr. Smith reply, "She's still in the powder mag, Captain."

"Send the runner for her, Smitty," Kidd ordered.

"Aye, Cap'n," Smith answered, then shouted, "Runner to the bridge!"

As the door closed behind Kidd, Marcus glanced at the stack of dishes and tools. "If it's alright with you, Captain Lowe, I was going to return these items to their proper places."

"Nay, mate," Captain Kidd interjected firmly. "Belle is going to take care of this mess herself."

"As you wish, Captain," Marcus said, stepping back and folding his arms.

Moments later, Annabelle entered the room. "Aye, ye wanted to see me, Cap'n?" she asked. Her eyes fell on the cluttered table, confusion crossing her face.

"Aye, Belle," Kidd replied, motioning to the mess. "What's all this foolishness doin' in me map locker?"

"I... donna know, Cap'n," Annabelle answered reflexively, though the hesitation in her voice betrayed her guilt.

Kidd narrowed his eyes. "How many times have I told ye not to stow your foolishness in me map locker?"

Annabelle winced, recalling the many times she'd been caught stuffing random items in there. "A lot of times, Cap'n," she admitted sheepishly.

"And yet, here we find ourselves yet again," Kidd said, his voice taut with frustration. He exhaled slowly to steady himself. "Get all of this back to where it belongs. Now."

"Aye, Cap'n," Annabelle mumbled, glancing down in embarrassment. She turned to Marcus and gestured toward the table. "Come on, Brother Marcus. Let's get this stuff movin'."

"Nay, nay," Kidd cut in sharply. "Marcus didn't put any of this here. Yer gonna take it all back where it belongs... by yerself"

"But Cap'n, he's me servant," Annabelle protested.

Kidd raised an eyebrow. "Do ye pay him?"

"Nay," Annabelle replied hesitantly. "It's his duty from the Order."

"If Marcus touches one thing on that table, I'll give him yer pay for the day," Kidd said, his voice hard.

Marcus, sensing the tension, stepped forward. "Captain, I appreciate the offer, but it's my duty. I couldn't accept the avatar's pay. She's clearly been contributing to the ship's work."

Captain Kidd sighed, pinching the bridge of his nose. He closed his eyes, took a deep breath, and slowly exhaled before fixing Marcus with a firm gaze. "Brother Marcus, you may have rented the Stormfang, but I ask that you not interfere with its operations. Let's discuss this further over a cup of coffee on the observation deck."

Annabelle frowned and checked her pocket watch. "But Cap'n, I still have twenty minutes," she protested.

Kidd shot her a look, the kind that warned there would be no further arguments.

"Never mind, Cap'n," she muttered, stepping back.

Kidd turned to Marcus. "Shall we?"

Marcus glanced at Annabelle, noting her deflated expression, then nodded. "Yes, Captain."

The two men left the operations room, leaving the door open behind them. Annabelle sighed, reluctantly grabbed the stack of plates from the table, and followed them out. As she walked, she silently cursed to herself for assigning Marcus the task in the first place.

[-----✝-----]

Captain Kidd and Marcus made their way to the observation deck, stopping briefly in the galley to grab fresh cups of coffee. The pot, still warm from resting on the stove, had brewed just enough heat to make the drink satisfying. As they arrived at the deck, they spotted two night-shift crew members sitting at a table, casually chatting.

"Oi, go find somewhere else to socialize," Kidd ordered, his tone leaving no room for argument.

The crew members glanced at him, recognized his serious expression, and quickly rose from their seats, offering respectful nods as they passed.

Kidd gestured toward a table on the starboard side. "Let's sit and discuss a few things, Brother Marcus," he invited.

Marcus followed the captain to the table, which was outfitted with four chairs secured to floor rails, designed to keep them in place but still movable. He pulled one out, took a seat, and sipped his warm coffee, allowing Kidd to start the conversation.

The captain settled in, leaned forward slightly, and asked, "Tell me, Brother, how many privateer ships have ye been on?"

Marcus thought for a moment. "More than five or six" he answered. "I traveled on them while serving with the College of Sages. Privateer vessels often go to places off the regular shipping lanes, so they were useful for my duties."

"And when you were aboard those vessels, how often did you work with the crew?" Kidd asked, his gaze sharp.

"I spoke to the crew quite a bit," Marcus replied.

"That wasn't me question," Kidd said, correcting him. "How often did ye *work* with the Crew? I'm talkin' about movin' bags, cookin' food, workin' the deck, or fixin' tings on the ship."

Marcus hesitated before answering honestly, "I can't say that I ever did."

Kidd nodded slightly, as if expecting the answer. "So, what did you do when you sailed with privateers?"

"Mostly, I wrote in my journal," Marcus admitted. "If the ship had a workout facility, I'd use that. I toured the ship on occasion, but... honestly, it was pretty boring when I think about it."

Kidd chuckled softly. "Let me explain somethin' to you about privateer culture. Everyone on a privateer vessel has one goal: *make as much coin as possible*. If you're a crew member, you wanna make that coin while doin' as little work as you can get away with. But if you're the captain, you've got the opposite goal. You wanna get as much work outta the crew as possible while keepin' their pay low, 'cause you've gotta cover all the ship's expenses: food, repairs, supplies, you name it."

Marcus nodded thoughtfully. "Makes sense," he replied, starting to understand the balancing act privateer captains faced.

Captain Kidd took a sip of his coffee and murmured, "Wow, that's really good." He set the cup down and continued, "Do you know what makes a privateer different from a *legit* sailor on a conscripted vessel? Other than the obvious, I mean."

Marcus thought back to his experiences aboard both types of ships. He considered mentioning the uniforms, cleanliness, or living conditions, but none of those seemed relevant to Kidd's point. Finally, he said, "I don't know."

"On a conscripted vessel, from the captain to the lowest runner, you earn a set wage, no opportunity to make any more than that," Kidd explained. "It's their way of fightin' skullduggery. I once crewed a ship called the Saint Michael out of Verdantia, right after the Espada Sovereign was sunk. They had stacks of rules for the crew: no talking to passengers unless ye was the captain or a porter, no gambling on board, and no second chances. Ye step outta line once, yer gone. No three-strikes rule. Captain says you're out, and you're out."

He took another drink of coffee before continuing. "Now, on a privateer ship, it's a whole different story. We take every opportunity to get our hands on a few extra coin. We double-book our cargo holds, run flim flam. Privateers exploit every loophole we can: import laws, tariffs, arrests, customers, passengers, even each other. Why? 'Cause the number one goal is to make as much coin as possible."

16

Marcus nodded slowly, absorbing the explanation. "I see."

"Do you?" Kidd asked, his eyes narrowing slightly.

"I think I do," Marcus replied. "The deal we made to rent your ship... I paid too much."

"Is that all?" Kidd asked, leaning back with a knowing smile.

Marcus went still, his mind switching to an analytical mode honed through years of investigative work. He began silently reviewing the situation aboard the Stormfang.

Lisa essentially managed the galley, creating recipes and handling service without pay. Sophie worked on deck alongside the Crew, contributing to its daily operations. Regina assisted Sparks in maintaining and improving the ship's systems, providing engineering support at no cost. Any one of these roles would reduce the captain's need for additional paid crew members. Marcus realized that these contributions should have been grounds for renegotiating the terms of the rental. Kidd had been getting substantial free labor, on top of an very high rental fee.

Marcus pushed aside the sting of being taken advantage of and focused on the most pressing question. "Captain, why are you telling me this?"

"Fer Belle," Captain Kidd replied simply. "You're supposed to do what's best for those girlies, right?"

"Without a doubt, yes," Marcus answered firmly. "There are tenets I serve by, and they make it clear: I'm to support the avatars in every way possible, giving them what they need to carry out the will of the goddesses."

"Then ye ain't doin' what's best for Belle," Kidd said bluntly.

Marcus frowned, caught off guard. "How do you mean?"

"Belle's a privateer through and through," Kidd explained. "She's got the same goals and tactics as the rest of us, make as much coin as possible and take advantage where ye can." He took another sip of coffee. "Do ye know why she went down to the powder mag earlier?"

Marcus hesitated, remembering that he hadn't questioned it. He'd simply chalked it up to Annabelle wanting to avoid more mundane tasks. "I didn't really think about it," he admitted.

"They play *crew* down there," Kidd revealed with a chuckle. "When they're supposed to be workin'. It's why I keep extra jobs lined up for 'em when I need it. Funny thing is, that boy Jeffie in the galley? He started off in the powder mag." He shook his head, amused by the memory.

Marcus began to feel a sinking weight in his chest. Annabelle wasn't just taking advantage of him, she was using her duties as an avatar to trick him into mundane work he would normally refuse. He felt both frustrated and disappointed, in Annabelle and himself.

"If ye let Belle take advantage of ye, she will," Kidd said, his voice more serious now. "Every single time. I know you're meant to be her servant, but don't be her dupe, not willingly, anyway."

Marcus gave a slow nod as the words sank in.

"The thing about Belle," Kidd continued "is she'll do the work if you make her. But first, she'll yell, complain like a banshee, maybe even throw a punch, I watched her hit a bloke for his troubles before. But once she realizes none of that'll get her out of it, she'll hunker down and get the work done."

"I see," Marcus murmured thoughtfully. "I've got a lot to learn about Annabelle... probably all of the avatars."

"Not an easy job, I reckon," Kidd said, draining the last of his coffee. "Word of advice, mate: *Don't make ship's business part of your duty. If the girlies wanna work to keep from getting bored, that's their choice. But yer payin' to be here. At least enjoy yourself a bit.*" He gave Marcus a quick wink before standing.

"Thank you, Captain," Marcus said with a respectful nod. "You've given me an important perspective I hadn't considered."

"Aye, have a good day." Kidd replied casually as he strode off toward the bridge.

Marcus watched him go, feeling the gears in his mind shift as he reconsidered his approach to Annabelle, and to his broader duties concerning the avatars.

[-----✝-----]

Marcus spent the remainder of "Miss Annabelle's time" sitting quietly on the observation deck, contemplating how best to serve the avatars. His conversation with Captain Kidd weighed on him. He realized that he had been selectively following the guide's tenets, prioritizing what was more comfortable for himself over what was truly best for the avatars.

His mind drifted to past talks with Sister Ingrid. She had tried to guide him toward this very realization before he stumbled into error. He sighed, finishing the last of his coffee and silently recommitting himself to the avatars' mission, vowing to stay focused on their purpose as vessels of the goddesses' will.

After his reflection, Marcus sought out Miss Fournier, intending to spend her allotted time with her. However, she was deep in discussion with Mr. Sparks. The two of them were theorizing ways to install an oven in the galley without compromising the ship's safety. Marcus observed their communication dynamic with interest.

Regina spoke in long, structured paragraphs, carefully building her case with layers of facts, options, and possibilities, although she often veered off on tangents. Sparks listened intently, his responses short but impactful, usually a single sentence that clarified or dismissed key points in Regina's detailed analysis. It was a curious balance of thought and brevity that worked surprisingly well between the two.

Deciding his presence wasn't needed, Marcus left them to their work and returned to the observation deck. The two crew members from earlier had reclaimed their spot, now engaged in a lively game of crew, a popular privateer card game. They sat near the wall, each with a small stack of coins. Marcus guessed they were using one-coin denominations for their wagers.

He approached and took a seat with them. The first man, a pudgy olive-skinned deck mate named Harmon from Islewind, nodded in greeting. The other, a skinny blonde runner named Popper from Opulentia, grinned as they continued playing. Marcus recognized the card game from his time aboard other ships, he had seen crews play it in groups ranging from two to six players, but he had never played himself.

"Mind explaining how the game works?" Marcus asked, watching the cards as they were dealt.

Both men exchanged glances, then shook their heads. "It's a bit too complicated to explain all at once," Harmon said.

"Aye." Popper agreed. "Ye'd be better off just learnin' as ye go."

They offered to deal Marcus into the next hand to show him the ropes. Marcus paused, recalling Captain Kidd's advice about not being taken advantage of. He decided instead to negotiate.

"Tell you what," Marcus said. "I'll give each of you five coins to teach me the basics properly. Once I've got the hang of it, we can see about dealing me in."

The two men grinned, clearly pleased with the offer. Popper collected his stack of coins and leaned forward. "Alright, Brother Marcus, let's teach ye how to play crew."

The game of crew was surprisingly complex, with layers of strategy that reflected the life of a privateer. Each player was dealt five cards, referred to as their "debt" rather than a hand. The game offered three distinct ways to win, each yielding different rewards from the pot of coins in the middle of the table.

The first method was by creating a run. A player could lay down three of the same card across different suits, such as a run of queens. Alternatively, a player could form a sequence of three or more consecutive cards in the same suit, for example, a run of four, five, and six of clubs. Players could continue building on their run if they had the right cards, extending it with a seven and possibly an eight to achieve what was called a "sweetheart run." However, runs came with a risk: *piracy*. Another player could disrupt a run by playing a corresponding card to claim its benefits. For example, playing the nine of clubs would hijack someone's sweetheart run, and there was no way to steal it back.

The second way to win was by "telling a story." This involved pairing two cards, subject to specific requirements. Each suit had a "personality" that shaped the story's theme: clubs represented violence, diamonds symbolized wealth or treasure, hearts referred to love, and spades meant law enforcement or being caught by the authorities. A story had to begin with a low card (any card below a seven) and end with a high card (seven or above).

The third path to victory was by "retiring" with the least amount of debt essentially, having the lowest-value cards on the table at the end of the game. For example, if one player had two twos while another had a three and a four, the player with the twos would win the hand.

The payouts were equally intricate. If a player had both a winning run and a successful story, they could claim half the pot, which was the pool of coins in the center of the table. However, if a player managed to achieve two three-card runs or a single five-card consecutive run, they will take the entire pot.

If a player retired with the least debt, they would only claim half the pot, leaving the other half for the next round symbolizing *that there was always more money to be made on the sea*. Players who played all their cards through stories alone wouldn't get any payout, as "stories don't make a man any coin."

Marcus was fascinated by the game's depth, but he lacked the time to apply his newfound knowledge. Miss Sophie's rotation was about to begin, and he didn't want to risk being late. He stood, thanked Harmon and Popper for their time and instruction, and left a five-coin piece on the table to start their next pot.

With a nod of farewell to the crewmen, Marcus made his way off the observation deck, his mind turning from the strategies of Crew to the duties ahead with Miss Griffin.

[-----✟-----]

Marcus arrived on the Stormfang's deck and moved to the edge of the work area. From his vantage point, he observed the deck crew in constant motion, each task flowing seamlessly into the next. There is always something to do: *adjusting rigging and sails to maximize speed, clearing ropes and equipment from the deck, and maintaining overall cleanliness.* It reminded Marcus of a large, choreographed dance routine, much like those performed at chamber events, every crew member knew their role and timing.

Among them, Sophie Griffin worked diligently, keeping pace with the others. Despite her effort, her inexperience was evident. She had to stay hyper-aware of her surroundings, making sure not to collide with anyone or trip over scattered ropes or machinery. Marcus stood at the edge of the bustling activity, patiently waiting for Sophie to notice him and decide whether to wave him off or approach.

After a few minutes, Sophie grabbed a block and tackle from the deck and carefully carried it to a nearby storage bin close to where Marcus stood. She dropped it inside, dusted off her hands, and approached him.

"Hi there, Brother Marcus," she greeted with a bright smile.

"Miss Griffin," Marcus replied warmly. "What shall we do for the hour?"

"I need your help working something out," Sophie explained. She gestured for him to follow and began leading the way past the bridge and toward the stairs. As they walked, she continued, "I've been working on my mana control ever since the goddess blessed me. But I need your help refining my magic techniques."

Marcus hesitated. "I'm not sure how I can help. I don't have any magic."

"Don't worry about that," Sophie reassured him with a casual wave of her hand. "You'll do just fine."

Marcus followed, curious and eager to assist, though still unsure how he could contribute to her training. He considered what might be troubling her. *It's similar to Miss Fournier's situation*, he thought. After receiving the goddess's blessing, Sophie likely found herself with much larger and more efficient mana reserves, making it difficult to control the power output of her spells. What might have once been a knockout blow could now become lethally overpowered if not carefully managed.

"So, I'm guessing you're trying to find the right spell strength," Marcus ventured.

Sophie paused on the stairs, glancing back at him in surprise. "Yeah! How did you know?"

"Miss Fournier was having a similar issue after her time with the Goddess of Change," Marcus explained as he followed Sophie down the stairs. "Though, based on her account of the fight with Hema, being overpowered might've actually helped her win that battle."

"How so?" Sophie asked, curiosity sparking as she shifted into analytical mode.

"According to her, her 'Child's Play' spells aren't designed for fighting. But with the surge of mana from her goddess, she ended up channeling so much power that her spells created confusion, something Hema wasn't prepared for. That gave her the upper hand," Marcus explained. "And with Regina's natural genius and adaptability, she caught Hema off guard by combining portal rituals in ways Hema didn't expect."

"Sounds like Regina only won because of beginner's luck," Sophie remarked thoughtfully.

"In a way," Marcus agreed. "She overpowered Hema, yes, but Hema was far more experienced in combat. If the fight had gone on longer, I fear Hema would've pressed that advantage and killed Miss Fournier."

Sophie frowned. "Maybe. But Regina might've found another way to beat her."

"Oh, I don't doubt that," Marcus replied. "The problem is, she might not have had the chance to use any new tactic in time."

"Like finding bullets for a gun you're not holding," Sophie said, adding the metaphor to make sense of the situation. "I hadn't thought about it that way."

They reached the birthing floor, and Sophie opened the door to the exercise room. Inside, she walked to a plank of wood standing about four feet tall. The front was padded with cushioned material, fastened securely with pegs and stitching.

"This," Sophie said, setting the plank down on the deck, "is a training dummy." She turned it around, revealing two large straps on the back that ran vertically from the top down. The straps formed a handle wide enough for an adult to put their arms through.

Marcus immediately understood. He took the dummy from Sophie, slipped both arms through the straps, and lifted it into position. "Ready when you are, Miss Griffin," he announced.

"Okay, I'm going to start soft," Sophie said with a smile.

She turned her full focus to the training dummy, carefully lining up her stance and positioning for a basic punch. She threw it with controlled strength, her fist crashing into the padded cushion. The force pushed Marcus back slightly, but he braced himself and easily compensated. Glancing over the dummy, he gave Sophie a nod to signal he was ready for more.

Sophie nodded in return and took a deep breath. Her expression sharpened as she concentrated on casting her HARDKNUCKLE spell. Slowly and deliberately, she shaped the spell circles, channeling what she estimated to be five percent of her mana into the first and second layers. She threw the enhanced punch, and this time, the result was far more dramatic, her fist slammed into the dummy with a flash of violet energy, the impact knocking Marcus clean off his feet.

He hit the deck with a loud thud. Lying flat on his back, Marcus stared up at the ceiling, momentarily dazed as his mind tried to process what had just happened. One moment, he had been standing, ready for the punch; the next, he was flat on the floor.

"Oh, uh... sorry!" Sophie called out, stepping forward when she saw him stir.

Marcus groaned softly but waved a hand to reassure her. "I'm okay," he said, sitting up and then getting back on his feet. He retrieved the training dummy and slipped his arms back through the straps. Once in position, he nodded again. "Ready when you are, Miss Griffin."

Sophie blinked in surprise, a bit impressed that he'd recovered so quickly from the hit. "Sorry about that, Brother Marcus," she apologized again. "I'll cast it again, but with less mana this time."

She took another stance and carefully shaped the spell circles once more. This time, she pulled her mana back drastically, reducing it to what she thought was only one percent of her reserves. With another HARDKNUCKLE punch, she struck the dummy. The impact barely moved Marcus, who absorbed the blow with ease.

"I'm guessing that one was too weak," Marcus observed from behind the dummy.

"You guessed right," Sophie admitted with a sigh. She reset her stance and prepared for another attempt.

This time, she aimed to channel five percent again, but she switched arms, her momma had taught her that using HARDKNUCKLE repeatedly with the same hand could easily break a bone. Carefully shaping the circles, she unleashed another enhanced punch.

The force of the blow pushed Marcus back a step, but he steadied himself quickly. He noticed the difference immediately, this punch was far more controlled. The previous hit had felt like the power had rushed in unevenly, but this one delivered a smooth and concentrated impact.

As he reset his position, Marcus offered his assessment. "I think that one might be about right."

Sophie smiled, feeling a sense of progress. "Good. Let's do a few more like that to make sure."

Marcus gave a nod, bracing himself once more. "Whenever you're ready."

She nodded, adjusting her stance in front of the training dummy. "Now for the fun part. I need to get used to using that spell in regular combinations."

She threw a quick combination—left punch, right punch—and then followed it up with a surprise HARDKNUCKLE from her left hand. The sudden impact hit harder than Marcus expected, knocking him to the floor once again.

As he got to his feet, Marcus shook his head. "Maybe a bit too much," he said, dusting himself off. "Close, though."

Sophie grinned mischievously. "Nah, it was about right. You just weren't expecting it."

Marcus chuckled, setting up behind the dummy again. "maybe."

Sophie lined up another combination—regular right punch, left, right, left—before unleashing another HARDKNUCKLE with her right. The force pushed Marcus back, making him straighten up, but this time he managed to stay on his feet. He adjusted his stance and nodded.

"See? Told you," Sophie teased. "You just weren't ready the first time."

"I stand corrected," Marcus said with a grin.

Sophie smirked and launched into another series of punches. She moved fluidly through her combination, but this time she paused before casting the HARDKNUCKLE. She noticed Marcus raise an eyebrow over the top of the dummy.

"I could tell you weren't ready," she explained, lowering her fists. "Didn't want to knock you down again."

"How very kind of you, Miss Griffin," Marcus replied with mock flatness before stretching his arms and repositioning himself behind the dummy. "Alright, ready."

For the next half-hour, they repeated the process. Sophie cycled through punch combinations, refining her mana control with each HARDKNUCKLE. Over time, she found a balance, learning how to properly channel her enhanced reserves without overwhelming herself or her target. Marcus endured each blow with steady resolve, offering occasional feedback while bracing for impact.

Eventually, Sophie slowed, wiping a light sheen of sweat from her brow. She could feel her mana reserves dipping below her comfort level. "Alright, I think that's enough for now," she said, stepping back from the dummy.

"Agreed," Marcus replied, shaking out his arms.

"Go ahead and take a break for lunch," Sophie told him. "I'm gonna grab a shower and then head there myself."

"Sounds like a plan," Marcus said, slipping the straps off his arms and setting the dummy down.

With a nod and a smile, Sophie left the room, feeling accomplished from the progress she had made with her spell control.

[----- ⚓ -----]

22

In the galley, Annabelle and Regina sat across from each other at a table, chatting over lunch. Behind the counter, Lisa was busy handing out bowls of chicken stew to the line of crew members eagerly waiting their turn.

"Everybody loves Lisa's cooking," Regina observed, taking a spoonful of stew and savoring it.

"Aye," Annabelle agreed. "She's got a tongue like the devil, but her cookin' is straight from the heavens." Raising her bowl, she called out, "To the Green Princess!"

The crew responded with an enthusiastic and chaotic cheer of "ARR!"

"Aww, thank you," Lisa replied with a smile, placing a hand on her chest in mock modesty.

"No, Princess, thank you for all the tasty grub!" Annabelle added on behalf of the crew.

At that moment, Sophie walked up to the counter, watching Lisa bask in the crew's appreciation. "What's for lunch, Princess?" she asked playfully, teasing her.

Lisa smirked and reached behind her, grabbing a bowl of chicken stew. She handed it to Sophie. "Chicken stew," she answered, hiding her grin.

"Thanks," Sophie said with a grin, grabbing a spoon from the pile on the counter before making her way to the table where Annabelle and Regina sat. She sat down and greeted them. "Afternoon, ladies."

"Hello again," Regina chirped.

"Afternoon, Copper," Annabelle replied, her sharp orange eyes studying Sophie closely.

Sophie stirred her bowl. "How's the stew?" she asked before taking her first spoonful.

"Delicious!" Regina responded enthusiastically.

"Aye, Copper. The princess can sure whip up a miracle," Annabelle added, though her gaze never left Sophie. She leaned in slightly, curiosity glinting in her eyes. "Copper, I gotta ask, why would you volunteer to work the decks?"

Sophie noticed Annabelle watching her a little too closely. She paused just long enough to be aware of it, but didn't let it show on her face. Instead, she casually ate a spoonful of stew, and she immediately knew why Annabelle was watching her so closely. She forced herself not to react to the stew; she instead answered the question, "I need to do physical training every day to stay strong. Working the decks is great for that."

Annabelle frowned slightly. She couldn't understand it. Most crew did everything they could to pick up a skill and move off the hard labor on the main deck. Yet here Sophie was, volunteering to stay in the grind just because it was *good exercise*. Annabelle kept staring as Sophie took another bite, seemingly unaffected by the stew. Slowly, Annabelle glanced over to Lisa and gave her a silent look that asked: *Did ye do it?*

Lisa met her gaze, gave a quick nod, then shrugged nonchalantly as she handed another bowl of stew to a crewman.

"How do ye like the stew, Copper?" Annabelle asked, suspicion in her voice.

"It's good," Sophie replied, taking another spoonful. "But it could use more spice."

Annabelle's eyes narrowed as she looked between the bowl of stew, Sophie, and Lisa, who continued serving the crew as if nothing was out of the ordinary. Annabelle's temper began to flare.

23

She fouled it up! The stew was supposed to knock Copper off her feet! And now she's playin' dumb!

Lisa shrugged again in response to Annabelle's glare and returned to her work.

"Can I have some of that?" Annabelle asked suddenly, holding up her spoon.

Sophie raised an eyebrow. "Wow, you must really love the chicken stew," she teased, pulling her spoon from the bowl and leaning back to let Annabelle have a taste.

"Thanks." Annabelle said, leaning forward. She scooped a generous spoonful and popped it into her mouth. For a moment, she was sure Lisa had failed her prank entirely. But as she swallowed, her eyes widened. A fiery heat exploded across her tongue and throat, like she'd just swallowed a burning coal.

"Something wrong?" Sophie asked, managing to tolerate the heat burning her mouth with a straight face.

"It's so hot!" Annabelle yelped, jumping up from her chair. She rushed behind the counter in a panic, desperate for something to put out the fire raging in her mouth.

The galley erupted with laughter as the crew watched Annabelle frantically gulp down three cups of water from the serving counter. It didn't help. If anything, the water only seemed to spread the inferno that Annabelle was sure was melting her teeth.

Lisa was laughing so hard she had to catch her breath. Remembering the cup of milk she had stashed on the shelf under the counter, she called out, "Hey, Anna! Here, this will help." She reached under the counter and pulled out the milk.

Annabelle didn't hesitate. She grabbed the cup from Lisa and downed it all in one go, not even pausing to breathe. When she finally came up for air, she gasped, "Oi, that was hot, missy!"

The room filled with more laughter as Annabelle wiped her mouth, still looking a little rattled.

Meanwhile, Sophie approached the counter, feeling the burn herself. "Hey girl, can I get some of that milk?" she asked, fanning her mouth slightly.

"Sorry, that was my only cup," Lisa replied, still grinning. "I will go grab more from the pantry."

"No nee...I'll get it!" Jeffie eagerly offered, grabbing an empty cup and hurrying off past Annabelle.

Lisa turned to Sophie, puzzled. "Wait... why are the peppers not burning you as badly?"

"Oh, they are," Sophie admitted, her voice steady. "But in the Aurorium, we learn discipline. We don't let it show." She glanced over at Annabelle, raising an eyebrow with a teasing smile. "We try not to look like... that." She says, pointing her chin at Annabelle

Lisa snorted, and both girls broke into giggles.

"So," Sophie said after a moment, "you and Annabelle made up?"

"Yes," Lisa replied with a smile. "My goddess' animal spoke to me, he told me I should work on my relationships."

Sophie perked up. "Wait, your goddess has an animal too?"

"Yes," Lisa said. "A baby elephant named Erisol."

"War has a pet badger," Sophie told her. "I think his name is Titus... or maybe Timothy."

"My name is Titus," She hears the violet badger say in her mind.

24

Just then, Jeffie returned with a cup of milk. Sophie accepted it gratefully and drank it all in one go, finally soothing the heat from the peppers in her stew.

Annabelle, now fully recovered from her ordeal, sauntered up to the counter and leaned over toward Sophie. "That was a dirty trick, Copper," she said accusingly.

Sophie put on a mock innocent expression. "I have no idea what you're talking about," she replied in an exaggerated imitation of Annabelle's proper voice. "I was just enjoying Lisa's delicious stew."

Annabelle narrowed her eyes but couldn't help the smirk tugging at her lips. Lisa chuckled softly behind the counter as the crew continued laughing in the background. The three avatars stood together, the playful rivalry between them easing into a funny camaraderie.

Chapter 2

Journal Entry: April 20th, 1910

Themedium The Stormfang will dock at the Laminae port of Arcanum at midday to deliver the information boxes to Apex Tabitha Sanderlin. Through Brother Theodore, Captain Lowe conveyed the schedule with the calm certainty of a man who knows both the sea's mercy and its fury.

The Avatars continue to find their rhythms aboard the ship. Miss Fournier has taken to physical conditioning under Miss Griffin's disciplined guidance, their camaraderie growing with each session. Miss Salazar, ever diligent, sharpens her magical talents alongside Miss Nozaki, whose quiet mastery has not gone unnoticed by her mentor, Mr. Smith. This dynamic, these bonds, feel like threads tightening, a formation of purpose that is bound to grow.

[----- ⚓ -----]

Annabelle stood on the observation deck with Smitty, the ocean stretching endlessly beyond them. The salty wind tousled her hair as she demonstrated her progress with Maelstrom Mastery. Focused, she extended her hand and summoned a waterspout. Using mana shaping, she meticulously controlled the spell's structure, nearly perfect... until, just as the spout reached its peak, it burst apart with a chaotic spray of seawater. Droplets shimmered in the air like shattered glass.

Annabelle flashed a confident grin. "I just gotta work that last part out."

Smitty crossed his arms, brow furrowed. "What did ye do wrong, Belle?"

Her smile faltered. "I ain't doin' the mana shaping right," she admitted sheepishly.

Smitty snorted. "Aye, yer shaping mana like the green lass over there." He jerked a thumb over his shoulder toward Lisa, who glared daggers at the back of his head. "She dominates the sea, thinks she's only water."

"But it *is* only water," Lisa muttered under her breath, clearly insulted by the comparison.

"See." Smitty says to Annabelle with a grin.

Annabelle tapped her finger to her lip, mulling over his words. "So... I think I understand what yer sayin', but... what am I supposed to do different?"

"Less mana shaping," Smitty replied with a sigh. "Yer magic's not about forcing control. It coaxes the power of the sea, it flows with it, dances with it. Watch."

Smitty took a deep breath, centering himself. As he raised his hand, the water behind the ship surged upward in a graceful spiral. The spout rose like a polished cone, cresting in a plume of frothing white water shaped like a flower blooming in midair.

Annabelle studied every detail, recalling Smitty's earlier lessons: the rush of water drawn upward, spiraling with a natural rhythm. The plume danced at the top like a hat, itself a symbol of mastery and finesse.

"Now ye try," Smitty said.

Annabelle swallowed a witty remark, knowing Smitty's patience was thin. Instead, she nodded. "Aye." She took a steadying breath, exhaling slowly to calm her nerves.

This time, she pictured guiding hands, not rigid but fluid, like a dance partner, positioned at the waterline to direct the flow. The waterspout responded, spiraling higher than Smitty's had, powerful and elegant... until it reached the top. Instead of forming a plume, water exploded outward in all directions, raining down onto the Stormfang's observation deck with an audible splatter.

Annabelle groaned softly. Her arms ached, though not as sharply as before. The strain from all that mana shaping eased. She wiped a few droplets from her face, shaking her head.

"Well," she muttered with a hint of self-mockery, "at least it didn't hurt this time."

Smitty chuckled under his breath. "Progress, lass. Ye'll get it yet."

"And how was that?" Smitty asked, his tone curious but testing. He wanted to hear her explanation, to gauge how much she truly understood.

Annabelle considered his question. "It was easier to shape it this time. I got the spout to do almost what I wanted... but I couldn't get that fancy shape at the top like ye did." She flexed her fingers. "And my hands don't hurt like before."

Smitty nodded approvingly. "Aye, that takes practice. Everyone puts their own flair on spells. Yer daddy, Cap'n Salazar, used to create a full ship on top of his spouts."

Annabelle's face lit up at the mention of her father. She imagined how she might create a ship of her own...perhaps with sails made of frothing spray and a hull of spiraling water. The thought warmed her spirit.

"Yer learnin' real good, Belle," Smitty continued. "Once ye master this last bit, I've got a good spell for ye next."

Annabelle beamed with pride. "Well, I am a natural," she declared.

Smitty chuckled, shaking his head. "If ye say so, girlie." He pulled out a pocket watch from his vest and checked the time. "Any last questions? I've got duty in a bit."

Annabelle tapped her chin thoughtfully. "Hmm... oh! Hey, Smitty, when ye were on vacation at Islewind…"

"Magic, girlie," Smitty interrupted with a grin. "Questions about the magic. Got any o' those?"

Annabelle sighed, frowning playfully. "Nay, I think I got it."

"Good. See ye in a bit on the bridge, then." He stepped toward the door but paused to add, "Remember, ten spouts, ten waves. Alternate 'em: wave, then spout."

"Arrr!" Annabelle gave a cheeky salute.

Smitty shook his head with an amused smirk.

As he turned to leave, he passed Lisa, who was seated at a back table, sipping tea. He gave her a polite nod. "Miss."

Lisa glanced up and returned his greeting with a smile. "Have a good morning, sir," she said softly before taking another sip of her tea.

The door to the deck creaked shut behind him, leaving Annabelle to her thoughts, and her training.

Annabelle raised her hands and cast a wave spell. Using mana shaping, she coaxed the water into a high, broad crest that rolled with perfect form. She understood now, this training was meant to teach her the balance between mana channeling and shaping. The wave spell required steady channeling but only minimal shaping to control its breadth and height.

The wave crashed down with a satisfying roar. Annabelle took a breath and prepared for the next spell. This time, she summoned a waterspout. The exercise was the reverse of the wave: minimal channeling but a lot of shaping. It was a delicate balance, and while her gift from Chaos gave her plenty of mana, relying too heavily on channeling left her drained after each session.

She shaped the waterspout, letting it rise from the ocean like a spiraling column. Determined to get it right, Annabelle attempted to form the water at the top into a ship, just like her father used to. But instead of graceful sails and a hull, the water erupted clumsily, as if forced through an invisible boulder. She sighed. Shaping was more complex than she'd thought, especially when trying to create something too complicated.

After finishing the waterspout, Annabelle wiped her brow and decided to take a break. She made her way to the deck table where Lisa had set breakfast, a bowl of oatmeal topped with an array of fruit.

"Are you taking a break?" Lisa asked, arching a brow as she sipped her tea.

"Aye," Annabelle replied with a grin. "Been casting all morning. I need a breather." She grabbed the spoon and stirred the oatmeal, inspecting the contents. Strawberries, blueberries, and diced apples, though the apples had turned a curious shade of brown. Annabelle knew Lisa wouldn't serve anything spoiled, so she wondered what gave the apples that look.

She scooped up a generous spoonful and took a bite. The oatmeal's rich, comforting warmth melted across her tongue, the sweetness of the fruit perfectly balanced by the caramel-like flavor of the apples. Annabelle couldn't stop herself from closing her eyes and letting out an involuntary "Mmm."

Lisa giggled softly. "Glad you like it, Anna."

Annabelle blinked and tilted her head. "Anna?" she echoed. She was sure Lisa had heard Smitty and Kidd call her Belle, but this nickname was new.

"Um-hmm," Lisa said with a playful smile. "I like it. It suits you… sometimes." She gave Annabelle a wink.

Annabelle chuckled. "I don't know about all this." she joked before shoveling another spoonful of oatmeal into her mouth.

Lisa shook her head, still smiling, and continued eating her breakfast in companionable silence. The ship swayed gently beneath them, the calm sea a quiet witness to their growing friendship.

Sophie and Regina strode onto the observation deck, dressed in their workout clothes. They spotted Lisa and Annabelle at a table near the back wall, enjoying their breakfast oatmeal.

"Good morning!" Regina greeted them with her usual high-energy cheerfulness, shining as she waved.

"Hey," Sophie added more casually.

"Mornin'." Annabelle replied, swallowing a bite of oatmeal.

Lisa raised a hand in greeting while sipping her tea.

"Sophie and I had an idea," Regina said, practically bouncing on her heels. "While we're in Laminae, we should visit the Luminous."

"For what?" Lisa asked, curious.

"I need to find a ritual book," Regina explained, "something that'll show me how to tie Galahad to me. And Sophie wants a book to help her use her dad's magic." She flashed an eager smile. "The magic section in the Luminous is huge. I'm sure they've got stuff on Maelstrom Mastery and Earthbloom magic too."

Annabelle perked up, grinning at Sophie. "You can't do yer magic?"

Sophie rolled her eyes, smirking. "I can do the punching magic just fine. Want me to show you?" She playfully raised a fist as if ready to demonstrate.

"It may be fun," Lisa interjected smoothly, aiming to diffuse the playful tension between the two. Though she didn't have any pressing need to study her Earthbloom magic, the thought of spending time with her new friends appealed to her. Building stronger connections with all of them seemed more important than any book right now.

"Oh, we should tell Brother Marcus and Smitty," Annabelle said, shifting focus back to the idea. "Let 'em know we want to stop by the library before they start offloading Brother Al's boxes."

"You have to ask permission?" Sophie teased, raising a brow at Annabelle.

"Nay," Annabelle retorted, narrowing her eyes in mock defiance. "We just have to use the crane to get the boat out of the hold. Once they start offloading the boxes, we'll have to wait 'til they're done."

Sophie shrugged in mock surrender. "Fair enough." Hoping to steer the conversation elsewhere, she turned to Lisa. "So, what's for breakfast?"

"Oatmeal with caramelized apples and berries," Lisa answered, her face bright with pride.

"It's so good," Annabelle chimed in enthusiastically, scooping up another spoonful.

Sophie glanced at the steaming bowl of oatmeal and grinned. "I think I'm gonna need to get me some of that."

[-----✛-----]

"Is there somewhere we can hide Miss Griffin while the Aurorium Clan is aboard?" Marcus asked Yancy "Smitty" Smith, who stood calmly at the ship's wheel.

In his usual slow, melodic tone, Smitty replied, "There shouldn't be any reason for the Coppers to come aboard... 'especially since the purple girlie can't see 'em."

"Unfortunately, it's part of the deal," Marcus explained with a sigh. "Apex Sanderlin agreed to grant your crew passage, but only after we deliver the information they want. If any of your crew steps onto Laminae, they risk being detained, especially Miss Fournier and Miss Nozaki. They're separated from their families, which makes them vulnerable."

"I see," Smitty murmured thoughtfully. "But the Coppers and farmers don't wanna work together."

"True," Marcus acknowledged. "But that's the problem. Because they lack diplomatic ties with the Kingdom of Verdantia, the Aurorium will act faster, without giving us a chance to explain. No room for deference means no room for negotiation."

"Sounds complicated," Smitty muttered, shaking his head.

Before Marcus could respond, the avatars arrived on the bridge—Annabelle and Regina leading, with Lisa and Sophie close behind.

"Good morning, ladies," Marcus greeted warmly.

The avatars responded in their own ways:

"Hi!" Regina said with her signature enthusiasm.

Sophie gave a small wave, her expression serious.

Lisa waved with a smile.

"Brother Marcus," Annabelle added, "We're going to the library. Before ye offload Brother Al's boxes to the Coppers, ye'll need to put the pretty boat in the water."

Marcus paused, frowning slightly at her phrasing. Referring to his late mentor's name as *Brother Al* felt disrespectful. He opened his mouth to speak, but Smitty beat him to it.

"Did ye okay it with the Cap'n?" Smitty asked, looking past Marcus to Annabelle.

"I don't gotta ask," Annabelle said confidently. "'Tis goddess business."

Smitty silently stared at her, his eyes holding her to account.

Annabelle's bravado faltered. "I'll go and ask 'im," she muttered, turning to head into the captain's operations room.

Marcus took the opportunity to ask the others, "What will you ladies do at the Luminous?"

"There are some books we need to read," Regina answered.

"I doubt we'll have enough time to read multiple books," Marcus noted.

"Oh..." Regina's face fell as she pondered their options. "I guess we'll have to check books out then."

Marcus thought about the logistics and the complications awaiting them with the Aurorium. "It might be better if we drop the boat while we're out at sea. Then we can meet you at the Luminous after the offloading is done."

"Possible," Smitty replied. "We'd have to drop sails and anchors... but you're the customer, Brother."

Annabelle reappeared from the Captain's room. "The Cap'n says I can go if ye say it's okay," she said to Smitty, looking down at the deck in frustration.

"Did ye do yer exercises?" Smitty asked.

"Aye" Annabelle answered quickly.

"All yer exercises?" he pressed, his gaze flat.

Annabelle hesitated, her offense showing in her expression before she admitted, "No..."

"Ye can go after ye finish all yer exercises," Smitty said firmly. He turned to Marcus. "So, ye want to stop and drop the pretty boat?"

Marcus nodded. "Yes, if that's what the avatars want." He glanced at the remaining three, who exchanged looks and nodded their agreement.

Smitty gave the command in his slow, steady cadence. "Lower sails, drop drift anchors, and ready the crane."

The deck crew immediately set to work. Knots were untied, allowing the sails to drop to their crossbars with a soft thwump. The crew split into two teams: one managing the drift anchors, the other heading below deck to prepare the crane. The steady rhythm of coordinated labor echoed across the ship as they moved efficiently to carry out their tasks.

Regina and Sophie returned to their room to change into their outfits. Meanwhile, Lisa stayed behind in the galley, working with Jeffie to prepare for lunch service. She showed him how to reheat the gumbo she'd made earlier, ensuring that all he'd need to do was warm the pot and serve while she was gone.

On the observation deck, Annabelle focused on her training, casting her remaining nine waves and nine waterspouts in quick succession. Each one required precision and focus, but she pushed through, determined to meet Smitty's expectations.

Meanwhile, the crew worked efficiently, assembling the crane they had retrieved from below deck. With practiced coordination, they mounted it on the ship and hoisted the so-called "pretty boat", a mana-leeching vessel provided by the Order, out of the hold. Once the boat was lowered into the water, the crew released it from the crane's moorings. Hooks, one of the deckhands, rode down with the boat and secured it to a loop on the ship's hull to keep it steady. Afterward, he climbed back aboard using a rope ladder dropped over the side.

Marcus stayed aboard the Stormfang to oversee the transfer of Brother Albert's information boxes to the Aurorium Clan's investigators. Before the avatars departed, he pulled Sophie aside with a serious expression.

"If any member of the Aurorium Clan identifies you," Marcus warned, "they'll separate you from the others. Please, I beg you, exercise discretion while you're ashore."

Sophie nodded solemnly, understanding the gravity of his words.

The avatars then boarded the "pretty boat." Regina took the controls and, with a steady hand, guided it away from the ship and toward the Luminous. The early light glinted off the water, the boat cutting through gentle waves as they headed toward their destination.

[-----✿-----]

Regina brought the boat to a halt about 100 meters from the Luminous, her eyes narrowing at the sight of people standing around the docks and guarding the library's entrance.

"What's wrong?" Annabelle asked from the co-pilot seat.

"People are standing around the Luminous," Regina answered, her tone cautious.

Annabelle gave her a look that silently said, *So what?* Without a word, she reached into the boat's utility compartment and pulled out a small telescope. She extended it and surveyed the dock area, paying particular attention to the guards. "Aye, yer right. Looks like they've got people watching the pier."

"Let me see," Sophie said, holding out her hand.

Annabelle passed the telescope over, and Sophie peered through it. She scrutinized the formation of the guards, recognizing it instantly. It was a transportation hub formation, standard Aurorium protocol. To the untrained eye, it would seem random, with guards alternating between roving patrols and static posts. In truth, the formation followed precise timing intervals set by a command leader. Sophie adjusted the focus, zooming in on one of the people stationed as a lookout. Her stomach tightened when she spotted a Sentinel badge glinting on the guard's chest.

"The clan has this place locked down," she muttered aloud.

"Why is that a problem?" Lisa asked, confused by Sophie's reaction.

"They're Aurorium Sentinels," Sophie explained, lowering the telescope. "They're running a standard protection formation. For a building this size, there are probably multiple groups inside, led by a Shadow. If I go in there, there's no way they won't spot me."

Annabelle smirked. "Well, it was nice knowing ye, Copper. I'm sure we'll meet again someday," she teased, voicing what the others were silently thinking.

"Annabelle!" Lisa scolded, before turning back to Sophie. "What if they do not recognize you? Could you not just hide your badge in your pocket?"

Sophie shook her head. "It's not that simple. Marcus told me he spoke to Apex Sanderlin about me, meaning she warned Apex Molina meaning a detain on sight order would have gone out. They know my face by now." She ran a hand through her hair, frustration building. "Not to mention violet hair isn't exactly common."

"What if you didn't look like you?" Regina suggested brightly.

"Definite improvement," Annabelle quipped, only to receive a swift kick to the back of her chair from Sophie.

"No, no, no!" Regina exclaimed with a laugh. "I mean it. What if we change how you look so they don't recognize you?"

"That... could work," Sophie admitted, thinking it over. "But I don't have anything to disguise myself."

"I can handle that," Regina said with a grin. "I know a spell called Child's Play: Dress Up. It can change your appearance temporarily. No one would know it's you."

Sophie sighed, resigning herself to the idea. "Alright. Let's give it a try. What do I need to do?"

"Just sit still," Regina instructed. She pulled her wand from her dress pocket and began focusing her mana. The spell required visualization, so she imagined Sophie as a younger girl in a flowing blue dress with white accents. She pictured her hair as black, styled in full curls instead of its usual violet color.

Regina waved her wand and cast the spell. A shimmer of mana enveloped Sophie's body, forming an illusion that matched Regina's mental image. In a flash of light, Sophie's appearance transformed. Sitting where she had been moments before was a little girl, wide-eyed and dressed as Regina had pictured.

Lisa stared at Sophie in awe, marveling at how completely Regina's spell had transformed her. Only Sophie's skin tone and violet eyes remained the same. If Lisa hadn't witnessed the change firsthand, she would have thought this was an entirely different person. She considered the disguise thoughtfully and then asked Regina, "Won't her eyes give her away? Can you change their color?"

"If I do, she won't be able to see," Regina explained matter-of-factly.

Annabelle glanced back at Sophie, took one look at her childlike form, and burst into uncontrollable laughter.

Sophie ignored her, keeping her composure. "Thank you, Regina," she said. But the moment she spoke, she noticed something off, her voice had changed to match her appearance.

Annabelle doubled over, laughing even harder.

Sophie scowled. "How long will this spell last?" she asked, her tiny voice only making Annabelle laugh more.

"The spell will last as long as I keep channeling mana into it," Regina explained. "So, you'll have to stay close to me, or it'll fade."

"Okay," Sophie replied in her high-pitched voice, her irritation growing as Annabelle cackled all over again.

Lisa rolled her eyes. "Come on, Anna. That's just mean."

"Yeah, Anna," Sophie chimed in, crossing her arms and pouting theatrically. "Don't be a big dumb meanie."

Regina pushed the throttle lever forward, guiding the boat toward the pier at the Luminous. She mimicked the moves she'd once seen Sister Sallie make when docking here, steering with precision. She headed for the slip reserved for the family on duty, but her heart sank when she noticed a different boat already in the spot. It was a stark reminder, her family isn't on duty anymore. Her father and little brother were missing, and her mother, June, was hidden under Apex Sanderlin's protection.

Regina wondered which family was managing the Luminous now. It was likely the Phillips; they had four children, Michelle, Megan, Monique, and Katheryn. Six people to share the workload. It must have made things so much easier. The Fourniers had only been three, and when Regina was ten, library duty had kept them endlessly busy, especially at the Arcane Vault in Lorendale, a smaller town just a few hours from the capital.

She thought of her mother's solution back then: casting her Mystic Manifestation spells to create magical clones that dusted shelves and took out trash. Regina had struggled to master the magic system. Its rigid hexagonal mana patterns were too tricky for her to master, though her mother had reassured her she'd understand them when she was older. Mommy June wasn't magical at all, but was a genius when it came to crafts. She had cared for Regina's mom when illness had struck.

Lost in thought, Regina pulled the boat into a slip beside the reserved one. She misjudged the approach, and the boat struck the pier harder than intended. Everyone aboard lurched forward with the impact, then rocked back as the boat came to a stop.

"Oi!" Annabelle yelped. "Ye came in too strong, Regina."

"Sorry," Regina said, embarrassed as she reached to shut off the mana-leeching system. Before she could dwell on her mistake, she felt Sophie's hand on her arm, a firm but reassuring touch.

"Don't worry, Regina," Sophie said softly. Despite the childlike tone her spell gave her voice, the sincerity in her words was evident. "We'll find your family."

Regina turned and met Sophie's eyes. The illusion may have changed Sophie's appearance, but her unmistakable violet gaze carried the weight of her promise. Regina smiled, her heart lifting. "Thanks, Sophie."

"Aye," Annabelle added confidently. "There won't be a place in the Seven Kingdoms where they can hide from us."

Regina's smile widened. She felt fortunate that the Goddess of Change had brought these girls into her life. "Thanks, Annabelle," she said quietly.

Lisa placed a hand on Regina's shoulder, squeezing gently in silent support. No words were needed, her presence said enough. Together, they would face whatever came next.

The four girls disembarked from the boat and walked down the pier. Annabelle couldn't resist one more playful jab at Sophie.

"It's a bit scary out here, little missy," she teased, looking at Sophie's childlike disguise. "Wanna hold me hand?" Annabelle extended her hand dramatically.

"Okay," Sophie replied sweetly in her spell-altered, high-pitched voice. Without hesitation, she grabbed Annabelle's hand.

Annabelle grinned. "I've always been good with the wee ones..." Her words cut off abruptly as Sophie's grip tightened like a vice. Annabelle yelped and dropped to one knee in pain. "Oi!" she cried, loud enough to draw the attention of one of the Aurorium Sentinels patrolling nearby.

Lisa noticed the Sentinel glance their way, his eyes narrowing as he observed the commotion. Alarmed, she turned back toward Annabelle and Sophie and hissed, "Hey! Can you stop?"

Sophie immediately loosened her grip, returning to a standard handhold. "Sorry," she said, her childlike voice fitting perfectly with the innocent apology.

Annabelle stood, rubbing her hand. "Aye, sorry," she muttered sheepishly. The Cap'n and Smitty had always warned her that she played around too much. Now, Lisa's silent disapproval was drilling the lesson home.

Lisa quickly composed herself, wiping away any sign of frustration. She put on a polite smile, one she'd perfected through her finishing training, and glanced at the Sentinel to dispel any suspicion. The guard eventually looked away.

The four girls continued walking through the pier and past the guards. Most of the Sentinels paid them little attention beyond quick second glances. However, Sophie noticed one Sentinel holding his gaze a moment longer than the others. He whispered a question to a nearby teammate, his eyes occasionally flicking back to her.

Feeling uneasy, Sophie asked the others, "Do people ever stare at you because of your hair colors?"

Lisa turned and looked thoughtfully at Sophie, realizing this was probably the first time Sophie wasn't attracting attention due to her signature violet hair. "I do not know," Lisa replied with a hint of subtext. "I cut my hair once and I do not remember anyone paying me any less attention."

"The stupid boys at my school call me *old lady girl*!" Regina muttered bitterly, recalling that obnoxious boy Andy, who always teased her.

The others glanced at Annabelle for her thoughts. She shrugged and said, "I like it when people look at me. I don't waste my time askin' why."

The group reached the entrance of the library, climbed the stairs, and entered the main hall. Regina's eyes immediately fell on a boy about ten years old sitting at the reception desk. Her stomach tightened with anger as memories surfaced...Mattie, her little brother, had been here when that blood witch Hema threatened him with a giant transforming axe.

Regina clenched her fists until Sophie's firm hand gripped hers. "I'm sorry, Regina," Sophie whispered gently, squeezing her hand in quiet solidarity.

Regina took a calming breath and returned the squeeze. "It's okay, Sop—Suzie," she corrected herself, mindful of Sophie's disguise.

She approached the counter and spoke to the young attendant. "Good morning. Is there a ritual room open today?"

The boy looked up and frowned. "What's wrong with your hair?" he asked bluntly.

Annabelle bristled. "Oi, ye little..." She caught herself before swearing at the child. "I outta take you outside," she told him, eyeing him sharply. She noticed one of the Aurorium Sentinels nearby, turning his attention to her and quickly changing her tone. "If ye weren't so cute," she added with a grin that resembled a smile from a shark.

Lisa silently glared at the boy, clearly offended by the rude question.

"Nothing's wrong with our hair," Regina said firmly, then added, "What's wrong with your hair?" The boy shifted uncomfortably under her stare.

Before he could dwell on the insult, Regina smoothly changed the subject. "Is there a ritual room open today?"

The boy mumbled something under his breath, then pulled a large book from beneath the desk. After flipping through a few pages, he looked up. "Room four is open all day. Would you like to sign it out?"

[-----✝-----]

Marcus stood on the deck of the Stormfang, gazing down at the pier. Brother Theodore was there, flanked by a group of young Aurorium members, a horse-drawn cart positioned at the edge of the dock, facing toward the city. The deck crew worked efficiently, assembling the gangplank to lower it to the pier so the Aurorium work crew could begin unloading the boxes meant for Apex Sanderlin's team, The Investigators.

"Brother Marcus, how goes the day?" Captain Lowe's voice called out from behind.

"Good morning, Captain," Marcus replied as Lowe stepped up beside him at the railing, both men watching the activity below.

"Hell of a mornin'," Captain Lowe added with a wry grin. "Didn't expect I'd ever have a bunch of coppers on me ship."

Marcus nodded, offering a knowing smile. "The situation does make for strange bedfellows." He hesitated for a moment, studying the captain more closely. "Captain Kidd, if you don't mind, I have a question."

Lowe took a sip of his coffee and gave a nod, signaling for Marcus to continue.

"I've noticed that both you and Annabelle refer to the Aurorium Clan members as *coppers*. Where does that nickname come from?"

Lowe paused, clearly caught off guard by the question. He mulled it over for a moment before answering. "Among us privateers, there's always been fear of the Aurorium Clan arrestin' us for nothin'…lockin' us up in their copper handcuffs. We even have a sing-song about it."

Marcus considered this, then replied, "From what I understand, the Aurorium can't arrest anyone without an official order from one of the kingdoms."

"Sure thing, Brother Marcus," Lowe said with a shrug, not entirely convinced but not arguing the point.

On the pier, Brother Theodore reached the top of the gangplank and called out, "Permission to come aboard!"

"Granted," Smitty answered from the ship's bridge.

Theodore strode across the deck toward Marcus and Captain Kidd. He checked his watch and offered a polite smile. "Good morning, Brother," he greeted Marcus before turning to Lowe and extending his hand. "Good morning, Captain, Brother Theodore Massey."

"Top o' the mornin'," Captain Lowe replied smoothly, shaking Theodore's hand with a voice free of his usual patois. "Captain James Lowe."

35

Marcus raised an eyebrow, quietly amused. He recognized that shift Annabelle's tendency to adopt a *proper voice* when mocking others must have been learned from Lowe.

"Good to see you, Brother," Marcus said to Theodore, shaking his hand next.

"How have you been?" Theodore asked, his handshake firm and warm.

"Busy as always," Marcus replied. "And you?"

"Much the same. I've got an appointment with Apex Sanderlin later this evening. She's eager to learn everything she can about the avatars, their guide, and the Order."

At that moment, an Aurorium Eclipse reached the top of the gangplank, leading a small contingent of Aurorium members. The Eclipse was tall and broad-shouldered, dressed in denim pants, a white button-down shirt, and a brown leather jacket with his Eclipse badge pinned to the left breast. His olive complexion and jet-black hair gave him an imposing, dignified presence. He called out in a commanding voice, "Permission to come aboard!"

"Granted," Smitty responded from the bridge.

The Eclipse gestured silently, directing his group to gather at a spot out of the way on the deck before approaching the bridge himself. He halted in front of Marcus, Theodore, and Captain Lowe, his gaze locking onto Marcus.

"Brother Marcus?" he asked.

Marcus extended his hand. "Yes, that's me."

The Eclipse shook his hand firmly. "Eclipse Simmons," he introduced himself, then added, "Is the avatar Regina Fournier available?"

"Sorry," Marcus replied, "the avatars are off the ship right now. Is there something I can help you with?"

Simmons reached inside his coat and pulled out a sealed letter, handing it to Marcus. "A letter for young Miss Fournier from Apex Sanderlin."

Marcus accepted the letter, noting the red wax seal stamped with the Aurorium's "A." "I'll make sure she gets it," he promised.

"Thank you, Brother," Simmons said with a nod before turning and continuing toward the bridge to speak with Smitty.

"Brother Marcus, I've got a favor to ask," Captain Kidd said, his tone casual but thoughtful.

"Of course, Captain," Marcus replied, tucking the letter for Regina inside his journal for safekeeping.

"You see, Belle's got a birthday coming up, and I wanted to do something special for her," Kidd explained. He maintained his more refined voice, free of his usual pirate drawl. "I was hoping you could help me keep her in the dark about it."

Marcus smiled. "I'd be happy to help. But you should know... they all have a birthday coming up."

"What's that now?" Kidd asked, raising an eyebrow.

Marcus considered the Captain for a moment before replying. "You'll have to forgive me, Captain. You're so close to Miss Salazar that I sometimes forget how little you know about the other avatars." He paused to let the words settle. "All the avatars were born on the same day. They share a birthday."

"Is that always the case?" Brother Theodore interjected curiously. "Whenever there's more than one avatar?"

"It is," Marcus confirmed.

"Brother Theo, is your duty similar to Brother Marcus' here?" Captain Kidd asked, shifting his gaze to Theodore.

"No, Captain, it is quite different," Theodore explained. "While Brother Marcus is responsible for guiding and assisting the avatars, my duties focus on observing and recording the history of the Aurorium Clan. The Order has maintained a special relationship with the clan since shortly after they freed themselves from the Seven Kingdoms' control."

"So, you and Brother Marcus are like captains of different ships," Kidd suggested with a grin.

The two monks exchanged a glance before Marcus responded. "Not quite. Since I'm the avatars' guide, monks assigned to other duties are required to accommodate any requests I might make."

Brother Theodore said nothing but gave Marcus a flat, unimpressed look.

"Oh, so you could order him around," Kidd chuckled.

"I'd rather not," Marcus replied smoothly. "In my experience, people who are forced to help aren't usually very helpful. I'd much rather ask for their cooperation or convince them to assist willingly." He maintained a dignified smile, but there was a touch of humor behind his eyes.

Captain Kidd chuckled again, shaking his head. "Ye make a good point there, Brother Marcus."

[-----✝-----]

The three men made their way to Captain Kidd's operations room behind the bridge. The captain propped the doors open, wanting to keep an eye on everything happening aboard his ship. The Aurorium Clan or "Coppers", as Kidd referred to them organized themselves with precision and quickly got to work.

Eclipse Simmons took a position on the bridge, calmly overseeing the operation. He dispatched a shadow to manage the efforts in the hold, while splitting his team of twenty Sentinels into groups. Nine went below to load boxes onto the crane platform, five worked the crane to hoist and lower the boxes, and the remaining six transported boxes from the deck to the cart waiting at the far end of the pier, roughly a hundred meters away by Marcus's estimate.

The efficiency of the operation impressed Marcus. The patrol worked like a well-oiled machine, their movements swift and purposeful. Each crane lift brought a new platform, complete with Brother Albert's mountain of boxes from the hold. The deck team unloaded the boxes in unison, cleared the platform, and sent it back below for the next load. While they worked on deck, the transport team hauled boxes to the cart without delay.

Marcus found himself reflecting on Miss Griffin. The Sentinels reminded him of her, always focused and disciplined, wasting no time between tasks. He surmised that the constant presence of both an Eclipse on the bridge and a shadow in the hold likely motivated such focus.

Despite the sheer volume of cargo, the patrol filled the cart surprisingly quickly. Once loaded, the cart was sent off toward the village to be offloaded for Apex Sanderlin's team of investigators. Marcus expected the operation to pause at that point, but to his surprise, the Sentinels kept working. They continued to bring up boxes, stacking them neatly along the roadside as they waited for the cart to return.

Their tireless coordination gave Marcus a deeper appreciation for the structured nature of the Aurorium Clan. There was no wasted motion, no confusion, just constant, efficient progress.

[-----✿-----]

Inside the Luminous, Regina guided the other avatars through the library's extensive magic section, which was still under repair after her battle with Hema the Blood Witch. Familiar with the library's layout and systems, Regina naturally assumed the role of tour guide. She showed the others how to navigate the book indexing system.

Lisa needed the least help. As a student at Valorcrest Academy, she was already familiar with Laminaen indexing techniques. Annabelle and Sophie, however, required more detailed instructions, especially Annabelle, who had never dealt with anything more complex than ship logs and navigation charts.

Once oriented, Lisa headed straight for the section on Earthbloom magic, eager to find more information on her unique abilities. Annabelle sought out books on Maelstrom Mastery, her confidence growing now that she better understood mana shaping. Sophie found her Alrunia book near the ritual magic section.

Curious, Sophie dove into the text. She quickly learned that Alrunia operated through runes, which functioned like ritual circles. These runes allowed casters to perform a wide range of spells: engulfing targets in fire, creating portals, or even placing someone in a web that suspends their movements. For Alrunia's magic to work correctly, balance was crucial. The system required a careful relationship between several factors: the subject's size and density, the rune's dimensions, and the amount of mana infused to activate and sustain it.

The book cautioned against infusing too much mana into a rune, warning of a dangerous phenomenon known as mana backlash. To cast a rune-based spell on an inanimate object, the rune had to be carved or stamped directly onto the item. For human subjects, however, direct carving was forbidden due to the risk of erratic and unpredictable results.

One example described using a fire rune to thaw a block of ice measuring 7 centimeters by 7 centimeters. A two-centimeter-diameter rune, when infused adequately with mana, could melt the block in two minutes. A larger rune would complete the task more quickly but at a much higher mana cost proportional to the rune's size.

The final section of the book contained a catalog of runes, twenty pages in total, each rune accompanied by a short description of its function. Sophie counted them carefully, her mind already racing with ideas. If this magic truly came from her father's side of the family, she had much to learn, and even more before she could call herself a capable Alrunia mage.

Satisfied for the moment, she bookmarked the page on fire runes and continued flipping through the text, eager to discover more.

Meanwhile, Regina had her own challenges. She was certain her father had used a combination of ritual magic and his Artist's Majesty magic. This ability allowed him to create intricate ritual circles without physically drawing them. Regina had not inherited this magic, so she had to learn it like every other system. Complex rituals still required her to painstakingly draw the circles by hand. Her father had reassured her many times that, with practice, she'd eventually reach his level.

At the moment, Regina was focused on deciphering the symbols on the leather bracelet she had borrowed from her mommy June. The bracelet featured three distinct symbols intricately combined: a bonding sigil embedded within what looked like a summoning circle, both encased by an outer circle Regina couldn't quite identify. She scoured the ritual books for a match but found only fragments similar circles but never a complete replica.

It wasn't until Sophie suggested that the other circle might be a combination of two different ones that the solution clicked into place. Regina realized her father had merged a draining circle with a conduit circle. The draining circle leached mana from anyone it was attached to, while the conduit circle funneled that mana directly into the summoning circle. This setup kept Galahad's sigil active, allowing the guardian spirit to remain bound and ready to manifest as long as the wearer could provide him with mana.

On the reverse side of the bracelet's strap, Regina found a bonding circle imprinted with an ink fingerprint, most likely June's. This fingerprint bound her to the entire magical ensemble, linking her mana to the ritual system. The net effect was ingenious: the bracelet would drain a small, steady amount of mana from June while she wasn't in danger. However, when a threat arose, Galahad would manifest to protect her, requiring more mana until the danger had passed.

For someone like June, who wasn't a mage and had no other use for her mana, this system was perfect. Regina, however, was a mage. She needed her mana for a variety of spells and may have to use Galahad to protect her father and maybe Mattie if she felt like it.

After some thought, Regina devised a plan. She would modify the ritual so anyone wearing the strap could use it. Instead of altering the bracelet permanently, she would recast the summoning ritual with the same circles but add a new step: grafting the bonding circle to both the strap and a separate ritual mark placed on her own body. This modification would allow her to channel mana to Galahad without needing to wear the strap, making the system adaptable for both her and anyone else.

With her plan forming clearly in her mind, Regina smiled to herself. If this worked, it would enable her to create a protective item that allows Galahad to manifest around anyone with the strap in their possession.

Annabelle and Lisa had both found books about their respective magic disciplines, Maelstrom Mastery and Earthbloom, and decided to dive into their reading while Regina and Sophie continued their search. Annabelle excitedly noted a list of spells she couldn't wait to try and surprise Smitty with. One spell, Siren's Scream, disoriented enemies with a deafening, magical wail. Another, Riptide Strike, concentrated the raw force of the sea into her fists and feet, enhancing its impact. There were even summoning spells that could call upon sea creatures like octopuses, whatever those are, and sharks to attack foes. Annabelle resolved to ask Regina about them when they were alone again. Annabelle grinned, her imagination already racing with ideas.

Meanwhile, Lisa skimmed through the third Earthbloom manual, which focused heavily on combination methods. The entire volume emphasized using multi-layered spell circles to create more versatile effects. This conflicted with what her mistress, Hestra, had always taught her. Mistress Hestra had drilled into her that combination circles were "magic of the locusts", unnecessary complexity that diluted a mage's skill. According to Hestra, a truly skilled Earthbloom practitioner could achieve any effect with a single circle enhanced by carefully arranged runes. Yet, as Lisa turned the pages, she discovered techniques she had never considered before, new possibilities that challenged the rigid teachings from her upbringing.

After some time, Regina decided they had gathered enough materials. She fetched a cart and began stacking the books she needed for the Galahad ritual: four books on ritual circles and magic theory, a volume on Kiroku-Mbili magic, and a guide to Crystalmancy. Sophie added her book on Alrunia magic, while Annabelle placed her Maelstrom Mastery guide on the cart. Lisa added the third volume of the Earthbloom series.

At the front desk, the young attendant used a pair of side-by-side ritual circles to check out the books. He placed each book in the first circle and a stack of blank paper and ink in the second. With his hand between the circles, he activated the ritual spell. A flash of light and a puff of smoke later, a perfect copy of the book appeared in the second circle. The young man read a script to the girls, explaining that the books would only be good for a month; after that, they would break down and disintegrate.

Once all the books were copied, the four avatars climbed the staircase to the third floor and found an open door with the number four painted on it. They entered the room, closing the door behind them.

Regina turned to Sophie. "I'm going to end the disguise spell now," she said, raising her wand. The *Dress Up* illusion around Sophie dissolved in a flash of soft light. Sophie exhaled, making sure to stay out of sight from the door just in case someone happened to walk into the room.

Regina wasted no time preparing for the ritual. She retrieved a grease pencil from the room's materials kit and began drawing the concentric circles she had devised based on her research. Each circle had to be precise, the runes carefully positioned for the ritual to function correctly.

Once the preparation was complete, Regina tied the leather strap with Galahad's sigil around her wrist and stepped into the center of the circles. She took a steadying breath and raised her wand, methodically activating the spell circles one by one, starting from the outermost ring. The lines of each circle began to glow softly as the mana flowed into them, forming a web of magical energy around her.

With all the circles active, Regina began the summoning chant. Her voice echoed in the small room as she called forth Galahad, the guardian spirit bound to the sigil. The ritual would not only summon him but also forge a new bond between them. This was her father's legacy, and she was determined to get it right.

The glow of the circles intensified as the spell progressed, filling the room with a radiant, otherworldly light. The summoning was underway.

Regina closed her eyes and took a deep, steadying breath. The room fell into a tense stillness as she began the chant:

"From the depths of legend, where knights of old reside,
Arise, Galahad.
Avec un cœur d'acier et un bouclier de lumière,
Protecteur des innocents, dans la nuit la plus sombre.

I call upon your spirit, noble and true,

Bind yourself to me, for my aim is true.
Avec un lien incassable, nous ne ferons qu'un,
Défenseurs de la justice, sous le soleil couchant.

Galahad, Galahad, hear my vow,
To honor your name, I offer my strength without limits.
Avec un honneur inébranlable, avec une bravoure indomptée,
Le gardien, monsieur le chevalier Galahad."

The concentric spell circles flared with intense light, their runes glowing with brilliant light. The leather strap on Regina's wrist shimmered in unison, its sigil radiating a pulse of energy that synchronized with her mana. A sudden warmth spread from the sigil, as though threads of magic were stitching themselves into her very essence.

Then she heard him, not with her ears but within her mind.

"I am at your service, young mage," a deep, resonant voice declared.

Regina smiled, her eyes still closed, savoring the success of the ritual. "I am glad to have you, Sir Galahad."

The light of the circles gradually dimmed as the ritual completed, but the bond remained strong, a quiet hum of power connecting her to the guardian spirit with which she is now bonded.

Chapter 3

"So, I have to ask," Eclipse Simmons said, turning to Captain Kidd. "Why would anyone choose to stay a pirate? Is it just for the money?"

Captain Kidd chuckled, his voice warm and gravelly. "Privateer, matey," he corrected. "And the answer is simple…freedom. Oh, don't get me wrong, the coin's good, but some of these scallywags would sail for free if ye let 'em."

Eclipse glanced at the crew, watching as they moved tools and mended ropes. He raised an eyebrow. "They don't look too free to me. They crew your ship and answer to you. I've heard tales of pirate captains throwing men overboard on a whim."

"Pirates!" Captain Kidd scoffed. "Now that's a cursed lot, alright. We're privateers, different entirely. Pirates prey on their own, stirring up trouble with the law and making it hard to earn an honest coin. Callin' us pirates is like callin' you Aurorium folks Jiberau."

That word hit its mark. Eclipse's jaw tightened, and a spark of anger ignited in his eyes. Marcus noticed the tension as the captain's words hung in the salty air. Yet, Eclipse didn't rise to the bait. Instead, he exhaled slowly and replied, "Point taken."

Without missing a beat, Brother Theodore chimed in. "Perhaps what Eclipse Simmons meant, Captain, was: if a privateer values freedom so highly, why submit to anyone else's rules?"

"Aye, that's a fair question," Captain Kidd admitted, leaning back on the railing. "It's simple, really: *freedom ain't free*. Ye still need a safe place to sleep and a belly full of food. The seas are full of thieves and liars, and a lone man won't last long. Find a crew ye trust, and ye've bought yourself a fighting chance."

Eclipse nodded slowly, observing his sentinels at work. "It sounds like a hard life for a… privateer. Not all that different from the Aurorium clan in a way."

Captain Kidd grinned. "Aye, the coppers I met understand the trade-offs of freedom better than most."

Eclipse burst into hearty laughter, the earlier tension dissolving. "Privateers have been reciting that same rhyme since I was a Sentinel," he said, wiping his face.

"Rhyme?" Marcus asked, puzzled.

Captain Kidd nodded. "Aye, like most things, there's a rhyme about dealing with Aurorium folk. Care to recite it, Mr. Simmons?"

Eclipse thought for a moment before raising a finger. "*Watch ye step on dry land, 'cause them Coppers be ready to pinch, woman or man. If ye're fool enough to test their might, them Coppers will bind ye in cuffs day or night.* That about right?"

Captain Kidd's eyes sparkled with approval. "Close enough, matey. Where'd ye hear it?"

"I've traveled with more than a few privateer ships in my time, Captain." Eclipse replied with a knowing smirk.

"How is the life of an Aurorium similar to a privateer?" Marcus asked, mentally comparing Sophie and Annabelle as he tried to piece together their experiences.

"From the moment we're promoted to Sentinel, we have a mission quota to meet," Eclipse Simmons explained. "Missions bring income both to us and the clan. If you slack off, the whole clan suffers. That quota increases once you become a Shadow, and if you're promoted to Eclipse, it gets even worse."

"Like a captain's ledger," Captain Kidd said thoughtfully. "See, a captain may own their ship, but when they take on a crew, they're responsible for housing and feeding 'em. Everything costs, dock fees when you sit in port, supplies when you sail. And, of course, there's wear and tear on yer ship. So it's in your best interest to have a contract lined up before you leave port."

"Oh yes, that's how it is for us," Simmons continued. "Eclipses have Shadows and Sentinels under their command, and you're accountable to the village Apex for your patrol's quotas, not just your own. Depending on the Apex, you can spend hours poring over reports, making sure every last quota is covered before you can even think about handling your own."

The men nodded in understanding, empathizing with the burden of leadership.

Simmons paused, noticing a shadow signaling him from the deck, pointing toward a cart arriving at the End of the pier. He gave a quick thumbs-up before raising his voice. "Alright, you Coppers! Enough malingering! Get moving and finish the job!" His commanding tone sent the Shadows and Sentinels into action.

He then reached into his jacket and pulled out an envelope, sealed with the Aurorium's emblem, a stylized "A" in a wax seal. He handed it to Captain Kidd.

"This is a clearance order from Apex Sanderlin," Simmons said. "It protects you and your crew from arrest for past crimes. But let me be clear: this only applies to what's already on the record. If you start kidnapping or robbing banks, this becomes null and void."

Captain Kidd accepted the letter with a grin. "Aye, thanks, mate. We'll be sure to keep our noses clean."

[----------]

The Stormfang sailed to the Luminous to pick up the four avatars shortly after the Auroriums had secured Brother Albert's records. The avatars had completed their business at the Luminous and were already en route to rejoin the ship, making the reunion seamless. Wasting no time, the Stormfang set a course for Verdantia to fulfill its dual purpose: returning Lisa to her parents—who had been sending urgent messages to the Order demanding her return, a clue from Brother Albert's stack of boxes.

Once out on the open sea, the avatars reintegrated into the ship's daily life, passing the time by working on the ship.

Regina and Sparks collaborated on a project to build an oven, scavenging spare parts from Sparks' workshop. Regina augmented their efforts with a magical ritual from a book she had borrowed from the Luminous. It took her five attempts to get the spell just right, but in the End, the oven functioned perfectly. Delivering it to Lisa brought great excitement, though installation proved more complicated than expected.

The two had to modify the ship's structure, covering a nearby porthole to vent excess heat safely out to sea.

Meanwhile, Annabelle and Sophie transformed the cargo hold. With no cargo to store, Annabelle suggested standing up one of the two fighting rings. They rigged up the ropes and posts to form sturdy, square arenas, ready for sparring and training exercises. The hold now resembled a competitive training ground, perfect for honing combat skills during the voyage.

[-----✿-----]

The next morning, Regina and Sophie faced off in the fighting ring. They had already completed their weight training and a run around the hold, a bonding experience Regina enjoyed, though she found running insufferably dull.

Both wore boxing gloves, just big enough to prevent Sophie, the *purple people beater*, from knocking out Regina, the *foxy silver boxer,* with a single clean shot. Regina had removed her Galahad strap for the session; the spirit couldn't distinguish between a training punch and a real threat, and she didn't want it activating mid-spar.

In the ring, both young women held their hands high in a defensive stance. Sophie's posture was tight and deliberate, her movements fluid like a dancer's. Her violet eyes scanned over her gloves, searching for any large opening in Regina's defense. She wasn't planning to go easy, sloppiness would be punished, but she also didn't want to discourage her new training partner by going too hard.

Regina's stance, by contrast, was more rigid. Her arms were raised straight up and down, shielding her face and chest. Galahad had advised her that this position would minimize damage against someone as skilled as Sophie. Peering through a small gap in her hands, Regina looked for any weakness she could exploit.

Sophie tested Regina's guard with a series of jabs, once, twice, three times. Regina's defense surprised her. Though Regina didn't shift her body to absorb the punches, she also didn't falter under the blows to her forearms. Sophie threw another probing jab, but this time Regina saw her chance. Timing her counter perfectly, she stepped in with a quick straight punch as Sophie retracted her hand.

The punch landed square on Sophie's chin. Caught off guard by the speed and proximity, Sophie stumbled slightly, eyes widening.

"Not bad," she muttered, recovering quickly. But now it was her turn. She retaliated with an overhand right, aiming to make Regina pay for the chin shot.

Regina saw the punch coming and tried to duck under it, setting herself up for another counter. However, she didn't duck far enough. Sophie's fist grazed the top of her head, sending a sharp jolt of pain through her skull. The impact disrupted her focus, and as her downward momentum continued unchecked, Regina lost her balance and tumbled awkwardly to the mat.

"Regina!" Sophie gasped, her stance dropping as she rushed forward, eyes wide with concern. "Are you okay? I didn't hurt you, did I?"

Regina shook her head quickly, blinking through the throbbing ache. "No, I just tripped," she lied, trying to sound nonchalant.

Sophie frowned but stepped back, giving her space. Regina inhaled slowly, willing the pain to subside. She wasn't about to let one glancing punch end their sparring session.

Regina adjusted her gloves and nodded. "I'm ready. Let's go."

44

The pair silently agreed to resume the round. Regina shifted her stance, widening the gap between her forearms slightly to improve her view of Sophie while maintaining a solid defense. Sophie noticed the adjustment and threw a probing jab toward the opening. Regina quickly brought her arms in to block, successfully defending, but unable to counter.

Regina retaliated with a pair of quick jabs. Sophie blocked them and returned fire with a jab of her own, which Regina deflected easily. They circled each other, testing and probing with short, tactical punches.

As they danced around the ring, Sophie noticed Regina's left arm dropping slightly. Fatigue, she assumed. Seeing an opportunity, she moved swiftly, aiming a straight right punch for Regina's chin.

But Regina had been baiting her. With a calculated step to her right, she dodged the incoming punch and trapped Sophie's arm with a quick right jab. Before Sophie could recover, Regina followed up with a left hook to her ribs. The strike landed cleanly, making Sophie wince. Fortunately, Regina didn't have Sophie's raw punching power...but still, *it stung*.

Sophie backed up, gathering herself.

"I got you again!" Regina cheered, bouncing in place and pumping her fists in the air triumphantly.

Sophie sighed, shaking her head with a half-smile. *Okay, that's enough playing around.* She knew she had been going too easy on Regina, but that wouldn't help her partner improve. She was going to have to step it up not out of embarrassment, of course. No, definitely not.

"Alright, alright," Sophie muttered, resetting her stance and narrowing her eyes.

They stepped in again, trading punches. This time, Sophie didn't hold back. She led with two sharp jabs, putting more force behind them. Regina blocked but struggled to counter, forced to maintain her guard. Sensing the pressure, Regina tried to step back and reset, but Sophie stayed on her, closing the distance and hammering her guard with another punch.

With a quick follow-up, Sophie unleashed a three-punch combination. The flurry broke through Regina's defense, creating an opening. Sophie capitalized instantly, driving a straight punch into Regina's chin.

The hit landed hard. Regina's head snapped back, and her legs gave out beneath her. She fell to her knees on the mat, tears welling in her eyes from the shock and pain.

Sophie froze, guilt flashing across her face. She hadn't meant to hit that hard. Stepping closer, she softened her voice. "I'm sorry... I didn't mean to...are you okay?"

Regina blinked rapidly, trying to shake off the pain. "I'm fine," she called out, though her eyes told a different story.

Sophie sighed, offering her a hand. *Tough girl*, she thought, admiring Regina's determination despite the obvious hurt.

Regina raised her hand to stop Sophie from pulling her up to her feet. She couldn't let herself break down...*not now*! If she couldn't endure this, how could she hope to save her father and Mattie?

"No," she said firmly, even as tears streamed down her face. "It's okay. I'll be okay." Wiping her face quickly, she stood tall, determination pouring from her like a geyser. "I want to keep going."

Sophie hesitated. "Maybe we call it a day with the hitting practice," she suggested, raising her gloved hands in a gesture of surrender.

But Regina had already set her stance, her body tense with resolve. Tears, still hot and defiant, traced down her cheeks. "I'm good. LET'S GO!" she barked, launching a straight punch.

She meant to aim for Sophie's raised glove, but her strike veered slightly and landed squarely on Sophie's chin. The impact froze Sophie in place. The pain shot through her jaw, forcing her to reevaluate the situation. *Damn*, she thought, shaking her head slightly. *When Regina wanted to, she could hit with the power of a mule kick.* Tears threatened to rise in Sophie's eyes, but she pushed them back, hearing her mother's voice echo in her memory: We are Aurorium, we don't solve our problems with tears.

Sophie's eyes sharpened, her focus homing in on her silver-haired sparring partner. "Fine, then," she said, resetting her stance with a serious expression.

Regina's heart skipped. She'd seen Sophie fight before. *Had she crossed a line?* Quickly, she raised her guard, keeping a wary eye on Sophie, who stepped in with two jabs, light but probing. Regina blocked them easily, but Sophie followed up with a powerful right straight, crashing into her guard and knocking her arm away from her face.

The force of the blow sent Regina stumbling back on her heels. She saw Sophie winding up for another punch, this time a left straight aimed directly at her. Regina knew she wouldn't be able to block in time. Her instincts told her to brace for impact. Eyes squeezed shut, she waited for the hit that never came.

After a few seconds, she cautiously opened her eyes. Sophie stood frozen, her gaze fixed on something behind Regina.

Sophie's face was blank, her violet eyes wide with shock. Behind Regina, she saw him…Titus, War's purple badger, standing as battle-ready as he had been the last time she'd seen him in War's castle. He stared at her silently, his presence both unsettling and familiar. Slowly, Titus faded like smoke on the wind.

"Sorry," Sophie whispered, her voice barely audible as she blinked away the vision. Shaking her head, she looked at Regina and added, "I... I think I need to stop for today. I'm not feeling so good all of a sudden."

Regina blinked, still confused but inwardly relieved. She had narrowly avoided a brutal punch. "Okay," she said, her voice cautious. "Are you sure you're alright?"

"Yeah," Sophie replied, though her voice lacked its usual steadiness. She tugged her glove off with her teeth and exhaled deeply. Walking to the ropes, she sat on the middle one and held it open, creating a path for Regina to leave the ring.

Regina hesitated for a moment, studying Sophie's expression, but then stepped through the opening. The training session had taken an unexpected turn, and she wasn't sure what to make of it.

Regina slipped through the ropes and exited the ring, pulling off her gloves as she went. Sophie followed, removing her second glove with her hand. They stored their gloves in a small, floor-locked cabinet near the ring.

Regina glanced at Sophie, unsure what had just happened. Sophie seemed distant, her expression clouded with thought. Hoping to break the tension, Regina spoke up. "Hey, I've been thinking about that punch spell you use. I think you could modify it to make it a more powerful hit."

Sophie blinked, pulled from her swirling thoughts. "What? How?" she asked, her mind still half-stuck on the vision of Titus.

Regina crossed her arms and explained analytically, "If you add a second spell circle, after the stabilizing one, facing outward from your fist, it should detonate directly into your target."

Sophie raised her hand in front of her, concentrating. She slowly wove two spell circles in the air, one facing inward and the other outward, as Regina described. The second circle proved more difficult than she expected; its shape faltered and became uneven. Cautiously, she didn't channel any mana through them, unsure what might happen with the unstable formation. Feeling the strain in her hand, Sophie frowned. "Yeah, that's tricky," she admitted, letting the circles dissipate.

Regina nodded. "If you can get it to work, though, it'd be like punching with an exploding fist."

Sophie mulled it over for a moment, flexing her fingers. "Exploding fist, huh?" she considered, a slight grin tugging at the corner of her mouth despite the earlier unease.

The tension between them eased a little as they continued walking together.

[----- ⚓ -----]

On the observation deck, Annabelle was deep into her morning training with Smitty. She conjured waves and waterspouts in rapid succession, alternating hands, waves from her left, spouts from her right. She was still trying to form the shape of a ship atop her spouts, but so far, all she could manage was something vaguely resembling the underbelly of a vessel.

As she cast each spell, she noticed Smitty watching her closely. He seemed impressed by her progress.

"And that makes ten," Annabelle panted, catching her breath after the relentless casting session.

"Yer gettin' better with yer magic," Smitty complimented, nodding in approval. "But ye still haven't decided the shape of yer spout."

"I have!" Annabelle shot back confidently. "I'm gonna make a ship. Just like me, da."

Smitty scratched his head and gave her a thoughtful look. "That's a tough one, Belle. Maybe ye should try somethin' simpler first. Work your way up to a ship."

"Nay," she replied firmly, crossing her arms. "No half steps."

Smitty chuckled. "Alright, alright. If ye're that determined, I'll teach ye a new spell. This one's fer fightin', so pay close attention."

Annabelle's curiosity piqued. She wondered which spell he had in mind. Over the last night, she had been secretly studying the Maelstrom mastery book she borrowed from the Luminous with Regina. Maybe Smitty was about to teach her one of the advanced spells she'd read about like that Riptide Strike, Summon Sea Monsters, or perhaps even the legendary storm spell hidden behind a warning that only masters should attempt it.

Smitty conjured a stream of water from his palm. "First, ye're gonna do a basic water conjurin'," he explained. The water shot forward, but before it could reach Annabelle, Smitty swirled his hands, guiding the water to encircle him. The column expanded, forming a protective bubble around his body.

"Then, ye coax the sea to protect ye," he continued, his voice distorted by the rushing water. "If ye do it right, the sea's protective love will shield ye from any attack. Go ahead, try and hit me."

Annabelle saw this as her chance to show off. She recalled the Riptide spell from her studies, the one where a mage summons the sea's power to enhance their attacks. Focusing her energy, she concentrated the spell's force behind her left ankle and heel. With a swift roundhouse kick, she aimed for Smitty's protective seashell shield.

Her kick connected, and the impact was explosive. The spell caused a torrent of seawater to burst across the observation deck, soaking everything, including Lisa, who stood on the far side of the deck in a dress gifted to her by the Order. The wave sent Annabelle flying into a distant table, knocking it and a nearby chair loose from their secured clamps. Smitty, however, remained firmly in place, his shield intact.

Seeing Annabelle sprawled on the floor, Smitty rushed over to her. "What were ye doin', girlie?" he asked, kneeling beside her to check if she was alright. "Are ye okay, Belle?"

Still lying on the floor, Annabelle gave him a thumbs-up, her signature devilish grin spreading across her face. "I'm good," she said, brushing off the crash. "Almost got ya, Smitty."

Smitty's concern faded, replaced by an exasperated look. He crossed his arms. "And who taught ye the Riptide strike?"

"No one taught me," Annabelle replied as he helped her to her feet. "I read it in a book."

"Oh, so ye read magic books now, do ye?" he asked, his tone accusing.

"Just me magic books," Annabelle shot back with a smirk. "No point readin' about stuff I ain't gonna do."

Smitty gave her a skeptical look. "Did ye read about the seashell shield too? Because, girlie, ye ain't ready for Riptide yet."

"Looked pretty good to me," she said, adjusting her bandana to keep her wild hair in place.

"If it was that good, ye wouldn't have lost the clash," Smitty pointed out. "I'd be the one on me back, and ye'd be standin' tall."

Annabelle huffed but didn't argue. The pair returned to their original positions, ready to continue training.

"Alright then," Smitty said, a grin creeping onto his face. "Show me this sea shell spell, Miss book reader."

"Aww, Smitty," Annabelle groaned, "this spell is so boring. I can't even use it to hit people!"

Smitty raised an eyebrow. "Are ye complainin'... again?"

Annabelle saw him preparing to walk away and quickly backtracked. "Sorry, First Mate," she said sheepishly.

"Don't be sorry, girlie," he corrected her. "Get busy. *Sea shell*, let's see it."

Annabelle sighed and focused. She thought back to Smitty's demonstration and what the book had said about conjuring water into a protective sphere. She waved her hands, summoning seawater with one hand and guiding it into a bubble around herself. The book had explained that a proper sea shell was a perfect sphere, reinforced by the caster's mana to become nearly impenetrable. Regina had even explained that word to her...impenetrable. Annabelle smirked, feeling proud of herself as she infused more mana into the swirling water.

She noticed that by making the walls of the shell thicker, she could increase its strength, though it meant sacrificing some space inside. The more mana she pumped into it, the sturdier the shell became.

"Let's see ye get m—OW!" Annabelle yelped mid-sentence as water unexpectedly surged into her foot with the force of a rock. The sharp pain broke her concentration, and the shell exploded, drenching both her and Smitty in a wave of seawater.

Small splashes reached Lisa, who was hunched over nearby, trying to keep her fresh croissants dry. She recoiled and screamed, "Why does it smell so bad?! It is just water!"

Smitty chuckled. "Nay, missy. 'Tis not just any water—it's the sea, same as what we're sailin' on."

Annabelle burst out laughing as Lisa sniffed her hair and grimaced. "By the harvest, I'm going to need another shower," Lisa muttered in dismay.

Annabelle grinned mischievously. "I don't think that'll help, princess. The sea won't wash away with just a bit o' water."

Lisa shot her a glare. "Oh, you think that's funny, huh?" With a huff, she grabbed Annabelle's croissants and shoved both into her mouth in one swift move.

"Oi! Princess, don't be like that," Annabelle groaned, disappointed. "I was lookin' forward to those! Bet they tasted like a piece o' the good life."

Lisa, still fuming, stood up with her oatmeal. "Hmph," she huffed, and as she walked away from the observation deck, she deliberately knocked over Annabelle's oatmeal bowl, spilling it across the planks.

"Oi! Now ye're just wastin' food!" Annabelle cried in exasperation. She turned to Smitty. "Can ye believe her?"

Smitty shook his head, laughing. "Aye. Yer sister's quite the handful."

"Sister?" Annabelle repeated, eyes wide. "What do ye mean?"

[-----✝-----]

After breakfast, Marcus settled at a table on the observation deck, setting out a pad of paper separate from his journal. He used this pad to organize the facts he and the avatars had uncovered.

Despite his efforts, an uneasy thought gnawed at him: *if he could just figure out the conspiracy's true goal, maybe he could shake the feeling that they were being stalked.* It was as if the conspiracy's agents lurked just out of sight, waiting to strike.

Marcus knew *one thing for sure, the avatars are targets, just as Isabella and Gretta had been.* But the question that haunted him was whether the conspiracy existed long before the discovery and recruitment of the avatars, or if their emergence had triggered its formation. According to Brother Albert, the conspiracy was connected to a series of crimes and clandestine actions across the Seven Kingdoms. One recurring thread was the involvement of the overpowered witches, like the case of a prince who had died mysteriously in his sleep, his heart frozen solid as though he'd been abandoned in the icy peaks of Stoneridge.

His thoughts were interrupted by the familiar voice of Popper, one of the crew members who had taught him how to play crew. The man strolled over with a grin.

"Good mornin', Brother," Popper greeted. "Fancy gettin' in on a couple of hands of crew?"

Marcus smiled, closing the pad. "Sounds like fun," he replied, standing to join Popper and Harmon. A few rounds of cards might be precisely what he needed; a distraction that could help him connect dots he hadn't seen before. Sometimes, insight came when you least expected it.

With that thought, he joined the game, leaving behind his scattered notes and the cold cup of coffee on the table.

The trio of men sat at the table as Popper dealt each player five cards, then turned over the top card to start the discard pile.

Marcus picked up his hand, careful to keep the cards hidden from view. He had the Queen of Hearts, Queen of Clubs, Five of Diamonds, Ten of Hearts, and Seven of Spades. From what he knew of the game, his best chance lay in the pair of queens, but he decided to play it safe and see what fortune would bring.

Harmon drew a card from the top of the deck, examined it briefly, and placed the Ten of Spades on the discard pile.

Marcus saw an opportunity. He picked up the Ten of Spades and discarded his Seven of Spades, feeling more confident now with two possible pairs, queens and tens, giving him a path to victory.

Popper drew from the deck and, after a few moments of consideration, discarded the Eight of Diamonds. Harmon followed, pulling a card from the deck and placing the Jack of Clubs onto the discard pile.

When Marcus drew next, luck was on his side. He pulled another Queen—Queen of Diamonds—and smiled as he placed it on the table in front of him, followed by his other two queens, leaving him with the ten of hearts and spades. He discarded the Five of Diamonds and sat back. One more ten would give him a double load and clinch the pot.

Popper drew from the deck and discarded the Jack of Hearts. Harmon pulled a card next and discarded the King of Diamonds. Marcus drew with anticipation, hoping for a ten, but pulled the King of Hearts instead. Frustrated, he placed it on the discard pile.

On his next turn, Popper picked up the discarded King of Hearts and laid down his load: three kings, the King of Hearts, King of Spades, and King of Diamonds. He discarded the Ten of Diamonds, just out of Marcus's reach. Harmon didn't hesitate and snatched the Ten of Diamonds, laying down his own load of three cards, the Eight, Nine, and Ten of Diamonds. Now, all three players had only two cards left, each hoping to complete a second load and maximize their winnings.

Marcus felt the tension build. He needed that final ten, but the plan he had banked on now felt like a noose tightening around his neck. Still, he was in for a coin, might as well go all in for a gold. He drew from the deck, revealing the Five of Diamonds. *Not my card*. He placed it on the discard pile.

Popper paused, considering the card. He chose to draw from the top of the deck instead, then discarded the Eight of Spades. Harmon followed suit, discarding the Nine of Hearts.

Marcus pulled another card, the Four of Diamonds. His frustration deepened. He placed it on the discard pile and exhaled sharply.

Popper drew the Four of Diamonds, smirking as he discarded the Seven of Diamonds and made the play of selling his debt: the Three of Spades and Four of Diamonds, for a total of seven. Harmon laid down his remaining cards, a Six of Clubs and Five of Diamonds, totaling eleven. Marcus was left with the two tens in his hand, totaling twenty.

"Come home to daddy," Popper grinned, dragging three of the six coins in the pot toward him. He left three coins for the next round, then tossed an extra coin onto the table to raise the pot to four.

Marcus sighed but smiled. The game wasn't over yet.

Marcus and Harmon each added a coin to the pot in the center of the table. Harmon collected the cards and began shuffling.

Marcus reflected on his previous mistake, he'd been too rigid in his planning, putting himself in a position where he needed a single card to win. *I won't let that happen again, he resolved.*

Once the shuffle was complete, Harmon dealt out new cards, and each player picked up their hand. Marcus reviewed his: Five of Diamonds, Seven of Diamonds, Eight of Hearts, Two of Clubs, and Jack of Spades. His only viable strategy appeared to be building a run with the five, six, and seven of diamonds.

Since Harmon was the dealer, Marcus had the first turn. The face-up card on the discard pile was the Queen of Spades, which didn't help his plan. He drew from the deck and received the Seven of Hearts. Deciding it might be helpful later, he kept it and discarded the Jack of Spades.

Popper drew a card, added it to his hand, and discarded the Ten of Diamonds. Harmon followed by drawing and discarding the Eight of Clubs.

On his next turn, Marcus drew from the deck and pulled the Nine of Hearts. His eyes lit up, he now had a run he hadn't considered: Seven, Eight, and Nine of Hearts. Feeling optimistic, he placed the run on the table and discarded the Seven of Diamonds, holding onto the Five of Diamonds and Two of Clubs.

Popper drew his next card, kept it, and discarded the King of Clubs. Harmon drew a card, kept it, and placed the Nine of Diamonds on the discard pile.

Marcus drew again and found a Two of Hearts. A run of twos could work, he thought. It would also prevent him from being stuck with high cards at the end. He kept the card and discarded the Five of Diamonds.

Popper picked up the Five of Diamonds and laid it down with two more fives for a full load. He then discarded the Four of Diamonds. Harmon drew from the deck and, after a moment, discarded another Nine of Diamonds.

Marcus pulled a card from the deck. It was the Three of Spades. Seeing no use for it, he placed it on the discard pile. He glanced between Popper and Harmon, weighing his options, then decided to sell off his hand. He placed both of his twos on the table for a total of four points.

Popper revealed his remaining cards: the Four of Diamonds and the Ten of Clubs, giving him a total of fourteen.

Harmon sighed, waving his hand in defeat. He placed his cards face down on the table. "Ye got me, mate," he grumbled, shaking his head.

Marcus chuckled, feeling more confident in his strategy this time. Half of the pot remained, and the game continued.

Feeling satisfied with his win, Marcus collected two coins from the pot and began shuffling the cards. Harmon and Popper each tossed a coin into the pot, bringing the total back to six. As he shuffled, Marcus reflected on how he'd secured the victory. His success stemmed from adapting his strategy to capitalize on opportunities rather than waiting for ideal circumstances. That shift had caught his opponents off guard and left them scrambling to adjust.

Dealing cards to Popper, Harmon, and himself, Marcus pondered how they might play this round. Both he and Popper were ahead, while Harmon was down two coins. Marcus figured Harmon might get aggressive this hand, trying to win some of his coin back.

After dealing the final card, Marcus placed the deck on the table and flipped over the top card to reveal the Seven of Diamonds.

He reviewed his hand: Ten of Hearts, Ace of Spades, Six of Diamonds, Jack of Clubs, and Two of Hearts. Not much to work with right now.

Popper led the round, drawing a card from the top of the deck. He added it to his hand and discarded the Eight of Clubs. Harmon drew next and placed the Queen of Diamonds on the discard pile.

Marcus surveyed his hand, seeing no immediate use for the Queen. He drew from the deck and pulled the Four of Spades. *Not bad*, he thought, keeping it and discarding the Ten of Hearts. Without a clear strategy yet, he decided to trust the deck and see what came his way.

Popper snatched up the Ten of Hearts and laid down a run of three tens, Hearts, Clubs, and Spades. He discarded the King of Hearts, causing Harmon to shake his head in frustration. Harmon drew from the deck, glanced at his card, and smiled before laying down a four-card run: Five, Six, Seven, and Eight of Hearts. He discarded the Three of Spades.

Marcus's mind raced. Why would Harmon drop the Three of Spades? He reasoned that Harmon was likely holding either an Ace or a Two and planning to sell his debts soon. Marcus needed to move fast. He drew from the deck and found the Ace of Hearts. Perfect. He added it to his hand and discarded the Six of Diamonds. Still, he wasn't confident it would be enough to secure the pot.

Marcus caught the grin on Harmon's face when he didn't lay down a load. *He's planning to cash out*, Marcus thought grimly.

Popper drew next, placed a card in his hand, and discarded the Nine of Spades. He leaned back with a grin. "I gots me a story," he said, laying down the Two of Diamonds.

"Once, when I was workin' on a ship, I found me a treasure map pointin' to a faraway island." He added the Queen of Hearts to the table. "When I got there, I never found the treasure, but I did find the love o' me life. She was such a good woman, I quit the privateer game and settled down with her on a farm."

Harmon tossed the Ace of Clubs onto the table with a frustrated sigh. "These damn cards. That's it for me," he muttered before standing. "I'm gonna get me some sleep." Without another word, he walked off.

Popper leaned over and swept three of the six coins from the pot into his pocket. He then gathered his other coins and the cards. "I think I'll call it a day too. Good day to ye, Brother Marcus," he said with a grin.

"Have a good day, Mr. Popper," Marcus replied, handing back his cards.

Once the deck was cleared and the men left the observation deck, Marcus turned his attention to his notes. He hoped to find new insight, but the tangled web of the conspiracy remained maddeningly opaque. His thoughts drifted, and he imagined himself seated at a different table, a symbolic game of crew, with Brother Albert,

Hema, Mage, Isabella, and Gretta, plus a shadowy figure he dubbed "The Conspirator."

In this mental game, the players revealed their cards in turn, each one representing a key event:

-Gretta laid down a card signifying the attack on the Aurorium village.

-Mage followed with a card representing the assassination attempt on Miss Salazar.

-Isabella's card depicted her role in the village attack.

-Hema, however, placed her card face down—Marcus had no information about her actions during that time.

-The Conspirator played an unknown card.

-Brother Albert laid down a card indicating the first contact with the avatars.

When it was Marcus's turn, he skipped it; at that stage of the game, he had not yet entered the conspiracy's orbit.

Marcus pondered the motives behind Gretta and Isabella's actions. He knew that Gretta's village had suffered after the Aurorium Clan arrested many of its people for counterfeiting Verdantian Harvest Crowns. The village's collapse led to Gretta's disappearance, but she re-emerged as part of the conspiracy. But was that enough to justify such large-scale violence?

And Isabella, was her presence at the massacre evidence that the attack was central to the conspiracy's goal? Were they freeing a prisoner, preventing the clan from taking action, or accomplishing some other hidden objective?

Next, Marcus imagined Mage's role. Miss Salazar's assassination clearly seemed to serve some purpose, as Mage hadn't attacked anyone else on the Stormfang. Salazar must have been her priority target.

As the game progressed in his mind, Gretta, Isabella, Mage, and Hema played unknown cards. The Conspirator played a card symbolizing the attack on Miss Griffin. *Why had the Conspirator sent an unknown assassin in a leather hat instead of deploying Isabella or Gretta?* Could the attack on the Aurorium village have been so high a priority that resources were diverted, leaving Miss Griffin's fate to a secondary force? Perhaps the situation had shifted, forcing the Conspirator to adjust their strategy on the fly. That might also explain why the attack on West's Tavern had been so chaotic, allowing the avatars to escape even though it cost Brother Albert his life.

Brother Albert's next card in the game represented him explaining the conspiracy to the avatars.

The following turn saw more unknown moves from Gretta, Mage, and Hema. Isabella played a card showing her role in the attack on West's Tavern and her attempt to seize Brother Albert's journal. The Conspirator countered with a card symbolizing the second assault on the tavern—this time by the mysterious man in the leather hat. *What was the purpose of that second group?*

Marcus found it hard to believe Isabella couldn't overpower the avatars before they received their goddesses' gifts. *Was the second wave meant to ensure Isabella's success? Or did the unknown attackers have their own objective—perhaps to capture or kill the avatars?*

More unknown cards followed. Isabella played one depicting her near-fatal attack on Brother Albert with her machine creature. The Conspirator played another card with the same leather-hat faction. *Why had they persisted? Marcus could only assume that the second group had its own goal, one separate from Isabella's.*

Finally, Brother Albert played his last card, representing his sacrifice to wound or kill Isabella and give the avatars time to escape. In Marcus's mind, Albert silently stood from the table and walked away.

Marcus exhaled, trying to piece together the grander plan. *Was the attack on the Aurorium village meant to cripple the clan's ability to stop Isabella from obtaining the journal?* That seemed excessive for a single objective. There had to be more at play.

The next imagined turn saw Gretta, Hema, and the Conspirator laying down more unknown cards. Isabella did not play—she could be dead. Mage's card showed her failed pursuit of the avatars.

Marcus leaned back, staring at his notes. *Was the Conspirator running out of options? Where did Hema fit in all of this?* Gretta, Mage, and Isabella had all been involved in various parts of the plan, but Hema's actions remained a mystery. Why had the Conspirator outsourced the attack on Miss Griffin to a local criminal entity instead of using Hema?

The answers may reveal themselves when they reach Verdantia. For now, Marcus could only hope.

[-----✠-----]

Over the next few days, the Stormfang sailed steadily toward Verdantia, day and night. During the voyage, the avatars immersed themselves in ship life, each contributing in their own way.

Lisa added biscuits and dumplings to her meal rotations, making good use of the oven Mr. Sparks and Regina had installed in the kitchen. The crew appreciated the variety, and Sparks beamed with pride every time someone complimented the improvement.

Annabelle, on the other hand, grew increasingly frustrated with Marcus. She repeatedly scolded him for not doing her share of ship work, loudly declaring that he was a "terrible servant." When Marcus still refused to comply with her demands, she even took her complaints to Smitty. Despite her protests, Marcus remained steadfast, unwilling to be bullied into performing tasks outside his responsibilities.

Sophie threw herself into ship duties to make up for her lack of formal training. She worked with the deck crew, assisting with sails, maintenance, and even filling in as a runner, delivering messages and supplies across the ship. Her effort didn't go unnoticed, earning respect from both the crew and Smitty.

Regina worked alongside Sparks on various projects. After finishing the oven installation, they brainstormed ways to improve the lighting in the ship's hallways. Unfortunately, most of the best ideas required magic, which wasn't practical for everyday ship operations. In her free time, Regina focused on understanding her Earthbloom sense, hoping to learn how to activate it consistently. With Lisa's guidance, she developed a clearer understanding of its nature and appearance, but she still struggled to trigger the magic sense in her mind.

Marcus served the avatars as best he could, enduring Annabelle's constant admonishments with quiet patience. It was the price of adhering to his tenets of service. Each morning, he trained with Miss Griffin and Miss Fournier. He admitted to himself that his skill level was closer to Fournier's than Griffin's. Griffin was relentless in her training regimen, her determination evident in every session.

"I was preparing for the shadow promotion tests before I met Brother Albert," Griffin explained one morning. "If the clan still holds the Shadow exams, I plan to take them this year. I feel ready, I'm confident I'll be promoted."

Marcus nodded, recognizing the fire in her eyes. The journey continued, each avatar quietly honing their skills for the challenges ahead.

The day before reaching Verdantia, the Stormfang sailed through a perilous storm. Concerned for the safety of both crew and passengers, Captain Kidd restricted access, only essential personnel were allowed on the bridge and main deck, and no one was permitted on the observation deck.

The avatars, except for Lisa, appreciated the forced downtime. Lisa, however, found herself busier than ever, with everyone now free to stop and enjoy her meals. Her kitchen bustled as she worked to keep up with demand.

Later, between lunch and dinner service, all four avatars and Brother Marcus gathered at a large round table, passing the time with a game of crew. The ship rocked from the storm-tossed waters, but the five of them paid it little mind, laughing and bantering as they played.

Annabelle drew a card from the deck and discarded another with a confident grin. "This pot is as good as mine."

Sophie drew her card, dropped one on the discard pile, and glanced at Regina. "Your go, Regina."

Regina grabbed Sophie's discarded card and laid down a run of three on the table. Without missing a beat, she placed another card on the discard pile and nodded at Lisa. "Your turn."

Lisa drew from the deck and added a run of three cards to the table before discarding a high card. She smirked at Annabelle. "Maybe that pot will escape you after all."

"Shoulda never let you join with those crop crowns," Annabelle muttered, glaring at her five-card debt and silently willing the cards to transform into something useful.

Lisa sat proudly, smiled smugly, and fanned herself with her two remaining cards.

Marcus smiled quietly as he drew and discarded a card. He chose to stay in the background, content to watch the avatars banter and bicker like old friends.

Annabelle tapped the deck with her pointer and middle finger. "Time fer you to pay off," she declared, drawing her next card. Her eyes lit up, exactly the card she needed. With a triumphant flourish, she slammed all five cards onto the table. "Aye, matey! Double coin!" she exclaimed, discarding her final useless card.

The others groaned as Annabelle stood, grinning and holding her hands out in a pulling motion. "Bring me dem coins, girls."

Reluctantly, the avatars and Marcus passed two more coins to the pot. Annabelle made a show of dragging the pile to her side of the table. "Come sail with mama!" she crowed.

Everyone chuckled as they each tossed two more coins into the new pot. Annabelle playfully kissed two coins in her hand and slid them over. "You two be safe now," she said with a mock sniffle, then held one coin up dramatically. "And you, look after yer little sister. Don't let anyone mess with her."

"No need to worry," Lisa teased. "I will give them a good home."

"Says you," Annabelle shot back, smirking as she shuffled the deck for the next round.

Regina dealt the cards to everyone, and the group silently reviewed their hands. Lisa was the first to draw, pulling a card from the deck before discarding another. Marcus followed suit. Annabelle repeated the action, mumbling, "Be good to mama," as she looked at her cards. She pouted dramatically before placing one in the discard pile.

Sophie drew her card, then confidently laid down a run of three before discarding another. "It's on you, Regina," she said, gesturing for her turn.

Regina grabbed a card from the deck and stared at her hand, weighing her options. *Could I make a run of sevens? Or fives?* She hesitated, overthinking the possibilities.

"Oi!" Annabelle protested. "Make a play, girlie! The storm's only gonna last so long."

Regina narrowed her eyes at Annabelle. "I'm thinking, thank you."

"Uh-oh," Sophie muttered, giving Annabelle a side-eye glance. "You don't wanna make her mad."

"Bah," Annabelle scoffed, waving a dismissive hand.

Finally, Regina made her choice, discarding a card. "Your turn, Lisa," she said.

"'Bout time," Annabelle teased.

Regina stuck out her tongue at her in reply.

Lisa pulled a card from the deck and laid down a run of fives, discarding another card. She smirked at Annabelle. "They are almost mine," she taunted, her voice dripping with playful malice.

Marcus drew his card but found no use for it in his hand. He discarded it, saying, "It's to you, Miss Salazar."

"All right," Annabelle said with a grin. "Time to show you girls some real magic." She tapped the deck with her fingers. "Alla-ka-bam," she intoned as if casting a spell. Drawing the top card, she frowned in disappointment, it is utterly useless. With a pout, she tossed it onto the discard pile.

"What happened to the real magic?" Sophie teased.

"Didn't feel like it," Annabelle replied with a dismissive shrug.

Sophie laid down her pair of cards and announced, "Seven."

"Beats me," Regina said, tossing her cards onto the table in defeat.

"I have fifteen," Lisa declared triumphantly.

Marcus sighed and quietly handed his cards to Lisa without a word.

"Cheap move, copper," Annabelle muttered, glaring at Sophie. "Should've held out for a double run."

Sophie grinned and collected half the pot. "One of these coins is yours," she teased Annabelle. "I'll make sure to buy something you don't like with it."

"Bah," Annabelle scoffed again, waving her hand. She flicked a coin into the pot, and the other players followed suit.

Marcus rotated his shoulder as he slid his coin back into the pot.

"Are you okay, Brother Marcus?" Lisa asked, sliding her own coin into the pile.

"Oh yes, Miss Lisa," Marcus reassured her. "Just a little sore from training with Sophie and Regina."

"Marcus is really good at working out," Regina added. "He can even handle the weights on the highest settings."

"I never saw the point of working out and training," Annabelle chimed in with a playful smirk. "I'm naturally strong."

"You don't say," Sophie replied, raising an eyebrow and grinning slyly.

"That's right," Annabelle shot back confidently. "Shame yer goddesses didn't bless ya with the same gifts of strength," she taunted.

"Yeah," Sophie said, narrowing her eyes as she leaned slightly forward. "It's a shame. Maybe you should join us for morning training. You know, show off those *gifts* of yours."

"I would," Annabelle replied, tossing her hair dramatically, "but I wouldn't want to discourage you. It's hopeless for you to catch up to me."

Lisa chuckled softly as she dealt cards to everyone for the next hand.

"What do you think, Regina?" Sophie asked, glancing at her friend. "Would you want to work out with Annabelle too?"

"Umm..." Regina hesitated, remembering her promise to Sophie. She forced a smile. "I think it'd be good for all of us," she said, her grin feeling as stiff as wallpaper plastered on too thick.

Sophie gave her a sly look. "What do you say, Regina? Who would win in a fight, me or Annabelle?" Her expression carried an unspoken reminder: *Remember your promise.*

Regina paused, glancing nervously between them. Finally, she answered, "Well... you're the better fighter, and your magic's stronger, so... I'd have to say you would."

Sophie chuckled and gave Annabelle a playful wink, her look clearly saying, *See? Even she knows you can't beat me.*

"By the sea!" Annabelle exclaimed, throwing up her hands. "This is the biggest travesty I've ever seen!" She turned to Regina, her eyes wide with mock betrayal. "How could ye, girlie?"

"Sorry?" Regina replied sheepishly. "I mean, you can fight. Just... not as well," she added, trying to placate her orange-haired friend.

Annabelle sneered but crossed her arms defiantly. "Bah! I could beat ye, that's all I know," she muttered.

Regina decided not to argue, hoping the situation would blow over.

Lisa, meanwhile, had been silently observing the exchange. As she finished dealing the cards, she shook her head. "I still do not understand all this fuss about fighting," she said. "I mean, Regina beat that axe-wielding woman, Hema, and she doesn't even fight."

"If ye can't fight, princess, ye can't keep yer stuff," Annabelle said matter-of-factly, giving Lisa a firm look. "That's just the way of the world."

"She's got a point," Sophie added. "If the Aurorium Clan weren't great warriors, we'd be enslaved in no time."

Lisa's eyes widened. "Sophie I think the Seven Kingdoms have moved beyond slavery," she protested.

"Mm-hm," Sophie retorted with a skeptical expression, giving Lisa a look that seemed to say: *Do You really believe that?*

Lisa frowned, but decided not to continue the debate. The avatars settled into the next hand as the storm outside roared. Despite the wind and rain, their laughter and banter flowed freely, keeping their spirits high like the ship riding the crest of a wave.

Chapter 4

The Stormfang glided into the bustling harbor of Ferryville, a key trade city in the Sacred Acres of Verdantia. Before docking, Captain Kidd ordered his crew to shed their pirate-like attire, bandanas and tights were swapped for plain trousers and neutral seafaring clothes. When Marcus asked why, the captain explained that Verdantia enforces a strict arrest-on-sight law against pirates. "They don't care for the difference between pirates and privateers," Kidd added grimly. "In the Sacred Acres, we play it safe, corporate sailors on a business contract."

Kidd entrusted Smitty with command of the ship and chose to accompany Marcus and the avatars ashore, particularly to keep an eye on Annabelle.

At the pier's end, they were met by a man in a dark, tailored coat: *Zachary,* the assistant to Lisa's father. He held a sign with her name on it and greeted them with a courteous nod before escorting the group to waiting carriages. As the avatars climbed inside, a porter loaded their bags onto a separate horse-drawn cart.

The ride toward Vendura's capital, Meadowbrook, offered a serene view of fertile landscapes. Orchards and rolling farmland spread across the horizon, tranquil and orderly under the warm afternoon sun. The avatars gazed out in quiet admiration of the land's beauty. After several hours of travel, they finally arrived at the gates of the Governor's mansion.

The estate grounds were meticulously arranged, a display of wealth and elegance. Stone paths divided vibrant flower beds into sections, each brimming with vivid blossoms, purple, yellow, white, and orange, forming a living tribute to the goddess of the Harvest. Towering, sculpted hedges encircled the grand mansion, which stood tall like a mountain of polished stone.

As the carriages halted before the grand entrance, a team of attendants emerged to greet them. They bowed politely and offered to escort everyone except Marcus and Lisa to their rooms. Though Captain Kidd was an unexpected guest, the attendants assured him that accommodations would easily be made for him.

"Governor Nozaki wishes to speak with you and Miss Lisa immediately," Zachary informed Marcus, leading the two toward the Governor's study within the mansion.

Lisa felt at home the moment she stepped into the Governor's study. Countless hours of her childhood had been spent here, sitting at her father's desk as he taught her about governance, law, and history. When she wasn't learning from him, she had her finishing lessons with Miss Brunhilda or magic training with Mistress Hestra. Those days felt so distant now. Since starting at Valorcrest Academy in Laminae two years ago, her visits to the mansion had become increasingly rare, her time consumed by her studies and academy life.

Marcus took in the room with quiet admiration. The study was both elegant and imposing, reminding him of the council chambers on Order Island. A sturdy wooden desk stood near a floor-to-ceiling wall of windows, their rectangular panes held in place by a brass framework. The center panel had a brass handle, revealing that it wasn't just a window, it was a door leading to a balcony. To the left of the desk, a globe rested atop a cabinet stocked with wine and spirits. Along the opposite wall, two-shelf bookcases were filled with leather-bound books. Above them hung detailed maps of Verdantia, Vendura, and other provinces of the kingdom. The right wall was lined with life-size statues of former governors, each one carved with striking detail. One statue caught Marcus's eye, a woman in a flowing dress, holding a pot tipped downward as if pouring something out. From his knowledge of Verdantian traditions, Marcus recognized the figure as a depiction of the goddess of the Harvest.

A side door near the statues opened, and Governor Conrad Nozaki entered. He wore a black suit, complemented by a crisp white shirt and a black tie. On his lapel was a small gold-trimmed pin shaped like a tree, a symbol of devotion to the Verdantian faith known as "Nature's Bounty." Behind him padded a lynx with sleek silver-gray fur. Marcus noticed the creature's intelligent gaze.

Lisa smiled as the lynx silently followed her father's movements. *Silverpaw.* She knew the familiar well, her father wasn't a mage, but her grandfather, a renowned explorer, had bonded the cat to Conrad during an expedition to Stoneridge.

"My little chipmunk," Conrad said warmly, opening his arms for a hug.

"Hi, Daddy," Lisa replied, rushing forward and embracing him. Her green hair brushed against his chest as he smiled softly.

After releasing her, Conrad turned to Marcus and extended his hand. "Governor Conrad Nozaki," he said with authority and pride.

Marcus shook the Governor's hand firmly. "Brother Marcus Igbindeion. It's a pleasure to meet you, Governor."

With the introductions complete, Conrad gestured for them to take a seat. "Please, both of you," he said, motioning to the chairs in front of his desk.

They settled into the comfortable chairs while Conrad perched on the edge of the desk, creating a relaxed, yet attentive atmosphere.

"So," Conrad began, his gaze sharpening as he pointed at his daughter, "why aren't you at school?"

Lisa hesitated, gathering her thoughts. *How could I explain the whirlwind of events that had turned my life upside down?* After a moment, she spoke carefully. "When I went to Granmark with my classmates, Brother Albert from the Order contacted me. He warned me that I was in danger. Later, I learned I was an avatar of the Goddess of Unity."

"Unity?" Conrad repeated, his brows knitting together. He gestured toward the statue along the wall. "Lisa, you know we worship and venerate the goddess of the harvest."

"I met the goddess, Daddy," Lisa replied firmly. "She told me she isn't the goddess of the harvest."

Conrad leaned back slightly, his expression skeptical. "And how exactly did you meet a goddess?"

"I went to Order Island," she explained. "There, I communed with her. She taught me so much."

Conrad folded his arms. "And how do you know you weren't just speaking to someone from the Order? It would be easy for them to stage something like that, make you think you were talking to the *Goddess of Unity*, just to influence you."

"I can assure you, Governor Nozaki," Marcus interjected calmly, "that is not what happened. Serving the avatars is one of the highest duties of the Order of Saint Lorraine. We would never deceive or manipulate them in any way."

"So you say, Brother Marcus," Conrad replied, his tone skeptical. "And where is this Brother Albert? I'd like a word with him; *luring a young girl into danger like he did.*" His accusation laced with thinly veiled outrage and disdain.

At the mention of Albert, Lisa's eyes welled with tears. Memories of his sacrifice surged forward, and her voice broke as she yelled, "He saved me, Daddy! He died protecting me from that woman!"

Conrad froze, stunned by his daughter's outburst. He stared at her as though she had suddenly begun breathing fire.

Sensing the rising tension, Marcus stepped in before things spiraled further. "Brother Albert Thompson was Lisa's original guide," he explained gently. "He gave his life to protect her, allowing her to escape an organization that sought to control her and exploit her powers."

Conrad clenched his jaw. "And why would anyone want my daughter?" he demanded. "Because the so-called goddess of unity *blessed* her?"

"I am not the lady of the harvest!" Lisa snapped, her frustration spilling over. She pulled a handkerchief from her purse to wipe her tear-streaked face. "I am Unity's avatar."

"Blasphemy," Conrad muttered, his voice low and sharp. "We didn't raise you with this nonsense. We honor the goddess of the Harvest. She's the one who blessed you with your powers."

"No, you are wrong," Lisa insisted. "I met Unity. I know my gifts come from her blessing, not the harvest goddess."

Conrad's eyes narrowed, his patience wearing thin. He turned on Marcus. "What has your Order done to my daughter? Filling her head with these ridiculous ideas?"

"I assure you, Governor Nozaki," Marcus said calmly, "we have done no such thing. I understand that Verdantia follows the Nature's Bounty religion and tradition. However, I personally witnessed Lisa communing with the Goddess of Unity." Hoping to ease the tension, Marcus added, "I hadn't considered how Nature's Bounty might relate to the world's ancient history, as passed down by the twelve goddesses."

Conrad waved a dismissive hand. "That pantheon nonsense? Nature's Bounty doesn't need to fit in with that mythology. The so-called twelve goddess pantheon is a farce, which is why their religion crumbled."

Marcus noticed Silverpaw prowling the room, his movements tense and watchful. The lynx's gaze never left Marcus. He measured his words carefully. "Perhaps this isn't the time for a theological debate. All I can say is that I saw Lisa commune with Unity. I understand it's difficult to believe, but it's the truth."

Conrad huffed in annoyance, waving Marcus off. He sat in the seat behind his desk, Silverpaw padding after him. The familiar settled on his bed but continued watching Marcus with an alert intensity.

"So," Conrad said, his tone clipped, "when are you going back to Valorcrest?"

"I do not know," Lisa admitted softly. "I have to help Regina find her family."

"Why can't the Order, or the Jiberau, handle that?" Conrad asked, pointing a finger at her. "I doubt they need you getting in their way."

Lisa frowned. "You should not call them that, Daddy. Sophie told me that *Jiberau* means *slave*."

"It means 'worker,'" Conrad corrected dismissively. "Now, back to the real issue. Are you returning to school with that pirate ship, or do I need to arrange travel for you?"

Lisa hesitated. She felt the same gut-churning discomfort she had when Erisol first appeared to her. She took a deep breath. "I cannot go back yet, Daddy. I have a mission from the goddess."

"From this goddess of unity," Conrad scoffed. He turned to Marcus with exasperation. "Brother, can you tell her she doesn't have to help this Regina? I am trying to get her back to the expensive school I pay so many crowns for."

Marcus straightened in his seat. "I feel I must clarify something, Governor Nozaki. I do not lead Lisa and the other avatars, I serve them." He continued, his tone steady. "If Miss Lisa told me she wanted to return to Valorcrest, I would make the necessary arrangements. But if she tells me her path lies in helping Miss Regina, I will do everything in my power to assist her."

Lisa blinked in surprise. She wasn't used to Marcus being so direct. He often tailored his words to fit the audience, but here, his honesty was striking.

"So," Conrad said, his eyes narrowing, "if I made her to return to Valorcrest and she chose to stay on that pirate ship, you'd help her lie to me about it?"

Marcus paused, weighing his response carefully. "I would advise Miss Lisa to try reasoning with you first, considering your political influence," he replied diplomatically. "Open defiance would not be in her best interest."

"Well," Conrad replied smugly, leaning back in his chair, "at least you haven't lost all your sense."

"Daddy, the other avatars and I need to go to Snyder to search for something," Lisa informed her father. "The goddess wills it."

"Oh, she does, does she?" Conrad replied, his tone skeptical. "And what exactly is in Snyder?"

Marcus noticed a flicker of surprise in Conrad's expression, subtle but telling. It was as if the mention of Snyder had caught him off guard.

"I am not entirely sure," Lisa admitted. "But it feels right, like it's what we're meant to do next."

"My predecessor's notes mention a facility in Snyder," Marcus added. "Unfortunately, without his journal, we can't pinpoint exactly what we'll find there."

Conrad crossed his arms. "And who's going to pay for this little *field trip* of yours?" he asked, fixing his gaze on Lisa.

"The Order will gladly cover any expenses related to the avatars' journey," Marcus responded smoothly.

Conrad fell silent, weighing the situation. Silverpaw, sensing the tension, strode to his side and nuzzled his hand for attention. Conrad absentmindedly scratched the lynx behind the ears as he spoke again. "Fine. You can go gallivanting with your little group of girls." He paused, his tone sharpening. "But after that, you will go straight back to Valorcrest Academy. No detours. And once you're there, you will stay there."

Lisa bit her tongue, resisting the urge to argue. She could see it in his eyes, *if she pushed back now, he would force her back to the academy immediately.* Instead, she forced herself to nod. "Yes, Daddy. As you say."

"I'm glad we understand each other," Conrad said, his voice carrying a note of finality as he continued to pet Silverpaw. "Oh, and one more thing, you'll attend your sister's birthday gala tomorrow. After that, you may leave for your trip."

Lisa swallowed her frustration and gave a polite smile. "Yes, Daddy."

Conrad nodded in approval and leaned back slightly. "Good. Now, if you'll excuse me, I need to speak with *Brother Marcus* alone."

Lisa rose from her chair and headed toward the door. As her hand reached the handle, Conrad's voice called after her.

"And Lisa," he added, "make sure you're presentable at dinner tonight."

"Of course," she said, her forced smile still in place as she left the room.

Once in the hallway, Lisa let her façade drop and exhaled slowly. Two men stood near the door; *Coleman and Marquis,* two of her father's enforcers. Unlike Zachary, they lacked polish and refinement, but they were highly effective. Their presence confirmed her worst fears: *had she defied her father just now, these men would likely have hauled her away by force, whisking her back to Valorcrest under lock and key.*

The weight of isolation pressed down on her. Sure, she and the other avatars could fight their way out of the mansion, steal a carriage, and race back to the Stormfang. But then what? Her father had powerful connections. He could call on the Verdantian navy to track her down and drag her back, ensuring she stayed exactly where he wanted her.

Lisa's thoughts swirled with uncertainty and doubt. She couldn't see a solution yet, but she wasn't entirely out of options. She still had the other avatars by her side. With them, there was at least a spark of hope.

For now, she needed to stay calm, play her father's game, and wait for her moment.

[-----✟-----]

As the door closed behind Lisa, Conrad turned his full attention to Marcus. His familiar, Silverpaw, prowled silently around the room, circling behind Marcus with deliberate steps.

"So, *Brother Marcus,*" Conrad began, leaning back in his chair, "what is all of this really?"

Marcus glanced over his shoulder at the lynx, who was stalking him with unblinking, predatory eyes. He returned his focus to Conrad.

"Exactly what I have told you," Marcus replied evenly. "The Goddess of Unity chose your daughter before she was even born to represent her will in this world. When a goddess selects an avatar, it means she foresees a threat significant enough to endanger her creation. For four goddesses to have chosen avatars simultaneously..." Marcus paused, gauging Conrad's reaction. "The threat must be particularly dire."

Conrad's eyes narrowed, his expression unreadable. "You say you have some idea of this threat. What is it, exactly?"

"The goddesses were vague on the details of where it can be found," Marcus admitted cautiously. He didn't want to overwhelm Conrad with the full weight of the conspiracy surrounding the avatars. "We have some leads, but no precise answers yet."

Conrad tapped his fingers on the desk, his face tightening. "And what if this threat kills my daughter?"

"The avatars have proven remarkably capable of defending themselves," Marcus assured him. "My main concern is that they are most vulnerable when separated. Together, they are far stronger."

Conrad's tone grew sharp. "Are you seriously telling me that being surrounded by a Jiberau, a pirate, and that other girl somehow protects my daughter?"

"Yes, actually," Marcus answered without hesitation. "Miss Sophie Griffin, as an Aurorium Sentinel, is highly trained in multiple forms of combat and tactics. Annabelle Salazar may be a privateer, but she's demonstrated exceptional skill and quick thinking under pressure. As for *that other girl*, Miss Regina Fournier, she has already defeated a formidable agent of the threat we face. Each of them contributes to your daughter's safety."

Conrad crossed his arms, scoffing. "My daughter isn't some kind of Jiberau warrior or a scrappy pirate. She's not cut out to do battle and wage wars. She'd be better off becoming a wife and mother. That's where her future lies."

Marcus leaned forward slightly, his gaze steady and unflinching. "Governor Nozaki, having spent time with your daughter, I can tell you with absolute certainty, you are gravely underestimating her."

Silverpaw growled softly from his place near the window, but Marcus didn't flinch. Conrad regarded Marcus in silence, as if weighing his words.

[-----✚-----]

Sophie was led to her room by a well-built man with striking white hair and chocolate black skin like her own, dressed in a crisp white suit and wearing a slightly askew cap. His commanding presence didn't go unnoticed as he guided her to the door.

"Here you are, ma'am," he said, holding the door open with a courteous gesture.

"Thank you," Sophie replied, stepping inside. Curiosity got the better of her, and she asked, "Is there a gym or somewhere I can work out around here?"

"Yes, ma'am. There's a running track behind the mansion and a gymnasium next to it," he informed her. "Oh, and just so you're aware, the governor is expecting you at dinner tonight."

Sophie's interest piqued, and she gave him a charming smile. "Sounds lovely. What's on the menu?"

"The chef is preparing roast chicken, potatoes, and a vegetable medley," he answered, keeping a professional demeanor despite her playful tone. "My name is Samuel, and I'll be at your service. If you'll excuse me, I'll unpack your things."

Sophie's expression hardened slightly. She wasn't keen on anyone going through her belongings. "No, that's alright. I'll handle it," she said, subtly removing her Aurorium badge from her bag to avoid any misunderstandings.

Samuel, however, was gently insistent. "Please, ma'am. You don't have anything I haven't seen before," he said, holding out his hand for her bag.

After a brief hesitation, Sophie relented, though a sense of unease lingered. "Alright, then," she said, watching as he carried her bag to the wardrobe.

As he placed the bag inside, Samuel turned back to her. "So, is it true? Are you really a Jiberau?"

Sophie winced at the term, her jaw tightening. "Aurorium," she corrected firmly. "Jiberau means slave, and I am nobody's slave."

Samuel raised his hands in apology. "I'm sorry. That's just what we've always called your people."

Sophie straightened, her voice taking on a calm but authoritative tone. "The Jiberau were once slaves to the Seven Kingdoms, yes. But after the *Night of Broken Chains*, they reclaimed their independence. We became protectors, warriors, and investigators under the name Aurorium, which means *light of freedom*."

An awkward silence followed as the gravity of her words hung in the air. Sophie's attention shifted momentarily when she heard a faint, oddly familiar ringing in her ears, though she couldn't quite place it.

Samuel broke the silence with a more casual question. "So, what will you wear to dinner tonight?" he asked, eyeing her neatly hung clothes.

Sophie glanced at her current outfit: purple pants, a white shirt, and a matching vest. "What's wrong with this?" she asked, a hint of defiance creeping into her voice.

Samuel paused thoughtfully before replying, "Here in Verdantia, women typically dress differently." His tone was polite but carried a subtle undertone of disapproval. "The tailor shop could prepare a dress for you. They're quite talented, and I'm sure they can make something purple for you."

Sophie's eyes narrowed, irritated by the suggestion. She never liked wearing dresses; she would battle with her mother when she forced Sophie to wear a dress, so these people didn't have a chance to force her compliance. "Actually, I'll be wearing this," she said firmly, leaving no room for debate.

Samuel inclined his head slightly in deference. "As you wish, ma'am." He resumed organizing her belongings before adding, "If you don't need anything else, I'll take my leave."

"I don't" Sophie confirmed curtly.

"Very good, ma'am," he said with a smile. "I'll be back at five o'clock to collect you for dinner."

"Sounds good," Sophie replied, watching him exit the room. Once the door clicked shut behind him, she exhaled slowly and shook her head. The lingering tension in the room told her that the night ahead would be just as complicated as everything else so far.

[-----✿-----]

Annabelle, Regina, and Captain Kidd followed two attendants down the corridor leading to their rooms. Both wore white uniforms typical of household staff. One was an older, thin man with his attendant's cap perfectly centered on his head; the other was younger, large and muscular, prompting Annabelle to wonder if they had stitched two uniforms together to fit him.

At last, they arrived at a room. The older attendant gestured politely to Regina. "Miss Fournier, your room will be here." He opened the door and motioned for her to enter.

Regina stepped inside and gasped softly. The state room was beyond anything she had experienced, easily surpassing the cramped cabins aboard the Stormfang. The decor gleamed in shades of white, green, and silver. A massive bed, framed with intricately carved wood and draped in heavy curtains, stood as the centerpiece. Across from it, a grand wardrobe loomed with ornate brass handles glinting in the light.

Curious, Regina walked over and flopped onto the bed. The plush mattress cradled her like a cloud, soft and comforting. She sighed, sinking further into the sheets, imagining herself closing the curtains and sleeping here for days.

The older attendant cleared his throat gently, breaking her thoughts. "Young madam, would you like me to unpack your travel bags and place your belongings in the wardrobe?"

Regina sat up slowly and waved toward her bag. "Sure, go ahead."

"As you wish." The attendant entered the room fully, allowing the door to close behind him as he retrieved her bag from the floor. He stood tall, exuding a calm professionalism. "My name is Otis," he said with a respectful nod. "I'll be your personal attendant during your stay. If there's anything you need, please feel free to ask."

Regina blinked, surprised. "Wow. I've never had a personal attendant before. Are you... Like a servant?" she asked, mentally comparing him to Brother Marcus.

Otis smiled good-naturedly. "A very good servant, I hope. Please don't hesitate to ask if you need anything."

Regina pondered for a moment, then asked, "Are you an Earthbloom mage?"

Otis paused in surprise. "I am, yes," he admitted. "Though I must confess I'm not a particularly skilled one."

"Great!" Regina perked up. "Can you tell me how to use *Earthbloom Sense*?"

Otis opened the wardrobe and began placing her clothes inside. He paused thoughtfully. "That's an interesting question. I've never had to consciously think about it. It's... instinctual. Like hearing birds chirping in the distance or watching a sunrise. I simply know what the earth tells me about the life around me." He resumed his task, carefully folding her garments. "Why do you ask?"

"I'm learning Earthbloom, but I can't do any spells, because I can't figure out how to use Earthbloom Sense," she explained, frustration slipping into her voice.

Otis nodded in understanding. "It can take young mages years to develop the sense. It's the foundation of our magic." He tilted his head curiously. "I've never heard of an Earthbloom mage coming from anywhere but Verdantia. Where are you from, Madam?"

"I'm from the Great Kingdom of Laminae," Regina answered proudly. "But I'm not an Earthbloom mage. I'm a Nexus Mage, some people call us *Learner Mages*."

"A Learner Mage?" Otis echoed, intrigued. "What sort of magic system is that?"

"It means I can use any magic system I want," Regina explained. "But I have to learn how each system works and how to shape my mana to cast spells."

"Now that's fascinating," Otis remarked, placing the last of her clothes in the wardrobe. "And what magic systems have you learned so far?"

Regina ticked them off on her fingers. "Let's see... EnfanceMagique, Arletto, Forge de l'espace aérien, Verboisance, and Maelstrom Mastery."

Otis rubbed his chin thoughtfully. "Impressive. But I wonder how deeply you understand each system. Take Earthbloom, for example. The sense is crucial to working with the elements, it informs us about the life forces we interact with. I could not imagine casting a spell without first connecting to Mother Earth."

65

Regina considered his words, a pang of doubt creeping in. He had a point. She could set up tier-two Earthbloom spells, but her mastery was nowhere near enough to cast. She had never stopped to think about how foundational the sense might be to everything.

"Madam?" Otis's voice gently pulled her from her thoughts. "You're invited to dine with the Governor this evening. He's generously offered you the services of the mansion's tailor to prepare a dress."

"Wow, he did?" Regina asked, blinking in surprise.

"Yes, the governor is quite generous," Otis replied with a smile. "Shall we visit the tailor now?"

"Sure," Regina agreed, glancing longingly at the bed one last time. She silently promised herself a long, uninterrupted rest in its comforting embrace.

[----- ⚓ -----]

Annabelle and Captain Kidd stepped into her room, passing the towering attendant who held the door open with a hand as large as a dinner plate. Annabelle was momentarily stunned by the grandeur of her surroundings. The room stretched wide, bathed in hues of white, green, gold, and rich mahogany.

In the center stood an enormous mahogany bed, draped with light, flowing curtains. It was so vast, Annabelle mused, *this her room could fit the entire Stormfang crew.* To one side, a large wardrobe stood like a work of art, its carved surface depicting a tree whose branches seemed to stretch organically from the floor.

"Now this is my kind of room," Annabelle exclaimed, dropping her sea bag at her feet and stepping further inside.

"Aye," Captain Kidd agreed, scanning the opulent space. "One could get quite used to this." He kept his own bag slung over his shoulder, knowing he wouldn't be staying in this room with Annabelle.

"I'm pleased the room meets your approval," the attendant spoke, his deep presence offset by a surprisingly high-pitched voice. "If you would like, ma'am, I can assist in unpacking your belongings."

"Yes, that would be appreciated," Annabelle replied, slipping into her *proper voice*.

"You may call me Emory," the man said as he stooped to retrieve her bag.

Annabelle sat on the bed, immediately enveloped by its softness. It felt like she was cradled in the arms of a gentle, loving mother. Meanwhile, Captain Kidd moved to the window and gazed out at the sprawling, perfectly manicured grounds.

Emory opened the wardrobe and glanced back at them. "I shall be your personal attendant during your stay at the mansion. Please feel free to make any requests, and I will see to them promptly."

Annabelle's eyes sparkled with mischief as she sat up. "Anything?"

"Anything within my capability," Emory answered smoothly, beginning to unpack her bag.

Grinning, Annabelle hopped off the bed, her half-twisted, half-braided hair bouncing around her shoulders. She silently cursed the strands, this is why she always wore a bandana. Approaching Emory, she challenged playfully, "Think you can lift me with one hand?"

Emory smiled faintly. "I believe I can manage that."

With a laugh, Annabelle raised her arms above her head, forming a makeshift handle. Without hesitation, Emory hoisted her effortlessly, his large hand supporting her beneath her ribs. He even tossed her gently into the air.

"Oi, Cap'n, look at me! I'm flyin'!" Annabelle called out gleefully, arms outstretched.

Captain Kidd chuckled from his vantage point by the window. "Aye, that ye are, Belle."

Grinning widely, Annabelle declared, "I am an angel of the seas!"

Emory lowered herself carefully to the floor and gave a polite nod. "If you'll excuse me, I'll get your clothes packed away."

"In that case, I'll await your return," Annabelle said, slipping back into her *proper voice*. She strolled over to where Captain Kidd stood, playfully bumping his arm.

Emory bent down to search through her bag. Pulling out a garment, he raised an eyebrow. "By the harvest, I think this ought to go straight to the laundry, ma'am," he remarked dryly.

"Ah, that's fine," Annabelle replied with a slight shrug.

Emory paused for a moment before retrieving a sturdy leather belt adorned with a chain attached to a miniature anchor. He held it up, studying it curiously. "What might this be?" he asked.

Feeling the captain's silent scrutiny on her, Annabelle quickly replied, "Oh, it's just for decoration. It ties me outfit together."

Emory gave a slight nod and placed the belt at the bottom of the wardrobe. "The governor has invited you to dinner this evening," he informed her. "He has also made the mansion's tailors available to prepare a suitable dress for you."

Annabelle raised a suspicious brow. "And how much is that gonna cost me?"

"Governor Nozaki would cover the expense, of course," Emory assured her with a smile.

Annabelle relaxed slightly and nodded. "Ah, well then. Lead the way, my good man." She turned to Captain Kidd with a wicked grin. "Think the captain could get a dress too?"

Emory remained composed. "I imagine the captain would prefer a fine suit," he replied diplomatically.

"Aye, that sounds more my style," Captain Kidd chuckled.

Emory opened the door and gestured for them to exit. As Annabelle stepped through, Captain Kidd gave her a light shove from behind. She spun around with mock innocence, her eyes meeting his in a silent exchange. His gaze drifted pointedly toward the wardrobe where her anchor belt lay.

Unable to come up with a convincing excuse, Annabelle shrugged with a sheepish grin, silently conveying, I might need it. Captain Kidd sighed but said nothing as they followed Emory down the hall.

[-----⊙-----]

Lisa strolled down the hallway of her family's mansion, heading toward her bedroom to freshen up. She wrinkled her nose at the lingering thought of the Stormfang's ever-present scent: *a mix of salt, wood, and unwashed fabric.* She liked being aboard the ship, but it always left her feeling grimy. Now that she was home, she yearned for a hot bath and a change into clean, comfortable clothes.

As she reached her door, she paused, hearing a flurry of voices and activity coming from across the hall. A loud commotion echoed from her sister Evelyn's room. Curiosity piqued, Lisa decided that getting cleaned up could wait *a little*. She crossed the hall and gently pushed the door open.

Inside, Evelyn stood at the center of controlled chaos. She wore a silk housecoat, her long black hair wrapped in large curlers, and her face coated in a mask of creamy mud. Around her, a team of tailors buzzed like bees, meticulously working on a stunning green dress adorned with gold highlights.

"Lisa! You're back!" Evelyn exclaimed, prancing over to her sister. Ignoring the tailors, she wrapped her arms around Lisa in a tight, enthusiastic hug. The mud mask smeared onto Lisa's cheek in the process.

When she pulled away, Evelyn's face was lit with excitement. "We were so worried about you! We heard all kinds of things, that you were kidnapped by pirates, then the Jiberau had you, and then The Order rescued you. Are you okay?"

Lisa blinked, momentarily stunned by how twisted the story had become. "Oh... yes, I am fine," she managed to say.

"Well, good!" Evelyn cut her off, already moving back toward the dress. "Mom and Dad have been impossible since you disappeared. I couldn't even get out to see Seth!"

Lisa stifled a knowing smile. Seth was Evelyn's boyfriend, the one their parents disapproved of because he wasn't from the right kind of family. They'd made it clear he wasn't worth Evelyn's time, but her sister clearly had not agreed.

"Sorry," Lisa said reflexively, though she doubted Evelyn was really listening. Her sister was now engrossed in the dress, scrutinizing every detail. Evelyn pointed to the shoulders, lined with gold trim, and frowned.

"What do you think?" Evelyn asked. "Should I keep the gold trim on the shoulders? Or maybe change it to red or silver?"

Lisa glanced at the tailors, who froze in horror. She could see the dread in their eyes at the mere thought of starting over again. Hoping to save them the trouble, Lisa offered a quick opinion. "I think the gold looks perfect. It'll tie everything together for your gala tomorrow."

Evelyn tapped her chin thoughtfully. "I guess..."

"Have you seen Mom?" Lisa asked, eager to reunite with her mother.

"She's probably setting up the banquet hall," Evelyn replied absentmindedly. Then, as if struck by inspiration, she turned back to Lisa with a hopeful smile. "Hey! You can make the tiger lilies bloom early for my party with your magic, right?"

Lisa hesitated. Tiger lilies didn't usually bloom until late May or early June. Forcing them to bloom early would burn through much of their essence, and the flowers wouldn't produce seed pods. "I can... but if I do, the lilies will not last through the summer," she explained carefully.

"But think of how beautiful the gala would be if the hall were lined with tiger lilies in full bloom," Evelyn said, clasping her hands together. "I will only have one goddess gala, and you could make it so special with your magic!"

Lisa sighed inwardly. The "goddess's gala" was a grand tradition for Verdantian girls on their seventeenth birthday. It symbolized their transition to adulthood, signaling they were ready for marriage and family. Socialites treated these galas as a

68

way to leave a lasting impression. Lisa vividly recalled the buzz around Constance Murray's gala, where she'd made a spectacular entrance during a dance number performed by a renowned troupe from Islewind. Although Lisa missed the event due to her studies at Valorcrest, she heard all about it upon returning home for winter break.

"I do not know..." Lisa murmured, uncertain of what Evelyn had in mind. She noticed her sister was once again fixated on the dress and clearly not paying attention anymore.

Deciding it was time to leave Evelyn to her preparations, Lisa smiled softly. "Goodbye, Evelyn."

Evelyn gave a distracted wave, her eyes never leaving the fabric.

Lisa stepped out of the room and headed to her own. The moment she crossed the threshold, she felt a wave of comfort and familiarity wash over her. She took in the sight of her room: her makeup table perfectly organized, her bathroom ready for a much-needed soak.

Closing her eyes, Lisa inhaled deeply, savoring the sense of peace. Finally, she thought to herself, 'Ahh, I am home'.

[-----❁-----]

Regina, Annabelle, and Captain Kidd arrived at the tailor's hall at the same time, escorted by Otis and Emory. They were greeted warmly by the establishment's manager, a woman wearing a light green linen dress. A sash crossed her chest, adorned with an embroidered symbol of a green tree encircled by a golden aura, resting just above her bosom.

With a graceful lean forward and a bright smile, the manager said, "Welcome to the Meadowbrook Tailor's Guild. May we create something beautiful for you today?"

Regina's heart lifted for a moment, her mind brimming with possibilities. Ideas for a dinner dress flickered through her thoughts, perhaps a black dress with a silver sash like the one the Goddess of Change had worn when she communed with her, or maybe a shimmering silver dress with a striking black bow. Or even a green dress, similar to the one worn by this kindly woman in front of her, with a subtle silver accent.

But then, as quickly as the excitement had come, it evaporated. Her thoughts turned to her father, who was being held hostage by the conspiracy. The memory of his captivity washed over her like a cold wave. Guilt gripped her: *how can I indulge in this when she hadn't done enough to find him and Mattie?* Her shoulders sagged as the weight of helplessness pressed down on her.

Before Regina could speak, Annabelle gently placed a hand on her arm, the warmth of the gesture breaking through her haze.

"Don't worry, Regina. We'll find yer peoples," Annabelle said softly, her voice steady with reassurance.

Regina's eyes softened as she turned to her friend. She placed her hand over Annabelle's. "Thanks, Annabelle," she whispered with a faint smile.

The moment caught the attention of everyone around them. Even the manager seemed momentarily frozen by the display, but quickly recovered, her years of experience handling debutantes shining through.

She turned her full attention to Regina, lightly grasping her hand to regain her focus. "Madam, I have just the tailor for you," the manager said with a gentle tug, drawing Regina's gaze to her face.

Regina found herself mesmerized. The woman had a beautifully manicured, round face, framed by a stylish bob of blonde curls. A beauty mark rested just below her left eye, and her piercing blue eyes sparkled with practiced charm. Caught off guard, Regina reflexively responded, "Okay."

The manager smiled and waved her free hand toward a nearby woman dressed in a white smock decorated with needles, thread, tape measures—and oddly, what appeared to be lollipops.

"This is Mistress Hannigan," the manager announced with a flourish.

Miss Hannigan offered a silent wave and a knowing smile.

"You'll swear she has tailor's magic," the manager continued enthusiastically, as if she were presenting a performer. "She can craft beauty from mere fabric rolls in ways you'd never imagine."

Regina barely registered the words. Guided by the manager's gentle tug, she found herself walking toward Mistress Hannigan, as if in a trance. Once there, she managed a quiet, "Hello."

"Please, come with me," Miss Hannigan said warmly, taking Regina's hand from the manager's with a reassuring touch. "I believe I have just the dress for you."

Hannigan led Regina to a spacious work area filled with towering rolls of fabric. The colors were meticulously arranged by hue. The darkest shades were near the top, gradually lightening row by row until the rolls near the floor were almost white, tinged with the faintest hint of color.

Miss Hannigan guided Regina to a square platform that lifted her a few centimeters from the ground. "Now, madam," the tailor said gently, "tell me, what are your favorite flowers?"

Regina blinked, momentarily taken aback by the question. Slowly, she began to consider her answer, letting herself relax in the warmth of Hannigan's presence.

[----- ⚓ -----]

The manager gently took Annabelle's hand and guided her to a man dressed in a tan smock, its many pockets bulging with tools of his trade. "Madam, this is Mister Berkshire," the manager introduced. "His talent has created some of the most exquisite attire for both royalty and the bravest souls alike."

Mr. Berkshire gave a respectful nod as he took Annabelle's hand. "A pleasure to meet you, Miss Salazar," he said in a dignified tone. His voice was calm but carried the weight of practiced refinement. He led her to his workspace, where neatly organized rolls of fabric stood in rows by color.

As he turned to her, he asked, "Tell me, miss, what do you want people to say about you when they see you?"

Annabelle blinked, momentarily caught off guard by the question. Memories of how people often treated her, like she was dangerous or destined to cause trouble, flashed in her mind. She thought of the fear and mistrust that followed her wherever she went, like a shadow she could never shake. But then she remembered how Brother Marcus looked at her, as if she were something special, someone worth believing in. That warmth filled her chest, and she knew exactly what she wanted.

"I want people to say: *This girl is special. I should treat her right.*" Annabelle said thoughtfully. Then, with a playful grin, she added, "then maybe: *I should give her as much coin as I can.*"

Mister Berkshire chuckled softly. "I think I understand," he replied, his eyes twinkling with amusement.

Meanwhile, Miss Hannigan approached her work with flamboyant flair and a keen eye for color. She circled Regina like an artist contemplating her canvas, swishing bolts of fabric with theatrical precision. She began with a sunny yellow that bathed the room in warmth, but it wasn't quite right. A soft blue followed, swirling around Regina like a morning breeze, but still, Hannigan was unsatisfied.

Then she found it, a deep, velvety purple that seemed to hold both strength and grace. The tailor's vision sharpened as she expertly measured and layered the fabric. Piece by piece, she created a three-part ensemble: a sleek purple silhouette as the base, topped by a matching vest-style bodice that fit Regina's figure perfectly. Beneath it, a crisp white shirt provided a clean contrast, lending the outfit a timeless elegance.

Regina hesitated for a moment, her mind flashing to Sophie's similar attire. But when she finally saw her reflection, those doubts melted away. The dress wasn't just elegant, it was hers. It imbued her with a quiet confidence she hadn't felt for a long time. Miss Hannigan's craftsmanship had given her more than a beautiful outfit; it had awakened something within her.

Mister Berkshire approached Annabelle's design with an understated finesse, allowing his intuition to guide him. His goal was to craft a garment that reflected Annabelle's daring spirit, striking a balance between vibrancy and subtle sophistication.

He selected a rich orange as the dress's primary color. It flowed gracefully from each side of the gown and down the sleeves, framing a pristine central panel of pure white. The contrast was striking, at first glance, it appeared as though Annabelle wore an orange coat draped over a white dress. Yet upon closer inspection, it became clear that the entire garment was a seamless masterpiece, meticulously crafted for elegance and movement.

When Annabelle slipped into the dress, she ran her hands over the fabric, marveling at how perfectly it encapsulated her. It wasn't just clothing, it was an embodiment of her strength, and fire. Mr. Berkshire had captured her essence without a single word of explanation.

The hall buzzed quietly as both young women stood in their new dresses, each a testament to the tailors' artistry. Regina's gown exuded grace and mystery, while Annabelle's radiated bold confidence.

Miss Hannigan and Mister Berkshire exchanged approving glances. Their work was done, and in the eyes of their clients, it was nothing short of magic.

[-----❀-----]

After their time with the tailors, Regina, Annabelle, and Captain Kidd stood before a row of tall mirrors, admiring the quick yet masterful craftsmanship of their new outfits.

"You look like the Copper," Annabelle teased Regina, referring to Sophie's signature color. "She ain't gonna like you wearing her color."

71

"I think she'll like how pretty my dress is," Regina replied confidently, smoothing the purple fabric. She glanced at Annabelle's vibrant ensemble. "You look like a queen."

"Aye," Captain Kidd agreed, his eyes twinkling with amusement. "The queen of mischief." He tied his hair back into a short ponytail, eyeing his reflection. His black slacks and crisp white shirt, paired with a tailored white jacket, gave him a surprisingly regal air.

Annabelle struck a dramatic pose, playfully admiring herself in the mirror. "Ah, so many people can't appreciate me true beauty when they see it. Such a shame, really." She twirled slightly, testing how easily the fabric moved. Despite the long sleeves, the dress was remarkably flexible.

"How is everyone liking their creations?" the tailor shop manager asked, her cheerful voice drawing their attention. Her smile seemed to radiate warmth, brightening the entire room.

The trio gave approving nods, voicing their satisfaction.

"Come to think of it," Captain Kidd said, glancing around, "where's Sophie Griffin?"

"She never came down," the manager informed them. "Perhaps something came up."

Annabelle shook her head, exasperated. "Only the Copper would pass up the chance for beautiful clothes like this, especially for *free*!"

The manager chuckled politely. "If everything meets your approval, we'll take your dresses and suit for cleaning and have them delivered to your rooms before dinner," she explained, her pleasant smile never faltering.

"Okay," Regina replied.

"Sounds good," Captain Kidd agreed with a nod.

Annabelle, however, cradled her sleeve as if it were a cherished pet. "Oh, my dear," she fake-sniffled, stroking the fabric with exaggerated tenderness. "No, no, don't cry. We'll reunite soon enough." She caressed the sleeve as though comforting a heartbroken lover.

Regina giggled at the display, while Captain Kidd chuckled and patted Annabelle's shoulder. "There, there," he said, playing along.

Annabelle shot him a playful glare through mock tears. "This is a very emotional moment, Cap'n. Show some respect!"

The lighthearted exchange left the room filled with laughter, their spirits high as they prepared for the evening ahead.

Chapter 5

As Lisa stepped out of the warm cascade of her shower, she felt more than just the water draining away—today's burdens melted with it. Her skin glowed with renewed life, a radiant testament to her liberation from the weight of recent trials. A bright smile tugged at her lips, a smile that had been hidden under the shadows of circumstance for too long.

Turning toward her vanity, Lisa reveled in the comforting familiarity of her beauty ritual, a routine she'd nearly forgotten in the chaos of recent events. The familiar scent of lavender and citrus oils filled the air, evoking memories of simpler, carefree moments. With a steady hand, she dipped into her collection of creams and scrubs, each step deliberate and grounding. The coarse salt scrub danced across her skin, carrying away fatigue as though polishing both body and spirit.

She rinsed, savoring the feeling of rejuvenation. As the astringent-soaked cloth cooled her skin, Lisa closed her eyes, leaning into the tingling sensation. It is not just cleansing, it is the rediscovery of herself, of the small rituals that had shaped her resilience over time. The final act of applying moisturizer was slow, meditative. Every gentle stroke reminded her of her worth, her strength.

Gazing into the mirror, Lisa saw more than a physical transformation. This is her, her identity reaffirmed in the quiet sanctity of her self-care. She whispered to her reflection, a silent promise to face what lay ahead with grace and fortitude.

Back in her bedroom, she found a white dress trimmed in light green hanging outside her wardrobe. A subtle reminder of her obligations later that evening. The clock on her vanity read two o'clock; *plenty of time to check on her guests, the other avatars.* She chose a simple blue sundress instead, something easy and comfortable, and styled her hair into a neat bun. With dinner preparations looming, makeup could wait.

Lisa stepped out into the hallway, her sandals making soft, rhythmic sounds on the polished floors. She knew where to find an attendant and quickly made her way toward the stairs, spotting a young man stationed at the far end of the corridor.

"Where are my guests?" she asked.

He hesitated for a moment, then recognition dawned. "Oh, those girls with the... uh, unique hair?"

Lisa's expression turned flat, her thoughts reflexively touching on her own hair's distinctive hue.

"Ah! No offense, miss," the attendant corrected quickly. "They're staying in the first-floor guest wing. Shall I go and get them for you?"

"No need," Lisa said with a smile. "I will head down myself."

"Of course, ma'am," he replied, giving a respectful nod.

Lisa descended the grand staircase, passing attendants, soldiers, and servants who glanced at her only long enough to notice her hair and eyes before respectfully averting their gaze. She strode through the mansion's ornate corridors, her presence commanding attention yet unintrusive. The path led her to the guest wing, where she found a stocky, dark-skinned attendant sitting in the servants' quarters. He wore his hat askew, engrossed in a book.

"Hello," Lisa called gently.

The man looked up, setting his book aside as he stood. His posture shifted immediately into respectful formality. "Good afternoon, Miss Nozaki. How can I be of service?"

"I am looking for my... guests," she said, hesitating. *Should I call the other avatars my friends yet?*

"What rooms are they in?"

"Sadly, only Miss Griffin is in her room," the man informed Lisa. "The other three haven't returned from the tailor shop yet."

"Oh," Lisa said, processing the news. "What room is she in?"

"Second from the end on the left," he replied. "Would you like me to show you?"

"No, that is all right," Lisa replied with a polite smile. She turned and left, her thoughts lingering on the attendant. Something about him intrigued her, though she couldn't pinpoint why. Pushing the feeling aside, she made her way to Sophie's room and knocked. A few muffled sounds and clatters came from inside before the door swung open.

"Oh, hey, Lisa," Sophie greeted, a little surprised. She stood in comfortable clothes provided by the Order. "What brings you here?"

"I wanted to check on you girls, see how you are settling in." Lisa explained. "Do you mind if I come in?"

"Sure, come on in." Sophie stepped back, holding the door open for her.

Lisa entered and glanced around the room. It was neatly arranged, almost like it hadn't been used, except for the desk where an open notebook sat next to The Alrunia Text, the book Sophie had borrowed from The Luminous.

"So, how is everything so far?" Lisa asked, crossing her arms lightly.

"This place is nice," Sophie said with a nod. "I've just been studying for now. How about you? Happy to be home?"

Lisa's skin flushed slightly under Sophie's gaze.

"Wow, girl, you are glowing," Sophie teased with a grin.

"Oh, thank you." Lisa gave a self-conscious laugh. "I had to do my beauty routine; my poor face was desperate for it."

"You'll have to share that with me some time." Sophie said, clearly intrigued.

"Okay." Lisa promised. "Are you coming to dinner tonight?"

"Yep, wouldn't miss it," Sophie replied, settling onto the edge of her bed. "It sounds amazing."

"Oh, you are in for a treat," Lisa said enthusiastically. "The kitchen staff here makes the most incredible dishes. Compared to them, my cooking is slop."

"What?!" Sophie balked. "Girl, you are lying. The meals you made on the ship were delicious! I can't imagine anything better."

"You will see," Lisa said with a knowing, playful smirk. "But dinner is a little formal. What are you planning to wear?"

"Just my usual," Sophie answered casually. "I figure slacks and a vest should work for semi-formal."

Lisa hesitated, knowing how things worked in Verdantia. "Here, women are usually expected to wear dresses or gowns. I am not sure if pants would meet the formal dress code…"

Sophie sighed. "Honestly, dresses just aren't my thing."

Lisa tilted her head, surprised. "Really? I have never met a girl who did not like wearing dresses."

Sophie chuckled, shaking her head. "Yeah, I've never been into them. My momma used to get so mad at me for it. Sometimes she'd call me her *lady son*."

Both girls laughed softly at that, but Lisa noticed a shift in Sophie's expression. The laughter faded, replaced by a deep sadness. Sophie's thoughts had drifted to her mother. After her encounter with War, she'd promised herself not to cry again. Sometimes, though, that promise was hard to keep.

Lisa gently placed her hand on Sophie's forearm. "I am sorry, Sophie. It must be really hard... after everything you have been through."

Sophie swiped a stray tear from her cheek. "It is," she admitted softly. "But I can't fix anything with tears." She inhaled deeply, steeling herself. "So, about that beauty routine... think you can show me?"

"Of course," Lisa agreed, embracing the change in topic. "It is going to change your life," she added with a playful smile.

The two girls, one with green hair and the other with violet hair, left Sophie's room. On the way out, they paused by the attendant's quarters to let Samuel know Sophie's clothes could be hung in her room once they returned from the laundry.

They continued toward Lisa's bedroom, navigating the busy halls of the governor's mansion as staff, guards, and officials hurried from task to task. The grand structure bustled like a hive, but in this moment, Lisa felt grounded by Sophie's presence.

Sophie stepped into Lisa's bedroom and paused, awestruck by the sheer size of the space. It was at least three times wider than her guest room, with wooden dividers sectioning off various areas. To the left, a cozy sleeping nook held a grand canopy bed. Beyond that was a dressing area, and near the far wall, a study space where an oversized desk was covered with neatly arranged books and papers. Directly opposite the desk stood Lisa's beauty station, a white, ornate vanity table with golden leaf-shaped patterns etched into a large mirror. The leaf's tip pointed upward, the veins of its design shimmering softly as the afternoon light caught the highlights. Where they now stood was clearly the sitting area, with two plush couches facing each other and a circular coffee table between them.

"Wow," Sophie breathed. "This is the largest bedroom I've ever seen," she said with conviction, knowing she was speaking the absolute truth.

Lisa blinked, taking in the room through Sophie's eyes. "I guess it is a large one," she said with a casual shrug, though the thought had never crossed her mind. Compared to her suite in Valorcrest, this room felt modest. Still, it was a palace compared to the tiny quarters she'd lived in aboard the Stormfang.

Sophie snorted, arching an eyebrow. "You guess? Lisa, all of us and Brother Marcus could live in here and never get in each other's way."

Lisa chuckled, picturing the scene Sophie described. It wasn't entirely far-fetched. Still, they'd probably need to put Marcus somewhere else. Smiling wryly, she quipped, "Maybe Brother Marcus would have to sleep in the hallway."

Sophie smirked and mimicked Marcus' serious tone. "He would be honored to sleep in the hallway if that's what you required, Miss Nozaki."

Both girls burst into laughter, their voices filling the vast room.

Lisa led Sophie to the bathroom, opening the door to reveal a sink surrounded by neatly organized jars of scrubs, oils, and cloths soaking in moisturizing solutions. The scents of herbs and floral essences wafted through the air.

"Well, let's get started," Lisa said, her tone excited. "Your first time using beauty magic might take a while." She flashed an exhilarated grin. "But trust me, it is so worth it."

Sophie eyed the array of products with cautious curiosity. "Okaay," she replied, dragging the word out as if it might buy her time to mentally prepare.

"What is the problem?" Lisa teased. "You shoot guns and fight people how can you be afraid of a beauty routine?"

"Your logic makes sense," Sophie deadpanned. "And yet, here we are."

Lisa shook her head, laughing softly. "Just sit down," she said, patting the back of the chair by the sink. "You will be fine."

Reluctantly, Sophie took a seat, gripping the armrests lightly. Lisa turned on the faucet, filling the basin with warm water. She handed Sophie a bar of soap and a soft rag.

"First things first—soap and water," Lisa instructed.

Sophie accepted the soap, dipped it into the water, and worked it into the cloth until it foamed with bubbles. Methodically, she began washing her face, scrubbing areas like the bridge of her nose and her forehead with care. After a final rinse, her skin glistened slightly under the light, clean and refreshed.

"Good," Lisa nodded, satisfied. She opened a jar of salt scrub and held it out. "Now use this to cleanse the impurities from your skin. Just take a little and massage it in."

Sophie dipped two fingers into the jar, scooping a modest amount of the gritty paste. She spread it across her palms and began gently rubbing it onto her face in cautious circles.

"Not like that, you really have to work it in," Lisa corrected. Watching Sophie's hesitant technique, Lisa's brows furrowed. Finally, she sighed and offered, "May I?"

Sophie hesitated but nodded. "I guess…"

"no need to worry," Lisa reassured her with a warm smile. "I will take good care of you." She projected as much encouragement as she could, hoping to ease her friend's nerves.

Lisa turned the chair so that Sophie was angled toward her, positioning her right side near the sink. Bending slightly, Lisa dipped her fingers into the scrub and began working it into Sophie's skin with small, firm circles. "You have to use a bit of pressure to get the scrub deep enough to really do its job," she explained, her hands moving expertly over Sophie's face.

76

Sophie wasn't prepared for how firm Lisa's touch was. The gritty sensation of the scrub pressed into her skin with a surprising intensity, but it didn't hurt. She focused instead on the thought of how much better her skin would feel afterward.

The minutes passed, Lisa working with thorough care until she had gone over Sophie's entire face. Finally, Lisa stepped back and smiled. "Okay, now rinse off," she instructed, gesturing toward the sink.

Sophie let out a small breath of relief, ready to move on to the next step.

Sophie turned in her chair, leaning over the basin to rinse the soap from the rag. Once clean, she used it to wipe away the salt scrub. As she worked, she noticed tiny particles on the rag, remnants of the scrub and grime that had been hiding in her skin. She frowned, surprised by how much was still there even after washing with soap.

"Yes, it is amazing how much gunk hides in those pores," Lisa said knowingly. "Okay, time to move on to the next stage."

Lisa reached for a jar filled with pre-soaked astringent rags. "We are going to lay these on your face for about a minute," she explained, removing the lid and placing it on the counter. She held the jar out toward Sophie.

Sophie pulled out a rag, squeezed out the excess liquid, and carefully spread it over her face. The rag stung lightly against her skin, the chemicals activating a faint tingling sensation. She began silently counting the seconds, the prickling sensation lingering but bearable. By the time she reached sixty, she tipped her head forward and peeled the rag off, instinctively moving to drop it into the basin of water.

"Whoa!" Lisa exclaimed, quickly grabbing the rag from her. "This rag goes back in the jar. If it gets mixed with water or soap, we'd have to clean and re-soak it all over again."

"Oh, sorry," Sophie said sheepishly as Lisa returned the rag to the jar.

"How does your skin feel?" Lisa asked, placing the jar back on the counter.

"Kinda stings," Sophie reported honestly, before raising an eyebrow. "So, what's next?"

"This is the best part," Lisa said with a grin. She replaced the jar of astringent under the counter and grabbed a sleek, cylindrical bottle of oil. "This is jasmine oil infused with emberroot. It'll moisturize and invigorate your skin." She gave the bottle a playful shake.

Sophie held out her hand, and Lisa poured a small amount of the warm, fragrant oil into her palm. Sophie rubbed the oil between her hands and gently spread it over her face. The sting from the astringent faded almost immediately, replaced by a comforting warmth that seemed to radiate from within her skin. It felt like sunlight softly glowing beneath the surface of her face.

"Mmm... that's nice," Sophie murmured, half to herself, as the soothing sensation settled in.

"Your skin is absolutely glowing," Lisa said, admiring the way Sophie's rich, chocolate-colored complexion gleamed under the soft lighting. The oil complemented the striking contrast of Sophie's violet hair and eyes, and her dark skin.

Sophie turned to the mirror and leaned closer, smiling as she admired her reflection. Her skin was clean and radiant, practically luminous. "I have to get some of this beauty stuff for myself." she said, turning her face from side to side and running her fingers over her smooth cheeks.

"Luckily, I know someone who can help with that," Lisa said with a playful wink.

The two of them laughed together, their friendship strengthened through this simple but meaningful moment of shared self-care.

[-----◉-----]

As twilight deepened, its golden hues streaming through the mansion's grand windows, three of the four avatars, Sophie, Annabelle, Regina, and Brother Marcus, along with Captain Kidd, assembled in the opulent dining room. It was a rare moment of camaraderie amidst their unfolding journey. Annabelle, Regina, and Captain Kidd radiated a newfound elegance, their recent visit to the tailor's shop evident in their attire. Each outfit seemed to reflect the essence of its wearer: Annabelle's fiery orange ensemble echoed her bold, untamed spirit; Regina's attire balanced grace with a core of quiet resilience, the silver sheen of her hair shimmering like liquid light; and Captain Kidd's refined yet adventurous look hinted at a man who moved effortlessly between high society and daring escapades.

Sophie, by contrast, embraced a subtler, tailored look. She wore neatly pressed purple slacks paired with a crisp white shirt, accented by a matching vest and tie. Her afro, perfectly rounded and luminous, gave her a regal air. Tonight, she had set aside her signature fedora a symbolic shedding of her usual armor, making a subtle statement of quiet elegance.

Brother Marcus had also deviated from his usual Order uniform. He wore simple slacks and a white shirt, blending in with the mansion's refined atmosphere. His ever-present journal, slung by a leather strap across his back, was a quiet reminder of the knowledge and burdens he carried. His pistol, concealed beneath his clothes, remained close, an unspoken requirement of his duty.

Guided by the mansion's attendants, the group moved toward the dining room with a quiet sense of expectancy. The table, draped in white linen and layered with dark red underlays, gleamed under the soft glow of chandeliers. Every detail, from the precisely aligned silverware to the perfectly positioned water glasses, hinted at unseen hands laboring with meticulous care.

Lisa's entrance turned every head. Draped in a flowing white gown accented with soft green trim, she moved with effortless grace. Her green hair was styled in a flawless bun, and the sash across her shoulder lent her an air of quiet regality. As she took her seat beside Brother Marcus, an unspoken alliance seemed to manifest in the arrangement. To her left, an empty chair remained, a silent placeholder for either an unseen guest or an unfulfilled role in this delicate tableau.

At the head of the table, the seat awaited Governor Conrad Nozaki. The pause in the proceedings added to the room's quiet tension, as if the mansion itself were holding its breath. Regina's striking presence was underscored by her shoulder length, entirely silver hair, a mark of her connection to the Goddess of Change, gleaming under the room's soft lighting like strands of moonlight. Her composed elegance contrasted against Annabelle's playful defiance; the hairdresser had woven white ribbons through her wild locks, as if symbolically taming her wild hair for the formal occasion. Captain Kidd, seated beside Annabelle, exuded calm assurance, his attire perfectly balanced between casual defiance and respectful poise.

As everyone settled into their seats, the soft clinking of glasses and low murmur of conversation filled the room. The setting sun painted long shadows across the polished floors, each shadow an echo of the hidden complexities within the gathered

78

company. Tonight, the air whispered promises of camaraderie and family togetherness.

Lisa broke the quiet anticipation with a warm, confident tone. "Good evening, everyone," she greeted, settling into her chair with a grace that belied her inner anticipation. The gentle hum of conversation stilled as her guests gave her their attention. "Mom and Dad should be joining us shortly," she continued. "Unfortunately, Evelyn might not make it tonight. She has been busy preparing for the Goddess Gala tomorrow. It has been a whirlwind for her."

Regina's eyes lit up, her smile radiant. "You look absolutely beautiful, Lisa," she complimented, her voice vibrant with admiration.

"Aye, Lisa," Annabelle added, her tone carrying the weight of sincere praise. "Yer a true vision of beauty."

A smile blossomed on Lisa's face, warmth radiating from her expression. "Thank you," she replied softly, her voice imbued with genuine gratitude. In this moment, surrounded by *friends*, she felt somehow grounded, anchored even by these girls.

The atmosphere shifted subtly as Lisa's parents, Conrad and Linda Nozaki, made their entrance. Conrad's attire, a simple grey suit with an open collar, absent a tie, exuded relaxed elegance. Beside him, Linda's sleek black dress, cinched at the waist with a striking yellow sash, added an air of refined sophistication.

"Good evening, everyone," Conrad greeted warmly, his presence putting the room at ease. "I trust everything is to your satisfaction?" He posed the question with a genial smile before moving to take his seat at the head of the table, Linda settling gracefully beside him, adjacent to Lisa.

"Good evening, Mother," Lisa greeted respectfully, her voice soft yet affectionate.

"Welcome home, my little chipmunk," Linda replied with a tender smile, using the nickname as a nostalgic echo of their shared moments. She reached out to gently squeeze Lisa's arm. "Did you get a chance to see Evelyn today?"

"Yes, ma'am. She's completely immersed in the gala preparations," Lisa replied.

"She's not the only one busy with preparations," Linda added cryptically, her tone laced with playful intrigue.

"Well then," Conrad interjected, his voice booming with jovial authority, "shall we begin the feast?"

"Aye!" Annabelle exclaimed enthusiastically. The volume of her response drew several amused glances, including a subtle nudge from Captain Kidd, gently reminding her of the formal setting.

Conrad chuckled and turned his attention to Annabelle with mild curiosity. "And who might you be?" he asked, his tone light but subtly inquisitive.

Annabelle, sensing an opportunity, straightened and adopted the polished demeanor of her *proper voice*. "Indeed, Lord Nozaki," she said, her voice smooth and respectful. "Lisa and I have forged a strong friendship." Her radiant smile aimed to ease any doubts her lively entrance had sparked. "Annabelle Salazar, at your service," she introduced herself with a graceful nod.

Marcus blinked in surprise, quietly admiring Annabelle's transformation. He'd never seen her deploy such poise before. *She's sharper than she lets on*, he thought to himself, recognizing the strategic charm she wielded.

"She's not just a friend," Regina added eagerly, supporting Annabelle. "She's an exceptional mentor in magic. And her cooking? Unmatched. The crew of the Stormfang always shows up when Lisa's in the kitchen."

Lisa's face warmed with a mix of pride and embarrassment as the compliments flowed.

"The Stormfang?" Conrad echoed, his brow furrowing in mild confusion.

Captain Kidd interjected smoothly. "The Stormfang is my ship, Governor," he explained, his voice carrying the authority of his title. "A vessel of significance on the seas."

"Ah, the pirate ship," Conrad mused, the pieces of scattered rumors falling into place.

"With all due respect, Governor," Annabelle corrected gently, maintaining her composed elegance, "we are privateers, not pirates. While pirates seek plunder and chaos, we operate by a different code. We navigate the seas on our own terms, without descending into lawlessness."

"So you claim, young lady," Conrad replied with measured skepticism. He turned his attention to Sophie, his tone gaining an edge. "And what of you, young one from Jiberau?"

Sophie's eyes hardened at the question. "I beg your pardon?" she said icily, her voice sharp with indignation.

"Daddy," Lisa interjected firmly, her tone carrying a mixture of correction and patience, "they are called the Aurorium Clan. *Jiberau* was a term from their darker days of enslavement."

"Thank you," Sophie said from across the table, acknowledging Lisa's support with a grateful nod.

The tension was interrupted as a kitchen attendant, clad in a crisp white chef's jacket, wheeled in a cart adorned with gleaming white bowls. "Appetizers are served," he announced with a practiced grace. Attendants swiftly distributed bowls of vibrant red soup to Captain Kidd, Annabelle, Regina, Brother Marcus, Lisa, and Sophie. At the same time, Conrad and Linda received theirs directly from the chef, a silent acknowledgement of their high status.

The room filled with the rich, savory aroma of the dish. Just as spoons were lifted in anticipation, Conrad raised a hand, commanding a momentary pause. "Shall we pray?" he proposed, instilling a reverent hush across the gathering.

Instantly, Lisa, Conrad, and Linda bowed their heads in solemnity. Lisa's eyes flickered open for a brief moment, scanning the table. She observed her companions' varying reactions: Brother Marcus folded his hands respectfully; Regina mirrored Lisa's posture without hesitation. Meanwhile, Sophie maintained a neutral stance, silently observing. Annabelle, however, remained relaxed, clearly unconcerned with the formality.

Lisa's gaze sharpened as she caught Annabelle's nonchalant posture. Annabelle blinked and shrugged lightly, her expression asking, *What's the issue?*

Lisa's eyes narrowed, silently conveying: *You know exactly what.*

With a resigned sigh, Annabelle waved a hand as if to say, *Fine*, and reluctantly bowed her head, making a token effort to participate.

Conrad's voice resonated through the room. "Oh, great Goddess of the Harvest, we extend our deepest gratitude for the bounty before us. We rejoice in Lisa's safe return to our fold." Linda gently squeezed Lisa's hand in a quiet gesture of solidarity as Conrad continued, "We seek your forgiveness for our missteps and implore your continued blessings. In your grace, we find our sustenance and purpose."

Though the words rang of gratitude, Lisa detected an undertone in her father's voice, a veiled criticism that stirred a silent frustration within her. Still, she chose restraint, refusing to rise to the provocation.

"May the harvests flourish," Conrad concluded, his words hanging in the solemn air.

Echoing Conrad's words, the assembled voices, including Lisa, Linda, and the staff, unified in their response, "May the harvests flourish," sealing the prayer with collective affirmation.

As the group began savoring the appetizer, the rich, vibrant flavors surprised Annabelle, Regina, Brother Marcus, and Sophie. Despite the simplicity of its tomato and spice composition, the soup's taste far surpassed their expectations.

"Lisa," Annabelle called out in her refined voice, curiosity sparkling in her eyes. "Can ye replicate this soup's magic?"

Lisa chuckled softly. "Maybe, if I could get my hands on the recipe."

Linda Nozaki smiled teasingly at her daughter. "Have you been playing chef for your friends?"

"Yes, Mother," Lisa admitted with a hint of pride. "While I was on the Stormfang, the galley became my refuge. It turns out my culinary exploits were pretty popular."

Conrad, his tone carefully measured, added, "It's good to know you kept yourself... occupied during your absence." His words alluded to the unspoken matter of Lisa's journey with privateers and her time alongside the Order of Saint Lorraine, a delicate chapter indeed.

"Serving the goddess demands my all, Father," Lisa replied with steady composure. She redirected her focus to the dish before her, choosing not to engage further.

The group finished their soup in silence, savoring every last spoonful. The attendants efficiently cleared the bowls, paving the way for the main course. With a flourish, the chef announced its arrival, personally serving the governor and his wife to emphasize their honored status.

The main course was a feast for the senses: perfectly roasted half-chickens accompanied by golden-crisp potatoes and vibrant seasonal vegetables. The aromas alone elicited awe from the guests.

Annabelle marveled at the chicken's flavor, wondering if there was magic hidden in the recipe. Regina relished the perfect harmony of spices and textures with each bite. Brother Marcus, eating quietly, reflected that he could only dream of meals this good back on Order Island. Meanwhile, Sophie enjoyed the variety on her plate, savoring each new flavor. *Do they eat like this every day?* she wondered.

Lisa glanced around the table and noticed the reverence in her companions' expressions. Their admiration for the chef's skill filled her with quiet humility. She recognized how far her own culinary journey had to go.

When the last of the main course had been cleared, the attendants returned with the next offering. The chef announced proudly, "Dessert is served."

The kitchen doors swung open to reveal plates bearing slices of fresh apple pie, each paired with a scoop of creamy vanilla ice cream and drizzled with caramel. As with the previous courses, the governor and his wife received their desserts directly from the chef, reinforcing their distinguished status.

"Captain Lowe," Conrad's voice carried down the table to Captain Kidd. "I'm curious about the nature of your ship's voyages."

"Indeed, Governor," Kidd responded formally. "The Stormfang primarily engages in the transport of passengers and goods between harbors, much like other privateer vessels." He paused to savor a bite of pie before continuing.

"Fascinating," Conrad said, leaning forward. "Can you share any particularly memorable assignments?"

"Excluding the current company," Captain Kidd began with a slight smile, glancing at Annabelle, "there was one time we transported a cargo of chicken eggs from Verdantia to Stoneridge. Midway through the voyage, the eggs began hatching."

Annabelle grinned mischievously. "The hold turned into a chaotic nursery," she added.

Kidd chuckled. "By the time we reached Stoneridge, the client was... less than pleased."

Annabelle mimicked the shopkeeper's indignant reaction, her voice high and exaggerated. "'I don't deal in chickens! What am I supposed to do with these?'"

The table laughed as Kidd continued, "Fortunately, Annabelle found a farm willing to take the chicks off our hands. Thanks to her determination, they found a new home."

Annabelle's cheeks flushed with a mixture of pride and modesty.

Conrad, however, grew somber. "These farms... They undermine the blessings of the Harvest Goddess. They steal sacred techniques to profit off our lands," he muttered darkly. His comment caused an awkward pause at the table. The group used the opportunity to focus on their desserts, letting the tense moment pass in silence.

Eventually, Conrad's gaze shifted to Sophie, his expression sharp with disapproval. "Miss," he began, eyeing her purple slacks and vest with thinly veiled disdain, "is it not customary for the Jiberau to wear dresses?"

Sophie met his gaze with calm defiance. "I wouldn't know," she replied coolly. "I'm from the Aurorium Clan."

Conrad sighed heavily, his expression momentarily distant. "The Jiberau were once a noble people," he mused. "They served willingly across all seven kingdoms." He leaned back, his tone darkening. "Then they chose that nasty business, against the royal families for their 'freedom'... and shattered the balance of our society." He shook his head, as though lamenting a tragic mistake, and took a bite of his dessert.

The atmosphere grew taut as Sophie leaned forward, her eyes burning with conviction. "Freedom," she said firmly, "is a universal right, not a privilege granted at the whims of the powerful." Her voice remained steady but charged with emotion.

"You're quick to speak of the Jiberau's 'service,'" she continued, "yet you ignore the horrors inflicted upon them. Their children were torn from their arms. Resistance was met with brutal violence and death. And despite those atrocities, they rose, stronger and more defiant than ever." She paused, her gaze unwavering. "They became a testament to justice, to the courage of those who refuse to live in chains."

A heavy silence followed, Sophie's words resonating in the space like a challenge waiting for an answer. Conrad said nothing at first, seemingly caught between defensiveness and reflection. The tension hung, palpable, as the evening's undercurrents surged closer to the surface.

"And that night of terror," Conrad said coldly, "when your people robbed us of our great royal family, King Calvin, Queen Aveline, and all the princes and princesses." His tone was almost accusatory, as though Sophie herself had been responsible. "All so the Jiberau could play soldier and constable." He shook his head with disdain. "What a waste."

Sophie's jaw tightened as she worked to suppress the fury rising in her chest. She calmly reached for her glass, taking a slow sip of water to center herself. When she finally spoke, her voice was measured but edged with quiet defiance.

"The Seven Kingdoms destroyed my people's future for the sake of a few extra coins," she began, her gaze locked firmly on Conrad. "The Jiberau petitioned the Council of Kingdoms, twice, for the right to freedom. Both times, they were denied." She paused to take another drink, her tone hardening as she continued. "That betrayal angered our ancestors so much that they rose from their graves, seeking justice for their children." She leaned back slightly, her eyes narrowing with a faint, dismissive sneer. "Unfortunately, the royal family died... but really, they could have just voted differently."

Conrad's face darkened at her casual dismissal. His nostrils flared, and Marcus, observing the exchange closely, noted the growing tension. Conrad had likely expected a philosophical triumph over Sophie, a chance to put her in her place, and instead, she had swiftly dismantled his argument. Marcus knew this conversation was heading toward disaster if it continued its course.

Attempting to steer the discussion onto safer ground, Marcus interjected smoothly, "Governor Nozaki, I wanted to ask, who on your staff should I speak to about arranging the avatars' trip to Snyder?"

Conrad, still fuming, turned toward Marcus, momentarily disoriented by the sudden shift. After a brief pause, he muttered, "My man Zachery can connect you with the right folks."

But Conrad was not ready to move on. His gaze swung back to Sophie, his voice low and sharp. "All those warriors of yours didn't keep Granmark safe, did they? It's a shame, really. If the Jiberau had just stayed in their proper place, that tragic event might never have happened."

Sophie's fingers clenched under the table. For a fleeting moment, she was glad she wasn't armed, if she'd had her pistol, she wasn't sure she could have resisted the temptation to shoot the man dead where he sat. Instead, she fixed Conrad with a glare of pure disgust.

Before Sophie could unleash the full force of her anger, Marcus spoke up, his voice stern and commanding. "Governor, with all due respect, that is completely uncalled for. *Miss Griffin is from Granmark*, and it is beyond offensive to speak of the massacre there with such disregard."

Conrad shook his head dismissively. "You see?" he said bitterly, waving a hand. "The world weeps for the Jiberau when their choices bring enemies seeking revenge. But no one shed a tear for the Verdantians who lost their farms and homes when their diligent workers disappeared overnight."

Sophie felt a tightness in her throat but swallowed it down. *He doesn't deserve my tears*, she reminded herself fiercely. Instead, she opted to hit back, her words as cold as ice.

"We should cry for businessmen so incompetent that they couldn't keep their farms running once their endless supply of free labor was gone."

Conrad's eyes narrowed, but Sophie wasn't finished. She leaned forward slightly, her voice dripping with disdain.

"Sounds like they should have been better businessmen... in my humble opinion."

83

The table fell into a tense silence. Sophie's icy sneer and unflinching gaze sent a clear message: *You don't intimidate me.*

Taking a moment to gather her composure, Sophie continued, her voice steady but charged with meaning. "It's a tragic irony that Verdantia, unlike the other kingdoms, has failed to learn from history's harsh lessons." She shook her head slightly and returned to her dessert, the sweetness on her tongue contrasting sharply with the bitterness of the conversation.

Governor Conrad Nozaki remained unfazed by her words, his tone turning patronizing. "You are quite mistaken, young lady. The Verdantian Jiberau experienced a far better fate than you're suggesting." He leaned forward, his posture suggesting authority. "While Verdantians shouldered the burdens of education and labor, learning the ways of the world, the Jiberau enjoyed their idyllic childhoods, playing on the farms until the age of ten. After that, their duties were limited to simple tasks, farm work mostly." He offered a thin, mocking smile. "Perhaps it's the school children who should be demanding liberation," he added with a dry chuckle, trivializing centuries of suffering with unsettling ease.

Sophie's response was swift and biting. "Oh, yes, treated so well," she echoed, her voice like ice. "Reduced to slaves. denied any and all rights, to their homes, their families, their very autonomy." Her frosty gaze locked on Conrad's, but she was momentarily distracted by a strange, familiar ringing in her ears. She couldn't place where she had heard it before, but she brushed it aside, determined to remain focused on the verbal battle at hand.

Conrad waved her off as though her words were a mere inconvenience. "So you claim, young lady. To me, they were simply indolent and ungrateful."

Sophie's eyes widened in disbelief. "Ungrateful?" she echoed, her voice taut with simmering rage. "When Jiberau women were subjected to unspeakable violations at the whims of their oppressors? When their husbands were sold or executed as public spectacles the moment they dared to resist?" Her words hit the room like thunder. "And when debts needed settling, it was their children who paid the price, traded like *animals* to satiate their masters' greed. Their desire for freedom wasn't a whim; it was survival."

The table fell into a stunned silence. The weight of Sophie's words lingered, their stark truth undeniable.

Conrad, however, was unmoved. "Your education in history seems woefully misguided," he remarked dismissively, turning his attention back to his dessert with a disinterested air, as if to downplay the gravity of her statements.

Lisa sat quietly, her discomfort growing with each passing moment. Her father's blatant disregard for Sophie's pain, and by extension, the suffering of her entire people, gnawed at her. She felt an urge to speak up, to defend her friend and denounce her father's ignorance, but something held her back. She chose, for now, to watch, her silence a calculated patience rather than agreement.

Across the table, Annabelle wordlessly raised her fork in a small gesture of solidarity with Sophie, her expression one of subtle but firm support.

The tension simmered beneath the clatter of silverware and the low murmur of conversations. Linda Nozaki, seated with a composed curiosity, let her gaze drift thoughtfully around the table. It eventually landed on Regina, who appeared unbothered by the tension. She calmly savored her pie and ice cream with a serene innocence that contrasted starkly with the gravity of the situation unfolding before them.

The surface civility barely masked the growing divide at the table. Words had been exchanged like blows, and though no one had raised their voice, the quiet was filled with unspoken conflicts yet to be resolved.

Breaking through the undercurrent of tension, Linda's voice rang clearly across the table. "Excuse me, young lady," she addressed Regina with a gracious smile, her curiosity evident. "Might I inquire your name?"

Regina paused, her spoon hovering mid-air, before responding with a warm, radiant smile that seemed to light the dimly lit dining hall. "I am Regina Fournier, Nexus mage from the esteemed academies of Laminae," she answered, her voice carrying a soft, melodic cadence. The unintentional rhyme drew a few light chuckles around the table.

Linda leaned forward slightly, intrigued. "And how many summers have you seen?"

"Fourteen—nearly fifteen," Regina answered, a glimmer of pride in her eyes. "I'll turn fifteen next month."

"A delightful coincidence," Linda observed, her smile deepening. "Lisa shares her birth month with you. May I ask the date?"

"May fourteenth," Regina said, her tone tinged with curiosity at the unfolding connection.

"That's my birthday as well," Annabelle interjected, her tone bright with wonder. The revelation drew the attention of everyone at the table.

Marcus, ever observant, seized the moment to explain. "All avatars share the same birth date," he noted, his voice calm but confident. "It's a peculiar and consistent feature when avatars are chosen."

Conrad, stroking his chin thoughtfully, leaned back in his chair. His gaze turned calculating as he pondered the revelation. "Such peculiarities... The Order certainly imposes unique conditions upon its avatars," he mused, his voice laced with skepticism.

"It isn't the Order's design," Marcus gently corrected. "They follow the guidance of the twelve goddesses themselves. The process ensures harmony between divine will and mortal duty."

Conrad's sharp gaze shifted toward Lisa, then swept across her companions. His voice grew firmer, protective instincts sharpening his words. "And what of my daughter? Is this truly the goddesses' desire for her, to become a warrior, or is it the ambition of the Order?"

Marcus met the governor's scrutiny with calm assurance. "With respect, Governor, both the Order and the goddesses recognize your daughter's unique potential. To guide an avatar is to align with divine will. Lisa's path serves not only her destiny but the balance and harmony the goddesses strive to maintain."

A heavy stillness fell over the table, Marcus's words resonating deeply. They carried the weight of ancient purpose, emphasizing the avatars' roles in shaping the world's future.

Conrad, however, remained skeptical. The traditions he held, those of strength and valor defined by men, clung stubbornly to his reasoning. "That makes no sense," he countered bluntly. "If the goddesses sought champions for battle, surely they would have chosen men."

Annabelle lifted her chin, her voice steady and dignified. "My goddess seeks a leader who can break chains, not with brute force, but with courage and style." Her words carried an air of conviction that silenced any immediate rebuttal.

Sophie followed, her voice calm but resolute. "My Goddess has entrusted me with the mantle of combat, but only as a last resort. Peace is always the goal, war is the final option, when every other path has been exhausted."

Lisa spoke next, her eyes gleaming with quiet hope. "My goddess envisions a world enriched by togetherness, where all are embraced, no matter their origins or differences."

Finally, Regina's voice emerged softly, yet with a determination that couldn't be ignored. "My goddess doesn't ask for warriors," she explained. "She desires agents of transformation. I am meant to guide the world into a new dawn, one where it thrives in harmony."

The table fell into a contemplative silence as each avatar's words echoed through the room. The scope of their destinies, so entwined with the divine, hovered over the gathering like an unseen force. Even Conrad, though skeptical, seemed momentarily at a loss for words. The weight of change was palpable, and for the first time that evening, the room shared a unified stillness, one that carried both awe and inevitability.

Conrad, scrutinizing Regina with a mixture of curiosity and challenge, posed a pointed question. "And what would you do when confronted with peril? When an adversary seeks your demise?" His voice carried skepticism, as though daring her to offer a credible answer.

Regina, momentarily focused on gathering the last bit of caramel onto her spoon, responded without looking up. "I'll use the magics at my disposal to defeat them." she said casually, though her words were imbued with quiet conviction.

Conrad scoffed, his tone thick with sarcasm. "I'm sure your journey will be long and full of vanquished foes," he remarked, though his curiosity betrayed him beneath the dismissal.

"I've already faced the Blood Witch and emerged victorious," Regina countered, her tone calm, as she savored the final bite of her dessert. The statement cut through the room like a blade, silencing any further mockery.

"The Blood Witch?" Conrad echoed, blinking in disbelief. Something flickered across his features.

Marcus stepped in, his tone diplomatic but firm. "Miss Regina faced and defeated a notorious criminal, a feat that saved her mother's life and proved her capable strength."

"And she's taken on more than that," Annabelle chimed in, her pride evident. "She rescued me from the Shadow Witch's clutches when we first met."

The weight of these revelations settled over the table. Conrad's gaze lingered on Regina, now sharper, probing as though trying to unravel the mysteries behind her calm exterior. Regina, feeling his intense scrutiny, retreated into the comfort of her dessert, letting the lingering flavors of pie and ice cream provide a momentary escape.

Linda broke the silence, her voice both concerned and resigned. "I do not believe my daughter is suited to the path of a warrior," she said softly, her gaze drifting to Lisa. "She is far better suited to nurturing roles like a mother. Facing down an enemy is not within her nature."

Lisa flinched inwardly at her mother's words. After everything she had endured, her divine encounter, the gifts bestowed upon her by the Goddess of Unity, such doubts stung deeply. Taking a steady breath, she composed herself and spoke with quiet authority.

"Mother, the Goddess has granted me abilities beyond your understanding. I have been empowered in ways you can't imagine," Lisa said, her voice steady and resolute.

Linda waved dismissively, clinging to her old beliefs. "Yes, dear, I'm sure she has. But your father is right, you are not a warrior, not like your companions here."

Lisa realized that words alone would never be enough to change her parents' minds. She would have to show them. Rising gracefully from her seat, she extended her hands, drawing on her mana. With practiced ease, she traced three glowing spell circles in the air.

An orange circle flared to life, drawing fire from the table's candles and shaping it into a hovering orb. A blue circle followed, pulling water from nearby jugs into a floating sphere. Finally, a green circle formed, coaxing the centerpiece's flowers to bloom and entwine in mid-air, forming a bouquet that drifted gently above the table.

Linda gasped, her alarm immediate. "Lisa! Displays of this magnitude are unnecessary!" Her tone was sharp, betraying her own knowledge of Earthbloom magic.

Lisa met her mother's gaze without flinching. "This is nothing compared to what I can truly do," she said calmly. "What you see here is a mere fraction of my reserves. I could cast more spells without diminishing these."

Conrad's voice cut through the moment like a blade. "Enough, Lisa."

At his command, Lisa gracefully dissolved the magic. The fire returned to the candles, the water flowed back into the jugs, and the flowers drifted gently back to the table. The room was left in stunned silence, the quiet now heavy with unspoken tension.

Conrad leaned forward, his tone sharp and authoritative. "You, young lady, are excused," he declared, his voice brooking no argument. "But before you go, I believe you owe everyone an apology for this... spectacle."

Lisa froze for a moment, disbelief flashing across her face. *An apology? For demonstrating the gifts bestowed upon her by the Goddess?* Slowly, her gaze hardened. The weight of her parents' expectations pressed down on her, but she stood tall, unwilling to be shamed for what she had become.

The room remained silent, every eye watching, waiting for her response.

The simmering frustration Lisa had been struggling with surged to the surface. This was a pivotal moment, one that demanded more than silent acquiescence. Slowly pushing her chair back, she rose to her full height, her posture embodying the strength and resolve that had crystallized within her.

"Indeed, it is time for me to leave," she said, her voice steady and calm. Offering a brief but courteous bow to the table, she continued, "I bid you all a good night." Her words carried a polite finality, signaling the end of her tolerance for the evening's hostilities. Turning on her heel, she made her way toward the door.

"Lisa," Conrad's voice cut through the air, sharp and commanding. "Your apology."

Lisa halted mid-step. Slowly, she pivoted to face her father, the spark of defiance in her eyes now burning with full intensity.

"Father," she began, her voice unwavering, "this evening has been marred by nothing but disparagement toward my companions and a complete disregard for their lives, beliefs, and experiences." She paused for effect, her words striking like steel. "I will gladly apologize to those present... after you offer your own apology to my fellow avatars."

The room fell into a tense stillness, the weight of her defiant stand palpable.

Marcus, ever the mediator, sensed the escalating tension and interjected gently. "It seems we have strayed beyond the bounds of productive discourse," he suggested, hoping to defuse the confrontation.

But Lisa remained firm, her gaze never breaking from her father's. She addressed Marcus without turning.

"Brother Marcus," she began, her tone pointed, "are you, or is the Order, engaged in any deceitful schemes? Do you conspire to overthrow this kingdom from the shadows?"

Marcus didn't hesitate. "I can assert with full confidence that we are not," he answered clearly and without ambiguity.

The room watched in rapt silence as Lisa continued, her words aimed as much at challenging her father's assumptions as affirming the integrity of the Order.

"And yet," she pressed on, her voice steady but tinged with both sadness and conviction, "since our arrival, both you and the Order have been subjected to grave accusations, accusations that do nothing but deepen distrust." She took a step forward, her gaze piercing through the tension like a beacon. "Do you not see how such claims only serve to fracture the unity we desperately need? The darkness we've all witnessed thrives on division."

Marcus nodded solemnly, recognizing the profound truth in her words. "Indeed," he agreed, his tone reflective. "Unfounded accusations weaken our shared purpose. They undermine the very harmony we seek to protect."

Lisa's expression softened, though her resolve remained intact. She turned her attention fully to Marcus now. "Brother Marcus," she said firmly, her voice resonating with quiet authority, "I must ask you to refrain from further intervention in this matter."

Marcus inclined his head slightly in deference, his respect for her leadership clear. "As you wish," he replied, offering a slight bow to acknowledge her directive.

With that, Lisa returned her gaze to her father, standing tall and unyielding. The message was clear: she would no longer tolerate being diminished or disrespected, *not by anyone, not even him*. The atmosphere in the room hung thick with unspoken tension, every member of the assembly silently processing the seismic shift in the dynamic between father and daughter.

Annabelle, who had once seen Lisa as the sheltered princess aboard the Stormfang, now witnessed a woman of unflinching resolve and strength, no longer burdened by fear.

Sophie cast a glance at Lisa, admiration flickering in her violet eyes. It wasn't just the elegance of Lisa's attire that impressed her, it is the fearless way she stood her ground against authority. That bravery became a beacon of inspiration.

Regina, though perhaps not fully understanding the complexities at play, grasped the significance of Lisa's defiance. This was more than a defense of herself; it was a stand for all of them.

Conrad's patience frayed to its limit. His voice, now sharp and thunderous, rang through the dining hall. "GO TO YOUR ROOM!" He jabbed a finger toward the exit, his frustration a physical force. Taking a deep breath to steady himself, he added more calmly, "We will discuss this later."

Lisa met his glare without a word, holding her ground for a moment longer before she inclined her head slightly in acknowledgment. She turned and resumed her departure, her steps echoing softly against the polished stone floor.

But a sudden, distinct sound halted her, paws clicking against the hard surface. Lisa's senses heightened as her Earthbloom sense alerted her to the approach of Silverpaw, her father's lynx familiar. Something was off. Its presence felt hostile in a way she had never known before.

"Father," Lisa called over her shoulder, uncertainty creeping into her voice. "Please call back Silverpaw?"

Conrad's response was tepid at best. "Silverpaw, enough," he muttered without conviction. The command held no absolute authority, and Silverpaw ignored it entirely. The lynx crouched, muscles coiling, before leaping directly at Lisa with startling ferocity.

Lisa had no time to cast a protective spell. Instinctively, she raised her arms to brace for impact.

The attack never landed.

A surge of seawater roared into the room, crashing into Silverpaw with the force of Annabelle's current spell. The lynx was flung against a marble column, the water swiftly reshaping into a swirling sphere that trapped the snarling creature within. The sphere shimmered ominously as Silverpaw clawed at the edges, powerless to escape.

Lisa's eyes darted to the source of her unexpected rescue. Annabelle stood with her right hand raised, her control over the spell evident in the way the water remained perfectly suspended. She gave Lisa a reassuring thumbs-up and a cocksure smile, her composure as steady as ever.

"Annabelle..." Lisa breathed, both astonished and grateful.

Conrad surged to his feet, alarmed. "What is this madness?! He'll drown in there!" he bellowed, his eyes wide with panic.

"Relax, Governor," Annabelle replied smoothly, her voice calm and confident. "The bubble contains a pocket of air. Your kitty can breathe just fine." She glanced at Captain Kidd, who watched her with a mixture of astonishment and approval. The captain's expression softened into a smile as Annabelle winked subtly at him, mate to mate, sharing a proud family moment.

The room was filled with tense silence as the avatars quietly reaffirmed their solidarity. In that moment, an unspoken vow passed between them: *they would stand by one another, against threats from both outside and within.*

"Release him immediately!" Conrad commanded, his voice brooking no argument.

Before Annabelle could respond, Marcus rose from his seat, his expression grave. "Governor," he began with firm resolve, "your familiar's attempt to harm Miss Lisa cannot be ignored. This was no accident."

Sophie crossed her arms and added dryly, "Maybe it's time to reevaluate who's really in charge between you and your familiar. Some extra training may be necessary."

Conrad hesitated, his gaze shifting between Marcus and Sophie. He appeared caught off guard by their unified front. Clearing his throat, he tried to downplay the incident. "At times, Silverpaw can be... overly zealous. Perhaps he simply wanted to play."

Lisa's eyes narrowed, seeing through the weak excuse. Silverpaw was no ordinary familiar, he was disciplined, loyal, and trained to act only on clear commands. The idea that he had acted on his own instinct was implausible. The more she thought about it, the more a painful realization settled within her: *the lynx had likely attacked under Conrad's silent influence*. The weight of that betrayal hit her like a stone.

Without a word, Lisa turned and resumed her departure. This time, her steps were steady but heavy with the weight of disappointment. The confrontation had revealed more than just tension; it had laid bare the growing chasm between her and her family.

The sound of her footsteps echoed through the hall, mingling with the unspoken emotions in the air. The pain of her father's disregard and the lingering sorrow of unacknowledged wounds clung to her like a shadow. But she did not falter. She walked with dignity, her resolve unbroken.

Behind her, the avatars watched in solemn understanding. This night had marked a turning point, not just in their journey, but in the bonds that held them together.

Chapter 6

Journal Entry, April 23rd, 1910

The storm that erupted between Lisa Nozaki and her father, Governor Conrad Nozaki, has shaken the very foundations of our mission. What once seemed like assured support now hangs precariously, frayed by familial conflict. The Governor, who holds significant influence over our next steps, may yet withdraw his favor, a development that could cripple our journey before it begins. Diplomacy will be critical in the coming days. Without Conrad Nozaki's cooperation, the expedition to Snyder and the mysterious site Brother Albert spoke of may be imperiled.

Lisa, however, has demonstrated a strength I had not fully appreciated. She stood tall in the face of both paternal control and societal expectation, refusing to be diminished. I worry that this defiance has deepened the rift between her and her father, though it has undoubtedly set an example among the avatars.

Annabelle Salazar's swift intervention during the altercation, using her magic to protect Lisa, caught me by surprise, but perhaps it shouldn't have. Despite their differences, there is an emerging bond of loyalty between the avatars, one forged in shared trials. Even Sophie Griffin, typically unflinching in the face of authority, bore the weight of Verdantia's patriarchal disdain with a calm resolve. Yet I fear that this land's unrelenting cultural shadows have touched a nerve deep within her, a reminder of injustices her people have long endured.

Meanwhile, Ladies Fournier and Salazar have embraced, if only temporarily, the luxuries and peculiarities of the Governor's mansion. Regina's grace and Annabelle's charm may prove vital tonight, as we navigate a more delicate arena: Evelyn Nozaki's Goddess Gala. This event, a grand celebration honoring Verdantia's deity, is poised to gather the region's elite under one roof. It will be more than an evening of pageantry; it is an opportunity—perhaps our only one—to mend the fractured ties between Lisa and her father, secure political support, and forge alliances that may tip the balance of our quest.

For now, we must play our roles carefully. The labyrinth of Verdantian politics offers both danger and opportunity. I suspect that tonight's festivities may hold more revelations than intended. As the avatars prepare for their introduction to Verdantia's upper echelons, I turn my attention to the logistics of our next journey. The path to Snyder will be paved not only with supplies and maps but also with trust—trust that remains fragile.

As the morning light spreads across this strange, beautiful land, I am reminded of the weight we carry. I can only hope that the Goddess Gala will illuminate a path forward, guiding us from the shadows of conflict into the promise of Unity and resolution.

[----- ⊕ -----]

At the sports track behind the Governor's mansion, Sophie and Regina jogged side by side. Regina strained to keep up with Sophie, who had slowed her pace out of consideration for her silver-haired training partner. As they completed their fifth lap, Sophie veered off toward the bleachers, grabbing a water bottle handed to her by the handsome attendant, Samuel. She took a long drink.

"Thank the goddess that's over," Regina sighed dramatically, collapsing onto the grass with her arms spread wide. She stared up at the sky, her breath coming in quick, ragged bursts.

Sophie wiped her face with a towel and smirked. "Over? That was only five laps. We've got five more."

"Five more?!" Regina shot upright, her face scrunching in disbelief. "What does all this running have to do with fighting and training anyway?"

Sophie capped the water bottle and sat beside her. "Endurance," she explained. "And discipline. If you can push past your limits here, you'll last longer in a fight when it really counts."

Groaning in protest, Regina dragged herself upright. "Ugh, fine. Guess I'll have to get used to being a morning runner now." She took the bottle Sophie offered, savoring a large gulp.

"Whoa, slow down," Sophie warned. "Too much at once, and you'll throw up."

Regina instantly stopped, wiping her mouth.

Sophie raised an eyebrow. "Ready?"

"Let's get it over with," Regina muttered, steeling herself as they returned to the track. They resumed jogging, their steps falling into rhythm. Despite her best efforts, Regina only managed three more laps before she stumbled to a stop, panting.

"Sorry, Sophie," she gasped, waving a hand. "I... I can't do any more."

"You okay?" Sophie slowed to a walk, concern flickering in her violet eyes.

"Yeah, I'm just wiped," Regina admitted, leaning forward with her hands on her knees.

"Alright. Rest up. I'll finish the laps, and then we'll move on to strength training," Sophie instructed before breaking into a quicker, more determined run.

As Sophie sped up, Regina watched in awe. Her friend's strides were long and powerful, her gaze focused solely on the track. Each lap she completed seemed effortless, her movements almost hypnotic. Regina lost count as Sophie circled the track again and again, passing the wooden bleachers multiple times without showing any signs of exhaustion.

"Is training with me holding her back?" Regina wondered aloud, a knot of doubt forming in her chest.

"Well, hello there."

Startled, Regina turned to find two boys approaching. They wore school uniforms and carried books. The blonde one looked a little shy, while his dark-haired friend exuded confidence. Both appeared to be around Regina's age.

"Hi," she greeted brightly, taking another sip of water.

The dark-haired boy spoke first. "Hey. I'm Toby, and this is Andrew. Are you and your friend new to the Kingdom?"

"Yep," Regina replied cheerfully. "We just arrived yesterday with Lisa."

"The governor's daughter?" Andrew perked up.

"That's right," Regina confirmed. Sophie flashed by in the distance, drawing their attention.

"Who is she?" Toby asked, eyes narrowing with curiosity.

"That's Sophie," Regina answered. "She's from the Aurorium Clan."

"Aurorium?" Andrew repeated, sounding impressed. "Look at her go... She is incredible."

"Yeah, such a vision," Toby added dreamily, watching Sophie sprint past again, her deep brown skin gleaming in the sunlight. Her afro-bun barely shifted despite the speed at which she moved.

"Does she have a boyfriend?" Andrew asked suddenly, snapping Regina out of her thoughts.

Caught off guard, Regina blinked. "I... don't think so."

"Oh, so she's free," Toby teased, nudging his friend with a smirk.

Before the could continue Regina redirected the conversation. "What school do you go to?"

"Meadowbrook Academy," Andrew answered.

"And you?"

"I was going to Laminae Public Number Seventy-One," Regina replied with a sigh. "But my family's on library duty at the Luminous, so I've been on home study. Now that I'm an avatar, who knows? Maybe I'll get permanent home study! No more dance classes, and I can have Mommy June cook me lunch every day. Her casserole's amazing. And her quiche—oh, goddess, her quiche..."

Toby and Andrew stared at her, dumbfounded by the flood of information.

"Quiche?" Toby echoed blankly.

"Home study," Andrew parroted, equally lost.

Regina tilted her head, scrutinizing their perplexed expressions.

Sophie slowed her pace, finally stopping by the bleachers where Regina and the two boys stood waiting. Grabbing a towel, she wiped the sweat from her face and neck.

"Well, hello there," the blonde-haired boy greeted with a charming smile. "Andrew Gibson, at your service." He extended his hand toward her, palm down, as though expecting her to accept it in some ceremonial fashion.

Sophie raised an eyebrow, momentarily caught off guard by the formality. Still, she reached out and shook his hand with her damp, sweat-slicked one. "Sentinel Sophie Griffin. Pleasure to meet you."

Andrew didn't seem fazed by her sweaty grip. "The pleasure is all mine," he said smoothly. Sophie found herself briefly appraising him: *well-dressed, confident, with an athletic build. Definitely easy on the eyes,* Sophie muses to herself.

"How are you enjoying our beautiful kingdom so far?" he asked her with a cute smile.

Sophie smirked. "Oh, I'm definitely liking the views. A girl could get used to this."

"Yes, we do have some breathtaking sights," he agreed with a grin. "Maybe I could show you around sometime?"

She tilted her head playfully. "Oh? You're a tour guide I couldn't have guessed?"

"For the right person, I just might be," he bantered back. "I have to ask—how did you get your hair and eyes to be purple?"

Sophie chuckled, tossing the towel over her shoulder. "Didn't you hear? I am so very special."

Andrew laughed, clearly enjoying the banter. Before the moment could deepen further, Regina interjected with a loud, innocent question: "Are you two going to kiss each other?"

Both Sophie and Andrew froze, eyes widening in shock. The tension shattered like glass, leaving them speechless as they stared at her. Toby snorted but quickly checked his watch, tugging Andrew's arm.

"Come on Drew, we have to get to class," Toby reminded him.

Andrew gave Sophie's hand a gentle squeeze before raising it to his lips and placing a soft kiss on her knuckles. "Sentinel Sophie Griffin," he said, voice warm, "I must take my leave. But I hope we meet again soon."

"That would be nice," Sophie replied, her smile returning. "Till next time, Mr. Gibson."

With a quick wave, Andrew and Toby hurried off toward the academy grounds.

Sophie watched them leave, then turned to Regina with an exasperated look. "Girl! we really need to work on your timing."

"Sorry!" Regina said sheepishly, rubbing the back of her head. "I didn't realize what was going on."

Sophie sighed, shaking her head in mock defeat. "It's fine, I guess." She gave Regina a good-natured pat on the shoulder. "Come on, we've still got training to do."

She paused mid-step, her expression shifting. That strange, familiar ringing noise echoed faintly in her ears again. Sophie scanned the horizon, her brow furrowing.

"Do you hear that?" she asked quietly, her gaze distant.

"Hear what?" Regina replied, looking around with confusion.

Sophie didn't answer right away. She stood still, listening, as the ringing persisted, like a whisper carried on the wind. Something was calling out there, something she had heard before.

[-----◉-----]

Confined to her room as punishment for yesterday's heated argument with her father, Lisa sought solace in the small comfort of breakfast alone. The morning sun streamed through her window, casting a soft, golden light over the tray of fruit salad and warm, buttery croissants. As she spread the last slice of butter across a flaky surface, watching it melt into the delicate layers, she felt some of the tension that had gripped her chest begin to ease. Yet, her mind refused to quiet. *Had I been too unyielding? Had I crossed a line?* She replayed the argument in her head like a bitter refrain.

With a final bite, Lisa set aside the remnants of her meal and turned her attention to her morning routine. The act of bathing was more than a simple ritual of cleansing, it was a quiet act of resilience, a way to refresh her spirit and shed the doubts clinging to her like shadows. Afterward, each stroke of the hairbrush was purposeful, each stretch and exercise a grounding ritual that helped center her amidst the uncertainty that clouded the day ahead.

Choosing her attire became a deliberate exercise in self-expression. The red dress with white trim wasn't just for aesthetics, it was a declaration. I am no one's prisoner and I will not be diminished.

Dressed and composed, Lisa crossed the room to the large window overlooking the mansion's lush garden. Vibrant greenery sprawled below, a stark contrast to the stifling walls of her confinement. She sank into the cushioned window seat, a favorite spot where she often let her mind wander. Today, however, she sought refuge in a different escape. She opened Earthbloom Magic: Volume Three, its fresh pages whispering of distant wonders and untold powerful techniques.

As she read, the garden beyond her window blossomed with quiet life. Flowers unfurled in the sun's warmth, and birds flitted among the trees, oblivious to the turmoil brewing inside her heart. The words on the page transported her into a different realm, a world where she wasn't constrained by her father's expectations but instead by the boundless possibilities of her magic.

Lisa was no novice to Earthbloom magic. Her talent was both innate and nurtured under the tutelage of a revered master, her lessons grueling and spiritual in nature. Yet, the basics she had mastered were merely the surface of an ocean whose depths she had yet to fully comprehend. As she delved further into the text, new ideas challenged her understanding. The book spoke of complex techniques like combining elemental circles, a method Regina had been working on. Lisa was not one to be a follower, but she would not let Regina upstage her in her own Earthbloom magic.

The concept of nested spell circles captured her imagination most vividly. A water circle nested within a plant growth circle, capable of conjuring a flourishing forest in an instant, such mastery hinted at a symbiotic harmony between elements she had never been taught to pursue. It wasn't just about faith or intuition. It was a blend of artistry and precision, a symphony of nature that required both elemental alignment and an academic understanding of magical theory.

Then came the section on rune alignment, which revealed a staggering truth: a spell's effectiveness could increase or fail by up to eighty percent based on the resonance of its runes. This detail reframed everything Lisa had once believed about magic as an intuitive craft. Precision, not just intent, held the key to true mastery. One misplaced rune, one error in alignment, and even the most promising spell could collapse into chaos or worse – mana backlash.

As Lisa absorbed these revelations, a sense of awe enveloped her. Magic wasn't just the flowing energy she had once thought, it is an intricate dance between forces, a balance between logic and the untamed energies of Mother Earth. There was still so much to learn, so many possibilities to explore. It was as though the book had unlocked a door to a new dimension of her craft, inviting her to step through and claim her potential.

Just as she prepared to turn the page, a knock at the door interrupted her thoughts. Lisa frowned, glancing at the clock on her desk.

Who would summon me at this hour?

With a resigned sigh, she slipped a delicate bookmark between the pages, preserving the place she longed to return to. Rising from the window seat, she moved gracefully toward the door, each step measured and composed.

Lisa approached the door, thoughts swirling about who might be waiting on the other side. She opened it to find a face she didn't recognize, an attendant, yet unfamiliar in the bustling household. Curiosity flitted across her mind as she took in his presence.

"Good day, Miss Lisa," he greeted, bowing slightly in a display of both respect and formality. His voice carried a warmth that softened the rigid decorum.

"Your presence is required in the main ballroom," he continued, his gaze steady but hinting at a quiet urgency.

Lisa nodded with polite detachment, masking her growing curiosity. "Of course. Shall we?" she replied, her tone measured and poised.

"Right away, madam," the attendant affirmed. He turned and led the way, his footsteps brisk but deliberate. Lisa followed in silence, her feet gliding over the plush carpeting as they made their way through the mansion's labyrinthine corridors.

The atmosphere was charged with anticipation. Attendants and workers hurried past, their hands laden with decorations and equipment. The flurry of preparations could mean only one thing: *the Goddess Gala*. Her mother, Linda, and elder sister, Evelyn, had undoubtedly thrown themselves into orchestrating every last detail. Lisa's gaze lingered on a group of military officials gathered near one hallway, their voices low and serious. Their presence spoke volumes, her father, the Governor, was likely convening with them over matters of great importance.

They finally arrived at the towering double doors of the grand ballroom. The attendant stepped forward and opened one of them with a reverent air.

"The Lady Nozaki awaits, ma'am," he announced.

Lisa inclined her head in acknowledgment. "Thank you," she said quietly before stepping into the ballroom. The door closed softly behind her, leaving her surrounded by a whirlwind of purposeful activity.

The vast space thrummed with life. Attendants moved like clockwork, their actions perfectly choreographed as they arranged decorations and constructed an elevated dance floor. Carpenters hammered in unison, their measured rhythm echoing faintly beneath the murmurs of bustling workers. Streams of silk, white, green, and gold, adorned the walls, evoking the splendor of a verdant garden in bloom.

In the midst of the commotion stood Linda Nozaki, a figure of quiet authority. Dressed in a simple gown with her hair tucked under a bonnet, she issued precise instructions to a group of servants. They were draping an opulent cloth over a massive portrait of Evelyn. The image captured Evelyn in radiant beauty, her white dress and serene smile embodying both grace and joy.

Lisa approached cautiously. "Hello, Mother," she said, her voice soft but deliberate.

Linda turned, her expression sharp with surprise and disapproval. "Hello, Mother," she repeated, her tone laced with reproach. "After yesterday's display, is that all you have to say?"

The words hit like a cold gust of wind, momentarily silencing the surrounding activity. Lisa hesitated, the sting of her mother's scolding lodging itself in her chest. Linda continued, the tension in her voice palpable. "Honestly, Lisa, with everything going on, why do you insist on vexing the family so?"

Lisa bit back a retort, unsure how to bridge the chasm between them. Silence seemed like her only viable defense.

Linda's eyes narrowed. "And now you've become a quiet little chipmunk. Those girls…" she gestured vaguely, her irritation simmering, "they are a bad influence on you."

The accusation stung. It was unfair, dismissive of what truly mattered. Lisa took a steadying breath. "That is not it, Mother," she said softly but firmly. She needed to make her understand. "It is about more than that."

"Oh? Then enlighten me." Skepticism dripped from Linda's words.

Lisa hesitated but pressed on. "Daddy was... cruel to the other avatars and to Brother Marcus, without any cause. The goddesses spoke to us, she said we have to work together, all of us. But daddy was trying to tear us down and drive us apart."

"The Goddesses?" Linda repeated, as though the concept were foreign and slightly absurd.

"Yes," Lisa confirmed, meeting her mother's gaze with quiet conviction. "When I communed with the Goddess of Unity, she warned of a threat, something only we avatars can prevent. That's why we need to stay united. She reached out to me because of my connection to her... that is why I have my green hair and eyes. It's not a coincidence."

Linda's expression shifted, flickering between concern and skepticism. "And here I thought I was your mother," she said, her voice softening slightly despite the bite of her words. "Where did you supposedly meet this goddess?"

"On Order Island," Lisa answered, her voice firm despite the tension. She knew her family's distrust of the Order ran deep, but she wouldn't falter now.

Linda's eyes darkened with caution. "You should be careful, little chipmunk," she warned gently. "The Order is not as virtuous as they would have you believe. If they had their way, they would rule all Seven Kingdoms. Your father knows that, it is why we fight to preserve our way of life here in Verdantia."

Lisa shook her head slightly. "I do not think they have those ambitions," she countered, her voice carrying a quiet but resolute hope. "What I saw... it wasn't about control. It was about collaboration, about working together to make the world a better place for everyone."

Linda sighed deeply, her gaze softening just a fraction. "Just be careful," she repeated, though her warning lacked its earlier edge. "You may see only what they want you to see."

Lisa didn't respond, letting the words hang between them. There was more to this conversation, more to her mother's fears than she fully understood, but for now, it was enough to stand her ground.

Linda barely masked her exasperation with a scoff, her attention abruptly pulled to a scene across the room. "No, no, no!" she exclaimed, her voice sharp as she spotted a group of attendants in the middle of a floral disaster. "The tiger lilies belong on the center tables, not the outliers!" With a firm grip, she seized Lisa's wrist and swept her into the flurry of activity. "Apparently, I must oversee everything myself."

They navigated the bustling ballroom together, weaving through a sea of workers. The air was charged with tension, and the attendants froze in place under the intensity of Linda's gaze as she approached. Her voice, though composed, carried the weight of command. "We have a limited number of tiger lily centerpieces," she stated, her tone brooking no argument. "Joseph, where is Joseph? We agreed, tiger lilies for the center, jasmine for the perimeter. Surely that is not too hard to follow?"

"I'm here, I'm here!" came a hurried voice from behind. A flustered man appeared, his face flushed from exertion. "What seems to be the problem?"

Linda turned to face him, her expression softening slightly without losing its edge of authority. "There you are, Joseph. We agreed on the arrangement, did we not? Jasmine on the outer tables, tiger lilies at the center."

"Yes, of course," Joseph replied, already scanning a set of notes in his hands. He turned to an older attendant, who hesitantly pulled a crumpled paper from his pocket. "Which version of the plan are you using?" Joseph asked.

"Seventeen," the attendant confessed sheepishly.

"Ah, that explains it," Joseph said with a sigh. "We're currently on version twenty-three." He offered Linda a reassuring smile. "Please, ma'am, don't trouble yourself further. I'll handle this. Perhaps you and Miss Lisa could take a moment to relax over some tea. You've already had such a long morning."

Linda's posture eased, the tension ebbing slightly as she placed a hand on Joseph's shoulder in gratitude. "What would I do without you?" she praised.

"Let's not dwell on such grim thoughts," he joked lightly, covering her hand briefly with his own. "Rest assured, everything will be in perfect order for tonight's festivities."

Taking the opportunity for respite, Linda turned and strode toward an exit, Lisa trailing quietly behind her. They walked in companionable silence, the din of the ballroom fading behind them.

"I cannot wait for all of this to be over," Linda admitted after a while, her voice softer, distant. Her gaze wandered as if searching for peace on the horizon.

Their steps brought them to a staircase crowned by a set of glass double doors. An attendant stood nearby and straightened at their approach.

"My daughter and I will be taking tea on the balcony," Linda announced with her usual command.

"Very good, ma'am," the attendant replied, quickly ascending the stairs to open the doors for them. The balcony beyond revealed a stunning panorama of the gardens and distant fields, the afternoon light casting a serene glow over the landscape.

The attendant worked with swift efficiency, pulling out chairs, draping a white cloth over the table, and arranging cups with precision. A tray of jars sat nearby, awaiting their selection. "Shall I fetch the jasmine tea, ma'am?" he inquired.

Linda nodded approvingly. "Yes, thank you."

Once he left, the two women took their seats. The moment felt suspended in time, the quiet offering them a rare opportunity for reflection.

"So," Linda began, her tone deceptively light yet edged with expectation, "tell me about your Goddess of Unity."

Lisa met her mother's gaze steadily. "She is not my goddess, Mother," she began thoughtfully. Then, after a pause, she reconsidered. "Well, in a way, she is. I am her avatar."

Linda leaned forward slightly, curiosity sparking in her eyes. "You don't say. And what exactly does an avatar do?"

Lisa drew in a deep breath, organizing her thoughts. "I'm meant to carry out Unity's will on Earth," she explained, her voice a blend of awe and responsibility. "Mother, there is a great threat approaching, one that requires us to act now, together."

Linda's brow arched in mild disbelief. "And this goddess of yours chose you to handle it? Not a soldier or a seasoned warrior? What's your plan, dear, cultivate peace through gardening and cooking?" she quipped, her tone half-mocking while challenging.

The words stung, but Lisa held firm. "Without unity, Mother, the world will be thrown into chaos," she said, her voice steady and resolute. "We'll be trapped in cycles of tyranny and destruction, with leaders masking their oppression as justice and prosperity. I might not be equipped to fight battles, but I can build the alliances that could prevent those battles from ever happening."

Linda remained silent for a moment, her expression thoughtful as the attendant returned with the tea. His movements were smooth and precise, a quiet interlude to their tense discussion. He poured the tea with care, then bowed before stepping away.

As they sipped their tea, Linda finally spoke, her voice quieter than before. "You're serious about this."

"I am," Lisa replied gently.

Linda nodded slowly. "Very well. I will hear you out." Turning to the attendant, she instructed, "Please summon Sir Santora."

"At once, ma'am," the attendant replied, leaving with swift purpose.

Lisa watched him go, then turned back to her mother, sensing the shift in their conversation. There was no longer outright dismissal in Linda's eyes, only a cautious consideration, as if she were finally beginning to understand that something much larger than either of them was at play.

As the attendant's footsteps faded, Linda and Lisa returned their attention to their tea, both blowing gently across the surface before taking a sip. The mirrored action subtly underscored the divide between them, Lisa's vibrant green hair and eyes a stark contrast to her mother's more traditional features. Yet beneath their differences lay a mutual, unspoken desire to understand each other.

Linda broke the silence, seeking clarity. "So, how exactly did you come to meet this goddess of yours?" Despite her lingering skepticism, curiosity glimmered in her tone.

Lisa's gaze grew distant as she reflected on the encounter. "On Order Island, there's a sacred place where our realm overlaps with theirs. The four of us avatars, connected deeply within ourselves and found pathways to our goddesses' domains." Her voice softened with awe. "Meeting Unity was like reconnecting with a part of my soul. She even had my green hair and eyes. It felt... familiar, like seeing a long-lost friend."

Linda's brows knit slightly in thought. "Did the Order provide any... refreshments before this mystical experience?" she asked, her voice laced with suspicion.

Lisa nodded. "Yes, they offered us tea, something unique to the island. It was delightful, unlike anything I've ever tasted."

"And the other avatars? They drank it too?" Linda pressed.

"Yes, we all did." Lisa frowned, perplexed by the line of questioning. "But what does that have to do with..."

"And your manservant? Did he drink any of this tea?" Linda interrupted, her gaze steady.

Lisa shook her head slowly. "No, it was only for us avatars."

Linda nodded, taking another sip, her expression thoughtful but unreadable. Silence settled between them for a moment.

"I do not understand what you are implying," Lisa admitted, her frustration seeping into her voice.

"I'm sure you do not," Linda replied enigmatically, leaving the comment to hang like a riddle.

The conversation was interrupted by the return of the attendant, now accompanied by a striking figure. The man's presence was magnetic yet understated, exuding a quiet authority. His long hair framed a face marked by an easy charm, and his crisp white shirt and tan pants lent him an air of relaxed refinement. Lisa's curiosity was piqued, she didn't recognize him, but Linda's welcoming smile revealed familiarity.

"Sir Santora," Linda greeted warmly, gesturing to the empty seat at their table. "Please, join us. It is an honor to have you here."

"It would be my pleasure," Santora responded, his voice smooth and pleasant. He waited as the attendant prepared his chair and place setting, his every movement composed and respectful. Once seated, the atmosphere shifted subtly, as though his presence brought a layer of quiet intrigue to the gathering.

Linda leaned slightly toward Lisa. "Sir Santora has recently become Vendura's Earthbloom master. His expertise is unparalleled," she explained with a touch of pride. Turning to Santora, she continued, "And this is my youngest daughter, Lisa."

"The pleasure is all mine," Santora said, extending a handshake. His smile was warm but assessing.

"Nice to meet you," Lisa replied, her handshake firm yet slightly hesitant. She was still trying to decipher the man's demeanor.

"You are truly a vision of the goddess," Santora remarked, his words laced with both admiration yet something similar to skepticism. "Even the finest portrait would fail to capture such presence."

Caught off guard by the praise, Lisa felt heat rise to her cheeks. She glanced away momentarily, unaccustomed to such direct compliments from someone of his stature.

Linda seized the opportunity to guide the conversation. "Lisa, why don't you share with Sir Santora the story of your journey and encounter with this *Goddess of Unity*?"

Encouraged by her mother's words, Lisa recounted the events, her meeting with Brother Albert, the voyage to Order Island, and the communion with Unity. She described every detail, including her later encounter with Erisol, each word carrying the weight of a profound transformational journey.

When she finished, Santora leaned back slightly, his expression thoughtful. "That *is* quite the tale," he remarked. "However... I fear you might be at the center of an elaborate deception."

"A deception?" Lisa echoed, disbelief tightening her chest. "How could that be? I met Unity. It was real."

Santora leaned forward, his gaze sharp. "Your so-called Goddess of Unity bears a striking resemblance to our own harvest goddess. The green hair, the aura of acceptance, these are not coincidences. And your encounters? No witnesses. Everything hinges solely on your word."

Lisa bristles, as her conviction wavers. "I know what I experienced," she insisted. "The other avatars saw their goddesses too."

Santora nodded slightly. "Consider the tea you drank. It's entirely possible that it was infused with herbs designed to induce vivid, even spiritual, dream states. I could brew a concoction right now that would convince you that you have been living on the bottom of the sea for the last year."

Lisa blinked, the foundation of her belief trembling beneath the weight of his words. "But... we all had the same visions. Could the Order really fabricate something so elaborate?"

Linda's calm voice interjected. "Did you know any of these girls before you arrived at Order Island?"

"No, Mother," Lisa admitted reluctantly.

"Pirates often weave elaborate lies to disarm their prey," Santora added, his tone measured but pointed. "What if one of these avatars, the girl with gray hair, perhaps, was also part of the deception? Designed to make you trust her, to pull you into a false bond?"

A shadow of doubt crossed Lisa's mind. All her experiences with the other three avatars

Could all of that have been a manipulation?

"We are meant to stand together, to protect the balance," Lisa muttered, her mind and voice plagued with confusion.

Linda's eyes narrowed slightly, her expression thoughtful. "Balance... or perhaps a subtle way of isolating you, making you prioritize their needs above the family's?" She paused, then suggested, "Or maybe even the Kingdom's?"

Lisa stared into her tea, the warmth of the liquid doing little to soothe the growing uncertainty in her heart.

The mention of Sophie, with her vivid violet hair and tragic history, cut through the fog of doubt swirling around Lisa's mind. "What about Sophie?" she challenged, her voice trembling slightly but resolute. "Violet hair is unheard of, and her village was decimated by Isabella and Gretta. That's not something anyone could easily fake."

Santora's expression darkened slightly, his voice tinged with both disdain and acknowledgment. "Ah, the Jiberau girl," he said, his tone betraying the centuries-old animosity between their peoples. "The Jiberau has always harbored enmity toward Verdantia. Envy of the Harvest Goddess's blessings festers in them like a deep wound. It wouldn't surprise me if their stories were crafted to manipulate you."

Lisa bristled, but before she could respond, Linda spoke, her voice measured yet cutting. "And you've never seen her village yourself, have you? All you have is her word. That tragic tale could just as easily be a fabrication."

A chill crept into Lisa's thoughts. *Could it be true? Could everything Sophie had told her be an intricate lie?* Lisa had seen the effect on Sophie with her own eyes, was Sophie that good at lying? *Was she part of an intricate deception?* Yet the memory of Brother Albert's torment haunted her. His injuries, inflicted by one of Isabella's mechanical monstrosities, had been raw and undeniable. She had seen all his wounds with her own Earthbloom sense. If it was all a ruse, what was the point of his suffering?

"Why would they go to such lengths?" Lisa questioned, confusion and dread twisting her voice. "What purpose does all of this serve?"

Linda's gaze sharpened, her explanation precise and unnervingly calculated. "The Order seeks influence, my dear. With your father poised to become Supreme Minister, you're a very valuable asset. They intend to control him through you, positioning you as their tool, willingly or not."

Santora nodded gravely, his tone dark with understanding. "It is a long game, Lisa. They embed their influence early, planting seeds of manipulation throughout the Seven Kingdoms. When the time is right, they harvest control from within. It is an insidious strategy built on patience and subterfuge."

Lisa's mind raced through the events of the past weeks. Every moment, every revelation, every bond she had formed was now tinged with suspicion. Could it all have been orchestrated? "But it does not make sense," she argued, clutching onto the pieces of her conviction. "Brother Albert's wounds were real. I saw his pain. I tried to heal him... I drained almost all of my mana doing it."

Linda tilted her head slightly, her next question striking with precision. "Had you consumed any tea before that incident?"

The inquiry hung in the air, its weight pressing down on Lisa. Slowly, the memory surfaced, she had indeed drunk a cup before attempting the healing. Her eyes widened as she whispered, "Yes, I had a cup of goddess tea."

The admission rippled between them like a silent revelation.

Santora leaned back slightly, his brow furrowed in thought. "If I had access to this tea," he mused, "I could analyze its ingredients. It might reveal whether you were influenced by more than just words and ritual."

Linda didn't hesitate. She turned and summoned the attendant once more. When he arrived, she delivered her instructions with a calm but unyielding authority. "Bring Brother Marcus from the Order here," she ordered. "oh and have him bring some of his *fabulous* tea with him."

"At once, ma'am," the attendant replied, bowing before leaving with urgency.

A brief silence followed. Lisa stared at the table, her thoughts tangling into an inescapable knot of doubt and fear. Were the experiences she had held so sacred nothing more than an illusion? Her world teetered on the edge of uncertainty.

Sir Santora, sensing the storm within her, reached out and gently took her hand. His touch was steady, offering a quiet anchor in the midst of her spiraling thoughts. "You mustn't blame yourself for this," he said softly, his voice filled with understanding. "You've been drawn into something far beyond your control."

Lisa's eyes met his, searching for reassurance. Despite the whirlwind of revelations, the warmth in his gaze offered a small but vital comfort, a reminder that she was not entirely alone in this. Yet, even with his empathy, the shadows of doubt refused to release their grip on her heart.

[-----✟-----]

In the grand dining hall of Meadowbrook, the air was rich with the aroma of a feast, evoking the bounty of a ship's galley after a long and arduous voyage. Annabelle, Marcus, and Captain Kidd sat around a table laden with food, their plates reflecting both their personalities and pasts. Annabelle's platter overflowed with bacon, ham, hash browns, pancakes drenched in honey, and lemon pastries, she ate with the gusto of plunder, savoring her spoils. Captain Kidd's breakfast mirrored his larger-than-life presence: a hearty omelet bursting with ham, cheese, peppers, and sausage links, and a towering stack of pancakes. Marcus, ever composed, opted for a simpler meal of oatmeal topped with fruit and brown sugar, accompanied by a steaming cup of coffee that whispered of calm seas and fresh beginnings.

Annabelle leaned forward, her tone playful but probing. "Brother Marcus, what adventures call to ye today? Will ye be attending the gala tonight?"

"I haven't decided," Marcus replied, taking a measured bite of oatmeal. "I need to prepare for our journey to Synder tomorrow. But perhaps I'll go. I've never witnessed a Goddess Gala before."

Annabelle's eyes sparkled mischievously. "Oh, ye should. I'll be wearin' a brand-new dress for the occasion," she declared with a grin, as radiant as any treasure.

"Aye, but before ye get too carried away, ye've got magic practice," Captain Kidd reminded her, his voice stern but laced with affection.

Annabelle groaned. "There ain't no sea around here," she protested.

"Smitty told ye plain as day, ye don't need no sea," Kidd shot back, meeting her fire with fire. "And don't forget, lass, ye still owe me five coin."

Seizing the opportunity, Annabelle turned to Marcus, eyes gleaming with mischief. "Marcus, lend me five coins, will ye?"

Marcus chuckled softly and shook his head. "All I have are Harvest Crowns."

"I don't take crop crowns," Captain Kidd interjected with mock indignation, raising an eyebrow. "Besides, I want her money, not yours."

"Yer a terrible servant, Marcus," Annabelle teased with a playful pout before returning to her breakfast.

"I'll strive to improve Miss Salazar," Marcus promised with a wry smile.

The trio continued their meal in good humor until an attendant approached their table and addressed Marcus with practiced formality. "Brother Marcus Igbinedion?"

Marcus set down his coffee. "Yes, that's me."

"The lady of the house has summoned you," the attendant explained, "and has requested that you bring your *fabulous tea.*"

"I'll need to retrieve it from my room," Marcus replied with a polite nod, his voice steady.

Annabelle's fork paused mid-air. "Oi, ye've been hidin' tea this whole time?"

Marcus offered a slight bow in her direction. "As always, I intend to improve my service to you, Miss Salazar."

Annabelle waved him off with a smirk. "See that ye do, and don't be too long about it."

Rising from the table, Marcus followed the attendant through the mansion's labyrinthine corridors. Silence stretched between them, though it was a companionable quiet; each man focused on his duties. Marcus, well-trained by the Order in observation and restraint, found himself noting the attendant's composed efficiency. Their unspoken understanding spoke of shared discipline, though from different worlds.

When they reached Marcus's chambers, he retrieved a small bag of the goddess tea. The scent of the blend brought a fleeting sense of calm, but his memories warned him of the danger it posed. The sight of carpenters and laborers bustling throughout the mansion heightened his curiosity. *Why such extensive preparation for a birthday gala?* The presence of military personnel near the Governor's office further deepened his unease. Lower-ranking soldiers rarely lingered without purpose. Were they here for security, or was something more significant underway?

As they ascended an ornate staircase, Marcus glimpsed a scene through a set of grand glass doors. Seated on the balcony beyond were Miss Lisa and Lady Linda, joined by an unfamiliar man in a crisp white shirt. Marcus's keen eyes noted the subtle intimacy between them, the man's hand resting lightly over Lisa's in a gesture of comfort or solidarity. The sight stirred questions within him, though he quickly refocused as the attendant came to a halt.

"We have arrived," the attendant announced quietly, signaling the End of their journey.

"Thank you," Marcus replied with sincerity, acknowledging the man's service. As he stepped forward, another attendant stationed at the glass doors turned to greet him.

"Brother Marcus Igbinedion, here for the Lady Nozaki," Marcus announced with formality.

"Excellent," the attendant responded with a courteous nod. He opened the doors wider and stepped through, his voice resonating through the space. "Brother Marcus Igbinedion has arrived."

As Marcus entered, the grandeur of the balcony, the presence of those gathered, and the charged atmosphere made it clear, this wasn't merely a request for tea. It was something else entirely.

The balcony unfolded like a sanctuary bathed in the warmth of the morning sun. Its light danced across the space, illuminating Lady Linda Nozaki's composed figure beneath the table's umbrella. Her attire, though simple, exuded an air of quiet authority. Beside her, Lisa sat lost in thought, her red dress with white trim catching the sun's rays as she stared into her tea, seemingly seeking answers in the depths of the delicate porcelain. Opposite them, a man in a white shirt clasped Lisa's hand in silent solidarity, his presence both comforting and enigmatic.

Marcus stepped onto the balcony, the light briefly enveloping him as he took in the tableau. "Good morning," he greeted with quiet warmth. His gaze naturally drifted to Lisa's downcast face, her turmoil almost palpable. "Is something amiss?" he asked, his concern genuine.

An attendant silently placed a chair for Marcus between Lady Linda and the unfamiliar man, completing the circle. "Good morning, Brother Marcus," Linda greeted with a graceful gesture toward the seat. "Please, join us." Turning to the attendant, she ordered with authority, "Bring a pot of boiling water for the tea."

Marcus took his place, his focus returning to Lisa. "Miss Lisa, is there anything I might do to assist you?" he inquired gently.

Linda leaned forward, the light accentuating the accusatory steel in her eyes. "My daughter has been weaving quite the extraordinary tale about her experiences with the Order," she said, her voice carrying both intrigue and accusing skepticism.

Marcus inclined his head. "Yes, it is a tale that stirs the heart, especially given her youth."

Linda's gaze sharpened. "And this Brother Albert," she continued, her words cutting with precision, "I would very much like to speak with him."

A solemn expression crossed Marcus's face. He paused to compose himself before replying. "Regrettably, Brother Albert Thompson has passed," he began softly. "He gave his life to protect the avatars, including Miss Lisa, from forces that would exploit or harm them."

A weight settled over the gathering. The mention of Albert's sacrifice hung like a specter among them, a sobering reminder of the dangers lurking in unseen corners of their world.

Linda's eyes narrowed, her following words glinting with quiet suspicion. "How convenient for you that he's no longer alive to corroborate your account," she accused.

Marcus met her gaze, his voice calm but resolute. "I assure you, Lady Nozaki, it was anything but convenient." His eyes softened as he glanced at Lisa. "Brother Albert was on the verge of uncovering the identities of those who threatened your daughter's safety. I would give anything for just one more moment with him, to learn what he discovered, if nothing else."

Linda's scrutiny intensified. "And how are we to verify his death?"

Without hesitation, Marcus reached into his shirt pocket and withdrew a pocket watch, its cover engraved with the emblem of the Order of Saint Lorriane. The chain glinted as he placed it gently on the table. "This is a monk's pocket watch," he explained, his tone imbued with the gravity of tradition. "It serves as a beacon to our Order, revealing our location and status. Each member of Saint Lorriane is entrusted with two sacred relics: our journal and this watch."

He paused, a shadow of grief crossing his features. "When I first met Miss Nozaki, it was in the aftermath of Brother Albert's death. His journal had been destroyed days earlier, and the avatars arrived at Order Island with his watch, stained with his blood. Though I did not witness his final moments, the passing of this relic was his last act, a message left in the alleys where he made his final stand."

The air grew heavier with his words, the silence stretching as the weight of Albert's sacrifice pressed upon them all. For a moment, Marcus seemed lost in the memory, his grief etched in the faint tremor of his voice.

Lisa broke the silence, her hand resting gently on Marcus's arm. "The goddess revealed to me that Brother Albert found joy in his time with us," she said softly, her voice a blend of sorrow and solace. "In the beyond, he shares tales of our adventures with others."

Marcus smiled faintly, his hand covering hers in gratitude. "Thank you, Miss Lisa," he answered softly, the warmth of her words offering him a brief reprieve from his grief.

But Linda's voice soon reasserted itself, steering the conversation back to more pressing matters. "Which brings us to the topic of the goddess and your mysterious tea," she stated, her gaze steady and inquisitive.

Marcus straightened slightly, his mind racing to understand the implication. "The tea is made from leaves harvested exclusively on Order Island," he explained. "It's a simple brew, though the plant itself is unique to the island."

Linda leaned back slightly, her expression contemplative. "Simple, perhaps," she repeated, though the weight behind her words suggested otherwise.

Marcus sensed the tension beneath her inquiry but sought to provide reassurance. "I can assure you, there's nothing inherently magical or intoxicating in its composition."

"We shall see," Linda remarked, her tone signaling that the matter was far from settled.

The conversation shifted as Mister Santora, newly introduced as the Earth bloom master and a connoisseur of flora, leaned forward with interest. "What species did these leaves originate from?" he inquired, curiosity glinting in his eyes.

Marcus met his gaze calmly. "They come from a tree we call the *goddess tree*. It's one of our sacred duties to protect and nurture these trees, ensuring they flourish."

Linda Nozaki's expression hardened, her skepticism solidifying into a pointed accusation. "So, my daughter alone is privileged to drink this mystical tea, this elixir that supposedly connects her to a goddess. And I'm to believe you haven't simply drugged her, planting these grand illusions of divine favor in her mind?"

Her words struck like a blade, but Marcus remained composed. He raised his hand slightly, signaling his desire to speak. "May I pose a question?"

Linda's patience was wearing thin. "What is it?" she demanded curtly.

Marcus leaned in slightly, his tone steady and measured. "How does your theory account for the marked increase in Miss Nozaki's magical prowess?" he asked. "Following their communion with their respective goddesses, each avatar experienced a significant enhancement of their mana reserves and shaping abilities. Miss Fournier, for instance, reported a drastic improvement in her mana shaping, accompanied by an increase in her mana reserves. These changes cannot be easily explained."

Santora, ever the scientist, offered a counterpoint. "There are alchemical solutions that could simulate such effects," he mused. "A mixture of Void root and Emberroot tea, for example, has been known to temporarily augment a mage's mana capacity, giving the impression of increased reserves."

Lisa's mind raced as her education at Valorcrest Academy surfaced to challenge this claim. But such an intervention *would inevitably cause mana toxicity,* she thought, silently dismissing Santora's hypothesis. *We didn't consume the tea daily.*

The realization struck her like a bolt of indignation. This line of questioning wasn't about truth; *it is about manipulation, an effort to undermine her experiences and sow doubt.*

The tension thickened as an attendant returned, pushing a portable boiler into place. The tea kettle perched atop it gleamed like a harbinger of the brewing confrontation. "The boiler, as requested by the lady," the attendant announced, oblivious to the escalating conflict in the room.

Linda seized the moment. "I wish to try this tea of yours, Brother Marcus," she declared, her gaze unwavering.

Marcus tensed, his voice edged with urgency. "I must advise against that," he began cautiously. "You must consider…"

Lisa interrupted, her voice calm but resolute. "Brother Marcus, we acknowledge your concerns. Please, proceed with the tea."

Santora's eyes gleamed with intrigue. "Actually, I'd like to handle the brewing myself," he interjected, clearly eager to observe the process firsthand.

Marcus hesitated before handing over the bag of tea leaves. He turned to Lisa, his concern evident. "Miss Lisa, recall what happened to Captain Lowe after he had just a sip of this tea," he reminded her. "And that was after my warning not to drink it."

A mischievous smile tugged at Lisa's lips as she recalled the incident. "Ah, yes. How could I forget?" she answered with malicious amusement.

Marcus wasn't amused. His voice grew more insistent. "Miss Lisa, I strongly urge you to reconsider." He pauses a moment to steady himself and then says, "I don't think you will be able to forgive yourself if you subject your mother to the goddess tea." Marcus did not have much concern for Santora.

Lisa met his concern with gentle authority. "Brother Marcus, I appreciate your advice," she replied, her tone polite but firm. "However, I must insist that you keep your further opinions to yourself."

Resigned, Marcus signaled to the attendant. "Please bring buckets and wet towels," he instructed, his request met with a puzzled look.

"Buckets?" the attendant echoed, brow furrowed in confusion.

"Yes, and wet towels," Marcus confirmed, his tone steady despite the undercurrent of apprehension. "Trust me, we'll need them."

The attendant nodded, though his expression betrayed lingering bewilderment, and hurried off to fulfill the request.

Meanwhile, Santora prepared to brew the tea, pausing to ask Marcus a practical question. "How much should I use for the pot?"

Marcus observed Santora's interest before replying. "For a pot of that size, I would use the entire bag."

Santora arched a brow, a trace of skepticism in his voice. "Won't that overpower the flavor?"

Marcus responded with measured indifference. "I wouldn't know. My experience with the goddess tea is limited to a single occasion."

Linda seized on the admission, her voice sharp. "And yet you deem it fit for young women like my daughter?"

"I do," Marcus answered without hesitation. "She embodies the goddess of Unity, and the tea facilitates her connection with the divine."

Marcus turned to Lisa, his gaze silently pleading for her to reconsider. But Lisa's smile, tinged with both mischief and malice, was her answer. She had made her decision. Whatever the forthcoming ordeal might bring, she believed it was a necessary step.

Marcus's thoughts churned as he observed the scene, his concern for Lisa colliding with his sense of duty. He wanted to trust her as an avatar of Unity, yet the escalating scrutiny of both Linda and Santora made him question how much longer he could stand by without intervening. He longed for unwavering faith in her path but remained burdened by the weight of his protective instincts.

Santora's brewing of the tea took on a ritualistic air, each movement deliberate and rhythmic, adding to the growing suspense. He served the tea methodically, first to Marcus, then Linda, himself, and finally Lisa. The tea's steam rose like a harbinger of revelation, while the attendant returned with buckets and wet towels, oblivious to the palpable tension.

Santora inhaled the tea's fragrant aroma, breaking the silence with a quiet acknowledgment of its potency.

Linda seized the opportunity to press Marcus. "Before we proceed, Brother Marcus, is there anything you'd care to disclose about your Order's true intentions for my daughter?" she demanded, her gaze piercing.

Marcus met Linda's gaze steadily, his tone stripped of formality. "No, Madam. There are no hidden agendas regarding Miss Lisa," he said, his voice resolute. His eyes flicked briefly to the tea. "However, Miss Lisa should drink first. She is the only one who can drink it without risk."

Linda's eyes narrowed in suspicion. "And if I agree to that condition, what then?"

Marcus didn't waver. "I'll drink the remainder of the pot," he answered evenly. He knew this was a dangerous gamble, but was prepared to take it if it meant protecting Lisa from herself. "If that's what you require."

Linda lifted her chin and addressed Lisa with authority. "Go ahead, dear. Have a drink of this *fabulous tea*."

Lisa nodded, cooling the liquid with a soft blow. Taking a deep sip, she felt warmth spread through her, the familiar presence of Unity wrapping around her like a comforting embrace. She closed her eyes, savoring the connection. "Mmm," she hummed softly.

"Lisa," Linda's voice cut through the calm moment. "is this the *goddess tea* you've spoken so much about?"

Lisa opened her eyes and met her mother's gaze. "Yes, Mother. It is," she affirmed and took another sip, her calm confidence evident.

Linda turned her attention to Marcus. "Brother Marcus, your turn."

Marcus glanced around the table, the expectant faces of Lisa, Linda, and Santora, and resigned himself to the inevitable. Memories from years ago surfaced unbidden. As a young novice eager to prove himself, he had joined the other scribes of Saint Lorraine in a reckless rite of passage: drinking a full cup of goddess tea. He remembered how Sister Sallie had gone first, fearless and bold. When it had been his turn, the tea had hit him like a storm. His body had violently rejected it, leaving him hunched over and retching for what felt like an eternity. He and Sallie had sworn never to touch the tea again.

Today, he would have to break that oath; hopefully, Sallie would forgive him for this trespass.

Blowing on the tea to test the temperature, Marcus steeled himself. He took a tentative sip, confirming it wasn't scalding, then drank the entire cup in one swift motion. The tea burned slightly on the way down, but he set the cup back on the saucer with a quiet resolve. He silently pointed at the cup, signaling Santora to refill it.

Santora obliged, pouring another round. "Doesn't seem so bad, Brother Marcus," he remarked, a note of challenge in his voice.

Marcus fixed him with a flat stare. "Just give it a minute," he warned, hoping, perhaps foolishly, that the tea's effects might spare him this time, he is the guide to the avatars after all.

With a smirk, Santora slid the refilled cup to Marcus and raised his own. "Bottoms up," he said casually, taking a sip Marcus did not feel the need to stop him. He is not the guide to Sir Santora.

The attendant returned just then, carrying buckets and damp towels. Marcus beckoned him over, grabbing a towel and one of the buckets. "Mr. Santora," he said gravely, holding out the items, "you'll want these soon."

Santora chuckled dismissively. He took another drink. "I really don't think so," he replied. With a grin, he jested, "Maybe I'm an avatar of a goddess myself, the goddess of the harvest, naturally."

Marcus felt a churn in his stomach, a familiar and ominous sensation; the tea is now angry, it is not inside the belly of an avatar. He let out a loud belch, momentarily clutching his abdomen. He looked toward Lisa, his concern etched deeply into his features. Quietly but firmly, he whispered, "Miss Lisa, please... don't put your mother through this."

Lisa hesitated, glancing between her mother and Santora, who continued to smile. "I think I will be just fine." Santora said confidently, raising his cup once more.

But Marcus knew better. His voice carried a final note of urgency. "You won't forgive yourself, Miss Lisa. Not for doing this."

She faltered, her gaze shifting uneasily to her mother.

Santora snorted and added smugly, "Come now. Look at me, I'm perfectly..."

The words died in his throat as a sudden cough seized him. He tapped his chest, trying to speak again, but only managed another fit of violent coughing. His face reddened, his breath coming in gasps.

Lisa's eyes widened. She motioned urgently for the attendant. "Get him a bucket. Now!"

Linda's skepticism began to crack, her eyes darting between the wheezing Santora and the grimacing Marcus, whose condition worsened by the second. Marcus's second cup of tea sat untouched, but he didn't dare hope for reprieve. Within moments, his body betrayed him thoroughly. He doubled over, and the contents of his stomach were forcefully ejected into the bucket. The sound echoed on the balcony, raw and painful.

"Excuse me!" Linda protested, scandalized by the scene. "What is the meaning of...?"

Lisa jumped from her seat and reached over to cover her mother's teacup with her hands. "Mother, please do not drink it!" she pleaded, her voice resolute. "I... I was going to let you suffer just to get you back for doubting me. I am so sorry, I was angry and confused, but I cannot allow you to do this."

Linda blinked, taken aback. "Lisa, you are caught in their manipulations. You can't..."

"No!" Lisa interrupted. Tears welled in her eyes as she continued. "I doubted myself. I let you and Santora make me question everything, my memories, my connection to Unity. But I cannot doubt this. I will not let you go through what they are."

Santora's coughing escalated to violent retching, and Linda flinched as he clutched the bucket, convulsing.

"Mother, please," Lisa pleaded. "Just look at me... with your Earthbloom sense. Please."

Linda hesitated for a long moment. Finally, she closed her eyes and extended her senses. When they flew open again, they were filled with shock.

"How...?" she breathed. Her voice failed her as she stared at her daughter, as though seeing her for the first time.

Lisa offered a tearful smile. "The Goddess of Unity blessed me, mother. This tea is only meant for avatars."

The reality slowly settled over Linda. She set the cup down gently. "Tell me about her," she said quietly, the disbelief in her voice giving way to wonder.

Lisa released a breath of relief, her heart lighter than it had felt in days. "Of course," she replied softly, returning to her seat.

Santora and Marcus continued to retch in the background, but for the moment, it no longer mattered. Understanding had finally begun to dawn.

Chapter 7

From dawn till dusk, the governor's mansion buzzed with electric fervor. Corridors and chambers pulsed with anticipation for Evelyn Nozaki's illustrious Goddess Gala. Staff members moved like a well-practiced orchestra, each step purposeful as they maneuvered the sprawling estate. Artisans in their craft, they convened in hidden nooks, gathering rare ingredients and finalizing arrangements for the evening's grand spectacle.

At the mansion's core, three kitchens, each a bastion of culinary ambition, sprang to life. United under the watchful eye of the kitchen's master chef, the challenge they faced was immense: to delight an expansive guest list with an array of appetizers, sumptuous entrées, and indulgent desserts. The air grew thick with the fragrant warmth of spices and ovens, a sensory testament to the scale and grandeur of Miss Nozaki's vision.

Amidst this frenzy, Marcus wrestled with a logistical crisis—there was no available transport to Synder for himself and the avatars. The unexpected savior was Linda Nozaki, the governor's poised and formidable wife. "In this household," she remarked with a smile edged in authority, "it is not a good idea to attempt to tell the first lady of the mansion no." Within moments, her influence secured a carriage for the avatars and their belongings, with assurances of further transport once the gala's demands abated.

In a rare moment of quiet, Linda offered Marcus a heartfelt apology. "I was too harsh regarding Lisa," she admitted, her voice softened by regret. Marcus dismissed the matter with grace, understanding her reaction as a mother's protective instinct. Touched by his empathy, Linda promised to advocate for Lisa's continued journey with the avatars, intrigued by Brother Albert's findings in Synder. Marcus expressed his deep gratitude, recognizing Linda's intervention as a crucial support in their unfolding story.

Meanwhile, the mansion revealed a hidden treasure to Annabelle, Regina, and Captain Kidd: a tailor's workshop where dreams took shape from fabric and thread. With a blend of excitement and curiosity, the trio embarked on a sartorial adventure.

Annabelle's initial disappointment was evident when she was presented with a modest dress, far simpler than the gown she had worn the previous day. Yet Mr. Berkshire, the tailor, quickly won her over with a promise to craft a shimmering floral corsage for her wrist—a delicate touch that transformed simplicity into understated elegance.

Regina's delight was immediate upon seeing her off-white dress. It was a blank canvas ready to be made her own. With Miss Hannigan's guidance, a silver bow was added to the left side of the dress, elevating the ensemble with a touch of bespoke charm.

Captain Kidd, ever the charismatic rogue, selected a sharp black suit paired with a crisp white shirt. He chose an orange tie and pocket square to inject a splash of vibrant flair, a reflection of his bold personality.

Sophie, on the other hand, embraced her defiance of tradition. She chose her purple suit, complete with the jacket, embodying her confident individuality. Her attendant, Samuel, hesitated at the sight. "There may be restrictions on attire," he warned delicately. Sophie remained unyielding. "If they turn me away, so be it," she replied, her indifference a testament to her steadfast identity.

As evening fell, the mansion's atmosphere shifted. The bustling corridors, once alive with the rhythm of preparation, now lay in hushed stillness. Only a handful of attendants lingered, stationed at key intersections to guide the night's distinguished guests.

Sophie took in the transformation, sensing that the mansion itself had paused to gather strength for the night's spectacle. The air of anticipation was palpable, like the collective holding of breath before the curtain's rise.

The avatars and their companions entered the grand ballroom, where chandeliers bathed the room in a glittering blanket of light. Their attendants guided them to a circular table near the room's heart, adorned with a centerpiece of fragrant jasmine flowers. The table awaited two more arrivals.

Lisa entered first, her green hair styled elegantly in a bun, softened by curled bangs. She moved with quiet grace, her attire a reflection of the evening's grandeur. Marcus arrived shortly after, his presence completing the gathering. Despite his slightly hurried demeanor, the day's logistical hurdles had not dampened his composure.

Together, they settled into a moment of shared purpose. Their table, a beacon of camaraderie amidst the gala's brilliance, marked the beginning of an evening that promised to weave new memories and unveil hidden fates.

[-----E-----]

At the stroke of seven, the grandeur of the governor's mansion ballroom transforms. The lights dim to a whisper, and the murmuring crowd recedes into shadows. A solitary spotlight pierces the darkness, illuminating Governor Conrad Nozaki at the center of the dance floor. His black tuxedo, offset by a green bowtie and cummerbund, symbols of the fertile land he governs, enhances his commanding presence. Conrad embodies solemnity and reverence, the weight of tradition resting on his shoulders.

He closes his eyes and inhales deeply, the gesture commanding the quiet focus of every soul in the room. His voice, resonant and steady, breaks the silence with a sacred invocation. "Great and generous goddess of the harvest, as your humble servant, I tend the fields and raise the livestock." His prayer rises and echoes to the vaulted ceilings, a pledge intertwining gratitude and duty, promising his unwavering commitment to the goddess' commandments and the prosperity of Verdantia.

As his hands lift in supplication, a second spotlight awakens, revealing Evelyn Nozaki at the summit of a shimmering staircase. The soft shimmer of silk streamers and precise lighting enshrines her in a radiant tableau. Evelyn's dress, an intricate

111

blend of emerald silk and golden fabric, is a masterpiece of elegance and heritage. The gown flows with regal grace, its sequins and beads catching the light like scattered stars, each movement enhancing the luminescent aura around her.

"Goddess, I present to you a testament of my service and dedication to your commandments: *my firstborn daughter, Evelyn.*" Conrad proclaims, imbuing the moment with sacred gravity.

With fluid grace, Evelyn begins her descent. Her steps are so light they barely whisper against the wooden stairs. At the base of the staircase, a young soldier stands at attention, clad in a ceremonial military uniform. This vibrant green uniform echoes the evening's theme of fertility and growth. He extends his left arm in a gesture of support. Evelyn accepts with poise, her arm threading through his as they proceed, their synchronized steps a seamless performance of ritual and Unity.

At the heart of the dance floor, they halt before Conrad. The young soldier salutes, a gesture met in kind by Conrad. Without a word, the soldier turns sharply and vanishes into the cloak of darkness beyond the spotlight's reach.

Now standing side by side with her father, Evelyn faces the assembly, a beacon of familial pride and devotion. She raises her voice, clear and unwavering. "Great and generous goddess of the harvest, I offer you my love to build a strong family, my bosom to feed them, and my service to guide them. I offer this freely, goddess, as freely you offer your great bounty to the world."

Her words echo through the vast hall, resonating with the elemental cycles of life, nurturing, giving, and leading, mirroring the goddess's own boundless generosity. Conrad and Evelyn embrace in a solemn display of respect and familial Unity. Then, with purposeful strides, Conrad departs the dance floor, following the path into the darkness taken by the soldier.

Evelyn remains alone in the spotlight, her gaze steady and filled with anticipation. From the shadows, a voice calls out, steeped in both reverence and authority. "The harvest goddess grants our great land her earth." As the words reverberate through the room, figures cloaked in darkness appear, guiding broad brown silk streamers down the aisles. These streamers, symbols of the fertile soil, reach the edges of the dance floor like extensions of the goddess's nurturing gift.

Evelyn's response is firm and resolute. "Goddess, I will dedicate my service to till and keep this earth." Her vow is a sacred contract, binding her to the stewardship of the land.

The ceremony continues. "The harvest goddess grants our great land her water." A second group enters, carrying vibrant blue silk streamers. Their movements mimic the graceful flow of water, animating the fabric with life as it ripples under the light.

"Goddess, I will dedicate my strength to gather the water and use it to grow your food and feed my brood," Evelyn declares, reaffirming her commitment to nurture and sustain life.

Finally, the ritual invokes fire. "The harvest goddess grants our great land her fire." Red and orange streamers appear, swirling in arcs around the tables. Their undulating movements create a vivid illusion of flames, fierce yet controlled.

"Goddess, I will dedicate my love to using your fire to cook the meals to feed my family and craft the things to improve your world and honor your name," Evelyn pledges, honoring the sacred hearth as a source of warmth, creativity, and transformation.

The voice in the shadows speaks again. "Through your work and dedication to the ways of the harvest goddess, you honor the goddess, and in return, she will reward you."

The figures with streamers advance in unison, encircling Evelyn in a mesmerizing dance of color and motion. The silken strands weave a dynamic tapestry around her, symbolizing the interplay of human effort and divine influence. The ritual climaxes with the streamers forming resplendent floral blooms that encase Evelyn like a living wreath, her transformation into womanhood celebrated in a breathtaking tableau.

As the lights gradually brighten, the full splendor of the scene unfolds. Evelyn stands poised and serene at the center, the embodiment of grace and purpose. The streamers slowly unfurl and recede, leaving her as the sole focus of the room's admiration.

"Great people of Verdantia, I give you the Lady Evelyn Nozaki. Receive her and love her as one of your own," announces a distinguished figure, his voice rich with authority and warmth. His ceremonial attire, blending tradition with vibrant gala motifs, reinforces his status as a revered leader.

The crowd rises in a wave of applause, welcoming Evelyn into her new role. The young soldier returns, offering his arm once more. Evelyn smiles, accepting the gesture, and together they make their way to the guest of honor table. The soldier pulls out her chair with a practiced elegance, and Evelyn takes her seat between her parents, Conrad and Linda. Once she is settled, the soldier joins her at the table, marking the conclusion of this pivotal rite of passage.

[-----✿-----]

"Wow, that was amazing!" Regina exclaims, her eyes still wide with awe. She turns to Lisa and asks, "Are you going to have a party like this?"

"I will, but I do not think it'll be as…" Lisa trails off, searching for the right word. "Much."

"When's your party?" Sophie inquires, her gaze wandering across the room, subtly assessing a few of the handsome young men scattered among the tables.

"Two years, next month." Lisa replies, sipping from a glass of water. "Our Goddess Gala is on our seventeenth birthday."

"Wait, your birthday's next month?" Sophie asks, blinking in surprise.

"Yes, May fourteenth," Lisa answers.

"Oi, that's me birthday too!" Annabelle declares, straightening in her chair.

"And mine," Regina adds with a grin.

"Same here," Sophie confirms.

The four girls exchange looks, their eyes, violet, green, orange, and silver, locking in an unspoken connection. They turn as one toward Brother Marcus, who is oblivious to their discovery until he senses their gazes. He glances up from his thoughts, confused.

"Apologies, ladies. It seems I missed your request," Marcus says, clearing his throat.

"Aye," Annabelle quips, grinning mischievously. "And that's why you're a bad servant."

"What do you need from me?" Marcus asks, amused by the playful accusation.

"Did you know all of our birthdays are on the same day?" Lisa inquires.

113

"I did," Marcus replies calmly. "I assumed you'd have figured it out by now. You talk to each other every day, after all. In fact, I believe we even discussed this yesterday before... the energetic exchange."

"Bah!" Annabelle dismisses with a wave. "Shows what ye know."

"I will strive to be a better servant, Miss Salazar," Marcus says with mock solemnity, his tone tinged with sarcasm.

Captain Kidd chuckles and winks at Marcus, sharing in the joke.

Lisa's gaze drifts to the raised table where her family sits, overlooking the festivities. She notices her father, Conrad, speaking to an attendant, gesturing in her direction. A knot forms in her stomach. She waves with a smile, attempting to ease the tension between them.

Conrad acknowledges her with a polite but cold wave before returning to his conversation. Lisa sighs softly. This tension may persist for a while. She wasn't sure how to bridge the growing rift between them, but that was a problem for another day.

Sophie's attention shifts to Andrew, the cute boy she had noticed earlier. She waves subtly, hoping to catch his eye, but he remains absorbed in a conversation at his table. She frowns slightly, resolving to find a way to draw him over after dinner.

A booming voice interrupts her thoughts. "Dinner is served!" the head chef announces from the center of the dance floor.

The kitchen staff springs into action, swiftly delivering plates to the tables. At the governor's table, a young woman in a chef's jacket pushes a cart laden with dishes and pitchers. She begins placing plates before Lisa, Sophie, and the others when Sophie feels a gentle tap on her shoulder.

It's Samuel, her attendant, his expression serious. "Excuse me, ma'am," he begins, his tone measured. "I need you to come with me."

"What? Why?" Sophie asks, confusion clouding her features.

"I promise I'll explain on the way," Samuel replies with a tone that leaves no room for argument. "But you need to come with me now."

Sophie glances around the table. "I guess I gotta go. I'll be back," she announces to the table before standing to follow Samuel.

"Is there anything I can assist with?" Marcus offers, eyeing the attendant warily.

"No, it's nothing urgent," Samuel reassures him before leading Sophie out of the banquet room and into the hallway. They walk in silence until they reach a quiet intersection where two corridors meet.

Stopping abruptly, Samuel turns to face her. "Miss, the governor has decreed that you cannot attend his daughter's gala in improper attire."

"Improper attire?" Sophie echoes incredulously. She glances down at her outfit, purple slacks, a matching vest, jacket, and a bowtie over a crisp white shirt. "How is this improper? I wear this to my clan's functions all the time."

"With all due respect," Samuel replies, carefully choosing his words, "this is not a Jiberau function. In Verdantia, women are expected to wear dresses, which is the only appropriate attire."

Sophie stiffens at the mention of the name *Jiberau*. *Oh this again.* She crosses her arms, her expression hardening.

"So, your orders are to escort me back to my room to change?" she asks icily.

"Yes, ma'am," Samuel confirms. "The governor has provided a suitable dress for tonight."

Telling herself that Samuel is now officially ugly, Sophie waves a hand dismissively. "Fine. Lead the way."

Samuel offers a polite nod. "Very good, ma'am." He turns and guides her back through the eerily silent mansion. Sophie is struck once more by how empty the halls feel compared to the hive of activity earlier in the day. The once-bustling estate now resembles a deserted tomb.

At her room, Samuel opens the door with a courteous gesture. "Here you go, ma'am."

"Thank you," Sophie replies coolly, stepping inside.

"Do you know how long it will take to change?" Samuel asks hesitantly.

Sophie glares at him. "I won't."

"Ma'am, you will not be allowed back to the gala without proper attire," Samuel reminds her gently.

"I won't be returning to the gala," Sophie states firmly.

Samuel hesitates. "But you haven't had dinner. The kitchen will be closed until breakfast."

"I'll manage," Sophie replies curtly.

Samuel frowns, clearly debating whether to press the issue. Finally, he speaks. "If you're retiring for the night, I'll take my leave."

"Yes, I think that's best," Sophie agrees.

Before leaving, Samuel pauses one last time. "Ma'am, may I ask, what's so wrong about wearing a dress?"

Sophie's patience snaps. "It's a Jiberau thing," she bites out before slamming the door shut.

Sophie enters her room, her gaze landing on the white dress displayed neatly on a hanger. It's adorned with a small purple ribbon tied into a bow at the chest, a delicate, elegant design. But to Sophie, it represents something far more sinister: this oppressive way of life. As she stares at it, the faint, familiar ringing returns to her ears, a sound she can't quite place. She shakes it off, focusing instead on her plan.

She peeks into the hallway to ensure it's empty, and as expected, silence reigns. Satisfied, Sophie retrieves a small bag from her luggage, containing square wood cutouts she had commissioned from the Stormfang's machinists. With the bag and dress in hand, she changes out of her purple attire into freshly laundered black training clothes. The ringing in her ears intensifies briefly, but she forces herself to ignore it.

Once dressed, she slips quietly through the mansion, heading to the courtyard behind the estate. The night air is cool, and she moves with purpose to the edge of the lake. Near the water's edge, a large log floats lazily, its surface broken by a branch that rises like the mast of a small ship. *Perfect.*

Sophie drapes the dress over the branch and pulls a fire rune from her pouch. Concentrating, she channels mana into the carved wood, causing the rune to glow faintly. She presses the rune to the fabric, and the moment she releases it, flames burst to life, consuming the dress. The fire crackles as it dances along the silk, the orange glow reflected in the still waters of the lake. With a gentle push, she sends the log adrift, watching in satisfaction as the burning symbol of oppression floats toward the lake's center.

A smile tugs at her lips. "Time to go home," she whispers.

Then it hits her ... the ringing in her ears. Recognition crashes in, sharp and sudden.

Memories flood in. As a child, when she played outside with her friends, her mother, Arisa, used her Aurorium badge to send a tone to call her home, a clear, insistent ringing that only Aurorium members could hear. "Too much dignity to shout down the street like some slave mom," Arisa would say with a smirk. Later, when Sophie trained as a Sentinel, Eclipse Baker had explained that the tone was part of a distress call spell, a signal designed to help locate lost or kidnapped comrades.

If Sophie was hearing it now, someone nearby, another Aurorium badge holder, was in distress, but how? The clan does not operate in Verdantia?

Adrenaline surges through her. Sophie sprints back to her room, the burning dress forgotten. Once inside, she retrieves her badge from the wardrobe. She opens the leather case and gazes at the silver "A" emblem of the Sentinels, its torchbearer insignia shining in the dim light. Pressing her fingers to the badge, she channels a small amount of mana and commands, "Locate."

The badge flares to life, emitting a sharp chirp in her ears. Sophie rushes to the window, scanning the landscape until her eyes land on a distant barn. The badge's signal aligns perfectly with the structure.

"What would an Aurorium be doing in Verdantia... in a barn?" she mutters under her breath.

She searches through her belongings but finds nothing suitable for a weapon. Frustrated, she settles on her inspection glasses, slipping them into her pocket before quietly sneaking out of the mansion again.

Navigating through the mansion is surprisingly easy; the attendants are all stationed to monitor internal areas, keeping guests from wandering deeper into the estate. No one seems concerned with preventing someone from leaving. Sophie moves swiftly through the courtyard and into the cover of the surrounding trees. The thicket offers ample concealment, and she utilizes her training to stay low and hidden, her violet hair the only conspicuous feature in the moonlight. She moves carefully, slipping from shadow to shadow.

As she nears the barn, the locator tone grows louder. Something feels off, there are no animal sounds coming from the building. The silence is unnerving.

Approaching from the rear, Sophie finds a small window and peers inside. Lanterns cast a dim glow across the interior, but the space appears deserted. There are no animals, no people, only the hollow quiet of an abandoned structure. Yet her badge insists the source of the signal is inside.

Sophie slips on her inspection glasses and makes her way to the front entrance. The large wooden doors creak slightly as she pushes them open. Her glasses immediately reveal traces of mana and residual body heat. Though the barn looks empty, the glasses show the ghostly outlines of movement: *five, maybe six or seven individuals,* who had been here within the past several hours. There are no visible warning spells or tripwires, but Sophie knows better than to assume safety. Concealment spells could mask hidden rituals. However, her glasses should detect any direct mana signatures.

She advances cautiously, senses on high alert. The locator tone pulses steadily in her ears, urging her forward into the depths of the quiet barn.

Sophie scans the barn, moving from stall to stall. Some have remnants of hay scattered across the floor, while others are clean and empty. Each stall features a large rug on the ground. The chirping in her ears from the locator badge fluctuates, growing louder at times, only to suddenly fall silent. It doesn't make sense. Why would the signal cut out if she hadn't found the badge sending the distress call?

She retraces her steps to an earlier stall, and the chirping resumes. Sophie removes her glasses, studying the space more carefully. The barn is illuminated by gas lamps hanging at each stall entrance, their flames casting flickering shadows on the walls. The stall where the signal fades seems unremarkable at first glance, just another floor covered in hay. But then Sophie notices something odd: none of the hay touches the rug with the intricate golden border and central design of the Verdantian tree. It's as if the rug was placed after the hay had been cleared.

Suspicion piqued, Sophie grips the rug and yanks it aside. The lantern light reveals a hidden door beneath it, with a large metal ring affixed vertically in the center. A faintly glowing ritual circle surrounds the door, the mana within it flickering weakly as though it's on the verge of dissipating.

Without hesitation, Sophie grabs the metal ring and lifts. The door creaks open, and the locator chirp returns at full volume, confirming she's close to the source of the distress call. A narrow staircase descends into an underground chamber.

Instinctively, Sophie reaches for her pistol, only to remember, *it's back on the Stormfang in the armory.* She mutters a curse under her breath. With no other option, she steps cautiously onto the staircase, her senses on high alert. The stairs lead to a short, dimly lit stone hallway. Torches flicker in metal holders along the walls, casting long, shifting shadows as she advances.

Turning a corner, Sophie finds a barred cell. Inside, a man with dark skin like hers sits on the floor. His hair is twisted into unkempt locks, his face obscured by a wild beard. His clothes are tattered, and he looks disoriented. At first glance, Sophie might have mistaken him for a drunk vagrant.

The man's head jerks up when he sees her. He leaps to his feet and grips the bars tightly. "You heard my call," he says urgently. "How many are with you? Have you dealt with the ogres?"

"Ogres?" Sophie echoes, startled. His intensity unsettles her, but she keeps her voice steady. "How did you send the locator tone?"

"I performed a ritual," the man explains, though his frustration grows as he struggles to articulate more. "The ogres... they took my..." He groans, banging a fist against his head in agitation. "Come on... I know this one..."

"Your badge?" Sophie offers, hoping to calm him.

"Yes! Badge!" He exhales in relief, as though the word had been on the tip of his tongue. "That's it. My badge."

"Who are you?" Sophie asks cautiously.

The man fiddles with his hair, then replies in a formal, practiced tone, "Antonio Lepele of the Aurorium Kutora Mora. I bring the light into the darkness."

Sophie's eyes widen in recognition. The introduction confirms his rank, he's an Eclipse. She remembers the clan's sayings: Sentinels are "torchbearers of the clan," Shadows "dance with both darkness and light," and Eclipses "bring light to the darkness."

"You're an Eclipse?" she asks.

"Yes," Antonio replies, as though he had momentarily forgotten the term.

Sophie's sense of urgency sharpens. "We need to get you out of here." She rushes to the cell door and tugs at the lock, finding it firmly secured.

"The tree man has the key," Antonio says.

117

"Tree man?" Sophie frowns. "What's wrong with you?"

Antonio only stares at her, confused by the question.

Sophie inspects the lock and says, "I might be able to kick this open."

"The tree man put his protection on the door," Antonio warns. "You need him to open it."

Ignoring his cryptic comment, Sophie raises her foot and drives her heel into the door. It doesn't budge. Frustrated, she channels mana into her hand and unleashes a HARDKNUCKLE spell. A shimmering, magical barrier materializes around the cell door, absorbing the impact without so much as a scratch.

"Dammit!" Sophie bellows, realizing the door is warded. She slips her inspection glasses back on, revealing the protection ritual, an intricate circle of mana surrounding the bars and walls of the cell. It's designed to repel both physical and magical force.

"You have to find the tree man," Antonio repeats. "Only he can break the barrier."

Sophie studies the ritual through her glasses and notices something: the area she struck with her spell is slowly repairing itself. A sufficiently strong hit might destabilize the barrier. Pocketing her glasses, she turns to Antonio. "Stand back. This is going to be a big one."

"Don't do it!" Antonio protests. "The tree man's barrier is too strong!"

"I'm pretty strong too," Sophie replies with a confident grin.

Antonio hesitates before backing up to the far wall and sitting down.

Sophie takes a deep breath and visualizes the sequence of spells she needs. She draws an outward-facing spell circle near her elbow and two more circles around her fist—one inward, one outward. She whispers the activation sequence under her breath, committing it to memory: "Elbow, inside, outside... elbow, inside, outside."

When she's ready, she rears back and channels her mana. "HARDKNUCKLE-EXPLOSION!!" she calls out in her mind, slamming her fist into the barrier. The impact generates a shockwave of force, sending a burst of light rippling through the ritual circle. Sophie braces herself, expecting the barrier to collapse.

Instead, the light reverses direction, racing back to the point of impact like a swarm of angry insects. The energy detonates outward, throwing Sophie violently into the stone wall behind her. She crumples to the floor, dazed and breathless.

Antonio sighs from within the cell. "I told you... The tree man..." he calls to her in a commanding tone.

Sophie groans as she pushes herself off the ground, her muscles aching from the impact. "Yes, Eclipse, you did tell me," she replies dryly. Dusting herself off, she asks, "how do I find this 'tree man'?"

"The ogres will lead you to him," Lepele says matter-of-factly. "Follow them, and they'll take you to him."

Sophie raises an eyebrow. "Ogres, right... Sure." She exhales, trying to decipher his cryptic words. "Seriously, what's wrong with you?"

"The demon cursed me," Lepele says, his frustration evident. He rubs his temples as though struggling to find the right words. "I've been vexed... by the demon."

Sophie frowns. *A demon curse?* She glances around the room, unsure what to make of his explanation. Needing more context, she slips her inspection glasses back on and scans the space again. Mana particles from the barrier swirl faintly in the air, but there are no other immediate clues. Turning her attention to Lepele's cell, she notices a bowl in the corner.

"How do you get food?" she asks.

"The demon brings it," he replies without hesitation.

Sophie's eyes narrow. "Can you describe this demon?"

"She wears white... and has evil eyes," he says gravely.

"Evil eyes. Got it," Sophie mutters, stifling her growing frustration. "And the ogres, what do they do?"

"They're the ones who keep me here," Lepele explains. "They also bring the tree man and the demon down here."

Sophie sighs and repeats sarcastically, "Okay. So... find the tree man or the demon by following the ogres. Great plan."

"Exactly. Follow the ogres," Lepele confirms earnestly.

Shaking her head, Sophie turns and makes her way back up the stairs. She needs a plan. She could stake out the thicket near the barn and wait for these so-called ogres. However, as she reaches the top of the stairs and steps out of the stall, a voice startles her.

"Well now, what do we have here?"

Sophie freezes and slowly turns. Four men in overalls stand near the barn's entrance, their silhouettes outlined by the lanterns. There's something unsettlingly familiar about them, but she can't quite place it.

"Looks like we got ourselves a Jibber who lost her way home," the second man sneers, his voice dripping with malice.

Found the ogres, Sophie thinks to herself grimly.

Chapter 8

The dinner service unfolded with a grace that mirrored the grandeur of the evening. The kitchen staff, in a display of culinary mastery, presented a pork roast steak that exemplified their craft. The meat was tender and perfectly seasoned, accompanied by golden-brown roasted potatoes whose crisp exterior yielded to a soft, fluffy center. A vibrant vegetable medley added both color and freshness to the meal. Animated conversation and bursts of laughter filled the avatars' table as they savored the feast. Only Sophie's plate remained untouched, a silent testament to her sudden departure, its contents cooling as the night progressed.

Lisa's curiosity piqued when her gaze crossed paths with the attendant who had escorted Sophie away. She called him over and inquired about Sophie's location and he explained that she would spend the remainder of the evening in her room. Concern rippled across the table as the group learned that Sophie would not be rejoining them for the remainder of the evening. In a gesture of camaraderie or perhaps appreciation of the delicious food, Sophie's meal was divided amongst her companions. Annabelle and Captain Kidd exchanged a knowing look, each taking half of the pork steak, while Reigna gracefully claimed the vegetable medley. Lisa followed suit, quietly taking the potatoes and rolls.

As the final plates were cleared, the air shifted in anticipation of the first dance. Evelyn, resplendent in a gown that shimmered like the night sky, took her place at the center of the dance floor. Her partner, a young soldier in a crisply tailored green uniform, stood tall beside her. The music began, a lively, celebratory tune that echoed the vigor of youth. Their feet moved in perfect harmony, weaving a story of transition, of stepping beyond the threshold of childhood into a world of greater responsibility and promise.

As the tempo evolved into a sultry rhythm, their dance deepened. The soldier drew Evelyn closer, their movements an unspoken conversation of daring and trust. They moved as though their combined silhouette had become a single entity, embodying grace and subtle passion. The climax came with a dramatic dip, Evelyn's form suspended in his arms, a pose met by a burst of applause from the enraptured audience.

Breathless, Evelyn and her partner held their final position for a moment longer before she stood upright, her arm instinctively resting on his as he remained at her side. She turned to face the gathered guests, her voice clear and commanding. "This is my gala," she declared with an infectious smile, "and I say everyone needs to get on the floor and dance this night away!"

The crowd responded with enthusiasm, rising as one. The dance floor soon transformed into a kaleidoscope of movement and color. Annabelle and Captain Kidd were among the first to join, their earlier composure dissolving into carefree laughter. Reigna followed, her fluid movements weaving a dance of light and shadow. Marcus remained seated, momentarily absorbed in the lingering taste of water, while Lisa sat beside him, lost in thought.

Marcus's gentle inquiry broke the silence between them. "Miss Lisa, how are you enjoying your visit home?"

Lisa looked at him, her expression a blend of joy and wistfulness. "The mansion... it has been comforting to see again," she admitted softly. "But I was not prepared for how different everything feels. The tension within my family... it is like I am a stranger in my own home."

Marcus nodded with understanding. "Serving the goddess, I imagine, comes with its share of sacrifices."

Lisa gave a slight nod before turning the question back on him. "And you, Marcus? How often do the ties of family pull at your heart?"

He hesitated for a moment, then answered with quiet certainty. "The Order is the only family I've ever known. From birth, we are given to the Order by our parents."

Lisa's eyes widened in surprise. "Given? Why would anyone give up their baby?"

"For many families, it's not an easy choice," Marcus explained, his voice measured. "The Order's compensation can be life-changing in a world where resources are scarce. It's often a matter of survival."

"So... you have never known your parents?" Lisa asked gently, her curiosity tinged with empathy.

"I haven't," Marcus replied. "to me, the Order is home, my family. My loyalty and connections are with them." His tone shifted slightly, signaling a reluctance to dwell further on the topic.

Sensing his discomfort, Lisa nodded, but there was something she still needed to say. "I need to apologize for this morning," she began, her voice steady but sincere.

"You never need to apologize to me, Miss Lisa," Marcus interjected smoothly.

But Lisa shook her head, determined. "No, I do. I ignored your advice and confronted my mother and... *that man*. I thought using the tea to retaliate was justified, but I did not consider the risk it would be to you. I regret that."

The weight of her words hung between them. Marcus, ever loyal, sought to ease her guilt. "It wasn't my first encounter with the tea," he said lightly, offering a small smile. "I've survived worse."

His attempt at reassurance drew a faint smile from Lisa, though her concern for him remained evident. In that unspoken understanding, a bond between them deepened a quiet acknowledgment of loyalty, trust, and shared burdens.

"You are sweet, Brother Marcus. Truly, you are a very good servant," Lisa said softly, her voice imbued with genuine respect and affection.

A warm smile lit up Marcus's face, gratitude shining through his usually reserved expression. In a simple but meaningful gesture, he briefly touched her hand, an act that spoke volumes about the camaraderie and mutual understanding they had cultivated.

Seeking to lighten the mood, Lisa asked with a playful grin, "Would you like to share a dance?"

Marcus hesitated, his humility rising to the surface. "I must confess, I'm not much of a dancer," he admitted, suggesting she might prefer someone more experienced.

But Lisa wasn't swayed. Her gaze held steady, a blend of kindness and authority. "Brother Marcus," she said gently but firmly, her words both invitation and gentle command. It was clear she wanted his company, regardless of his skill.

"As you wish, Miss Lisa," Marcus acquiesced with a respectful nod.

As they made their way to the dance floor, the music surged to life, the lead singer's voice cutting through the air with vibrant energy. His bandmates echoed each verse in perfect harmony, and the instrumental bridges throbbed with an intensity that seemed to electrify the entire room.

Marcus felt a rush of apprehension as the tempo quickened. The beat seemed almost overwhelming, a mirror to his internal nervousness. Yet, as Lisa guided his hands to the proper position, her calm presence eased his anxiety.

"Relax," she encouraged softly. "Listen to the rhythm, feel the beat, it will guide you."

Marcus drew in a deep breath and focused on her words. Slowly, he began to move, his initial steps awkward and hesitant. He misstepped once, then twice, but each error was met not with embarrassment but with a renewed determination. He trusted Lisa's steady guidance, and it anchored him amid the chaos of the lively music.

"Watch me," she said, her tone light and reassuring. Taking the lead, she became one with the rhythm, nodding her head with each beat, her finger occasionally pointing skyward to emphasize key notes. She was his compass, a visual guide through the shifting currents of the melody.

"Step forward with your right foot," she instructed. Marcus complied, though he overshot the movement. Lisa gently applied resistance, her hand signaling the need for a smaller, more measured step. Without words, their subtle push and pull became a dance of communication, each correction a silent message between them.

Gradually, Marcus's movements became more fluid. The mechanical awkwardness faded as he began to internalize the rhythm. Under Lisa's patient direction, he found a syncopation that felt natural, a pattern of motion that no longer required constant instruction.

"See? You can dance, Brother Marcus," Lisa beamed, her praise bright and warm.

"I seem to have a hidden talent," Marcus quipped, the lightness in his tone a reflection of his growing comfort. He smiled, feeling at ease for the first time in a long while.

The dance floor around them whirled with a kaleidoscope of color and movement. Laughter and joyful chatter punctuated the air as other couples twirled and swayed to the music. In that moment, for both Marcus and Lisa, the burdens of duty and expectation faded into the background. The dance became less about steps and technique and more about shared presence—a rare moment of levity in their otherwise complex lives.

As the song continued, Lisa observed a transformation in Marcus. His usually solemn demeanor softened as he surrendered to the music's pulse. His movements gained a quiet confidence, no longer guided by instruction but by the instinct of the rhythm itself.

122

It struck her then, just how much weight he carried every day, the quiet sacrifices he made, the stoicism he rarely allowed himself to break. And here, in this fleeting moment, he had found a measure of freedom, of joy. She felt a surge of gratitude for the connection they shared, knowing that tonight, amidst the laughter and music, they had both found something precious: a brief respite from the responsibilities that so often defined them.

[-----✠-----]

Sophie stands defiantly in the center of the barn, the musty scent of hay thick in the air, mingling with the sharper tang of fear. The four men approach her like hyenas, their coats discarded in a grotesque mockery of leisure. Their laughter reverberates off the wooden walls, warped by the barn's acoustics into something more menacing. The tools of work scattered around, the pitchfork to her left, an upside-down shovel to her right, each feels maddeningly out of reach. Her heart pounds, but her resolve anchors her. She has faced worse before. Yet every muscle tenses, coiled and ready for the clash she knows is coming.

The dim light filtering through the barn's cracked slats casts jagged shadows across the walls, making the men appear larger and more distorted. The barn, with its looming darkness and eerie stillness, transforms into an arena. Sophie's mind races, strategizing her next move with the cold precision of survival instinct. She is unarmed, outnumbered, and alone. But surrender was an inconceivable option.

One of the men, whom she mentally christens Ogre Number 2, steps forward. "Here, jibber jibber," he croons mockingly, his voice laced with condescension. His stubbled face shows the neglect of a man who lives for violence, but his eyes gleam with malice, betraying a cruel intelligence beneath the bravado.

Another figure shoves through the group, broad-shouldered, with shoulder-length hair streaked grey. "Oh no, boys. This one's mine," he declares with a grin that reveals teeth bared in predatory anticipation.

Sophie's breath catches in her throat. Recognition flickers at the edge of her mind. "You," Sophie says, her voice steady despite the storm in her chest. "You were dressed as a royal policeman in Granmark."

His eyes widen ever so slightly, a crack in his facade, before dark amusement takes over. He chuckles, a low, sinister sound. "Oh, would you boys look at this, she remembers little ole me." He takes a step closer, his presence looming larger in the dim light. "See, darling, the goddess made sure we'd meet again."

Sophie instinctively steps back, matching his advance with careful retreat. The tension between them is palpable, a dance of predator and prey. Yet as he moves closer, a strange calm washes over her. It's not resignation, it's clarity. She knows her limits; brute strength won't win this fight. But training taught her that battles are not decided by strength alone.

Her mind sharpens, calculating. *Let him think he has the upper hand.* Sophie allows fear to touch her features, her breath hitching just enough to sell the illusion.

"You don't want to do this," she says, her voice quivering expertly.

The man laughs, a vile, hollow sound filled with cruel anticipation. "Oh no, darling. I think I really do want to do this." He gestures for the others to stay back. "Yah, boys, this one's all mine." His words drip with arrogance; each step forward meant to intimidate and assert control.

Sophie mirrors his movement, taking another calculated step back. She keeps her eyes darting, as though seeking escape, further baiting his overconfidence. "Enjoy what?" she challenges, lacing her tone with just enough defiance to provoke him.

His grin widens, predatory and smug. "Oh, it's been a while since I had the chance to train a girl as pretty as you," he taunts, his voice slithering like venom. "Breaking the fight out of girls like you, that's my favorite part of the job. Watching the moment you realize you can't win... now that is oh so sweet."

He inhales deeply as though savoring her fear, his eyes narrowing in twisted pleasure. "It's such a beautiful thing."

Sophie's stomach churns at his words, revulsion rising like bile. But she doesn't flinch. She can't afford to. Instead, she amplifies her mask of fear, letting her expression shift to one of horror and helplessness. She knows better than to overplay it, her performance needs strike a delicate balance. Behind the facade, her mind works feverishly, cataloging every step he takes, every word he utters. Each detail is another piece of the puzzle she needs to solve if she's going to get out of this alive.

In her mind, she dubs him the evil ogre, a title earned not only by his actions but by the darkness festering within him. It's a silent vow to herself, a reminder of who and what she's fighting.

He steps closer, his arrogance blinding him to the trap she's setting. Sophie maintains her distance, every nerve taut but controlled. She knows the game now. *He believes he's already won. And that belief will be his downfall.*

With predatory quickness, the evil ogre lunges, closing the gap between them faster than Sophie expects. She pivots to retreat, but her foot catches on something buried in the hay. Time seems to slow as she stumbles and falls backward, her hands instinctively reaching out to brace herself. She hits the ground hard, the impact knocking the breath from her lungs. Dust and hay swirl around her as motes of light shimmer in the dim barn air.

"No, no, darling," the ogre sneers, looming over her with a twisted grin. "You can't be on the ground already. "You need to fight at least a little, make it a challenge for me."

His voice oozes menace, each word designed to unnerve her. But Sophie refuses to be shaken. Her pulse races, but she channels that fear into focus. She pushes herself backward, scooting across the rough barn floor with her hands and feet. Her eyes remain locked on the ogre, watching his every move.

He advances slowly, savoring the chase. His hand lashes out toward her face, but Sophie dodges, shifting her weight just enough to evade his grasp. He swipes again, missing by mere fingers. Each attempt is half-hearted, as if he's toying with her. His grin widens as he plays the predator, but Sophie's mind is already calculating.

Dust and hay cling to her scraped palms and the backs of her legs, but the pain is distant, overshadowed by the surging adrenaline in her veins. She maintains eye contact, her gaze sharp and unyielding, even as her body propels her backward in a frantic crawl. The ogre's slow, deliberate movements betray his arrogance. He believes this is a game that he has already won.

Sophie uses that assumption against him. Each time he reaches for her, she feints, her quick reflexes keeping him just out of reach. The flickering lantern light throws erratic shadows across his face, exaggerating his grotesque features. But she doesn't look away. Fear grips her, but she refuses to give in to it; she feigns despair on her face. Inside, she focuses all her thoughts on survival.

With a sudden burst of energy, Sophie scoots further back, steering herself toward a stall on the left side of the barn. The narrow enclosure offers a brief respite, a place to move her strategy to the next stage. She crosses the threshold just as the ogre slows, pausing a few feet away. His dark silhouette fills the entrance to the stall, and his voice slithers through the air like a serpent.

"Yes, yes. You're right, darlin'. No need for an audience," he says, his tone deceptively calm. "Let's keep this intimate moment between just you and me." The malice beneath his words is palpable. His smile, wide and sickening, sends a fresh wave of disgust through Sophie.

He steps forward, confident and unhurried, as though savoring every moment. But Sophie is no longer focused on showing fear. Her mind sharpens, scanning the stall for anything she can use to her advantage. She sees it all clearly not a cage at all, but a battlefield of opportunities. Loose planks, scattered tools, piles of hay, all potential weapons if used correctly.

The ogre's words are meant to intimidate, to weaken her resolve, but Sophie doesn't waver. He wants her afraid, helpless. He wants to break her spirit before he strikes.

Her breath steadies as she plants her hands firmly on the floor. Her face of fear transforms. Unleashing the weapon, sharpened by her defiance. The predator before her expects submission. Instead, she plots her next move with the cold precision of a hunter, the warrior.

He turns to his ogre comrades, his voice casual and laced with authority. "You boys stay outta here. This might take me a while."

"Oh, what the hell, Nate? How's that fair?" one of them calls back, frustration laced in his voice.

"Shut it, Tate! I'll let you dance with her first when I'm done," Nate snaps, his grin widening as he turns his full attention back to Sophie.

The moment he steps within reach, Sophie's coiled muscles release like a spring. Her leg lashes out in a precise, powerful kick aimed at his left knee. The impact locks the joint in an unnatural position, throwing him off balance and forcing a grunt of surprise and pain from his throat. His grin falters as he staggers forward. This isn't just a defensive maneuver, it's a message. She is on an ogre hunt.

Seizing the opportunity, Sophie surges forward. Her body is a conduit of kinetic energy, and she drives her forehead into Nate's nose with brutal force. The sharp crack reverberates in her ears, a jarring yet satisfying sound that sends a surge of adrenaline rushing through her veins.

Before Nate can recover or shout for help, Sophie strikes again, her fingers darting forward to jab his throat. The precise hit silences him with a choking gasp. She follows up with a rapid series of punches, her fists pounding his torso and face. Each hit carries her defiance, but she knows her limits; her punches lack the mass and power to cause any severe damage. Yet she will not be deterred. Adapting mid-combat, she switches to elbow strikes, each blow delivered with controlled ferocity.

The shift in her tactics catches Nate off guard. He reels under the relentless barrage, crumpling to his knees as he gags for air. His dazed, garbled attempt to call for help is met with mockery from his oblivious companions outside.

"Come on, Nate! Don't hurt her too bad, we want a go!" one of the other ogres jeers, their laughter filling the barn like a cruel chorus.

Sophie's eyes narrow. They think he's still in control. *Good.*

Anchoring herself firmly to the barn's rough floor, Sophie draws on the fire of her determination. With a surge of strength, she drives her knee upward into Nate's battered face. The sickening crunch that follows echoes through the stall, a confirmation of her dominance over the monster who had sought to break her. Nate instinctively raises his arms in a feeble attempt to block the next blow, but it's too late. Sophie delivers another strike, his scream reduced to a choked, gurgling sound.

Not content to leave him merely reeling, she pivots fluidly. Raising her elbow high above her head, she channels every ounce of strength, fear, and fury into one devastating blow. Her elbow crashes into the back of Nate's skull, and he collapses like a broken marionette, his groans fading into unconsciousness as his face meets the floor with a final thud.

A wave of cold contempt washes over Sophie as she stands over him. This man, this *monster*, who reveled in the pain of others, now lies defeated at her feet. Her lip curls in disdain as she crouches low, her voice a venomous whisper meant for his ears alone.

"You were right, this does feel good. Is it good for you?" she taunts, her words reclaiming the power he sought to steal from her.

Straightening, Sophie breathes deeply, her silhouette cutting a fierce figure against the dim barn light. The tension in her muscles doesn't fade entirely; she knows the danger isn't over yet. With a decisive motion, she drives her foot down onto the back of Nate's head, ensuring his unconscious state. The dull thud is punctuation, the final note in this brutal confrontation.

Her survival instincts sharpen, guiding her gaze to a pitchfork leaning against the far stall wall. Without hesitation, she moves swiftly, gripping the wooden handle. Planting her foot against the tines, she snaps the shaft with a sharp crack, fashioning a makeshift bo staff. The solid weight in her hands is both a comfort and a declaration. She's no longer unarmed, she's ready.

Sophie steps out of the stall, her footsteps measured and deliberate. The remaining ogres turn their heads at the sound, and the flickering light from the barn's cracked walls stretches her shadow long and imposing across the dusty floor.

"He promised me a good time," she announces, her voice steady and mocking. "But in the end, he couldn't even dance."

The words land like a slap. The laughter from before falters, the other men exchanging uneasy glances. Nate's defeat is an undeniable reality. Sophie wields her words like weapons, undermining their bravado and confidence.

"Any of you want to have a good time?" she continues, the challenge in her voice unmistakable. Slowly, she spins the staff in her hands, the motion fluid and precise, a warning of her readiness.

The ogres shift uncomfortably, their earlier eagerness wavering in the face of her defiance. Sophie stands tall, her posture exuding strength and control. She is no longer a survivor of. She has awoken something more, a hunter, a warrior, the Avatar of War.

[-----✿-----]

Under the shimmering glow of the ballroom's chandeliers, Regina stood at the edge of the dance floor, captivated by the mesmerizing performance unfolding before her. Captain Kidd and Annabelle moved with a grace that suggested the expertise of seasoned dancers. Their movements flowed effortlessly, each step weaving into the next with a synchronicity that hinted at countless hours of practice. The vibrant melody, alive with playful energy, seemed to animate not only the dancers but the entire room.

They began with deceptively simple steps, executed with a refined elegance. Captain Kidd led Annabelle through a series of spins, his touch firm but gentle. The hem of Annabelle's dress flared like liquid silver, catching the ballroom lights as she twirled. When her spin came to an elegant close, she instinctively found his hand again, their connection unbroken as they transitioned into the next series of movements.

Annabelle's solo moment came like a sudden gust of wind, she whirled in place, her form becoming one with the melody's exuberant rhythm. As she completed the spin, Captain Kidd was there, his hand extended to seamlessly draw her back into the shared rhythm of their dance. They shifted into a playful routine, circling each other with an almost theatrical swagger. Their shoulders bounced to the beat, fists raised in mock defiance, as they embodied the spirit of the lively tune.

The dance took a humorous turn when Captain Kidd exaggerated a flirtatious glance at another woman nearby. Annabelle, quick to respond, pantomimed an indignant slap and wagged her finger at him with mock severity before theatrically storming off. Captain Kidd followed with an equally exaggerated expression of remorse, his hands clasped in an over-the-top plea for forgiveness. Their playful exchange drew scattered laughter from the audience.

The reconciliation was swift, he tapped Annabelle on the shoulder, then offered his hand in a gallant gesture. With grins that spoke of shared mischief, they resumed their dance, the tension of their playful argument dissolving as quickly as it had begun.

Regina found herself swept up in the performance, clapping along to the infectious energy as the final notes of the song echoed through the hall. The room erupted in applause, but for a moment, all Regina could see was the joy radiating from her friends as they bowed dramatically to the cheering crowd.

As Annabelle approached with her arms wide, her eyes sparkled with both challenge and promise. Regina froze, suddenly aware of the attention shifting in her direction. "I... I don't know how to dance." she admitted quietly, her words barely audible amidst the lingering applause.

Annabelle's smile widened mischievously. "Don't ye worry, missy, I'll teach ye," she said, her voice full of playful confidence.

Regina hesitated, but before she could protest further, Annabelle gently but firmly took her hand and guided her onto the dance floor. "Now, watch me feet," Annabelle instructed, her tone both encouraging and lighthearted.

Regina focused on Annabelle's steps, nervously mimicking the movements. The lively music began anew, and though Regina's initial steps were hesitant, Annabelle's infectious enthusiasm soon had her moving more freely. Around them, the other dancers whirled and twirled, their laughter blending with the music's vibrant rhythm.

Step by step, under the watchful eyes of the crowd and the supportive guidance of her chaotic but caring friend, Regina embarked on a new adventure, one filled with laughter, movement, and the boundless joy of the dance.

[-----⛊-----]

In the dust-filled gloom of the barn, Sophie faced the trio of ogre-like men. Her posture, relaxed yet alert, conveyed both readiness and defiance. The tension crackled in the air like static as her voice, laced with mockery, shattered the silence.

"I'll tell you what, direct me to the demon or the tree guy, and I promise, I won't beat you too bad."

The men exchanged puzzled glances, the absurdity of her request hanging between them. The red-haired leader, his muscular frame straining against his white work shirt, stepped forward with a scowl. "What kinda jibber nonsense are you spoutin'?"

Sophie chuckled softly, shaking her head as if disappointed in herself for expecting more. "I knew there was something off about that man," she muttered under her breath. Raising her voice, she added, "Look, I need to free the prisoner you've got locked up downstairs. Which one of you is going to be the smart one and help me out?"

The red-haired man's growl deepened. He clenched his fists, the veins on his forearms bulging as he slammed one into his other palm. "The only *help* we're gonna give is tossing you in that cell right alongside him."

Sophie's eyes sparkled with challenge. "Really? That's the best you've got? Come on, you really don't want to disappoint me." Her smile widened ever so slightly, a deliberate provocation.

The words were a trigger. One of the men, more petite and wiry, lunged with reckless aggression. Sophie moved like lightning, her staff sweeping in a clean arc that cracked against his jaw. The impact echoed through the barn, a sharp punctuation mark of her defiance. She followed up with a snap kick to his sternum, forcing him to stagger back before a final strike swept his legs out from under him, sending him sprawling into a nearby stall.

"Get up, you idiot!" the red-haired man barked, his frustration mounting as his remaining comrades charged together.

Sophie danced out of their path, her body flowing with balletic grace. The staff spun in her hands, a blur of wood in motion, as she evaded the first man's clumsy punch. Pivoting smoothly, she tripped the second with a low sweep of the staff, sending him crashing to the floor.

Retreating to the front of the barn, Sophie seized the open space to reposition herself. Her staff twirled above her head like a storm in motion. She pivoted sharply, completing a one-eighty turn to face the trio as they regrouped. She stood near the barn wall, grounding her stance.

She anticipated their next move before they made it; *this time, they won't come at her one by one. They would try to overwhelm me in a coordinated rush.* And sure enough, they advanced in formation, two in front with the red-haired leader towering behind them like a battering ram.

Sophie's eyes narrowed as she surged forward, meeting their charge head-on. Her staff spun faster, gathering momentum like a coiled spring. She struck with ruthless precision, her weapon crashing down on the second ogre's head. The man crumpled to the ground with a groan.

The blonde ogre charged in next. Sophie's staff whistled through the air in a sweeping strike aimed at his face. To her surprise, he caught the weapon mid-swing, his grip tightening with a grin of triumph. "Gotcha now!"

Undeterred, Sophie unleashed a rapid pair of kicks, one to his sternum and the other, more devastating, to his groin. He doubled over in pain but refused to release her staff. Sophie barely had time to react as the red-haired man's fist shot toward her head. She ducked, the blow narrowly missing her as her mind raced for a solution.

Her fingers brushed the small wooden cutouts in her pocket: runes she had prepared to train with her Alrunia magic. Without hesitation, she pulled one free and infused it with mana. The air crackled as the block ignited, transforming into a fireball. Sophie hurled it at the red-haired ogre, the flames engulfing his head in a burst of heat and light. He stumbled back, roaring in pain and confusion.

Seizing the opportunity, Sophie launched herself into a double-footed kick that sent him crashing to the ground. She scrambled to her feet, adrenaline driving her forward. Her focus sharpened, she needed her staff back. The blonde still held it tightly, his face twisted in pain and anger.

Sophie feinted another kick, causing him to flinch, then brought her knee down hard on his head. The blow landed with precision, and his grip finally slackened. She ripped the staff free and spun it defensively, her senses on high alert.

"You're gonna pay for that," the blonde ogre snarled, coughing between threats.

Sophie didn't dignify him with a response. Her eyes tracked the red-haired leader as he staggered upright, his face smeared with soot from the fire spell. He growled, his gaze locking onto her with murderous intent.

Sophie moved with fluid grace, sidestepping to gain better positioning. Her staff twirled in a mesmerizing display, a complex kata that saw it loop behind her back before arcing overhead. The red-haired man charged, his smug expression betraying his overconfidence. He thought he had her rhythm figured out.

But Sophie was two steps ahead. She abruptly shifted the staff's motion from horizontal to vertical, catching him off guard. The weapon struck his chin with an upward blow, snapping his head back violently. Before he could react, Sophie followed through with a fierce downward strike, gathering all her momentum into the impact. The crack of wood against bone echoed through the barn as he crumpled to the floor, his massive frame collapsing like a felled tree.

For a moment, silence reigned. Sophie's chest heaved with exertion as she surveyed the remaining two ogres, who were now back on their feet. They shared a glance of mutual dread, the arrogance in their eyes replaced by fear and anger.

"We... we can't let her do this to us," the second man called out, his voice tinged with desperation.

The tension thickened in the barn as Ogre Man Number 2's declaration echoed in the stale air. He and his blonde-haired ally exchanged a glance, silently resolving to take Sophie down together. Their movements slowed, becoming deliberate and measured. They extended their hands, intent on ensnaring her or her weapon, advancing with the calculated precision of predators circling prey.

Sophie, standing her ground, remained poised, her staff gripped firmly in both hands. Though her posture exuded calm readiness, her mind worked rapidly, strategizing her next move. She slipped her hand into her pocket, retrieving another wooden square. As she channeled mana into it, uncertainty crept in, the familiar feeling of fire the fire rune was absent. Is *it water? Or stone?* If it were stone, she could end the fight swiftly, but she had no time for certainty.

Seeking to provoke them, Sophie's voice pierced the silence. "Sorry, when did you ever let me do... well, anything?" The challenge, laced with mockery, hung in the air.

The ogres hesitated, momentarily thrown by her defiance. Tension crackled between them like static, each side gauging the other, calculating risks. Then, with a mutual nod, the two advanced together, aiming to corner her.

Sophie's grip on the staff tightened. She had only seconds to act. With a fluid motion, she flung the wooden square at the blonde-haired ogre's face. As it hit, a torrent of water erupted, dousing him in a sudden splash. He staggered back, sputtering in shock. Though the rune's effect was not as forceful as Sophie had hoped, the momentary confusion it caused was enough.

Seizing the opportunity, Sophie launched a sweeping strike with her staff. Ogre man number 2 ducked under it, narrowly avoiding the blow. His agility surprised her, but she was no stranger to close combat improvisation. Pivoting on instinct, Sophie spun low and drove the staff upward with precision, connecting with his nose in a brutal crack.

The man reeled from the hit, but Sophie didn't relent. She followed with a rapid jab to his chest, knocking him off balance, and then a powerful spin kick to his head. The force sent him sprawling to the ground, his body hitting the floor with a heavy thud.

Breathing heavily, Sophie readjusted her stance and turned her focus to the blonde ogre, who was shaking off the effects of the water rune. His expression twisted in rage as he wiped water from his face.

"You're going to pay for that, you Jiberau—"

Sophie didn't let him finish. With her patience worn thin, she prepared a HARDKNUCKLE spell, channeling mana into her fist. The spell ignited with a faint glow around her hand. She lunged forward and drove the enchanted punch straight into his jaw. The force was overwhelming. His eyes rolled back, and he crumpled to the floor, unconscious before he even hit the ground.

"Who's a slave now!?!" Sophie shouted, her voice reverberating through the barn. The echo faded, leaving only the heavy silence of victory. She stood amidst the aftermath; four men, once so confident, now strewn across the barn floor, defeated.

For a moment, Sophie allowed herself to breathe, to revel in the triumph of her hard-won battle. But the moment was fleeting. She dropped her staff to the floor and retrieved her inspection glasses from her shirt pocket, relieved to find them undamaged. Sliding them on, she began methodically searching the fallen men, her hands moving with calm efficiency. She checked their belts, their pockets, even the discarded jackets strewn about the barn.

Nothing. No key. No clue.

Her stomach sank as realization dawned. Despite the intensity and success of the fight, she was no closer to freeing Eclipse Lepele from the magical prison below. The weight of the situation pressed down on her, turning the thrill of victory into bitter frustration. She had won the battle, but the mission remained incomplete.

Sophie clenched her fists, taking a steadying breath. The barn felt suffocating, the dust and stillness pressing in from all sides. Yet even in the face of this setback, a spark of resolve reignited within her. This was just a moment, a pause, not an end. The true strength she carried wasn't in the staff strikes or spells she had cast, but in her refusal to give up. Eclipse Lepele is still waiting for her, and she wasn't about to leave him trapped.

Her eyes hardened as she surveyed the barn once more. There had to be another way forward. She would find it. No matter what.

[-----⚙-----]

After a few dances, Lisa bid Marcus a gentle goodnight. His spirits had lifted from the evening's festivities, though a profound fatigue had settled over him. Opting for solitude, he retreated to his room, leaving the gala's vibrant energy behind. Lisa, however, wasn't yet ready to relinquish the night. The celebration still sang in her veins. She wandered back onto the dance floor, her laughter mingling with the music as she immersed herself in the revelry.

But the festive glow soon dimmed when yet another unwelcome hand brushed against her backside. A chill of discomfort spread through her, sharp and sobering. She withdrew immediately, retreating to the safety of her table, her earlier joy now tempered. From her vantage point, she surveyed the ballroom, a silent storm brewing behind her thoughtful gaze.

Amid the kaleidoscope of spinning dancers, she spotted Captain Kidd. He guided Madam Tanley, radiant in a sun-kissed yellow gown, across the floor with the effortless grace of a man who knew how to lead both on land and sea. The woman, fiery-haired and vibrant, glided in perfect harmony with him, a far cry from her husband's reserved demeanor as a grain merchant. Captain Kidd's leadership in this setting was subtler than the commanding presence he wielded with his crew. Here, a gentle touch or an exchanged glance conveyed his authority, a skill he wielded with finesse, except, of course, when it came to Annabelle.

Annabelle's approach to influence was anything but subtle. She bulldozed through social conventions with a boldness that mirrored Governor Nozaki's own style. As she watched her friend's antics, Lisa couldn't help but notice the striking similarities between Annabelle and her father. Yet these thoughts soon gave way to a more personal question: *what is my role in all of this? am I simply another thread woven into her family's legacy, or do I move to a rhythm uniquely her own?*

The music swirled around her, but Lisa's thoughts drifted to her sister, Evelyn. Even in her absence, Evelyn's presence lingered, her guidance a constant whisper in Lisa's mind. This night was more than just a celebration. It was a mirror, reflecting the many paths laid out before her. And in the quiet between the notes, Lisa grappled with an identity still in the making.

Her reverie was interrupted by Evelyn's sudden arrival. Without warning, her sister unceremoniously dropped into the chair at her side, her presence as striking as the green-and-gold gown she wore. "Hey, why are you not dancing? I thought I told everyone to hit the dance floor tonight," Evelyn teased, her voice light but carrying an unmistakable edge of expectation.

"Hello, Evelyn," Lisa greeted, a mix of affection and resignation in her tone. She quickly added, "I am just taking a break," hoping to deter further questioning.

Evelyn wasn't easily deterred. "Why are you sitting here all by yourself? There are plenty of boys out there dying to dance with you," she pressed, her eyes scanning the crowd as if scouting for potential partners.

Lisa sighed, the memory of unwanted hands in unwanted places still too fresh. "It is not about the dancing. They just want to touch my behind, it makes me uncomfortable." she admitted, her voice steady but guarded.

131

Evelyn chuckled, dismissing the concern with a casual shrug. "Oh, come on. They are just showing you they like you. Take it as a compliment."

Lisa frowned but chose not to argue. The silence that followed was punctuated by the distant hum of music and laughter.

Evelyn, never one to let a conversation die, leaned in conspiratorially. "So, no one out there caught your eye? All those boys out there?" she asked, her skepticism on full display.

Avoiding her sister's gaze, Lisa said reluctantly, "Maybe one or two." It was a half-hearted admission; Lisa did not want to reveal too much.

"There you go!" Evelyn exclaimed, latching onto the confession with glee. "Who knows, maybe you can recruit one of them for one of your charity missions." she teased, nudging Lisa playfully.

Despite herself, Lisa smiled, the annoyance easing as she swatted at Evelyn's arm. "Stop it," she said, laughter softening her voice.

The moment of levity passed as Evelyn's expression shifted, a mischievous glint in her eyes. "So, I heard you stood up to Dad," she began, unable to hide her amusement. "I wish I could've seen that. What were you thinking?"

Lisa hesitated, the question striking deeper than Evelyn intended. "I… I just could not tolerate how daddy was treating my…" She faltered, struggling to find the right words. How could she describe her bond with the avatars and Marcus? *Friends* did not seem right, but anything else felt too complicated.

"Friends?" Evelyn echoed skeptically, raising an eyebrow. She took a slow sip from her drink before continuing. "You were taken from us, Lisa. You don't need to stay with them anymore. You are home now."

Lisa stared at her sister, the idea foreign and unsettling. *Leave the avatars?* The notion felt impossible, as though it would strip away a part of her soul. "I want to be with them. I belong with them," she asserted, the conviction in her voice surprising even herself.

Evelyn regarded her for a moment, then hummed thoughtfully. Her gaze drifted to where Regina and Annabelle danced in carefree synchronization. "Like peas in a pod, huh, chipmunk?" she remarked, a mixture of curiosity and resignation in her tone.

Lisa followed her sister's gaze. Watching the others on the dance floor, she knew with certainty that she couldn't abandon them. "We may not be a perfect match," she admitted, "but together, we make sense…mostly"

"If you say so, chipmunk," Evelyn replied with a teasing smirk, finishing her drink. Her attention shifted past Lisa, her expression brightening as she spotted someone in the crowd.

Lisa turned to see Sargent Linwood standing nearby, a bouquet of roses in hand. His posture was both formal and inviting. "If you're ready, my lady," he said, his voice warm and respectful, extending an arm to Evelyn.

With a grin, Evelyn embraced Lisa tightly, whispering, "Go enjoy yourself, chipmunk. I am going to enjoy a moonlit walk through mom's garden with this good-looking military man." She squeezed her sister one last time before turning to link arms with Linwood. Together, they made their way toward the grand staircase, leaving Lisa to watch them disappear into the crowd, her emotions swirling in the wake of their departure.

As Lisa's gaze lingered on the retreating figures of Evelyn and Sargent Linwood, a thread of contemplation wove its way through her thoughts. Her mind drifted to her own goddess gala, a rite of passage still waiting on the horizon. *Would it be a betrayal, she wondered, to honor a goddess outside Unity's pantheon during such a sacred ceremony?* The question loomed in the quiet recesses of her mind, unanswered, a whisper of the deeper conflict that simmered within her.

Shaking the thought aside, she turned her attention back to the dance floor. Annabelle and Regina caught her eye, the two of them spinning and laughing in carefree harmony. Despite their stark differences, they had become fast friends, their bond radiating a warmth that stirred something in Lisa. She noted how Regina and Sophie had also grown close, their shared training sessions fostering a connection that seemed to deepen with each passing day. The idea of joining them crossed Lisa's mind briefly, but the thought of enduring such rigorous physical discipline quickly snuffed out the impulse.

Her gaze wandered across the crowd to Madam Tanley, who now danced alone. The absence of Captain Kidd suggested that another chapter of the evening was drawing to a close. It was the nature of such nights, beginnings, climaxes, and quiet resolutions playing out like acts in an intricate drama.

Lisa's eyes shifted to the stage, where her parents sat. Conrad stood, his gestures sharp and commanding, while Linda remained seated, her expression calm but resolute. The quiet tension between them was palpable, their conversation charged with unspoken disagreements. Lisa's chest tightened as she realized the subject of their debate could only be her. The weight of her earlier defiance pressed down on her, guilt creeping in as she pondered the strain her actions had placed on her family.

In that moment of reflection, Lisa found herself caught between two worlds; her duty to her family and her growing bond with the avatars. These competing desires clashed within her, each pulling her in opposite directions. Her family expected loyalty and obedience, a continuation of tradition. Yet, the avatars had become more than companions; they were a part of her identity now, tethered to her in ways she hadn't fully grasped until tonight.

The gala, with all its vibrant dances and whispered conversations, felt like a mirror reflecting her inner turmoil. Each interaction around her became symbolic a reminder that life was an intricate web of connections, choices, and allegiances. The question she faced was no longer just one of belonging, but of deciding who she wanted to be and which parts of herself she was willing to fight for.

Lisa sighed softly, her mind still caught in the crossroads of identity and expectation. The path ahead was unclear, but deep down, she knew that every step she took, whether in defiance or compromise, was leading her toward a greater understanding of herself and her place in this ever-complex world.

[----- ⚓ -----]

Amid the kaleidoscope of laughter and music filling Evelyn's Goddess Gala, Annabelle stood as a beacon of pride, watching Regina conquer the sequinta a dance as captivating as the stories of the seas Annabelle had sailed. The style was a treasure she had brought back from an unforgettable voyage, during which her crew had transported a dance troupe from Islewind to Opulentia. Their infectious joy had left an indelible mark on Annabelle, and now, she passed those memories on to Regina.

Regina's movements told a story in rhythm and grace. Her feet whispered across the floor in short, precise steps, only to launch into bold, sweeping strides that set her entire body in motion. Her hips swayed fluidly as her hands arced above her head, gliding down in elegant flourishes. Each turn and repetition was a testament to her focus and excitement for mastering something new. Annabelle clapped along, content to serve as both guide and admirer, her own steps simple yet supportive, a soft echo to Regina's spirited performance.

As Regina danced, Annabelle's gaze drifted toward their table. Lisa sat alone, her expression distant, lost in thought, a stark contrast to the vibrant energy surrounding them. Compelled to act, Annabelle excused herself with a decisive nod and made her way across the room, her steps purposeful and steady, like a captain steering her ship through turbulent waters.

When she reached the table, Annabelle extended her hand without hesitation. Mischief sparkled in her eyes, her grin warm and inviting. "Oi, missy," she teased, her voice carrying a blend of camaraderie and playful command. "The princess of the party has declared the dance floor mandatory."

Lisa blinked, momentarily caught off guard. Before she could form a coherent response, Annabelle took her wrist, the touch reassuring yet insistent. The warmth of Annabelle's hand dispelled the quiet chill of solitude that had settled around Lisa. With a gentle tug, Annabelle pulled her to her feet, the gesture a blend of understanding and stubborn determination.

"Anna!" Lisa protested, her voice laced with both laughter and reluctance. "I was just resting!"

"Yeah, well, yer not anymore," Annabelle retorted with a grin, her confidence unwavering. She guided Lisa through the bustling crowd with ease, her energy infectious.

The journey from the table to the dance floor was brief but symbolic, a transition from introspection to engagement, from isolation to shared celebration. Annabelle's grip on Lisa's hand wasn't just a physical connection; it was a lifeline, a reminder that joy could be found in letting go, even if just for a moment.

As they reached the floor, Annabelle released Lisa's hand only to spin her playfully, a lighthearted invitation to immerse herself in the celebration. Lisa allowed herself to be swept into the movement, her initial resistance fading as she mirrored Annabelle's steps. Their hands reconnected in perfect synchronicity after the spin, a gesture that spoke of trust and friendship built on their shared experiences.

Lisa quickly noticed the familiar rhythm in Annabelle's dance. The movements reminded her of the Kachae, a traditional dance of Verdantia. The realization bolstered her confidence, at least for a moment. But Annabelle's free-spirited improvisation soon pushed the boundaries of expectation. Each unexpected flourish demanded Lisa's full focus. She had no choice but to trust in the moment, to trust Annabelle, as the dance evolved into something uniquely their own. She is not going to falter in front of Annabelle and hear her mouth about it.

From across the floor, Regina observed the dynamic duo with admiration. Annabelle wasn't holding back, pushing Lisa to keep up with a whirlwind of steps and twists. Yet Lisa, to Regina's delight, rose to each challenge with resilience, her movements growing more assured with each turn. This wasn't just a dance, it was a testament to their friendship, a reflection of trust forged through their time together.

Lost in her observations, Regina barely noticed the tap on her shoulder. Startled, she turned to face a boy standing nervously before her. His black suit, accented with green lapels that echoed the gala's vibrant theme, fit him well. His smile, a mix of shyness and courage, revealed the effort it had taken for him to approach her. In that moment, Regina saw both his apprehension and an endearing charm that stirred something inside her.

"Hi," he greeted, his voice hesitant but earnest. "Are you having fun?"

"Oh yes!" Regina beamed, excitement bubbling over. "The gala is amazing!" Her enthusiasm was infectious.

He shifted on his feet, his gaze dropping briefly to the floor. "Oh... okay," he murmured, as though unsure how to proceed. He hesitated, then looked up, the band's music swelling around them. "I was wondering..." His words trailed off, swallowed by the sound of the gala.

Regina leaned in, her curiosity piqued. "What? I'm sorry, I can't hear you over the music," she said, raising her voice slightly.

"Oh, uh, sorry," he stammered, clearing his throat nervously. "I was just wondering..."

Seeing an opportunity, Regina decided to take charge. "Hey, do you know any good dance moves?" she asked brightly, pulling him in with her natural eagerness.

His face lit up, the tension melting away. "Sure! We have dance class at school, and..."

"Can you teach me?" Regina interjected, her eyes sparkling with interest. "I love learning how to dance!"

"Sure," the boy replies, his smile widening with reassurance as he extends his hand in invitation.

Regina takes it eagerly, allowing herself to be guided into a basic dance routine. At first, there is a spark of excitement, an anticipation that this moment will match the exhilarating spectacle of Annabelle and Lisa's performance. Yet, as the steps unfold in predictable simplicity, a creeping sense of disappointment takes root. The routine, though executed with care, lacks the complexity and flair she had hoped for. "Is this all you know how to do? It's boring," she blurts out, her candidness cutting through the buoyant atmosphere.

The transformation in the boy's expression is immediate. The brightness in his eyes dims, his posture wilting like a flower suddenly deprived of sunlight. Regina, caught up in her own high expectations, fails to grasp the weight of her words until it's too late. His enthusiasm, once buoyed by the opportunity to share something he knew, crumbles beneath her unintended dismissal.

"Sorry, I have to go," he mumbles, retreating quickly into the crowd, leaving Regina standing alone.

Confusion clouds her thoughts. She doesn't understand what went wrong, only that the moment slipped away before she could stop it. With a puzzled shrug, she allows herself to be carried once more by the rhythm of the music. Swaying to the beat, she claps her hands in time, her spirit rallying despite the fleeting connection.

Meanwhile, Lisa, breathless from her dance with Annabelle, gently extricates herself from her friend's relentless pace. "Okay, I need a break," she announces, taking a step back to catch her breath.

"What?" Annabelle's surprise is almost comical, her hands still outstretched as if expecting another spin. "I thought you liked to dance!"

"I do, but..." Lisa fumbles for an excuse, her eyes darting around the room for inspiration. Seeing her peers mingling and chatting, she seizes on a sudden idea. "There are all these cute boys here; we should really be dancing with them," she suggests, hoping it will distract Annabelle from pushing her into another exhausting round.

Annabelle cocks her head, puzzled. "Why?"

Lisa sighs internally, realizing she'll need a bit of creative persuasion. "It is part of the gala rules," she fibs with a playful grin, willing the lie to sound convincing. "You know, like a tradition."

Annabelle's eyes widen slightly in realization. "Oh! Well, why didn't anybody tell us?" She straightens with purpose, her adventurous spirit reignited. "All right then, let's go catch us some boys!"

Lisa chuckles, both amused and relieved. Annabelle's declaration propels them forward, and they approach a small group of boys with a mix of determination and curiosity. Regina, now rejoining them, is swept into the plan without protest. Together, the trio strides up to a group of boys gathered among themselves.

Annabelle, leading the charge, clasps her hands together and addresses the group with the authority of a captain summoning her crew. "Gentlemen," she declares, her voice clear and confident, "Which of ye be man enough to help one of us beauties fulfill our duties at this here gala?"

The boys exchange wide-eyed glances, caught off guard by the audacity of her approach. The air is thick with a mix of curiosity and awkward uncertainty.

Sensing the need to smooth things over, Lisa steps forward with a diplomatic smile. "What my *friend* is trying to say is, we would like the pleasure of a dance with some of you handsome gentlemen," she explains, her tone warm and inviting. The tension eases as a few of the boys chuckle nervously.

"I want to learn new dances," Regina adds earnestly, her enthusiasm shining through.

A black-haired boy steps forward, his sharp black suit and green lapel pin catching the light. He offers Lisa his hand with a mixture of courage and shyness. "I'll dance with you," he says, his voice steady yet gentle.

Lisa smiles, taking his hand. "Okay," she replies, a note of cautious optimism in her voice. As they prepare to leave the circle, she adds softly, "Please watch your hands." Her words are a gentle but firm reminder of her boundaries. The boy nods respectfully, and together, they move toward the main dance floor.

Annabelle, meanwhile, wastes no time in selecting her own partner. She spots a boy with a look of both apprehension and excitement. With a grin, she clasps his hand. "Ye look like fun. Let's shove off," she commands playfully, leaving no room for hesitation. With a tug, she leads him into the lively throng of dancers.

Regina, momentarily left behind, faces the remaining boys with a lighthearted challenge. "So, who got an 'A' in dancing class?" she asks with a playful grin, her tone inviting rather than competitive.

The boys exchange looks, their initial shyness beginning to dissolve. One of them, a tall boy with sandy hair, raises his hand sheepishly. "Uh, I got a B-plus," he offers.

Regina laughs, delighted by his honesty. "That's good enough for me!" she replies, holding out her hand. He accepts it with growing confidence, and they step together into the dance's embrace. The music, vibrant and infectious, becomes their guide as the trio of friends and their new partners dive into the rhythm of the gala, each dance a story unfolding with every spin and step.

[-----⊕-----]

Sophie's frustration echoed through the barn, her voice a mixture of desperation and resolve. "Come on, Sophie, think!" she yelled to herself, her eyes scanning the dimly lit interior, searching for anything that might dismantle the magical barrier imprisoning Eclipse Lepele. She would never leave him behind, he is from her clan and she will see him free. She reassured herself that Brother Marcus would find a way to explain Eclipse's presence later if needed.

She scoured the cluttered shelves near the entrance, ranch tools and equipment meant for managing horses and cattle. Everything was familiar but utterly useless in breaking through a magical seal.

The sudden crunch of footsteps on gravel snapped her to attention. Instinct took over. Sophie seized her staff and positioned herself beside the entrance, angling herself to stay hidden behind whoever was about to enter. She steadied her breathing, her grip tightening on the staff.

The barn door creaked open, and in stepped a figure whose appearance clashed with the rustic setting. A man in a white linen suit, his blonde hair tied neatly in a masculine ponytail, paused in the doorway. His eyes widened at the disarray before him—the unconscious men sprawled across the barn floor.

"By the sea, what happened here?" he exclaimed, his voice tinged with shock.

Sophie exhaled in relief. "Captain Kidd," she called out, stepping from her hiding spot.

The captain spun around, his expression shifting from confusion to surprise. "Sophie Griffin? What are ye doing here?" he asked, concern lacing his tone.

"They have a member of my clan locked up in the basement," Sophie explained quickly, her voice steady and urgent. "I need to get him out, but the barrier's sealed. I haven't found a way to break it yet."

"A basement? Here?" Captain Kidd arched a skeptical eyebrow, glancing around the barn as though seeing it in a new light.

Sophie pointed towards the hidden entrance under the stall floor. "It's down there," she said, her movements purposeful as she guided him. Captain Kidd carefully stepped over the unconscious men, his shoes crunching softly against the straw-covered floor. He paused at the top of the stairs leading into the basement and peered down into the darkness.

"What happened to them?" he asked, nodding toward the fallen men.

"We fought," Sophie replied simply, a mixture of weariness and pride in her voice.

Captain Kidd gave her a long, appraising look. "Ye did all this?" he asked, incredulous.

"Yep," she replied with a self-assured grin.

"Three of them?" Captain Kidd asked, his tone colored by both disbelief and admiration.

"Actually, four." Sophie held up four fingers before gesturing towards the far end of the barn. "There is one over there, unconscious in the back stall."

The captain let out a low whistle. "Oi, missy, remind me to never cross ye," he quipped, shaking his head in amazement. His admiration turned serious as he redirected his attention to the task ahead. "Let's see what we're dealing with down here," he said, descending the staircase.

Sophie followed close behind, her footsteps echoing softly in the enclosed space. As they rounded the corner, Captain Kidd and Eclipse Lepele sized each other up from opposite sides of the bars.

"Evening, Governor. The name's Captain James Lowe, of the good ship Stormfang," Captain Kidd introduced himself, his voice carrying the easy confidence of a seasoned commander.

"Evening?" Eclipse repeated, confusion clouding his expression. He turned to Sophie with a frown. "It's nighttime? Why didn't you tell me?"

"I'm pretty sure I did," Sophie replied, her tone dry, the corners of her mouth twitching in faint amusement.

Captain Kidd tilted his head, curiosity glinting in his eyes. "And ye are?" he asked the prisoner. "How'd ye end up locked in this here cell?"

Eclipse hesitated, frustration flickering across his face as he struggled to recall. "I'm Antonio Lepele of the Aurorium," he finally said. "I was on a ship when…" His voice trailed off, and he grimaced, raising a hand to his head in exasperation. "I can't remember," he admitted, his voice strained with the effort.

"Easy now, mate. No need to push it," Captain Kidd reassured him, though his interest in the story was evident.

"The demon woman put a curse on me," Eclipse muttered, his dreadlocks swaying as he shook his head. "You need to find the tree man to break the barrier before the ogres return."

"Tree man? Ogres?" Captain Kidd echoed, glancing at Sophie with raised eyebrows.

She smirked slightly. "I think I've already met the ogres," she said wryly. "Eclipse, how many were there again?"

The Aurorium prisoner counted off on his fingers, his brows knitting in thought. "Four… It's four," he said with certainty.

Captain Kidd chuckled. "Well, it looks like young Miss Sophie here is quite the ogre slayer," he remarked with admiration.

Lepele stared at Sophie, astonishment widening his eyes. "But… you're so young. And small. And only a torchbearer," he stammered, struggling to reconcile the image of the petite girl before him with the defeat of four men.

"I got lucky," Sophie replied modestly, though the glint in her eyes hinted at more than mere luck. She shifted the conversation back to their goal. "Eclipse, what do you know about the tree man or the demon woman? I need to find them if we're going to get you out."

Lepele's eyes darkened as he thought about the demon woman. "She's powerful… and cruel," he said quietly. "She placed this curse on me, and the tree man, I don't know …. he works with her and controls the barrier. They are after the clan's secrets."

Captain Kidd crossed his arms, his gaze thoughtful. "All right, then. We find this tree man and put an end to this mess. But we'll have to move quickly before they realize that these here ogres are down."

"The tree man is dangerous, he will bore into your mind!" Eclipse Lepele vented his frustration and resignation, his words bleeding into one another. "I tried everything to stir discontent among his ranks, but the ogres stay loyal. They saw right through me."

Captain Kidd rubbed his chin thoughtfully, his brows knitting. "Aye, mate, this *tree man* must have some potent magic to command that kind of loyalty," he remarked, his tone dripping with sarcasm. He turned to Sophie, his eyes narrowing. "Any chance ye can force the door open?"

Sophie shook her head, irritation flickering across her features. "No. There's a barrier spell, too strong to break."

Intrigued, Captain Kidd reached into his pocket and produced a gleaming gold coin. With a flick of his wrist, he sent it spinning toward the cell door. The moment the coin touched the barrier, it flared to life, glowing briefly before repelling the coin with an invisible force.

"Great... Magic," Captain Kidd said with a roll of his eyes, stooping to retrieve the coin. He gave Eclipse a wry grin. "Don't worry, matey. We'll figure something out."

Sophie crossed her arms, skepticism gnawing at her. Captain Kidd had openly admitted he had no talent for magic, so what exactly was his plan? As he ascended the stairs, she followed closely, curiosity and apprehension warring within her.

At the top of the stairs, Captain Kidd halted and faced her with a serious expression. "Ye sure about this guy?" he asked. "Yer friend down there... he seems a bit touched in the head."

Sophie nodded without hesitation. "Yeah, I've noticed. But he's one of us, a member of my clan. I'm not leaving him behind."

Captain Kidd studied her for a moment before relenting. "Aye, Missy. Loyalty's a fine thing." His gaze shifted to the unconscious men scattered across the barn floor. A mischievous glint entered his eyes. "I gots me a rather bad idea, that might just work."

Sophie frowned. "What do you mean?"

"Help me move these blokes outside," he said, rolling up his sleeves.

"What, Why?" Sophie asked, puzzled by the sudden request.

"Because I'd rather not carry the burden of their souls if things go sideways," Captain Kidd replied bluntly. He shot her a pointed look. "Unless yer goddess has given you some divine solution?"

Sophie hesitated, momentarily at a loss for words. Captain Kidd sighed in exasperation. "You're as bad as Belle sometimes," he muttered before stepping toward one of the prone men. He slipped off his jacket and grabbed the unconscious man's shoulders. "Get his legs," he instructed.

Sophie scoffed at being compared to Annabelle, but when she remembered her clanmate was in need, she complied, lifting the man's legs. Together, they carried him out of the barn and laid him down about two King's steps from the entrance. One by one, they hauled the rest of the men outside, arranging them haphazardly on the ground.

"Those guys are as heavy as ogres," Sophie remarked, wiping sweat from her brow.

Captain Kidd chuckled. "Aye, missy. Next time, try escorting them outside before knocking them out."

Despite herself, Sophie grinned. His humor, though dry, lightened the tension. Captain Kidd's expression grew more serious as he straightened his shirt. "Now, listen carefully. Grab anything ye left in the barn, then head back to the mansion. Get Brother Marcus. He'll need to handle this quietly, make sure no one knows yer involved."

139

Sophie nodded and quickly patted her pockets, feeling the familiar shapes of her inspection glasses and badge. "I'm good. I'll send Brother Marcus right away."

As she turned to leave, Captain Kidd's voice stopped her. "Oh, and one more thing," he added, his tone suddenly lighter. "If you see a lass in a yellow dress with red hair, tell her I regret that we will have to postpone our ... *dance lesson.*"

She hears him say, "Well, there goes the dancin' fer de night." With resignation.

Sophie blinked, momentarily thrown by the odd request. "Uh... okay," she replied hesitantly. With one last glance at the scene, she made her way toward the mansion, her mind buzzing with questions. Who was the woman in the yellow dress, and why did Captain Kidd care so much about a dance lesson in the middle of all this?

She shook the thought aside, focusing on her task. There was no time to get distracted—not with Eclipse Lepele's life and freedom hanging in the balance.

Chapter 9

After a final twirl through a cascade of melodies with Miss Lisa, Marcus felt the weight of the upcoming day press against his thoughts. The evening had been a welcome reprieve, but the looming journey to Snyder haunted the edges of his mind. Brother Albert's cryptic discovery echoed like an unsolved riddle. Offering Miss Lisa a respectful nod of departure, Marcus took his leave, excitement and apprehension mingling in his chest.

Navigating the mansion proved more daunting than expected. Though he was no stranger to navigating a labyrinth, the Governor's mansion twisted before him like an ornate puzzle. Hallways curved deceptively, each corner blurring into the next until Marcus felt ensnared in a web of marble and shadows. He retraced his steps several times, each turn deepening the mystery of the estate's silent architecture.

Finally, a passing attendant rescued him from his bewilderment. With a knowing smile, the attendant guided Marcus through the maze of corridors, their footsteps muffled by the plush carpets. At last, Marcus reached his quarters, where gratitude colored his polite farewell.

Before retiring, he paused at Miss Sophie Griffin's door. He knocked on the door, but there was no answer. Likely, she had already surrendered to the call of sleep. The lateness of the hour resonated in the mansion's stillness.

Marcus entered his room, performing the quiet ritual of night. The life of a guide to avatars demanded not only mental preparedness but physical discipline. After washing away the remnants of the day, he wrapped himself in the comfort of his night clothes and toyed with the idea of writing in his journal. Yet, the night's events, though joyful, hadn't offered anything he deemed worthy of record. Instead, he sipped cool water, letting his thoughts drift toward tomorrow's uncertainties.

Lying in darkness, Marcus mentally organized the tasks ahead. His eyelids grew heavier with each imagined item checked from the list. Sleep's gentle embrace tugged at him, and he surrendered, comforted by the knowledge that adventure, and the avatars, would wait for morning.

But sleep was short-lived.

A sharp, insistent knocking shattered the stillness, jolting him upright. The sound echoed in the quiet like a clarion call. "Brother Marcus!" The voice, unmistakably Sophie Griffin's, carried urgency.

"One moment," Marcus rasped, his mind struggling to shake off the remnants of slumber. He crossed the room, each step guided by instinct rather than thought, and opened the door to find Sophie standing before him, wearing her training attire, adorned with intricate symbols of the Order, caught the low lamplight, but it was the determination in her gaze that seized his full attention.

Without preamble, she pushed her way inside, her presence filling the room like a charged storm. "Close the door," she commanded softly but firmly.

Marcus obeyed, his curiosity sharpening. "What's the matter, Miss Griffin?"

She hesitated, her eyes flitting to the corners of the room as though assessing for unseen threats. "I need you to do something," she said, her voice edged with unease.

"Of course," he replied, his tone gentle but alert. "Anything I can."

For a moment, Sophie seemed to wrestle with herself. Then, her shoulders softened, and she spoke quietly. "Can I have a hug, Brother Marcus?"

The request caught him off guard. He hesitated. "Miss Griffin, I must decline. It wouldn't be appropriate for a guide to have such... familiarity with one of the avatars."

Sophie's jaw tensed, a flicker of frustration passing across her features. "It's not that," she whispered, her voice laced with something more profound. "Sometimes... I just miss my mother. She used to help me through moments like this." She glanced down, the vulnerability in her posture both genuine and carefully controlled.

Embarrassment flushed through Marcus. He had misunderstood her, his pride chastising him for the assumption. "I'm sorry, Miss Griffin. I forget how hard it has been for you sometimes."

After they embrace, Marcus comforts Sophie, saying, "You are safe with us, Miss Sophie."

She commands "*Please stop.*" with a cautious whisper.

He froze during their embrace, her arms still holding him close.

Sophie continued, her voice lowering to a near whisper. "Listen carefully. I think we're being watched."

Marcus stiffened. The idea of surveillance within these walls unsettled him. His mind raced through possibilities, his earlier oversight glaring now.

"I need you to do something," Sophie continued, urgency replacing the earlier vulnerability. "Get dressed and head to the barn across the lake. Captain Kidd is waiting there. You're to assist him with a delicate matter."

His gaze narrowed. "What's happening?"

"A member of my clan is trapped in a magical prison. The captain has a plan to free him, but he can't do it alone. Your help is essential."

The weight of her words pressed down on Marcus like a tangible force. He inhaled deeply, nodding. "I understand."

"Good." Sophie stepped back, her gaze steady. "And Marcus, don't tell anyone I sent you."

"I will keep that to myself." he assured her.

Sophie withdrew, her embrace dissolving like the echo of a forgotten dream. Marcus felt the chill of solemnity settle over him, the unspoken questions weighing heavier with her departure. Her eyes lingered on his one last time, shadowed with carefully woven sorrow. "Thank you, Brother. I'm sorry to trouble you like this," she whispered, her voice a fragile blend of regret and urgency.

Marcus met her gaze with the composed stoicism of a man shaped by duty, though beneath his exterior, curiosity churned like a restless tide. "No apologies necessary. It's my duty," he replied firmly. "Good night, Miss Sophie."

"Good night," she said softly, stepping into the hallway. Her silhouette faded into the dim corridor, leaving him alone with the silence and a gnawing sense of intrigue.

Marcus sat on the edge of his bed, a sentinel in the quiet darkness. He waited until the distant click of Sophie's door confirmed her departure. Rising with renewed purpose, he dressed swiftly, his thoughts racing through a kaleidoscope of possibilities. He slipped from his room, his footsteps cautious and precise as he entered the shadowed maze of the mansion.

Night had transformed the estate into a realm of heightened senses. The walls whispered in the stillness; every creak of the floor, every rustle of fabric seemed magnified. Marcus passed through the courtyard, the cool air sharp on his skin. Dew clung to the grass, and the lake's murmur carried on the wind. The mansion's training fields, silent and foreboding, stretched out under the moon's watchful gaze.

As he traced the moonlit curve of the lake, the barn appeared ahead, a glowing sanctuary defiant against the encroaching dark. Lantern light spilled from its windows and door, cutting through the night like a beacon. The sight sent a thrill of anticipation down Marcus's spine. The barn seemed alive, its illumination both a guide and a warning.

Questions danced in his mind, each one flickering like a distant star. *Why would a member of the Aurorium Clan be in Verdantia, and why is he locked up? And what role did Captain Lowe play in this clandestine affair?* Marcus wonders what else he was missing.

Approaching the barn, Marcus paused. A figure sat on a tree stump near the water's edge, a woman draped in a dress as bright as sunlight. Her red, fiery hair cascaded over her shoulders like molten copper. She seemed lost in thought, her gaze tracing the rippling reflection of the moon. When her eyes briefly met his, there was a flicker of recognition, calm and indifferent, before she returned to her musings.

Marcus nodded politely in acknowledgment, a brief moment of shared understanding passing between them. Both of their minds were clearly elsewhere, preoccupied with unseen burdens. With a distracted wave, he resumed his path, the barn's enigmatic glow growing nearer with each step.

The structure loomed ahead, its wooden frame casting jagged shadows against the silver-stained ground. As Marcus drew closer, the scene before him sharpened with unsettling detail. Flames licked at the interior walls, their fierce dance visible through the barn's gaps. Captain Lowe stood off to the side, jacket slung casually over one arm, his posture one of almost unsettling calm.

At the captain's feet lay four men, their unconscious bodies sprawled in disarray like discarded marionettes. The sight halted Marcus in his tracks, a surge of adrenaline quickening his breath. He closed the distance rapidly. "Captain! What's going on here?" he demanded, his voice taut with urgency.

Lowe turned with a slow, measured grace, his eyes gleaming with a spark of mischief. He greeted Marcus with a sly grin and an exaggerated air of formality. "Ah, Brother Marcus. Fancy meeting ye here," he drawled, tipping an imaginary hat. "A rather curious evening, wouldn't ye say?"

"Curious, yes," Marcus shot back, his gaze flicking to the prone figures. "What happened to them?"

Lowe chuckled softly, the sound oddly detached from the gravity of the scene. "Well, you see, after the gala, I took a stroll. Imagine my surprise when I stumbled upon this... spectacle. The barn, blazing like a bonfire, and these fine gentlemen here, overcome by the excitement, one might assume." He waved a hand theatrically at the unconscious men. "Naturally, I felt compelled to play the Good Samaritan and drag them out before they became kindling."

Marcus's eyes narrowed. "And the fire?"

"Ah, now we come to the heart of the matter," Lowe said, his voice lowering conspiratorially. "You see, beneath that barn lies a peculiar little secret, a prison cell, if you can believe it. And not just any cell. Our dear prisoner happens to be a member of Sophie Griffin's Aurorium clan."

Marcus froze. "You don't say, Captain?"

"Yes, indeed," Lowe confirmed, his tone almost playful. "He's still down there, protected by some infernal magic barrier. Quite clever, really. It keeps him safe from the flames but also prevents anyone from getting him out."

A shrill cry tore through their conversation. The woman in the yellow dress, her red hair a blazing beacon, sprinted from the lakeside, her voice cutting through the stillness. "Fire! Fire!" she shouted, alarm twisting her features. "The governor's barn is on fire!"

Marcus's eyes snapped to her retreating form, then back to Captain Lowe, incredulity etched into his expression. "You set the governor's barn on fire?"

Lowe raised both hands in a gesture of defense, his tone level but tinged with exasperation. "That is such an ugly accusation, Brother Marcus. I found this here barn ablaze and risked life and limb to drag those poor souls out. I'm many things, but an arsonist is not one of them."

Marcus hesitated before nodding. "Apologies," he offered, piecing together the implications of Miss Sophie's instructions. His mind raced to the trapped Aurorium prisoner. "But let's hope that fire doesn't choke out the air inside the barrier."

"Ohh," Lowe said with a blink, a shadow of realization flickering across his face. "Hadn't thought of that," he admitted, his nonchalance faltering for a moment. The unguarded response revealed something that tugged at Marcus's thoughts, a familial resemblance. He had always attributed Miss Salazar's calculated recklessness to the influence of the Goddess of Chaos, but now he wondered if the real inspiration stood right before him.

The barn's skeletal frame crackled as flames climbed higher, turning the structure into a searing pyre. The distant murmur of approaching help reached their ears. Law enforcement, firefighters, and Hydro magic mages converged swiftly upon the scene. The mages, clad in red coats, moved with precision, their presence commanding as magical glyphs bloomed at their feet. Water from the lake spiraled in graceful arcs toward the fire, crashing against the inferno in waves of conjured power.

"yer up, mate," Lowe says lowly so only Marcus can hear it.

Among the responders, a trio of government policemen strode toward Marcus and Lowe. The lead officer, a stout man with a badge depicting a harvest tree, spoke above the din. "Excuse me, gentlemen," he called, his voice steady and authoritative despite the chaos surrounding them. "What exactly is going on here?"

Taking a steadying breath, Marcus stepped forward, masking his nerves with practiced diplomacy. "Officer, after the gala, Captain Lowe and I decided to take a walk," he explained, gesturing to the barn. "We heard a commotion and found the structure already on fire. Inside, we discovered these unconscious men. We pulled them out before the flames could consume them."

Lowe added smoothly, "It was quite the ordeal. During our efforts, we made another unsettling discovery, there's a man trapped in a hidden cell beneath the barn."

144

The officer's brow furrowed. "Did you try to get him out?"

"We tried," Marcus confirmed, his voice calm despite the tight knot forming in his gut. "But the cell is protected by a magical barrier. We couldn't bypass it."

"Neither of us possesses any arcane expertise," Lowe said with a hint of frustration. "The barrier's design is beyond us."

The officer gave a thoughtful nod and turned to one of his subordinates. "We'll need a ritualist to dismantle that magic. Get someone from the mansion."

"On it," the subordinate replied, breaking into a brisk run toward the distant glow of the estate.

As the officer turned back to Marcus and Lowe, his gaze sharpened. "Do either of you know the identity of the prisoner?"

"No," Marcus answered truthfully. "He identified himself as a member of the Aurorium clan, but he offered no further details."

The officer paused, the mention of the Aurorium clan igniting a spark of recognition. "Aurorium… a Jiberau, then," he muttered, scribbling notes onto a pad. The name 'Jiberau' carried weight in his tone, suggesting the disdain between Verdantia and the Aurorium Clan implications. "What would a *Jiberau* be doing locked away in our sacred acres?"

Marcus remained composed, grateful that Sophie wasn't here to endure this line of questioning. "That's the same question we're asking, officer."

The officer hummed thoughtfully but let the matter rest for the moment. Meanwhile, the firefighting effort reached its crescendo. Columns of water extinguished the last stubborn tongues of flame, and the barn's blazing skeleton collapsed into smoldering ruin. Within half an hour, the inferno was quelled, and the darkness reclaimed its dominion over Meadowbrook.

A ritualist, clad in a tuxedo, missing the bow tie and cummerbund, an obvious attendant of the goddess gala, arrived with urgency and walked into the barn likely intent on dispelling the magic barrier. After a short amount of time likely after the barrier broke, the ritualist emerged followed by two police men carrying Eclipse Lepele, his identity confirmed by Captain Lowe was found unconscious within the cellar's depths. They deposit him onto a stretcher and an Earthbloom mage moved swiftly to his side. He weaves a red spell circle with red runes rotating around it, performing the same Earthbloom healing spell the same way Miss Lisa does. He worked diligently to clear the smoke from his lungs, which helped stabilize him. "He'll recover," the mage assured Marcus and the officer. "But he'll need rest. He won't regain consciousness for a few more hours."

Marcus exhaled in relief. The night's crisis was waning, but the questions it left behind were vast and tangled. Eclipse Lepele's presence, the hidden cell, and the fire formed a mystery that refused easy answers. Marcus glanced at Captain Lowe, who returned his gaze with a faint, knowing smile.

"Quite the adventure," Lowe exclaimed, patting Marcus on the back.

Marcus nodded grimly. The night had revealed its secrets in fire and shadow, but it was only the beginning.

The four unconscious men were swiftly attended to. Healers stabilized their injuries before law enforcement whisked them away for questioning, isolating them from the gaze of curious onlookers, including Marcus and Captain Lowe.

The arrival of Governor Nozaki heralded a shift in atmosphere. Surrounded by a cadre of assistants, he strode toward the smoldering scene, his presence commanding and composed despite the chaos that had engulfed his property. His gaze sharpened as he took in the aftermath. "Brother Marcus," he greeted with a tone blending curiosity and concern, "it seems you've found yourself entwined in yet another of Meadowbrook's extraordinary stories."

Marcus, his mind still caught between the lingering adrenaline and surreal nature of the night, responded with a dry tone. "Indeed, Governor. It appears the goddesses have seen fit to lead me through quite the exciting labyrinth tonight."

Nozaki arched an eyebrow at the invocation but did not comment. Instead, his attention shifted to the lead policeman. "And what of my barn?" he demanded, the question weighted by expectation. There was a readiness in his posture, as if bracing for a truth he would rather not hear.

The officer stepped forward, providing a succinct recount of the night's events. He described how Marcus and Captain Lowe had stumbled upon the burning barn, rescuing the incapacitated men before discovering a hidden cell beneath the flames. The mention of the prisoner, a Jiberau, added a layer of perplexity to the unfolding mystery.

The Governor turned to Marcus, his expression laced with both surprise and suspicion. "A Jiberau?" His voice carried the gravity of the word. "Did he come with you, Brother Marcus?"

"No, sir," Marcus answered firmly, meeting the Governor's gaze without wavering. "This is the first time I've encountered the man." He allowed his words to settle with calm finality, ensuring there would be no room for misinterpretation.

Still piecing together the narrative, Nozaki's eyes narrowed in thought. He gestured toward the direction where the four men were being interrogated. "Perhaps they can provide some clarity," he mused aloud. The lead officer gave a brief nod before issuing quiet instructions for Marcus and Lowe to remain nearby.

As the Governor's attention shifted, Lowe leaned toward Marcus, his voice low and laced with amusement. "Nice touch, bringin' up the goddesses back there," he remarked, offering a sly smile.

Marcus allowed a faint smirk in response, though his mind remained partially attuned to the ongoing interrogation. From a distance, Governor Nozaki stood like a pillar of authority, arms crossed, his gaze leveled at the four men who now faced his scrutiny. Their silence spoke volumes, defiant yet strained under the weight of the Governor's penetrating glare.

The tension in the air shifted subtly in Marcus's favor. The men's unwillingness to cooperate might inadvertently grant them an advantage, drawing attention away from their own involvement. The standoff played out like an intricate game, one where Marcus knew he had to tread carefully.

Governor Nozaki, his frustration evident, finally broke from the interrogation and returned to Marcus and Lowe. His gaze swept across the scene, lingering momentarily on the unconscious Eclipse Lepele. "By the harvest, I will unravel this mystery," he declared, his voice resolute. "I don't recognize those men. And as for him..." He gestured toward the Aurorium prisoner, his words trailing off as if unable to fully articulate his bewilderment.

Seizing the opportunity, Marcus stepped forward. He framed his request with quiet urgency. "Governor Nozaki, I respectfully request that you entrust Eclipse Lepele's care to me." He held the Governor's gaze, letting sincerity and diplomacy shape his tone. "I would consider it a true favor to the Order of Saint Lorraine."

The Governor's eyes narrowed in skepticism. His protective instincts, shaped by years of leadership, flared visibly. "How can I be certain he's not a spy for the Jiberau? And why do you see this as a favor to your Order?"

Marcus remained composed, understanding the delicate balance he was navigating. "I have no personal stake in this, Governor. However, Miss Griffin, and by extension, Miss Lisa, may view his safe release as a gesture of goodwill. It is in everyone's best interest to avoid any misunderstandings. I am sure that if the position were reversed and you found Miss Lisa in the hands of the Aurorium clan, you would expect them to release her to Verdantia immediately. Marcus takes calculated risks to ensure success in his persuasion. "I am sure that Miss Linda Nozaki would agree that it is far more advantageous diplomatically to turn over the Aurorium clan member without pretense in expectation of considerations later."

Governor Nozaki pondered the response, his gaze distant for a moment before returning with a calculated edge. He weighed the risk against the potential benefits and finally spoke, his tone steeped in pragmatism. "Very well, Brother Marcus. But if he is to be released into your care, there is one condition."

Marcus inclined his head, listening intently.

"He must leave my kingdom immediately," the Governor continued. "I care not where he goes, so long as he departs right now." His statement was firm.

Marcus contemplated the situation before offering a solution. "I can arrange for Eclipse Lepele to board Captain Lowe's ship, the Stormfang. The Order has retained its services indefinitely." He turned to Governor Nozaki, his tone resolute. "Eclipse Lepele will not set foot on Verdantian soil again. He'll depart with the avatars."

"Aye, Governor," Captain Lowe added with his usual charm. "I'll personally see to it. The good copper won't leave my ship until we've sailed far from your sacred shores."

Governor Nozaki sighed, weariness seeping into his voice. "Fine" he shakes his head and says "The things we do for family," resignation lacing his words like a weary mantra.

"Aye," Lowe echoed softly. "The things we do for family." The reflective weight of his tone resonated with the Governor, their shared burdens briefly understood in silence.

As the hour crept closer to midnight, Marcus, Lowe, and one of the Governor's aides worked swiftly to coordinate the departure. Lowe, ever efficient, prepared for the journey with the ease of a man seasoned in sudden farewells. He gathered his things quickly, but there was a moment of pause in his otherwise brisk demeanor. Sitting at a small desk, he wrote a letter, a message to adopted daughter Annabelle.

With a solemn expression, Lowe handed the letter to Marcus. "Make sure she gets this," he said quietly, his voice tinged with a vulnerability that rarely surfaced.

Marcus accepted the letter with a firm nod. "I will."

The carriage stood ready under the moon's gaze, its wheels creaking softly as Captain Lowe and Eclipse Lepele were helped inside. Marcus watched silently as the door shut with a decisive finality. The snap of the latch seemed to echo through the quiet estate, marking the first step of their escape toward the Stormfang, a promise of sanctuary beyond the reach of tonight's turmoil.

As the carriage disappeared down the path, swallowed by the night's shadows, Marcus remained where he stood, under the cold weight of uncertainty. The events at Meadowbrook had proven to be more than a passing incident; they were the prologue to a far more perilous journey. The looming mission to Snyder now felt charged with unseen threats and questions that demanded answers.

He lingered in thought, his mind circling the strange events that had unfolded within the Governor's mansion. Each revelation had added to a tapestry of intrigue more intricate than he had imagined. With Lowe and Lepele en route to safety, Marcus turned his attention to what needed to happen tomorrow.

With one final glance toward the darkened horizon where the carriage had vanished, Marcus turned back to the mansion. Dawn would soon rise, and with it, new challenges to meet head-on. He resolved to be more responsible and not maintain these late nights.

Chapter 10

Journal entry: April 24, 1910:

The festivities at Evelyn Nozaki's Goddess Gala, marking her seventeenth year, were overshadowed by an unexpected discovery. Sophie Griffin, somehow, unearthed the plight of Eclipse Lepele, an Aurorium compatriot ensnared within a concealed cell beneath the governor's barn in Meadowbrook. It was through a concerted effort, spearheaded by Griffin and facilitated by Captain James "Kidd" Lowe and I, that Lepele was extricated. My diplomatic affiliations were instrumental in ensuring his release and subsequent safe passage to the Stormfang. However, this operation precipitated Captain Lowe's withdrawal from our forthcoming venture to Snyder.

The circumstances surrounding Lepele's capture and confinement remain shrouded in mystery, particularly how he came to be detained within a hidden jail under the governor's estate—a fact that has eluded all parties involved. Governor Conrad Nozaki has since pledged to identify and reprimand those responsible for the blaze. Yet, given the known tensions between the avatars and Governor Nozaki, I think it is best not to delve further into this matter.

[-----◉-----]

With the help of their attendants, the avatars packed their belongings early in the morning, preparing for the journey ahead. Despite their late return from the previous night's events, they gathered for breakfast in the mansion's dining room. Only the First Lady, Linda Nozaki, joined them; both Governor Nozaki and Lisa's older sister, Evelyn, had opted out of the meal. The kitchen staff, still recovering from the laborious demands of Evelyn's Goddess Gala, had prepared a simple but flavorful breakfast: *pancakes, bacon, and a fresh fruit salad*. Though humble in presentation, the combination of flavors proved a welcome delight for the weary diners.

Lisa and her mother shared a lighthearted conversation, savoring their final breakfast together for the foreseeable future.

"So, does your Unity goddess like our food?" Linda asked playfully, a teasing smile curling her lips.

Lisa tilted her head, confused for a moment. "I do not know, Mom. I do not think she has ever had it."

"But you are her avatar," Linda pressed, the teasing glint in her eyes shining brighter.

Understanding dawned on Lisa. "She does not live in my body, Mom," she clarified with a chuckle.

Nearby, Regina quietly observed the pair, enjoying a sip of coffee. Their interaction stirred memories of her own mother, before illness had stolen those moments from her. A small, nostalgic smile touched her face as she briefly drifted into recollection.

Across the table, Sophie tried to block out the mother-daughter exchange. The loss of her own mother, Arisa, was a wound still raw. She focused intently on her meal, honoring the promise she'd made not to cry over losing her again.

Meanwhile, Annabelle paid no attention to the conversation between Lisa and her mother. Her focus was locked on Marcus, her amber eyes gleaming with suspicion.

"So, let me get this straight," she said, holding up a piece of bacon before biting into it. "The captain decided to leave with this *sundown fellow*, without talking to me first?" The tone of her voice sharpened with each word, her instincts as a privateer sniffing for deceit. "Why would he do a thing like that?"

Marcus, weary from his own late-night ordeal, carefully modulated his tone to avoid provoking Annabelle's temper. "That is correct, Miss Salazar. As I mentioned, time was of the essence. The captain couldn't find you after packing and had to leave quickly. He did, however, leave a letter for you, which I have here to address any concerns."

Annabelle's eyes narrowed. "And where's this letter now?" she asked, her tone challenging.

"I have it safely stored in my journal," Marcus answered steadily.

"I'd like to see it," Annabelle demanded, crossing her arms.

Marcus hesitated for a moment before responding diplomatically. "I believe it would be best if you read the letter after breakfast," he suggested, casting a glance at her hands—sticky with fruit juice and bits of bacon.

Annabelle opened her mouth to argue, but Sophie chimed in with a teasing lilt. "Give the man a break. You know you got back late. Captain Kidd wouldn't have had to leave a note if he didn't expect to be traveling all night."

Annabelle's eyes flashed as she turned to Sophie. "That's *Captain Lowe* to you, *Copper*." she corrected, a challenge in her voice.

Sophie smirked, unfazed. "He told me I could call him Kidd," she teased "because I am a valuable member of the crew."

Annabelle scoffed, waving her hand dismissively. "Bah! Yer not crew."

"The captain said I was," Sophie countered, taking a bite of pancake with exaggerated satisfaction. "And he *is* the captain."

Annabelle leaned forward slightly, glaring at Sophie for a moment before letting out a grunt of exasperation. "Yer full of it!" she replied, shaking her head.

Having spent the last month traveling with the avatars, Marcus had learned that it was often best not to intervene in their playful squabbles. Attempts to mediate only prolonged the bickering. Instead, he focused on his breakfast, savoring the perfectly balanced flavors while the avatars of War and Chaos continued their verbal jabs.

"Excuse me," Regina prompted Linda Nozaki, leaning forward slightly. "Misses Nozaki, may I ask you a question about your Earthbloom magic?"

"Of course, my dear," Linda replied warmly, offering a kind smile. "What is on your mind?"

Lisa, sipping her orange juice, smiled knowingly. *Knowing her mother wasn't quite prepared for the inquisitive persistence of Regina Fournier, the silver avatar of Change.*

"How does your Earthbloom sense work?" Regina asked, her eyes bright with curiosity. "How does it integrate with the world around you? Since it isn't exactly a spell, how do you tap into it?"

Linda blinked, momentarily caught off guard. She glanced at her daughter, who offered no support, only a smirk and a leisurely sip of her juice. Taking a moment, Linda closed her eyes as if focusing on her senses before answering thoughtfully. "That is... an excellent question. But I am not sure I can explain it. It is like trying to describe how hearing works."

Regina nodded but wasn't satisfied. "When you were teaching Lisa, how did you explain it to her?"

"Oh, I did not teach Lisa Earthbloom magic," Linda replied with a chuckle. "She learned it from a mistress at the Harvest Church." Tilting her head curiously, she asked, "Are you an Earthbloom mage yourself?"

"No, I'm a Learner mage," Regina answered before catching herself. Realizing she was using a term familiar only in Laminae, she quickly clarified, "I mean, a Nexus mage. In Laminae, we call ourselves *Learner mage.*"

Linda frowned slightly in confusion. "A Nexus mage... So, you learn multiple magic systems? But how is that possible? Everyone's born with an affinity for a specific type of magic. How do you use different ones?"

"I wasn't born with any affinity," Regina explained. "My mother was a Nexus mage, and she taught me how to adapt to magic systems. She always said learning magic is a marathon, not a sprint." Regina sighed softly, frustration creeping into her voice. "I've read that Earthbloom mages can't cast effective spells until they develop the Earthbloom sense, but none of the books explain how to actually gain that sense."

Linda considered this for a moment, studying the determined young woman in front of her. "Well... I can tell you that learning the sense was crucial for me to cast Earthbloom spells. It did not come quickly, it took time, and then one day, it just... started working."

"Yeah, everyone says that," Regina muttered with resignation, her shoulders sagging slightly.

"Wait," Linda said, intrigued by the challenge Regina faced. "What other magic can you do?"

"I've learned spells from a lot of magic systems," Regina answered. "Child's Play, Enfance Magique, Forge de l'espace aérien, Verboisance, Maelstrom Mastery, and Crystalmancy, which I've just started learning." As if to demonstrate, she summoned a silver crystal stake, holding it in her palm. "See? I can create a crystal with Crystalmancy."

Linda sipped her tea, her eyes narrowing in thought. "Impressive. Can you cast a spell from a different magic?"

"Sure," Regina replied easily. With practiced fluidity, she cast Child's Play – Hide and Seek, conjuring three projections of herself. The duplicates formed a circle behind her, each smiling and waving at Linda before vanishing in a shimmer of light. "That's one of my favorites."

Linda studied the display with a keen, appraising gaze. "That is so interesting."

151

Regina refocused the conversation. "The problem is that when I arrange my mana to mimic Earthbloom affinity and try to channel it, I don't know how to use the sense."

"Ah," Linda murmured, setting her tea down thoughtfully. "But that is the thing, you do not channel mana to activate the sense. When I use mine, I am not consciously channeling anything. It is more like… feeling Mother Earth's mana flowing around and through me. It is as if I am standing in a rainstorm, feeling the wind, the rain, listening as it explains what's nearby, like a mother describing her children."

Regina paused, her mind turning over Linda's metaphor. The manuals from the Order spoke of Earthbloom magic's deep connection to planetary energy. She visualized it now, not as a resource to harness, but as a natural storm flowing around her. "That… makes sense. I think," she said slowly, wondering how she might apply this perspective.

"Did that help at all?" Linda asked gently, concern flickering across her face.

"Every bit helps," Regina replied with a small smile, repeating a phrase her mother had often used during their training sessions. "Thank you, Mrs. Nozaki."

An attendant leaned down to whisper something to Linda, who nodded in understanding. She rose from her seat, smoothing her dress. "I do apologize, everyone. Duty calls, A woman's work is never done."

The table echoed their goodbyes and well-wishes as Linda departed. Moments later, the avatars and Marcus finished their breakfast and returned to their rooms to freshen up. They discovered that the attendants had already moved their belongings to the stables, readying everything for their departure.

[-----✝-----]

The five of them arrived at the stables where a long carriage, hitched to two sturdy horses, awaited them. Beside the carriage, four saddled horses stood tied to a retaining log, their bridles and saddlebags neatly secured. Nearby, the stable manager, a dignified man in a polished version of the house staff uniform, gently stroked one of the horses' heads as the group approached.

"Good morning, Mr. Convers," Marcus greeted with a polite nod. "How's the morning treating you?"

"Good morning, Brother Marcus," Convers replied cheerfully, gesturing to the carriage. "Life's good. The attendants have already loaded your belongings. Now, about the transportation… Unfortunately, we didn't have a second carriage or driver available, so I arranged a horse for each of the young ladies." He turned toward the tied horses, smiling proudly.

Regina hesitated before speaking up. "Um… I don't know how to ride a horse."

Convers responded without missing a beat, his tone reassuring. "Oh, it's easy. I'll show you how. Would anyone else like a quick riding lesson?"

None of the other avatars raised their hands.

Sophie leaned toward Annabelle with a teasing smirk. "Raise your hand, *Anna*. You know you can't ride a horse," she whispered.

"Shut yer trap, Copper!" Annabelle hissed back. "If ye can do it, how hard can it be?"

"You'll see," Sophie retorted playfully before stepping forward. "Which horse is mine?"

"Take your pick, ma'am," Convers replied with a courteous bow.

Sophie approached the third horse, a speckled brown-and-white mare adorned with brown leather accessories. Grabbing the reins firmly, she gently petted the horse's head. "Easy, girl," she whispered soothingly. The mare pulled back at first, but Sophie's steady grip and calm voice soon reassured it. With a soft sigh, the horse relaxed, its large eyes quietly accepting Sophie's presence.

"That's right," Sophie whispered, her tone soft and confident. "We're going to be good friends, you and I."

Lisa, meanwhile, approached the first horse, a sleek, black beauty. As she gently stroked its mane, the horse instantly relaxed, letting out a sigh and shaking its head playfully. Lisa smiled, reminded of the subtle influence her Earthbloom magic often had on animals.

Not to be outdone, Annabelle strutted over to the second horse, a handsome brown gelding. Shooting a glance at Sophie and Lisa, she placed a hand on the horse's head and gave it a firm pat. The horse snorted in response, tossing its head as if to reject her attempt at control.

"Oh, now don't be like that," Annabelle coaxed, her voice dipping into a persuasive lilt. "Ye can trust me, aye?"

The horse seemed unconvinced, shaking its head once more with a low, disgruntled nicker. Annabelle frowned but kept her composure.

Meanwhile, Convers led Regina to the final horse, a large brown stallion with a striking black mane. Regina hesitated, her nerves prickling as she took in the sheer size of the animal. Growing up in the city, she was accustomed to carriages, not towering beasts like this.

"Oh, don't worry," Convers reassured her with a gentle smile. "This here is Mango. He's a sweetheart." He stroked the horse's head soothingly. "You just have to show him you're friendly. Go on, give him a nice little pet."

Tentatively, Regina reached out and stroked Mango's head. The horse's hair was softer than she had expected, almost velvety under her fingertips. Mango nickered softly, letting out a deep sigh as his large brown eyes met Regina's. She felt her initial fear slowly ebb away.

"See? He likes you," Convers said encouragingly. He reached behind the hitching log and retrieved a carrot from a nearby bucket, slipping it into Regina's hand. "Here, give him this."

Regina accepted the carrot and held it out to Mango, who eagerly took the treat from her palm. The horse munched contentedly before snorting, as if offering a gentle thanks. Regina smiled, the connection between herself and the animal calming her further.

"You're doing great," Convers praised. "Now, when you're ready, I'll show you how to mount him."

Regina gave a slight nod, her confidence growing as Mango nuzzled her hand. Around her, the other avatars prepared their horses, each with their own unique style. Despite her nerves, Regina felt a flicker of excitement.

The stable courtyard buzzed with quiet activity as the avatars familiarized themselves with their horses. Marcus, seizing the opportunity for a rare moment of peace, climbed into the carriage's passenger compartment. The seat was wide and cushioned, a welcome respite from the constant whirlwind of the avatars' presence. He leaned back, closing his eyes for a brief moment, maybe making up a few minutes of sleep after his late-night service to Miss Sophie.

Outside, Lisa and Regina had returned in their riding clothes, having exchanged their gowns for more practical attire. Lisa's confidence radiated as she gently stroked the neck of her black stallion, speaking ever so softly to it. The horse responded with an affectionate nicker, nudging her arm playfully. Regina, meanwhile, took a deep breath, standing beside Mango, still getting used to his imposing size.

Sophie had already mounted her speckled mare "Kicker" and guided it into a gentle walk. She moved with ease, as though the two had been partners for years. "Good girl," Sophie cooed, giving the mare a light pat on the neck. The horse swayed gracefully beneath her, each movement in perfect sync.

Annabelle, on the other hand, approached her horse, a brown gelding with a temperamental gleam in its eyes. "Cantaloupe, eh? That's a daft name for a beast," she muttered under her breath, adjusting her grip on the reins. She flashed a confident grin toward Sophie and Lisa, then placed a boot in the stirrup and swung herself into the saddle.

The horse stood still for a moment, then suddenly snorted and tossed its head, its muscles tensing beneath her. Without warning, Cantaloupe reared slightly and bucked, sending Annabelle tumbling unceremoniously to the ground with a loud thud.

"Saints preserve me!" Annabelle yelled before hitting the ground. Brushing dirt from her sleeves as she scrambled to her feet. Sophie burst into laughter, covering her mouth as Annabelle shot her a glare.

"What's so funny, Copper?" Annabelle snapped, her pride stinging worse than the fall.

Before Sophie could respond, Annabelle's attention was drawn to a flash of orange. Sitting on the fence near the horses was a small, bright-eyed monkey with a broad, mischievous grin. Annabelle hadn't seen this annoying beast since visiting Chaos's realm; it was Chaos's pet monkey, *Simba*. The creature pointed at her and erupted into laughter, slapping its leg in amusement.

Annabelle blinked and rubbed her eyes. *Did I hit me head?* She asked herself, bewildered.

Simba cackled even louder, swinging from the fence with exaggerated glee. "You're a natural with horses!" he jeered. "Go on, do it again! I could watch this all day!"

Annabelle stumbled back a step, her jaw tightening. "Ye can't be real..."

"What was that?" Sophie called from atop her horse, noticing Annabelle's distracted expression.

"Nothing!" Annabelle barked, her voice strained. She glared at the monkey, who now rolled onto the ground, holding his belly.

"Go on!" Simba teased, wiping an imaginary tear from his eye. "Do it again! I ain't had this much fun in years!"

Annabelle scowled at him, hissing lowly under her breath. "Quit laughin', you daft little beast."

Simba only swung himself back onto the fence, his grin widening.

"What are you talking about?" Sophie teased, unaware of the spirit animal's presence.

"Nothing that concerns ye." Annabelle growled, marching stiffly back toward Cantaloupe.

With a smirk, Sophie added, "You make it look so easy, *Anna*. Want me to give you some pointers?"

"Nay, I gots this," Annabelle retorted, forcing herself back onto the horse.

But Cantaloupe had other ideas. Within seconds, he bucked again, sending her flying even harder than before. Annabelle groaned, lying on the ground in defeat as Simba howled with laughter.

"Are you all right?" Mr. Convers asked, stepping forward and offering her a hand.

"I'm fine," Annabelle muttered, rubbing her back as she climbed to her feet. She shot another glare at the horse, which stomped the ground defiantly and snorted.

"I have to say, I've never seen a trained horse reject someone quite so... forcefully," Convers remarked, scratching his chin thoughtfully.

"The bloody thing's jealous of me pirate swagger, that's all," Annabelle huffed.

"Perhaps it'd be best if you rode in the carriage with Brother Marcus," Convers suggested diplomatically. "This horse seems intent on putting you on the ground."

Annabelle crossed her arms but eventually relented with a sigh. "Aye, governor," she grumbled, wounded pride in every word.

"Don't worry, I won't tell the captain," Sophie teased, trotting gracefully around the track. "Unless I think it's funny."

With Annabelle's horse safely out of reach, Convers turned his attention to Regina. She had mounted Mango but struggled to maintain control. The horse moved in fits and starts, sensing her nervous energy. Each tug on the reins sent Mango sidestepping uneasily.

"Easy, easy," Regina murmured, trying to mimic the calm tones she had heard from Sophie and Lisa. But her tension betrayed her, and Mango refused to settle. The horse jerked sharply, causing her to clutch the saddle to avoid falling off.

"You're holding too tight," Convers advised gently. "Relax your hands and trust him to follow your lead."

"I'm trying," Regina replied through gritted teeth, loosening her grip. Mango snorted but continued moving unpredictably. After a few more failed attempts, Regina sighed heavily. "I think I'm better off in the carriage with Annabelle."

"No shame in that, miss," Convers reassured her. "Horses take time to get used to."

Relieved, Regina dismounted with Convers's help and led Mango back to the retaining log. Moments later, she joined Annabelle and Marcus in the carriage. Marcus arched an eyebrow at the sight of them both entering.

"Welcome aboard, Miss Fournier," Marcus greeted with a faint smile.

Annabelle crossed her arms and huffed, staring out the window. "Horses are stupid."

"I think I just need more practice," Regina added with a sheepish grin.

Marcus chuckled softly. "Well, looks like I won't be the only one enjoying this spacious seat after all."

As the carriage wheels creaked softly under their weight, Sophie and Lisa continued riding their horses in a steady trot around the track. The rhythmic sound of hooves echoed through the stable yard, their laughter drifting through the cool morning air. Marcus watched from the window, savoring the rare moment of calm as the journey ahead slowly came into focus.

Sophie and Lisa decided they would ride their horses all the way to Snyder. With everyone settled, Sophie and Lisa on horseback and the others in the carriage, the small caravan set off on their six-hour journey to the rural town.

The carriage driver, Mr. Davis, tipped his hat as he guided the reins. "It'll be a long ride, folks. We'll want to stop twice along the way to rest and water the horses," he advised.

"Sounds like a good plan," Marcus agreed from inside the carriage, glancing out at the road ahead.

Sophie and Lisa rode ahead, leading the procession. The main highway stretched before them, wide and well-maintained, cutting a path through the lush Verdantian landscape. As they left Meadowbrook's bustling capital behind, the scenery gradually shifted. Picturesque rural villages dotted the roadside, nestled beside sprawling fields of golden crops and orderly groves of fruit-bearing trees. The familiar refrain from her school days echoed in Lisa's mind: "The food that feeds the Seven Kingdoms."

They continued along the road, the rhythmic clip-clop of hooves blending with the distant sounds of village life.

Inside the carriage, Regina gazed out the window, marveling at the highway's design. Her eyes traced the two parallel lanes, one filled with large wagons carrying grain, produce, and livestock, while the other hosted passenger carriages and horseback riders.

"This highway system is impressive," Regina remarked. "Everything is so organized."

Marcus nodded, leaning forward slightly to explain. "Transportation is crucial here. Verdantia's primary economy revolves around exporting crops and livestock to the other six kingdoms. To keep things running smoothly, the Supreme Minister and Congress passed strict traffic laws. The inside lane on the kingdom highways is reserved exclusively for product transport, grain, livestock, goods. The outer lane is for passenger travel."

"Interesting," Regina said thoughtfully. "It's practical. Efficient."

"Aye, that reminds me of primary slips in port towns," Annabelle chimed in. "They're reserved for merchant ships. Legitimate ones, mind ye. No privateers allowed. Ships dock there to offload as fast as possible. Onloading's not permitted."

Marcus chuckled softly. "So even the seas have their own version of traffic control."

"Aye, they sure do," Annabelle replied with a grin.

The journey continued smoothly for another two hours before Mr. Davis signaled a stop. He pulled the carriage into a clearing near a tranquil lake at the edge of a small town.

"This'll be a good place to rest," Davis announced as he climbed down from the driver's bench. He began unhitching the carriage horses to lead them toward the water.

Sophie and Lisa dismounted and guided their own horses, Kicker and Grape, toward the lake's edge. The horses eagerly dipped their heads, drinking deeply from the cool water.

"Looks like they were thirsty," Sophie observed, stroking Kicker's mane affectionately.

"I cannot blame them," Lisa added. "It has been a long stretch without a break."

Mr. Davis led the carriage horses alongside Grape and Kicker. Like the others, the pair wasted no time plunging their snouts into the water, their thirst obvious as they drank greedily.

"How are you fine ladies doing today?" Mr. Davis asked as he guided the cart horses toward the lake.

"Good," Sophie replied, brushing a hand over Kicker's mane. "I haven't ridden in a while, I forgot how good it feels."

"Yes," Lisa agreed. "It feels good to shake the bones loose." She paused, glancing at Sophie thoughtfully. "I didn't think Jib—Auroriums would be big on horse riding."

Sophie caught the slip but appreciated Lisa's quick correction. "We ride a lot," Sophie explained, patting Kicker at the water's edge. "We patrol the rural towns to make sure the people living out there aren't forgotten."

"So... you Jiberau are police?" Mr. Davis asked curiously, his tone bordering on disbelief.

"Excuse me," Lisa interjected, her voice polite but firm. "Her clan is named Aurorium."

"It is?" Davis asked, his eyebrows raising in visible skepticism.

"It is," Sophie affirmed gently but with a firm edge. Deciding to elaborate, she added, "The Aurorium Clan isn't the police, but we're charged by the kingdoms to uphold laws and take on missions. We have specialized skills, investigation, people recovery, and personal protection. We don't replace the police; we fill in the gaps where specialized skills or extra manpower are needed."

"Ah, I see," Davis murmured, nodding slowly. "But you're so young."

"We start training in the clan when we're ten years old," Sophie explained. "From that point on, we're considered active clan members."

"You don't go to school?" Lisa asked, surprised by the idea of children entering the ranks so early.

"We do," Sophie replied. "During the initiate years, the clan brings teachers to the village to teach us. Once we're promoted to Sentinel rank, we return to regular school."

"How long does it take to get promoted to sentinel?" Lisa asked, her interest piqued.

"It depends on the person," Sophie said, giving a modest shrug. "To be promoted to sentinel, or shadow, you have to pass an exam."

"And what rank are you now?" Lisa asked, realizing she wasn't sure if Sophie had mentioned it before.

"I'm a Sentinel," Sophie answered, her voice steady with quiet pride. "We're the torchbearers, maintainers of the fire." She recited the phrase from her promotion ceremony, a solemn warmth in her tone.

Lisa smiled at the conviction in Sophie's words. "Torchbearers, huh? That sounds pretty noble."

"I guess," Sophie replied softly, her gaze drifting to the reflection of the sky in the lake. For a moment, the conversation gave way to peaceful silence as the horses drank deeply, their presence grounding the avatars and their companions in the serene beauty of the rural landscape.

Annabelle, Regina, and Marcus exited the carriage, stretching stiff muscles after the two-hour leg of their journey. The trio wandered along the lake's edge, away from Sophie, Lisa, and Mr. Davis, taking in the tranquil beauty of the scene. The gentle rustling of trees and the glimmer of sunlight on the water created a rare moment of peace as they walked and conversed.

"So, Brother Marcus," Annabelle began, her tone casual but curious, "What do we expect to find in this Snyder place again?"

"Brother Albert's report mentioned a cave and an old building," Regina answered before Marcus could. "Near an apple orchard with a big sign."

"Unfortunately, the details get vague after that," Marcus added. He glanced at Annabelle as they walked past a weathered picnic table near a water spigot. "By the way, if you don't mind my asking, what did Captain Lowe say in his letter?"

"Dunno," Annabelle replied, pulling the letter from her oversized jacket pocket. She twirled the envelope in her hand, admiring the gold trim around its edges. "Ain't read it yet."

Marcus frowned slightly. "Miss Salazar, I think you should. Captain Lowe wanted you to read it, probably for a good reason."

"Oi! I'm gonna read it!" Annabelle shot back, waving him off with a dismissive hand. "Ye two keep walkin'. I'll catch up once I'm done."

With a shrug, Marcus continued along the lakeshore. Regina followed, casting a curious glance back at Annabelle before returning her focus to the path ahead.

Annabelle carefully opened the envelope, taking extra care not to damage the gold trim. *This is too fancy to waste—maybe I can get some coin for it later*, she mused. She unfolded the letter and began to read:

Dear Annabelle,

I have to return to the Stormfang. Some business came up, so I won't be able to join you all on your *goddess adventure*. Make sure to have a good time and show those other avatars and Brother Marcus how to have some fun.

Love,
James Lowe

Annabelle smirked. To anyone else, this would have seemed like a lighthearted note, but she and the captain had worked out a code long ago. They knew how to send hidden messages in case their letters were ever intercepted by coppers or other authorities. Every detail in the letter carried a specific meaning.

The first clue: he addressed her as "Annabelle," not "Annabelle Salazar.", not "Belle", If he had included her full name, it would've been a signal of immediate danger, time to run and hide, if it was just "Belle" it would mean that she is good and safe, just using her first name "Annabelle" meant, Ye could be in danger, so stay sharp.

Next was the line, "Make sure that you have a good time." In their code, this warning alerted her to be on the lookout for suspicious activity, people might be watching. If he had told her to "be on your best behavior," that would have meant enemies were actively closing in.

Then there was the line about showing the avatars "how to have fun." That was the captain's way of saying she could trust the avatars and Brother Marcus, but should be wary of everyone else.

Finally, he had signed the letter "James Lowe." Not "Captain Lowe," not "Kidd." That was his way of saying, Be cautious. Don't take too many risks.

Annabelle sighed softly, a mixture of relief and gratitude warming her chest. Despite her affection for the avatars, the Stormfang was still her true home. She slid the letter back into her jacket pocket with a smile, her worries momentarily eased.

She caught up with Marcus and Regina as they continued their walk around the lake, the three of them enjoying the calm before the journey resumed. After a stroll, they returned to the others, and the caravan prepared to set off once more. Sophie and Lisa took the lead on horseback, with Mr. Davis driving the carriage behind them.

The highway stretched ahead of them, lined with sprawling farmland and small, scattered villages. Tall groves of trees and endless rows of crops painted the landscape in shades of green and gold. The rhythmic clatter of the wagon wheels mixed with the steady clop of hooves as the group traveled deeper into rural Verdantia.

As they passed through town after town, Sophie began to notice a steady decline in the quality of the settlements. The polished charm of the capital's outskirts gave way to older, worn-down villages. Stone facades visible from the highway were gradually replaced by plain wooden buildings that had clearly seen better days.

Lisa rode beside Sophie, her gaze drifting to the fields. "They still call these fields the *food that feeds the seven kingdoms*," remembering the phrase from her secondary school days. Despite the idyllic image that slogan painted, the reality of these rural towns was stark, years of neglect and overworked lands were etched into the very bones of the buildings.

Sophie surveyed silently, her mind lingering on the disparities between Verdantia's capital and its rural outskirts. It was a familiar sight, *different kingdoms, same patterns*. The further they traveled, the more it became clear that the glory of these once-thriving communities had long since faded.

The next rest area wasn't as pleasant as the first; its layout was purely practical. The area was divided into three sections: the central section featured a well, hitching posts, and a modest work shack. To the left, a row of picnic tables provided a spot for travelers to stretch and relax. On the right, several training apparatuses filled the space; cloth-wrapped trees served as makeshift punching bags, while a series of embedded logs formed a high-knee obstacle course. A short, stone-paved running track circled the training area.

Upon arrival, Sophie and Lisa dismounted and tied their horses to the hitching posts by the well. Mr. Davis unhitched the carriage horses and secured them to the posts opposite. "The watering buckets should be in the work shack," he informed them while adjusting the reins.

The girls retrieved the wide-mouthed metal buckets, filled them at the well, and brought water to all four horses. The animals eagerly dipped their heads and drank deeply after the long ride.

With the horses tended to, Sophie and Lisa found a nearby picnic table and rested their heads on their arms. Mr. Davis followed suit at a separate table, clearly tired from the journey.

Regina decided to make use of the training equipment. Having spent the last two hours sitting in the carriage and missing her morning training, she felt the need to get her blood pumping. Meanwhile, Marcus and Annabelle walked around the rest area, stretching their legs and enjoying the fresh air.

"So, Miss Salazar," Marcus began after a while, "I noticed you skipped your magic practice this morning."

Annabelle rolled her shoulders. "Aye, I did. Might as well catch up now, eh?" she said with a smirk. After some light probing from Marcus, she agreed to start her training session.

Not wanting to disturb the avatars, Marcus settled onto a bench to review his notes, his condensed version of Brother Albert's cryptic report. Knowing the reports were deliberately vague to avoid unwanted attention, Marcus reexamined his summary with a critical eye. He considered that he might have overlooked something important.

Brother Albert's report mentioned an apple orchard with a large red sign out front. Near the orchard, there was said to be a wild strawberry patch. Somewhere in that vicinity lay a hidden temple or facility of great significance. The lack of details gnawed at Marcus, but he reminded himself that Albert wouldn't have concealed information without good reason.

As the group settled into their respective routines, the rest area fell into a calm rhythm—only the sound of rustling leaves, distant bird calls, and soft footfalls on the stone track broke the silence.

After her training session, Regina sat cross-legged on the ground, assuming the same meditative posture she used when communing with Change. This time, however, she shaped her mana into Earthbloom. With slow, controlled breaths, she focused on maintaining the shape and flow of her mana within her body. Remembering her conversation with Lisa's mother, she resisted the urge to push her mana outward and instead sought to sense the earth's energy around her.

At first, nothing. She encountered the same resistance that Lisa had warned her about, the dangerous barrier that could cause mana backlash. Frustration tugged at the edge of her mind. *I'm so close*, she thought, unwilling to waste the opportunity.

She allowed her thoughts to drift. Her mind wandered back to the gala, where she had learned new dances with the boys the previous night. Ethan's hands had guided hers through the steps, his grip a little too firm, but his determination shining through his inexperience. *He led me with touch and rhythm.. That's what I need now: to let the earth lead me.*

Regina surrendered her control. Slowly, she felt it; the earth's presence gently weaving through her mana like a guide. Time became fluid as she focused solely on the connection. Sparkling impressions of energy began to form around her, not seen with her eyes, but perceived through some other sense. She didn't fully understand how it worked, but she allowed herself to flow with it, dancing in tandem with the earth's energy.

Minutes passed. Maybe ten maybe twenty. Regina felt exhilarated, a surge of triumph warming her from within. *This is it!*

Then, without warning, a blinding flash overwhelmed her senses. The shockwave shattered her concentration, and her mana snapped back violently, sending a sharp, painful jolt through her chest. She gasped, clutching at her heart as she collapsed to the ground.

Marcus noticed immediately. Horror flashed across his face. **"REGINA!"** he shouted, dropping his papers and sprinting past the picnic tables and horses.

His cry jolted everyone. Sophie, Lisa, and Mr. Davis sat shot upright, disoriented from the sudden commotion. Annabelle, in the middle of her sea dome spell, lost focus. The watery barrier collapsed, drenching her from head to toe.

"Oi! What the bloody hell?" Annabelle sputtered, shaking water from her face.

Marcus skidded to a stop and knelt beside Regina, his mind racing. "Miss Regina, what happened? Can you hear me?" He hesitated, unsure how to help or what she had done to herself.

Regina groaned softly and managed to raise a shaky hand, giving him a thumbs-up. "I'm okay…" she croaked.

Marcus let out a long, relieved breath and collapsed onto his backside, his hand running through his hair. "Thank the goddesses... I thought you had a heart attack."

Annabelle stomped over, dripping wet and glowering. "Oi, Brother Marcus! Ye got me all wet!" Despite her irritation, a grin tugged at the corners of her mouth as she glanced at Regina, now sitting up slowly.

Marcus looked over his shoulder, smirking. "Miss Salazar, as I understand it, water is the sea, which you, as a privateer, have a deep love for. So, I suppose you're thanking me?"

Annabelle rolled her eyes but chuckled. "Hmph. Cheeky bloke."

With the excitement over, everyone gradually settled back down. Regina stood, brushing off her clothes and shaking her head in frustration. She had been so close to understanding Earthbloom's sense, yet now she felt like she was back at square one.

As they resumed their journey to Snyder, Regina attempted to use Earthbloom to sense a few more times, but each attempt ended in backlash. The pain lessened with each try, but it remained enough to force her to stop. Eventually, she decided to let it go for now.

Annabelle, still damp from her failed spell, leaned against the carriage wall and dozed off during the final leg of the trip. Marcus sat beside her, quietly watching the passing landscape. His gaze occasionally drifted to Regina, keeping a protective eye on her to ensure she didn't push herself too far.

Ahead of them, the road stretched on, the distant town of Snyder waiting beyond the horizon. Hidden somewhere within that town lay the answers they sought—and perhaps more questions than they could anticipate.

[----------]

As the caravan veered off the main highway, a weathered sign arched over the road, proclaiming in faded letters: "Welcome to Snyder, the Jewel of the Harvest." The title seemed almost ironic, an overstatement compared to the reality that lay ahead.

The town of Snyder unfolded before them like a relic from another time, stubbornly intact yet visibly worn. Its main street stretched out sparsely, the buildings on either side resembling aged teeth in a weary smile, each one a testament to better days.

On the left and right stood the essential fixtures of any rural town: an inn whose once-charming facade had faded into a patchwork of peeling wood and chipped paint; a saloon with creaking swinging doors, whispering secrets of wild nights long past; government offices, their civic pride eroded by time; a general store stocked with farm tools and canned goods; and finally, the sheriff's office, is the best kept building in the small town that was just about one streets worth of buildings.

The relentless sun bore down on the scene, highlighting every crack and crevice in the weathered buildings. Snyder was a place that had endured without much fanfare, functional but fraying at the edges. The group's arrival seemed to stir the town from its slumber.

Lisa and Sophie guided their horses to a hitching post outside the inn, their hooves clopping softly on the sunbaked dirt road. Mr. Davis maneuvered the carriage into place at the center of the street, its worn wheels groaning in protest from the long journey. Dust kicked up gently around them, settling like a quiet greeting.

As the carriage rolled to a stop, the group disembarked and began retrieving their belongings from the storage compartment. Marcus, ever attentive, grabbed Mr. Davis's leather bag along with several pieces of luggage. He carried them into the shaded comfort of the inn's lobby, relishing the reprieve from the afternoon heat.

Inside, the lobby was quiet and calm, with the faint smell of aged wood and dried herbs hanging in the air. Marcus approached the innkeeper, who stood behind the counter, a ledger in hand. His voice echoed faintly as he arranged their accommodations, each word slipping easily into the stillness of the space.

Mr. Davis, with a polite tip of his hat, took responsibility for the horses and carriage. He led them around the building to the stable yard with practiced efficiency, his boots crunching softly on the dirt.

One by one, the avatars and Marcus collected their room keys and ascended the creaking staircase to their quarters. Each step groaned beneath their feet, a reminder of the inn's long service to weary travelers. Inside their rooms, the promise of a cool wash and fresh clothes was a welcome thought after the dust and fatigue of the road.

The agreement was simple: they would meet for dinner later, giving everyone time to clean up and rest. For now, Snyder waited quietly, its secrets and stories resting beneath the worn surface of its streets and buildings.

Chapter 11

Journal Entry: April 25, 1910

Our arrival in Snyder revealed a town clinging to echoes of former prosperity. The sign at the entrance called it "The Jewel of the Harvest," though time has tarnished that gem. Its cracked streets, weary buildings, and the weathered eyes of its few inhabitants tell a story of slow decline, a place both preserved and forgotten.

Along the way, we passed through villages and farmland that mirrored Snyder's quiet deterioration. Verdantia may feed the seven kingdoms, but its rural heartlands clearly suffer under that burden. The decline was apparent throughout our journey from Vendura's capital, Meadowbrook, to the Cornucopia city of Snyder.

Regina faced her own challenges. Her growing frustration with Earthbloom magic became apparent when she attempted a practice session at one of our rest stops. For a fleeting moment, she seemed to grasp the elusive connection between her mana and the earth itself, only for it to slip away, triggering a painful mana backlash.

The road has taken a toll on us all. Yet, this is only the beginning. Somewhere in this quiet, unassuming town lies the next clue to Brother Albert's mystery. The apple orchard with the red and gold sign. The hidden temple. The truth is buried within these dusty streets.

[-----✿-----]

The dawn ushered in a refreshing coolness over Snyder. Sophie and Regina seized the opportunity for a brisk training run, their steady breaths merging with the town's early stillness. As they paced down the country road, Sophie noted the stark contrast in their surroundings: the governor's mansion, a lush island of life with its immaculate gardens and vibrant foliage, stood in defiant contrast to this neglected, older crumbling town drying up while it toils forward.

On the main road, groups of laborers trudged toward their day's work. Their spirited cheers and whoops echoed as they passed the runners. Regina's brow furrowed in confusion at the attention, while Sophie flushed, an involuntary smile tugging at the corners of her mouth. She directed her gaze forward, letting the rhythmic cadence of her footsteps drown out the noise.

Their run concluded at the hotel, where Regina collapsed onto the dusty ground with exaggerated relief. She flopped onto her back, hands spread wide as she stared skyward.

"Sweet mercy! I've never loved the ground this much," she groaned dramatically.

Sophie, chuckling as she wiped her brow, extended a hand. "It wasn't that bad, just two king's journeys. You survived."

Regina rolled her eyes, accepting the hand. "Survived? Maybe, it's still…" she pauses to catch her breath, "it's still early."

From her seat at a shaded outdoor table, Lisa looked on with amused detachment. A cup of tea steamed beside her nearly finished breakfast plate.

"I will never understand why you two insist on torturing yourselves first thing in the morning," Lisa quipped.

Sophie shrugged as they approached, while Regina rose to her feet, catching her breath.

Lisa shifted her attention to a short distance away, where Annabelle stood in fierce concentration. Water danced and churned in a shimmering vortex around her, twisting in sync with her fluid movements. Each strike she threw into the air caused a surge around her fists, until she shifted to kicks.

"At least Annabelle is doing something useful," Lisa remarked, motioning toward the privateer mage. "All this running... what could be the point?"

Sophie grinned, stretching out in her stance. "Improved blood flow means enhanced mana flow. Better mana flow means stronger, faster casting and endurance during spell work. Not to mention mental clarity, pretty useful when crafting complex magic."

Lisa snorted softly, raising an eyebrow as she sipped her tea. "If you say so."

At that moment, Marcus stepped out from the hotel's back entrance, balancing a coffee cup and a bowl of oatmeal. He offered a polite nod to Lisa before gesturing to the seat beside her.

"Mind if I join you?" he asked.

"By all means," Lisa replied with a nonchalant wave.

As he settled in, Marcus turned his attention to Sophie and Regina. "Morning training done already?"

"Absolutely," Regina said quickly, a grin creeping across her face.

Sophie smirked. "Short run today. Some of us needed an easy start," she teased, nudging Regina.

"We ran enough," Regina shot back with severity, giving Sophie a playful push. Their laughter echoed as they strolled inside to freshen up.

Marcus's gaze wandered to Annabelle. Her focus remained sharp as she moved through her training regimen, a series of conjured waves and punches, each movement a perfect blend of martial precision and magical control. She finished with an impressive flourish, forming a dome of water that shimmered like liquid glass around her.

Marcus smiled quietly, reflecting on how far Annabelle had come. He recalled their first meeting, when she had filled the carriage the avatars were riding in with a torrent of seawater, unable to cast her magic bubble spell. Now, she was casting spell after spell with precision.

Sensing his eyes on her, Annabelle turned sharply, a brow arching in challenge. "What're ye starin' at, Brother Marcus?"

He raised his hands in a gesture of peace. "My mistake, Miss Salazar. Just admiring your skill."

Annabelle's gaze softened slightly, her pride barely concealed. "Well, maybe next time, ye'll admire wit' a coin or two, eh?" she teased, turning back to her training.

Marcus chuckled and returned to his meal as Sophie and Regina reappeared, now refreshed and carrying plates of breakfast. They claimed seats at the table next to Marcus and Lisa, their chatter light and easy in the morning sun.

Annabelle, still under the sun's growing heat, powered through her demanding routine. Smitty had assigned her a relentless sequence: a waterspout, a crashing wave, two riptide punches, two riptide kicks, and finally the complex *seashell* spell. Ten times around.

With each repetition, Annabelle's arms ached, muscles trembling from exertion and the steady drain of mana. She clenched her jaw, determined not to falter. Drawing a deep, calming breath, she summoned the sea's essence once more. Mana coursed through her veins like a current, pooling in her hands as seawater spiraled upward, forming a towering spout.

"Come on then," she muttered, narrowing her eyes as she attempted to mold the water into the shape of a ship. The currents twisted, resisting her control. The ship's silhouette shimmered briefly before collapsing into formless waves. Frustration gnawed at her, but she kept her composure, releasing the water in a graceful cascade that soaked the grassy field behind the hotel.

Annabelle reset her stance, grounding herself with a deep inhale. Mana surged anew, and this time she conjured a sweeping wave, sending it crashing across the open space. Each movement tested her stamina. Without a natural water source nearby, she had to pull the element from her own magic, giving it an orange tint, a costly endeavor that drained her reserves faster than usual.

A waft of breakfast aromas, eggs, bread, and something tantalizingly sweet drifted from the hotel, accompanied by the distant clink of forks against plates. Annabelle's stomach growled in protest. She grimaced, shaking off the distraction, and launched into the next phase of her training. Her right fist shot forward, summoning the sea's force in a powerful riptide punch. She mirrored the motion with her left hand, amplifying the impact of her strike with the surge of conjured water. She then performed a riptide kick with her left foot and repeated the magical strike with her right foot.

Finally, she leaned back, summoning a substantial mass of water and meticulously shaping it into a dome around herself. The surface shimmered like liquid crystal as she activated the *seashell* spell, infusing the barrier with reinforcing mana. Beads of sweat trickled down her temple as she maintained the structure, pushing her limits. Slowly, she let the dome dissolve, the water cascading in delicate streams that soaked into the earth.

Breathing heavily, Annabelle acknowledged the familiar warning signs of heavy mana use. It was time to stop. The promise of breakfast lured her as she marched back toward the hotel, her steps slow but steady.

She arrived in time to catch a snippet of conversation at one of the tables. Regina leaned in close to Marcus, her tone curious and tinged with urgency.

"Brother Marcus, how are we going to find the building Brother Albert mentioned?" Sophie asks before eating a fork full of eggs.

Marcus set his coffee down, his expression thoughtful. "His report described a structure near an apple orchard. Across from it, there should be a large red sign with gold trim. There's also supposed to be a wild strawberry patch nearby." He paused, glancing at the others. "The innkeeper mentioned several orchards in the area, but he didn't know of any wild strawberry patches."

Annabelle, plate in hand, joined the group. She'd chosen eggs and steamed vegetables with a cup of juice, though she sighed at the absence of bacon. The eggs were a step above what Jeffie usually managed, but they still paled compared to the fare from the mansion's cooks. She gave a philosophical shrug, her hunger overruling her disappointment. At least it was warm.

A cooling breeze swept over the deck as Annabelle settled into her seat next to Sophie and Regina. She tuned into the ongoing conversation, her spirits lifting as she ate.

"We should split up," Sophie suggested, practicality guiding her tone. "We've got two single horses. If we divide the area, we can cover more ground."

She turned to Marcus, who nodded thoughtfully.

"Do you have a map of the area?" Sophie asked.

"I don't," Marcus admitted, his brow furrowing in thought. After a moment, an idea sparked. "But the general store might have one."

Sophie nodded approvingly. "If you can get a map and a pen, we can use it to coordinate our efforts and make sure we don't search the same area twice." She outlined the plan between bites of bacon, her tone calm and matter-of-fact, as if strategies like this were second nature in her clan.

Annabelle, overhearing the discussion, narrowed her eyes. Her gaze drifted to Sophie's plate, now glaringly piled with the last of the bacon. Annabelle's irritation bubbled over. "Who cares how ye coppers do things," she muttered under her breath. The frustration in her voice was unmistakable. "This is sacred acres territory. Coppers don't do nothin' here."

Sophie paused, confused. "What?" She glanced up and noticed Annabelle's plate, conspicuously devoid of bacon. A slow grin spread across her face. "Oh, *Anna*, what's the deal? Vegetables for breakfast? Are you eating healthier now?" She smirked and made a show of popping another crispy piece of bacon into her mouth with exaggerated relish.

Annabelle's glare sharpened. "Some stinking copper took the last of the bacon," she said, her voice tight with barely restrained annoyance.

Sophie feigned sympathy, her eyes twinkling mischievously. "Oh, that's tragic. The bacon is so good today, *Anna*." She leaned back, clearly savoring both the bacon and the banter.

Annabelle straightened, determined not to rise to the bait. She picked up a piece of steamed vegetables and replied coolly, "It's fine. There'll be bacon tomorrow."

"Doubt it'll be as good as today's." Sophie teased, her smirk widening as she sensed Annabelle's patience fraying.

Annabelle's composure finally cracked. With a flick of her fingers, she summoned a small burst of seawater, sending a splash straight into Sophie.

Sophie froze for a moment, then tilted her head back in mock acceptance. "Ahh, thanks, *Anna*. The water's so refresh…" She abruptly stopped mid-sentence, her nose wrinkling as the briny scent hit her. "Goddess above! Why does this water reek like that?"

Sputtering, Sophie stood, shaking droplets from her clothes in dismay. "I have to wash this off, right now." She shot Annabelle a glare before striding toward the hotel's entrance, muttering under her breath. "By the ancestors, that smell…"

166

Annabelle watched her retreat with a satisfied grin. She spotted Sophie's abandoned plate and leaned over, snatching the remaining pieces of bacon. Taking a triumphant bite, she murmured, "Aye... tis good bacon."

[-----+-----]

Marcus's visit to the town's general store took on a sense of quiet urgency. The aisles bustled with life, packed with locals and lined with everything from homemade jams to hand-woven baskets. He navigated through the crowd with singular focus, his goal clear: to find a comprehensive map of Snyder.

As he searched, his gaze landed on something valuable nestled among local artifacts—an updated directory of the village's businesses. Each entry was a vivid snapshot of Snyder's identity, showcasing the entrepreneurial pride woven into the fabric of the town. The descriptions painted stories of bustling orchards, resilient farms, and family-run shops, all thriving in this remote corner of the region.

Marcus's focus narrowed on the agricultural section. He knew their target was tied to an orchard or a farm, and this new information would help streamline the search. Pulling out the map he'd acquired, he marked three orchards and three farms that seemed the most promising. On the eastern side of Snyder, he highlighted one orchard and two farms. To the west, another cluster caught his attention, two orchards and one expansive farm, each brimming with possibilities.

Satisfied with the plan, Marcus returned to the hotel to share the findings.

[-----+-----]

The group convened on the deck, leaning over the spread map as Marcus explained their next move.

"We've got six potential locations," he began, tapping the map. "Three to the east, three to the west. If we split up, we can cover them all faster."

Regina's eyes gleamed with a mixture of hope and determination. For her, the search was personal. Somewhere among the orchards might be answers about her family—answers buried in time like forgotten seeds beneath the trees.

"I'll take the west," Regina volunteered immediately, her tone steady but charged with emotion.

Lisa glanced at her and nodded. "I will go with you. We will check the orchards first."

Meanwhile, Sophie and Annabelle prepared to handle the eastern sector. Sophie's methodical nature shone through as she studied the map, mentally charting the most efficient routes between their targets. Annabelle leaned in beside her, absently toying with the corner of her plate, her focus already drifting to the challenge ahead.

"Alright," Sophie concluded, straightening. "Let's stick to the plan. We'll meet back here by sundown to compare notes."

With their roles assigned and the search mapped out, the team prepared to set out, the weight of both history and destiny pressing quietly on their shoulders.

[----- ⚓ -----]

Sophie guided Kicker down the gravel-strewn road leading to the eastern edge of the rundown town. Annabelle sat close behind, her arms wrapped securely around

Sophie's waist. The morning sun cast long, stretching shadows as they rode past a sprawling, neglected farm. Tomato plants clung desperately to rusted metal supports that jutted from the cracked, sunbaked earth. The air was thick with the mingling scents of ripe tomatoes and the faint metallic tang of old iron.

Further along the road, the scenery shifted. Dust-coated potato plants drooped under the relentless heat, their leaves sagging like weary laborers. Actual workers moved steadily between the rows, wide-brimmed hats shielding their faces as they tended the crops with quiet diligence.

Annabelle broke the rhythmic clatter of hooves with a curious question. "So where did ye learn to ride these here beasts, Copper?"

"Initiates learn to ride and care for horses during the early phases of training," Sophie explained, her voice calm despite the jostling ride. "We use them regularly in the clan for transport and patrols."

Annabelle adjusted her hold slightly. "Do ye see anything yet?"

"Not yet," Sophie replied, tapping gently on Annabelle's arms. "And can you loosen up a bit? I'd like to keep breathing."

"Oh," Annabelle murmured, easing her grip. Her gaze swept over the fields they passed. "These folks work hard."

"Farm work isn't easy," Sophie remarked with a hint of nostalgia. Memories of her time as an initiate resurfaced, long, grueling days in the fields under an unrelenting sun. There was pain in those memories, but also a sense of quiet pride. Shaking off the thought, she refocused on the mission. "We're looking for a red sign with gold trim and a wild strawberry patch. Keep your eyes peeled."

A lull passed between them before Sophie's curiosity piqued. "How long were you a pirate?"

"Privateer," Annabelle corrected with a sly grin. "I've been a privateer all me life."

Sophie arched a brow. "All your life? How does that even work? You were a privateer at eight?"

Annabelle's playful demeanour dimmed as her voice softened. "Aye. I was with Kidd before he became captain of the Fang. He looked after me after... well, after me, papa and his crew..." Her words trailed off, her gaze distant.

Sophie remained silent, sensing Annabelle slipping into the painful recesses of her past. In her mind's eye, Annabelle was back in the lifeboat, salty spray mingling with tears as she watched the Stoneridge military faction gun down her family and crew. The Espada Sovereign vanished beneath the waves, swallowed by the dark sea.

"How did you end up with Captain Kidd?" Sophie asked gently, steering the conversation away from the depths of sorrow.

Annabelle's voice was steady but subdued. "When I was a wee little girl me Papa's ship the Espada Sovereign was sunk by a rouge navy." Annabelle recounted "After me peoples died, Kidd and I stuck together. We didn't have no one else."

Sophie hesitated, then spoke softly. "I didn't know that's how your parents had died."

"They were on the Espada Sovereign," Annabelle replied, her voice cracking slightly. "Those Stoneridge bastards... they just opened fire and sent her to the bottom."

"By the ancestors…" Sophie whispered, horrified by the stark brutality of the tale. She reached back and gently tapped Annabelle's hand. "I'm sorry. That's… unspeakable."

Annabelle sniffed, attempting to suppress the vulnerability creeping into her voice. "You know what might ease the pain?"

"What's that?" Sophie asked, her voice a blend of concern and warmth as she placed a comforting hand over Annabelle's.

"I need five coin," Annabelle declared, a playful smile curling her lips.

Sophie laughed softly, swatting at Annabelle's arm. "Oh, you."

"No, really," Annabelle continued with mock seriousness. "Ten coin would help even more. This grief... it's unbearable."

"I don't know how Captain Kidd puts up with you," Sophie teased, shaking her head. Just then, her eyes caught sight of a large sign up ahead. Painted a vivid green with white letters and trim, it read Goldleaf Orchards.

"Not red with gold trim," Sophie muttered with a sigh of disappointment.

"Nope," Annabelle echoed with a chuckle.

Sophie nudged Kicker's flanks. "Hyah, Kicker!" she called, urging the horse into a faster pace. The steed responded eagerly, its hooves kicking up clouds of dust as the wind rushed past.

Annabelle broke the exhilarated silence with another teasing remark. "About them ten coins..."

"Sorry, no coin," Sophie quipped, amusement glinting in her eyes. "Just Harvest crowns. You'll have to find another way to pay off Captain Kidd."

Annabelle's eyes widened playfully. "Oi! How'd ye know about that?"

"Captain Kidd told me," Sophie shot back with a grin. "Right after he said I was crew."

"Bah!" Annabelle protested, laughing as the wind carried their banter across the open road.

They passed a rustic stand labelled Wilde Fruit and Pies, the warm, inviting scent of freshly baked goods mingling with the earthy sweetness of ripe fruit. Sophie inhaled deeply, momentarily savoring the pleasant contrast to the dust and dry heat around them. Soon, they reached an apple orchard enclosed by a simple wooden fence. Workers bustled about, some picking apples directly from the branches while others carefully gathered fallen ones into woven baskets.

"So seriously, how did you and Kidd end up together?" Sophie asked, glancing at Annabelle. Her curiosity was genuine, sensing that Annabelle hadn't shared the whole story before.

Annabelle sighed, her voice roughened by the weight of memory. "Well, after the Sovereign was sunk, Kidd and I had to row like hell to get outta there, so those Stoneridge bastards didn't spot us. They fired on me papa and the crew, not caring about anything but sinking the ship." She paused, her grip unconsciously tightening around Sophie's waist. "Next morning, we got picked up by a puppet ship. Those blokes had the nerve to make us buy tickets to ride to the next port."

"Seriously?" Sophie asked over her shoulder, disbelief evident in her tone.

"Aye," Annabelle confirmed. "Me papa gave me the ship's chest to hold before those bastards showed up. He must've known they were gonna shake the ship down. Kidd and I snuck off in a lifeboat under cover of the mist. That's why they didn't see us when they opened fire."

"Wait... that story was real?!?" Sophie blinked, stunned as she glanced back at Annabelle.

"Oh yeah, missy. Wouldn't lie about that," Annabelle replied gravely.

Sophie observed the orange-haired girl clinging to her, the usual mischief in Annabelle's voice replaced by a haunted, reverent tone. A new layer of respect and empathy settled in Sophie's mind as she considered how much Annabelle had endured. The silence between them deepened, filled only by the rhythmic clatter of Kicker's hooves and the whisper of wind stirring the dry landscape around them.

They rode on, the road a blur of dust and scattered stones beneath them. The occasional wooden sign punctuated the barren scenery. Finally, they came upon another farm sign, this one painted green with bold white letters: Red River Farm.

"Green again," Sophie muttered with a frustrated sigh. She nudged Kicker forward. "Hyah!" The horse picked up speed, dust kicking up behind them as they raced toward the last marked location.

"Oi, how'd ye become a copper anyway?" Annabelle shouted over the thudding of hooves, her words barely reaching Sophie through the wind.

"What?" Sophie yelled back, twisting slightly to hear better.

"I said, how'd ye join the Aura?" Annabelle clarified, adding a hint of respect to the term.

"You mean the Aurorium?" Sophie corrected with a smile. "It's not something you join. You're born into it."

Annabelle raised an eyebrow. "So ye didn't choose to be a copper?"

"Nope," Sophie answered simply.

"Yer whole life, huh?" Annabelle continued, her voice curious, as if trying to piece together a life so different from her own.

Sophie chuckled. "You haven't seen any children wearing badges, have you?" She leaned forward, adjusting her grip on Kicker's reins. "After your tenth birthday, you become an initiate. Think of it like being a copper-in-training. We learn how to wear the uniform, use weapons, and practice the basics of magic."

"Sounds like a dream," Annabelle teased, her voice laced with sarcasm.

"Wrong," Sophie shot back sharply. "It was hell. You're basically a slave. From dawn to dusk, it's nothing but work and training. No games, no fun. Just constant drills and chores."

Annabelle grew quiet, absorbing the harsh reality Sophie described.

"The only way out is to pass the Sentinel test," Sophie added, her voice softening as she remembered the long, grueling process. "It took me a year, but I passed on my first try."

The road ahead widened as they reached the entrance to another farm. A large, rustic sign greeted them, its letters painted green on a weathered wooden background: The Reeves Estate.

"Curses," Annabelle muttered under her breath, clearly disappointed. "No luck here either."

"Maybe Lisa and Regina are having more luck," Sophie suggested, steering Kicker around. With a quick nudge to the horse's sides, she urged him into a gallop once more. Dust swirled behind them as they raced back down the path, wind whipping through their hair.

As they passed the fruit stand again, Annabelle suddenly called out, "Oi, we gotta stop!"

Sophie tugged Kicker's reins gently. "Whoa, girl." The horse slowed to a stop, and Annabelle quickly dismounted, striding over to the stand with a purposeful expression. Sophie, curious but bemused, guided Kicker closer. Annabelle stood in front of the sign, her gaze sharp and calculating as if trying to decode a hidden message.

"What are you doing?" Sophie asked as she tied Kicker to the hitching post and dismounted. "You can't be hungry; we just ate breakfast."

"It ain't that," Annabelle replied, barely paying Sophie any mind. Her eyes darted left toward the Red River Farm sign, then right to Goldleaf Orchards. "Tell me, Copper, ye ever find a pirate map?"

Sophie folded her arms, intrigued. "Can't say that I have. What's your point?"

Annabelle turned, her face lighting up with excitement. "See, pirates and privateers don't trust banks. They keep their coin on the ship. But if they think they're about to get arrested, they need a way to hide their stash a coin. So, they bury it somewhere only they can find and leave themselves a map."

"Okay..."

"But here's the trick," Annabelle continued, her grin widening. "They don't make it easy to read. Greedy coppers, or, ahem, police could just snatch the map and steal the loot. So, they encode it with clues only they can understand."

Sophie processed the explanation, her eyes narrowing thoughtfully. "But Brother Albert didn't leave us a map," she pointed out.

"Didn't he, though?" Annabelle said with a confident gleam. She pointed to the Red River Farm sign. "Red." Then, she gestured toward Goldleaf Orchards. "And gold." Finally, she swept her hand toward the fruit stand. "Near a wild strawberry patch. This is it. We're here."

Sophie's eyes widened as the pieces fell into place. She scanned the area, her anticipation rising. "So where's the building?"

Annabelle turned completely around, facing a grove of trees that bordered the property. "This way, me thinks," she said with a conspiratorial grin, beckoning Sophie to follow.

They entered the grove, dappled sunlight filtering through the canopy above. Shadows danced on the ground in shifting, ghostly patterns. Sophie's hand instinctively brushed the empty spot at her side where her pistol would usually rest. The feeling of vulnerability pricked at her nerves.

Annabelle frequently glanced back toward the fruit stand, ensuring they maintained the right direction. Sophie, meanwhile, kept her eyes on the woods, alert for any sign of the structure they sought.

After a short walk, they emerged into a clearing. At its center, a hill loomed, with an odd wooden structure built into its side. The sun cast eerie, twisting shadows across a stylized black sun, deeply burned into the wood. The dark lines swirled in intricate, cryptic patterns.

Approaching the structure, they found a large door carved into the hillside. It featured four shallow slots, resembling small shelves. Around the door, stone blocks jutted from the hill in seemingly random positions. To the side, a paragraph of unfamiliar text was etched into the wood.

Annabelle stepped closer, tracing the carvings with her fingers. After a moment, she turned to Sophie with a frown. "Oi, Copper, can ye read this?"

Sophie shook her head, studying the script. "Nope. I've never seen anything like it." She paused thoughtfully. "Maybe Lisa or Regina can read this."

"Aye, maybe yer right." Annabelle agreed. She pushed against the door, testing it. The door didn't budge an inch. She leaned her full weight into it, then stepped back in frustration. "There ain't no kickin' this door in," she muttered.

"We need to report back and let the others know what we've found," Sophie said, glancing toward the dense treeline. "Can you manage if I leave you here?"

Annabelle's eyes narrowed in mock indignation. "Leave me? What're ye on about?"

"I want to bring Brother Marcus here too," Sophie explained, nodding toward Kicker. "And the horse can only carry two."

"Oh, aye okay." Annabelle conceded, her expression softening. Then she pressed a hand to her forehead dramatically. "But what am I supposed to do while ye abandon me here to fend for meself in these wild lands?"

Sophie sighed, already bracing for the inevitable negotiation. "Alright, Annabelle. What'll it take to soothe your worries?"

With a mischievous grin, Annabelle replied, "A couple of crowns fer a drink... and maybe a slice a pie."

Sophie rolled her eyes but reached into her pocket, pulling out a handful of coins. She dropped ten Harvest crowns into Annabelle's waiting hand. "There. Happy now?"

"Thank ye, me dear Copper," Annabelle said with mock solemnity, her eyes sparkling. "Yer generous donation will greatly improve the lives of those in need," she added with a theatrical flourish.

Sophie shook her head, unable to suppress a smile. "Just make sure you're at the fruit stand when I get back," she instructed, turning toward the grove.

"Don't worry, I'll be here!" Annabelle called after her, already pocketing the coins as she sauntered back toward the clearing.

Sophie pushed through the trees, her mind racing with anticipation. They were close, she could feel it. Now, it was time to regroup and bring everyone together to unlock whatever secrets this place held.

Chapter 12

Sophie raced back to the hotel, her thoughts swirling with the latest revelations she couldn't wait to share. Meanwhile, Annabelle sought a moment of quiet at the fruit stand nestled between an apple orchard and a sprawling farm on the outskirts of the rural town. She ordered a slice of strawberry pie, its sweet, sun-warmed aroma blending with the earthy scent of ripening fruit. A glass of chilled lemonade, beads of condensation glistening on its surface, completed her Order.

She selected a table beneath the broad arms of an ancient oak tree, where dappled sunlight danced across the tabletop. From her vantage point, the orchard stretched to her right, its trees heavy with red apples that occasionally dropped to the ground with soft thuds. Ahead, farmhands, Earthbloom mages, wove their elemental magic, guiding water from a mobile reservoir. With fluid gestures, they conjured shimmering arcs of liquid that fell gently onto the fields, each droplet catching the light in a dazzling display.

Annabelle took a sip of lemonade, savoring the tart chill that contrasted with the summer heat, while each bite of pie felt like a comforting indulgence. Yet her peace was interrupted by a commotion near a fruit stand. A young man strode forward, his posture and presence unmistakably that of a collector. Hardened and cold-eyed, he radiated an unspoken warning, his movements sharp and deliberate as he confronted a young girl behind the counter.

Annabelle watched as he seized the girl's arm with practiced aggression, leaning close to mutter something meant to intimidate. A spark of anger flared within Annabelle. Her fingers tightened around her empty glass, its smooth surface grounding her as she observed the scene. In this place of beauty and simplicity, such acts felt like an offence against such a beautiful day.

She exhaled slowly, her mind whispering an all-too-familiar truth: *This is how it is here*. It was a complex reality she had never entirely accepted. Still, her gaze returned to the farm where the mages continued their work with serene focus. Their harmonious dance of water and growth stood in defiant contrast to the harshness playing out nearby. Annabelle mused over the limits of her own powers. Her Maelstrom Mastery magic could summon storms, yet it was not useful to personal combat scenarios, that tier-three spell was meant for ship to ship combat it's destructive force could sink an enemy vessel with little time.

The weight of the moment pressed on her, and she rose, seeking distance from the confrontation. She unwrapped the anchor chain from around her waist just a little, its metallic sheen glinting in the afternoon light. With a deft hand, she looped it onto its retaining hook on the side from the back a habit born of countless sods that wanted a piece of her where preparation meant the difference between losing coin or gaining coin.

Carrying her plate and glass, she moved toward the far end of the counter where a large tub of soapy water waited. She deposited her dishes with a quiet splash and muttered under her breath, "Smart setup," appreciating the efficiency of the self-serve system.

Annabelle's gaze drifted back to the fruit stand just as the girl reached beneath the counter, retrieving a battered box, the same one where Annabelle had earlier paid for her refreshments. The makeshift cash register. The man, still radiating authority and menace, released his hold on the girl just long enough to dump the box's contents into a worn leather coin bag. His casual entitlement grated on Annabelle's nerves. *The fox must eat*, she thought cynically, recognizing the all-too-familiar cycle of exploitation.

With a sharp gesture, the man tossed the now-empty box back onto the counter and pointed toward the bushels of fruit stored at the rear of the stand. The girl hurried off without a word, her steps quick and uneasy.

"Get me a bushel of apples too," he commanded, his tone devoid of gratitude.

Annabelle caught his gaze shifting to her, his eyes narrowing as he barked, "What are you looking at, girl? Beat it."

Feigning confusion, Annabelle cupped her hand to her ear. "What's that then?" she called out with exaggerated curiosity. "Didn't quite hear ye there."

The collector's eyes hardened. In three decisive strides, he was upon her, seizing her arm in a vice-like grip meant to intimidate. "I said, get out of here before something bad happens to you."

Annabelle's lips curved into a smirk, though the anger simmering beneath the surface remained steady. "Yer doin' it all wrong," she replied calmly, pulling her arm free with a quick jerk. "If ye take the money and the product, ye'll run this place straight into the ground. They'll have no choice but to hike up their prices to make up for what ye took. That'll run off customers, and soon enough, there won't be no coin left for yer *payment*."

The collector's jaw tightened in response. His hand found her arm again, squeezing harder this time, before he shoved her backward, he said. "This isn't any of your business, girl." Annabelle stumbled but quickly caught her footing, her defiant glare never wavering. She brushed off her sleeve and stood her ground.

"Ah, but here's the rub," she continued, her voice casual but edged with steel. "This is my business. See, Captain Jack's decided he's done with the sea. He's settin' up shop right here, and this land be *his* territory now. I'm here for his coin." *People this far from the sea always complain that pirates sometimes set up bandit gangs when they can't cut it at sea, so Annabelle decides to use their prejudice and ignorance to her benefit.*

The man's eyes narrowed as her words registered, suspicion and irritation flashing across his face. "Captain Jack, huh? Let me give you a message for your *captain*." he sneered, stepping closer.

Annabelle didn't wait. The moment he was in range, she slipped the anchor from her belt and struck. A rapid series of blows landed on his face, chest, and neck, each strike a practiced movement drilled into her by Captain Kidd. The man staggered, caught off guard by her ferocity, and she finished with a solid kick to his stomach, sending him sprawling onto the dusty ground.

Before he could recover, Annabelle was on him. She pressed a knee into his chest and positioned the anchor beneath his jaw, its sharp edge just grazing his throat. Her eyes blazed with intensity as she leaned in. "Time to pay up," she said, her voice low and deadly.

The man coughed, his defiant glare still intact. "You have no idea who you're messing with," he spat, literally, aiming a wad of saliva at her face in a feeble attempt to regain control.

Annabelle wiped her cheek with the back of her hand, fury flashing in her eyes from the disrespect. "Oh, I gets it just fine," she said coldly, pressing the anchor a fraction deeper into the soft flesh beneath his chin. "But here's what ye don't understand. Yer time's up, mate. The crew of the Sovereign don't take no mess from nobody."

The man's hand shifted subtly, inching toward her weapon. She caught the movement instantly and swatted his hand away with a sharp blow from the anchor. He winced as she leaned in further, her voice dropping to a dangerous whisper.

"Now, if ye want to keep all yer teeth, I suggest ye hand over the coin. And do it quick-like."

His breathing grew labored under the pressure of her knee, his bravado visibly cracking. With a resigned scowl, he reached into his bag and fumbled for the coins.

"That's more like it," Annabelle muttered, her voice tight with contempt.

Reluctantly, the man snatches the leather coin purse from his belt and drops it onto the ground with a growl. "You and your *captain* are going to pay for this," he snarls.

Annabelle presses the anchor slightly deeper against his neck, her eyes steady and cold. "Mate, did ye forget somethin'? That bag there be Captain Jack's crowns. Now, where's mine?"

The man's defiant glare falters as he realizes further resistance is pointless. With a reluctant huff, he pulls out a smaller cloth coin bag and places it beside the leather one.

"There now," Annabelle says with mock cheer. "That's how ye square yer debts." She straightens and steps aside, giving him just enough space to stand. Her voice drops back to a steely tone. "Now be a good lad and tell yer friends this here belongs to Captain Jack."

Grimacing, the collector struggles to his feet, one hand cradling his bruised face. He casts a wary glance over his shoulder as he stumbles toward the neighboring farm's fence. Annabelle offers him a lazy wave, a silent reminder that he no longer matters and she'd be ready to prove it to him again.

As the man slinks away, Annabelle crouches to pick up the bags of coins. Just as her fingers close around the leather bag, the sound of pounding footsteps rushes toward her. She doesn't bother to turn. Instead, she casts the seashell spell; in an instant, a dome of swirling water encircles her. The collector's fist strikes through the barrier, slowed and partially deflected by the rushing current.

"Ye just don't learn, do ye, mate?" Annabelle quips, glancing over her shoulder with an infuriatingly smug grin.

With a fluid gesture, she channels her power, directing the water into a forceful current spell. A column of pressurized liquid slams into the man, sending him crashing into the fence with a satisfying smack. For good measure, Annabelle intensifies the flow, ensuring he's thoroughly drenched and humbled.

She shakes the bags of coins in her hand and calls out, "Don't let me catch ye here again, boyo!"

The man sputters, his clothes soaked and clinging to his frame. Coughing and beaten, he staggers away without another word, though not without one last venomous sneer.

Annabelle dusts off her hands and strides back to the counter. "Bring me that box," she says, her tone gentler now as she gestures toward the makeshift cash register.

The girl, still a bit shaken, retrieves the box and places it on the counter. Annabelle opens the leather coin bag and pours half the contents inside.

"Fer operating expenses," she explains with a wink. Leaning in conspiratorially, she adds, "Find yerself a second box, aye? Keep a few coins in it as a decoy."

The girl nods eagerly. "Okay, I will," she replies, a small smile breaking through her lingering fear.

"Good lass," Annabelle says, then gestures toward the bushel of apples on the counter. "Put that back where it belongs, would ye?"

The girl quickly carries the bushel to the back of the stand. When she returns, Annabelle rests her elbows on the counter, adopting a more thoughtful expression. "How often does the law come out this far?" she asks casually, her eyes scanning the distant horizon.

"The sheriff? Never," the girl replies with a mix of relief and resignation. "He stays in town. We're on our own out here."

"Ye don't say," Annabelle murmurs, filing the information away. She extends a hand with a friendly smile. "Name's Annabelle, and what's yers?"

"My name is Milly," the girl answers, her voice steadier as she shakes Annabelle's hand.

"Pleasure to meet ye, Milly," Annabelle says warmly. "Don't ye worry now. Things'll be different from here on out."

Milly smiles, this time without hesitation. The fear in her eyes is fading.

Annabelle says, "About Captain Jack's payments." With a wink and a toothy grin.

[-----⊙-----]

The trek to the "Wilde Fruit Stand" dragged on, the landscape blurring in the slow march of time. By the time Sophie, Lisa, Regina, and Brother Marcus arrived, the sky was a canvas of amber and gold, shadows stretching long across the fields. They spotted Annabelle lounging by the stand, a large glass of lemonade in hand. She basked in the warm glow of the late afternoon sun, her expression peaceful as she took a slow sip. It was the very image of ease, though the glint in her eye hinted at untold mischief.

Together, the group walked toward a clearing just beyond the stand, their footsteps muffled by the underbrush. In the heart of the clearing stood an ancient wooden structure, weathered but sturdy, its surface adorned with an intricate sun design burned deep into the timber. The craftsmanship bore the mark of an age-old tradition or artisans, lost to time. Inside the wooden structure, a door had been carved directly into the rock face. Stone blocks, each marked with a number, rested in recessed compartments beside the door, as if guarding a forgotten secret.

Lisa approached the wooden enclosure, her gaze tracing the cryptic letters scorched into the timber. She frowned in thought, recognizing the script as old

176

Grantic, a language once spoken by a small Verdantian community before the adoption of the king's English.

"I must be rusty," Lisa murmured, scratching her head in frustration. "This does not make any sense."

"What does it say?" Regina asked, curiosity flickering in her eyes as she glanced between the carved letters and the stone blocks.

Lisa shook her head slowly. "It is tricky. It could mean one of two things, either 'the combination to open the door is the radius of the earth,' or just 'This is not the door.'"

Brother Marcus, standing on the opposite side of the enclosure, spoke up, his voice touched with awe. "Miss Lisa, what's that symbol?" He gestured toward the burned sun emblem, its radiant lines casting faint shadows in the fading light. The design bore an uncanny kinship to the insignia of the Order of Saint Lorraine.

"I do not know, please come have a look at this." Lisa called, her voice echoing slightly within the wooden structure.

Marcus made his way around Regina, offering her a polite nod as he passed. He examined the script closely, the ancient letters stirring memories of his early studies with the Order. "It's been years since I've read Grantic," he admitted, squinting as he tried to decipher the message. "But what does it say?"

Lisa repeated the options, her frustration evident. "Either 'This is not the door' or 'the combination is the earth's radius.' But the phrasing's weird. It does not quite fit."

Marcus's eyes widened slightly with realization. "It means both."

"Both? How could that even work?" Lisa asked, her voice edged with impatience.

"It's a cipher," Marcus explained, his tone shifting to that of a teacher. "We use a similar method in the Order. Brother Albert must have figured it out when he found this place as well."

Sophie, who had been quietly listening, crossed her arms and frowned. "So, this is an Order facility?"

"I don't believe so," Marcus replied somberly. "If it were, Sister Alameda and I would have found records of it in Brother Albert's reports."

"But someone's using your cipher," Sophie pressed, suspicion sharpening her voice.

"It is… unusual," Marcus admitted. "First question, does anyone here know the earth's radius offhand?"

"Six thousand three hundred seventy-eight kilometers." Regina answered promptly.

Annabelle blinked in surprise. "Girlie, how do ye know that?"

Regina shrugged, her voice calm and matter-of-fact. "You need to know the earth's radius and circumference to perform certain rituals, like opening portals."

Marcus's mind flashed to a haunting memory: Regina lying on the ground, injured and screaming in pain after forcing Hema, the Blood Witch, through a portal to the tallest mountain in Stoneridge. The image lingered, a chilling reminder of her hidden strength.

Clearing his throat, Marcus refocused on the puzzle. His gaze travelled to the numbered blocks embedded in the stone wall. "It looks like these blocks are meant to input the combination," he observed.

Without hesitation, Regina stepped forward. She selected the blocks marked six, three, seven, and eight, pressing them into the door's recessed shelves. Each block clicked into place with a firm, mechanical sound.

The stone blocks click into place but nothing happens. The group watched in tense silence, waiting to see what if anything would happen.

"It cannot be that easy," Lisa muttered, her skepticism evident as she eyed the mechanism. "Why would they carve three separate sections for the numbers if they only intended for someone to use the top one?"

Annabelle tilted her head, considering the setup. "Well, the radius of a circle is the distance from the center to the edge, right? Maybe we ought to try the middle row," she suggested, though uncertainty laced her voice. The group turned to look at her in mild surprise, prompting her to shift awkwardly. "What?" she added defensively.

Marcus chuckled warmly. "Miss Salazar, you do have a knack for the unexpected."

Encouraged, Regina removed the blocks from the top shelf and repositioned them in the middle row. Each block slid into place with a soft click. This time, when she pressed the sequence in, a deeper, more deliberate click echoed from within the rock face, suggesting progress. Yet, despite the sound, the door remained inert.

"So... this still isn't the door," Sophie sighed, her frustration creeping into her voice. She glanced around the clearing, tension simmering beneath her composed exterior. "So where is it?"

"That would be the question." Lisa mused aloud, her gaze sweeping over the ancient structure and the surrounding woods.

"Oi! Brother Marcus!" Annabelle called, her voice breaking the contemplative silence. "If you were the one building this, where would ye hide the door?"

Marcus exhaled thoughtfully, rubbing his chin. "That is precisely what I've been pondering. And there's another question that haunts me, why choose the earth's radius? They could have selected any significant number. Why six thousand three hundred seventy eight kilometers?"

Meanwhile, Sophie retrieved a small notepad and jotted down the number "6378." She stared at it intently, as if the digits might rearrange themselves into a solution. Muttering under her breath, she asked herself, "What are they trying to tell me?" Noticing Annabelle looking distant, Sophie decided to rope her in. "Annabelle, got any ideas?"

"Huh?" Annabelle blinked, snapping back to the present. "What're ye askin', Copper?"

Sophie gestured toward the note. "We're trying to find the real door. The only clue we have is this number."

Annabelle approached, hand outstretched. "Lemme see that paper of yers," she said. Sophie handed it over, watching as Annabelle studied the digits with a navigator's focus. Annabelle's eyes lit up suddenly, and a grin broke across her face.

"I think I've got it," she declared, tapping the paper with newfound enthusiasm.

"What do you mean?" Lisa asked, leaning closer. Regina also looked up from her deep thoughts, curiosity piqued.

"Me dear Lisa," Annabelle began, her excitement mounting, "on a ship, when you chart a course, ye need two pieces of information: azimuth and distance. I don't think the number is six thousand three hundred seventy-eight. Look at it as two separate values: *sixty-three* and *seventy-eight*." She pointed at the digits. "Turn sixty-three degrees, then travel seventy-eight... something?"

"Kilometers?" Regina raised an eyebrow. "That seems a bit much. We'd be halfway across the region."

Sophie nodded in agreement. "Yeah, a nearly hundred kilometers is impractical I think. The mechanism wouldn't make sense if the door were that far away."

"What about paces?" Lisa suggested. "You could measure that without tools."

Regina's eyes narrowed as she contemplated the arrangement of the puzzle. She studied the symbols on the wooden structure and the positioning of the false door, reasoning through the puzzle's design. "The creators would have assumed anyone solving this would face the door when beginning," she concluded. She raised her hand and pointed toward the faux door. "We should start in that direction."

"Alright," Sophie said, pulling a small compass from her jacket. She aligned the dial with sixty-three degrees and pointed forward with confidence. "That way."

With renewed purpose, the group prepared to follow the heading, the ancient puzzle slowly yielding its secrets one step at a time.

The group set off in the direction Sophie indicated, Marcus moving ahead while she stayed back to check her compass at intervals, ensuring their path remained steady.

Annabelle initially took the lead, striding forward with her usual confidence. But after a few course corrections from Sophie, who pointed out that she was drifting off the path, Annabelle huffed in annoyance and ceded the lead to Regina. "Fine, Copper, ye steer the ship," she muttered, rolling her eyes as she fell back in line.

Their journey eventually brought them to a secluded cabin deep in the woods, hidden beneath a canopy of thick trees and overgrown shrubbery. It would have been easy to miss had they not been specifically searching for it. The door creaked ominously as they pushed it open, revealing an interior shrouded in years of neglect. Dust blanketed every surface, and cobwebs clung to the corners like spectral veils.

"Oh, goodness," Lisa groaned, covering her mouth and nose. "Please tell me this is not where we are supposed to be."

"This place is..." Sophie wrinkled her nose, scanning the decrepit surroundings, "...challenging."

"Unfortunately, ladies," Marcus said with a resigned sigh, "I believe this is our destination."

They cautiously moved through the dim cabin, their footsteps stirring motes of dust in the stagnant air. Regina paused, closing her eyes to maybe extend her Earthbloom senses She had been training to sharpen this ability, but it was still an unpredictable skill. As she reached out with her mana, a surge of overwhelming input slammed into her mind, causing a sharp, stinging backlash in her chest. She winced, gasping as she stumbled slightly.

"Why are you so determined to hurt yourself?" Lisa scolded gently, though there was admiration hidden beneath her concern.

Regina grit her teeth, catching her breath. "There's... something back there," she managed to say, gesturing weakly toward the rear of the cabin.

Annabelle quickly stepped to her side and offered an arm, steadying her friend. "Oi, Missy, that Earthbloomer magic of yers must be somethin' else," she teased lightly, hoping to lift Regina's spirits.

"I almost had it," Regina muttered, frustrated by her faltering control. She was determined to master this ability, setbacks or not.

Marcus glanced toward Lisa and whispered. "Miss Lisa, why is she struggling with such intense reactions to Earthbloom magic? Shouldn't it be easier by now?"

Lisa sighed and gave Regina a knowing look. "She is rushing it. the sense is a passive spell, but Regina is forcing it like an active one. That is why she's getting backlash."

As they approached a dusty dining area with a long table, Lisa made a face of pure disgust at the thick cobwebs draped across its surface. "Ugh. No! I am not touching any of that."

While the others inspected the room, Sophie's gaze fell on the floor beneath the table. Something seemed off. The rug in that area was noticeably cleaner than the rest of the cabin's filthy floor. "Hmm..." she mused, slipping on a pair of inspection glasses from her jacket. Through the enhanced lenses, she spotted a faint mana trail leading to the rug. "What do we have here?" she mused aloud. Without hesitation, she yanked the rug aside, revealing a trapdoor concealed beneath it. "I think this might be what we're looking for."

"No, no, no," Lisa protested, stepping back with a look of horror. "I am not crawling down there."

"Sounds good," Sophie replied cheerfully. "Someone should keep watch, anyway." Before Lisa could protest further, Sophie spotted a ladder leading down into the darkness and ducked beneath the table, beginning her descent.

"Aye, girlie, ye keep watch," Annabelle chimed in, grinning as she followed Sophie under the table. Meanwhile, Regina, feeling steadier, took a deep breath and focused on shaking off the last remnants of mana backlash.

Sophie carefully climbed down the ladder, her feet feeling for each rung as the darkness swallowed her. When she reached the bottom, she extended her hands, probing the void around her. "Be careful, it's pitch black down here," she called up, her voice echoing faintly.

Annabelle soon joined her, fishing a rock shaker tube from her jacket. With a few brisk shakes, the tube's stones began to glow with an eerie green light, casting spectral shadows across the chamber walls. The glow revealed a torch mounted on the wall just out of Sophie's reach.

"Hold on," Sophie said, stretching to grab the torch. Her fingers brushed the head of the torch, and she noticed it was still wet with oil. "Lucky break," she muttered, pulling out her flint striker. Sparks flew, and after a few blows, the oil caught flame. A warm glow replaced the cold green light, revealing more details of the hidden chamber.

Regina climbed down next, joining the others as they cautiously advanced down a narrow corridor. Their footsteps echoed softly as they moved deeper into the underground space. The passage opened into a large room filled with cluttered tables. Papers and books lay strewn across the surfaces in chaotic disarray. Along the walls, rows of bookcases housed dusty books, and several green chalkboards displayed a mix of diagrams, calculations, and scribbled notes.

Six doors lined the perimeter of the room, each bearing the symbol of the black sun burned into the wood. Words in the ancient Grantic script were etched below each sun emblem, their meanings obscured by time and language. As Sophie and Annabelle shifted their lights around the room, the interplay of flickering shadows heightened the eerie atmosphere. The girls exchanged glances, each silently acknowledging the gravity of the discovery before them.

Marcus descended the ladder into darkness, his footsteps echoing softly. The dim light from Sophie's torch and Annabelle's glowing shaker cast long, shifting shadows that gave the underground chamber an eerie atmosphere. As he stepped fully into the room, he took in the sight of the cluttered tables and chalkboards.

"What have we found, ladies?" he asked, his voice tinged with awe and curiosity.

"Not sure," Sophie replied, holding her torch higher to survey the scene. The firelight revealed a chaotic array of papers and books strewn across a large circular table. "Looks like some kind of classroom."

"I don't think so," Regina countered, gesturing toward a chalkboard. "It's more like a research room. I need more light here."

Sophie moved closer, raising the torch to illuminate the board. Regina pointed to a series of equations and diagrams. "See this? Someone was working on something they couldn't quite figure out."

Marcus studied the setup, his expression thoughtful. "There are rooms like this on Order Island," he said, nostalgia creeping into his voice. "Sister Sallie does her research in a similar space."

"Yeah, I remember," Regina said, her voice soft, as if the familiarity of the scene tugged at something within her.

Sophie's gaze sharpened. "*Just like on Order Island.*" she muttered, suspicion tightening her tone.

Marcus nodded slowly, his brow furrowed in thought. "I can't deny the similarities. If this was an Order facility, though, there should be a way to properly light the room. They wouldn't rely solely on torches, it's too impractical for detailed work."

His observation spurred the group into action. They spread out to search for anything that might activate a lighting system. In the dim glow of Annabelle's rock shaker, Regina noticed a crank near the entrance. She traced a cable running from the crank up into a conduit in the ceiling, which appeared to connect to hidden mechanisms.

"Worth a shot." Regina said, exchanging a glance with Annabelle before grasping the crank and turning it. As she wound the cord around the spool, a series of mirrored panels in the ceiling slid open. Sunlight, redirected through a series of glass reflectors, poured into the room. The sudden flood of warm light transformed the space, revealing its contents with startling clarity.

The central table was covered with open journals, diagrams, and annotated sketches. Despite the dusty cabin above, this room appeared well-maintained, a hidden sanctuary for serious research.

With the main room fully illuminated, the group split up to explore the adjoining chambers. Sophie entered the first room on her left and found shelves lined with empty glass jars, each marked with a numerical code similar to the blocks they had seen at the cabin door. She examined them, puzzled by their meticulous organization. "Serial numbers." she murmured, though the jars' exact purpose remained unclear.

Annabelle wandered into a stark, sterile room. At its center stood a gurney table, and the surrounding countertops gleamed with cleanliness. A tall glass cabinet on the far wall stood empty. The scene reminded her of the sick bay on the Stormfang, where Gary kept supplies meticulously stocked. But here, everything was bare. Annabelle frowned. *Does their doctor bring his own supplies?* She wondered.

181

Marcus, meanwhile, discovered another room that sent a chill down his spine. Like Annabelle's room, it featured a gurney, but the countertops here held jars filled with organs suspended in a strange yellow liquid. The Grantic labels on the jars hinted at organized research, grim research. Marcus's jaw tightened. He had seen rooms like this before, facilities dedicated to experiments too horrific to be spoken of openly. He exhaled slowly, steadying himself as he grappled with the implications.

Regina entered a room that resembled a laboratory. A large table in the center held a machine with a viewing aperture at the top. Beside it was another device, partially filled with water, designed to separate materials through heat. Shelves lined with jugs of water suggested routine use, though for what purpose, she couldn't be sure. It reminded her of equipment used for mineral analysis or botanical studies in school.

The four reconvened in the main room, just as Lisa appeared from the ladder hallway.

"Oi, ye were supposed to keep watch, girlie," Annabelle teased with a grin.

Lisa's eyes narrowed, her green hair practically bristling with indignation. "I should go back upstairs." she shot back, crossing her arms.

"Relax," Sophie interjected with a chuckle. "She probably just got lonely."

"Hmph," Lisa huffed, though a faint smile tugged at the corner of her lips. She turned away from the ladder, clearly unwilling to return to the grimy cabin above. "So, what did you find?" she asked, eager to shift focus.

Sophie was the first to respond. "A storage room full of jars with numbers."

"Found an empty sick room," Annabelle added. "Clean as a whistle, but no supplies."

Regina spoke next, her tone thoughtful. "Mine looked like a lab. There's equipment for processing materials, but I don't know what exactly they were studying. Maybe plants, rocks... or animals." She paused, her gaze distant. "But why go to the trouble of building all of this underground?"

The question hung in the air like a shadow, each of them silently contemplating the hidden purpose of the facility.

Marcus took a deep breath, his expression heavy with the weight of grim knowledge. "I think I know why this place is underground," he began, drawing the group's full attention. "In the room I checked... there were jars. Organs preserved in some kind of solution." His voice grew quieter, shadowed by painful memories. "I've seen facilities like this before, though not hidden like this. Whoever operated here... they were experimenting on people, extracting organs, probably searching for something inside their bodies." He gestured toward the cluttered table in front of them. "All of this may tell us what they were looking for."

Sophie swallowed hard, then spoke with resolve. "Let's see what's on the table." The group gathered around, the musty scent of aged paper and ink mingling with their growing apprehension. They began sifting through the documents, each member hoping to uncover clues to the facility's dark purpose.

Regina flipped through a stack of pages, her mind half-focused until a drawing caught her eye. Her hands froze, the world tilting as recognition washed over her. It was a crude yet familiar sketch, two figures, a boy and his father, standing under a tree. It mirrored her little brother Mattie's style exactly. Below it, the caption read: _Matthew Fournier, April 23, 1910._

Her heart clenched tight. Tears blurred her vision as she whispered, "Oh no... no, no, no." The memories came crashing down. Just a year ago, Mattie had taken pride in signing his drawings after an art exhibit their father had brought them to. He had called them his *portfolio*. Now, that same signature was staring back at her like a cruel specter of fate.

"We missed them..." Regina choked out, her voice trembling with grief. Tears streamed freely as sobs wracked her body. "If we hadn't wasted time at that stupid party..."

Marcus quickly moved to her side, his gaze scanning the date and name on the paper. He placed a comforting hand on her shoulder. "Miss Fournier, I am so sorry. We couldn't have known."

"Known what?" Sophie asked, alarmed by Regina's sudden breakdown.

Marcus turned to face her, his expression grave. "Based on the date on this drawing, her stepbrother was here... just two days ago."

"What!?" Sophie's voice was sharp with disbelief.

"No way." Annabelle muttered, her face a mix of shock and confusion.

"But how?" Lisa whispered, covering her mouth as her wide eyes reflected her horror.

Regina's anguish erupted into a piercing scream. "**THEY WERE HERE!**" she cried. "**THEY WERE HERE AND WE WASTED TIME AT A PARTY!**" Her voice echoed, raw with guilt and rage.

Sophie hurriedly slipped on her inspection glasses, her hands shaking as she scanned the room. The lenses revealed faint trails of heat and mana converging on one of the unexplored doors. "There's a trail," she announced, her voice trembling with a fragile blend of hope and urgency. "Someone might have been here yesterday."

Annabelle wrapped her arms around Regina, pulling her into a tight embrace. "It'll be okay, Missy," she murmured gently. "We'll find them."

Regina sobbed into Annabelle's shoulder, her mind racing with desperation. But the thought that her family might still be within reach ignited a spark of resolve. She pulled away, wiping her face roughly with her sleeve. Taking a deep breath, she summoned more mana than she had ever dared before. Her Earthbloom sense flared to life, expanding outward in waves as she sought out any trace of her family.

"Regina, stop!" Lisa shouted, panic surging in her voice. "You are going to hurt yourself!"

But Regina wouldn't listen to her. She pushed her senses further, feeling the echoes of life around her, Marcus and her companions, the bustling workers near the fruit stand, and the subtle vibrations of the natural world. Trees, crops, animals, and roots all became vivid impressions in her mind. Yet, there was no sign of Matthew or Jules.

Desperation clawed at her. She drew in more mana, her senses straining under the intensity. Every heartbeat pulsed like a drum in her ears. Still... nothing.

Suddenly, her body jerked backward as Lisa grabbed her and shook her firmly. "**Stop it!**" Lisa commanded, her voice sharp and trembling. "You won't find them if you kill yourself!"

Regina gasped, tears streaming anew as exhaustion and grief overwhelmed her. "I have to find them," she whimpered, collapsing into Lisa's support. Fresh sobs wracked her as she crumpled under the emotional weight.

Lisa held her steady, her grip firm yet gentle. "We will," she whispered fiercely. "But you cannot do it like this. We will figure it out. *Together.*"

The room fell into a tense silence, broken only by Regina's quiet sobs. One by one, the others closed in around her, their presence a silent vow of solidarity. They would not let this darkness swallow her family.

Chapter 13

Journal Entry: April 24, 1910

Today's discoveries at the hidden facility hinted at by Brother Albert have unveiled unexpected twists. The most shocking being that Matthew Fournier and most likely Jules Fournier had indeed been brought to this very place, only to vanish just before our arrival. In their wake, Sophie Griffin and Annabelle Salazar are now combing through the remnants of their presence, eager to find any trace that might lead us towards the conspiracy.

The facility itself bears the hallmarks of a sinister laboratory, designed with the intention of human experimentation. While the purpose of their research eludes us still, I am confident that unlocking these secrets will expose the true objectives of the conspiracy, particularly their reasons behind the abductions of Jules and Matthew Fournier.

In a parallel effort, Regina Fournier and Lisa Nozaki are meticulously sifting through the documents we've found. Each document holds the potential to reveal the conspiracy's forthcoming moves or the destinations they might be headed towards.

Amidst these investigations, I stumbled upon an insignia that closely resembles that of the Order of Saint Lorriane. It's increasingly clear that the Black Sun organization not only mimics our Order in appearance but also adopts similar practices and strategies. This unsettling discovery suggests they might have once been among us or have had access to our doctrinal texts. Below is a sketch of the emblem, a testament to their eerie familiarity with our ways.

[Sketch of the Black Sun Insignia]

Sophie adjusted her inspection glasses, the lenses glowing faintly as they picked up dissipated traces of mana and heat. The trails wove between trees and bushes like ghostly threads, guiding her through the forest. Annabelle followed close behind, scanning their surroundings with sharp, curious eyes.

"The trail's getting stronger," Sophie said to herself, noting the denser concentrations of mana ahead. It was a good sign, they are heading in the right direction.

Soon, Sophie spotted a narrow path worn through the undergrowth. "This must be the route to their hidden facility," she murmured, leading the way down the trail. Eventually, the trees opened up into a large clearing where devastation greeted them, entire trees lay crushed and shattered across the ground.

Sophie adjusted her glasses, focusing on the center of the clearing. A thick, swirling residue of mana hovered over the wreckage, evidence of a powerful ritual's aftermath. She picked up a rock and hurled it into the clearing. It sailed through the air before landing with a dull thud atop the crushed trees. No hidden barrier revealed itself.

Annabelle grinned mischievously, scooping up a handful of stones. "Guess it's time to have some fun." She flung the rocks in various directions, her laughter breaking the eerie quiet.

"What are you doing?" Sophie asked, eyebrow raised.

"Throwing rocks, obviously," Annabelle replied between tosses. "What were you doing?"

"Checking for something in a cloaking spell," Sophie answered. "But I didn't find anything. You're just..."

"Having a rock-throwing contest with meself," Annabelle finished with a smirk, launching another stone.

Following her investigative training, Sophie shook her head and began pacing the perimeter of the clearing. As she studied the surroundings, a pattern emerged: the trees at the edges had been cut down cleanly, unlike those crushed at the center. There was no residual mana on the stumps, indicating they'd been felled by mundane means, tools or elemental magic that dissipated quickly.

Her steps brought her to a large dirt mound, taller than herself. The reek hit her instantly, the unmistakable stench of waste and decay. She gagged and covered her nose with her sleeve. It was a trash and latrine pit, no doubt dug by hand. Wheel tracks and drag marks leading to and from the mound provided additional evidence of manual labor.

Sophie turned back to the clearing, her gaze thoughtful. This was more than just the aftermath of a single event. "Someone set up camp here," she murmured, "but what kind of structure did they build... and how was it dismantled?"

Annabelle's voice broke her thoughts. "Find anything cool, Copper?"

"Just a mound of stink," Sophie said, still analyzing the scene. "But I'll figure out the rest soon enough."

[----- ✿ -----]

In the facility, Regina skimmed through one of the journals on the table, ignoring Lisa and Marcus as she focused intently on the text. The entries described a series of experiments aimed at extracting mana from a subject. The author had initially tested on cadavers, something the author confirmed as a doomed approach. After numerous failed attempts, the author concluded that mana could not be extracted from a dead body. Frustrated, they ordered their "local servants" to procure live subjects for further testing.

The first subject was an old man whom the servants had found at night. According to the journal, the man reported being sixty years old. His appearance was described as grizzled and unkempt. During the intake interview, he explained that he had been expelled from a local community workhouse for being too old to work and had been living in the forest while searching for another place to stay. The author designated him as Subject 27207. After the intake, the author used a suspension ritual to freeze the man's bodily functions in time.

The author then began a vivisection, seeking to identify where mana was generated and stored within the body. Although it was commonly believed that mana resided in the heart, the author disregarded such assumptions and conducted the study from scratch. Using a tool referred to as a "peering scope," the author examined the subject's opened body but found no evidence that the heart played any role in producing or storing mana. The journal noted that due to Subject 27207's advanced age, his mana levels were likely too diminished to draw any meaningful conclusions. Ultimately, the author removed the man's organs, preserved them in liquid, and cataloged the jars for further study.

The following entry detailed the author's growing frustration with the local servants, who were ordered to obtain a younger subject. The author noted their complaints and suggested they should be disciplined by "The Order" at a later time. Another entry described continued analysis of Subject 27207's organs, which revealed no traces of mana. The author theorized that mana could not exist outside a living body but admitted that the lack of mana in the old man's remains made it difficult to verify this hypothesis.

The following journal entry expressed the author's irritation over the local servants' continued delay in acquiring a younger subject. They strongly suggested that "The Order" replace the current servants due to their incompetence. Eventually, however, the servants delivered a new subject, a man who claimed to be thirty years old. During the intake interview, Subject 27208 revealed that he was a worker from the Umbrathorn Empire who had travelled to Verdantia to learn skills and earn money to bring back to his home kingdom. This man was far more physically capable than Subject 27207, to the point that the author had to use both restraints and magic to subdue him. The author expressed frustration with the subject's refusal to accept that the experiments were intended for study rather than harm.

Despite the initial difficulties, the author was pleased with Subject 27208's physical condition. Preliminary tests confirmed that his healthier body produced a far greater amount of mana. After performing a subduing ritual, the author placed the subject under the suspension spell, which slowed time to a near standstill. During the vivisection, the author observed through the peering scope that mana flowed through the heart, but originated in the pancreas and was stored in the liver. The discovery was recorded alongside detailed diagrams of the organs, mapping the flow and production of mana in different colors. Regina could sense the author's

187

pride in this breakthrough, as they noted that few in "The Order of the Black Sun" had the determination to make such a discovery.

The following entry documented the author's efforts to extract mana from the subject's body. They gathered needles made from a variety of materials: wood, iron, aluminum, glass, lead, nickel, and more. A local servant assisted by holding the peering scope while the author began with a wooden needle, pricking the subject's liver. The result was minimal, only a small puncture with no mana extraction. The author meticulously repeated the test with each needle, encountering the same failure until they reached chromium. When the chromium needle pierced the liver, mana surged into the metal, causing it to heat rapidly. The author described how the needle became too hot to handle, melting through their gloves. they needed pliers to remove the needle safely.

Once removed, the mana dissipated quickly, the glow vanishing before the author could examine it further. The experiment led them to conclude that chromium could temporarily conduct mana but could not store it. To verify the findings, the author repeated the test using a titanium needle, which yielded no results. Further tests on the pancreas showed that none of the materials could draw mana from the organ, supporting the theory that the pancreas was solely responsible for creating mana and did not store it.

As the suspension ritual's timer neared its end, the author prepared to remove the subject's organs for study. Before beginning the procedure, they ordered the local servants to acquire another subject. However, the head servant objected, warning that further abductions might draw the attention of the local sheriff. The author, increasingly irritated, dismissed the concerns and commanded them to find a solution before returning to the task at hand.

In the next entry, the author noted that once the liver was removed from the body and the suspension ritual ended, the mana within it quickly dissipated, making mana harvesting from the organ impossible. They concluded that mana could not be extracted from the liver outside of a living body. Since the liver lost mana so rapidly, any effective mana extraction would require keeping the subject alive, either through a suspension ritual or by carefully accessing the liver without killing the subject. Further tests on other organs confirmed that none contained any residual traces of mana.

In the following entry, the author recounted having an epiphany over breakfast. Since Blood contained iron, they theorized that a vessel constructed from a specific composite of iron might be capable of storing extracted mana. As the local servants took their time procuring another subject, the author focused on designing prototypes. They planned to create multiple iron-nickel composite bottles, each fitted with a chromium needle at the mouth to channel mana into the vessel.

The journal detailed the construction of seven such prototypes. However, a local servant questioned how the author would verify whether the bottles successfully stored mana. When the author explained their intention to use the peering scope for this task, the servant warned that the method might not work. The author expressed their growing frustration, accusing the servants of obstructing progress on the goals established by the Black Sun elders. They then ordered the servants to hasten the acquisition of another subject, sharply rebuking them for the delays. The entry concluded with the author expressing their intention to express dissatisfaction with the local staff to an official during an upcoming meeting.

In the next entry, the local servants delivered a new subject, a twenty-four-year-old woman with fair skin and golden blonde hair, features typical of the Kingdom of Stoneridge. During the intake interview, she explained that she had come to Verdantia to work as a nanny for a wealthy family. The author labelled her as Subject 27209. They noted that while the woman had a persistent cough from a childhood bout with scarlet fever, she was otherwise healthy. However, the author expressed irritation with her constant crying, which hindered the intake process. When instructed to disrobe, Subject 27209 threw herself to the floor, refusing to cooperate. The author resorted to using a compliance ritual, which consumed a significant amount of mana just to force her onto the table. The mana expenditure delayed the casting of the suspension ritual, prompting the author to order the servants to prepare ember root tea to speed up their mana recovery.

The entry then described the author's tests on the vessels designed to store mana. The first vessel, made from an iron-lead composite, allowed mana to flow from the subject's liver but failed to contain it. The mana escaped almost immediately as glowing particles. The second vessel, composed of an iron-nickel alloy, produced the same result, with mana particles leaking out in a shimmering wash.

The third vessel, made from an equal mix of iron and titanium, initially succeeded in containing the mana. However, after prolonged extraction, the particles began to escape at a slower rate than before. The fourth vessel, composed of ten percent iron and ninety percent tin, failed spectacularly—the mana surged out in a brilliant torrent of rainbow-colored particles almost as soon as it entered the container.

The fifth vessel, containing forty percent iron and sixty percent copper, showed promise. It successfully held the mana without any visible leakage at first, but after accumulating a large amount of mana, the vessel exploded, tearing open from the side. Despite the failure, the author saw this as confirmation that a copper-iron alloy could be the key to success.

The sixth vessel, made of forty percent iron and sixty percent aluminum, failed outright, with mana particles escaping rapidly through the joint between the needle and the ship. The seventh and final vessel, made from sixty percent iron and forty percent chromium, captured a significant amount of mana but ultimately burst apart under the strain, leaving only shattered pieces behind.

The author concluded the entry by noting plans to create a new series of vessels with varying concentrations of iron, Copper, chromium, and titanium alloys for their next round of experiments.

In the following entry, the author described their efforts, with the help of a few local servants, to construct seven new vessels made from various composite alloys of iron, Copper, chromium, and tin. The breakdowns were as follows:

-Vessel 1: 50% iron, 30% copper, 10% chromium, 10% tin
-Vessel 2: 40% iron, 20% copper, 20% chromium, 20% tin
-Vessel 3: 60% iron, 20% copper, 10% chromium, 10% tin
-Vessel 4: 40% iron, 30% copper, 10% chromium, 20% tin
-Vessel 5: 50% iron, 10% copper, 10% chromium, 30% tin
-Vessel 6: 50% iron, 30% copper, 10% chromium, 10% tin
-Vessel 7: 40% iron, 50% copper, 5% chromium, 5% tin

The author also noted a confrontation with the leader of the local servants, who firmly refused to gather any more subjects for at least a fortnight. The leader explained that the local sheriff had begun investigating the disappearances in the neighboring town. Frustrated, the author recorded their belief that the servants needed "retraining." The situation escalated when the author suggested abducting the sheriff as a subject, only for the servant leader to flatly refuse and walk away without further discussion.

With no immediate access to new subjects, the author used their downtime to review their findings. They concluded that younger subjects had a much higher capacity for mana storage in the liver. Based on this, the author proposed setting an age limit for future subjects, ideally between ten and twelve years old. They also expressed concern that the facility's official inspection might occur before the vessel tests were completed, placing the blame squarely on the uncooperative servants.

Convinced they were close to a breakthrough, the author approached the servant leader once more, suggesting alternative methods to obtain another subject— perhaps from a nearby town or through a deceptive scheme. However, the servant leader refused to entertain any of these ideas. The author's frustration mounted, and they vowed to push for the replacement of the entire servant staff, whose resistance was hindering their progress.

The entry ended with the author expressing outrage when one of the lower-ranked servants suggested developing a way to measure the mana stored in the vessels. The author took this as an insult, believing the servant had no understanding of the research's priorities and undermined the importance of their work.

In the next entry, the author recounted a trip to town to gather provisions. While there, they observed numerous potential subjects and saw no sign of the sheriff or his deputies investigating any disappearances. There were no missing-person posters or any indications of concern. Convinced that the local servants had lied about the situation, the author became certain that the servants were deliberately sabotaging their project's goals.

The following entry chronicled a confrontation between the author and the local servants. The author accused them of fabricating the story about the sheriff's investigation. In response, the servants reprimanded the author for speaking with townsfolk and potentially drawing unwanted attention. Enraged by their defiance, the author invoked a disciplinary ritual referred to as "the follower" to assert dominance over the staff. Despite this, the servants refused to procure any more subjects until after the official's upcoming visit.

Determined to continue their research without further delays, the author documented their decision to take matters into their own hands. Around dusk, they ventured out and encountered a young girl with red hair. Using a compliance ritual, they compelled her to follow them back to the facility. During the intake interview, the author learned that the girl, now labelled Subject 27210, was nine years old and came from a local farming family.

As the author began casting the suspension ritual on the girl, something extraordinary occurred. She spoke in a voice that was not her own, otherworldly and filled with authority. The voice questioned the author, asking what they hoped to accomplish with their experiments. The author, shaken but resolute, chose not to engage and proceeded to place the girl under the suspension spell. Regina feels a pang of sadness run through her chest. Somehow, she knows that the red-haired girl was a chosen avatar of the goddess of creativity, taken from the world before she could commune with her goddess.

The experiments that followed tested the seven newly constructed vessels. The results were largely disappointing. Vessels one, three, and five failed immediately, releasing mana particles in a burst of rainbow-colored light. Vessel two initially held a significant amount of mana but began to slowly leak particles, prompting the author to conclude that the alloy was inadequate despite it being airtight. Vessel four also showed early promise but eventually crumbled into dust as the mana broke down the alloy.

Vessel six shattered in the author's hand during the filling process, further proving its instability. However, vessel seven was a success. It flawlessly contained the mana particles without leakage or structural damage. The author expressed satisfaction but lamented the lack of time to craft additional vessels, realizing that this breakthrough could have advanced their work considerably if not for the many setbacks they had faced.

In the final journal entry, the author expressed anticipation for the upcoming visit from the official representative of the Order's leadership. They were eager to showcase the significant accomplishments achieved during their time at the facility. The author also made it clear that they intended to report the constant interference and insubordination from the local support staff, ensuring that those responsible would be held accountable for their lack of loyalty to the Order's vision. Swearing "soon all in the Order will come to honor the name Neptune."

[-----✿-----]

Regina looked up from the journal, finally noticing that Sophie and Annabelle had returned.

"There was some kind of structure out there," Sophie began.

"Out where?" Regina asked, blinking in confusion.

Sophie paused, frowning slightly. She had already explained what they found, a site almost a king's journey away. Wasn't Regina paying attention while reading? "The clearing. About a king's journey from here," Sophie clarified.

Marcus, noticing Regina's disorientation, stepped in. "Miss Sophie and Annabelle found a clearing with what looks like the footprint of a large building or vehicle. Something rectangular left a deep impression in the ground."

Annabelle tapped Sophie on the arm and chuckled. "Don't fret, Copper. She's like that when she's readin'. Ye can't tell her a thing, her mind's somewhere else entirely."

"The real question is, where did they go next?" Lisa mused aloud.

"I didn't see any clues at the clearing," Sophie admitted. "But it was obvious a small-to-medium-sized group lived there. If we ask around, we might learn something useful."

"But why this place?" Marcus wondered. "What was in this facility that the conspiracy needed? What were they trying to accomplish here?"

"Research," Regina answered bluntly, tapping the journal she'd just finished. "They were researching how to extract and store mana from the human body."

"That explains the organs in the storage room," Marcus said, glancing toward one of the facility's doors. A quick look at his watch showed it was six o'clock. With the sun due to set in an hour, he turned to the group. "Ladies, I think we should wrap this up for now. Let's head out before nightfall."

"Good idea," Lisa agreed.

"I'm staying," Regina said firmly.

Marcus hesitated. "Miss Fournier, we don't know if this place will be safe after dark. I don't think spending the night here is a good idea."

"Then don't," Regina replied glibly. "I'll see you in the morning."

"Regina, girl," Sophie spoke gently, stepping forward. "This could take days. If we push too hard, we might miss something important."

"They were just here." Regina countered, her voice tightening with emotion. "If we wait too long, we could lose them forever."

"Miss Fournier, I implore you, let's leave this until morning," Marcus urged again, his tone cautious but sincere.

"I don't have to do what you say," Regina snapped, frustration boiling over. "I don't have to do what any of you say!" Her eyes blazed as she pointed toward the door. "Go or stay, I don't care. But I am staying here until I FIND MY FATHER!"

"Missy, we're just sayin'…" Annabelle began.

"I don't care!" Regina shouted, cutting her off. "We're wasting time while those people still have my family!"

With a huff, she stood abruptly, knocking her chair to the floor. Without another word, she stormed toward the bookcases at the back of the room, her movements sharp with frustration.

Lisa sighed, exchanging glances with the others. "I will stay with her," she offered, hoping to ease the tension.

"I will as well," Marcus added. "I'll do what I can to assist Miss Regina." He turned to Sophie and Annabelle, both still processing Regina's outburst. "Ladies, will you be all right at the inn on your own tonight?"

"Aye," Annabelle replied softly, still stunned. She stared after Regina, as if seeing a side of her she hadn't known before.

"Shouldn't be a problem," Sophie said with a nod. "We'll head back in the morning. I want to talk to the sheriff and see if there's anything he knows about this group." She gave Annabelle a light tap on the shoulder. "Come on."

With that, the two young women climbed the ladder and made their way outside, heading toward Sophie's horse Kicker.

[-----✚-----]

The next morning, Sophie decided to handle her training alone since Regina was *occupied*. As she ran through the town, she mentally reviewed the information they had gathered the previous day. Her plan was to speak with the sheriff and see if he knew anything about the group that had recently come through town. If she were polite enough, he might share something useful, especially since the Aurorium clan had no official relationship with Verdantia's law enforcement.

After a hotel breakfast and a quick shower, Sophie dressed in her plain clothes uniform, pants, a vest, a tie, and her signature hat, minus her Aurorium Sentinel badge of course. As she descended the stairs into the lobby, she spotted Annabelle gazing out at the street, her eyes alert and searching.

"Looking for a date?" Sophie teased as she approached.

192

"Huh?" Annabelle blinked, startled by the question.

"What are you looking for?" Sophie asked, stepping closer.

"Oh, ye know... people watching us," Annabelle lied casually. "Maybe we can catch one of those conspirators keeping an eye on us."

Sophie raised an eyebrow, knowing full well Annabelle wasn't telling the truth. Still, she didn't want to start an argument first thing in the morning. "Good thinking," she replied smoothly.

Annabelle grinned and tousled her messy hair. "So, Copper, where are we headed?"

"I was thinking," Sophie began, "a vehicle that large would have to be for a sizeable group. I want to see if the sheriff can tell us if any strangers passed through town recently and aren't around anymore."

Annabelle shrugged. "Sounds like a solid Copper's plan."

"How's that?" Sophie asked.

"Nothin'," Annabelle said with a dismissive wave. "lead the way, Copper."

Sophie shook her head and then led the way out the front door, Annabelle following closely behind. As they crossed the street, Annabelle asked, "What do you think Regina's up to?"

"Not sure," Sophie admitted. "I mean... I can't imagine how I'd feel if I were in her shoes. If we hadn't stopped at the governor's mansion, maybe we would've caught up to her family by now. Maybe this whole mess would be over."

"Yeah. Then I wouldn't have a copper hanging around on me ship like a stool pigeon," Annabelle muttered to herself. "Wouldn't have no copper actin' like she's part of me crew."

"And you wouldn't be getting a fat fee from the Order," Sophie added with a smirk. "You'd most likely be arrested."

"Nope." Annabelle shot back. "No dumb coppers tryin' to lock me up for nothin'."

They reached the sheriff's office, where an older man in overalls sat on the porch, gently rocking in his chair while sipping a cup of what looks like sweet tea. Sophie nodded politely to him, tipping her hat. "Morning, sir."

The old man smiled warmly. "Morning, miss. Are you lookin' for the sheriff?"

"Yes, sir," Sophie replied. "I'm trying to track down some people who may have come through town recently."

"Well, go on in," the man said kindly. "Sheriff's inside."

"I'll wait out here," Annabelle announced.

"Afraid they'll arrest you?" Sophie teased.

Annabelle chuckled. "Come on now, Copper. No self-respecting privateer's gonna walk into a police house. I'll stay out here and chat with this fine ol' soul here," she said, flashing a smile at the old man.

"Suit yourself," Sophie said, stepping through the door of the sheriff's office.

The interior of the building was rustic, with wooden slats aligned lengthwise across the ceiling, creating a pattern that resembled a mural. Behind the counter hung a large flag of Verdantia, featuring the Mother Tree in the center. The tree was flanked by a bowl of crops on one side and a sword resting on a shield on the other, with the entire flag bordered by golden fringe. The welcome counter, also made of wooden slats, prominently displayed the word "Sheriff" in large letters, flanked by five-point stars. A logbook lay open on the counter, its middle page visible.

Behind the counter stood a young woman in a modest traditional dress. Her blonde hair was neatly pulled into a low ponytail by a hair clip. She greeted Sophie with a warm smile, her blue eyes sparkling.

"How can I help you?" the woman asked kindly.

"I was hoping to speak to the sheriff," Sophie replied, returning the smile to ease any tension. "I'm looking for someone."

"The sheriff is in a meeting at the moment, but you're welcome to wait," the woman said, gesturing toward a bench by the wall without looking up.

"Thank you," Sophie said, removing her hat as she walked over to the bench.

As she sat down, the woman suddenly exclaimed, "By the harvest! How did you get your hair such a beautiful color?"

Sophie turned, surprised. "It's always been this color," she answered cautiously, unwilling to delve into the truth and offend their religious sensibilities. "I'm not really sure why, to be honest."

"Oh," the woman said, looking a bit disappointed as she returned to her work.

Sophie sat quietly for a moment, thinking about the clearing from the previous day. She calculated how many people it would take to do that much work and maintain a camp of that size, including the human waste mounds she'd seen. Deciding not to waste time, she stood and approached the counter again.

"I was wondering, do you remember a large group of people coming through town recently?" Sophie asked. "Maybe a traveling circus or an acting troupe?"

The woman didn't look up from the logbook. "Can't say that I do," she answered casually.

"How about someone buying a lot of supplies, food and such?" Sophie pressed.

"Not sure. You'd have to check with the general store," the woman replied, still focused on her writing.

Sophie considered what it was like when Eclipse Baker led fieldwork in the rural areas of Opulentia. That expedition had about thirty people, thirteen Sentinels, sixteen Shadows, and Baker himself as expedition commander. She recalled how the townsfolk had noticed their presence, especially after they arrested a bandit gang. With that in mind, she asked, "Has the local tavern been having any trouble lately?"

The woman paused her writing and looked up. "That's really a question for the sheriff. What did you say your name was?"

"Sentinel Sophie Griffin," Sophie answered automatically before realizing that this was Verdantia, where her Aurorium Clan had no jurisdiction.

"Sentinel," the woman repeated thoughtfully. Her eyes lit up. "Oh, wait…are you a Jiberau?"

Sophie winced inwardly but maintained her composure. "You could say that. We go by Aurorium now," she explained cautiously.

"Oh," the woman said with mild indifference. "Well, we still call it Jiberau here."

"Of course you do," Sophie muttered with a forced smile, deciding to use the woman's ignorance to her advantage. "I'm here on a job from Opulentia. There's a group of people traveling between kingdoms, kidnapping women and children, and ransoming them to their families. When the families can't pay... they leave the bodies behind in towns like this one." She leaned in slightly. "The last ones were cut up so badly their families had to identify them by hand."

The woman's eyes widened in shock. "There hasn't been anyone like that around here... at least not that I've heard. Maybe the sheriff knows more."

Sophie pressed further. "A group like that would have a lot of members. Someone might've come into town with a suspicious amount of money. Maybe a facilitator, someone who doesn't ask too many questions?"

The woman shook her head. "The sheriff would know. I just handle the books."

At that moment, the sheriff entered the room, a large man with a broad midsection clad in a tan uniform. His badge, a five-point star encircled by a thick golden ivy-like border, gleamed on his chest. Beside him walked a man in a white shirt and tie, holding a briefcase and a rancher's hat.

"We'll look into it, Mr. Reeves," the sheriff said as they came in, his tone reassuring. "We can't have bandit gangs extorting our small business folk."

Both men stopped short when they saw Sophie, momentarily captivated by her violet hair and eyes. The sheriff recovered first. "Well, hello," he said, smiling as he approached. "What can I do for you, miss?"

"This is Sentinel Sophie Griffin," the woman at the counter explained. "She's looking for a group of kidnappers that might be hiding in the area."

"You don't say," the sheriff murmured, glancing at Mr. Reeves, who was now leaving the office but still looking back at Sophie with a look that says something is going on in his mind but she cannot tell what yet.

"Please, come back to my office," the sheriff said, gesturing down the hall. "Let's compare notes."

"Yes sheriff." Sophie agreed, following him behind the counter.

The sheriff's office was an ample space with walls, floors, and ceilings made of the same wooden slats as the rest of the building. His desk, large and imposing, dominated one-third of the room. Sophie walked into the room, ready to continue her investigation.

"Please, take a seat," the sheriff said, gesturing to the plain wooden chair in front of his desk as he eased into his large, cushioned chair. Sophie noted the contrast, her chair had no cushioning, just bare wood.

"Sentinel," the sheriff mused, leaning back comfortably. "With a title like that, you must be a Jiberau?"

"Aurorium, actually," Sophie corrected, doing her best to suppress a wince at the mention of her clan's slave name.

"Ah, Aurorium," he repeated, stumbling slightly over the unfamiliar word. "So, what brings an Aurorium Sentinel to Verdantia, alone, no less? And so young, I might add."

"I have special authority from the kingdom to investigate these criminals," Sophie lied smoothly. "My team recently rescued and returned Governor Nozaki's daughter. After we explained what we uncovered, the kingdom allowed us to investigate, though not to engage." Sophie crafted the lie carefully, keeping it simple. "My team leader, Marcus from the Order of Saint Lorraine, is speaking with farm owners right now. He sent me to talk to you, since we're both in law enforcement." She deliberately played to his ego, keeping her tone deferential but not overdone.

"I hadn't heard that the governor's daughter was found," the sheriff said, curiosity piqued. "What did your team discover?"

Sophie hesitated briefly, wondering how Annabelle always made lying seem so effortless. "We're part of a special investigative unit that's uncovered a conspiracy spanning the Seven Kingdoms," she said, watching as the sheriff leaned forward, clearly engaged. "This group has orchestrated a series of kidnappings and murders targeting powerful families."

"That's how they got the Nozaki girl?" he asked.

"Exactly," Sophie replied. "We're still piecing together how they operate and move between locations. We think we may have just missed them here but hope to pick up their trail."

"Do you think they've got pirates involved?" the sheriff asked.

"It's possible," Sophie answered. "This organization hires whoever they need to advance their goals. Pirates wouldn't be out of the question."

The sheriff nodded thoughtfully. "Ever heard of a Captain Jack?"

"Can't say that I have," Sophie replied honestly.

"Well," the sheriff continued, "I've got reports of a pirate calling himself *Captain Jack*. He's been setting up an extortion racket on the west side of town, targeting small businesses."

"That might be related," Sophie speculated. "Though the group we're after usually doesn't settle anywhere for long. Still, they could have used Jack's crew to get supplies and left him flush with coin afterward. What's on the west side of town?"

"The Reeves Estates," the sheriff said with a sweeping hand gesture, as if invoking grandeur. "Orchards and farms all owned by the Reeves family. Their representative was just here, saying pirates intimidated a local produce stand and lunch spot into handing over nearly all their crowns for *protection*."

"Sheriff," Sophie asked, trying another angle, "if I needed to obtain a large amount of supplies for a group of people without drawing attention, who in town would I speak to?"

"No one comes to mind," he answered, pausing in thought. "How big is your team?"

"Six strong," Sophie replied, making sure to keep the number believable. "Have you noticed any unusual activity lately, people spending more than usual or suddenly flush with coins?"

The sheriff furrowed his brow, searching his memory. "Sorry, that doesn't ring a bell," he admitted. "I don't think I can be much help with your investigation. But I'd like to speak with your superior, this Brother Marcus."

"I'll let him know," Sophie said, standing and extending her hand across the desk. "Thank you for your time, Sheriff."

The sheriff stood and shook her hand. "It was a pleasure, Miss Sentinel."

As Sophie left the office, she realized she had given the sheriff more information than she'd gained. With little to show for the meeting except the knowledge of a pirate gang's activities, she passed by the welcome desk and waved politely to the attendant before stepping outside.

On the porch, Annabelle was perched on the railing across from the old man in the rocking chair, cracking jokes about fish. Sophie caught only the tail end of it and shook her head, slipping her fedora back on.

The old man chuckled, his gregarious smile aimed at Sophie.

"How'd ye make out, Copper?" Annabelle asked, hopping down from the railing with a clatter as the anchor chain on her belt jingled at her waist.

"Terrible," Sophie replied with a sigh. "The sheriff hasn't come across anything that fits. But there must be something here to find."

196

Annabelle exchanged a knowing glance with the old man before turning to Sophie. "Well, then... I'm not sorry about this."

"About what..." Sophie asked suspiciously, bracing herself for whatever Annabelle was about to pull.

Without warning, Annabelle gave Sophie a firm shove. Sophie staggered backward and tumbled straight into the old man's lap. Flustered and indignant, she scrambled to right herself, her face flushed.

"What the hell, *Anna*?!" Sophie shouted, standing and brushing herself off.

The old man chuckled good-naturedly, helping her to her feet. "There you go, ma'am," he said with a warm smile.

"Thanks, sir," Sophie muttered, straightening her clothes before glaring at Annabelle. "What is wrong with you?!?" about to use the *One Free punch* that War granted her.

"Hold on now," Annabelle defended herself with a mischievous grin. "I knew ye wouldn't get nothin' out of that there sheriff, so I made a deal with Mr. Cassidy here. He promised me information if I got you to sit on his lap."

Sophie turned to the old man, who rocked contentedly in his chair with a broad grin, then back to Annabelle, who raised her hands in mock surrender.

"You can't be serious!" Sophie said, disbelief in her voice.

"A deal's a deal," Cassidy said, standing and stretching. "Now why don't you two young ladies buy an old man a cup of coffee, and we'll have ourselves a proper conversation?"

Annabelle followed Cassidy off the porch, glancing nervously at Sophie's fuming expression. Sophie stalked behind them, shoving Annabelle lightly in the back.

"Why didn't you sit on his lap if it's so harmless?"

"He didn't ask fer me," Annabelle said with a sneer. "Guy clearly has no taste, Copper."

"No! You're not calling me Copper for the rest of the day," Sophie snapped. "Or I'll knock you out cold."

Annabelle turned to retort but froze at the sight of Sophie's glare. Her violet eyes burned with restrained fury. Annabelle gulped. "Okay, okay! I'm sorry."

"Sorry what?" Sophie prompted sternly.

"I'm sorry, Sophie," Annabelle muttered, like the name tasted foul in her mouth.

"Good." Sophie said, glaring for a moment longer before relaxing.

Cassidy chuckled over his shoulder. "Tough one, aren't ya?" he teased.

Sophie bit her tongue, vowing that if Cassidy crossed the line like that again, he'd regret it. The trio walked to a small restaurant at the edge of Snyder's solitary street. They took seats at the third table, positioned near a window overlooking the street.

A waitress approached with a welcoming smile. "What'll you have, darlins?"

"A cup of coffee for me," Cassidy said, grinning. "And orange juice for these fine young ladies."

"Sure thing," the waitress said before heading off to fulfill the Order.

Cassidy turned to Sophie and Annabelle. "I've been in this town my whole life. Seen all kinds of folks pass through, bandits, reformers, you name it. But I've never seen anyone quite like the group that was living out near the Reeves Estates."

The waitress returned, placing a coffee in front of Cassidy and orange juices in front of Sophie and Annabelle.

"Thank you," Sophie said with a polite smile.

"Much obliged," Annabelle replied

"Can I get y'all anything to eat?" the waitress asked, her notepad ready.

"I'll take bacon and eggs with a side of pancakes, thanks," Cassidy chirped.

"Nothing for me, thanks," Sophie declined.

"Nay, I'm good and fed" Annabelle said tersely, crossing her arms, though irritation simmered beneath her calm exterior. The old man had just conned her out of a full breakfast, on top of the coffee.

"Alright then," the waitress said, walking off.

Annabelle leaned forward, tapping the table. "Right then, back to yer story, mate," she urged, determined to get something out of this deal.

"Of course, of course," Cassidy said. "My cousin Nathaniel, he works at the general store, got mixed up with these folks. About a month ago, some new secret customer started paying him real good. They gave him lists of supplies to buy and told him to keep quiet about it. Nate didn't mind; he needed the extra coin with a new baby on the way."

"How much did they have him buy?" Sophie asked.

"A lot," Cassidy replied. "He'd clean out the bakery once a week for them. And the butcher? He paid off all his debts from my cousin's little side hustle."

"This is all well and good," Sophie said after taking a sip of her juice, "but how do I know these are the people I'm looking for?"

"Well," Cassidy continued, "one day, Nate was overwhelmed, juggling work at the store and those deliveries, so he asked me to help. He needed a second wagon to haul everything out to the drop-off point. Paid me a few crowns and gave me a bottle of the good stuff to help him out."

He paused to sip his coffee. "When we got to the Reeves' estate, a woman appeared, looked like she was wearin' shadows, and her eyes... glowing red like rubies. It was like she could see right through me. The way she looked at me? I swear she was daring me to step out of line."

He paused again, taking another sip. "There was another girl with her beautiful, just like you, ma'am." He raised his mug in Sophie's direction with a respectful nod.

Sophie would normally blush at Cassidy's comment, but after how she ended up here, she refused to give him the satisfaction. Instead, she maintained a calm, interrogative expression.

"This girl," Cassidy continued, "had a look in her eye like she couldn't wait to kill me. You know, like how a cat looks at a mouse when it isn't even hungry." He paused, shivering slightly at the memory. "And her magic, ice magic. I've never seen anything like it."

Sophie's interest sharpened. She noted *Ice Magic,* then asked, "What color was her hair?"

Before Cassidy could answer, the waitress returned with his breakfast, placing the plate in front of him. "Anything else for you all?"

Everyone at the table shook their heads, allowing the conversation to resume.

"Now, what color were the ice girl's hair and eyes?" Sophie pressed, eager to confirm whether they had narrowly missed Gretta, just like Regina had missed her family.

"Brown," Cassidy replied, cutting into his pancakes. "But not your regular brown. Darker. And her eyes? Same color. It was... unnerving, really." He shuddered at the thought.

"How'd ye know she had ice magic?" Annabelle asked, leaning forward.

"She froze a tree," Cassidy said between bites.

"Wait, what?" Sophie asked in disbelief. "What do you mean she froze a tree?"

Cassidy set his fork down and explained, "I was waiting by the wagon when I caught the brown-haired lady looking at me. She smiled, one of those gentle inviting smiles, you know? Some women like older men." he said with a wink. "But then she touched a tree with her finger. In a second, the whole thing froze solid, squirrels and all. They just fell out in little ice blocks." He paused, reliving the moment. "And the whole time, she kept smiling. She liked seeing how scared I was. She even dragged her finger along the wagon as she walked by, touching my leg a few times. When I flinched, she laughed." Cassidy's voice trembled, and beads of sweat appeared on his brow.

"That sounds like Gretta to me," Sophie murmured thoughtfully. "Did your cousin mention the last time he made a delivery for them?"

"Four days ago, I think," Cassidy answered. "He's been drowning his sorrows at the saloon ever since, losing all those extra crowns."

"Is there anything else you remember?" Sophie asked.

Cassidy hesitated for a moment, then said, "I saw that brown-haired girl one more time. I was sitting in my rocking chair in front of the sheriff's office when she walked right up to the door. She gave me that same smile before going inside."

"What did she do in the office?" Sophie asked, curiosity piqued.

"She met with the sheriff," Cassidy replied. "Stayed for about half an hour. On her way out, she touched my shoulder and said something like *next time* before walking away. It still gives me the chills."

"When was that?" Sophie asked urgently.

"Two days ago," Cassidy confirmed. "Oh, I'm sure of it. I haven't felt that close to death in all my years. I won't forget it anytime soon."

The waitress returned and placed the bill on the table. "Whenever you're ready, darlins."

Annabelle snatched up the bill and raised an eyebrow, sixty-five harvest crowns. She instinctively started to slide it toward Sophie but stopped when she saw the lingering smoldering anger in her violet eyes. With a sigh, Annabelle reached into her newly acquired leather pouch with the Verdantian Mother tree on it and pulled out a few of her newly acquired crop crowns, leaving extra for a tip. *No harm in earning a bit of goodwill.*

Sophie stood, placing her fedora back on. "Good day, Mr. Cassidy," she said curtly before walking out of the restaurant.

Annabelle followed, giving Cassidy a half-hearted wave as she went.

[-----⊕-----]

Sophie and Annabelle rode Kicker from the town center, heading toward the Wilde Fruit stand. Annabelle had insisted on the stop despite Sophie's protests. When they arrived, Annabelle offered to buy her a slice of strawberry pie and a glass of lemonade as a peace offering. Reluctantly, Sophie accepted in the name of peace among the avatars.

As they ate, Sophie had to admit the pie was excellent. Still, that didn't mean Annabelle was off the hook if she dared call her *Copper* today.

"Honestly, Sophie, I don't know why yer still mad," Annabelle said over her empty plate. "Ye got the information ye were after, right?"

Sophie twirled her fork, staring at Annabelle from across the table. "Yeah... and that's the only reason I'm not punching you right now."

"Come on," Annabelle said with a grin. "He didn't even do anything to ye. Ye just sat on his lap fer not even a minute."

As soon as the words left Annabelle's mouth, she realized her mistake. Sophie's grip on her fork tightened. For a moment, Annabelle wondered if Sophie was about to stab her with it.

"I swear to War..." Sophie muttered through clenched teeth, stopping herself to take a deep breath. "...You should just stop there, Anna."

"Oi! If I can't call ye the 'C' word, then you can't call me *Anna*!" Annabelle protested.

"Sure thing. Let me just push you onto some creepy old guy's lap and see how you like it," Sophie shot back, her violet eyes narrowing. She scanned the seating area and pointed to an older, heavyset man enjoying a sandwich nearby. "How about him?"

Annabelle groaned in frustration. "Fine," she declared, standing suddenly. "Let's get this over with!" She strode across the seating area, ignoring Sophie's stunned expression.

"Annabelle, what are you..."

Before Sophie could finish, Annabelle tapped the man on the shoulder. "'Scuse me, good sir. I'm gonna sit on yer lap. Mind scootin' back a bit?"

The man blinked in confusion. "What?"

"Come on, mate," Annabelle said as she tugged his chair back and plopped herself onto his lap. "There we go. We good now, Sophie?" she called out, smirking.

The man fidgeted uncomfortably. "Miss, I just want to eat my sandwich..."

"Hold on," Annabelle continued, grinning mischievously. "Mate, I need ye to grab my bum. That's part of the deal."

"What?" the man stammered, baffled.

Annabelle grabbed his free hand and placed it on her behind. "Okay, Sophie! We square now?"

Sophie groaned, burying her face in her hands. She stood up and stormed over. "I'm so sorry, sir," she said, pulling Annabelle off him. "Come on, Annabelle. Now."

"Not 'til ye say we're square," Annabelle declared, bouncing slightly on the man's lap for emphasis.

"Seriously?!"

"Aye," Annabelle confirmed with a grin.

"Please, miss," the man begged. "If my wife sees us, I'll be in a heap of trouble..."

Frustrated, Sophie threw up her hands. "Fine! We're square. Now get up!"

Annabelle hopped off the man's lap and hugged Sophie gleefully. "I'm so happy, Copper!"

"Yep, me too," Sophie muttered, rolling her eyes.

The man sat frozen, sandwich in hand, staring at the two women in bewilderment.

"Oi, what are ye starin' at?" Annabelle snapped at him.

"Can I eat my sandwich now?" he asked weakly.

"Yes, sir. Enjoy your sandwich, and try the lemonade. It's first-class," Sophie said with a forced smile before dragging Annabelle back to their table. "Come on. We've got to get moving."

After finishing their drinks, they cleared their plates and glasses, placing them in a basket for washing. They then set off on foot toward the facility, passing through the false-door puzzle at its entrance.

"Annabelle," Sophie whispered, glancing around. "We're being followed."

Annabelle's eyes lit up with excitement. "Why don't ye quit hidin' in the shadows and come collect this butt-kickin' like a man?!?" she shouted.

Sophie sighed, regretting that she'd mentioned the followers at all.

"There she is." a familiar voice called out from the trees. Six men emerged into the clearing, and Annabelle immediately recognized the bandaged thug from the previous day.

"Back for more, eh?" Annabelle taunted, crossing her arms.

Sophie glared at her. "What the hell have you gotten me into now?"

"One moment, Copper. I'm conductin' business here." Annabelle replied, waving her off.

The bandaged man sneered. "Not so tough without your pirate gang, huh?"

"Gang?" Annabelle burst into laughter. "Is that what ye told them? That a whole gang beat yer sorry arse? Oh, ye lyin' sod. Listen up, boyos, he took that beatin' from yours truly. Just me alone!" She jabbed a thumb at her chest with a smirk.

Sophie noticed the men closing in around her and Annabelle. She shot a sharp look at her companion. "What did you do to these people, *Anna*?"

"Oi! I didn't do a thing," Annabelle protested, pointing at the injured thug. "He started this with me! Bloke's got a memory like a goldfish."

Sophie wasn't entirely convinced but chose to stay silent.

"Just take us to Captain Jack," one of the other men said, his tone smug. "We don't want to hurt you two little girls too bad."

"Captain Jack?" Sophie's eyes narrowed as she recalled the sheriff's report. "Annabelle... what have you been doing out here?"

Annabelle gave her a sly grin and winked. "The Cap'n don't like people spreadin' his business all out in the open."

Before Sophie could respond, the men rushed at them. The closest thug lunged at Sophie, trying to grab her. She sidestepped quickly and delivered a swift uppercut to his chin. Though not her most powerful strike, it stunned him long enough for her to trip him with a sweeping foot, sending him to the ground.

Annabelle met another thug head-on, crashing her shoulder into his midsection and knocking him down. In a fluid motion, she pulled her anchor from its hook and swung it around her body, slamming it into an attacker who had tried to sneak up behind her.

Sophie missed the weight of her pistol in moments like this, but she had other tools. She reached into her jacket and pulled out an Alrunia Square, feeling it pulse with mana as she infused it. It was a 'rock' square. She hurled it at another attacker, and mid-flight, the square conjured a melon-sized boulder that crashed into his chest, knocking him to the ground.

A sudden grab from behind yanked Sophie off her feet. Another thug had her locked in a bear hug from behind and is now lifting her up.

Annabelle spun, intending to bring her anchor back to her hand, but the injured thug grabbed the chain and delivered a hard punch to her face. The impact staggered her, but instead of retreating, Annabelle followed the force, letting him pull her closer before smashing her forehead into his nose. Blood spattered from the impact.

Meanwhile, Sophie wrapped her legs around the head of the man approaching her and used the leverage to headbutt the man holding her from behind under the chin. He released her with a grunt of pain. Not wasting the opportunity, Sophie tightened her grip with her legs, grabbed the front man's head, and yanked him down with her. She rolled and drove her elbow into his nose with a satisfying crunch.

Annabelle tried to free her anchor, but the thug held firm, refusing to let go. She heard another attacker approaching and spun to throw a Riptide punch, but the thug jerked her chain, causing her to stumble and miss. Seawater sprayed into the air as her riptide punch missed its mark. Off balance, she took a solid punch to the face, followed by another to the chest, knocking her backward into the thug's waiting arms.

Sophie got back to her feet, spotting the thug she had tripped earlier rushing her again. His posture gave away his plan, a kick aimed at her midsection. She sidestepped it with ease and retaliated with a HARDKNUCKLE strike to his nose, dropping him flat.

Annabelle struggled in the grip of her captor. She stomped at his feet, but he lifted her off the ground to avoid the attack. Another thug grabbed her chin with a sneer. "I really don't want to mess up your pretty face. Just tell us where to find Captain Jack."

Annabelle's response was swift, she bit down hard on his hand, making him yelp in pain, and kicked him with both feet.

"Ahh, you little harlot!" the thug snarled, backhanding her across the face.

Sophie saw red. Her vision narrowed as rage built inside her, War's words echoing in her mind: *Keep those girls safe.* She channeled mana into her feet, weaving a pair of spell circles beneath them. Releasing the stored energy, she launched herself forward in a blur, flipping into a downward kick that struck the thug's skull with bone-crunching force, driving him into the ground.

Annabelle watched in awe as Sophie stood over the crumpled man, her violet eyes blazing with fury. The remaining thug holding her began to drag her backward, but Annabelle couldn't help warning him. "Listen, mate... you might wanna just let me go."

"Shut your loud mouth." he snarled, pulling her away from the advancing Sophie.

Sophie's voice was low and lethal. "I'll say this once. Let her go. Or start praying to the Harvest Goddess…or whoever you think will save you."

Annabelle felt a shiver run down her spine. She would never admit it, but in that moment, Sophie terrified her. Sophie took another slow, deliberate step forward.

The thug hesitated for a moment, then dropped Annabelle and released the anchor with a metallic clatter. Without a word, he turned and ran so fast he created a cloud of dust behind himself, no doubt running for his life.

"You okay?" Sophie asked, her voice steady but laced with concern.

Annabelle, uncharacteristically quiet for a moment, blinked and turned to face her. "Huh? Oh... yeah, Copper. I'm good. They hit like they just left their momma's arms."

"Good to hea…" Sophie suddenly swayed and collapsed mid-sentence, hitting the ground hard.

"Copp…?" Annabelle began, but dizziness overwhelmed her. The world spun as her knees buckled, and she crumpled to the ground beside Sophie.

[-----⊕-----]

"It's just two little girls," a man's voice said, irritation lacing his tone.

202

"That's all I saw," replied another voice—calm, deep, and intimidating. It sounded muffled, as if the man was wearing a mask.

"This doesn't make any sense," the first man objected, clearly exasperated. "Where's this Captain Jack hiding out?"

"No idea," the masked man replied. "But one of these two probably knows."

"Was all that spellcasting really necessary?" the first man asked, frustrated. "Braithwaite and Conners are out cold."

"I watched them in action," the masked man explained coolly. "The purple one, especially. She uses two different types of magic. If she manages to break free, that'll be a problem."

"Ugh," the first man groaned. "First, those *damned people* show up with all their demands, and now this? How long until they wake up?"

"My capture spell depends on their resilience," the masked man said. "But they should be waking up soon."

"Fine. Go back out there and see what you can dig up on this pirate trying to muscle in on us," the first man ordered.

The masked man sighed, the sound of his boots echoing off wooden stairs as he walked away. The remaining man began pacing, his footsteps clacking rhythmically across the floor.

Sophie stirred as her head was lifted roughly. The man leaned in close and yelled in her face, "Wake up!"

A sharp slap followed, snapping Sophie fully out of her daze. Her head throbbed, and her senses remained dulled from whatever had knocked her out. Her vision blurred, but as it cleared, she made out a fat young man standing impatiently in front of her. He wore denim pants and a plaid shirt, his expression tense and irritated.

"Where's your boss?" he demanded.

Sophie blinked, trying to steady her thoughts. That's when she noticed the ropes binding her to a chair. The room around her looked like a dimly lit basement.

She groaned softly and muttered under her breath, "What has that damn pirate girl got me into now?"

Chapter 14

At the hidden facility, Marcus woke in a surprisingly comfortable bed. The room, though clearly defunct, retained a strange charm, as if the abandoned space clung to echoes of a once-vibrant operation. He stretched, clearing the fog of sleep, and began piecing together what he'd learned so far. The facility's records hinted at experiments focused on extracting and storing mana from human bodies, though their greater purpose remained frustratingly elusive.

After dressing, Marcus made his way to the main room. There, he found Regina buried in a journal, her eyes scanning each line with an almost feverish focus. He hesitated before speaking, concern gnawing at him. Ever since they discovered that the conspiracy had held her father, Jules, and little brother, Mattie, here, missing them by just one or two days, Regina had thrown herself into relentless research. She'd barely eaten, much less rested.

"Good morning, Miss Regina," Marcus greeted her gently.

No response.

Marcus knew this side of her well, how she could lose herself so deeply in study that she tuned out the world entirely. Usually, though, she could still hold conversations on autopilot, her mind half-aware. This was different. She wasn't even pretending to listen.

He approached and placed a hand on her shoulder. "Miss Fournier, are you alright?"

Regina flinched slightly, then blinked as though pulling herself from a deep haze. Her silver hair framed her face, accentuating the dark circles under her eyes.

"I'm fine," she mumbled, her voice soft and strained. "I think... I'm close to figuring it out."

"Did you sleep at all last night?" Marcus asked, his tone edging into stern concern.

"I don't have time for sleep," she replied curtly. "We have to catch up to them."

Marcus frowned. He admired her drive but couldn't ignore the toll it was taking. He had seen this pattern in her before in members of The Order , the unyielding determination to master knowledge, but this time, it was more desperate, given their situation it is much more reckless.

"Miss Fournier," he said carefully, "it isn't wise to push yourself like this, especially with such dense, technical information. You..."

"I won't find my dad in my sleep!" Regina snapped, her voice cracking with raw emotion.

Marcus paused, weighing his following words. He shifted tactics, softening his approach, hoping to get her to realize on her own she should change tactics "What were you just reading?"

Regina looked down at the journal in her hands. She opened her mouth to answer, then faltered. The words she'd absorbed mere minutes ago now felt distant and foggy. "I... I can't remember."

"Alright," Marcus said gently. "What about the journal before this one?"

She slid the current book aside, revealing the previous journal beneath it. The name "Jupiter" was etched into its cover. She stared at it, willing the contents to resurface in her mind. Nothing. The realization hit hard. hours of frantic effort, wasted. Tears welled in her eyes as the weight of failure pressed down on her.

"Miss Regina," Marcus murmured, kneeling to meet her gaze. "I have no doubt you'll figure out where they've taken your family. But you must let your mind rest. You'll be no good to them if you push yourself to the point of collapse."

"But they're getting away!" she cried, the tears streaming freely now. "Every second I waste..."

"And I have faith that the four of you will find them," Marcus interjected firmly. "But how long do you think they can survive if you lose yourself in the process? Your father is a scholar, a man of knowledge. I doubt they took him simply because he's your father. They need him for something. That means, for now, he and Matthew are probably... relatively speaking, safe."

Regina sniffled, processing his words. "Mattie," she corrected softly. "His name is *Mattie*."

"My apologies," Marcus said with a nod. "But please understand, Miss Regina, you have an incredible mind, but even you need rest to function. Exhaustion clouds your thoughts. Take a short nap, or at least a break. Recharge."

"I... don't know," she muttered, wiping her tears with trembling hands.

Marcus stood, offering her an out. "If you don't want to sleep, how about a walk? Clear your head."

"I don't want to leave," Regina whispered, her voice barely audible. The fog of exhaustion wrapped tighter around her.

Marcus sighed inwardly. He had no authority to force her to rest, bound as he was by his duty to support, not command her. Watching someone self-destruct in pursuit of a noble goal was a burden he hadn't anticipated, and he quickly found it unpalatable.

"Can I at least get you something to eat?" he asked gently.

"That... would be okay, I guess" she said, stretching slowly. The slight movement seemed to release some tension from her frame.

Satisfied for now, Marcus prepared to head out. "I'll be back soon, Miss Regina," he said over his shoulder, stepping through the double doors at the rear of the facility. The cool forest air greeted him as he made his way toward the nearby farm stand.

As he walked, the weight of Regina's despair lingered. He prayed silently that she would find the strength to listen, to her body, or to him, or reason, before the mission's demands consumed her entirely.

[-----⚙-----]

Lisa woke up in a modest room, likely intended for a servant or worker. The small space was functional but quiet, its second bed untouched and neatly made. She sighed, her gaze lingering on the empty bed. Regina hadn't slept here. The girl was pushing herself too hard again.

Lisa swears to herself that she will break her own bad habit of wearing yesterday's clothes, Lisa slipped into the dress from the day before anyway, vowing to do better next time. A quick stop at the community washroom followed, where she washed her face hastily, just enough to remove the sweat and grime. Feeling slightly refreshed, she made her way to the main room.

There, Regina paced restlessly, her silver hair damp and clinging to her face as she flipped through the covers of various manuals and journals. Lisa watched the scene for a moment before calling out, "Good morning, Regina."

There was no response. Regina's focus was unbreakable, or at least, it seemed that way. Frowning, Lisa crossed the room and gently placed a hand on her shoulder. "Regina, are you okay? Did you get any sleep?"

Regina turned around sharply, her exhaustion written in every line of her face. The bags under her eyes stood out against her pale complexion. "Sleep isn't going to find my dad and Mattie," she muttered, pulling away from Lisa's touch.

"Killing yourself will not find them either," Lisa shot back, her tone firm but kind.

Regina ignored her, moving to the next book on the table. She scanned its label, shook her head in frustration, and set it down. Lisa watched her repeat the process with another journal, the tension rising in the room like a coiled spring. Memories of Order Island surfaced, specifically, the moment she lost control and pushed Regina down for using her magic. After Erisol showed her how unkind she was to Regina, Lisa vowed to change her ways, especially in her treatment of Regina. Lisa considered leaving Regina to her own devices and eventually burning herself out, but the same feeling in her stomach tells her that Unity disagrees with that plan.

Why do you test me so, goddess? Lisa thought with weary resignation.

She stepped forward again, taking Regina's hand gently. "Please, Regina," she said softly. "You are going to hurt yourself if you keep this up."

Regina yanked her hand away. "You don't understand. Your family is fine!" she snapped.

Lisa took a deep breath, swallowing her irritation. "You are right. I cannot fully understand what you are going through. But I do understand pain. I know you are afraid that if you stop, your family will slip further away. But I will stay here and keep reading through..." she gestured around at the scattered journals and papers, "...all of this, until you wake up. You told me once that you love sleep, remember?"

Regina's face twisted as tears welled in her eyes. "What are you going to do, push me down again?" she challenged bitterly and she stands up to confront. "Just leave me alone!"

Lisa's patience snapped. In a swift motion, she shoved Regina to the floor and pinned her down. "Now You Listen!" Lisa growled, her voice low and fierce. "You are going to lie down and sleep. I will wrap you in tree roots if that is what it takes! You are not the only smart one here, Regina! We are all in this together, and you are no help to anyone if you run yourself into the ground chasing shadows!"

Regina glared up at her, a different fire in her eyes this time, stubborn, not wounded. For a moment, neither spoke. Then a soft voice broke the silence in Regina's mind.

"You must adapt your strategy," said Tiktik, the Goddess Change's silver fox pet, calmly seated nearby.

Regina's defiance crumbled. "Okay. Fine." she muttered, conceding to both Lisa and Tiktik at once.

Lisa stood and helped her to her feet. Without a word, she guided Regina to the dormitory and pointed to the freshly made bed. Regina hesitated, then quietly apologized. "I'm sorry, Lisa."

Lisa watched as Regina stripped off her clothes and collapsed onto the mattress. "And... sorry, Tiktik," she mumbled before passing out almost instantly.

'Tiktik?' Lisa blinked, wondering if the girl was delirious from exhaustion. But the question faded as she saw how deeply Regina had already sunk into sleep. With a quiet sigh, Lisa left the room, pulling the door closed behind her.

Back in the central area, the sheer disarray of journals and reports weighed on her. They had been combing through documents left by a different order than The Order of Saint Lorraine, but a new thought nagged at her: *why did the conspiracy care about this place? Why had Brother Albert come here? What had he found so significant?*

Lisa recalled the *Alchemists' Laws of Prosperity*, particularly the third: *Dedicate your resources equal to your immediate return*. The conspiracy had invested considerable effort in this location. *But why?*

Determined to find answers, she began inspecting the facility's rooms. The first one, a sterile space with an empty examination table, felt eerily unused, like a butcher's shop that had been shut down but now thoroughly cleaned. Dust coated every surface, a sign that the conspiracy hadn't been here recently.

The next room was filled with strange, unrecognizable machinery, all equally covered in dust and grime. Lisa dismissed it and moved on. The third room made her pause. Inside were preserved organs floating in yellow liquid, each one encased in a glass cylinder like some kind of macabre shrine. Yet there was only one of each organ, and each of the jars had a label that read "Neptune", and no signs of additional storage.

What in the name of the harvest was this for? she wondered. Still, the dust suggested it hadn't been disturbed in years.

She bypassed the dormitory, already familiar with its untouched state from her earlier cleaning efforts. But the last examination room was different. Unlike the others, it was devoid of dust or grime. It was empty now, but clearly, something had been here, something the conspiracy had taken.

What was in this room? Lisa thought, her curiosity sharpening into resolve. Whatever it was, it had to be significant enough to warrant all this effort. And she intended to find out.

[-----✛-----]

Marcus arrived at the Wilde Fruit stand and immediately noticed *Kicker* the familiar brown-and-white speckled mare tied near the seating area. His gaze swept the tables, hoping to spot Sophie Griffin or Annabelle Salazar. They could all walk back to the facility together. But there was no sign of either avatar. Dismissing the horse as a sign they'd gone ahead to the cabin entrance of the hidden facility, Marcus turned his thoughts toward catching up with them. *Hopefully, Miss Griffin had learned something valuable from the Sheriff or townspeople.*

Approaching the stand, Marcus was greeted by a smiling girl behind the counter. "What'll it be, sir?"

Marcus offered a polite nod. "Actually, I was wondering, have you seen two young women pass through here? One with violet hair and the other with…"

"Orange hair?" the girl finished, her smile brightening.

"That would be them," Marcus confirmed.

"They were just here," she chirped. "Had a slice of pie and a glass of lemonade. They mentioned having something to work out, then left through the forest like they had a destination in mind."

Marcus nodded, accepting that he'd likely find them back at the facility. Shifting his focus, he asked, "What's your lunch special today?"

"A turkey and cheese sandwich, with lemonade and an apple," she replied.

"That sounds perfect. I'll take three," Marcus said. He paused, realizing the challenge of transporting three glasses of lemonade through the woods. "Though… I'm not sure how to carry all the drinks."

Without missing a beat, the girl produced a large jug from beneath the counter, filled it with lemonade, and placed three metal cups alongside it. "There you go! Easy fix for friends of *Captain Jack*." she said with a playful wink.

Marcus blinked, puzzled but grateful. Annabelle Salazar had made a favorable impression in town. He watched as the girl carefully wrapped the sandwiches, hand-picked three apples from the bushel, and packed everything neatly into a cloth bag.

"That'll be one hundred and twenty crowns, sir," she said.

Marcus pulled out his coin pouch, counted out the amount, and handed it over. "Thank you," he said, taking the jug and food bag.

As he walked past the speckled mare, an idea struck him. He secured the jug and bag in the left saddlebag and untied the horse. "Alright, let's put you to use," he said, taking the reins and guiding the horse back toward the facility's larger rear entrance. Grape, Lisa's horse, was already hitched there.

Inside the facility, Marcus found Lisa seated alone at a table, papers spread out before her. "Good afternoon, Miss Lisa. Have you seen Miss Annabelle or Miss Sophie? Or Miss Regina, for that matter?"

Lisa looked up and gave a small wave. "Good afternoon, Brother Marcus. Regina's sleeping. I haven't seen Sophie or Annabelle today."

Marcus frowned. He had expected the pair to arrive ahead of him. Setting the food bag and jug on the table atop some scattered papers, he said, "I brought lunch for the three of us. Please, help yourself. I'm going to look for Miss Annabelle and Miss Sophie."

"Thank you, Marcus," Lisa replied, already turning back to her work.

Marcus crossed the main room, climbing the ladder that led to the dilapidated cabin aboveground. From there, he followed the forest path, searching for any sign of the two avatars. His ears strained for their playful bickering, but the forest remained quiet except for the natural rustling of leaves and distant birdsong.

Eventually, the path led him to a clearing, and the first clue that something was wrong. Scattered across the ground were several unconscious men. Judging by the scene, it was undoubtedly Sophie and Annabelle's handiwork. His eyes landed on Sophie's signature long-billed purple fedora and suit jacket, lying upside down near one of the downed ruffians; she never left those clothes behind, suggesting something was seriously amiss.

Marcus scanned the area further and spotted Annabelle's anchor-chain belt, a prized possession she would never abandon so carelessly. Alarm surged through him. He gathered both the items, his mind racing. Something had happened to them.

With a determined breath, Marcus returned through the hidden entrance in the cabin. He needed to regroup with Lisa and Regina. The situation had just become far more urgent.

[-----⊙-----]

Lisa nibbled on her turkey and cheese sandwich while absentmindedly flipping through papers scattered on the table. One sheet caught her attention, a child's drawing. She smiled softly, recognizing it as Mattie's work. But when she turned the page over, her smile vanished. On the other side was an official-looking edict, likely a directive from "The Order."

Her eyes scanned the text, and dread seeped into her gut. The edict outlined a mission for Order-affiliated facilities: to research methods of extracting and storing mana from human beings. It was marked as a top priority for all subsects and science outposts under the authority of something called the "Shadow Elders."

Lisa's thoughts raced as the reality of the facility's purpose hit her. The experiments here involved extracting mana from people. The idea twisted her stomach. She set the half-eaten sandwich aside, her appetite gone. *Could this be why the conspiracy was interested in the facility? Were they trying to harness mana extraction for their own ends?* And was this "Order" the same group Brother Albert had warned them about back at West's tavern?

The familiar clink of Annabelle's anchor-chain belt echoed from the ladder leading to the cabin entrance, breaking Lisa's grim thoughts. Relief began to flood her, until she looked up and saw not Annabelle, but Marcus, descending with the belt slung over his shoulder.

"Marcus, what is going on?" Lisa demanded, concern sharpening her voice.

Marcus hesitated before responding. "Miss Lisa… I'm not entirely sure. But I believe that Miss Salazar and Miss Griffin are in trouble."

Lisa's heart dropped. "What?!"

"I followed their likely path through the forest," Marcus explained. "I found a group of unconscious ruffians, clearly after a fight with the pair. In the middle of the clearing, I found these." He held up Annabelle's anchor-chain belt and Sophie's purple clothing.

Lisa's stomach tightened further. Neither Annabelle nor Sophie would ever leave these possessions behind unless something was seriously wrong. "I agree," she said grimly. "They would not abandon those. Something is most definitely wrong."

Lisa thought for a moment, weighing their options. "How about we go and talk to those ruffians," she finally suggested.

Marcus frowned, his brow furrowing. "Is that really a good idea?"

Lisa gave a dry chuckle, shrugging. "Probably not, but it is all we have to work with."

Marcus nodded, though the tension in his expression didn't ease. Together, they prepared to head out, both silently bracing for what they might discover next.

Lisa and Marcus moved through the forest from the double-door entrance. Lisa flatly refused to go back through the filthy cabin. As they arrived at the clearing near the false door puzzle, several of the unconscious men began to stir. Determined to learn what had happened to Annabelle and Sophie, Lisa strode toward them without hesitation.

"Excuse me, Miss Lisa, those men are dangerous," Marcus called out, concern evident in his tone.

"It will be fine," Lisa assured him over her shoulder. "Trust me."

Lisa weaves a brown spell circle with intricate brown runes, materializes it, and coaxes the earth beneath each of the five men, binding their hands and feet with controlled coils of earth. With a deep breath, Lisa used her Earthbloom sense, scanning the men for injuries to determine which one was most likely coherent enough to answer her questions. She approached the first man to wake, noting the blood streaming from his nose and mouth. His eyes darted around in panic.

"What's going on?" he stammered, his voice hoarse.

"Calm down," Lisa said soothingly. "I am not going to hurt you."

The man's gaze sharpened as he took in her appearance. His eyes widened in awe. "Lady Harvest..." he breathed, as if seeing a divine figure manifested before him.

Lisa fought the urge to sigh. *Another one of those superstitious types*, she thought. But instead, she leaned into the misconception, knowing it might help. "Oh my dear, you are hurt," she said gently. She weaved a red spell, a circle appeared as she focused her Earthbloom healing on his injuries. Through her sense, she identified a broken nose and a minor brain trauma, likely from an impact. Slowly, she began the process of repairing the damage.

"Have you seen my friends?" she asked softly while working.

"Miss Lisa..." Marcus began to interject.

She turned her head and shot him a silent '*Sssh*' look. He wisely fell silent.

"Your friends?" the man echoed.

"Yes, the other ones… like me, one orange and the other violet," Lisa clarified, her green eyes steady as she continued mending his broken nose.

"They had to go to the boss," the man muttered, still disoriented. He sniffled and expelled bloody mucus from his nose as the pain subsided.

Lisa maintained her calm, nurturing tone. "And where is the boss?"

"The big house," the man replied sluggishly.

Lisa frowned, then reminded herself that he had been struck in the head. She finished healing his nose and turned her attention to the subtle damage in his brain. Her magic worked slowly and methodically, knitting the affected tissue with great care.

"Stay with me," she softly coaxed as the man's eyes fluttered open again. "Who owns the big house?"

"The Sheriff," he mumbled before slipping back into a stupor.

Lisa blinked in surprise. "*The Sheriff?*" she softly repeated, turning to Marcus.

Marcus frowned, his gaze sweeping across the other fallen men. He speaks in a soft voice, doing his best to dismiss Miss Lisa's scenario in the downed man's mind. "These men… work for the Sheriff? That doesn't seem likely."

Lisa considered the possibility. "Maybe we should go and ask him ourselves," she suggested with a smile.

[-----⊙-----]

Lisa and Brother Marcus rode her horse, Grape, back to town, tying the reins to the hitching post outside the Sheriff's office. As they approached the building, they passed an older man sitting in a rocking chair. He wore worn overalls over a green and white striped shirt, and a rancher's hat was tilted low to shield his eyes from the setting sun.

"Hello," Lisa greeted instinctively, unsure if the man was asleep or awake.

The man stirred, glancing up at her. His eyes widened as he took in her green hair and striking eyes. "Lady Harvest," he breathed in reverence. "You are a vision."

Lisa flushed, suddenly self-conscious of her day-old sundress and muddy shoes. "You are too kind," she replied with a shy smile.

They continued inside the Sheriff's office, where a young woman behind the counter appeared to be wrapping up her work for the day. She froze mid-motion as her eyes landed on Lisa, her expression turning awestruck.

"Lady Harvest…" she whispered, clearly overwhelmed.

Marcus cleared his throat, stepping forward. "Good afternoon, ma'am. Is it possible to speak with the Sheriff?"

The woman blinked as if noticing Marcus for the first time. "The sheriff's been busy today," she said, hesitantly. "And honestly, this isn't a good time. We're just about to close up for the evening."

Undeterred, Marcus pressed on. "I must insist. I believe two of my charges have been kidnapped, and we need his assistance immediately."

The woman straightened, her pen pausing over her logbook. "Kidnapped?" she echoed, her voice sharpening. "What can you tell me about these charges?"

"They are two girls, fourteen years old," Marcus began, his voice measured but urgent. "Annabelle Salazar is a privateer by dress, with orange hair styled in braids and locs, orange eyes to match, and a distinctive anchor-chain belt. Sophie Griffin has violet hair, dark skin, and wears a matching purple suit and fedora."

Lisa found herself taken aback by the poetic way Marcus described the other avatars. It was accurate, of course, but she never realized how vividly he observed them. She couldn't help but wonder how he might describe her or Regina.

Adding her support, Lisa stepped forward. "Please, I fear they are in terrible danger," she said, channeling her father's negotiation lessons. *Never undersell your needs*, he would always say. She let her concern show on her face, hoping to sway the attendant's sense of urgency.

The woman jotted down notes before pulling a separate notepad from a drawer. "First things first," she said, her tone shifting into something more official, almost scripted. "What is your name, sir?"

"Brother Marcus Igbinedion, of the Order of Saint Lorraine," he replied with a note of pride in his voice.

"And you said two girls are missing?" she confirmed, jotting the names down.

"That is correct," Marcus affirmed. "Annabelle Salazar and Sophie Griffin."

The woman scribbled for a moment, then looked up again. "When was the last time you saw them?"

"Last night," Marcus answered, thinking carefully. "They were supposed to sleep at the inn and meet with the Sheriff this morning. Have you seen them?"

211

The woman shook her head slowly. "No, I don't recall anyone like that coming through here."

Marcus sensed a subtle shift in her demeanor. He couldn't quite place it, but it unsettled him; he held back from describing the exact scene where he'd found the girls' possessions, no need to *overcomplicate* the report.

"I know they made it through the night safely," Marcus said carefully. "I found some of their belongings in a clearing near where we planned to meet this morning."

"Where exactly is this clearing?" the woman asked without looking up from her notes.

"On the west side of town, near a fruit stand," he answered cautiously.

"Wilde Fruit Stand," Lisa added, earning a nod of approval from Marcus.

The woman wrote this down, then asked, "And when did you first realize they were missing?"

Marcus pulled out his watch and checked the time. It was nearly 5:00 PM. "It had to be around four o'clock," he replied.

The woman tapped her pen against the desk, then asked, "Mr. Igbinedion, what is your business in Snyder with your... charges?"

The question caught Marcus off guard. He hadn't anticipated needing an immediate answer to that. Quickly gathering his thoughts, he replied, "As a member of the Order of Saint Lorraine, I have a special duty to assist these young women in investigating a network of international kidnappers." He recalled Lisa's story about her own kidnapping and added, "Miss Nozaki here was a victim of this group and is now aiding the investigation."

Lisa nodded along, though she felt a sting of frustration at being portrayed as just a helper in his story. Still, she kept her composure.

The woman tore off the top sheet from her notepad and said, "Please wait here." Without further explanation, she disappeared into the Sheriff's office.

The attendant tore off the top sheet from her pad and said, "Please wait here," before heading into the Sheriff's office.

While they waited, Marcus took in the details of the station's front area. The space was rustic, its wooden furniture worn but functional. However, one item stood out: the opulent Verdantian flag mounted prominently on the wall, behind the counter. It seemed out of place in such a humble setting, more suited for the Governor's mansion than a small-town office. Usually, such a display might signal national pride, but to Marcus, it felt more performative, as though someone were trying too hard to proclaim their loyalty.

The attendant soon returned, hurrying them inside. "The sheriff will see you now."

Lisa and Marcus entered the office, Lisa stepping through first. Sheriff Jeffery Downs, a stocky, middle-aged man, rose from his chair and froze momentarily as he laid eyes on Lisa.

"Lady Harvest." he muttered reflexively, momentarily transfixed by her presence.

Marcus noted the reaction with mild curiosity, wondering how often Lisa was mistaken for a divine figure during her travels. To break the awkward silence, he stepped forward and extended his hand. "Thank you for seeing us, Sheriff. I'm Brother Marcus Igbindeion, of the Order of Saint Lorraine."

The Sheriff shook his hand firmly. "Sheriff Jeffery Downs. Please, have a seat," he said, motioning to two chairs in front of his desk before settling back into his own.

"So," Downs began, scanning the paper his attendant had given him, "you say two girls have gone missing?"

"Yes," Marcus confirmed. "They were supposed to meet with you this morning to discuss some recent activity in town. Did you have a chance to see either Miss Griffin or Miss Salazar?"

The Sheriff shook his head. "Can't say that I did," he replied, glancing at the paper again. He frowned. "This says one of them has violet hair and the other orange. That can't be right."

"No, it's correct," Marcus assured him. "Like Miss Nozaki here," he gestured to Lisa, "the others have distinctive appearances."

Sheriff Downs leaned back in his chair, his expression thoughtful. "That's... unusual," he muttered. "Do you have any idea what those girls were doing before they disappeared?"

"They were conducting an investigation," Marcus explained. "They planned to follow up on information we'd uncovered regarding our quarry. The plan was to meet with you and then regroup on the west outskirts of town to compare notes."

"Quarry, huh?" the Sheriff repeated. "And what exactly is that?"

"The group that kidnapped me," Lisa interjected, her voice steady. "We followed their trail here, but they vanished just before we arrived."

The Sheriff's eyebrows rose. "You're Governor Nozaki's daughter, the Lady of the Harvest, aren't you?"

"I am," Lisa confirmed.

"So tell me," Downs said, his gaze narrowing, "why would the governor's daughter be mixed up with the Order, chasing pirates with a Jibber girl?"

"I have special skills and information," Lisa began, before pausing, her mind catching on his last words. Her eyes sharpened. "How did you know Sophie was Aurorium?"

"Aurorium?" The Sheriff feigned ignorance. "What's that?"

"Miss Griffin's clan's name," Marcus interjected calmly. "They no longer use the term 'Jiberau.' It occurred to Marcus that the Sheriff would not have known that Sophie was Aurorium. She doesn't wear her badge here, and neither he nor Lisa mentioned it to the Sheriff or the attendant outside.

The Sheriff shrugged casually. "Well, okay then. And the other girl—Salazar—is a pirate, right?" He tapped the paper in front of him.

"She's a privateer," Marcus corrected.

Downs gave a faint, disbelieving chuckle. "Brother Marcus, I've got reports from multiple businesses around town claiming they've been extorted by a group of pirates. That wouldn't happen to be your Miss Salazar, would it?"

Marcus stiffened. *Annabelle could be brazen, but starting a crime spree? That was ... unthinkable.* "I can assure you; Miss Salazar has no involvement in such activities."

The Sheriff leaned forward, resting his elbows on the desk. "And if she's got a Jibber backing her up? That'd be a powerful combination. Sounds like the beginnings of a full-fledged criminal enterprise to me." He smirked. "Looks like you've been taken for a ride, Brother Marcus."

"Sophie would never do that!" Lisa burst out, her voice rising with indignation.

"Why?" Downs shot back, his tone mocking. "What makes you so sure, Little miss Lady Harvest? How long have you known this Jibber girl? A week? A month? Couldn't be much longer than that. I remember the communication from Granmark

213

when you disappeared. What, maybe around that time? I doubt they let Jibbers into Valorcrest."

Lisa faltered under the Sheriff's glare. "A month," she admitted softly. "About a month."

Downs snorted. "Exactly my point."

Lisa clenched her fists, biting back a retort.

"Sorry, little lady, but a month's not long enough to be a character witness," Sheriff Downs sneered, continuing to mock Lisa. "Looks to me like the Order got played. Pirates and Jibbers used you and Brother Marcus here to worm their way into our sacred Kingdom. Now they've probably teamed up with some local gang of hooligans and are planning to rampage across the countryside, pillaging our great home." He shook his head, his expression hardening. "But I'm not going to let that happen. I'll gather a posse and hunt down this *Captain Jack*. If I come across your girls, I'll be sure to let you know."

"No! That cannot be right!" Lisa objected, her voice tight with emotion. She couldn't believe her fellow avatars would betray them like that.

Sheriff Downs fixed Marcus with a cold stare. "Are we going to have a problem here?"

Marcus immediately read the unspoken threat. "No, Sheriff. No problem," he said quickly.

"What?!" Lisa blurted out, staring at Marcus in shock. She couldn't believe what she was hearing.

Marcus saw the Sheriff's gaze intensify and knew he had to play along. Turning to Lisa, he spoke deliberately, hoping she would catch the hidden message in his words. "Lisa, we've been fooled by Annabelle and Sophie's skullduggery. Sheriff Downs has helped me see the truth. We're fortunate we came to him before his office closed, or we might have fallen victim to their schemes. Praise the Harvest Goddess for her grace."

Marcus could see the Sheriff's suspicion easing, but Lisa was utterly bewildered. "I do not understand," she whispered, her voice cracking with confusion.

"We can talk about this later," Marcus said firmly, his tone leaving no room for argument.

"But why—" Lisa started to protest.

"**Not another word, Lisa!**" Marcus cut her off. From the corner of his eye, he saw the sheriff nod in approval. But his heart sank when he noticed Lisa's expression. Tears shimmered in her eyes, her face reflecting hurt and betrayal. The sight nearly broke him, but he had no choice, this was the only way to protect her and buy them the time.

The Sheriff leaned back in his chair, satisfied. "We can meet tomorrow I need to mobilize my posse before away from us." he said. "I'm sure I'll have a good update for you to take back to the Order and the governor."

Marcus masked his emotions behind a polite smile. "Thank you, Sheriff. That means a lot. We won't keep you any longer. I know you have important work to do." He rose from his seat and extended his hand to shake hands.

Lisa stood as well, visibly shaken. She glared at Marcus, her eyes full of anger, frustration, and pain, before storming out of the office without a word.

As the door slammed behind her, the Sheriff chuckled. "You've got your hands full with that one," he said, standing up, giving his hand a shake.

Marcus forced a tight-lipped smile and gave a half-shrug. He needed a way to steer the conversation in his favor. An idea sparked in his mind. "Sheriff, I really appreciate you saving me from those two," he said, keeping his tone warm and deferential. "I'd like to offer you a gift to show my gratitude. I don't want to bring it here, though, I wouldn't want to cause any... conflicts of interest."

The Sheriff grinned smugly. "Totally understandable, Mr. Marcus. You can bring it to my house. It's on the east side of town near the Johannson Apple Farm. Just past the gate, there's a big rock out front." He paused. "How long will you be in town?"

"A few more days, maybe a week," Marcus replied with a forced smile. "I must go. Have a good evening, Sheriff."

He gave a brief wave and held his composed expression until he stepped outside. Once on the porch, Marcus let out a slow breath. His eyes found Lisa standing at the top of the stairs, her back to him, gazing silently over the rooftops of the small town. For a moment, he hesitated. He knew the power Lisa wielded, and the fierce resolve behind it. The memory of her unflinching stand against her father flicker in his mind, a warning not to underestimate her.

With a steadying breath, he approached. "Miss Lisa," he said quietly. "We need to talk... away from here."

Lisa turned on him, her eyes blazing with fury. "How could you?!?" she hissed, her voice ice-cold and trembling with hurt. Tears shimmered at the edges of her vision.

Marcus straightened under her gaze, his tone calm but firm. "I swear to you, and to all twelve goddesses, I did what was necessary to keep you, Miss Regina, Miss Annabelle, and Miss Sophie safe."

"Sophie?" a gravelly voice interrupted from the side.

Both Marcus and Lisa turned, startled. The old man in the rocking chair was watching them now, the chair creaking slowly as he swayed back and forth.

The man adjusted the brim of his rancher's hat, his weathered face amused. "Please tell her I apologize for that bit of fun earlier," he said casually.

Lisa blinked, confusion overtaking her anger for a moment. "I am sorry, but... I do not think we are talking about the same person," she said cautiously.

"Oh, sure we are," the old man said, straightening in his chair. "Tall, slender girl with dark skin and purple hair."

"Violet, actually," Marcus corrected gently, narrowing his eyes in suspicion. "Where did you meet her, the sheriff says he hadn't seen her?"

The old man grinned. "Then I think you want to buy me dinner," he said with a wide, inviting grin.

[-----+-----]

Marcus and Lisa spoke to the old man named Cassidy in the diner for thirty minutes. He told them about his cousin's side business and how he delivered out to the place on the west side of town, where he met the ice witch, who enjoyed taunting and threatening him at the same time. He also explains to the pair that Sheriff Downs' son is leading a gang of young ruffians that dominates the crime scene in the beautiful town of Synder; mainly, the gang is filled with rejects who couldn't cut it working on a farm.

Over a steak dinner with mashed potatoes and vegetables, Cassidy explains that the Sheriff's dual role as local magistrate and town executive allows him to run the town with an iron fist. Since no one from higher government offices ever visits Snyder, Ol' Sheriff Downs uses his position to line his pockets with Ill-gotten crowns. If anyone snoops around his cash cow, then the Sheriff would dispatch his gang to take care of them. If that doesn't work, a quick arrest and 'an accident in custody' makes the problem go away.

Marcus and Lisa bid Mr. Cassidy adieu, leaving him to finish his second helping of peach pie. They leave the diner and gather themselves in the hotel, concluding that Sophie and Annabelle have run afoul of the local government, Marcus. Lisa agrees that the best course of action is to leave town as quickly as possible, retrieve everything valuable from the hidden facility, and return to Meadowbrook to review what they can deduce about where The Conspiracy has taken Jules and Matty Fournier next. Marcus tells Mr. Davis to get ready to return to Meadowbrook at first light; Meanwhile, Lisa gathers provisions from the general store in preparation for a meal cooked in transit back to the Governor's mansion. They pack not only their things from their hotel room but also Regina, Sophie and Annabelle's things, making sure they are ready to leave first thing in the morning should things with the Sheriff escalate abruptly.

Once the preparations in the town were completed, the pair returned to the facility after verifying that Regina is still fast asleep, Marcus takes Sophie's horse Kicker, and Lisa Mounts back up on her horse Grape and the pair ride across the town to the east side in the city to possibly negotiate with the crime boss sheriff for the release of the ladies Salazar and Griffin.

Chapter 15

Sophie winced as her cheek throbbed, the sting of the slap still fresh. She glared at the young man with unruly brown hair and patchy facial stubble. Turning her head slightly, she caught sight of Annabelle beside her, slumped forward with her wild orange hair cascading like a curtain, concealing her face. Both girls were tied to old and worn wooden chairs, likely taken from an old kitchen.

"Where is Captain Jack?" the man demanded again, frustration simmering in his tone. "Where's he hiding?"

"I don't know," Sophie replied curtly, shifting her gaze back to him.

His expression darkened. "Do you think I'm stupid?" He stalked toward her and grabbed a fistful of her violet curls, yanking her head back painfully. "I saw you with that one!" He forced her to look at Annabelle. "Don't tell me you're not mixed up with pirates!"

Sophie gritted her teeth through the pain. "Why don't you ask her? She's the only pirate I know!"

The man shoved her head away and crossed to Annabelle. He seized a handful of her chaotic hair and barked, "Wake up!"

Annabelle stirred with a groan. "Mate... could you keep it down? Me head's pounding."

The man yanked harder. "You're going to tell me about Captain Jack. Now."

Annabelle tilted her head lazily, blinking as though through a hangover. "Oh, him? What d'ya wanna know?"

"Where can I find him?" he growled, his patience wearing thin.

She whispered something under her breath, words that were too quiet for him to catch. Irritated, he leaned in, bringing his knife to her throat.

"Speak up!" he snarled.

Annabelle whispered again, this time describing a favorite spot in Umbrathorn that served the best fish and pasta.

"What are you going on about?" he snapped, leaning closer to hear her better, just like she wants him to.

In a flash, Annabelle lunged and sank her teeth into his ear. He screamed, wrenching himself away as blood spurted between her clenched jaws. He stumbled back, dropping the knife, hands flying to his now-mangled ear.

"You crazy cow!" His eyes widened at the sight of the blood coating his hands. "You almost took my ear off!"

Annabelle spat out the Chunk of flesh and grinned darkly. "Tastes like chicken. C'mon over boyo, I'm famished!"

Rage contorted his face as he staggered forward, oblivious to Sophie's foot jutting out. He tripped hard, crashing face-first onto the dusty floor with a grunt of pain. Blood from his torn ear dripped like red tears onto the planks beneath him.

He staggered upright, trembling with fury. "You'll pay for that. Both of you cows!" He looks down and sees the blood running down his shirt and says, "Oh no, did she bite it off?" he runs up the stairs to find aid or something.

"Don't be shy, mate!" Annabelle jeered as he limped up the stairs, clutching his ear. "Got plenty of appetite left!"

As soon as he disappeared, Sophie shifted in her chair, testing her restraints.

"We need to get out of here, Copper," Annabelle said, tugging at her ropes.

"Yep." Sophie struggled to her feet but collapsed back into the chair, causing it to creak ominously.

Annabelle glanced at the discarded knife on the floor. "Can ye reach that knife, Copper?" she asked, eyeing it hungrily.

"Not yet. Give me a minute." Sophie braced herself and threw her weight backward again. The chair groaned but held. Determined, she leaned forward to catch her breath.

"Maybe ye could grab the knife with yer teeth," Annabelle suggested, her tone half-teasing. "Then we'll hand it off, mouth-to-mouth, like proper pirates."

"Sure, because that'll solve all our problems," Sophie retorted, rolling her eyes. She slams herself down again with a loud crack. This time, the legs splintered and the frame crumbled beneath her. Sophie hit the floor hard, but her hands were free within moments.

She stood, brushing off splinters, and retrieved the knife. "Want me to stick this in your teeth you know like a proper pirate?"

"Bah! Ye just got lucky," Annabelle huffed as Sophie cut her first arm loose. She took the knife, and Annabelle finished the job herself while Sophie searched the room for a weapon.

"He'll be back soon," Sophie muttered, her violet eyes narrowing.

"Aye," Annabelle said, cracking her neck. "I needs me a proper meal."

[----- ⊕ -----]

Now free from their bonds, Sophie and Annabelle armed themselves. Sophie picked up two broken chair legs; one long, the other half its length, while Annabelle opted for a sturdy table leg, testing it with a few casual swings.

"So, the plan," Sophie began, "is to track down that guy you took a bite out of, get our stuff, and ask him a few questions."

"Okay," Annabelle replied, half-listening, eyes still on her makeshift weapon.

"*Anna*, we don't know how many people are in this place or where exactly we are. We can't charge ahead with your usual *care to the wind* way of doing things." Sophie's tone sharpened. "If we get tied up again, we won't get free a second time."

"Right. Don't get tied up. Got it," Annabelle said absently, still swinging her weapon.

Sophie sighed, glancing around the basement one last time before signaling with her head. "Let's move. I'll take the front; you cover the back."

As they crept up the stairs, Annabelle broke the silence. "So, why don't me magic work?"

"They probably used a suppression ritual," Sophie whispered back. "It's designed to block mana flow. We use similar techniques when transporting criminals."

Annabelle follows Sophie's lead to the stairs and then says, "All I know is they better gimme back me ting." Malice in her eyes, like Sophie has never seen before.

At the top of the stairs, Sophie cracked the door open and scanned the hallway beyond. Annabelle stomped up the last steps on purpose, making Sophie shoot her a scowl. Without a word, Sophie pressed a finger to her lips, motioning for quiet.

Annabelle smirked and raised a single finger in a mock salute, clearly enjoying herself.

The door led into a large kitchen. Sophie entered cautiously, holding her shorter stick horizontally in a defensive stance. Her eyes darted to a tea kettle and an open soup pot on the stovetop, no steam, no heat. The kitchen stretched at least four King's reaches in length and two in width, suggesting they were in a sizable farmhouse, likely still in the Snyder region of Verdantia.

Sophie silently committed the room's layout to memory. Counters and cabinets lined the walls, with a table and two chairs in the center. She advanced through to the dining room with Annabelle in tow.

Suddenly, a young man burst from the shadows and grabbed Sophie's arm, yanking her into a vicious knee strike to the stomach.

Gritting her teeth through the pain, Sophie retaliated, slamming the longer chair leg across his head. She twisted free and unleashed a series of rapid strikes, hammering his head, chest, and torso. A final spin kick sent him crashing into the wall.

"They're in here!" a voice shouted from deeper in the house.

"Hey there, tasty!" Annabelle called gleefully, then her voice turned fierce, "Where's me ting?!?" before leaping onto the table and sliding across it. She crashed feet-first into the man with the missing ear, knocking him to the ground; the force of her attack slid her off the table to the floor, surrounded by the other thugs.

"Hello, mates!" she quipped, lying beside him on the floor. "Any chance you can point a lass to the commode?"

One of the thugs raised a boot to stomp on her chest, but Annabelle blocked him with her table leg, straining under his weight. The man's size and gravity were working against her, until Sophie intervened. Sophie hurled her short stick into the thug's head and followed up with a crushing elbow strike, sending him sprawling.

Annabelle rolled to her feet and swung her table leg into another thug's back. He staggered but didn't drop, launching a wide haymaker. Annabelle dodged with a fluid spin and delivered a punishing strike to his spine, knocking him into the wall. Before she could catch her breath, another attacker grabbed her from behind, spinning her around and causing her to lose her weapon.

"Not smart, boyo." Annabelle growled. She stomped down hard on his foot, earning a pained scream. Sophie capitalized on the moment, smashing her remaining stick into the side of his head, knocking him unconscious.

Sophie glanced around quickly, noting that their original target, the earless man, is now fleeing up a flight of stairs. Annabelle moved to give chase, but Sophie grabbed her arm.

"Hold on!"

"What? He's getting away wit me ting!"

219

"And unless he can fly, I'm not worried," Sophie replied. She tested her mana flow and found she could channel it to her hand, though not enough to form a complete spell. They must be near the edge of the suppression field.

As Sophie searched the downed men, she swapped her broken chair legs for a pair of refined sticks wrapped in leather grips. Annabelle snickered.

"Stealing, Copper? Didn't know ye had it in ye."

"Collecting the spoils of war," Sophie replied, watching as Annabelle rifled through pockets, eventually pulling out a pouch of crowns.

Annabelle tossed the pouch in her hand. "Aye, spoils."

"Crowns won't help you fight," Sophie remarked dryly.

"Correction: *they won't help ye fight*." Annabelle's expression shifted as she touched her chest. "Those sods took me wee ting and they are gonna pay fer it!"

"Yeah, and your anchor belt." Sophie added.

Annabelle scowled. "Bastards."

"Find anything useful?"

"Just more coin." Annabelle pocketed another pouch.

Sophie sighed. "Let's go."

"Right behind you, Copper." Annabelle winked. "Just stocking up."

"You privateers really are pirates," Sophie muttered, heading for the stairs.

"Excuse ye tis fee collection," Annabelle corrected with a devilish grin.

The pair ascended to the second floor, moving cautiously along a dim hallway. One end was completely dark; the other was faintly lit by a half-open door bathed in dusky auburn light. Sophie motioned toward the door and crept forward.

Without warning, another thug burst from a nearby room, slamming Sophie against the wall. Annabelle reacted instantly, smashing her table leg across his back and following up with a sharp kick to the ribs. Sophie pushed him off and delivered a brutal series of strikes with her twin sticks, each hit precise and relentless, ending with a devastating blow to his knee.

"You're good with that," Sophie noted.

"Aye," Annabelle grinned. "it suits me."

Their banter was cut short as more thugs entered the hallway from both directions, boxing them in. The lead attacker sneered. "Well, boys, looks like we've got a two-for-one special: a jibber and a pirate."

The group jeered, hurling insults.

Annabelle and Sophie exchanged a knowing look. Without warning, Annabelle conjured a water surge, knocking down the men behind Sophie. Sophie charged forward, her sticks a blur as she laid out four attackers with ruthless efficiency.

Annabelle took advantage of the chaos, spearing one thug with her table leg and using a current spell to send two more crashing into the wall. When one grabbed her arm, disrupting her spell, she retaliated with a kick to the knee and a punch to the face.

"Move, Anna!" Sophie shouted, stepping in to deliver a final crushing blow to an advancing thug. Sophie's mana surged as she invoked a spell from her training with her momma: *Drillkick*. Her foot connected with a forceful strike, blasting the thug so hard that the wall caved in around him.

The three remaining thugs stared at the carnage in disbelief. One shook his head and muttered, "Never mind this," waving both hands in surrender. They dropped their weapons and quickly ran down the stairs.

Sophie and Annabelle exchanged dumbstruck looks before Annabelle shrugged. "Well, that was easy."

"Too easy," Sophie muttered warily as they stepped over the unconscious thugs. When they reached the door to the next room, Annabelle retrieved her table leg from the floor. The two nodded silently, steeling themselves for the next fight.

Sophie kicked the door open, storming in with her twin sticks raised. Annabelle followed, table leg at the ready. Their confidence faltered instantly.

The room was a study, dominated by a large desk. Behind it stood Sheriff Downs, broad-shouldered and calm, levelling a six-shooter at them. At his side was the thug Annabelle had bitten; Sophie had mentally nicknamed him *Chunk*.

"Hello, girls," the sheriff greeted, his expression cold. "Fancy meeting you here."

Sophie scowled, dropping her sticks and raising her hands. "Now it all makes sense."

"Oh? What's that, Jibber girl?" Chunk sneered, his grin infuriatingly smug.

Sophie's jaw tightened at the slur. "I couldn't figure out how a bunch of weak thugs were running a crime ring without the sheriff shutting them down," she said evenly. "Turns out, it's his gang."

"It's **MY** gang!" Chunk barked, bristling with pride.

"Calm down, son," the sheriff ordered. "She's just trying to get under your skin."

Annabelle, grinning mischievously, stepped out from behind Sophie. "Aye, see? Coppers are the real criminals, just like I told ye." She blew Chunk a mocking kiss, watching him seethe.

"What now?" Sophie asked, her eyes scanning the room.

"Now?" Chunk sneered as he approached Annabelle with an evil grin. "Now, we get rid of you both."

He reached for Annabelle's face, but she snapped at him like a feral dog, forcing him to flinch back.

Sophie caught the sheriff shifting his aim toward Annabelle and Chunk. Without thinking, she darted to the right, forcing him to adjust. The first shot went wide, ripping into the wall. Sophie dropped flat to the floor, her training mantra echoing in her mind: **Run one, run two—DROP!**

The second shot missed, hitting just above her. She exhaled shakily. Avatar of War or not, she wasn't bulletproof.

Annabelle, meanwhile, smirked as an idea hit her. She summoned a waterspout beneath the sheriff, launching him into the ceiling. He flailed helplessly, pinned by the swirling column of water.

Chunk gawked at the display, momentarily stunned. Annabelle seized the moment, delivering a pair of rapid Riptide punches, right then left. The force hurled him over the desk, where he crashed headfirst into the wood. As the waterspout ended, the sheriff fell with a thud, his pistol skidding across the floor.

Sophie saw her chance. She sprang from the floor and dashed forward, her fist glowing with channeled mana.

HARDKNUCKLE!

She cast the spell, driving her punch into the sheriff's face. The blow sent him hurtling across the room, where he crumpled in a heap.

Sophie grabbed a pair of handcuffs from his belt and secured his right hand to his left ankle. The sheriff didn't stir, but Chunk groaned, slowly regaining consciousness. Annabelle loomed over him, eyes narrowed dangerously.

"*Where's me ting?*" she demanded, eyes burning with malice.

"What's a ting?" he asked in a mocking, disrespectful tone.

"*Me necklace.*" she replies

Chunk snickered, mocking her accent. "Can't tell ye."

Annabelle's fist slammed into the desk beside his head, cracking the wood. "Yer gonna give me back what's mine."

"I would, but I can't remember where we put it," he taunted.

Before Annabelle could escalate further, Sophie placed a calming hand on her shoulder. "Hold on, Anna. Let me try."

Annabelle hesitated, then stepped aside with a grin as Sophie picked up the sheriff's pistol.

"Look," Sophie said patiently. "If you give us the necklace, we'll leave. Believe it or not, we have better things to do."

Chunk sneered. "You're bluffing. Jibbers don't have it in them to pull the trigger. *Cowardice is your fatal flaw.*"

Sophie gritted her teeth in frustration. *Ancestors, give me strength*, she thought. Inspiration struck, and she tossed the gun to Annabelle. "You're right. I won't shoot you. But it is *her* necklace."

Annabelle caught the gun with a wicked grin and cocked the hammer. "Aye. So, about me ting…"

Chunk paled, fear washing over him, scrambling to his feet. "Forget this!" He darted behind the desk, frantically rifling through the center drawer. "I know I put it in here…"

"Yer running out of time, mate," Annabelle warned, her voice turning cold, laced with murder.

Sophie started to regret her decision. "Anna, calm down."

"oh I'm calm," Annabelle replied casually, though her eyes told a different story. "I just want me ting back…*good and now.*"

Chunk dumped the drawer's contents onto the desk. "It's gone! I don't know where it went!"

Without warning, Annabelle fired a shot into the furnace vent to his left. The bang echoed through the room, silencing everyone. Chunk froze, his fear palpable. Annabelle's playful demeanor vanished, replaced by a killer's focus.

"Mate, ye'd better…" She paused mid-threat, patting her tights. Her eyes widened in surprise. Reaching into a pocket, she pulled out her necklace. "Oh. Her it is."

Sophie stared in disbelief. "Wait… how… when…"

Annabelle flashed an innocent smile. "Oops."

Recovering, Sophie sighed and shook her head. "Fine. But now what about your anchor belt?"

"Aye, right." Annabelle levelled the gun at Chunk again. "Now, mate, where's the belt?"

Chunk swallowed hard, realizing his nightmare wasn't over.

[-----✝-----]

Marcus rode Sophie's horse, Kicker, while Lisa followed on her own horse, Grape. As they neared the sheriff's house, a plume of black smoke rose beyond Johannson

Apple Farm. Marcus eyed the direction and urged Kicker into a gallop. Lisa spurred Grape to keep up. The closer they got, the worse things looked.

Ahead of them, Sophie rode a black steed with Annabelle seated behind her, arms loosely wrapped around Sophie's waist. Both young women looked disheveled and weary.

The four of them pulled up in front of the sheriff's burning house.

"Hey, guys. Fancy meeting you here," Sophie greeted, her tone weary but casual.

"What happened here?" Marcus asked, eyeing the flames and the wreckage.

"Those bastards stole me anchor belt!" Annabelle declared.

Sophie rolled her eyes. "He said they didn't have it. I don't think he was lying."

"Likely story," Annabelle huffed.

"Girl, the man pissed himself. I doubt he was holding back," Sophie retorted.

Marcus raised a hand. "Actually, I have your anchor belt, Miss Annabelle. It's back at the facility, waiting for you to reclaim it."

Annabelle blinked, then grumbled. "Oh. Well, why didn't ye say so earlier? Bad form, servant." She shot Marcus a playful glare, which he took as a good sign she was recovering from their ordeal.

Lisa crossed her arms, nodding toward the blaze. "Okay, but what happened in there?"

"They ambushed us out in the field near the fake door," Sophie explained. "Next thing I knew, we were inside that house", she gestured to the flaming structure, "and we had to fight our way out. Then the house caught fire after Annabelle shot the furnace."

"Oi, ye don't know that's what started the fire!" Annabelle protested.

"It wasn't burning before you shot it," Sophie countered, smirking slightly.

"Bah!" Annabelle waved her hand dismissively.

"Ladies," Marcus interjected, "we should head back to the facility. I suspect this fire might attract unwanted attention."

"Aye, good point, Brother Marcus." Annabelle gave him a thumbs-up.

With that, the four rode through town, passing the closed Wilde fruit stand under the cover of night. Upon arriving at the facility, they tied their horses at the back entrance and slipped inside through the double doors. There, they found Regina seated at a table piled with papers, eating a turkey sandwich.

"Hey, where were you guys?" Regina asked, her words muffled by a mouthful of food.

"Oi, missy, we've been through it!" Annabelle began, launching into a dramatic recounting of their day. But she trailed off when she noticed Regina looking past her, eyes narrowing in concentration.

Sophie's instincts kicked in. "What is it?" she asked, turning to glance over her shoulder toward the forest.

"I think..." Regina said, setting down her sandwich and stepping forward slowly. "It feels like..." She deciphered what her Earthbloom sense was telling her, which she had become more adept at using after days of painful practice. Her eyes widened in realization. "Someone is out there!"

The group turned toward the forest edge. Lisa used her own Earthbloom sense but struggled to pinpoint anything unusual. "Where?" she asked, focusing hard.

"Over there," Regina said, pointing to the left. "Maybe... ten, no, maybe thirty meters away."

"Meters?" Sophie repeated, puzzled. In Opulentia, they measured distance in the King's systems.

"About twenty-five King's Reaches," Marcus supplied absentmindedly, doing the conversion in his head.

Lisa frowned. "How are you sensing that far?"

"I dunno," Regina replied, stepping toward the trees. "I'm going to check it out."

"I'll come with ye," Annabelle said, drawing the pistol she had taken from the sheriff's house.

Lisa blinked, startled. "Where did you get that?"

"From the sheriff," Annabelle answered with a grin. "Said he wouldn't be needing it no more."

Lisa gave Sophie a wide-eyed, questioning look. Sophie merely shrugged, silently conveying, *not precisely, but close enough.*

Turning to Marcus, Sophie ordered, "Stay here, Brother Marcus."

Sophie and Lisa followed Regina and Annabelle into the woods. Lisa continued using her Earthbloom sense, mulling over how Regina's reach seemed so vast. *Is it because of all the mana backlash she endured?* she wondered.

Regina, meanwhile, focused on what felt like a stationary presence ahead. Lisa's earlier advice echoed in her mind, Earthbloom wasn't about actively concentrating on something but rather about filtering out everything else. Over-focusing often led to painful backlash.

"It's not moving much," Regina murmured, narrowing her eyes.

Lisa, sensing her friend's unease, raised her voice. "Oh, Regina, there's no one in the trees watching us."

Regina spun around, startled. "What?! But I can..."

"It's like the muffins," Lisa interrupted, referencing their strange encounter at the docks in Granmark. "Here, I'll show you." She waved Regina over, her tone light and coaxing.

"Muffins?" Annabelle echoed, arching a brow as she strolled over to Lisa. "Not sure what yer talkin' about, missy."

Lisa gave her a dismissive shrug and focused on casting two spell circles. one green, the other brown. Runes shimmered along their edges. Regina, curious, studied the inscriptions. Around the green circle were runes for Grow, Capture, Ensnare, Stiffen, and Expand twice. The brown circle bore the runes for Open, Shallow, Capture, Hole, Ensnare, and Solid.

With a knowing wink at Regina, Lisa activated both circles. The green circle pulsed, releasing a wave of energy that commanded nearby tree vines to spring to life. They snaked toward a man concealed within the forest, wrapping around him mid-leap as he tried to flee. Suspended in mid-air, he struggled against the vines until the brown circle manifested beneath him. The earth opened, and when he finally broke free of the vines, he dropped into the pit. The spell sealed around him, leaving only his head exposed above the hardened soil.

"We should go and have a discussion with him." Lisa said, leading the group toward the trapped man. The four young women formed a semi-circle around him, their expressions ranging from curious to hostile.

The man's gaze fixed on Lisa's vivid green hair and eyes. "Lady Harvest," he muttered reverently.

Sophie stiffened, recognizing his voice. "You're the one who kidnapped us," she said coldly.

The masked man ignored her, his attention wholly on Lisa.

"Oi! We talkin' to ye!" Annabelle snapped, pulling the sheriff's pistol from her waistband. "Ye might wanna focus, mate."

"You won't hurt me," the man replied calmly. "Lady Harvest won't allow harm to come to her faithful followers."

"Why are you here?" Sophie demanded, stepping closer.

The man remained silent, still staring at Lisa.

"Why are you here?" Lisa echoed, her tone firmer.

Again, no response.

"Oi!" Annabelle kicked a clump of dirt at his head. "Ye hearin' us or what?"

Lisa took a deep breath, recalling lessons from the Harvest church. "You misunderstand," she said softly but firmly. "The harvest demands that we tend our fields... ensuring they are free of aphids and locusts."

At this, the man's gaze finally faltered.

"Our Lady Harvest commands us to remove the weeds that threaten our crops," Lisa continued. She conjured a glowing brown spell circle without activating it. Three green runes hovered around it ominously.

The man's eyes widened in fear. "Are you... saying Lady Harvest considers me a burden? A weed?"

Lisa's voice remained calm but cold. "A weed doesn't always know it's a weed."

"I'll talk!" he blurted, panicking as he recognized the runes in the circle. "I'm just a hired gun! Those local boys paid me to keep watch on a group that had been staying near here for a month. They took off a couple of days ago."

Sophie knelt to his level, narrowing her eyes. "And what can you tell us about them?"

The man hesitated. "Like what?"

"Like how many of them there were," she replied, tapping his head with her finger.

"I don't know," he admitted, looking away.

"You watched them for a month and don't know how many there were?" Sophie scoffed. "What, did they pay you in *beans*?"

"It's not that simple," he snapped, frustration creeping into his voice. "They always had someone on perimeter watch, like that lady with the machines, or the Ice witch, or the one who stayed hidden in the shadows. Any time I got close, I had to dodge one of them to avoid getting caught."

"Why would the local boys pay you to watch that group?" Lisa asked, dispelling her circle. "They were working together, were they not?"

The man shrugged. "I get paid to do what I'm told. Asking *why* isn't part of the job description."

"So, what did you see?" Sophie pressed.

"I saw the Shadow, Ice, and Machine witches. And then there was the one woman in a bloody dress," he explained. "One morning, I got close enough to see her leading a little kid and a man from their house toward the place you're staying at."

"They had a house back there?" Annabelle asked, pointing toward the clearing. "Where'd it go?"

"No idea. It just... disappeared a couple of days ago."

Marcus strode up just as the masked man continued talking. He took in the strange sight of the man's head sticking out of the ground and glanced around at the group.

"Is everything alright, ladies?" he asked calmly.

"Aye," Annabelle replied with a smirk, crouching on the opposite side of the trapped man's head from Sophie. "We're just gettin' acquainted with this poor sod here." She playfully rubbed the top of the man's hood, causing him to flinch.

"Please! You have to help me!" the man pleaded. "They're going to kill me!"

The avatars turned their attention back to him.

"He's not going to help you," Sophie informed him with a glare. "Now, tell me about that house."

The man hesitated, glancing between Marcus and Sophie.

Marcus gave a helpless shrug. "I really can't do much for you, my good man."

With a heavy sigh, the man relented. "It was like a mansion, a big house. I couldn't get too close, though. The shadows and machines would've torn me apart."

"How do you know that?" Marcus asked, his eyes narrowing.

"I saw them," the man explained. "The shadow creatures, they hunted animals in the forest. I watched them chase down raccoons, deer, birds, squirrels. They'd rip them apart for no reason. Didn't even eat them. Just killed them and left the bodies. Haven't you noticed how quiet the forest is? No animals around. They got the message."

"Yes... Mage is known for her violent sadism," Marcus muttered grimly. He crossed his arms. "Where do you think they went after leaving here? Did you hear anything?"

"I didn't hear where they were headed," the man replied nervously. "That's all I know. I swear!"

"Mate, I got a question," Annabelle interjected. "How'd ye knock me and the purple copper out?"

The man hesitated before sighing. "My magic. I have a spell that can put people to sleep."

Annabelle growled under her breath. "You sneaky little..." She stopped herself and glared at Sophie. "We can't let him go. He'll just try to take us hostage again!"

"You said you worked for the sheriff's gang, right?" Lisa asked.

"Yes, madam. Just a hired employee," he answered, his voice edging toward panic.

"How much are you owed?" Lisa continued.

"Five hundred crowns," he said sheepishly.

Lisa's green eyes widened slightly. That was enough to rent a luxury suite for a day or two, with meals included. Her disbelief was plain on her face.

The man rolled his eyes and sighed. "For you, Lady Harvest, I'll give you a discount. Three hundred crowns."

Sophie turned to Annabelle, who threw up her hands. "Why're ye lookin' at me? This is Lisa's idea."

Annabelle leaned in and tapped the man's head. "Two-fifty," she bargained.

The man scowled, then turned to Lisa. "Is Lady Harvest not generous?"

Lisa and Annabelle shared a look before Lisa replied with a grin. "Generosity begets generosity."

Defeated, the man sighed again. "Fine. Two-fifty."

Sophie leaned in, her voice low and deadly. "If you even think about crossing us again, I want you to remember the pistol my friend here is holding."

Annabelle showed off the sheriff's pistol with a flourish. "Nice, innit?"

The man's eyes bulged as he looked at it. "Oh, I promise! After I get my crowns, I'm heading straight back to Vinderville. You will never see me again."

Satisfied, Sophie and Annabelle stood, giving Lisa room to undo the spell circle. The ground opened, releasing the man. He climbed out, dressed in a dark blue outfit with numerous covert pockets. Annabelle handed him two hundred crop crowns and started to walk away.

"Ahem," the man coughed meaningfully.

Annabelle turned, eyes narrowing. "What's ye problem?"

"We agreed on two-fifty."

Marcus and the others gave her disapproving looks. With an exasperated groan, Annabelle pulled out her money pouch. "By the sea, ye girls are expensive!" She counted out fifty more crowns, grumbling, "This ain't fair, I earned every crown!" She dropped the coins into the man's hand.

"Thank you kindly," the man said with a mocking bow.

"Yeah, yeah. Just make sure we don't see ye again," Annabelle warned, tapping the pistol on her belt. "Ye might find yourself payin' a tax next time."

"Trust me, you'll never see me again," he promised, retreating into the forest toward the fruit stand and farms until he vanished into the darkness.

Once they were sure he wasn't coming back, the group returned to the facility. After securing the door, they sat around the table where Regina had been earlier.

Marcus cleared his throat. "Ladies, I believe things have escalated to a point where we need to leave town immediately, especially since the sheriff's house burned down." He gave Sophie and Annabelle a pointed look.

They both glanced away, guilt flashing across their faces.

"I'm sure reprisals will come swiftly," Marcus continued. "Our best course is to take what useful information and supplies we can and leave by first light. We can sleep on the way back to Meadowbrook."

"Back to Meadowbrook..." Lisa echoed softly, a wave of sadness washing over her.

The others noticed her shift in mood.

"Well, now, what's this then?" Annabelle asked bluntly.

Marcus hesitated before explaining. "Governor Nozaki only allowed Lisa to accompany us here, but he made it clear she wouldn't be returning to the Stormfang. She's to stay in Meadowbrook."

"What?!" Sophie protested.

"This is terrible," Regina murmured.

"What're we gonna do?" Annabelle began to scheme. "We could just blow past the mansion and head straight for the Fang. Run outta port like we did in Granmark!"

"That is not going to work," Lisa said gently. "Your ship will not leave port."

"Our ship, girlie," Annabelle corrected with a grin. "Yer crew."

Sophie gave Annabelle a hard look, tired of the ongoing bickering about Annabelle constantly saying she was not a member of the Stormfang crew. In response, Annabelle stuck out her tongue, taunting her playfully.

"Be that as it may," Lisa interjected firmly, cutting off the argument. "My father has eyes everywhere. If we tried to get me back to the ship, they'd likely stop the transport, arrest everyone, and charge the entire crew with conspiracy to kidnap me."

She scanned the table before adding, "Brother Marcus and Regina might be spared, but Annabelle and Sophie? You'd both be as good as locked up."

"And the Aurorium's clear passage wouldn't hold any weight here in Verdantia," Marcus added. "The local authorities would assume the crew participated in the conspiracy."

"Eclipse Lepele would get arrested too," Sophie muttered.

"Who's Eclipse Lepele?" Regina asked.

"He's a member of my clan," Sophie explained. "I found him in a hidden chamber under the barn near the governor's mansion."

"Captain Lowe escorted him back to the Stormfang," Marcus added.

Annabelle gasped dramatically. "So that's what's goin' on! Ye snuck another copper on me ship!" She pointed an accusatory finger at Sophie.

Sophie glared back. "Yep. We're plotting your downfall," she deadpanned.

"Focus!" Lisa snapped, exasperated.

"Right, focus!" Regina echoed, glaring at the pair.

Marcus steered the conversation back on track. "Can we determine where the conspiracy took Jules and Matthew Fournier with what he have here?"

"We could guess," Sophie admitted, "but we have nothing solid. It'd just be speculation."

The group fell silent for a moment. Seeing no suggestions, Marcus continued, "Then our next question is—what did the conspiracy want with this facility?"

"I know that the *Order of the Black Sun* was using it to extract mana from someone's body," Regina explained. "They were trying to find a way to store it for future use."

"The Order of the Black Sun?" Sophie repeated, her brow furrowing. "What's that?" She looked to Marcus for an answer.

"I can't say," Marcus admitted. "I've never heard of it. All the journals and reports I've read only refer to *the Order* without naming it. Miss Fournier, how did you come across that name?"

"It's in this journal," Regina replied, rummaging through the stacks of papers. She eventually found the journal, its cover missing a nameplate.

Marcus examined it. "The name's been deliberately removed…" He paused, recalling details from the reports he had sifted through earlier. Suddenly, he pulled a report from the pile, a set of papers bound by a metal ring. Flipping through it quickly, he said, "This explains it. According to this report, written by someone named Orion, the journal belonged to a member of the Order called *Neptune*. Orion punished Neptune for breaking their Order's tenets by erasing his name from his works and putting him *on display as an example*. Whatever that means…"

Lisa gasped remembering the name written on the jars holding organs "Oh by the harvest, this Neptune person those organs are his" Lisa says pointing to the room. "That is what this *Orion* means by putting him on display."

Everyone shared a ghastly glance acknowledging the macabre logic of the display in the storage room.

Eager to move the conversation forward Marcus suggests "So maybe *the conspiracy* is really just the Order of the Black Sun."

"Sure, why not," Sophie said with a shrug, unfazed by the name.

"So why would the Black Sun come here?" Lisa asked. "Why bring Regina's family and stay for weeks?"

"Maybe they just needed somewhere to hold them?" Regina suggested hesitantly.

"That doesn't make sense," Sophie argued. "If they just needed a holding place, why not use their magical moving house? Less risk, no evidence left behind."

She gestured at the table, accidentally flipping over a piece of paper among the scattered drawings. It caught her eye, a crude sketch of Matthew punching a woman in red, wielding a large axe. Beneath it was a written order. Sophie picked it up and read it silently.

"Stop actin' like ye can read, copper," Annabelle teased, crossing her arms.

"Shhh," Sophie snapped, focusing on the document. It appeared to be an official edict from something called the Council of Shadows, directing their legions to prioritize efforts under a mysterious Pathway Initiative. The Order spoke of planets, moons, and constellations being mobilized to fulfill a "holy goal."

"Pathway Initiative..." Sophie whispered, her eyes narrowing as she rifled through more of the papers for clues.

"What's that?" Regina asked.

"Get all of Matthew's drawings," Sophie instructed urgently. "I think your father was trying to send a message, maybe call for help."

"With kid's drawings?" Annabelle scoffed. "Copper, ye're really reachin' here."

"Just do it." Sophie said, her voice steady but firm.

Regina grabbed one of Matty's pictures. It depicted her father casting a spell to set a woman wielding a large axe on fire. Turning the page over, she found another edict, this one signed by someone named Orion. The message ordered planets and moons within this quadrant to dedicate themselves to solving the "Storage Problem" while maintaining the utmost secrecy. It also warned against the sin of pride, advising that anyone who believed themselves central to the Order's goal should visit *Storage Room 2* to learn from Neptune's downfall.

"Storage Problem," Regina thought aloud. She looked up and added, "I think Sophie's right. We need to gather all these papers with Mattie's drawings."

The group spread out, collecting all of Matthew's sketches. There were fifteen in total. They carefully stored them between the pages of Marcus' journal before gathering their belongings. Moments later, they stood outside the facility's main doors in the clearing, the oppressive quiet of the night pressing in on them.

"We cannot just leave this place here," Lisa said suddenly, her voice trembling with unexpected outrage. "The evil of this place... it makes me feel so..."

"Aye," Annabelle cut in, her expression twisted in discomfort. She looked around, trying to find the right words. "It feels like..."

"disgust," Sophie supplied, her violet eyes hardening. "We have to do something about this place."

Without a word, Regina stepped forward and arranged her mana into Earthbloom. She took a deep breath, allowing her senses to map the facility's full size and structure underground. Once she understood its layout, she conjured two interconnected spell circles, one brown and one green.

The brown circle glowed with runes: *Churn, Open, Crumble, Engulf, Sink, and Compact.* Around the green circle were the runes *Summon, Grow, Strengthen, Reach, Entangle, and Pull.* Regina wove the circles together and executed the spell.

The ground trembled beneath their feet as the earth churned violently, cracking open beneath the facility. Tree roots surged upward like living tendrils, snaking through the building's foundation and pulling the structure apart. Walls groaned and collapsed as the entire facility began to sink into the earth. Dust, dirt, and debris exploded into the night sky.

Realizing the horses were panicking, Marcus and Sophie quickly hurried to free Grape, Kicker, and the sheriff's horse from the crossbars. They led the frightened animals a safe distance away from the spell's radius.

The facility crumbled completely, the hill around it collapsing into a massive crater. When the dust finally settled, nothing of the building remained. Regina exhaled, dispelling the circles with a sense of accomplishment.

Lisa stared at the scene in awe. That wasn't just a random spell, it was Regina's first major Earthbloom success. Inspired, Lisa decided to repair the landscape. She conjured a synergistic spell circle, layering a brown circle inside a blue one. The blue circle shimmered with runes for Summon, Fill, and Contain, while the brown circle held Shape, Solidify, and Smooth.

Lisa activated the circles. The earth shifted, reshaping itself according to her command. Water surged from underground, filling the crater and forming a lake in the clearing. The terrain smoothed and stabilized, nature responding eagerly to Lisa's mastery of Earthbloom.

"Wow," Regina breathed, eyes wide with admiration. "Can you show me how to do that?"

Lisa let out a slow breath, feeling the high mana drain. "I will have to show you later. That spell was... alot."

"Well," Marcus said, his voice filled with awe, "that was incredible. Both of you."

"All that power, and not a single flower," Annabelle teased with a grin, earning a scowl from Lisa.

Always ready to meet a challenge, Regina focused her Earthbloom sense on dormant plant life around the new lake. She conjured a green spell circle, etched with five runes: Summon, Grow, Drink, Expand, and Strengthen. Energizing the circle, she watched as vibrant green particles radiated outward, coaxing hidden seeds and roots to sprout. Flowers bloomed rapidly, forming a lush, colorful border around the lake.

"Pretty flowers, as requested, missy" Regina teased, flashing Annabelle a grin.

Annabelle blinked in surprise, then laughed. "Aye, now that's more like it."

"Wow, Regina, you've really gotten the hang of Earthbloom magic," Sophie remarked. "Well... after a while, anyway."

Regina chuckled. "It definitely got easier once I learned how to use Earthbloom sense properly."

Marcus, holding Kicker's reins, glanced up at the moon before pulling out his pocket watch. The time read 11:45 p.m. under the silvery light. He considered how little rest they'd get if they returned to the inn and how much better it might be to reach their next destination directly.

"Ladies," he began thoughtfully, "we should ride through the night to the governor's mansion. We could sleep there instead."

"Sounds good to me," Annabelle agreed immediately.

"It would," Sophie retorted, crossing her arms. "You'd just sleep in the wagon, Anna."

"We can switch out," Marcus suggested. "I'll ride *Kicker* to the first rest stop. Sophie, you could get some sleep during that stretch. Then I'll take Miss Lisa's *Grape* to the second stop, giving her a chance to rest from there until we reach her home."

"But you will be exhausted if we do that?" Lisa asked, frowning.

"It's my duty to serve," Marcus replied earnestly. "I'll manage."

Annabelle furrowed her brow. "Wait... are we leavin' already?"

"Yeah, girl. Were you even listening?" Sophie asked with an incredulous look.

"Bah." Annabelle waved off the comment. "I just need to make a quick stop before we head to the mansion."

Sophie groaned. "What now? Haven't we been through enough for one day?"

"No, no, it's nothing like that," Annabelle reassured her. "It'll be quick. I promise." She flashed an innocent smile that didn't quite convince Sophie.

"Fine," Sophie sighed, shaking her head. "but I swear by the ancestors, if this turns into a mess, I'll let them take you this time."

"It'll be fine, I swear," Annabelle insisted. "Hey, Brother Marcus, can I borrow a pen and some paper?"

"Of course," Marcus replied, handing her a small scrap notebook and a pen from his pocket.

"Shall we?" Marcus said, gesturing for the avatars to begin their long journey back. The group exchanged looks of shared exhaustion but silently agreed. It was time to move forward.

[----- ⚓ -----]

Following Annabelle's directions, Sophie rode Kicker to the Wilde fruit stand. Annabelle hopped off and scribbled a note on a page from Marcus's scrap notebook:

Dear Fruit Stand Folks,
Save me a ten percent cut 'til I come back for it.

Fair winds and following seas,
Captain Jack

With a satisfied grin, Annabelle slid the note under the door at the back of the fruit stand. She then trotted around to the front, where Sophie waited, visibly annoyed, on the other side of the seating area, still astride Kicker.

Annabelle approached and climbed up with Sophie's help, settling into her spot behind her.

"Are you good now?" Sophie asked, her patience clearly worn thin.

"Aye." Annabelle replied cheerfully.

"You know, one day you're going to have to explain this whole Captain Jack business to me," Sophie pressed.

"Nothin' ta tell," Annabelle said nonchalantly.

"Oh really? How does *nothing* end with us tied up and you burning down the sheriff's house?" Sophie shot back.

Annabelle sighed, exhausted from the day's events. "Look, Copper, I'll cut ye in," she offered with a smirk. "If ye let it go."

Hearing the weariness in Annabelle's voice, Sophie decided to drop it for now. Nudging Kicker with her heels and a soft "kik kik," she urged the horse into a steady trot. They picked up speed as they reached the main road, heading toward the inn, their semi-final stop for the night.

[-----◉-----]

Lisa and Regina rode Grape back to the inn in Snyder, a town that was more of a single street than anything else. Marcus followed closely on the sheriff's unnamed horse, his ease in the saddle clear throughout the thirty-minute journey.

When they arrived at the inn, everyone dismounted. Marcus quickly tied the unnamed horse to a hitching post on the side of the building. Without wasting time, he hurried inside to wake Mr. Davis and deliver the bad news: they would need to leave immediately.

Meanwhile, Lisa tied Grape to a post on the opposite side of the inn's door and turned to Regina. "We packed everyone's stuff and left it in the rooms. Help me get it all down to the carriage while Mr. Davis gets ready," she suggested.

"Okay," Regina agreed, heading inside toward the second floor where their rooms were located.

Lisa climbed the stairs to room fourteen and unlocked the door. Her belongings were neatly piled on the bed, along with a burlap sack of ingredients she had gathered earlier. Grabbing both her travel bag and the sack, she made her way downstairs. She passed the empty check-in desk, taking care to avoid the saloon entrance. The last thing they needed was any attention this late at night.

Exiting through the backyard, she arrived at the wagon, parked in the lot where they had shared breakfasts the past few days. Regina was already there, placing her bag into the cargo compartment. Lisa followed suit, setting her travel bag in the compartment and securing the sack of ingredients in the food storage area near the front of the wagon.

Curious, she opened the compartment containing the cooking materials. Inside, she found a modest set: a medium-sized pot for open-fire cooking, one bowl, one plate, a single fork, a spoon, a butter knife, and a sharp knife. She stared at the limited supplies in dismay. *Oh no...* Lisa had been looking forward to making campfire stew for everyone before they parted ways, but she hadn't prepared for the fact that there weren't enough dishes. Unsure of what to do, she headed back inside, deep in thought.

[-----✠-----]

Inside the inn, Marcus knocked on Mr. Davis's door, waking the innkeeper.

"What happened to first light?" Davis protested groggily, rubbing his eyes.

"Unfortunately, Mr. Davis, we have to leave now," Marcus explained politely. "It can't be avoided."

Davis shook his head with a tired sigh. "Fine, okay," he muttered, giving a nod before retreating behind his door. Marcus heard him grumble something about "these damn people" before the door closed.

"Thank you," Marcus called after him, hoping Davis wouldn't be too upset. He then headed to his room, swiftly gathering his overnight bag. On his way back down the hall, he stopped by Sophie and Annabelle's rooms to collect their bags as well.

With the luggage in hand, he carefully maneuvered down the staircase and through the narrow hallway. As he passed the back door, he noticed Lisa pacing, clearly preoccupied with some kind of problem. He debated asking if she needed help, but decided to give her space for now. Instead, he continued outside and stored the bags in the wagon's compartment.

After securing everything, Marcus glanced around and noted that Lisa had returned to the inn. Whatever was bothering her, she seemed determined to figure it out on her own.

Sophie and Annabelle arrived at the inn to find Regina standing near the entrance, petting Grape.

"Hey, girl," Sophie called out, waving.

"Hi!" Regina chirped, her energy as bright as ever.

"What's the word, girlie?" Annabelle asked with a grin.

"I dunno…" Regina replied, tilting her head. "What word am I supposed to know?"

"Are we leaving?" Sophie asked.

"Not yet," Regina said, scratching behind Grape's ear. "I don't think we're ready."

Sophie and Annabelle exchanged a look before heading inside. They found Lisa pacing back and forth in the inn's serving area, clearly distressed. The room, usually filled with breakfast trays and plates, was eerily quiet and empty.

"Hey, Lisa," Sophie called as they walked toward her.

Lisa stopped pacing and sighed. "I need to find some bowls and silverware," she muttered.

"Bowls? For what?" Sophie asked. "What's going on?"

Lisa hesitated, then admitted softly, "I wanted to make us some campfire stew... just one last time together." Her voice wavered, and tears welled in her eyes.

Understanding dawned on Annabelle, and an idea struck her. "Go on, missy," she said with a devilish grin. "I'll meet ye outside." The grin clearly said, "I'ma fixer."

Sophie raised a brow but didn't question it. She gently guided Lisa out of the room and into the back area of the inn. Lisa gave Sophie a knowing look.

"What's she going to do?" Lisa asked cautiously.

"No idea," Sophie replied, watching Marcus inspect the carriage nearby. "but I am sure we don't want to a witness against her later."

"Hi there, Brother Marcus," Sophie called.

Marcus paused his work and turned to face them. "Hello, Miss Griffin. Are you ready to go?"

"Sure am," Sophie replied.

Just then, Annabelle emerged from the inn, carrying a stack of bowls and silverware. She strolled over to the back of the carriage, leaning in to place the items in the storage compartment alongside the pot and food.

"'Scuse me," she said to Marcus before clapping her hands together with satisfaction. "Problem solved!"

Sophie's eyes narrowed suspiciously. "Annabelle... Don't tell me you stole those bowls from the inn."

"*Stole* is such an ugly word, Copper" Annabelle said with mock indignation.

"Did you leave any crowns for them?" Sophie pressed, crossing her arms.

Annabelle blinked. "Why would I leave crowns? They got plenty o' bowls."

Sophie stared at her in exasperated silence.

"By the sea, ye girls are so damned expensive!" Annabelle grumbled, throwing up her hands as she turned and headed back toward the inn. "This is comin' outta yer cut!" she called over her shoulder.

Interlude 1 – Duncan and Cassidy

D uncan had served as an agent of the Emerald Veil, the secretive intelligence network of the Kingdom of Verdantia, for just under five years. His latest assignment had brought him from his home territory of Clarksdale to the small, unassuming town of Snyder. The local crime gang had been hiring, putting out feelers for an out-of-towner to shadow a group of strange newcomers who had arrived with a lot of money and magic that defied explanation. Duncan had been selected for the role, adopting the persona of a masked hitman called *Juniper*. His ability to put targets to sleep with magic made him a valuable choice.

For six weeks, Juniper worked for the gang, which was surprisingly led by the town's sheriff, Matthew Downs, and his son, Lincoln. Without the sheriff's influence, the gang was a disorganized mess; but they paid well. The group they wanted Juniper to monitor, however, was a different story altogether. These people were professionals. Organized, elusive, and highly capable, they had a network of low-level operatives but were also protected by witches unlike anything Duncan had seen. One witch moved through shadows, another conjured animals from metal with her striking blue hair, and the third, an ice witch, was terrifyingly sadistic, freezing anything and everything in her path solid. Duncan knew better than to get too close. Being discovered by any of them would almost certainly end his life in a gruesome way.

Things changed when that mysterious group suddenly disappeared. Almost immediately after, another group arrived: four girls with oddly colored hair, accompanied by a black man from the Order of Saint Lorraine, a known global intelligence agency. Before Duncan could collect his final payment and return to Clarksdale, the sheriff's gang got themselves into trouble. They were duped by rumors of a pirate captain invading their territory, rumors instigated by the orange-haired pirate girl with the anchor belt.

Duncan witnessed two of the girls take down six gang members in a matter of minutes. Realizing the danger of the situation, he captured them, delivering them to Lincoln Downs as ordered. He was then tasked with keeping an eye on the other two girls. At that point, Duncan was ready to cut his losses and leave without his money, but the local Veil agent ordered him to stay and gather intelligence on the girls and the strange facility hidden in the forest.

That assignment didn't end well. He found himself buried up to his neck in earth at the mercy of the four girls. After convincing them to let him go in exchange for 250 crowns, he watched them destroy the facility, reducing it to rubble and leaving behind a serene lake surrounded by blooming flowers. His mission was undoubtedly over.

Duncan decided it was time to retire his Juniper persona. Now, all that remained was to file his report with the local Veil contact and head home. He approached the town diner, knocking twice, waiting thirty seconds, then knocking three more times. After a brief pause, the door unlocked. Inside, Cassidy, the local agent, sat in the middle of a row of five booths along the wall and waved him over.

"Duncan, please, have a seat," Cassidy said, casually perusing the menu. His green shirt peeked out from beneath his well-worn overalls.

"Mr. Cassidy," Duncan greeted as he sat down across from him.

Cassidy glanced up. "You hungry?" he asked, still focused on the menu. "Sherrie, can we get a meal?"

"Sure, if you're payin', hon," the waitress, Sherrie, called from behind the counter.

"Great," Cassidy replied with a rare smile breaking through his grizzled exterior. He turned to Duncan. "You are gonna order something, right?"

"Yes sir, that sounds like a good idea," Duncan admitted, considering the fried chicken dinner.

"So," Cassidy began, lowering the menu, "what does Mr. Juniper know about that strange place in the forest?"

"It's destroyed," Duncan reported. "After those funny-haired girls let me go, they tore the place down. They turned it into a lake... with flowers around it."

As if on cue, Sherrie walked over to take their Order, her pad and pen ready.

Cassidy gestured for Duncan to go first. "What'll you have?"

"Fried chicken dinner," Duncan said, "with sweet tea."

Sherrie nodded and jotted it down. "And you?" she asked Cassidy.

"Chicken-fried steak with mashed potatoes and gravy and sweet tea," he confirmed.

"Got it," Sherrie said, collecting their menus and heading back to the kitchen.

Once she was gone, Duncan leaned in slightly. "What happened to those girls? I lost track of them after they left the forest."

"They came back to town late last night and then disappeared," Cassidy explained. "Most likely headed back to Meadowbrook. They cleaned out the inn. Even Mr. Davis left earlier than he'd planned, left me a note saying as much."

Duncan nodded thoughtfully, already formulating the report he'd need to send to his superiors. "What's the deal with that mansion? Did you ever figure out how it moved or where it went?"

Cassidy shook his head. "No clue," he admitted. "They've gotta be using some serious magic to move it like that."

"Who are those people?" Duncan asked, his tone incredulous. "I've never seen anything like them."

Cassidy gave a slight shrug just as Sherrie returned, setting two cups of sweet tea on the table.

"Your food will be up shortly," she informed them with a smile.

"Thank you," both men said in unison before she walked away.

"So, what became of our illustrious Sheriff Downs?" Cassidy asked, taking a sip of tea.

"His son's gang got pruned by those two girls," Duncan replied. "And, oddly enough, his house caught fire while his so-called gang was being beaten down by the pair." He gave Cassidy a pointed look, referencing their previous conversation where Cassidy had instructed him to disrupt the sheriff's criminal operations.

"That'll definitely do," Cassidy said with a satisfied grin.

"I have to ask," Duncan said, leaning forward slightly, "why did you tip those girls off about the mansion people and the sheriff?"

Cassidy's face hardened with quiet disdain. "Sheriff Downs lost control of his son's band of misfits," he explained, his contempt seeping through his otherwise calm demeanor. "They were already on a collision course with those girls. And they were outclassed at every turn. The smart move would've been to lie low and wait for the girls to leave town, then resume business as usual. But instead, they kept escalating."

Duncan shook his head slowly. "This town's rough."

Cassidy leaned back, his expression sharpening. "You know what the leadership expects from places like this?" he asked, then answered, "A well-tended crop, free of weeds and pests. No one at the governor's mansion cares what Downs was doing, so long as things stayed quiet and the crops keep flowing. Governor Anderson has enough on his plate without dealing with noise and nonsense from Snyder."

Duncan said nothing, opting instead to sip his tea.

Cassidy continued, his voice level but firm. "If Downs had reined his idiots in, made them calm down, everything could've gone back to normal. But no, they tried to expand operations to make up for the money they lost when those mansion people arrived. And you know what happens when the dog starts killing livestock?" Cassidy paused for effect. "The dog gets put down."

Duncan nodded slowly. "What's going to happen to the sheriff now?"

"Sadly," Cassidy said with a mock solemnity, "Sheriff Downs died a hero... trying to save his son from the house fire." The implication was clear: *the sheriff was already dead, his fate sealed alongside Lincoln's.* "The governor will have to appoint a new sheriff soon, given these tragic circumstances."

Duncan remained silent, taking another sip of tea.

"Don't worry. It's a local matter," Cassidy reassured him. "You'll get a glowing report. Thank you for your exemplary work."

At that moment, Sherrie returned with their plates. She placed Cassidy's fried chicken dinner and Duncan's chicken-fried steak on the table before asking, "More tea?"

Both men handed over their cups, thanking her as she walked away.

Cassidy cut into his steak and took a bite. "So, what's going to happen to our friend Juniper?"

"He's going to fall into a garbage can somewhere between here and Clarksdale," Duncan replied dryly, scooping up a spoonful of mashed potatoes with a bit of gravy.

Sherrie returned with fresh cups of tea and set the bill on the table. Cassidy glanced at it, then looked at Duncan with a sly grin.

"You're going to take care of that, right?"

Duncan sighed, pulling out his pouch of crowns. "No problem, sir."

"The goddess provides," Cassidy said with a chuckle, taking another bite of chicken.

Duncan shook his head in jovial defeat, but couldn't help smirking as he counted out the crowns to cover the bill. Thinking to himself *I can't wait to get back home.*

Chapter 16

Once Mr. Davis finishes getting ready, the six of them mount up and depart from Snyder. According to Marcus' watch, it's two-thirty in the morning. If they keep a steady pace, they should reach the Governor's mansion by nine o'clock.

Under the moonlight, Sophie and Lisa lead the caravan on horseback, guiding the carriage down the highway. Inside the carriage, Marcus and Annabelle fall asleep almost immediately as the wheels begin to roll, and Regina soon succumbs to sleep despite her efforts to stay awake.

After two hours, the caravan reaches the first rest stop along its route. Sophie, Lisa, and Davis water the horses and make use of the facilities. With a short break in mind, Sophie and Lisa find a picnic bench and lie their heads down for a quick nap.

Meanwhile, Marcus stirs from his sleep, realizing the carriage has stopped. Blinking away drowsiness, he glances out the window and recognizes the familiar rest stop. Annabelle is sprawled awkwardly across a seat, sleeping soundly, while Regina dozes with her head tipped back. Marcus stretches, noting Davis' feet propped up on the driver's bench, clearly, he's also napping.

Marcus checks his watch. Five-thirty. They've already spent an hour here. Sighing, he steps out of the carriage and walks to the picnic tables, where Sophie and Lisa are resting peacefully. Deciding not to disturb them, he pulls out his scrap notebook and settles on the ground. With careful strokes, he begins sketching the *talking pen* ritual Brother Albert had taught him.

"The avatars and I are returning to Meadowbrook after a series of events that culminated in the Snyder sheriff's house burning down. I have no doubt this incident will eventually trace back to them if we remain in Verdantia."

The inked words disappear from the page, absorbed into the pen and sent through the magical conduit to Sister Ingrid. Marcus silently counts the seconds, not expecting a reply. It has been two weeks since he last heard from her.

To his surprise, the pen rises from the page and begins to write: *"We have received word from the Aurorium Clan concerning Sophie Griffin. You are summoned to the Aurorium village in Magitekopolis posthaste. It is fortunate you have completed your investigation in Verdantia."*

Marcus reads the Message with a slight frown. He quickly writes back, *"Message received. Lisa Nozaki will not accompany the other avatars due to her father's restrictions."*

The words dissolve, vanishing into the pen. Moments later, a reply forms. *"What do you estimate for your ETA to Aurorium Magitekopolis?"*

Marcus takes a moment to calculate the journey. He considers both the geography and the time needed for sailing. "*I estimate it will take two weeks by ship to reach Magitekopolis from Verdantia and an additional day to travel to the Aurorium village from the port. I cannot be certain of our departure time from the Governor's mansion in Meadowbrook, but it should be within a day or two.*"

Again, the pen absorbs his Message and, after a short pause, it writes: "*Message received. Is there anything else?*"

Marcus hesitates, then picks up the pen and writes, "*Do you have any knowledge of an organization called the Order of the Black Sun?*"

After a long pause, the pen responds: "*I do not.*"

He quickly pens his subsequent request: "*I believe this may be the true name of the conspiracy. Please have Sister Alameda investigate this organization.*"

The words vanish, and after another brief delay, the pen writes its final reply: "*I will pass it along. Good day, Brother.*"

The glow fades as the ritual concludes. Marcus exhales quietly, tucks the pen and notebook away, then rises. He walks to the picnic tables and gently shakes Sophie, Lisa, and Mr. Davis awake. Annabelle and Regina remain undisturbed; there's no need to wake them since neither will be driving the carriage or riding a horse.

"We'll be moving soon," he says softly. "Get ready."

They stir groggily, the calm silence of the rest stop lingering in the cool early morning air.

[-----✠-----]

As Sophie, Lisa, and Mr. Davis prepared their horses, Marcus offered, "I can ride for one of you if needed."

Lisa raised her hand. "You can ride for me. I would like to get some more sleep before the next rest stop."

"Go ahead and lie down, miss Lisa," Marcus agreed.

Lisa climbed into the carriage, lying down on the bench where Marcus had been resting earlier. The caravan resumed its journey along the highway under the fading night sky.

Riding ahead, Sophie observed Marcus in the saddle. His movements were smooth and natural, as if he'd been riding for years. She figured he must have learned horseback riding during his duties with the Order, how else could they navigate the expansive archipelago at Order Island?

Hours passed before they reached the next rest stop. The horses showed clear signs of exhaustion from the overnight trek. Marcus, Sophie, and Mr. Davis dismounted and tied the animals up without bothering to water them just yet. Rest was the priority now.

Lisa stirred as the carriage came to a stop. Stretching, she suggested, "You all can get some sleep. I want to make something for us to eat."

Marcus gave her a questioning look. "Miss Lisa, are you sure?"

"Yes," she affirmed with a smile.

"You won't have to tell me twice," Mr. Davis announced, already heading for the carriage. He pulled a red, black, and white thick flannel blanket from the storage compartment and wrapped it around himself. "The horses need rest anyway. A few hours should do before we tackle the last leg of the trip."

Marcus nodded and found a spot by the carriage wheel. He leaned against it, letting Sophie have the bench so she could stretch out. Sleep overcame him quickly, and he was soon dozing with his head resting on the wheel.

While the others slept, Lisa quietly set to work. From the side compartment of the carriage, she pulled out the awkward contraption that served as their portable cooking tripod. It consisted of four metal legs with hinged joints and a central ring to hold a pot. She fumbled with it, muttering curses as she tried to figure out how it fit together. Finally, she managed to secure the legs, each digging into the earth just outside the stone fire ring. The pyramid-like frame stood stable, with the ring positioned perfectly to support the pot.

Satisfied, Lisa placed the pot in the ring, its lip fitting neatly over the edge of the support. She gathered her supplies: vegetables, spices, and the meat she purchased in Snyder, but quickly realized she had forgotten to pack proper knives. Grumbling to herself, she resorted to smashing the vegetables with rocks. Once the ingredients were in the pot, she rubbed two sticks together, trying to spark a fire. It took much longer than she would have liked; her patience was wearing thin, but she refused to give up.

Earthbloom magic could control fire but not create it. She and Regina could brainstorm a way to use their magic to ignite flames, but that was a problem for another time. Regina was dead to the world and not worth waking up. Finally, Lisa got the fire going.

An orange spell circle with six glowing runes appeared under the pot as she commanded the flames to intensify and consume more wood. With a second, blue spell circle, she summoned water from the well and poured it into the pot, mixing it with the ingredients. The stew began to boil steadily.

"A stirring spoon," Lisa muttered to herself, realizing she had overlooked that detail. She sighed, searching the area until she found a decently sturdy stick. It was covered in dirt, but she carried it to the well and scrubbed it clean. "Nothing ruins food faster than dirt," she muttered, shaking the excess water off the stick.

The stew simmered for the next hour as Lisa set out bowls and silverware. Despite the hiccups, she took pride in her efforts. This meal might not be perfect, but it would certainly make everyone happy.

"In for a crown, in for a sack," she murmured with a small smile, stirring the bubbling stew.

Annabelle woke to the inviting aroma of something cooking. Sitting up in the carriage, she rubbed the sleep from her eyes and noticed Sophie stretched out on the bench where Brother Marcus had been resting earlier. Regina was still asleep, head back and mouth open.

Annabelle grinned and nudged the two girls. "Oi, 'tis breakfast time, girlies."

Sophie stirred, groaning as she wiped her eyes.

Regina, however, recoiled and muttered, "No, go away," somehow managing to stay asleep.

Laughing softly, Sophie and Annabelle exited the carriage, leaving Regina behind. They passed Marcus, curled up against the carriage wheel, his head resting awkwardly on the wood.

"Poor guy couldn't even get a pillow," Annabelle muttered, crouching beside him. She gently ran her hand over his thick black hair. "Oi, Brother Marcus," she called softly.

Marcus stirred at the touch and sound of her soothing voice. When he opened his eyes, Annabelle's orange gaze and tangled hair were the first things he saw, her face smudged with dirt.

"Ye been slacking long enough," she teased, her voice mock-stern. "Time to get back to work."

Marcus scowled briefly, then relaxed with a smirk. "Good morning, Miss Salazar. What can I do for you?"

Annabelle stood and crossed her arms. "Don't know yet, but I'll figure it out soon enough."

Sophie chuckled at Annabelle's antics and headed toward the campfire, where Lisa was stirring the pot with a long stick.

"Are you making stick stew?" Sophie teased.

Lisa glanced at the improvised stirring stick and gave a sheepish grin. "Yes. Stick stew. The secret is in the stick flavor. Really brings out the ingredients." she joked.

"Wash up for breakfast," Lisa added with a playful wave.

The group gathered around the fire. Lisa passed out silverware, quickly realizing there were only forks and butter knives, no spoons.

"A fork?" Sophie protested, holding up the utensil. "Is this some kind of campfire tradition eating stew with a fork?"

"No, we just do not have spoons," Lisa explained with a shrug.

"You didn't grab any spoons?" Sophie shot an accusing look at Annabelle.

Annabelle waved off Lisa's attempt to hand her a fork and dug into her jacket pockets. "I guess I didn't." She pulled out the 3-in-1 utensil she had bought in Granmark and smirked as she separated it into a spoon, fork, and knife. She wiggled the spoon mockingly at Sophie.

Sophie glared but said nothing, her irritation simmering beneath the surface.

Regina quietly accepted a fork from Lisa, then eyed her bowl of stew. An idea sparked in her mind. With a focused arrangement of mana, she reshaped the fork with her crystalmancy, encasing it in a hexagonal crystal to form a makeshift spoon. She began eating, clearly pleased with her own ingenuity.

Lisa, meanwhile, remembered Mr. Davis' camp kit. She glanced at him sleeping in the shade, bundled in his flannel blanket. Without waking him, she retrieved a spoon from his supplies and returned to her seat by the fire.

Sophie, admitting defeat, finally started eating with the fork. She took a bite and immediately brightened. "Oh, this is good!" she said with a smile. "Girl, I've missed your cooking," she added, her violet eyes softening as she looked at Lisa.

"Aye," Annabelle chimed in, raising her bowl. "'Tis been too long, prin..." She caught herself as Lisa shot her a warning look across the fire; the look in her eyes made Annabelle sure that Lisa would use some Earthbloom spell to knock the bowl from her hands, so she corrected herself, saying, "Lisa," Annabelle corrected with a grin.

Lisa nodded smugly with approval.

Marcus, seated between Regina and Annabelle, added, "Miss Nozaki, we'll definitely miss your cooking once we're back aboard Miss Annabelle's ship." He took a forkful of stew and sipped some broth.

His comment brought a sudden hush to the group as the reality of Lisa's eventual departure sank in. The avatars quietly pondered the thought of losing one of their own on their journey.

Regina was the first to break the silence. "Brother Marcus," she began hopefully, "we don't have anywhere urgent to be, right? Maybe we could stay at the mansion for a while... you know, to do some research?"

"Sadly, Miss Regina, that's not the case," Marcus replied, shattering her hopes. "The Aurorium Clan has summoned us to Magitekopolis, and we need to get Miss Griffin there as soon as possible. This might be our last chance to spend time with Miss Lisa for a while."

The group fell into a somber stillness, staring into their bowls.

"Damn coppers ruin everything," Annabelle muttered, breaking the silence. "Why can't they wait a week or two?" She shot a glare at Sophie.

Sophie retorted sharply. "What do you know? You didn't have to give up your life for all of... this." She waved her arms in frustration, then set her bowl down and crossed her arms, retreating into silence.

"Please, not this again," Lisa snapped, her voice tense with irritation.

"Ladies," Marcus interjected calmly. "Miss Lisa put in a lot of effort to make this meal. Let's not ruin it with bickering and bad tidings."

"What are you going to do after we leave, Lisa?" Regina asked, setting her empty bowl aside.

"Most likely head back to Valorcrest and finish the semester," Lisa replied, taking another spoonful of stew. She silently regretted that the general store hadn't stocked any basil.

"Hey," Annabelle interjected, "why don't we just come pick ye up from that land of libraries after yer papa sends ye there?"

"Will not work," Lisa said, shaking her head. "I am sure my father will station guards to make sure that doesn't happen."

"And the Order would be in an impossible position," Marcus added. "We'd have to return Miss Nozaki immediately. Verdantia would not tolerate the Order, or anyone hired by us, kidnapping her from school to live the dangerous life of adventure."

"Well, this sucks," Regina sighed.

Annabelle scanned the group and sensed the melancholy hanging over them. Deciding to lighten the mood, she licked her spoon clean, reassembled her 3-in-1 utensil, and tucked it into her jacket pocket. She then slipped off the jacket, stood, and extended her hand toward Lisa. "Come 'ere, missy."

"What? Why?" Lisa recoiled slightly, eyeing Annabelle warily. By now, she knew better than to trust this chaotic girl without knowing her plan.

Undeterred, Annabelle reached across the fire and grabbed Lisa's hand, pulling her to her feet. "If this is our last time seeing each other, then I'm gonna show ye the proper way to dance," she declared with a devilish grin. "Can't have ye out here embarrassing us avatars with yer jerky moves."

"Jerky moves?" Lisa scoffed, stepping up to the challenge. "And what about your dance moves? You look like you are having a conniption fit."

"Oh, really?" Annabelle said, narrowing her eyes playfully.

"Uh, how are you going to dance without music?" Regina asked curiously.

"Girlie, ye don't need music, just a beat," Annabelle replied, thinking back to the dancer from Islewind who had taught her crew to dance during a voyage to a festival in Magitekopolis. She clapped her hands in a steady two-three rhythm. "Come on, help me keep the beat."

The others hesitated, but eventually joined in, clapping along. Annabelle exaggeratedly offered her hand to Lisa in an elaborate pantomime.

Lisa sighed dramatically and took her hand. "Keep your hands off my backside this time, I mean it." she said with a stern look.

Annabelle teased. "That's how the dance goes."

The two began moving to the beat, Annabelle leading as she turned Lisa back and forth. They stepped rhythmically, their movements fluid but playful, like a spinning whirlwind of energy. Annabelle guided Lisa into a turn, then positioned them to face the others while stepping in sync. After a few more twists, Annabelle tried to spin Lisa out to reset the dance, only to squeal when Lisa pinched her hand hard.

"Ow, *Princess*!" Annabelle exclaimed, breaking the rhythm.

Lisa pointed at her with a grin. "I told you to watch your hands. My behind is off-limits."

Annabelle stuck her tongue out in mock offence but quickly recovered. "Fine. I don't have to take this abuse." She glanced at Sophie and reached out. "Come 'ere, Copper."

"What?" Sophie looked startled as Annabelle pulled her to her feet. "I don't know how to dance like this."

"Oh, Copper, tis easy," Annabelle assured her, positioning Sophie's hands and feet. "Just follow me lead."

Lisa, meanwhile, reached for Regina's hand. "Your turn, Regina. Let me show you the correct way to dance."

Regina groaned but stood up. "Annabelle already showed me how to dance Sequinta," she informed Lisa.

"Oh, not that heathen nonsense," Lisa teased, glancing at Annabelle with a playful glare. "I am going to teach you the goddess' own Kachae. It is how ladies dance."

Annabelle shook her fist at her, and Lisa responded by lifting her chin in a regal, disapproving pose.

The campfire scene came to life with laughter and movement as the two pairs began dancing to the clapping beat. Annabelle clumsily led Sophie, whose awkward steps made her giggle. Lisa's teaching style was more structured as she guided Regina with precision. The girls' banter and playful rivalry filled the cool morning air, pushing away the earlier sadness.

Marcus clapped steadily, watching them with a warm smile. These girls avatars of the goddesses of Unity, War, Chaos, and Change, had already faced so much, yet here they were, sharing a peaceful, carefree moment together. For once, he allowed himself to let go of the looming worries about what challenges lay ahead. This moment, he decided, was one worth holding on to.

[-----✝-----]
Journal Entry: April 26, 1910

Recent events have left us with no choice but to depart Snyder swiftly. The corruption of the local sheriff and the unjust imprisonment of Ladies Griffin and Salazar have only reinforced the urgency of our journey. The Avatars and I have now returned to the Governor's mansion in Meadowbrook.

Unfortunately, our time together with Miss Nozaki is coming to an end. Once we arrive in Meadowbrook, she will be returning to Valorcrest as per her father's directive. It is a bitter reality, but one we must accept. The remaining three Avatars and I will press on to Aurorium Magitekopolis.

We plan to spend one last day at the Governor's mansion, making the necessary preparations. Tomorrow, we will embark on the next leg of our journey aboard the Stormfang.

The path ahead remains uncertain, but we are resolute in our purpose.

[-----✿-----]

The avatars and Brother Marcus arrived at the Governor's mansion at ten o'clock, according to Marcus' watch. Exhausted from their journey, everyone except Marcus made their way to Lisa's room to sleep, knowing they would return to the Stormfang the next day.

Regina awoke on the comfortable couch in Lisa's spacious bedroom. Sitting up, she rubbed her eyes and glanced around. Annabelle and Lisa lay fast asleep under the canopy of Lisa's large bed, their breathing slow and steady. The cot the staff had brought in for Sophie was already folded up, indicating that she was awake and moving about somewhere in the mansion.

Stretching, Regina rose from the couch and wandered to the adjoining bathroom. She paused in front of the large oval mirror above the sink, her silver hair still tousled from sleep. Shelves filled with bottles of lotions and various other products lined the space next to the sink. She stared at the unfamiliar items, unsure what to make of them, and decided to stick with what she knew washing her face with soap and water.

As she splashed water on her face, a thought crossed her mind. She hadn't had a proper bath in days. With their departure for the Stormfang looming, this might be her last chance to soak in a luxurious tub for a while. Smiling to herself, she decided to take advantage of the opportunity.

After her bath, Regina wrapped herself in a soft towel from the rack and stepped into the hallway. She spotted a young attendant in a crisp white uniform and matching beret, embroidered with the insignia of the harvest goddess.

"Excuse me, sir," she called softly.

The attendant noticed her and quickly approached, his expression a mix of professionalism and mild embarrassment. "Miss, you really should be... more decent when stepping out like this," he said gently.

Regina flushed, clutching the towel tighter around herself. "Sorry," she mumbled, "but could you bring our bags to the room? I need some clean clothes."

"Of course, ma'am," he reassured her, keeping his tone polite. "Let's get you back inside your room. I'll have your bags delivered ever so quickly." He guided her back to the door of Lisa's bedroom and, with a firm but courteous push, closed it behind her with a loud click, sending a clear message to stay put until he returned.

The sound of the door closing stirred Lisa, who yawned and sat up groggily, her face framed by a tangled mess of green hair. Still half-asleep, she stumbled off the bed and made her way to the bathroom. Moments later, Regina heard running water. Curious, she walked to the bathroom doorway and found Lisa rubbing what looked like salt on her face.

"What are you doing?" Regina asked, her voice breaking the quiet.

Lisa paused mid-scrub and turned, noticing Regina standing there wrapped in a towel, her wet silver hair clinging to her head. "Oh, Regina," she said with a sleepy smile. "This is my morning beauty routine."

"With salt?" Regina blinked in surprise. "What's next—pepper?" she quipped with a grin.

Lisa chuckled. "No, *I'm not cooking.*" She glanced in the mirror, seeing that the salt scrub was starting to dry and harden on her skin. "Let me finish this, and I'll show you how to do it. Trust me, your skin will glow afterward."

Regina raised an eyebrow but smiled back. "Glow, huh? Maybe that'll help me see in the dark on the Stormfang," she joked.

Lisa laughed softly, the warm sound echoing in the tiled room. The two girls shared a quiet moment of camaraderie, enjoying the peace before the challenges of their journey resumed.

[----- ⊕ -----]

Sophie was running laps on the track behind the Governor's mansion. She had woken up an hour earlier on the cot in Lisa's room. Preferring not to share a bed or squeeze onto the couch, she had claimed the cot without much argument from the others. Now, with the steady rhythm of her feet pounding the track, she let her mind clear, focusing only on maintaining her speed and form. This was a practice Eclipse Baker had called "running meditation." He would take his patrol of Sentinels and junior Shadows on dawn runs around Aurorium Granmark's perimeter, chanting cadences and reviewing orders from Apex Molina. Sophie had come to find it centering.

Her thoughts drifted to the facility they had discovered in Snyder. *What could the conspiracy, The Order of the Black Sun, want with the knowledge of mana extraction? Why had they brought Regina's father and little brother there?* More troubling still, the conspiracy's structure felt eerily similar to the Order of Saint Lorraine. Sophie wondered how such a powerful organization could construct and operate a hidden facility like that without the townspeople knowing. She shook her head, questions piling up in her mind.

The biggest mystery gnawed at her: *Why did the Order of the Black Sun need Jules Fournier and his stepson Matthew for almost a month?* She noticed herself slowing and pushed harder to regain her pace.

As she rounded the track again, Sophie recalled what Marcus and Regina had shared about Jules. He was a revered ritualist scholar, someone who Regina had half-joked was always striving to keep up with her mother, a Nexus Mage renowned for mastering and enhancing multiple magic systems. If that was true, the next question was obvious: *What task required a mystical scholar like Jules? Perhaps they wanted him to improve the mana extraction process. They may need him to adapt the compliance and capture rituals that were integrated into the facility's floors and walls.* Sophie mulled over these possibilities as she passed her towel and the steel water bottle that an attendant had provided earlier.

She remembered her training under Eclipse Suchi, who had drilled the fundamentals of investigation into her:

What was the goal?

Why was it done that way?

Who benefits?

And finally, what question am I not asking?

Sophie recited these questions mentally as she ran, trying to piece the puzzle together.

What was the goal? *To get Jules Fournier to do something for them.*

Why was it done that way? *Because Jules wouldn't have served them willingly. They kidnapped his stepson to ensure his cooperation.*

Who benefits? The conspiracy or the Order of the Black Sun.

What question am I not asking?

This last question haunted her as she rounded the curve near the well-kept bleachers. Her feet pounded the track as she tried to clear her mind and let the question form naturally. The Five W's and How: who, what, when, where, why, how, cycled through her head like a mantra.

Then it hit her. She came to an abrupt stop, her breath catching. She had been too focused on Jules and Matthew, too caught up in tactical thinking from her Sentinel training. The real question had been right in front of her: *How did the Order of the Black Sun know when to leave Snyder?*

Had the avatars missed them purely by chance? Or had the conspiracy anticipated their arrival? Are they tracking us? Sophie's thoughts raced. *If so, how are they tracking us, and how can we avoid it?*

She took a deep breath and scanned the estate grounds. The track stretched a good half a king's journey from the mansion's back door, and nearly a full king's journey from the barn where they had found and rescued Eclipse Lepele. In the distance, she could see a kingdom school for the wealthy and privileged children of nearby powerful households. This estate stood right along the path that those children and young adults travelled between their homes to the west and the school to the east.

A familiar sensation crawled over Sophie's skin, the same uneasy feeling she'd had when she found Eclipse Lepele under the barn. She glanced around but saw nothing out of place. Still, she trusted her instincts. Someone or something is watching her.

Deciding not to push her luck, Sophie walked briskly to collect her towel and water bottle. She wiped the sweat from her face, slung the towel around her neck, and started heading back toward the mansion, her thoughts racing faster than her feet had moments before.

When Sophie reached the back door of the mansion, she was greeted by a familiar face. The attendant, Samuel, stood waiting with his signature beret cocked to the side. His black skin and striking white hair made him physically appealing, but in Sophie's mind, his frequent and annoying use of the "J" word had long since destroyed any chance of him being attractive.

"Good morning, Miss Griffin," Samuel greeted her warmly.

"Morning," Sophie replied flatly, brushing sweat from her forehead.

"The First Lady would like to speak with you," Samuel informed her.

"Me?" Sophie blinked. "Why would she want to talk to me?"

"I couldn't say," Samuel answered with a polite smile. "But if you would follow me, please." His tone was both an order and a request wrapped in formality.

Sophie glanced down at her training clothes, still damp from her run. "Shouldn't I change first?"

"No, your training attire will be fine," he assured her.

With a shrug, Sophie waved her hand dismissively. "Well, lead the way."

Samuel guided her through the back entrance and into the mansion, past attendants dressed in pristine white uniforms. They stood like sentinels at their posts, nodding respectfully as the two passed. Sophie followed him up a grand staircase that led to a balcony overlooking the estate grounds. From this vantage point, she could see the running track, the sprawling gardens, and the barn where they had rescued Eclipse Lepele being rebuilt by worker men feverishly impersonating an ant colony.

"If you need anything, Miss, I'll be at the attendant's station just inside the door," Samuel said, his polished courtesy shining through.

"Thank you," Sophie replied curtly, stepping onto the balcony.

There, she spotted Linda Nozaki, Lisa's mother, seated at a small table, sipping tea with Brother Marcus. Linda waved to the empty chair beside her.

"Good morning, Sophie," Linda called with a warm smile. "Please, come and join us."

Sophie accepted the invitation, taking a seat across from Brother Marcus.

"Good morning, Miss Griffin," Marcus greeted her.

"Morning," she returned.

"Thank you for accepting my invitation," Linda said politely.

"Thank you for inviting me." Sophie replied, unsure if she'd had much of a choice.

Linda took a sip of her tea and leaned forward slightly. "I wanted to speak to another avatar, someone like you, about your situation," she began, her voice hesitant, as though searching for the right words to describe Sophie's connection to her goddess.

"If you don't require anything else from me, Miss Griffin, I'll attend to preparations for our departure aboard the Stormfang tomorrow," Marcus offered.

"That sounds good," Sophie said with a nod.

"Very well," Marcus replied, standing. He inclined his head respectfully toward Linda. "If you'll excuse me, Mrs. Nozaki."

"Of course," Linda replied. "If you encounter any difficulties, please don't hesitate to seek me out."

"Thank you," Marcus said before departing.

Once he was gone, Linda turned her full attention to Sophie. "So, what can you tell me about your goddess of Unity?"

The question caught Sophie off guard. She paused, then replied simply, "Nothing." Seeing Linda's confusion, she clarified, "My goddess isn't Unity."

"Oh," Linda said, genuinely surprised. "Who is your goddess, then?"

Sophie leaned back slightly, a self-assured smile crossing her face. "The Violet Goddess of War."

Linda's eyes widened as the realization sank in. She took a moment to process the revelation, then asked, "And the other girls? Who are their goddesses?"

Sophie took a long drink from her water bottle, quenching her thirst before answering. "Regina's goddess is Change," she explained, "and Annabelle's is Chaos."

Linda nodded slowly, still absorbing the information. "Regina," she mused. "She's the one learning Earthbloom magic, right?"

"That's her," Sophie confirmed with a grin. "I think she's got it down now."

"What? Really?" Linda asked in disbelief. "She couldn't even use the sense a few days ago."

"I saw her cast a few spells while we were in Snyder," Sophie said, her tone casual but impressed. "She talks a lot, sure, but that girl is very intelligent."

Sophie finished off the last of her water as Linda took a thoughtful sip of her tea. They both fell silent for a moment, reflecting on the conversation and the abilities of the avatars they had come to know.

"How do your parents feel about you being an avatar of the War Goddess?" Linda asked gently.

Sophie stiffened at the question, her mind flashing to memories of her deceased mother and father. Keeping her composure, she replied quietly, "My parents are gone." She worked hard to maintain her promise to her mother, to shed no more tears over her losses.

Linda's face softened with sympathy. "Oh, I'm so sorry, sweetie," she said earnestly. After a brief pause, she hesitated before asking tentatively, "Did your goddess...?" She let the question trail off, unwilling to finish it.

Sophie shook her head, the suggestion catching her off guard. "What? No. She wouldn't do that," she replied firmly. "She values life too much to throw it away like that." Sophie was sure, her goddess of War was far from reckless when it came to life itself.

Linda let out a quiet breath of relief. "I suppose it makes sense for the War Goddess to choose someone from the Aurorom Clan," she mused. "Your clan's fighting prowess is well-known throughout the Seven Kingdoms."

Sophie smiled faintly. Although Linda had mispronounced the clan's name slightly, she appreciated the effort. "As the goddess explained to me, the domain of War isn't just about fighting and combat. It's about creating alliances, understanding conflict, and knowing when to fight and when not to."

"I never thought about it that way," Linda admitted thoughtfully. "That kind of wisdom sounds... well, very powerful in its own right."

For a moment, they sat in quiet reflection before Linda added, "You know, you remind me so much of my daughter, Lisa."

Sophie's smile widened. "In a good way, I hope."

Linda chuckled softly. "Yes in a very good way."

[-----◉-----]

After Lisa's beauty routine, Regina found herself seated in front of the vanity mirror, inspecting her reflection. She was slightly disappointed that the "glow" in her skin wasn't literal illumination, but she had to admit, it looked amazing. Her skin was clear, soft, and vibrant, making her feel as pretty as she did on the special hangout days when her Mommy June did her makeup without her dad and Mattie.

"See? Look how much you glow." Lisa said proudly, standing behind Regina and smiling at her in the mirror. Her green hair was messily tied up out of her way.

"Yep. Even better than when Mommy June does it," Regina replied with a big grin.

Lisa glanced at her own reflection and suddenly realized she hadn't even started getting ready for dinner. "What time is it?" she asked herself aloud.

"Oi, it's time to stop makin' all that racket!" Annabelle's voice groaned from the bed. "I'm tryin' to sleep!"

Lisa grabbed the pocket watch from her vanity table and checked the time. "Anna, it's almost six o'clock. You have slept long enough."

Annabelle groaned again but sat up, stretching in the long nightshirt she had borrowed from Lisa. She shuffled over to grab her clothes from the previous day.

"You are not just going to put those back on, are you?" Lisa asked, wrinkling her nose in disgust.

"Yeah, why, Princess?" Annabelle said, raising an eyebrow. "They smell fine to me."

"By the harvest! We have free laundry here in the mansion," Lisa exclaimed. "It will not cost you a single crown."

"Fine," Annabelle grumbled, tossing the clothes onto the floor in Lisa's direction.

"The attendant brought our bags up," Regina pointed out, gesturing toward the pile of luggage from the carriage.

Annabelle walked over to grab her bag and pulled out a fresh outfit. Without a word, she stepped behind the trifold screen to change.

Lisa sighed and formed a glowing green spell circle in the air. Runes shimmered as the plants behind the screen responded to her magic, snapping a leafy vine at Annabelle's backside.

"Ow!" Annabelle yelped. "What's yer problem now, Princess?"

"The bathwater is free too, Anna," Lisa said, her tone a mix of stern and teasing.

"I took a bath on Monday, so I'm good," Annabelle replied, rubbing the spot where the plant had hit her.

"It is Thursday!" Lisa protested. "You are supposed to take a bath every day."

"Maybe if yer rich," Annabelle muttered. She called to Regina for backup. "Right, Regina?"

Regina blinked, confused. "I take a bath every day."

Annabelle sighed dramatically in defeat and trudged toward Lisa's large bathroom. "You two are weird," she muttered before slamming the door behind her.

Lisa and Regina exchanged a look, then burst into quiet giggles.

Moments later, there was a knock at the door. An attendant informed Lisa, "You are invited to dinner at seven-thirty tonight."

Lisa thanked him politely, closing the door before turning to Regina with a thoughtful look. "We better get ready," she said. Regina nodded in agreement, both girls still smiling from Annabelle's antics.

[-----✪-----]

After an uneventful dinner, quiet due to Governor Conrad Nozaki being away on provincial business, the avatars retired to Lisa's room. Despite all the sleep they had gotten earlier, exhaustion still tugged at them. Lisa insisted on a group nighttime beauty routine, much to Annabelle's annoyance. Annabelle protested and tried to flee multiple times, but was ultimately dragged into compliance. Afterward, the avatars promised to keep in touch and went to bed for the night.

The next morning, breakfast was subdued. The weight of their impending separation hung heavily over the table. There was nothing they could say to change the fact that three of them would soon part ways with Lisa, the avatar of Unity.

The next morning at breakfast Marcus quietly finished his meal early, excusing himself to oversee the packing of their belongings and ensure the carriage and wagon were ready for the trip to Ferryville.

The avatars remained seated in silence, slowly finishing their scrambled eggs, sausage, hashbrowns, and orange juice. None of them spoke, afraid that if they did, reality would hit them harder than they could bear.

When breakfast ended, Lisa escorted the others outside to the carriage where Brother Marcus waited for them.

"Ladies," Marcus greeted them with forced enthusiasm, "are we ready to depart?"

The avatars didn't respond, their gazes fixed on the ground.

Lisa gathered her courage, pushing through the sadness in her voice. "We should not drag things out. You all have to go." She opened her arms, offering a hug. "Come on. Give me hugs so you can get going."

Regina stepped forward first, wrapping her arms around Lisa. "Goodbye, Lisa. I'll visit you in Valorcrest after we find my dad," she promised softly.

Lisa hugged her tightly, fighting back tears. "I look forward to it."

Regina let go of the embrace and walked to the carriage, glancing back at the mansion. In one of the large windows, she saw Linda Nozaki watching them silently. Regina waved to her before climbing inside the carriage.

Sophie was next. She approached Lisa and pulled her into a firm, comforting hug. "I'll see you, girl," Sophie whispered in her ear. "Keep yourself safe."

"I will," Lisa replied, her voice cracking slightly. Tears welled in her eyes. "Don't forget me."

Sophie released the hug and gave Lisa a reassuring smile. "Not possible." she said with a wink before heading to the carriage and taking a seat next to Regina.

Without a word, Annabelle stormed toward Lisa, throwing her arms around her in an almost crushing embrace. Tears streamed down Annabelle's cheeks, falling freely as she held on tightly.

"I know," Lisa murmured softly, her own tears now flowing. "I'm going to miss you too."

Annabelle didn't speak, clinging to Lisa as if words would betray her.

"Anna... I cannot breathe," Lisa chuckled lightly through her tears, giving Annabelle a playful nudge.

"Oh." Annabelle quickly let go, wiping her eyes. "I…"

"I know," Lisa interrupted gently. "I wish I could go with you too."

Annabelle nodded mutely, wiping her face once more before walking to the carriage.

Finally, Marcus stood before Lisa. Tears streaked her face, but she met his gaze with quiet strength. He defaulted to his courtesy training, stepping forward and offering his handkerchief, emblazoned with the emblem of the Order of Saint Lorraine.

Lisa took the handkerchief and dabbed her tears, then suddenly leaned into Marcus, wrapping her arms around him and resting her head against his chest.

"This isn't goodbye, Miss Nozaki," Marcus assured her gently. "I'll visit you at school. Maybe I'll even find a way to bring the others with me."

Lisa sobbed into his chest, finally allowing herself to release the emotions she'd held back.

"It's okay," Marcus said softly, patting her back. "Cry as much as you need to."

After a few moments, Lisa pulled away, using the handkerchief to dry her tears. She smiled weakly. "I will give this back when you visit," she said, forcing herself to smile through the sadness.

"It's a deal, Miss Nozaki," Marcus replied, his own smile tinged with melancholy. "If there's nothing else, we'll be on our way."

"Very well, Brother Marcus," Lisa answered dutifully.

With one final, sorrowful look, Marcus returned to the carriage. He waved to Lisa and glanced up at the mansion. Linda Nozaki still stood at the window, her expression unreadable. He gave her a slight, respectful nod before stepping inside and sitting beside the quiet, grief-stricken avatars.

Once seated, Marcus knocked twice on the carriage ceiling, signaling the driver to depart.

Lisa stood on the estate grounds, watching the carriage and wagon roll away. Tears streamed down her face as she waved after them, making sure they knew just how much she would miss them.

As if reflecting her sorrow, the sky darkened, rumbling ominously before releasing a steady rain. Lisa remained where she stood, defiant against the downpour.

She had been wondering for some time now if she should call the other avatars her friends and she accepts that is not correct as her arm continued to wave until the carriage disappeared from sight, it occurred to her friends is not high enough she waved until her other family was gone.

Chapter 17

The journey to Ferryville stretched on, the rhythmic patter of spontaneous rain drumming softly against the carriage roof. One by one, sleep overtook the group, lulled by the quiet and the lullaby of rain. When the carriage finally rattled to a stop near the docks, the air was cool and damp with the scent of salt and earth.

Annabelle was the first to stir. Stepping down onto the wet cement walkway, she straightened her coat and gestured for the others to follow. They grabbed their bags, the fog-shrouded masts of the Stormfang rising like shadows ahead.

Annabelle led the way up the gangplank, her boots thudding in a steady rhythm. Reaching the deck, she announced firmly, "OPSO Annabelle Salazar requesting permission."

From the bridge, Smitty's voice carried through the drizzle. "Permission granted!" He watched from his post, deckhands below moving swiftly to prep the ship for departure from Verdantia.

Annabelle offered him a brief nod and descended toward her quarters. Behind her, Regina followed with an air of mischief. "Permission to come aboard, matey!" she called out with a grin.

"Welcome back, little missy!" Smitty chuckled, tipping his cap from the helm. His wave was warm but commanding, like the seasoned sailor he was.

"Arr!" Regina joked with exaggerated enthusiasm, before striding off toward the lower decks. She was eager to find Sparks and see what trouble, or genius, he might have stirred up during her absence.

Sophie came next, pausing at the top of the gangplank. "Permission to board," she said politely, though her voice wavered slightly with self-consciousness.

Smitty smirked. "Ye can come aboard, missy, but ye can't board us."

Sophie flushed, heat rising to her cheeks. She gives a nervous smile in apology.

"Granted, missy," Smitty said with a playful wink. "Yer guest is waiting for ye on the observation deck."

"Thank you," she answered, composing herself before heading toward the stairs.

Marcus was the last to arrive, his footsteps deliberate. He halted at the top of the plank and declared, "Permission to come aboard."

"Granted, mate," Smitty replied, shaking his head slightly as though amused by the formality.

Once on deck, Marcus scanned the surroundings. "Where can I find Captain Lowe?" he asked.

Smitty pointed to a door near the bridge. "Ready room, he's in there. Just go right in."

Marcus rapped on the door before stepping inside. Captain Lowe, better known as Captain Kidd, rose from a wooden table, his khaki pants and crisp white shirt lending him a sense of understated authority.

"Brother Marcus! How's it going, mate?" Kidd grinned as he approached. "Brought them girlies back with ye?"

"Three of the four," Marcus admitted with a sigh. "Miss Nozaki had to stay behind with the governor."

"Ah, that's a shame," Kidd said softly, his jovial demeanor giving way to concern. He shifted the conversation briskly. "Where to next?"

"Magitekopolis, the port city of Gearhaven. We have been summoned to the Aurorium Village there." Marcus stated. His voice was steady, though there was an undertone of urgency. "The Avatars didn't take Nozaki's departure too well."

Kidd frowned. "How soon are ye needin' to leave? Some of the crew's on shore leave."

"We should head out as soon as possible," Marcus emphasized.

"Alright, I'll send a runner to round them up. But we'll need to wait until tomorrow, we're running low on supplies and have to restock."

Marcus gave a curt nod. "Understood. And how's our new guest?"

"Settlin' in well. Jeffie's food worked its magic, he stopped talking gibberish after a few days. The man's got quite the tale to tell." Kidd's eyes gleamed with curiosity as he spoke, already mulling over the mysterious guest's potential stories.

Marcus smirked faintly. "Sounds like I have a lot to catch up on."

[-----✚-----]

Sophie placed her belongings neatly in her cabin and affixed her Sentinel badge to her vest. The metal was cool against her fingertips, a grounding reminder of her duties. With a deep breath, she made her way to the observation deck, her steps light but purposeful.

Pushing open the double doors, she found him: the man from the governor's barn cell. He sat at a table, his black-and-blond dreadlocks tied into a ponytail, looking far more presentable in a clean white shirt compared to the tattered rags he'd worn before. A book rested in his hands: *The Glory of Verdantia*. He appeared absorbed in its pages.

"Good afternoon," Sophie greeted, standing at ease with her hands clasped behind her back. "Eclipse?" she ventured, testing the title he had given before.

The man glanced up, his eyes momentarily distant as if searching his memory. "Sentinel..." he echoed thoughtfully, before pausing. "Forgive me, I'm still having trouble remembering things." He closed the book, stood, and extended a hand. "Eclipse Lepele, Aurorium Kurotora Mura."

Sophie shook his hand firmly, replying, "Sentinel Sophie Griffin, Aurorium Granmark." The words brought a rush of unwanted memories; her ruined village, lifeless bodies scattered like frozen, discarded dolls. She stiffened to maintain her composure, forcing herself to focus on the present.

"Thank you for pulling me out of that hell," Lepele said with quiet sincerity. "But tell me, torchbearer, how are you here... alone?" His tone was both curious and authoritative, the weight of his rank unmistakable.

Sophie swallowed hard, forcing her voice steady. "After the events in Granmark..." She faltered briefly, emotion tightening her throat. "I fled the village. The Order of Saint Lorraine found me and revealed that I'm the Avatar of the Violet Goddess of War."

Lepele tilted his head, confusion in his expression. "Granmark? What happened there?"

Sophie hesitated but saw no reason to hide the truth. She recounted the devastation she had witnessed; the lifeless bodies of her comrades and classmates, victims of a brutal assault led by Gretta and Isabella. Her voice trembled, though she fought back tears. She described her meeting with Brother Albert, the other Avatars, and her encounter with the Goddess and her mother, Arisa, from the land of the dead. Lepele listened intently, his expression darkening as the story unfolded. When she concluded their journey to Verdantia, she carefully omitted the secret deal with Aurorium Laminae.

Lepele remained silent for a moment, absorbing the weight of her words. "You met your dead mother?" he finally asked, his voice tinged with incredulity.

"I did," Sophie confirmed softly.

He shook his head and exhaled a slow breath. "Alright. Why not," he muttered. Then, clearing his thoughts, he fixed her with a pointed look. "When was the last time you checked in with the clan?"

Sophie straightened instinctively. "The Order sent a message when I first arrived at Order Island," she reported.

"That wasn't my question, Sentinel," Lepele replied, his tone sharpening. "When did you last check in?"

Sophie shifted uncomfortably. "I... haven't."

"And how long have you been with the Order?"

"Just under a month," she admitted.

Lepele let out a low, disapproving hum. "We must do things differently in Kurotora Mura. If one of my Sentinels went missing for a week, they'd know to report in as soon as possible. Daily, even. No exceptions."

Sophie stared at the deck, shame welling within her.

"But I suppose things are done differently in Granmark," he said with a mocking edge.

"I wouldn't know who to report to," Sophie blurted, a weak defensive despite herself.

Lepele glanced over his shoulder, his expression unimpressed. "What are the six Aurorium villages, torchbearer?"

Sophie straightened and recited by reflex, "Laminae, Kurotora Mura, Magitekopolis, Stoneridge, Islewind, and Granmark, Eclipse."

"Even if Granmark was wiped out, do you think one of the other villages might have accepted your message?"

"It makes sense that they would," Sophie replied hesitantly.

"So, you did know who you could contact," he concluded flatly.

"I suppose I did," she murmured, chastened.

"I'm glad I could illuminate that for you," Lepele chided, his tone dripping with sarcasm.

Seeking to shift the conversation, Sophie asked, "Eclipse, if I may—how did you end up in that cell?"

Lepele sighed. "I have no idea," he admitted. "I was on a mission with a Sentinel, Joseph Sharrock, aboard the Sequin Dancer. Pirates attacked us. We fought back, but they overwhelmed us. The ship sank, and... the next thing I remember is waking up in that cell."

"You're certainly doing better now," Sophie observed. "You seem less disoriented than before."

"They were trying to break me," Lepele explained grimly. "I believe they were poisoning my food, something to drive me mad so I'd give up our secrets."

"I'm sure you didn't tell them anything," Sophie said with conviction.

Lepele met her gaze, his expression weary. "I wish I shared your confidence. But... thank you, torchbearer."

[----- ⚓ -----]

After getting herself situated, Annabelle changes from her skirt and vest combo into a pair of tights with a white T-shirt. She wraps a bandana around the top of her head to keep control of her hair. She walks to the deck and meets with Smitty, who tells her that the captain brought a new copper as a passenger. The captain was speaking with Brother Marcus, so she decided to pay the new copper a visit and make sure he knew how they do things were done on the Fang.

She makes her way to the observation deck and sees the man wearing one of the captain's outfits, his hair dreadlocked and tied into a ponytail. He is speaking to the purple copper, but the conversation ends abruptly when Annabelle walks onto the deck. She takes the opportunity to insert herself into their conversation, "Greetings and salutations, mates," she says in a welcoming voice.

Sophie looks at Annabelle with a sneer, and the new guy, looking over his shoulder, is obviously impressed by Annabelle's leadership and sense of style.

"If that is all Eclipse." Sophie says to the new guy.

"Carry on, Sentinel," He says to her.

Sophie walks off the observation deck, giving Annabelle an unmistakably jealous look.

"Is yer name Eclipse?" Annabelle asks the new guy, "Tis an odd name."

He sits down at a table and smiles before saying, "My rank is Eclipse, my name is Antonio."

"So is your rank higher than the copper's?" Annabelle asks, referring to Sophie

"Don't you call all of us Aurorium *coppers*?" Lepele asks

"Oh, yeah," Annabelle says, stumbling a bit. "Sorry about that, I meant the purple copper."

With a smile and a shake of his head, Lepele says, "Yes, I am a higher rank than Sentinel Griffin. More importantly, who are you?"

Annabelle smiles and says, "Oh me, I am the daughter of Javier Salazar, Avatar of the beautiful Goddess of Chaos, currently the operations officer of the good ship Stormfang, this illustrious Annabelle Salazar." Striking a pose with her hands to her sides, a devilish grin, and a heroic glint in her eye towards the man, gauging her introduction.

Lepele, obviously impressed by Annabelle, sits back in his chair and says, "Wow, quite impressive." He continues, "But I have a question, usually the only bigger contract ships have operations officers. I have never seen a privateer vessel of this size have an Ops O. Why does this ship have one?"

Not sure how to answer, Annabelle says, "Aye, the Stormfang is special, ye see."

"I am sure it is." Lepele tells her. "This ship is quite the sight, it even has an oven in the galley, too bad the boy Jeffie can barely cook."

Annabelle's thoughts drift to when Lisa ran the kitchen, and she feels a pang of sadness, an uncontrollable frown weighing down her face.

"Oh, I'm sorry, I must have touched a nerve," Lepele says, bluntly teasing Annabelle.

"Nah tis fine mate." Annabelle shrugs off the feeling.

"So, Miss Salazar, what can I do for you?" he asks, clearly seeking to uncover her secrets.

"Nothin' much," She tells him, sitting down at the table across from him. "Heard we had a new passenger and I decided to, you know, check things out. So tell me, Mr. Eclipse, what are ye plannin' on me ship?"

"I've had to change my plan." Eclipse Lepele explains, "I was going to take over the ship with Sentinel Griffin and claim her for the Aurorium clan. But since you are the Ops O, then I think I just go along for the ride until we get to Magitekopolis." He explains to her with a wink.

Taken aback, Annabelle stutters for a moment and then says, "Glad you figured it out, before things got ugly," raising her fist with a cocksure smile.

[----- ✿ -----]

Regina quickly dropped off her belongings and swapped her dress for a pair of blue coveralls that Mr. Sparks had given her long ago to protect her "pretty dresses." She was eager to get back to work and see what new invention Sparks had dreamed up this time. Practically skipping through the halls, she soon reached his workshop.

Inside, Sparks was hunched over a box with a long wire connected to it. As she watched, he turned a crank on the side. The wire began to heat, glowing red-hot until it sizzled against the floor, leaving a singed black mark.

"Dammit!" Sparks cursed under his breath. He straightened when he noticed her. "Hey, Regina! Yer back!"

"Yep, just got back," Regina chirped, stepping into the room. She pointed at the contraption, now crackling faintly. "What's this?"

Sparks wiped his hands on a rag. "Got bored, so I started tinkerin'. It's one of our ideas for lighting up the hallways, if I can ever get the damn wire to stay properly lit. Problem is, it overheats and burns out."

Regina frowned in thought. "That's tricky," she admitted, stepping closer to inspect the contraption. "Maybe you could drain the heat into something else, like a water barrel?"

Sparks shook his head. "Thought of that. Too risky. If the barrels run dry, next thing you know, fire. And fire at sea…"

"Is bad," Regina finished with a grin. She'd heard that refrain enough times when they first started working together.

Sparks nodded. "Exactly."

Regina's mind wandered to her lessons in Earthbloom magic, particularly the concept of ambient mana floating through the air. An idea began to take shape. "What about mana lamps?" she asked suddenly.

"The captain already said no mana-drainin' tech," Sparks reminded her, giving her a sidelong glance. "I know you and yer 'sisters' have plenty of mana, but the rest of us ain't so lucky."

"Not draining," she corrected quickly. "I'm talking about lamps that use the earth's ambient mana, like a self-sustaining system."

Sparks raised an eyebrow. "Ambient mana? Huh. Never seen anything like that before. How's it supposed to work?"

Regina pursed her lips in thought, mentally sifting through spells and formulas she'd learned. If she could create a combination of ritual circles, one for gathering ambient mana, another for converting it to light, it might work. But it would need a touch activation system to be practical for everyday use. That would mean layering multiple circles in a compact design, which isn't easy.

"Can I use a notebook?" she asked, thinking she might be able to sketch out a prototype.

Sparks rummaged around his cluttered workspace and handed her a half-used pad and a pencil. "'Ere ye go, missy," he said, carefully stepping around the still-hot wire.

"Thanks!" Regina replied with a bright smile, her Laminaen accent slipping through in her excitement. She climbed onto a stool at the workbench and began sketching.

She worked methodically, theorizing how to blend Earthbloom magic with ritual runes. Drawing on Mrs. Tillman's magic lessons, she calculated the size and configuration of the circles, figuring out how much mana would be needed to keep them running. The design grew more complicated as she went. The central ritual required five infusion points, with an extra for the draining mechanism itself. But when she tried to integrate a touch activation system, the circle became too large, something the size of a shirt or pillowcase at minimum.

Regina sighed in frustration. She wasn't ready to give up just yet. With a determined glint in her eye, she erased part of the sketch and started reworking the components.

Sparks, meanwhile, was busy dunking his hot wire contraption into a bucket of water to cool it off. Steam hissed and rose in lazy tendrils around him. Regina glanced up from her notes.

"Mr. Sparks, can I keep this notepad?" she asked, holding up the notebook filled with her calculations.

"Aye," he replied with a nod. Then, with a grin, he added, "Just don't read the pages at the beginning."

"No problem," she said, laughing softly. She hopped down from the stool and tucked the notebook under her arm. As she made her way toward the door, she gave him a playful grin. "See ye later, Mista Sparks!" she said, her pirate patois still a work in progress.

"I'll see ye 'round, missy," Sparks called after her with a chuckle, shaking his head fondly as he watched her go.

[-----◉-----]

Lisa arrived at the banquet hall dressed in a simple blue gown, the silk-like white bow on the chest giving a touch of elegance. She spotted her family immediately, her father, mother, and older sister Evelyn, already seated. Evelyn's date appeared to be her escort from the recent goddess gala. Sir Santora, the Earthbloom *master* of Vendura, sat beside her mother, wearing a green shirt adorned with the harvest tree emblem.

"The Lady Lisa Nozaki," the attendant by the entry doors announced formally.

Heads turned toward her as her presence was acknowledged. Lisa walked gracefully to the table and took the seat offered to her beside Linwood, unfolding her napkin onto her lap.

"Good evening, Lady Harvest," Linwood greeted, extending a hand. "Sergeant Michael Linwood."

"It is a pleasure, Sergeant," Lisa said politely, shaking his hand. "Lisa Nozaki."

"Where are your friends tonight?" he asked, apparently unaware of recent events.

"They had to continue on to Magitekopolis. The Aurorium Clan needed Sophie's presence there," Lisa explained smoothly.

"Well, we're glad to have you here," Linwood said warmly.

"Yes, quite glad," her father, Conrad, added, his words laced with underlying meaning. "Our youngest flower bud, free at last from the influence of those pirates and the Jiberau."

Lisa met his gaze but said nothing.

"Sophie seemed nice enough to me," her mother, Linda, offered gently.

"It was all an act, my dear," Conrad interjected, his voice hardening. "That's how the Jiberau operate. They worm their way into your trust, only to stab you in the back when you least expect it."

"Nasty business," Santora murmured in agreement, swirling his wine. "The enemies of the harvest are insidious."

"Well said." Conrad nodded approvingly.

"Sophie is not like that," Lisa spoke firmly. She knew Sophie well enough her friend wouldn't waste time on manipulation when she could confront her problems head-on with punches, elbows, and kicks.

"The Jiberau are masters of subterfuge and espionage," Linwood chimed in, his tone almost robotic, as if quoting a training manual. Conrad nodded in agreement, clearly pleased.

Linwood added with a thin smile, "Honestly, I'd trust that pirate girl more than the Jiberau one."

Lisa chuckled softly to herself. Annabelle would likely pick his pockets for the fun of it, while Sophie would make her put the coins back.

"Our duty is to protect the garden from any who would harm the harvest," Conrad declared, quoting a line from the Book of the Harvest with a flourish. His words rang hollow to Lisa. Once, she would have admired such sentiments, but now they seemed more like a mask for tyranny, a false *unity* that demanded unquestioning submission to authority.

"You're an inspiration to us all, sir," Santora said, raising his glass in a show of deference.

Conrad returned the gesture with a pleased smile. Lisa felt her stomach twist in disgust at the display. *Sycophancy is a sickness*, she thought a corruption of Unity that forced people to kneel beneath the will of another.

258

"Lisa, dear," her mother interrupted her thoughts. "Are you looking forward to returning to school?"

Lisa kept her tone light to avoid provoking her father. "Yes, Mother. I am eager to catch up with my friends at Valorcrest."

"Not to mention your studies," Conrad added pointedly.

Lisa smiled politely, offering no response.

"Does that grey-haired girl attend school with you, Lady Harvest?" Santora asked.

"No," Lisa replied, taking a sip of water. "She attends a public kingdom school."

"When do you expect to see the other Avatars again?" Linda asked, cutting off Santora before he could press further.

"I am not sure, mother," Lisa admitted, her voice softening. "They are busy searching for Regina's family, so I won't see them in Laminae for a while." The thought saddened her.

"It's probably for the best, Lady Harvest," Santora said, smiling in a way that made Lisa's skin crawl. "Those girls could have stunted your development in Earthbloom magic."

Lisa's emerald eyes narrowed slightly. "You do not say, Sir Santora." She kept her voice neutral, masking her contempt. "Tell me, what's your opinion on nesting spell circles in Earthbloom casting?"

"Nesting circles?" Santora scoffed, waving the notion away. "Impossible. Rumors, perhaps, but even I can't do such a thing. Why do you ask?"

Lisa leaned forward slightly, her tone casual yet pointed. "Oh, I used a nested circle spell in Snyder to create a lake and I have been wondering why we do not use them more often."

Santora's eyes widened, clearly caught off guard. "I... would like to see that sometime."

Lisa smiled sweetly. "Of course."

She raised her hand and slowly traced a finger through the air. A shimmering blue circle with three intricate runes appeared, followed by a second green circle wrapping around the first. Each rune glowed faintly as they synchronized, the inner circle drawing on water while the outer circle enhanced plant growth. The air in the room shifted subtly as the spell took shape, and vines in the room's décor stirred, ready to sprout.

Before she could complete the casting, her mother cleared her throat sharply. Lisa glanced at Linda, whose stern gaze warned her: *Don't you dare.*

With a slight, conciliatory smile, Lisa waved her hand and dispelled the magic.

"That was quite the sight," Santora said after a long pause. "Can you explain the requirements for such a casting?"

"Certainly," Lisa replied, her tone cool. "Each circle requires its own mana pool, and the runes must be in harmony. The element in the inner circle creates a synergistic effect with the outer circle's spell."

"I'd like to see the full effects sometime," Santora admitted, unable to hide his curiosity.

"It would be my pleasure to show you," Lisa replied smoothly. Behind her composed demeanor, she was already planning how best to use a more powerful nested circle to make an impression.

The kitchen staff began the appetizer service, presenting elegant plates of deviled eggs, lobster bisque, and crisp garden salads. The flavors were rich and balanced, maintaining the kitchen's reputation for excellence. As the evening progressed, the main course followed: perfectly roasted beef with gravy, creamy mashed potatoes, collard greens with ham hocks, and buttered corn on the cob. Each dish was prepared with care, drawing appreciative murmurs from the guests.

Throughout the meal, Lisa watched the table dynamics with a detached air. Everyone, except her mother, paid constant homage to her father, gently stroking his ego with praise and deference. It was a dance Lisa refused to join. She focused instead on savoring the food, her polite smile concealing her growing disdain for the sycophancy that filled the room.

By the time dessert arrived, a decadent pecan pie served with vanilla ice cream drizzled in caramel, the atmosphere had settled into an uneasy rhythm. The guests savored every bite of the rich, sweet flavors with polite enthusiasm, evident in their enjoyment of the dessert.

As the plates were nearly cleared, Lisa seized a lull in the conversation. "Father," she began calmly, "when will I return to Valorcrest?"

Conrad Nozaki's eyes sparkled with amusement. "Already planning your next escape, are you?" he teased with a smirk. "To run off to your friends again?"

Lisa maintained her composure. "Father, you know I have no such plans."

He leaned forward slightly, his tone hardening. "Oh, I imagine the Order and that pirate ship of yours have some scheme in mind."

Lisa said nothing, knowing that any response would be met with more accusations. Words of reason held no power here, only her silence could keep the peace.

"You have no place on a battlefield," he continued, his voice edged with condescension. "Leave that to the Jiberau girl and your pirate friends. You are better suited for the life of a wife and mother."

The words clawed at Lisa's pride, the very identity nurtured by the teachings of the Goddess Unity. Still, she kept her expression neutral, refusing to let him see how deeply his dismissal stung.

"One day, you'll understand I'm right, Chipmunk," Conrad said softly, a rare note of affection slipping into his voice. His shift in demeanor, from accusing to tender, only unsettled her more.

Before the weight of his words could fully sink in, Lisa caught a look from her mother. Linda Nozaki was always the consummate diplomat, her emotions carefully masked in public. Yet Lisa and Evelyn had learned to read the subtle cues, the brief tightening of her eyes, the slight downturn of her lips. They knew those looks well, having endured enough hidden consequences when the public eye wasn't on them.

Drawing strength from her mother's silent warning, Lisa smiled gracefully and replied, "May the Goddess heed your words, Father."

Conrad seemed content with her answer, but Lisa knew this battle, like many others, would continue to be waged quietly beneath the surface.

[-----⊙-----]

The morning after the other avatars departed was a difficult one for Lisa. Her bedroom felt unnervingly empty, and the silence pressed down on her like a weight. Determined not to dwell on her sadness, she forced herself out of bed and into her daily beauty routine. As she washed her face, her thoughts wandered to the times she'd bathed aboard Annabelle's ship. She scrunched her nose, recalling the ship's persistent stink that clung to the air.

Moving on to her salt scrub, a memory of Sophie's horrified expression during their first beauty session made her smile briefly before the sadness crept back in. She missed them all, her chosen family. The absence was a hollow ache in her chest. After finishing her routine, she soaked in the bath, scrubbing her green hair in hopes that the simple act might wash away some of her loneliness.

Once she was dressed in a plain green dress, she checked the clock on her vanity. It was time for breakfast, but her appetite was gone. Instead, she settled at the small table on her balcony, staring at the horizon. The Stormfang was probably setting sail today. It would be a long time before she saw her friends again. Tears welled in her eyes as the longing overwhelmed her. Her father Conrad made it clear, she wasn't going anywhere. She was trapped in Meadowbrook, confined to the mansion with no means to immerse herself in studies or work.

Eventually, she wiped her tears, deciding she had cried enough for now. After a quick face wash, she sat down at her desk and opened the advanced Earthbloom magic manual she had checked out from the Luminous. She focused on a section about mana balancing, immersing herself in the complexities of advanced spell techniques.

A knock at the door pulled her from her thoughts. The governor entered without waiting for permission. "Good morning, Chipmunk," Conrad Nozaki greeted warmly.

"Morning, Father," Lisa replied, her voice subdued as she closed the manual. "What can I do for you?"

"I missed you at breakfast," he said, moving to stand near her desk.

"I am sorry. I did not realize attendance was mandatory," she responded evenly. "I was not hungry."

Conrad's expression hardened slightly as he cut to the heart of their ongoing dispute. "Chipmunk, listen. It's my duty to the *Harvest Goddess* to keep you safe. I can't let you sail off to Goddess knows where, doing who knows what. I wouldn't be a good steward of the gifts the Goddess has entrusted to me."

Lisa's jaw tightened, her emotions simmering beneath the surface. "The *Goddess of Unity* entrusted me with a holy mission," she said quietly, her voice gaining strength. "The world is in danger, and I have to do something to stop it."

Conrad said nothing, simply watching her.

"You've never met the Goddess of the Harvest," Lisa continued. "But I've met the Goddess of Unity. She explained so much to me."

"You were drugged by the Order," Conrad argued.

Lisa closed her eyes, drawing strength from the presence of Unity's power within her. "No, Father. I wasn't," she assured him firmly.

His expression softened slightly, but the fear in his voice remained. "And what am I supposed to do if you get hurt or... die out there, running with pirates and Jiberau? How am I supposed to be okay with burying my daughter?"

Lisa paused, truly hearing the vulnerability in his words for the first time. She sensed his fear, the anger he showed toward her and her friends had been born from that terror. Her empathy, a gift from Unity, allowed her to see the depth of his fear of such pain. But she also knew the price of doing nothing. If she remained safe in her father's cage, others would suffer as a result of her inaction.

With gentle strength, she met his gaze. "If the world burns because I kept myself safe while others risked their lives... how am I, *the Avatar of Unity*, supposed to reconcile that?"

Conrad was struck silent, contemplating her words, something Lisa rarely saw him do.

Finally, after a long pause, he asked, "If I told you to stay in school at Laminae, would you sneak off to the Order?"

"No, Father. I would accept visitors like Brother Marcus or Sister Alameda, but I would not leave," she said, understanding how much trust she needed to instill in him.

"Why?"

"Two reasons," she replied thoughtfully. "First, I gave you my word that I would stay at Valorcrest. Second, I know you would have someone watching me. And if I did try to leave, you would send the military to capture me."

She smiled slightly, and Conrad couldn't help but grin back, amused by her sharpness.

"Very astute, my Lady Harvest," he said, clearly pleased.

Lisa's expression softened. "I just hope I can prevent the world from burning, or the Seven Kingdoms from dying, before I become a woman with the authority to make decisions for myself."

Conrad's smile faded as he looked around her room in quiet thought. "How long would it take you to pack all your things?"

Lisa blinked, surprised. "I would not need much. Most of my belongings are still at Valorcrest. I am basically already packed."

He nodded slowly. "So... if I trust in the Avatar of Unity to keep her word and **stay safe**," he said, lowering himself onto the edge of her desk, "I could consider allowing her to travel on that privateer vessel with the other Avatars."

Lisa's heart leapt. A warm surge of happiness filled her chest, and before she could stop herself, she rushed to him, throwing her arms around his neck. Tears of joy streamed down her face. "Thank you! Thank you, thank you, thank you, Daddy!"

Laughing, Conrad gently pushed her back. "Hold on now," he said, trying to temper her excitement. "You need to hear me on this. Zachery will teach you a communication spell, and you're to write me a letter every single day. About what you're doing and how you're doing."

"I promise, Daddy. Every single day, even on the boring days," Lisa vowed, nodding eagerly.

His smile widened as he shook his head fondly. "That's my girl."

"Alright, let's get you packed," Conrad said, opening the door to Lisa's room. Standing in the hallway, arms crossed and her expression serious, was Linda Nozaki, Lisa's mother. She wore her signature *mom 's-not-playing-any-games* look, aimed squarely at her husband.

"Well?" Linda prompted him sternly.

Lisa noticed the tension and quickly realized her mother had played a role in persuading her father to change his mind. Smiling to herself, she wisely chose to stay silent.

"Well, what?" Conrad replied defensively. "She has to pack and learn the pen and water bowl spells."

"Oh, great," Linda said, clapping her hands twice. A team of attendants promptly appeared from the stairway. She gave her husband a sweet smile and hugged him, whispering something into his ear before stepping back. "Go on, dear. You have *important governor* work to do. Us Nozaki girls can handle things from here."

With a wave to his wife and daughter, Conrad descended the staircase without another word.

Linda turned to Lisa, her expression softening. "Show the attendants what needs packing, sweetie. That ship of yours must be preparing to set sail, we must hurry."

Giddy at the thought of seeing the other avatars again, Lisa glanced around her room before looking back at her mother. "Pack everything. I want to send them a telegram so they do not leave without me!"

Linda smiled approvingly. "Easy enough, I guess. You heard the girl, pack it all, gentlemen!" she ordered.

One of the attendants stepped forward hesitantly, glancing at the overflowing shelves and wardrobes inside Lisa's room. "Ma'am, there's a lot in here. What should we do if we run out of luggage?"

Linda's smile turned commanding. "I am sure you will think of something," she said, her tone leaving no room for further questions.

Behind her, Evelyn's door creaked open. Peeking out, Evelyn scanned the hallway with a frown. "What's going on here?" she asked.

"Your sister is shipping out with the other avatars," Linda explained, pride evident in her voice. "they are going to need her."

"What?" Evelyn exclaimed, her tone sharp with indignation. "She gets to sail with pirates? First, she gets into Valorcrest, my dream school, and now this? It's not fair, Mommy!" She stomped her foot in frustration.

Linda paused for a beat, then calmly knocked on Evelyn's door. "Good morning, Sergeant Linwood," she called sweetly.

A long moment of silence followed before a sheepish voice responded from inside the room. "Good morning, ma'am."

Evelyn flushed with embarrassment. "He... came over early to have breakfast with the family," she mumbled awkwardly.

Linda arched an eyebrow. "Such a shame the two of you missed breakfast," she remarked quietly, her tone dripping with subtle admonishment.

"It's still not fair!" Evelyn protested, retreating into her room and shutting the door behind her.

Lisa chuckled softly at the scene, but as she opened her mouth to speak, her mother raised a hand for patience. Linda knocked on then opened Evelyn's door once more. "Lunch will be on the west balcony at twelve-thirty sharp," she announced. "Both of you make sure to be there."

"Yes, Mom," Evelyn called back, clearly annoyed.

"Yes, ma'am," came Linwood's muffled, contrite reply.

Satisfied, Linda turned back to Lisa, her demeanor light and cheerful again. "Now, what were you saying, dear?"

"Mom, I will be..." Lisa began, only to be cut off again.

"Go, go! Send your message," Linda urged with a smile. "I'll handle things here until you get back. Hurry up, Chipmunk, there is much to do before you leave."

Lisa didn't need to be told twice. She dashed down the hallway toward the media room, determined to send a telegraph to the Stormfang before they set sail without her.

[-----✝-----]

The morning felt oddly different without Lisa aboard. The remaining Avatars and Brother Marcus gathered for breakfast in the Stormfang's galley without even discussing it beforehand. The absence of Unity's Avatar may have led them to compensate by strengthening their own sense of Unity. Sophie, Marcus, Annabelle, and Regina sat around the central table, quietly eating bowls of oatmeal, except for Regina, who was lost in her work. Jeffie had clearly put effort into the meal, but it couldn't quite compare to the high standard set by Miss Lisa Nozaki.

Regina, meanwhile, furiously sketched another version of her combination spell circle in Mr. Sparks' notebook. She had nearly exhausted every page in her efforts to design a functional ritual for her mana lamps, but none of her attempts had succeeded.

Brother Marcus broke the silence. "What's everyone's plan before we ship out today?"

"I've got training with Eclipse Lepele," Sophie replied between bites. "After that, I'll be working with the crew on deck."

"Sounds… challenging," Marcus said thoughtfully.

"Yeah, he's going to make sure I *do my training right*." Sophie muttered, a note of indignation in her voice.

Annabelle rolled her eyes and grinned. "Nobody cares about yer copper stuff, Sophie. I'm makin' sure the ship's ready to sail soon as the Cap'n gives the word."

"Now that you've got all that money, you can finally pay him the five coin you owe him," Marcus reminded her with a raised eyebrow.

Annabelle's smile faltered. "Yes… I can," she muttered reluctantly, clearly intending not to.

"He mentioned last night he's looking forward to that payment," Marcus added, his tone mild but pointed.

"Oh, so nice of ye to be tellin' me business, Brother Marcus," Annabelle hissed through clenched teeth, annoyed. "Ye need to be a better servant."

"As always, I strive to do so," Marcus replied smoothly.

He turned to Regina. "What about you, Miss Fournier? Do you have any plans?"

"Yep. Big plans," Regina mumbled, her focus locked on the notebook. She barely registered his presence.

Sophie chuckled. "I don't think she's paying attention to you, Brother Marcus." She stood, brushing her hands off. "Well, a torchbearer's work is never done." She dropped her bowl in the wash bucket and strode out of the galley.

Annabelle soon followed, finishing her oatmeal and stretching. "Time to get the day started," she said, before depositing her bowl and leaving Marcus alone with Regina, who remained deep in thought, oblivious to her surroundings.

Annabelle headed to the bridge, where she found Smitty giving instructions to Graves.

"Make sure ye fill up the tank," Smitty was saying, turning the wheel to test the ship's responsiveness. "Can't count on these lasses changin' the battery every day."

Graves, dressed in mismatched boots, black tights, and an open white shirt, nodded with a gruff "Arrr" as he passed Annabelle on his way to the deck.

"On yer way back, tell Flint I need to see him," Smitty called after him.

"Arr," Graves replied over his shoulder, descending the stairs.

Smitty turned his attention to Annabelle as he adjusted the helm. "What do ye need, Belle?"

"Just checkin' in fer work, First Mate," she replied with a bright smile.

Smitty gave her a scrutinizing look. "Have ye been practicing yer magic?"

"Sure have," Annabelle replied confidently, her pride evident.

"And when was the last time ye did yer practice?" he pressed.

Annabelle hesitated, silently counting back the days. She hadn't practiced this morning, and the day before had been spent travelling from Snyder. She bit her lip. "Been kinda busy lately," she admitted.

Smitty crossed his arms, his gaze hardening. "So ye've got magic trainin' to catch up on. How many days did ye skip?"

Annabelle looked down at the deck, feeling like a scolded child. "Two days," she confessed.

Smitty nodded knowingly. "Sounds like ye need to do three times the training, then."

"Three times?" Annabelle yelped. "But First Mate, I only missed two days!"

His eyes narrowed. "Four times."

Her mouth opened to protest, but she snapped it shut when she saw the seriousness in his expression. "Ye don't skip practice, Belle." Smitty said sternly. "It sets yer development back."

Annabelle bit her tongue, swallowing any further arguments. She knew better than to push it. Smitty wasn't one to budge once he'd made a decision. "Aye, First Mate," she said begrudgingly.

Satisfied, Smitty gave her a curt nod. "Good. Now get to it. The Goddess wants ye to master yer maelstrom magic, and ye don't do that by skippin' practice."

Annabelle sighed but knew he was right. Begrudgingly, she made a mental note to spend extra time on her training.

"Oi, Cap'n," Smitty called, leaning out from the bridge.

Captain Kidd emerged from his operations room, adjusting his hat. "What do ye need, First Mate?"

"The steering column's startin' to give. When we reach Magitekopolis, we should see about gettin' it fixed," Smitty reported.

"Aye," Kidd replied, nodding. Then he spotted Annabelle and grinned. "Belle! Where's me coin?"

"Oh yeah," Annabelle muttered, pulling her leather purse of harvest crowns from her belt. She began counting the coins when Captain Kidd held up a hand to stop her.

"Hold on now, Belle. We don't use crop crowns on this here ship. I want coin, universal gold coin," he emphasized. "Ye'd best head to the assayer's office and trade those in before tryin' to pay me."

Annabelle saw her chance to dodge unfair magic training and quickly saluted. "Aye, Cap'n!" she chirped and hurried down the gangplank onto the pier. Once there, she slowed her pace, remembering the no-running rule. Besides, there was no rush, she wasn't eager to spend the day doing endless spell drills for Smitty.

The pier led to a long building labelled Services. Annabelle passed a few vacant offices before spotting an open door with a man sitting behind the counter, reading a book. She stepped inside and addressed him in her most charming, proper voice.

"Excuse me, sir. Is this where I can exchange harvest crowns for universal gold coins?"

The man, who looked to be in his early twenties, set down his book after marking his place. He glanced up and froze for a moment, his gaze lingering on her bright orange hair. "What's wrong with yer hair?"

"Nothing," Annabelle said with a sweet smile. "I was blessed by the Goddess, which is why me hair's so beautiful." She flared her orange locks with a flourish. "Now, I'd like to exchange my harvest crowns. My ship's leaving today."

"Alright," he said, his tone shifting to a practiced professionalism. "How many harvest crowns do ye have?"

"I haven't counted them yet," Annabelle admitted, shaking her leather purse lightly.

"Well, hand 'em over and I'll tally 'em for ye." He held out his hand.

Annabelle passed him the purse, and he poured out the coins, arranging them by denomination, 1, 5, 10, and 25 crowns. As he worked, Annabelle glanced at his book, which lay open on the counter. A large illustration caught her eye. It depicted a man on a ship's deck, wind blowing his long black hair as he stood shirtless, a giant sail bearing the image of the Verdantian Harvest tree behind him. Beside him was a pirate woman with flowing black hair, an eye patch, and a cocksure smile. Her blue vest hung open, revealing a shirt marked with a Jolly Roger.

"What are ye readin'?" Annabelle asked, genuinely curious.

"This?" He perked up, holding the book slightly higher. "The Adventures of Percival Pennyworth. This is book four. Right now, Percival's caught up in a mystery, someone's killed a Verdantian senator and stolen sacred texts. He's tricked a pirate crew into helpin' him recover them."

"Sounds exciting," Annabelle said. "Who's the woman on the cover?"

"That's Alexis, the pirate captain's daughter. She fell for Percival after watchin' him beat her father in a duel."

"How dramatic," Annabelle teased. "And now they're both arrested, I suppose?"

"Yep," he replied enthusiastically. "By corrupt Jiberau trying to stop his mission."

"Wow," Annabelle deadpanned. "Sounds like a real hero."

"Oh, he is! In the first book, Love of the Goddess, Percival was recruited by the Verdantian military to uncover a conspiracy. The Jiberau and pirates were usin' corrupt officials to overthrow the world's royalty. Great read!"

"Like the story's straight outta the headlines," Annabelle muttered under her breath, amused by the fantasy's absurd parallels to real life.

The man chuckled, then turned back to his work. "You've got seven hundred harvest crowns," he said after a moment. "That converts to two hundred gold coins. After the conversion fee, you'll have one hundred eighty-five."

Annabelle's jaw dropped. "Fifteen gold coin for a fee? Are ye serious?"

"Sorry, but we have to take a percentage," he explained with a shrug, counting out the gold coins. As he recorded the transaction, he glanced at her again. "Which ship did ye say you were from?"

"The good ship Stormfang, good sir," Annabelle replied, slipping back into her proper voice.

The man perked up slightly. "Oh, there are messages for your ship." He gestured to a row of boxes above the telegraph machine. "Would you like to receive them?"

"Sure," Annabelle agreed, only to recoil in horror as he casually plucked ten coins from her pile. "Oi! What gives, mate?" she blurted out.

The man blinked, confused. "It costs five coins per message, and your ship has two messages."

Annabelle glared at the now-diminished pile of coins. "Might I see those messages before I buy them?" she asked, her proper voice returning.

"Sorry. Company policy." He shrugged again, unapologetic.

"Fine," Annabelle grumbled, crossing her arms. She had little choice.

The man completed the paperwork and slid a wooden tray with the remaining coins toward her. Two sealed envelopes, both marked Stormfang, sat atop the stack.

Annabelle accepted the tray and carefully counted the coins to ensure she received the full one hundred seventy-five. Satisfied, she slid them into her leather coin pouch. Taking the envelopes in hand, she turned to leave.

"Enjoy yer book, mate," she said casually over her shoulder as she walked out of the office.

Once outside on the pier, she broke into laughter, shaking her head at the absurdity of that Percival Pennyworth series. The idea of pirates following a bloke just because their captain lost a sword fight was ridiculous enough, but the thought of pirates and coppers working together? Completely laughable. Annabelle's chuckles echoed softly across the pier as she made her way back toward the Stormfang.

She didn't feel the need to rush. Smitty was likely going to have her stuck doing Maelstrom mastery training all day anyway, so she figured she might as well read the messages she'd just paid a small fortune for. Strolling leisurely, she opened the first envelope and unfolded the note inside:

Message to: Stormfang Captain
Please be advised that I will be returning to the ship with the Avatars tomorrow (April 28th). Please ready the boat for departure to Magitekopolis.
Signed: Brother Marcus Igbinedion

Annabelle raised an eyebrow. Why didn't the captain just send someone to fetch these messages earlier? She shrugged it off and opened the second letter.

Message to: The Stormfang
Lisa Nozaki is rejoining the crew. Please do not depart before she arrives.
Signed: Lisa Nozaki

Annabelle's eyes widened, and excitement surged through her. *Lisa is coming back!* A grin spread across her face, and she picked up her pace, hurrying toward the gangplank. The others would want to hear this, *the green princess was returning to the Fang!*

[-----⊙-----]

After sending her message to the Stormfang, Lisa returned to her room, where Zachery was waiting. He was ready to show her two communication spells. The first was a ritual that enchanted a pair of pens, once linked, anything written by one pen

267

would appear on the other. The second was a water bowl ritual, which allowed two connected bowls to transmit sound, using water as the medium. Zachery handed her a pen and a bowl for the rituals, along with a notebook embossed with the Verdant Mother Tree on the cover.

"On the first page," Zachery explained, opening the notebook, "you'll find the symbols for the water bowl ritual. The matching bowl will stay in the governor's study, so it'll serve as a direct line to your father."

Lisa nodded in understanding. Once the demonstrations were done, Linda took charge of packing all the essentials for Lisa's journey. Suitcases were filled and loaded into a carriage, and Linda ensured the kitchen staff prepared a lunch basket, knowing Lisa had skipped breakfast. Within ninety minutes, everything was ready, a testament to her mother's efficiency and attention to detail.

Now, Lisa stood beside the carriage, saying her goodbyes to her loving mother.

"Why do you not come with me, Mother?" Lisa asked softly.

Linda glanced over her shoulder briefly before turning back to her daughter. "I would, but I have a few things to handle here, your sister and her new boyfriend, for starters. But that's nothing you need to worry about. You just take care of those girls." She pulled Lisa into a firm, loving hug. "And keep yourself safe, my little Lisa."

Lisa held her tightly, savoring the warmth of the embrace. "I will, Mother. I am going to miss you so much."

"I will miss you too, sweetheart," Linda promised, her voice soft with emotion. "Visit when you can?"

"Yes, ma'am," Lisa said, her voice catching slightly.

"Now go, before your father changes his mind," Linda teased with a smile.

Lisa chuckled. "I am sure you will not let him, Mother."

Linda raised an eyebrow, feigning innocence. "I have no idea what you are talking about," she said with a wink. Despite her playful tone, tears began to well in her eyes.

Seeing her mother cry, Lisa couldn't hold back her own tears.

"Don't cry, sweetheart. You'll ruin your makeup," Linda said gently, lightening the moment with a smile.

Lisa blinked quickly and laughed softly. Looking up at the mansion, she spotted her father standing on the balcony of his study. He was watching them with a quiet, reflective expression. When Lisa waved, Conrad smiled and returned the gesture before retreating into his office.

Taking a deep breath, Lisa climbed into the carriage and settled into the plush seat. With plenty of space to herself, no Avatars crammed in beside her, she knocked on the roof and called out, "I am ready."

The carriage began to roll, taking Lisa toward the Stormfang and her friends. As they travelled, she gazed out the window, drinking in the beauty of Verdantia. Lush greens stretched across the landscape like a rich canvas, accented by bursts of vibrant reds, violets, browns, and whites. The sight calmed her, a vivid reminder of the home she cherished.

About halfway to Ferryville, Lisa opened the lunch basket her mother had prepared. Inside was a fresh salad of tomatoes, onions, olives, and peppers, along with a small container of vinaigrette. Lisa smiled at the thoughtful touch, her mother knew she preferred lighter meals free of meat, even if she wasn't a strict vegetarian. She poured the dressing over the salad and ate quietly, savoring each bite.

When she finished, she neatly placed the empty dish back in the basket and leaned back against the seat. The carriage continued its journey through the rolling fields and painted forests of Verdantia. Lisa's gaze drifted out the window once more, her thoughts turning to the Stormfang, her duty, and the friends she would soon be reunited with. Warm anticipation filled her chest as she imagined the green sails of the ship waiting at the docks.

[-----⚙-----]

"We've arrived, ma'am," the driver called out, knocking gently on the carriage window. He moved to the cargo compartment in the back to retrieve Lisa's luggage.

Lisa blinked awake, realizing she had dozed off after lunch. Stretching slightly, she looked out the window to see the entrance to the pier. Stepping out of the carriage, she watched the driver haul the first of many suitcases, his face already strained from the weight.

She grabbed her purse and walked alongside him. The driver paused at a chalkboard near the entrance to the pier, scanning the list of ships. "The Stormfang... spot seven," he muttered, sighing heavily. "Great, near the end of the pier."

With a resigned smile, he turned to Lisa. "Shall we, ma'am?"

"Of course," Lisa said with a nod, following his lead.

They made their way down the bustling pier. Workers were everywhere, carrying crates, logging cargo on clipboards, and directing goods between ships. Lisa marveled at the organized chaos, but her focus soon returned to the driver, who wrestled with the bulky suitcase as they approached the Stormfang's gangplank. Once they reached it, she hesitated briefly, her childhood fear of tripping and falling into the water tugging at the edges of her mind. Taking a deep breath, she steadied herself and carefully walked up the gangplank.

At the top, she stopped and spotted Captain Kidd on the bridge, standing behind the helm with a clipboard in hand.

"Excuse me, Captain," she called out politely, projecting her voice across the deck. "I'd like to request permission to come aboard your ship."

The captain looked up, a smile spreading across his face. "Welcome back, missy. Permission granted."

Lisa stepped onto the deck, smoothing her dress. "Can someone help with my bags, please?" she asked, glancing back at the driver, who was still struggling with the first suitcase.

From the bow, Annabelle called out, "Oi! We ain't butlers here, princess. Carry yer own bags." She crossed her arms, smirking beside Smitty.

Lisa sighed and glanced toward the carriage, thinking of the many bags still waiting to be hauled. Putting on her most winsome expression, a skill her sister Evelyn constantly teased her for not having, she spoke sweetly, "Oh, I understand. But with all those bags, if I had to carry them all myself, I will be too tired to cook anything for dinner tonight."

The effect was immediate. The entire deck crew paused, exchanging glances before nodding in silent agreement. Without a word, they abandoned their tasks and hurried to help the driver.

Phelps, a familiar face from the crew, reached the top first and grabbed the suitcase from the driver. "Let me take that fer ye, mate."

269

Collins, another deckhand, joined him. "Hey, show us where the rest of yer cart is. We'll get it loaded, no problem."

"oh... okay then." The driver said gratefully, relinquishing the suitcase to Phelps. "Follow me, gentlemen."

The crew followed the driver back down the gangplank, leaving only Phelps behind as he carried the suitcase toward the lower decks.

Annabelle scowled as she watched the scene unfold. "Those scurvy-ridden scallywags!" she muttered. "We pay them good coin, and they still run to do the green princess' bidding."

Smitty chuckled and clapped her on the shoulder. "Ah, Belle, one day ye'll come to learn there are things more valuable to a man than coin."

Annabelle crossed her arms, still fuming. "I don't get it."

"Ye will," Smitty said with a grin. "now, back to yer practice."

Chapter 18

Journal Entry: April 27, 1910

Fortune has smiled upon us, and Governor Nozaki has allowed Lisa Nozaki to rejoin the other avatars on our journey. The news has lifted the spirits of the entire crew. I suspect, beyond the bonds of friendship, it's her skills in the galley that they're most excited for—her presence has always meant an improvement in the quality of food aboard the Stormfang. Morale has undoubtedly improved since she rejoined the crew.

Of course, food isn't the only matter on everyone's mind. Eclipse Lepele has firmly inserted himself into Sophie Griffin's and Regina Fournier's training regimen. His skill as a trainer has proven itself, as has the worth of being trained by someone at his rank. Sophie, ever the loyal member of the Aurorium clan, appears to bristle at his strict oversight, though she follows orders without question. Regina, on the other hand, is absorbing the new training while working with the ship's engineer, Mr. Sparks.

Lepele's presence has also shifted the power dynamic aboard the ship. He's assumed a more active role in guiding Sophie, which is no surprise given his rank as Eclipse. However, his influence may extend beyond mere training; his commanding presence has a way of reshaping the priorities of those around him.

[----- ✠ -----]

Sophie and Regina's morning training was grueling under Eclipse Lepele's watchful eye. The Eclipse designed their routine to push both girls equally to their individual levels, driving them to the brink of their endurance. In the ship's hold, their workout area, they sprinted in tight circuits broken by sets of squats, push-ups, and leg raises. The thuds of their footsteps and labored breaths echoed off the ship's wooden walls, merging with the steady cadence of Eclipse Lepele's voice urging them on.

After the punishing session, Sophie and Regina exited the hold, their bodies aching and damp with sweat. The crisp sea air outside felt both a relief and a reminder of their exhaustion. They were about to part ways when Eclipse's voice cut through the sounds of the bustling deck.

"Sentinel Griffin." he called, his tone commanding yet restrained.

She halted, squaring her shoulders and slipping into formal composure. "Yes, Eclipse, what can I do for you?" she asked.

"You are to assist your green friend in the kitchen today," he instructed without preamble.

Sophie blinked in confusion. "Sir? I usually work with the deck crew."

Eclipse Lepele sighed and gathered himself before saying, "I apologize. Since my return, I find I sometimes struggle to express myself clearly," he admitted. "To be precise, you will not be working the deck today. You *will* help your friend in the kitchen. That is your assignment."

"Yes, sir," Sophie replied, her voice steady despite her curiosity.

[----- ✠ -----]

Sophie arrived at the galley in her purple pants, white shirt, and matching purple vest. She adjusted the tie at her neck before knocking on the back door of the galley three times.

The door creaked open, revealing Jeffie in a food-smeared chef's jacket. His wide eyes registered surprise at her presence. "Can I help you, ma'am?" he asked, his accent making the word *ma'am* sound more like *mom*.

"Actually, I'm here to help you," Sophie replied calmly.

"Ma'am?" He blinked, then glanced over his shoulder toward Lisa for clarification.

"Eclipse Lepele sent me to assist you both," Sophie explained, stepping aside so she could meet Lisa's gaze.

"Perfect!" Lisa said with a grin. Her green hair was pulled into a perfect bun on the back of her head, and the Verdantia tree emblem on her chef's jacket stood out prominently. "Come on in."

Jeffie stepped aside, letting Sophie into the preparation area. Two long rectangular tables bolted to the floor were covered in neatly organized bowls and kitchen tools. Despite the ship's subtle sway beneath them, the bowls remained firmly in place as though unaffected by the motion.

"You will need to change," Lisa said, already moving to a cabinet beneath the counter.

As if on cue, Jeffie tapped Sophie on the shoulder. "Ma'am," he said, while holding out a clean chef's jacket and a hair net.

Sophie accepted the clothing, cleared her throat, and gave him a pointed look. He quickly turned around, giving her privacy to change. Once she was dressed appropriately, Lisa took command.

"All right. For lunch, we are serving salted fish stew with hardtack. Jeffie, head to cold storage and grab the salted fish," she instructed.

"Sure thing, ma'am," Jeffie replied and walked briskly out of the kitchen.

"Sophie, I need you to grab onions, carrots, and potatoes from cold storage," Lisa added, already mentally planning how to prepare the rest of the meal.

"Got it," Sophie said, committing the list to memory before heading off.

While Sophie and Jeffie were gone, Lisa gathered the ingredients to make biscuits, only to realize she'd forgotten to ask for milk. As Jeffie returned with a box of salted fish, she paused her prep and called out to him.

"Oh, Jeffie! Can you grab me a bottle of milk, please?"

"Sure thing, ma'am," he answered, carefully placing the box into a tabletop indentation that locked it securely in place. He disappeared again toward cold storage.

"Thank you, Jeffie," Lisa called after him with a warm smile.

Sophie returned, arms cradling a bowl of vegetables. Approaching the second table, she hesitated, unsure how to place the bowl without it sliding off. She tried setting it into one of the indentations, but the bowl popped back up immediately. "What is wrong with this dumb thing?" she muttered, frustration creeping into her voice.

"Need some help?" Lisa asked, glancing up as she mixed ingredients in a bowl that was sealed to the countertop.

"Yeah... I can't figure out how to get this bowl to stay put," Sophie admitted, pushing the bowl down only for it to pop up again.

"When you press down, you have to twist it into place," Lisa explained patiently. "there is a locking mechanism. Cooking on a ship can be tricky since the movement can throw everything around. These tables are designed to keep bowls and equipment secure."

Sophie followed Lisa's advice, twisting the bowl until it clicked into place. It stayed firmly where it was.

"Okay, got it. Now, what do you need me to do?"

"Dice those vegetables for the stew," Lisa said, turning back to her station just as Jeffie returned with a bottle of milk. She took it from him with a nod of appreciation. "Thank you, Jeffie."

"Of course, ma'am," he chirped.

Sophie glanced around the galley, unsure where to start, when Jeffie called out, "Ma'am, the knives and cutting boards are on the wall over there." He nodded toward the far wall, where rows of pots, pans, utensils, and cutting boards hung neatly from hooks.

"Thanks, Mr. Jeffie," Sophie replied with a grin as she crossed the room. She grabbed a cutting board and knife, then wrestled with the board to lock it into the countertop's rectangular indentation. After a few awkward attempts, it finally clicked into place.

With a relieved sigh, she grabbed a carrot and began slicing, only to flinch as the knife nicked her finger lightly. She hissed under her breath, surprised by how sharp the blade was. Determined not to lose focus, she carefully finished chopping the carrot, but as she gathered the pieces, several chunks slipped from her grasp and tumbled to the floor.

"Ye gotta keep an eye on yer food if ye want to keep it off the floor, ma'am," Jeffie quipped, glancing over as he stirred a pot on the stove.

"Thanks," Sophie replied with a sheepish chuckle. "What should I do with this?" She pointed to the carrot pieces scattered on the floor. "Should I rinse them off, or...?"

Lisa scrunched her face in distaste. "I would say no. I would not eat anything that's touched *this floor.*"

Sophie looked down and understood what Lisa meant. Despite the galley being swept and mopped regularly, the floor had that stubborn, well-travelled layer of grime that seemed to be etched into the ship's bones. She nodded in agreement. "You might have a point there."

She headed to the utility wall, grabbing a small broom and dustpan. With quick, practiced motions, she swept up the carrot remains and dumped them into a trash can bolted near the back wall.

"Good call," Lisa said approvingly as she continued working on the stew. Sophie returned to her station, ready to learn from her mistakes and try again.

[----- ⚓ -----]

On the observation deck, Annabelle and Smitty practiced magic while Regina stood on the far side of the deck, flying the kite she had made with Sister Sallie. The breeze tugged playfully at the kite's string, but the small metal ring attached to it, a clever addition by Sister Sallie, allowed Regina to easily keep control.

Annabelle focused on her training, moving through her spell routine. First, she summoned a wave, its crest shimmering under the morning light. With a fluid motion, she shaped the wave into a waterspout, still perfecting the form. She concentrated, attempting to sculpt the top of the foamy spout into a trident. It wasn't quite there yet, but she felt herself getting closer. Determined, she continued, unleashing a series of riptide punches, one with her left fist and then her right, each imbued with the surging power of the seas. She followed with two precise riptide kicks, making sure her feet reached above her waist, one of Smitty's unrelenting requirements.

Finally, Annabelle summoned water from the surrounding air and sea to form a protective dome. The shimmering barrier glistened like a giant ball, the signature spell marking the end of her routine. She straightened and bowed to Smitty, her expression bright with pride.

"All right, Belle," Smitty said, crossing his arms with a grin. "I admit it, yer gettin' better with the Maelstrom."

Annabelle beamed. "What'll ye teach me next, First Mate?"

"I reckon I'll teach ye two new spells," Smitty replied, stroking his chin thoughtfully. "*The Morning Mist* and *The Gust at Sea*."

"Ooh!" Annabelle's eyes sparkled with excitement. She imagined the possibilities, new spells meant new ways to control the elements around her.

"Now, listen close," Smitty began. "We'll start with the Morning Mist. Picture it, early fog rolling off the sea, coverin' everything with her love, like a gentle blanket."

He moved gracefully, almost like a dancer, his arms swirling in a rhythm that coaxed mana from his body. Wisps of mist began to rise from his skin, growing denser until fog enveloped the observation deck. Annabelle watched intently, studying how his movements channeled the magic.

"This spell's all about subtlety, Belle," Smitty continued. "Ye don't force the sea; ye let her cradle ye in her mist."

With a sudden flourish, Smitty created a gust of wind, scattering the fog in a sweeping arc, straight toward Regina.

"Heyyyy!" Regina yelped as the mist billowed around her.

"Sorry, missy!" Smitty waved apologetically.

"Yeah, sorry, Regina," Annabelle added, biting her lip to stifle a laugh.

Regina lowered her kite slightly and turned to Annabelle with a curious expression. "Why do you call me by my name?" she asked out of the blue.

Annabelle blinked, caught off guard. "What're ye talkin' about?"

"You call Sophie *Copper*," Regina pointed out.

"Aye, she's a copper all right," Annabelle replied easily.

"And you call Lisa *Princess*." Regina continued.

"Yep. Sometimes she acts like she's better than us," Annabelle said with a smirk.

274

"But you only call me *Regina*. Why's that?" Regina asked, her eyes narrowing with playful suspicion.

Annabelle's face flushed as she fumbled for an answer. "It's... hard to explain."

Smitty chuckled, shaking his head. "It's 'cause she likes ye, missy."

"First Mate!" Annabelle protested, her cheeks reddening further as Regina giggled and returned her attention to the kite.

"We need to get back to the magic training, Belle," Smitty said with a hint of impatience. "Lemme see you do the Morning Mist spell. I'll give ye a hint, ye want yer mana thin."

"Aye." Annabelle replied, relieved to leave the awkward conversation behind. Closing her eyes, she pictured the sea within her, coaxing a small, thin layer of mana from it. She channeled it through her body, carefully controlling the flow as Smitty had instructed. As the mana rose to her skin, she thought she had it under control, until a sudden surge of sea water soaked her from head to toe.

Caught off guard, Annabelle froze, water dripping from her sleeves and hair. "What in the blazes...?"

"What did ye do wrong, Belle?" Smitty asked, folding his arms.

Annabelle frowned. "I didna shape the mana thin enough," she admitted reluctantly.

"That's part of it," Smitty said, giving her partial credit. "What else?"

"Nothin' else, that's it," she snapped, frustration mounting.

Smitty remained silent, his disapproving stare saying more than words could. Annabelle pouted, sifting through her memory of the spellcasting attempt. After a moment, she sighed. "I lost focus... right before I cast it."

"There we go," Smitty nodded. "Try it again. Keep yer mana thin, Belle, and focus on what yer doin'. Don't worry about lookin' dashing till after ye master the magic."

Annabelle bristled at the jab but kept her thoughts to herself. She shut her eyes, visualizing the sea inside her once more. Carefully, she summoned a thin layer of mana, shaping it as it passed through her body. She concentrated harder this time, refining the mist as it seeped from her skin. For a moment, it looked promising until, once again, water drenched her, dripping onto the deck below.

"Damn it!" she cursed, shaking the excess water from her hands and face.

"Better," Smitty remarked, raising an eyebrow. "There was a bit of mist that time." He settled into a chair at a nearby table and opened a weathered book. "Again."

Annabelle clenched her teeth and tried five more times, each attempt bringing her closer to success. On the sixth try, a fine mist spread across the observation deck, thinner than Smitty's demonstration but still impressive.

"Not bad, Belle," Smitty praised. "Ye'll be as good as yer papa was in no time. Add the Morning Mist to yer practice routine. Now, we'll move on to the Gust at Sea. This one's a bit trickier, so ye'll have to really focus."

Annabelle's ears perked up, eager to learn.

"The Gust at Sea," Smitty began, his tone shifting to that of a seasoned instructor, "is used by sailors and scallywags to fill their ships' sails. Ye need to picture the wind blowin' over the surface of the sea, like it's filling the sails with its power."

Annabelle closed her eyes, imagining the sea inside her and the wind sweeping across its surface.

"Good," Smitty continued. "Now, channel yer mana inside yerself and shape it into small particles, free-flowin' like air around ye."

As Annabelle watched closely, Smitty demonstrated the spell. He rubbed his hands together, a playful grin on his face, and a gentle breeze began to swirl around him. With a deliberate motion of his left arm, a strong gust shot outward, capable of filling a sail with ease.

Annabelle studied his movements intently, memorizing every detail.

"It's more complicated than it looks," Smitty warned, his grin widening. "Take yer time. Now, give 'er a try."

Annabelle nodded, shutting her eyes once again. She visualized her mana forming tiny particles, swirling over the surface of the sea inside her. When she felt ready, she opened her eyes, pointed her arm toward the horizon, and released the energy. A powerful gust burst forth—but instead of pure wind, water sprayed alongside it, soaking the deck railing.

"Dammit!" she swore, glaring at the watery mess she'd created.

"That's a good first try," Smitty reassured her. "This spell takes a while to master, so ye'll have to keep at it." He checked his pocket watch before pocketing it again. "Let's try it together. I'll go slow this time."

Facing her, Smitty began rotating his right hand in a slow, circular motion across his torso. "Cycle yer mana inside yerself," he instructed. "And while yer doin' that, use mana shapin' to break it down into particles smaller than water drops."

Annabelle visualized a swirling vortex of air inside her, the sea within supporting it like a cyclone. She carefully shaped the mana, reducing it to finer and finer particles.

"Keep spinnin' yer mana," Smitty said, maintaining his circular motion. "And don't lose focus, Belle. Are ye with me?"

"Huh? Aye, I'm with ye," Annabelle said, snapping her focus back to the task. "Spin the mana and use me shapin' to break it down smaller and smaller."

"Good. Now release it, let it swirl around ye, and send it out," Smitty demonstrated, a spiral of wind encircling his body before he extended his arm, releasing a clean blast of air out to sea.

Annabelle followed his lead. Wind and fine droplets of water swirled around her, drenching everything nearby, including Smitty and herself. She mimicked his motion, releasing a blast of wind mixed with water droplets over the back of the ship.

"Better," Smitty said, wiping his soaked face. "But ye've still got a ways to go. Do ye know why yer wind's full o' water, Belle?"

"Because I love the sea," Annabelle quipped with a grin.

"That ain't it," Smitty replied dryly, rechecking his watch with a disapproving look.

Annabelle pondered everything she knew about Maelstrom Mastery. Each spell had required different balances of mana channeling and shaping. The bubble spell required only simple channeling. The current demanded steady, continuous channeling. The wave spell required moderate shaping, while the waterspout took a much more precise control of mana shaping to perfect. Morning Mist, on the other hand, relied almost entirely on shaping with minimal channeling.

So, this Gust at Sea must be a test of balance, channeling and shaping working together in harmony.

"Ohhh," Annabelle muttered, the realization dawning on her. "I have to balance both channeling and shaping equally to keep the spell stable."

Smitty gave her a look of genuine surprise. "That's exactly right, Belle," he said, blinking as though he couldn't quite believe it. He glanced over his shoulder at

Regina, who was still flying her kite, before looking back at Annabelle. "Did yer sister help ye?" he asked, jerking his thumb in Regina's direction.

"Nope. Figured it out all by meself," Annabelle replied with a proud grin.

"I'm just havin' fun with me kite," Regina chirped. She raised her free hand and released a gentle burst of wind with a subtle flick of her fingers, sending the kite soaring a little higher. She giggled as the string tugged lightly in her hands.

Smitty froze mid-thought, his eyes narrowing in disbelief. "Wait... Missy, when did ye learn how ta do that?" he asked, pointing at her.

Regina shrugged casually. "I listened to you explain everything to Annabelle, then I paid attention to what she said about her spell. After that, I made my mana like Maelstrom Mastery, worked it around and around until it was in teeny tiny pieces, like Earth's mana, and then I released it from my hand." She babbled, her words flowing effortlessly as though reciting a list. "Your magic is kinda like Earthbloom but a little different. Actually, it might even be harder. At first, I thought it was like Crystalmancy because it looks simple, but it really isn't. Oh! Come to think of it, what kind of magic does Mr. Sparks have? I bet it's similar to Isabella's magic. I'll have to ask him after I finish flying my kite."

Smitty stood in stunned silence, blinking rapidly as he processed the torrent of information she'd just unleashed. His gaze slowly shifted to Annabelle, his mind clearly struggling to catch up.

"Aye, she does that when she's excited." Annabelle said with an amused smirk. "But I promise ye, First Matem she didn't help me with this."

Smitty blinked a few more times, then shook his head. "Well... okay then," he muttered. Checking his pocket watch, he cleared his throat and turned his attention back to Annabelle. "I want ye to practice both the Morning Mist and Gust at Sea spells before ye start yer shift today."

"Aye, First Mate," Annabelle responded, standing a little straighter.

Regina, catching the serious tone, decided to chime in with a playful grin. "And what should I practice?"

"Everything," Smitty answered with a wink. "I'll check yer progress later, missy." With that, he walked off the observation deck, leaving both girls to their tasks.

[-----┼-----]

After breakfast service, the galley's dining room was an ideal spot for Marcus's investigation. He sifted through a collection of papers tied to the conspiracy known as the Order of the Black Sun. Hidden among Matthew Fournier's drawings, the documents appeared either intentionally or accidentally disguised. Ten drawings in total, each one revealed an unsettling truth on its reverse side.

The first drawing depicted a woman in red, wielding a massive axe. Marcus suspected that Hema, the Blood Witch, was looming over Matthew and Jules. Hema appeared to be screaming, while the boys frowned deeply. The sketch was dated April 23, 1910, and signed by Matthew. On the back was a memo labelled "EDICT," stating, "paving our way to the Grand Design." The directive ordered all facilities under the sect of harvesters to halt current projects and focus on something ominously named the "Essence Initiative." A shiver ran down Marcus's spine as he noted unsettling parallels between the Black Sun Order and his own Order of Saint Lorraine. What was this "Grand Design," and how had the Black Sun risen to such power and influence?

The second drawing depicted a young Matthew punching the woman in red. Stars hovered above her head, emphasizing the force of the blow. Jules cheered in the background with both arms raised triumphantly. The reverse side revealed a requisition request for rare magical herbs, void root, Moonshade, Fae Cinnamon, Dragon's Breath, and Umbral Spice. These were to be shipped from a facility in the Umbrathorn Empire to two locations: a Stoneridge facility called Drago and one in Islewind known as Seacan.

A third drawing depicted a girl with grey hair, dressed in black, holding a wand similar to Miss Fournier's. She had angelic wings and was casting colorful spells. Dated April 21, it too bore Matthew's signature. The back of the page contained a shipping manifest describing the transfer of equipment to a hidden dock in Islewind, with details about the secrecy and security measures. However, the hosting town remained frustratingly unidentified.

As Marcus continued reviewing the artwork and documents, patterns of secrecy, coded orders, and conspiratorial connections between facilities across the kingdoms emerged. Each piece hinted at hidden operations, forbidden experiments, and clandestine shipments tied to the Black Sun's machinations.

His train of thought was interrupted by a voice. "Mind if I join you?"

Marcus looked up to see Eclipse Lepele standing by the table with two cups of coffee. The Eclipse was dressed in brown pants and a loose white tunic style shirt with untied laces at the neck, revealing a glimpse of his chest. His dark skin contrasted subtly with the bright shirt, and his long hair was tied in a makeshift ponytail.

"Yes you can." Marcus replied, quickly gathering Matthew's drawings to keep them safe.

Lepele handed Marcus one of the mugs before sitting across from him. "I was told you appreciate a good cup of coffee."

Marcus smiled faintly. "Well, sir, you've clearly done your homework."

"Well, I am an investigator." Lepele said, taking a sip from his mug.

Marcus blew on his coffee and took a cautious sip, letting the warmth settle before responding. He waited, giving Lepele room to speak.

"From what I hear, I have you to thank for getting me out of that cell," Lepele said, glancing around the dining area. "And into this fine situation."

"Think nothing of it," Marcus replied. "Miss Griffin was quite insistent about seeing you to safety. As her humble servant, I was duty-bound to improve your circumstances."

Lepele raised an eyebrow. "Servant? How does that work, exactly?"

"Miss Griffin was chosen by the Goddess of War to serve as her avatar on Earth," Marcus explained. "The Order of Saint Lorraine is sworn to protect and support avatars. Through them, we serve the goddesses."

Lepele frowned in disbelief. "Griffin's fourteen years old. She's a Sentinel. In the clan, Sentinels don't get that much freedom. How could she possibly be ready to have a full-fledged servant at her beck and call? Not to mention members of the clan live dangerous lives. She could get you killed just following her."

"To be honest, avatars live equally dangerous lives," Marcus answered with a knowing look. He took another sip of coffee. "The last group of avatars, a trio—died in battle at seventeen. Their path is never an easy one."

Lepele remained silent, lost in thought.

"The goddesses raise avatars when there is a great threat to the world," Marcus explained gently, hoping to offer context.

"Either way, thank you for all your help," Lepele finally said, extending his hand across the table.

Marcus accepted the handshake, recognizing the familiar strength that all Aurorium members seemed to possess. Even the women in the clan had grips that could rival soldiers. Choosing humility, he replied, "There is no need to thank me, Eclipse. I am but a humble servant of the avatars."

"So you say, Brother," Lepele responded with a knowing glance. He paused, then added, "I wonder how the clan will handle this whole *avatar* situation."

"I share your concern," Marcus admitted. "Miss Griffin's loyalty to the Aurorium Clan runs deep. I doubt she would ever willingly leave, but what happens if the will of the goddess conflicts with the will of the clan?"

Lepele leaned back slightly, his expression thoughtful. "I can tell you this much, the clan isn't used to being denied by its own members. Especially not by a torchbearer like Griffin."

"Torchbearer?" Marcus repeated, unfamiliar with the term.

"Sentinels carry the torch, they light of the clan's future." Lepele explained. "We call them torchbearers as a nickname."

Marcus nodded, appreciating the insight.

Lepele's eyes shifted to the stack of papers and drawings beneath Marcus's notebook. He gestured toward them. "What's with the drawings?"

Marcus sighed, glancing at the sketches. "We discovered that the people who took Miss Fournier's father and brother hostage were operating out of a hidden facility in the Verdantian town of Snyder. We think Jules Fournier gave his son these papers to draw on, maybe disguising them as clues to help secure a rescue. But I'm struggling to piece it all together."

"Mind if I take a look?" Lepele asked, holding out his hand. "Fresh eyes might help."

Marcus handed him the drawings. Lepele carefully examined each one, flipping between the illustrations and the communications on the reverse sides. He arranged them into groups, reading the documents with a focused intensity. Every so often, he murmured, "Hmm," as he studied the material.

After a few minutes, Lepele placed the papers, with the communication side up, on the table. He took a slow drink from his coffee and said, "Here's what I gather: about three years ago, your Verdantia facility was involved in something called the 'Harvest Initiative.' It seems to be part of a larger project referred to in these documents as *The Grand Design*. From the way these communications are worded, this *Harvest Initiative* sparked competition among multiple groups. Each was trying to solve the same problem, but your Verdantia facility fell behind and was eventually absorbed into a facility in Islewind."

Lepele set his cup down and met Marcus's gaze. "Do you know what your order's *Grand Design* is?"

Marcus shook his head. "*The Order* in these documents isn't the Order of Saint Lorraine," he clarified. "Miss Fournier discovered that the group behind these operations is called *The Order of the Black Sun*. I had never even heard of them before our mission in Snyder."

"Hmm. I can't say I've heard of them either," Lepele admitted.

"They seem committed to absolute secrecy," Marcus continued. "We have no idea how extensive their reach is or what their capabilities are."

Lepele frowned in thought. "Based on these communications, they seem to have a presence not just in Verdantia, but also in Islewind, Stoneridge, and my home kingdom of Umbrathorn. I'd wager their influence spans all seven kingdoms."

"I would assume the same," Marcus agreed solemnly. "If only we could find them."

[----- ⚓ -----]

That night, Annabelle stood at the bow of the ship, listening to the rhythm of the sea. Ever since hearing Regina and Lisa talk about their Earthbloom senses, she had wondered if she could attune herself to the ocean in a similar way. The book she had borrowed from the library offered no insights on a "sea sense," but pirates, and privateers by extension rarely documented all of their secrets.

Closing her eyes, Annabelle let the sound of the waves fill her mind. She felt the ship move with the ocean's push and pull, rising and falling, swaying port to starboard and back again. She imagined herself as the ship, her inner mana like the sea, ready to connect with the vast waters surrounding her.

A faint snicker pulled her out of her focus. Annabelle's eyes snapped open, and she turned to see two members of the night deck crew adjusting the sails. They looked surprised when Annabelle quickly turned around to look at them, as if they were unsure why she was looking at them. Annabelle rolled her eyes and let it go, deciding it wasn't worth getting worked up over. Instead, she got back to her training.

Starting with a wave spell, she conjured a surge of water and smoothly followed it with a waterspout. She focused intently on shaping the foam at the top into a trident, determined to master that detail. She pushed herself further, throwing a series of riptide punches and kicks, each strike imbued with mana and precision. Leaning back, she summoned a dome of water around her, the seashell spell, and once it was complete, she respectfully returned the water to the sea.

Time for the hard part.

Annabelle channeled her mana and broke it down into the smallest particles she could manage, coaxing a cloud of mist to spread across the deck.

"Oi, what's with all the fog?" came a disgruntled shout from one of the deck crew.

"Aye, aye," Annabelle muttered dismissively. She refined her mana shaping, pushing harder, and cast the gust a sea spell through her hand. As she waved it toward the crew, a light spray of seawater misted over them, drawing louder complaints. Annabelle snorted and shook her head. "Scallywags can't even handle a bit of training," she grumbled.

Deciding she'd had enough of their whining, she made her way toward the bridge to see how Captain Kidd was doing.

She found him manning the helm, his gaze on the horizon, steering the ship with a calm, confident grip.

"Evenin', Cap'n. How goes the day?" Annabelle asked, her tone light and plucky, the way Kidd liked it best.

Kidd turned to her with a roguish grin. "Made a bit of coin, had a bit of fun," he replied with a wink. "Saw ye doin' yer magic out there. Yer getting pretty good."

Annabelle pulled her shoulders back in mock pride. "Why, thank ye for noticin', Cap'n," she said with an exaggerated, playful bow.

"Figured ye'd be spendin' the night with yer sisters," Kidd remarked, his eyes still on the helm as he kept the ship steady.

Annabelle's expression shifted slightly. "Them three ain't me kin," she corrected. "Javier and Ada Salazar weren't their folks."

Kidd raised an eyebrow, giving her a curious look. "I dunno... ye kinda look like that motor-mouth girl," he teased.

"Bah!" Annabelle scoffed, waving him off. "She wishes she looked as good as me."

Kidd laughed heartily and gestured for her to come closer. "C'mere, Belle," he said warmly.

Annabelle stepped between him and the wheel, placing her hands on the pegs. Moments like this always brought a smile to her face. She remembered standing by his side when she was just ten years old, back when Kidd was the night helmsman for the Juniper Night. His guiding hands on hers had made her feel safe and valued, and even now, she cherished that bond.

"Why don't ye like yer sisters?" Kidd asked in his usual playful, nonchalant tone.

"I like 'em fine," Annabelle replied. "They just ain't me sisters. I'm sure I can do better."

"I dunno, Belle," Kidd mused. "I've gots a few sisters meself. Ye could do worse than the motor-mouth, the princess, and Sophie."

"Sophie," Annabelle scoffed, rolling her eyes. "Bite yer tongue, Cap'n!"

Kidd chuckled. "I'm just tellin' ye."

Annabelle changed the subject with a sly grin. "Y'know, Cap'n, I gots me a birthday comin' up."

"Oh, do ye now?" Kidd teased. "Ye sure about that? Sounds like ye might've gotten yer dates mixed up."

"Nope," Annabelle said with certainty. "All us avatars have the same birthday."

"I'll have to check with Brother Marcus on that," Kidd said, turning the wheel slightly to adjust the ship's course.

"Brother Marcus," Annabelle scoffed again. "if I told him me birthday was every day, he'd believe me. He's me servant."

"I don't think he'd lie to ye, Belle," Kidd replied, resting his head playfully on her shoulder. Annabelle giggled at the gesture, her frustration fading.

"So whatcha gettin' me for me birthday?" she asked, nudging him.

"I might've gotten ye somethin' nice," Kidd said with a mischievous grin. "But after seein' how ye treat that poor anchor belt I gave ye, I'm not so sure."

"Cap'n, I love me belt!" Annabelle protested, leaning back comfortably against him.

"Here, ye wanna steer?" Kidd offered, stepping aside slightly. He pointed to the compass mounted behind the helm. "Keep us on one-eighty-five."

Annabelle gripped the wheel tightly and focused, determined to show how much she'd improved. At first, she kept the wheel steady, but soon, the force of the sea fought back. The wheel began to shift under her hands, the ocean asserting its will.

Kidd chuckled. "Of all people, ye should know the sea won't be tamed," he said, placing his hand back on the wheel to help her find the rhythm. "Ye gotta listen to the sea, Belle. Doesn't yer magic teach ye how to hear her?"

"It don't work like that," Annabelle admitted, feeling embarrassed. Steering the Fang wasn't something she had mastered, at least, not yet.

"You don't have to hold the ship perfectly straight," Captain Kidd said in a calm, practiced tone, adopting his *proper voice*. "Just make small adjustments to keep the ship on course." He tapped Annabelle lightly on the side. "Here, let's work together. Gimme yer hand."

Annabelle obliged, placing her left hand in his. Now, with her right hand still on the wheel and his left hand resting beside hers, they stood together in a kind of ship-runner's embrace.

She held on tightly, determined not to lose control again. Kidd gave the wheel a gentle shake.

"Nope, nope. Loosen yer grip," he instructed with a playful grin.

Annabelle hesitated but eventually relented, relaxing her hold on the pegs. She felt uncertain, but she followed his lead.

"That's better," Kidd reassured her, steadying the rhythm of the wheel with her. After a few moments, he spoke again. "Ye know, Belle, ye never talk about yer goddess."

Annabelle blinked. "What's that now?"

"Yer sisters," Kidd said, his grin widening as he continued to tease her, "they let their goddesses slip into conversation now and then. You hear it all the time—'Unity says this,' or 'Change can fix that,' or 'War wouldn't like this.' But you, ye never say a word about yer goddess. Ye keep yer lips shut tight about her."

Annabelle frowned thoughtfully. He isn't wrong. She rarely talked about her goddess, though it wasn't something she did consciously. Still, nothing was ever free out on these seas. "What do ye want to know?" she asked cautiously, feeling that familiar pull between curiosity and secrecy.

"Oi, ye're a tough one, Salazar," Kidd complained with an exaggerated sigh. "All right, first of all, what's she the goddess of?"

"*Chaos*," Annabelle answered, her voice softening as she spoke the word. A sly smile tugged at her lips. "And she's a pirate, just like me."

Kidd chuckled, shaking his head. "Figures. Of course yer goddess is a pirate."

Together, they stood at the helm, steering the Stormfang through the night sea as the stars shimmered above them. The rhythm of the waves echoed like a distant melody, and for a moment, Annabelle felt perfectly in tune with both the sea and the wheel under her hands.

Chapter 19

After a thorough review of the papers from the Black Sun facility in Snyder, Eclipse Lepele offered valuable insights. He identified possible destinations where Jules and Matthew Fournier might have been taken: Islewind, Stoneridge, and even the Umbrathorn Empire. However, one troubling discovery stands out: *all the documents are three to four years old. If the Black Sun's operations have shifted in that time, tracking them down may prove even more difficult than we believed.*

For now, our course is set. Once we complete our business with the Aurorium Clan in Magitekopolis, the avatars will determine our next destination. The journey ahead promises to be perilous, but there is no turning back. The world may not yet grasp the danger it faces, but the Order of the Black Sun cannot remain hidden forever.

[-----✠-----]

In the swaying hold of the Stormfang, Sophie and Regina continued their training under the watchful eye of Eclipse Lepele. Today's session was different, they were sparring for points, with Lepele acting as their judge.

The two girls circled each other, exchanging probing jabs. Sophie noted how much Regina had improved since they started sparring a few weeks ago. Back then, Sophie had to hold herself back to avoid injuring her. Now, Regina was holding her own, her defenses becoming quicker and more instinctive.

Sophie launched a quick jab, aiming to catch Regina off guard, but the silver-haired girl blocked it with ease and backed away. Sophie pressed forward, hoping to break through Regina's guard, only to find herself deflecting counterattacks. *Impressive*, she thought. Still, Sophie's experience gave her an edge. She feinted with a jab, then swiftly followed with a straight punch and a cross. Regina, caught off balance, stumbled as Sophie's cross came in hard, until a flash of energy erupted between them. Galahad, Regina's guardian spirit, manifested to block the attack.

"Point, Griffin," Lepele called, prompting the girls to separate. He stroked his chin thoughtfully before adding, "Let's make this more interesting."

Regina tilted her head, confused, while Sophie's heart sank. She had a bad feeling about this. *He's going to handicap me*, she thought grimly. Probably tie one of my hands behind my back.

"Regina," Lepele said, his voice calm but firm, "you can use whatever magic you want. Griffin, no magic for you."

Sophie scoffed. "How is that fair?" she protested, earning a sharp look from Lepele.

"You hear that, Regina?" he said with a smirk. "She's afraid of all your magic."

Regina grinned, raising her fists. "I've got lots of magic," she said, playing along with the taunt.

Sophie scowled. *I should've known training with Regina would come back to bite me*, she thought bitterly.

"Starting positions!" Lepele boomed. The girls took their spots on opposite sides of the mat. He raised his hand and commanded, "Begin!"

Regina quickly cast her go-to spell: Kids' Play – Hide and Seek. Multiple copies of herself shimmered into existence and spread out across the hold. Sophie, however, wasn't fooled. She knew the clones weren't real, so she charged straight for the honest Regina. She threw a pair of punches, forcing Regina to dodge back.

Regina's mind raced for a new tactic, but she hesitated too long. Sophie stepped in with a quick straight punch aimed at her face. Another flash of light, Galahad's shield, stopped the blow.

"Point, Griffin," Lepele announced, his voice echoing off the hold's walls. He gave Regina a stern look. "You do know you can still throw punches, right?"

"Sorry," Regina muttered, shaking off her distraction. "Got lost in my own thoughts." She silently vowed to stay focused this time.

"Looks like it was fair after all," Lepele remarked, throwing a subtle jab at Sophie as they returned to their positions.

Sophie clenched her jaw and held her tongue. Lepele was an Eclipse, and he wouldn't take too much backtalk. Lepele raised his hand again and called, "Ready!" With a sharp drop of his hand, he shouted, "Begin!"

Sophie launched a cross punch. Regina ducked beneath it and quickly cast Envoûtement des Cercles Éternels, pointing her pointer and middle finger inside her glove directly at Sophie. Four glowing rings materialized around Sophie, binding her limbs in place. Sophie strained against them with all her strength but couldn't break free. Smirking, Regina tapped Sophie lightly on the nose with her boxing glove.

"Point, Regina," Lepele called. "That makes it 3–3. Game point, girls."

Regina dispelled the rings, and Sophie dropped to the mat with a grunt. Embarrassed but determined, Sophie let out a steadying breath and returned to her starting position.

"Positions!" Lepele commanded. The girls raised their fists, ready for the final clash.

"Begin!"

This time, Sophie rushed forward, but instead of attacking head-on, she dodged to her left, avoiding another attempt at Envoûtement des Cercles Éternels. A flash of energy passed harmlessly to her right as she circled around for an opening. Sophie threw a punch, which Regina ducked, retaliating with a jab of her own. Sophie dodged to the side and countered with a rapid combination. Regina blocked and weaved, staying on her feet but giving ground.

"Stay focused, Regina," Lepele called out, breaking through the noise in her mind.

Regina reset her stance and threw a jab, which Sophie blocked. They exchanged blows, each girl testing the other's defenses. Then, Regina had an idea. Drawing on her Maelstrom Mastery training, she cast the Morning Mist spell. A dense cloud of mist and water droplets rose around her, filling the hold and obscuring Sophie's vision.

Sophie froze, taking a step back to center herself. She couldn't see anything, so she tuned into her other senses. Calmly, she listened for movement. From her left, she heard the faint squeak of Regina's shoes on the mat. *I don't know if this mist is giving her any advantage*, Sophie thought. Still, she kept her body angled to the right, feigning inattention.

The moment Regina stepped into range, Sophie pivoted sharply to the left and closed the distance. She threw a powerful straight punch, her fist connecting with Regina's guard. Galahad appeared again, manifesting a shimmering mana barrier to protect her, but the force of the punch knocked Regina off her feet. She landed hard on the mat with a thud.

"Point, Griffin... I think," Lepele said, glancing between the two girls.

Regina sighed, disappointed that her tactic had failed. She dispelled the mist with a quick Gust at Sea spell, revealing Sophie standing tall, glove raised above her head.

"Griffin wins the day," Lepele announced.

Sophie reached down to help Regina up. They tapped gloves, a gesture Sophie had taught her early on in their training. "Good work," they said in unison, grinning despite their exhaustion.

"Good effort out there, both of you," Lepele said, nodding in approval. "Griffin, where are you off to today?"

Sophie felt the familiar pit in her stomach rise. She knew what this question meant, Lepele had no intention of letting her return to her usual deck duties. Bracing herself, she replied, "I was going to help Lisa and Jeffie in the kitchen, Eclipse."

"I don't think they need your help today," Lepele replied evenly. "I want you to fill in as the ship's runner. After you get changed, report to the first mate, Mr. Smith."

"Yes, Eclipse," Sophie responded, though her voice was stiff. The pit in her stomach grew heavier as she realized what that meant, she'll be at Annabelle's mercy all day. Her shoulders slumped as she turned to leave, silently asking herself, *Why is he messing with me so much?* In one sharp motion, she yanked her gloves off and flung them to the floor with a frustrated huff.

"See you later, Sophie," Regina called cheerfully, removing her own gloves.

"See you, girl," Sophie replied over her shoulder, walking briskly toward the ladder to exit.

Lepele turned to Regina. "And what about you? What are you up to today?"

"There's nothing to fix right now," Regina answered as she loosened the knot on her glove with her teeth. "Mr. Sparks already repaired everything while you were all waiting for us in Verdantia. Sooo... I guess I'll fly my kite and practice Kiroku-Mbili magic, or maybe Earthbloom. I haven't really decided." She paused and tilted her head playfully. "How about you, Mr. Eclipse? What are you planning to do? Gonna mess with Sophie some more?" She gave him a teasing grin. "Why do you keep doing that, anyway? Do you want to make her mad or something? Is that some Aurorium thing, or are you just having fun?"

Lepele blinked and stared at her, processing her rapid-fire questions. After a few moments, he finally said, "How would you like to do me a favor?"

"Sure!" Regina replied eagerly, though part of her was still curious if she'd ever get an answer about Sophie.

After finishing her morning training with Regina, Sophie changed into her day clothes and headed to the bridge. She checked in with Smitty, quietly offering her thanks to War that Annabelle wasn't there…yet. At Smitty's direction, Gimble, the regular runner, gave Sophie a crash course on how to be an effective runner: *repeat the message to the sender, ensure the receiver confirms it, and return promptly to the sender. When not running a message, help out on the bridge and main deck.* Simple enough.

Smitty handed her a few practice messages to deliver, one for the powder deck and another for the infirmary. Sophie assumed these were just warm-up tasks to help her get comfortable in the role. So far, things didn't seem so bad—until Annabelle Salazar strolled onto the bridge.

"Copper! Yer the runner?" Annabelle asked, her voice laced with malicious mischief. Sophie immediately felt a wave of suspicion. *She's already scheming.*

"Yes," Sophie replied stiffly. "Eclipse Lepele ordered me to fill in."

Annabelle grinned wickedly. "I'll have to thank him for that." She rubbed her hands together gleefully.

Sophie sighed inwardly. *And so her day began.* Usually, runners helped out on deck between messages, but Annabelle made sure Sophie had no spare time for such tasks. First, Annabelle sent a message to the powder mag, asking when the sailors planned to play Crew. They sent back a reply: after lunch, the captain has something for us to do. Sophie dutifully delivered the response, but Annabelle wasn't done.

"Next message," Annabelle said. "Ask the galley what's for lunch."

Sophie delivered the message, and Lisa replied: Pork belly skewers with rice and mixed vegetables. Sophie returned to the bridge, only for Annabelle to hand her another task, this time a message to Gary, the ship's doctor, asking for a medical inventory. Sophie searched the infirmary but didn't find him there. Instead, she discovered Gary in the hold, tightening down straps on a mountain of Lisa's luggage with Bobby and Ethan.

"Arr," Gary said when Sophie delivered the message, signaling that he received it. Sophie returned to Annabelle, who immediately sent her back to Ethan with a ridiculous message: Annabelle sticking her tongue out. Sophie shrugged and delivered it. Ethan chuckled, shook his head, and sent a hand gesture in reply, one Sophie was all too happy to return to Annabelle.

Undeterred, Annabelle sent another message: Sophie the Copper is ugly. However, Sophie somehow forgot the original message, delivering it as Annabelle's hair looks like an unruly mop. Ethan let out a belly laugh and boomed, "Arrr!" in approval.

By the time Sophie returned, Annabelle was pestering Smitty, begging him to let her steer the ship. He shut her down with a simple, "No." Annabelle grumbled, then tasked Sophie with delivering another inventory request to Gary. Sophie found him in the infirmary, counting bottles. He confirmed the message with another "Arr."

As if that wasn't enough, Annabelle sent Sophie to the kitchen to ask about dessert. Lisa's response was quick: Peach cobbler, if we have time. The day stretched on as Sophie ran message after message. Her legs began to ache from all the back-and-forth, but the Crew's playful banter kept her spirits up.

286

Annabelle eventually sent Sophie to deliver a message to "that sunlight copper guy," clearly referring to Eclipse Lepele. When Sophie hesitated, Annabelle complained, "The purple copper is making too many faces and moving too slow. Maybe she needs a beating."

Grumbling under her breath, Sophie made her way to the hold. There, she found Lepele training with Regina. A red aura surrounded his body as he propelled himself forward in a flash, his shoulder driving toward Regina like a battering ram. The spirit of Galahad manifested just in time to block the hit, keeping Regina on her feet despite being pushed back several steps. Sophie waited for an opening and finally delivered her message, albeit incorrectly: "Sophie is doing a great job as the ship's runner."

Lepele chuckled and replied, "Message acknowledged," before returning his focus to the training session.

When Sophie returned to the bridge, she found Captain Kidd and Smitty standing under the midday sun, talking with Annabelle. Kidd turned to Annabelle and asked, "Got the infirmary inventory?"

Annabelle called for Sophie, but Kidd waved her off. "I don't want the message. I want the actual inventory. Go help the doc sort it out."

Annabelle huffed in frustration but complied. Sophie couldn't resist taking a jab. "See you later, *Anna*." she teased with a smug grin.

"Stupid copper," Annabelle muttered under her breath as she stomped off.

Smitty checked the pocket watch in his shirt. "It's almost lunchtime, Cap'n."

"So it is," Kidd replied. Both men turned to Sophie expectantly.

"I don't know what to do," she admitted, feeling a bit out of place.

Kidd flashed his cocksure smile. "It's customary for the runner to have lunch with the Captain. So run along to the galley and get our food." He waved her off casually before retreating to his ready room.

Sophie made her way to the galley, where Jeffie was waiting with an ornate porcelain tray. The rectangular plates and covers were intricately painted with black designs and trimmed with gold. The two trays were stacked and interlocked like a puzzle.

"Make sure ye don't break it, yeah?" Jeffie warned seriously.

Sophie nodded, gripping the handles firmly. She carefully carried the tray up to the captain's operations room. Smitty held the door open, his usual indifferent expression watching the deck crew as they worked. Sophie entered to find Kidd relaxed at his table.

"Ohhh, what's fer lunch?" he asked with a grin.

"Pork belly skewers with rice and mixed vegetables," Sophie recited as she set the trays down. She hesitated for a moment, unsure which tray was hers.

"I get the top one," Kidd clarified, helping her out with a smile and a wink.

She slid the top tray across the table to him and took her seat. Lifting the cover from her tray, she revealed the delicious meal beneath, along with a covered cup of tea.

"So, runner," Kidd said as he leaned forward, "what's been happenin' on me ship?"

Sophie recounted her day, detailing the endless messages and the mishaps along the way, including her mistakes with Annabelle's notes. Kidd threw his head back in laughter.

"Ye know she does that 'cause she likes ye, aye" he said, shaking his head in amusement.

"I'm pretty sure you're wrong about that," Sophie said, shaking her head. "She likes Regina."

"Aye, she likes the motor-mouth girlie too," Kidd replied, pausing to spear a piece of pork belly. He chewed thoughtfully before continuing, "But she can't go back and forth with her like she can with you." He took another bite, savoring the meal. "Ohh, that green sister of yers sure can cook."

Sophie frowned slightly. "Why does everyone keep calling us sisters? We don't look anything alike, and we don't even have the same color," she said, her tone laced with curiosity. "I have a brother, and he's nothing like Annabelle."

Kidd chuckled as he wiped his mouth. "Missy, I've got sisters of my own. And the four of ye...yer like a rainbow family. All ye need now is a pet, like a dog or something," he teased.

Sophie thought of Titus and giggled quietly to herself.

"What were those scallywags in the powder mag up to?" Kidd asked casually, his eyes twinkling with mischief.

Sophie hesitated, not wanting to get the sailors in trouble. "They were, uh... working on the cannons. I wasn't sure exactly what they were doing," she said, trying to sound convincing.

Kidd immediately stopped eating and gave her a pointed look. "Sophie, do ye know why the runner has lunch and dinner with the Cap'n?"

Caught off guard, Sophie shrugged. "I'm not sure. To keep you company?" she guessed.

Kidd shook his head. "I got plenty of company, missy," he said curtly. "The runner is all over the ship. Ye're me eyes and ears out there, running around everywhere. I know those scallywags were playin' Crew all day." He leaned back in his chair, his gaze sharp. "The one-person ye don't lie to is the Cap'n. Understand?"

Sophie's cheeks flushed in embarrassment. "Aye, Captain," she said quietly. "They were playing crew in the powder mag."

"Good," Kidd said with a nod, his tone softening. "Now we gettin' somewhere."

The two continued their conversation over lunch, with Sophie sharing details about everything she had observed aboard the Stormfang. Kidd listened intently, his casual demeanor masking a keen interest in the ship's operations and the Crew's activities.

[-----☩-----]

Journal Entry: May 3, 1910

During our travels, the avatars have remained occupied with the various operations of the ship. Sophie Griffin's days have been directed by Eclipse Lepele, who has assigned her a variety of tasks. Under his guidance, she has assisted Lisa Nozaki and the kitchen staff, acted as the ship's runner, cleaned the powder magazine area, which likely hadn't been touched since the ship was built, and serviced every weapon in the ship's armory, ensuring they are ready for immediate use.

After her work in the armory, Eclipse Lepele tasked Sophie with learning five new runes for her Alrunia Magic: void, lightning, web, duplicate, and shockwave. She has successfully integrated some of these runes into her rifle and pistol bullets.

Subsequently, Lepele assigned her to assist Mr. Gary in the infirmary, where she has been helping to treat the Crew and organize the medical area.

Regina Fournier has been assisting me in investigating the papers we retrieved from the Snyder facility. We have confirmed Eclipse Lepele's conclusion that the Order of the Black Sun either took her family to the Islewind or Stoneridge facilities. This leaves our pursuit of the Fourniers at a standstill until we gather more information. Regina has also been working with Mr. Sparks to fix various systems he has installed around the ship and has started her own combat training with Eclipse Lepele, showing great aptitude in her learning.

Lisa Nozaki continues to dedicate most of her time to the kitchen, creating delicious dishes that sustain the Crew.

Annabelle Salazar remains busy with her magic training and duties as the operations officer, ensuring the smooth running of the ship's activities.

[-----✿-----]

"I'm really sorry," Regina said, her voice tinged with guilt as she stood in Sparks' workshop. Sparks was busy scrubbing caked-on grease from a circular piece of metal. "I'll get you another book. I promise, as soon as we get to port."

Sparks glanced at her briefly. "No, really, tis fine," he replied.

But Regina wasn't convinced. His tone seemed too dismissive, and he continued wiping the equipment with intense focus, moving the rag soaked in degreasing fluid back and forth as if venting his frustration on the metal. It reminded her of how her father, Jules, would silently work through his anger when upset with her. Sparks might not be yelling, but Regina couldn't shake the feeling that he was upset.

"I didn't mean to fill up your whole notebook," she added, shifting nervously. "I just thought maybe I could figure out how the mana lamps on the decks work."

Sparks said nothing, his furious scrubbing making Regina feel worse by the second. She sighed quietly and removed her glasses, wiping at the tears that threatened to form. Her thoughts drifted to her dad and Mattie. She still had no idea where they were or how they were going to find them, and the sadness hit her all over again.

After a moment, Sparks finally broke the silence. "Blaze was tellin' me there's somethin' wrong with the cannon loaders," he said without looking at her. "Think ye can take a look at it fer me?"

Regina's eyes brightened immediately. "Yes! Of course!" she answered eagerly, relieved that he trusted her again. "I'll get it fixed right up. Arrr!" She exaggerated the pirate tone for a joke.

Sparks chuckled softly. "Arrr, Little Missy," he said, shaking his balding head in amusement. "I'll come check on you when I'm done with this."

Channeling Annabelle's confident swagger, Regina smirked. "I'll probably have it all sorted before ye even get there!" She hopped off the stool and gave a playful salute. "Arr, matey!" she added with a grin before heading out.

Regina made her way through the lower decks, passing the sick bay and the machine shop before descending the stairs to the cannon deck. She knocked once on the door and entered, finding the room empty. Of course, she realized, they're probably playing Crew in the powder mag. She checked the adjacent room and, sure enough, found Gimble, Blaze, Flint, and Gary gathered around a table, deeply engrossed in their card game.

"Excuse me, Mr. Blaze," Regina called, stepping into the room. The men paused, looking up from their game. "You told Mr. Sparks you were having trouble with the cannon loader system?"

"Aye, missy," Blaze replied, playing another card without much concern. "When ye turn the crank, the mag drops, but the cannonball doesn't."

"Crank?" Regina asked, not recalling any crank mechanism in the cannon room.

"Hold on, missy," Blaze said, raising a hand. He laid down his final card. "Can anyone beat six?"

The others groaned in defeat, shaking their heads.

"Thanks fer the coins boyos." Blaze said, scooping up his winnings. He stood and motioned for Regina to follow him into the cannon room. Walking to the center of the space, he pulled down a crank mechanism that was hidden in the ceiling and folded out the handle. "Ye see, missy, when I turn this crank…"

He began rotating the handle, and a steady clicking sound echoed through the room as gears engaged. The eight cannons rotated upward, pointing toward the ceiling. As he continued cranking, a white package that looked like a pillow fell neatly into the mouth of every one of the cannons.

"The cannons tilt up, and the mag drops into 'em," Blaze explained. The mechanism gave a series of loud bangs above them. "That's the cannonballs hittin' the ceiling instead of fallin' into place."

He cranked the handle until the cannons rotated back to their original positions, aimed outward toward the sea. "Think ye can fix it?"

"Hope so," Regina said with a determined smile.

"That's the spirit, girlie." Blaze said, nodding approvingly.

Regina walked around the cannons, taking in their construction. She wondered aloud, "How do you light all eight cannons? Do you have a special candle or something?"

Blaze grinned. With a snap of his fingers, a circle of small flames appeared in midair around him and Regina. "They call me Blaze for a reason." he said with a wink.

Regina's eyes widened in admiration. "What type of magic is that?" she asked, curiosity sparking in her voice.

Blaze gave Regina a brief explanation of his Pyromancy magic before bidding her farewell to return to his card game.

Regina grabbed the ladder attached to the wall and climbed into the maintenance hatch in the ceiling. Once inside the confined space, she surveyed the intricate network of conveyor belts, chains, and platforms designed to move the white gunpowder bags and cannonballs. The machinery appeared to be a complex system of synchronized mechanisms, with openings cut into the metal floor for the powder and cannonballs to drop through. When functioning correctly, these openings would align with the holes in the roof of the cannon deck below.

She spotted another maintenance hatch near the crank Blaze had demonstrated earlier. Regina unhooked the ladder from the wall and reattached it to ceiling-mounted eyelets. Climbing up, she inspected the mechanism closely and found a set of tightly drawn chains. Testing one, she pulled it down and watched as the machinery advanced slightly. As she continued to experiment, she saw the powder bags follow their intended path, dropping through the openings perfectly. However, when it came time for the cannonball to drop, a harness retained the heavy metal sphere. The machine stuttered mid-cycle, causing the holes in the machinery and ceiling to misalign. The harness then retracted the cannonball back into the ceiling instead of releasing it into the cannon.

"Hmm... that must be the problem," Regina muttered to herself, noting how the machine seemed to catch at the same point in its cycle every time.

Determined to fix it, she crawled further into the cramped space, her small stature making it easier to navigate the narrow gaps between the machinery. The ceiling area was dim, and she couldn't see clearly, so she fished the small shaker from her dress pocket, the one Annabelle had given her during their first sail aboard the ship. She gave it a firm shake, activating the light-producing elements inside the rocks. The area was bathed in a faint green glow.

With the improved visibility, Regina felt around, testing various components. Most moved smoothly, but one, a specialized gear with alternating teeth and loops, refused to budge. Running her fingers over it, she realized it was covered in rust, the rough surface confirming her suspicion. She tugged on it, but the gear remained stuck.

"Great," she complained, her brow furrowing in frustration. "I need a tool for this."

Regina searched through her purse, well, Sparks called it a toolkit, but it was definitely more of a purse. A beautiful purse, in her opinion. Digging through its contents, she found a small screwdriver that might work as a makeshift pry bar. Carefully, she inserted the screwdriver under the gear and tried to lever it loose. The tool bent under the pressure.

"Ugh," she sighed, glaring at the bent screwdriver. She hit the handle against the rusted gear a few times, recalling how Mr. Sparks always said he wasn't angry when doing this, just "beating out the rust."

She tried again, but the screwdriver bent even more, and Regina knew she couldn't risk breaking one of Sparks' tools. She tapped the gear repeatedly, hoping to loosen the rust. After a few moments of persistence, she felt the gear shift—just a little, but it was progress.

"Okay... come on," she whispered, determination flaring in her chest as she prepared for another attempt.

Regina had an idea. A hook might do the trick. She rummaged through her tool purse but found nothing resembling a hook. However, she did find a spool of wire. Inspiration struck. She cut a length of wire, looped it around two of the gear's open teeth, and twisted it to form a makeshift handle. Sitting back for leverage, she pulled with all her strength. The gear shifted slightly, but not enough, and then the wire unraveled, sending Regina tumbling onto her backside.

She sighed in frustration, knowing she was close. *I just need a stronger handle.* This time, she wrapped the wire around the gear's loops multiple times and twisted it tightly. To prevent the same issue, she tied a second wire around perpendicular teeth, creating a cross-shaped handle for extra grip. Satisfied with her work, she braced herself and pulled with everything she had, gritting her teeth. The stubborn gear resisted but finally popped off the peg with a loud clink.

Though she fell back again, the handle held firm, keeping the gear safely in her hands. Regina smiled triumphantly and gathered her tools and light shaker. Descending the ladder carefully, she carried the rusted gear to the powder mag.

At a free table near the door, Regina laid out a white cloth, her wire brush, a piece of steel wool, and the gear. She began scrubbing the central hole where the peg had been, working the wire brush in firm, circular motions. The rust clung stubbornly to the metal despite her efforts. Frustrated, Regina remembered one of Sparks' sayings about "breaking the rust."

With a shrug, she spat into the hole and attacked it again with renewed vigor. The brush scraped furiously as the "rust breaker" did its job. Slowly but surely, the corrosion gave way. Once the core was clean, she switched to steel wool to smooth out the remaining rust on the surface and in smaller areas. The metal gleamed faintly by the time she finished.

Regina climbed back into the ceiling and reinserted the gear into the assembly. She pulled on the chain to advance the mechanism, observing as the machinery went through its cycle. The white powder bags dropped neatly through each of the eight openings. Then the cannonballs, wrapped in their custom harnesses, lowered perfectly from the ceiling. This time, the gear moved smoothly, allowing the metal plates to align. The cannonballs passed through the holes without issue, landing inside the cannon barrels below.

"Yay!" Regina cheered, raising her fists in victory.

As she descended the rope ladder, Sparks entered the room.

"Oi, missy! How's it going?" he asked, wiping his hands on a rag. "What's broken this time?"

"Nothing now," Regina said proudly. "I fixed it! One of the gears was rusted down, and the cannonballs couldn't drop from the ceiling."

"Really? How'd ye fix it?" Sparks asked, curiosity gleaming in his eyes.

Regina eagerly recounted the process, how she found the rusted gear, used the chain system to troubleshoot, and ultimately got the machinery working again.

Sparks raised an eyebrow. "Did ye really get everything working without usin' any of yer magic?"

Regina blinked, realizing the truth of his words. "Huh... I guess I didn't," she said, surprised. She wondered why she hadn't even thought to use her magic during the repair process.

"Well, look at that," Sparks said with a grin. "Seems like ye've got a knack for this."

Regina beamed with pride.

"Let's give it one more test—after we clear out all the powder bags and cannonballs," Sparks suggested with a chuckle.

"Arrr tis a good notion matey!" Regina replied, ready to double-check her work.

[-----⊕-----]

Sophie walked onto the observation deck, Annabelle trailing annoyingly close behind. She quickly spotted Brother Marcus and Eclipse Lepele seated at a table near the open area of the deck, likely enjoying the sea breeze.

Without pausing, Sophie made her way to their table, Annabelle sticking to her like a shadow. When she arrived, she stood at attention and announced, "Message for you, Eclipse."

"Make sure ye get it right, Copper," Annabelle chimed in, folding her arms and giving Sophie an exaggeratedly stern look.

Lepele raised an eyebrow, his curiosity piqued. "What's the message, Torchbearer?"

With a long, frustrated sigh, Sophie began, "The operations officer passes along that the *Purple Copper* is a poor messenger and has a stupid face."

"Mm-hmm," Annabelle hummed, nodding approvingly, still playing the part of a strict supervisor.

Sophie let out another sigh, her voice tinged with irritation. "She also thinks you should beat the *Purple Copper* with a stick to make her a better messenger. And don't worry about damaging her looks…since, according to the operations officer, her *ugly mug of a face* could only be improved by any marks you might leave."

"I don't recall all those sighs, Copper," Annabelle said, smirking.

Sophie glared at her, silently promising herself she'd find a way to pay Annabelle back for this nonsense.

"Message received, Torchbearer," Lepele said, sharing a playful wink with Annabelle.

Sophie groaned under her breath. "Do you have a reply, Eclipse?"

"No, Sentinel, I do not," Lepele replied calmly.

Annabelle straightened up, adopting a more refined tone. "Eclipse Lepele, would ye care to join me in the powder mag for a few games of Crew? I suspect there's a good opportunity to win some coins today, and I'd be happy to spot ye a few coins to get ye started."

Lepele smiled warmly. "Why thank you, Ms. Salazar. I'd be delighted, but I need to have a word with this *Purple Copper* here first. Could I meet you there?"

"Of course," Annabelle replied with a playful grin, curtsying dramatically.

Lepele turned to Marcus. "Brother Marcus, would you mind escorting Miss Salazar?"

Marcus rose gracefully. "Certainly. Miss Salazar, may I?" he asked with a courteous nod.

Annabelle rolled her eyes. "I ain't payin' for no escort, Brother. But ye can walk with me all the same."

Together, the two of them left the deck, leaving Sophie and Lepele alone.

Lepele remained seated as he addressed her. "Sentinel, can you explain *bearing* to me?"

Sophie took a deep breath and recited what she'd learned from Eclipse Baker. "Sir, bearing refers to maintaining one's outward appearance, composure, and control over emotions."

Lepele nodded slowly. "And would someone constantly sighing in frustration or glaring at others be considered a good example of bearing?"

"No, sir, I wouldn't," Sophie admitted, her voice low. "My behavior was out of line. But Annabelle is just so…" She trailed off, searching for the right word to describe the chaos that seemed to follow the wild-haired privateer everywhere.

"Is Salazar a member of the clan Torchbearer?" Lepele asked, his tone sharper now.

"No, sir," Sophie answered sheepishly, realizing where he was going with this.

"Then why is her behavior any concern of mine, or yours?" Lepele asked pointedly.

Sophie had no answer. She stood there silently, knowing she had no excuse.

"Awfully quiet now, aren't we?" Lepele said, his voice edged with disapproval. "You told me you were ready to take the shadow test, yet here you stand, acting like an unruly child fresh out of first phase initiate training."

The comparison stung. Sophie bristled. "That's not fair, Eclipse!" she blurted out, before biting her tongue when he gave her a cold, piercing look.

"No, please," Lepele said, his tone icy. "Continue. Enlighten me to your grievances."

Feeling cornered, Sophie hesitated but decided to voice her frustrations. "Ever since you got here, you've been pushing me from one job to the next; jobs that have nothing to do with my training. You even made me clean the powder mag, which I'm pretty sure hasn't been cleaned in the entire history of ever!" She paused to catch her breath, then pressed on. "Then you had me clean and maintain all the weapons in the armory. And worst of all, you always take Annabelle's side when she's mocking me, calling me ugly and telling you to beat me with a stick!"

"Are you finished?" Lepele asked, his expression unreadable.

"Yes, sir," Sophie replied, bracing for the inevitable reprimand.

"First of all," Lepele said, standing and walking over to the railing, "the last person I need to explain myself to is you, *Sentinel*. Your duty is to follow orders and learn from those above you." He gazed out at the horizon, his voice softening slightly. "The reason I assigned you those tasks was to broaden your experience. When you reach the rank of Eclipse, you'll find that many Sentinels fail their shadow test because they hyperfocus on what they're already good at. They neglect the areas they need to improve and, as a result, are unprepared for the full scope of skills the exam demands."

Sophie absorbed his words, the truth of them settling heavily on her shoulders. "I see," she murmured, feeling a mix of understanding and embarrassment.

"You're enjoying a lot of freedom with your little group right now," Lepele continued. "More freedom than any other Torchbearer in the Clan. But here's a word of advice, don't expect that to last when you return to us."

Sophie nodded in acknowledgment.

"Well then," Lepele said, turning back toward her, his usual sternness softening slightly. "I'm off to play a few hands of Crew. You're dismissed—report back to the bridge." With that, he strode off, leaving Sophie standing alone on the observation deck.

[----- ⚓ -----]

Annabelle stood proudly at the helm of her ship. Captain Salazar ran a tight vessel with a hold full of valuable cargo and passengers filling every bunk. Of course, it was a far better ship than the Stormfang … though the name of this vessel escaped her. Her loyal Crew serenaded her with a shanty:

"Oh, we sail the seas so wide and free,
For the love of coin, that's our decree.
With the wind in our sails and the stars to guide,
We chase the gold, and we won't be denied.

For the coin, the adventure, and our Captain's ever so fair,

294

We'll brave the storms and the salty air.
Captain Salazar, with a heart so bold,
Leads us to treasures and legends told..."

She was jolted from her dream by a firm shake to her leg.

"Belle, wake up," a soft voice called.

Annabelle instinctively grabbed her amulet, ready for trouble, until the voice clarified, "No, Belle! it's me."

She blinked and recognized Captain Kidd standing beside her hammock. "Cap'n?" she mumbled, still groggy. Glancing at the porthole, she saw it was still dark outside. "What gives? I was having the best dream."

"Well, too bad," Kidd replied with a smirk. "Get dressed, wake up yer sisters, and meet us in the galley."

Annabelle groaned and sat up. "What did Jeffie do this time?" she muttered.

"Just hurry up," Kidd said before walking out of the room.

Annabelle cursed under her breath as she got to her feet, wondering what nonsense had dragged Kidd from his quarters in the middle of the night. *It's something trivial, like a missing fork.*

"I heard that," Kidd called from down the hall, his footsteps fading away.

Grumbling, Annabelle pulled on a pair of tolerably clean tights, a short-sleeved white shirt, and the oversized jacket she'd inherited from Kidd when he'd bought a new one. After tying her hair up with a tie, a few stray locks escaping, she added a bandana, checked herself in the mirror, and nodded. "Aye, tis good enough," she muttered before heading out.

First on her list was waking Lisa. She knocked on the door to the star room and found it slightly ajar. *Princess really doesn't value her things*, Annabelle thought as she stepped inside. Lisa lay peacefully on her cot, her green hair spread out like seaweed on the shore.

"Lisa, girl, wake up," Annabelle whispered, giving the cot a gentle shake. "We gotta meet the Cap'n for something."

Lisa stirred, blinking sleepily. When she saw Annabelle standing over her, she frowned. "Anna, what...?" Her expression darkened as she noticed Annabelle's gaze drifting. "Hey!" Lisa grabbed a pillow and smacked her.

"Oi, the Cap'n sent me," Annabelle said, raising her arms defensively. "Told me to wake ye up and get everyone to the galley."

Lisa narrowed her eyes. "Why? What did you do?"

"I didn't do a thing, Princess! I was sleepin' just like you." Annabelle backed toward the door. "Just get dressed and meet us there." She slipped out before Lisa could throw another pillow, hearing the soft thud against the door behind her.

Deciding Sophie would be easier to rouse than Regina, Annabelle headed to the Fang room. She knocked firmly. "Oi, Copper! Get up!" She tested the door but found it locked.

After a second knock, Sophie yanked the door open, scowling. "What? What do you want?!"

"The Cap'n says we're to get dressed and meet in the galley," Annabelle informed her.

Sophie groaned. "What did you do this time?"

295

"Oi, why does everyone think I did somethin'? I was havin' the best dream till he woke me up."

"Fine," Sophie muttered, closing the door in Annabelle's face.

Two down, one to go. Annabelle sighed and headed to the sunroom, where Regina slept. She knocked and called out, "Regina, time to wake up." Testing the door, she found it unlocked. *Doesn't value her things either*, Annabelle thought with a shake of her head.

Inside, Regina lay sprawled in her hammock, limbs dangling in all directions like a storm-tossed rag doll. Annabelle knew from experience that Regina slept like the dead, so she didn't waste time being gentle. She grabbed Regina's hand and gave it a firm shake. "Regina, girlie, wake up!"

Regina's eyes snapped open, and without warning, she cast her favorite sleeping spell: Envoûtement des Cercles Éternels. Four glowing circles manifested around Annabelle, trapping her and lifting her off the ground.

"By the sea," Annabelle groaned. "Girlie, it's time to get up!"

Regina remained out cold, her grip on consciousness as loose as her hold on reality in dreams.

Annabelle wriggled in the magical restraints, recalling how that blue-haired girl, Isabella, had once broken free of this same spell using her own mana. "*If she could do it, I can too!*" Annabelle muttered. She closed her eyes and focused inward.

In her mind's eye, she summoned the storm within her. The sea churned violently, waves rising and crashing in a chaotic dance. Winds howled, and lightning crackled across the darkened waters. She let the storm rage, gaining strength with each passing moment.

A faint voice echoed within her, guiding her thoughts.

"*Not yet, Bella... Let the storm rage and consume the ocean. Let it gain the power it needs to fully serve ye.*"

Annabelle held onto the image of the storm, letting the voice's words wash over her as she prepared to break free.

Annabelle commanded the storm within her to expand, ordering the sea of her internal world to surrender entirely to its fury. The winds intensified, forming a colossal tornado infused with storm clouds, water, and crackling lightning. Power surged within her core, raw and untamed, not like her usual spells where she gently coaxed the sea into obedience. This was pure Annabelle, a force rising to shatter the glowing rings that dared entrap her.

A bubble of orange seawater erupted from her body, crashing against the magical restraints. The surging water assaulted the structure of the glowing circles, causing cracks to spiderweb across their surface. They flickered, dimmed, and finally shattered in an explosion of seawater, dispelling the spell entirely.

Regina was splashed awake, sputtering as she wiped her face. "What...what's happening?!"

Annabelle dropped to the floor, momentarily drained from channeling so much of her power at once. She gasped for breath, then muttered, "Thanks, Mat..." She stopped mid-sentence and turned around, expecting to see someone behind her. The room was empty. Frowning, she whispered, "Where did that voice come from?"

Regina blinked groggily, her silver hair a tangled mess. "What voice?" she asked, sitting up in her hammock.

Annabelle shook her head, dismissing the thought. "Never mind. Ye gotta get dressed, missy. The Cap'n wants to see us in the galley."

"Arr, girlie! I'll be seein' ye there!" Regina replied in an exaggerated pirate accent.

Annabelle paused, narrowing her eyes. She wasn't sure if Regina was teasing her or just playing around. With a shrug, she said, "Just hurry up and get ready, it's gotta be important." She stepped out into the hallway, deciding to give Regina some privacy to dress.

A few moments later, Lisa emerged from her room, wearing a breezy white sundress. She barely acknowledged Annabelle as she headed for the stairs. Not long after, Sophie pushed past Annabelle.

"Excuse me, *Anna*." Sophie taunted, throwing a smug glance over her shoulder.

"Oi, watch where yer goin', Copper," Annabelle shot back. "This here's me favorite coat."

Sophie scoffed but didn't reply, disappearing down the stairs. Shortly after, Regina stepped out, now wearing a pair of coveralls with the sleeves and legs rolled up to fit her short frame.

"Coveralls?" Annabelle asked, raising an eyebrow. "No dress?"

"Eh, coveralls are easy. I'm going back to sleep after this is over anyway," Regina explained casually.

Annabelle shrugged. "Good plan, let's go." Together, they headed for the galley.

[----- ⚓ -----]

Annabelle and Regina were the last to arrive in the galley's seating area. The rest of the Crew, including the avatars, Brother Marcus, and Eclipse Lepele, were already seated at various tables. Captain Kidd stood near the serving counter, his presence commanding attention despite the lively chatter.

Annabelle quickly found a seat with Blaze, Flint, and Gimble, while Regina joined Mr. Sparks, Mr. Gray, and Jeffie. Once they were settled, Kidd clapped his hands loudly, silencing the conversations with a sharp echo that filled the room.

"We've gots us a problem, gents," Captain Kidd began, his tone grave yet steady. "Our night runner, Mr. Popper, spotted a ship bearing down on us. We're far from any regular shipping routes, so it's safe to assume we're being followed by a skull ship."

The statement drew murmurs from the Crew. Brother Marcus raised a hand. "I don't understand. What's the issue exactly?" he asked. "Pirate ships aren't exactly new to us."

Kidd nodded as if expecting the question. "Aye, excellent point. Here's the thing, out here, especially at night, ships keep their distance. But this one's bearing down on us fast enough to overtake us before dawn. That's a classic skull tactic."

Lepele raised his hand, waiting to be acknowledged.

"Yes?" Kidd gestured for him to speak.

"What's our plan?" Lepele asked.

"We're gonna try to lose them in the fog ahead," Kidd replied. "Can't loot what ye can't find."

Lepele's eyes widened, and he quickly shook his head. "No! It's a trap, Captain!"

"A trap?" Kidd asked, frowning. "Explain."

Lepele leaned forward, his voice urgent. "It's the same thing that happened to the Sequin Dancer. We spotted a ship following us and tried to lose them in a fog bank.

But hidden within the fog was a snare, something that stopped the ship dead in its tracks. Once we were immobilized, waves of marauders boarded us. We couldn't fight them off; they overwhelmed us with sheer numbers."

The room fell into a tense silence as Kidd processed the warning. He pointed to Gimble, who stood immediately and made his way toward the stairs, heading for the bridge.

"Any suggestions while we wait for a report?" Kidd asked, stalling for time.

"We avoid the fog," Lepele suggested, his composure unfaltering. "But we don't let them realize we've caught on. We need to steer clear without giving ourselves away."

"Aww, Copper's scared of a fight!" Phelps taunted from across the room, drawing laughter from some of the Crew.

Lepele didn't react, maintaining an air of calm and discipline. His restraint only amplified his authority, though the room continued to chuckle at Phelps' joke. Kidd remained silent, letting the humor run its course as he waited for Gimble's return.

Ten minutes later, Gimble reappeared and whispered something into the captain's ear. Kidd's eyes widened slightly.

"Oh," he muttered, straightening up. He turned to Lepele and grinned. "Mr. Lepele, ye might just be our good luck charm."

The Crew quieted as Kidd raised his voice. "Listen up! There are ships hidden in the fog bank. If we hadn't known to look, we would've sailed right into their trap."

The tension in the room deepened, a hush falling as the Crew came to grips with the looming danger.

"This is what we're gonna do," Kidd continued, his commanding presence filling the space. "First, we prepare for a fight. Grab yer arms and make sure they're ready. Green missy," he pointed to Lisa, "ye and Jeffie cook up some good food, we'll fight better on a full stomach." His gaze shifted to Lepele. "Can we count on you coppers to defend the ship?"

"Absolutely!" Lepele answered firmly. Sophie nodded in agreement.

"Good," Kidd said. "Find the best places for yerselves to fight and feel free to take what ye need from the armory."

Blaze spoke up from his table. "We ain't sailin' into that fog, are we, Cap'n?"

Kidd chuckled. "Mate, I'm crazy, not stupid. I've got a bad idea, but it just might work. We're gonna run the engines up to half-max speed and make it look like we're headin' straight for the fog. At the last minute, we'll turn away, skimming the fog's edge, then crank the engines all the way up and speed off. We make ourselves too slippery a target, those skulls might leave us alone."

Annabelle caught the word *might*. Kidd wasn't as confident in the plan as he wanted them to believe.

"Cap'n, what if we don't got enough fuel to run the engines like that," Blaze warned. "We'll run out if we push 'em too hard for too long."

Kidd nodded. "Mate, ye forget, we've got that battery system Mr. Sparks set up in the workout room. We'll recharge it as we go."

Sparks nodded silently from his seat.

"Once we turn, we go to battle stations," Kidd continued. "The ship'll raise her defenses if those skulls come too close. For now, arm yerselves, eat well, and start makin' power in the workout room."

He raised his fist high. "FER THE FANG!"

"FER THE COIN!" the Crew roared in response, Annabelle among them, grinning as she shouted the refrain.

Kidd smirked, shaking his head. "Scallywags, every one of ye," he said with affection.

The Crew scattered, each member moving with purpose. The battle preparations had begun.

Chapter 20

The Stormfang buzzed with activity below decks, away from the prying eyes of the ship pursuing them. Eclipse Lepele led Sophie to the machine shop on the crew deck, where the two of them got to work crafting bullets for her rifle. As they worked, Sophie asked about his choice of weapon for the upcoming fight.

"I'm more effective with melee weapons in close combat," Lepele explained, inspecting a newly forged bullet. He then gave her a crucial task. "You'll man the crow's nest before the turn. Use your rifle to keep their sharpshooters off us. I'll fight on the main deck."

Meanwhile, Regina and Mr. Sparks headed to the workout room with Blaze, Phelps, Ethan, and Flint. Each crew member took a machine, working to keep the engine batteries charged as the ship pushed forward. After some time, they rotated stations to target different muscle groups, keeping themselves fresh for the long haul.

[-----✪-----]

In the galley, Lisa and Jeffie moved like clockwork, efficiently preparing sandwiches and chowder. They hardly spoke; each was focused on their tasks. One would stir the chowder while the other chopped vegetables or retrieved ingredients from the cold room. When the food was ready, Brother Marcus and Annabelle began delivering meals to crew members at their posts. Those in the workout room would have to grab their food when they could.

[----------]

The entire ship vibrated with energy as the engines roared to life, accelerating to half of max speed. Popper soon confirmed what everyone suspected: the pursuing ship had also increased speed, staying on their tail. Pirates or "Skulls" were hunting the Stormfang.

[-----⊞-----]

Halfway to the fog bank, Sophie finished loading bullets into every rifle and pistol cartridge they had. She filled her own ammo pouches to capacity, tucking spare rounds into the loops on her gun belt and jacket. The rest she brought to the armory, organizing them neatly in drawers labeled for each type of ammunition.

Annabelle arrived shortly after. She tested several bullets to find the right caliber for the pistol she'd *earned* from the crooked sheriff in Verdantia. Once she saw the fit, she grabbed a handful of rounds and dropped them into her jacket pocket. Sophie frowned at the sight.

"Are you really just going to keep bullets loose in your pocket like that?" Sophie asked.

"Aye," Annabelle replied casually.

"That's not secure," Sophie said flatly.

With an exaggerated sigh, Annabelle fastened the buttons on her pocket flap. "There, secure enough for ye? Thanks for the input, *Copper*." She gave Sophie a cheeky grin before walking off.

Lepele inspected the armory's inventory and selected a cutlass and a short sword for the battle. He also grabbed a pair of flintlock pistols. Though reliable, they were frustratingly single-shot weapons, a limitation he would have to work around.

[-----✿-----]

Regina and Sparks, slightly winded from the workout room, headed to the hold to inspect the engine fuel tanks. They verified that both tanks were full and that an extra drum of fuel stood ready beside each engine. The battery display glowed green, not fully charged, but sufficient for their plan.

[-----◐-----]

Back in the galley, Lisa and Jeffie cleaned up the kitchen, washing pots and utensils. Lisa's hopeful nature shone through as she spoke quietly. "Maybe this will all be for nothing," she said. "Maybe we will just sail around the fog, and the pirates will give up."

Jeffie wasn't so optimistic. "We can hope," he replied, though his tone betrayed his doubts.

[-----⊞-----]

As the Stormfang neared the edge of the fog bank, Gimble, the ship's Runner, found Sophie in the machine shop. "It's time," he said. "Ye need to get set up in the crow's nest."

Sophie nodded, grabbed her rifle, and made her way topside. The cold night air nipped at her skin as she climbed the rigging to the crow's nest. Once inside, she strapped herself securely into a bucket seat, tying a rope around her waist. The drop below was deadly, she didn't need to remind herself that falling from this height would end one of two ways: *splattering on the deck or drowning in the vast, dark sea.*

With her rifle across her lap, Sophie scanned the horizon. The fog loomed ahead like a ghostly predator, its shifting mass full of hidden dangers. From behind the ship, the lights of the pirate ship drew closer. She took a deep breath to steady her nerves. *Soon, the gambit would begin.*

Captain Kidd took the helm as they approached the edge of the fog bank, freeing Smitty to ensure the crew was ready for the maneuver. Below decks, the organized chaos continued.

[-----◉-----]

Lisa and Jeffie secured the kitchen, locking away dishes and supplies before heading to the armory to assist Mr. Gary. Jeffie carried a pot under his arm.

"What is that for?" Lisa asked.

"Fer me head," Jeffie explained with a grin. "Gotta keep the brain safe."

[-----╬-----]

Meanwhile, Brother Marcus worked in the powder mag, meticulously sewing cloth bags of gunpowder. He handed them off to the ceiling loader system, ensuring the cannon loaders would have plenty of ammunition ready.

[-----✿-----]

In the engine hold, Sparks shook Regina awake. "We're making the turn soon," he said before taking a swig from his flask, something Regina had never seen him do before. As Regina rubbed the sleep from her eyes, she asked, "How long can the batteries hold at full throttle?"

"Not long," Sparks admitted, watching the fuel gauges with a concerned eye. "These engines run best at three-quarters. Full power burns through fuel too quick, it's just not efficient."

[----------]

The entire crew was at their battle stations fifteen minutes before the turn, a testament to the leadership of Captain Kidd and Smitty. The Runner reported that the pursuing ship was closing fast, no longer hiding its intentions. The Stormfang was being hunted.

As the bow of the ship grazed the fog's edge, Kidd made his move. He cut the engines and swung the helm hard to port, spinning the Stormfang in a near-complete turn. The ship groaned under the strain, but as it straightened out, Kidd shoved the throttle to full power. The engines roared, and the ship surged forward with incredible force.

Wind lashed at the deck crew as they scrambled to pull up the sails, making sure nothing worked against the ship's momentum. Every bit of speed counted now.

Behind them, the pursuing pirate ship faltered. It hadn't anticipated the sudden maneuver and struggled to keep up. The larger vessel had to swing wide to make the same turn, losing precious time. The Stormfang, being smaller and more agile, now had the advantage.

[-----✿-----]

In the hold, Regina watched the battery gauge drain like water through a sieve. Her eyes darted to the fuel tank gauge, and her heart sank, it was dropping just as quickly. "Sparks!" she called across the hold.

"Crank the fuel in!" he yelled.

Regina grabbed the crank on her side and turned it with all her strength. Fuel rushed from the reserve drum into the tank, slowing the gauge's descent. Across the hold, she could hear the clicking of Sparks' crank as he did the same.

[-----⊕-----]

The ship's engines roared at maximum output long enough to put serious distance between them and the pirates. The enemy ship dwindled in size on the horizon, barely a speck in the distance.

"Ease it back to half, Cap'n?" Smitty suggested.

"Aye," Kidd agreed, throttling down to half power. With more control over the helm, he kept the Stormfang skimming the fog's perimeter, careful to avoid any potential traps. The worst seemed to be behind them...for now.

Kidd yelled up to the crow's nest. "Griffin! What do ye see back there?"

Sophie scanned the waters with her rifle scope. The fog churned ominously, and for a moment, she saw nothing. Then, like a nightmare rising from the mist, the pirate ship's black flag emerged, snapping in the wind.

"They're still on us, Captain," Sophie yelled back grimly. "and they're closing fast."

The curses of the crew echoed across the ship. Kidd barked new orders. "Gimble! Get down to the hold and check the fuel!"

[-----✿-----]

The Runner took off at a sprint, disappearing below deck. Sparks and Regina were waiting when he arrived. Sparks knocked on the side of the empty barrel with a hollow clang.

"Dry as a bone," he confirmed.

Regina tapped her own barrel for good measure. "Same here. Dry."

"How much fuel is left in the tanks?" Gimble asked.

"Three-quarters," Sparks answered.

Gimble nodded and ran as fast as he could back to the bridge to deliver the report.

[-----⊕-----]

Captain Kidd listened quietly before admitting, "There's no runnin' from 'em now." He issued swift orders. "Prepare for battle! pulling the throttle to one-quarter."

"Captain! I see ships ahead!" she yelled.

Kidd's hopes rose for a moment. "Can ye see their flags?"

Sophie hesitated, then her voice came back, somber and low. "Black flags. Two of them."

A collective weight seemed to drop on the entire crew. Any chance of outside help had vanished. The Stormfang was now outnumbered, outgunned, and cornered.

303

The deck crew moved like clockwork. Kidd backed down the engines to one fourth, and the tension mounted, wrapping around everyone.

"Convert the ship," Kidd ordered, his voice steady. "Gimble, get to it."

The Runner sprinted for the stairs as Kidd pulled the throttle back to zero. The engines fell silent. There was no point wasting fuel.

The deck crew armed themselves and braced for what was coming. The Stormfang floated quietly at the edge of the fog, surrounded by predators. Now there was no choice but to fight.

"Listen to me," Captain Kidd commanded, his voice cutting through the tension like a blade. The entire crew turned to him, the air heavy with unspoken fear. "That feeling crawling up yer spine? That's fear. The lump in yer throat tryin' to steal yer voice? She's fear too." He paused, letting the words sink in. Then, his tone shifted as he fell into his natural patois, deep and rhythmic like the sea itself.

"But fear ain't yer enemy! Dem damn Skulls, they be yer enemies! And it ain't right for dem to put fear in us," he growled, eyes flashing. "Cause who are we?" He pounded his fist on the helm for emphasis. "We de Fang!"

Smitty stomped his boot, his single, decisive step reverberating like a drumbeat. The crew followed, stomping their feet or slamming their fists against the ship's railings and bulkheads. The rhythm grew louder, shaking the deck like a battle cry rising from the belly of the boat.

"We're the ones who robbed Stoneridge clean!" Kidd roared, his voice carrying across the deck. "We're the ones who ran off coppers, crooked navies, and sea monsters alike!" He grinned fiercely, the gleam in his eyes igniting the crew's spirit.

The rhythm intensified, fists pounding and boots stomping. The Stormfang itself seemed to come alive, groaning under the pressure as though it shared the crew's fire.

"We'll leave 'em with nothin'!" Kidd bellowed. "Not even the shirts on their backs!"

With a resounding metallic clang, the ship began its transformation. Heavy plates of reinforced metal rose along the sides, encasing the Stormfang's hull in a protective shell. The crew cheered wildly as the bulkheads locked into place, the ship lowering deeper into the water, braced for battle.

"'CAUSE WHEN YE MESS WITH THE FANG," Kidd roared, drawing his cutlass high above his head, "YE GET BIT!"

The crew erupted in a frenzy of bloodthirsty enthusiasm, shouting their approval. The rhythmic pounding continued like a war drum.

"COME ONE, COME ALL!" Kidd declared, his voice booming over the sea. "WE GOTS DEEP POCKETS TO FILL!"

"FOR THE FANG!" the crew roared in response, their voices merging as one.

The Stormfang charged forward, armoured and defiant. The battle was coming— and the Stormfang would meet it with teeth bared.

[----------]

"GET READY!" Captain Kidd bellowed from the helm.

The tension was thick as the enemy ships drew nearer, their silhouettes sharp against the rising sun. Suddenly, a booming voice echoed across the waves, magically amplified.

"Good ship Stormfang," the voice called. "We've got ye dead to rights. Do the sensible thing, lay down yer arms and surrender!"

Kidd scowled, eyes narrowing as he scanned the approaching vessels. Without a word, he strode into his operations room and returned moments later, holding a rolled-up map. He stepped to the edge of the bridge, raised the makeshift megaphone to his mouth, and shouted back, his voice dripping with defiance.

"AND WHO ARE YE, MATE?"

There was a pause. Then the voice answered with an air of smug authority. "We are The Accursed Raider, terror of the seas!"

Kidd grinned wolfishly. "AND WHO ARE THEY?" he hollered, gesturing over his shoulder toward the two ships closing in from the front.

Another pause followed, as if the man on the Raider couldn't quite believe the question. Finally, he answered. "The Crazy Horse and The Hornet."

"THANKS, MATE," Kidd called back, scribbling the names onto the back of his map.

The amplified voice hesitated before asking, "Stormfang, why'd ye want our names?"

Kidd gave a wicked chuckle. He took his time before rolling the map back up and replying. "'CAUSE WHEN WE SINK YE," he roared, "I WANNA KNOW WHAT NAME TO WRITE ON ME WALL!"

A tense silence followed. Then, with a burst of crimson light, the Raider's deck erupted as a red flare shot skyward, signalling the attack.

"OPEN FIRE!"

Chapter 21

Gunfire exploded from the decks of all three pirate ships. Rifles cracked, and a barrage of bullets peppered the Stormfang's hull. The crew scrambled into cover, taking shelter behind the ship's reinforced walls. Muzzle flashes lit the air like bursts of lightning.

"Return fire!" Smitty ordered, his voice booming over the chaos.

The crew of the Stormfang answered with volleys of their own. Rifles barked as sailors leaned out from cover, sending rounds whizzing toward their attackers.

Smitty glanced at Annabelle and gave her a nod. The two of them took action, each summoning their magic. Smitty, ever the secretive type, unleashed a spell Annabelle hadn't seen before. The ocean roared in response as a massive wave surged forward, crashing into the Crazy Horse and pushing it off course.

Annabelle grinned and raised her arms, channeling her own power. "Let's see ye handle this," she muttered. A series of towering waterspouts erupted beneath The Hornet, tossing the ship violently to the side. Its riflemen, caught off balance, fired wildly into the sky, their shots sailing harmlessly over the Stormfang.

[----- ✠ -----]

Meanwhile, Sophie took aim from the crow's nest, her rifle steady despite the swaying of the mast. She fired a series of shots at the Raider's deck, alternating between regular, fire, lightning, and shockwave rounds. The chaos on the Raider was immediate.

The fire bullets flared brightly but fizzled out too quickly to do lasting damage. The shockwave bullets, however, proved devastating. Each impact sent crew members flying from the deck, crashing into railings or plummeting into the churning waters below.

"Gotcha," Sophie whispered, watching the disorder unfold through her rifle's scope. But after eight shots, her rifle clicked empty.

Sophie ducked down, quickly pulling open the stock of her rifle. She reached into her ammo pouch and began reloading, alternating regular and shockwave rounds for maximum disruption. The din of battle roared around her; gunfire, shouting, and the crash of waves blending into a cacophony of war.

With the last bullet loaded, she snapped the stock shut, cocked the charging handle, and chambered a fresh round. Sophie pushed herself back onto her knees and took aim once more.

The Accursed Raider loomed in her sights. Calm and focused, Sophie exhaled slowly and squeezed the trigger. The fight was far from over.

[----- ⚓ -----]

The crew on the deck of the Stormfang huddled behind cover, rifles in hand, firing at the Crazy Horse and the Hornet. Annabelle crouched low, reloading her weapon, when she noticed Smitty a few feet away. His lips moved as he sang a sea shanty under his breath. At first, she couldn't make out the words, but strangely, she felt their presence like a reassuring warmth. It was as though he was right beside her, calming the fear and reminding her to keep pushing forward.

A sudden boom shook the air, followed by a resounding, resonant gong. The Hornet's forward cannon had fired a round directly at the Stormfang. It slammed into the ship's armored shell, ricocheted off, and plunged harmlessly into the ocean. The impact left the deck vibrating beneath their feet.

"Griffin!" Captain Kidd's voice roared from the bridge. "Can ye do somethin' about that cannon?"

[----- ⊕ -----]

Sophie glanced toward the Hornet and saw the offending cannon protruding from its compartment. With a nod, she gave the captain a thumbs-up. *Time to shut that thing down.*

She shifted her aim, steadying her rifle as she tracked the cannon port. Her first shot, a regular round, missed the opening, striking the exterior hull of the Hornet. Sophie gritted her teeth, worked the lever smoothly, and adjusted her stance. Taking a deep breath, she calmed herself, focusing through the scope.

As she pulled the trigger, she felt the familiar pulse of the shockwave rune, drawing mana as it charged. She exhaled slowly, sighted in the small window above the cannon, and fired. The shockwave bullet streaked from the barrel in a burst of white-blue light, flying straight into the cannon's barrel.

The results were immediate. A powerful concussive blast erupted from the cannon port, throwing the heavy weapon out of position and sending chaos into the Hornet's cannon room. Taking advantage of the confusion, Sophie kept firing, alternating between shockwave and regular bullets. Each shot pounded the interior of the room with explosive force.

When her rifle clicked empty, she ducked back down into the crow's nest and reloaded swiftly from her stock. As she worked, an idea struck her, one inspired by her own work maintaining the Stormfang's powder mag and cannon room. Cannon rooms were rarely cleaned thoroughly. If the Hornet was anything like the Stormfang's had been, it might be full of old, volatile gunpowder. Sophie clenched her jaw with determination.

Pulling eight fire bullets from her pouch, she loaded them into the rifle's stock. This time, when she rose to take aim, she wasn't looking to disable the cannon. She was looking to ignite a firestorm.

The cannon port was still open. No one had repositioned the weapon yet. Sophie blocked out the surrounding battle noise, the crack of rifles, the shouts of sailors, and focused solely on the target. It was just like her practice sessions with Eclipse Logan on the firing range. Breathe in, exhale, steady...

The first fire bullet left her rifle, glowing with an orange flare. It soared through the port and struck something within the cannon room, sparking an instant flash of fire. Sophie didn't wait for confirmation. She squeezed the trigger again and again, firing all eight rounds.

From her vantage point, Sophie watched the flames inside the cannon room grow rapidly, feeding on something highly flammable, probably all that caked in gunpowder. The fire spread with alarming speed. Moments later, a massive explosion tore through the Hornet, sending debris flying from the portholes. Secondary explosions followed in quick succession, flames roaring out of every opening.

"FIRE ON THE SHIP!" came panicked cries from the Hornet's crew. The damaged vessel veered off course, smoke and flame billowing from its decks. In desperation, it turned and steered into the fog bank, its fate unknown.

Sophie let out a breath she hadn't realized she was holding. Now she truly understood why Eclipse Lepele had insisted they keep the Stormfang's powder mag and cannon rooms spotless. One careless mistake could turn a ship into a floating tinderbox.

"Griffin! Good work!" Kidd shouted from behind the helm, ducking as he loaded bullets into his rifle. "Can ye do it again, please?"

"I'll try, Captain!" Sophie called back, leaning over the edge of the crow's nest. She quickly reloaded her rifle with a mixture of lightning and shockwave bullets, preparing for another volley.

"Focus yer fire on the Crazy Horse!" Kidd ordered the crew. "One down, two ta go, boyos!"

The two remaining pirate ships pressed their attack. The Crazy Horse loomed to the Stormfang's port side, while the Accursed Raider advanced from the rear. Gunfire intensified as the skull ships drew closer, their crews now within effective rifle range. But it wasn't just bullets coming at them now, mages aboard the enemy ships unleashed spells. Small bolts of lightning crackled across the deck of the Stormfang, followed by a shower of sharp crystal shards the size of bullets.

The shards tore into the wooden deck, splintering planks, but most of the crew remained unscathed, taking cover behind the ship's reinforced walls. Phelps, who was huddled behind the mast, activated a stone armor spell. His body shimmered briefly before being encased in a rocky protective shell that deflected the crystal barrage with ease.

Annabelle noticed immediately when Smitty's shanty came to an abrupt halt. The atmosphere shifted; the comforting warmth she hadn't realized she was relying on vanished, replaced by an eerie chill. *Was that shanty some kind of magic spell?* She narrowed her eyes. *Was Smitty holding out on me all this time?* Oh aye, she was definitely going to question him later.

But for now, Smitty had bigger concerns. With a commanding gesture, he summoned a massive shield of water around the Stormfang. The watery barrier expanded to cover the entire deck, even encasing the crow's nest where Sophie was stationed. Magic spells from the Crazy Horse and Raider splashed harmlessly against the shield, their energy dissipating in ripples of water.

"I can't keep the Nautilus Shell runnin' fer long!" Smitty warned. His voice echoed with strain as he channeled his mana into the protective spell. "Mount yer counterattacks!"

Annabelle's eyes widened in realization. The Nautilus Shell spell reminded her of the sea bubble spell she had learned, though on a much larger and more complex scale. She clenched her fists, tempted to try it herself, but before she could even start, Smitty's voice rang out across the deck.

"No, Belle!" he barked, his gaze never leaving the spell's center. "Ye ain't ready for dis one!"

Annabelle gritted her teeth but didn't argue. Instead, she prepared to support the crew with her own spells.

As the Raider pulled alongside the Stormfang, Captain Kidd shouted from the bridge, "Runner! Tell the cannon room to open fire!"

"Aye, Cap'n!" Gimble answered, activating a spell circle. His body shimmered and transformed into a half-man, half-jungle cat form. He sprinted toward the stairs with incredible speed, disappearing below deck.

"Anyone got any good magic, like fireballs or lightning bolts or somethin' flashy?" Kidd asked while reloading his rifle.

Annabelle leaned out from her cover with a grin. "I can shout some really powerful curse words!" she quipped, earning a round of laughter from the crew.

"Aye, every little bit helps, Belle!" Kidd chuckled as he cocked his rifle and took aim.

A few moments later, the Stormfang's portside cannons roared to life. Heavy cannonballs pummeled the Crazy Horse, blasting through its hull and sending splinters flying into the air. Smitty dropped his Nautilus Shell spell, and the crew immediately resumed their rifle fire. Shots rang out in rapid succession as both sides exchanged relentless volleys.

The Stormfang was holding its ground, but the battle was far from over.

[----- ✿ -----]

Meanwhile, Regina and Mr. Sparks hurried down the stairwell toward the utility deck after securing the ship's "metal skin," as Sparks called it, around the bulkheads. The Stormfang jolted hard to starboard as the portside cannons fired a deafening volley.

"We gotta hurry," Sparks urged, quickening his pace. "They must be real close now."

"Okay," Regina replied nervously, doing her best to keep up. Her footsteps echoed faintly against the wooden stairwell as the tension of the battle pressed down on her.

When they reached the landing for the utility deck, the door suddenly swung open. A figure stepped through; a half-man, half-leopard creature with spotted fur and sharp yellow eyes.

Regina froze, her heart hammering. "*A cat-man?!?*" she gasped before letting out a panicked scream and running back up the stairs. She didn't stop until she reached the next landing, her breath ragged and hands shaking.

Glancing down, she saw Sparks still standing calmly near the leopard creature. He hadn't moved.

"What is wrong with you, Regina?" Sparks asked, baffled.

"What's wrong with *me*? What's wrong with *you*?!?" Regina countered, staring wide-eyed at the strange being. "You're just standing there with that cat-man! He's probably from one of those pirate ships! He's here to get us all, why are you just standing there?!"

Sparks raised an eyebrow as if she were speaking in riddles. He glanced between her and the feline figure. Then, with an exasperated sigh, he said, "This is Gimble, Regina."

The leopard-man made a sound somewhere between a deep purr and a growl, as he waved. Regina couldn't understand the words, but then she noticed the clothes the creature wore; *Gimble's usual outfit.*

"Oh... you use beast transformation magic," she realized. Gimble nodded, his feline face softening with amusement.

"Hi, Mr. Gimble," Regina said sheepishly, descending the stairs again.

The ship shook violently with another cannon volley. Gimble sniffed the air and growled out more unintelligible words, his feline instincts apparently on high alert.

"Ye know ye never did learn how to talk when yer like this," Sparks said, shaking his head.

Gimble let out a low, frustrated snarl and jabbed a clawed finger at both Sparks and Regina, then pointed toward the door leading into the utility deck corridor. The fierce growling that followed made his message crystal clear: *Get to safety. Now!*

"Okay, we got it," Sparks responded. He turned to Regina and grabbed her hand. "Come on, missy. Let's move!"

Reluctantly, Regina followed Sparks. But as they approached the hallway leading deeper into the utility deck, she felt something. A cold, hollow sensation crawled over her skin. It reminded her of the strange presence she sometimes sensed around the other avatars, Annabelle, Sophie, and Lisa, but where that feeling was warm and familiar, this was the opposite. It was dark, and hollow ... unnatural.

She halted suddenly, pulling her hand free from Sparks. Her gaze drifted toward the door leading to the observation deck across from them.

"Regina, what are you doing?" Sparks asked, frowning.

"I feel... something," Regina muttered, her voice distant. She took a hesitant step toward the source of the ominous presence.

Gimble noticed immediately. He growled and extended his clawed hand in front of her, his leopard eyes narrowing with a protective glare. The warning was unmistakable.

"Come on, Regina," Sparks urged urgently. "There's somethin' bad out there." He grabbed the collar of her coveralls and tugged her firmly behind the door.

"No, wait..." Regina protested, but Sparks didn't stop. He pulled her into the corridor, guiding her toward the armory where they'd be safer from any attackers. Regina relented, following quickly as her heartbeat pounded in her ears.

They hurried past the machine shop entrance when a loud crash echoed behind them. The stairway door burst open with a deafening smash. Gimble roared, grappling with a creature that resembled a metallic wildcat. The glowing blue beast snapped its jaws around Gimble's arm, its body surging with mana energy. Sparks froze, eyes widening in shock.

Regina stared, recognition dawning. *The blue mana energy... the metal animal construct... it was just like...Isabella is here!* The feeling from earlier, it was her.

310

She'd survived the encounter behind West's Tavern. Brother Albert hadn't killed her after all.

"Isabella," Regina whispered, her breath catching in her throat.

Two more mana-infused metal monsters burst through the doorway, glowing with the same eerie blue energy that surrounded the wildcat. One resembled a human-sized dinosaur like the ones Regina had seen in Laminae's museums, sharp-toothed, hunched, and almost reptilian. The other was a grotesque hybrid of man and crocodile, its long, gaping maw snapping as razor-sharp claws dug into Gimble's spotted arm, drawing fresh blood.

"I have to help him!" Regina declared, her resolve hardening. She silently confirmed with Galahad that he was ready. The guardian spirit answered with a strong, dutiful **yes**.

As she ran toward Gimble, Regina pulled her wand from her coveralls. She concentrated, arranging her mana for Crystalmancy. With a swift touch of her wand, silver crystal surged over the dinosaur monster's head, encasing it entirely. Gimble seized the opportunity to wrench his arm free. Roaring in pain and fury, he smashed his fist against the wildcat monster's head, but the creature didn't register it at all.

Regina quickly shifted her mana to Maelstrom Mastery. A torrent of water erupted from her wand, blasting the wildcat with such force that it was hurled into the crocodile hybrid. The impact knocked both creatures into a momentary heap, halting their assault on Gimble.

Taking advantage of the opening, Gimble delivered a powerful kick to the wildcat's side, sending both monsters crashing through the doorway of the portside crew sleeping quarters. Gimble turned and growled something unintelligible to Regina, pointing urgently at the bunkroom door.

Got it—I think, Regina thought as she ran toward the door. She shifted her mana back to Crystalmancy and quickly sealed the entrance with a thick barrier of silver crystal, locking the creatures inside.

Gimble stumbled back, his shoulders and arm now soaked with blood matting his spotted fur. Sparks hurried to his side, offering support.

"Here ye go, me man," Sparks said softly, wrapping Gimble's uninjured arm around his shoulder.

Regina's skin prickled with cold dread. The ominous presence she had sensed earlier grew stronger. Slowly, she turned to look through the door they had entered moments before.

Isabella Morales.

The corrupted avatar emerged from the observation deck door with calm, deliberate steps. Her long blue hair was braided neatly into a ponytail, except for a single bang that fell across her face. Her left eye glowed faintly, casting an eerie light over her emotionless expression.

"The Stormfang must be destroyed," Isabella announced, her voice cold and devoid of emotion. Blue mana particles emanated from her metallic left hand, shimmering like ghostly fireflies as if they were controlling the mechanical monsters that followed her.

Regina's heart pounded in her chest. She had seen Isabella before, but something about her presence now was even more terrifying. The glowing hand, the calculated steps... This woman was far beyond any ordinary enemy.

311

Without thinking, Regina pressed her wand to the doorway between them, conjuring a thick crystal barrier as wide as the doorway and equally as tall as the door, in a panic. She staggered back, breathing heavily as the crystal formed an impenetrable wall.

Isabella stopped in front of it and examined the barrier with a cold detachment. Slowly, she placed her metal hand against the crystal, as if testing its strength. Then, without warning, she drew her fist back and punched it. The impact was deafening, creating a large crack in the crystal's surface.

Regina gasped. That single punch had nearly shattered the wall, she felt the mana travel through her mana... somehow. She can't fight Isabella alone.

She turned and sprinted down the corridor, her shoes thudding heavily against the floor. The Stormfang rocked violently as another cannon volley rang out. The metal shell of the ship reverberated like a giant gong under the impact of enemy fire.

Sparks and Gimble reached the armory door, pushing through as Sparks half-carried the injured Gimble. Behind them, Regina could feel her crystal barrier fracturing further as Isabella struck it again, the force reverberating through her mana connection.

When the trio barreled through the doorway into the armory, the crew inside immediately turned their weapons on them, startled by the sudden intrusion.

"Whoa, whoa!" Sparks called, raising a hand in defence. "It's us! Don't shoot!" He glanced at Gimble's bleeding arm. "They're here, these bastards did this to Gimble!"

Gimble growled in agreement, his deep voice rumbling through the room.

"*It's Isabella!*" Regina gasped, her words directed at Brother Marcus and Lisa. "She has more of those metal monsters with her!"

Brother Marcus froze, his eyes widening in alarm. He sat up from where he had been tending supplies, clutching the bag of medical gear Gary had given him. He let out a breath of disbelief. "Goddess help us... She's here."

Lisa paled, her green eyes widening with shock. "Isabella...?" she whispered, her voice trembling. She raised a hand to cover her mouth, visibly distressed by the revelation. Memories of their last encounter with the corrupted avatar haunted her expression.

"She's going to kill us all," Regina said softly, her fear barely contained.

"All this for one girl?" Ethan scoffed, casting a mocking glance toward Marcus and the avatars. "She must be some good time."

His comment drew a round of laughter from several crew members, their nerves finding brief reprieve in humor.

Brother Marcus, however, didn't flinch. He stepped forward, his expression darkening as he addressed the room. "I have personally seen Isabella tear through trained sheriffs and deputies with ease," he said, his voice low but commanding. The laughter died almost instantly, replaced by an uneasy silence. "She doesn't leave many alive to tell the story of meeting her."

The weight of his words hung in the air, suffocating any further attempts at humor.

[-----⊕-----]

Meanwhile, on the bridge of the Stormfang, the crew continued to trade rifle shots with those aboard the Crazy Horse. Magic fireballs and lightning bolts sporadically struck the deck, crackling bursts of heat and energy forcing the crew to keep their heads down between volleys.

From her perch in the crow's nest, Sophie did her best to suppress the Accursed Raider's deck crew, which was approaching fast from the rear. She fired continuously, alternating between fire, shockwave, and lightning-infused bullets. Each shot drained her mana reserves, but she kept the Raider's crew from organizing an effective attack strategy.

Below her, the Stormfang and the Crazy Horse exchanged cannon fire. Sparks' reinforced metal shell deflected the Crazy Horse's shots, each impact ringing out like a giant gong. In contrast, the Stormfang's cannonballs tore into the Crazy Horse, leaving visible damage across its hull and deck. Yet the ship pushed forward, undeterred by the pounding.

After emptying her rifle, Sophie dropped to a seated position to reload. She inserted a fresh set of rounds, fire and regular bullets this time. She was running dangerously low on shockwave bullets, her new favorite. With her rifle restocked, Sophie quickly returned to her shooting stance, aiming back at the Raider. Her shots drove the deck crew into cover once more.

Mid-volley, Sophie's right arm suddenly went numb with a biting chill, as though she'd been plunged into the heart of a Granmark winter. Before she could react, ice rapidly encased the crow's nest, trapping her rifle. She jerked her arm free from the growing frost and knocked ice chunks from her jacket sleeve. Her eyes narrowed. The mage who did this was no mage; it was a witch, *the Ice Witch... **Gretta Blomqvist***.

Thinking fast, she grabbed a fire rune cutout from her vest pocket and channeled her mana into it. Slamming the rune into the ice surrounding her rifle, she watched as a burst of flame erupted, cracking and melting the ice. Sophie kicked at the weakened shell, breaking it apart and retrieving her weapon.

Instead of focusing on the Raider, she now scanned the deck of the Crazy Horse, searching for the mage responsible. It didn't take long. A woman in a long brown leather coat stood near the mast, her hood pushed back to reveal fair skin and brown hair. She raised her arms, summoning a column of arctic ice that surged across the deck. The magic collided with the mast, freezing Phelps in place, his legs, torso, and arms up to his elbows trapped in a frozen crystalline prison.

Sophie's breath hitched. Gretta. The woman who had taken her mother and countless others from her clan. The same woman who haunted her nightmares.

Without hesitation, Sophie aimed her rifle and fired. The regular bullet struck Gretta's right arm, causing her to whip around and lock eyes with Sophie. The woman's expression hardened as she raised her left hand, conjuring a an ice construct, shaped in Gretta's likeness, materialized, a defensive spell, perhaps similar to the armor spells used by Eclipse Tomalin.

Before Sophie could figure it out, another blast of ice magic struck the crow's nest, encasing it once again. This time, she kept her rifle close as she hit the floor of the bucket, teeth chattering from the freezing cold.

I'll fix this, but I need to be quick, Sophie thought, already pulling another fire rune from her vest pocket. She glanced up at the ice overhead and came up with a plan. Instead of using a ready-made slat, she would carve a new rune into the ice itself. She removed a bullet from her belt and used its tip to etch the fire rune design into the thick layer of frost. With slow, deliberate strokes, she deepened the carving, ensuring every line matched the rune slate's pattern perfectly.

313

"Let's hope this works," Sophie said under her breath. She touched the carved rune with her pointer and middle fingers, channeling her dwindling mana reserves into it. The fire run in ice responded instantly, glowing with fiery energy just like her wooden slats did.

As the rune absorbed her mana, Sophie felt the familiar drain of constant spell use. When the rune reached full charge, she pulled her fingers back, letting the magic take effect. A wave of heat spread across the ice, cracking and melting the layer that imprisoned her. She kicked the remaining shards free and gritted her teeth against the mana exhaustion washing over her.

Sophie seized her chance, breaking the weakened ice canopy with a hard kick. Rising to a kneeling shooting position, she scanned the deck of the Crazy Horse for her target. Bingo...*Gretta*. The woman now stood just to the right of her previous position, a block of ice covering her forearm where Sophie's earlier bullet had struck. Her ice construct still loomed nearby like a guardian.

Gretta's eyes locked onto Sophie with a searing fury. Without hesitation, she cast another freezing spell, but this time, the flames surrounding the crow's nest shielded Sophie from the ice's grip. Sophie quickly sighted in and fired a fire-infused bullet, aiming for Gretta's chest.

Before the bullet could hit its mark, an ice barrier materialized in its path, detonating on impact. The explosion sent shards of ice flying in all directions, some embedding themselves in the deck and into Gretta herself. Sophie cursed under her breath, already lining up her next shot.

Gretta retaliated with a new spell, raising her hand. Ice shards. *Great,* Sophie thought. Large, spear-like shards of ice erupted from Gretta's palm, hurtling toward her. Sophie squeezed the trigger just as the projectiles reached her, her bullet smashing one shard in mid-air but failing to stop the others. Two of the shards pierced the crow's nest, shaking the entire structure with a violent jolt and knocking Sophie flat onto the floor of the bucket.

Before Sophie could recover, she heard more shards slam into the wooden planks around her. She froze, realizing something critical: *She's not aiming at me, she's trying to destroy the crow's nest.*

The boards beneath her groaned ominously, creaking under the strain. Another trio of shards struck, splintering more planks. Sophie's mind raced. *Okay... this isn't going to hold. Time to move.*

Quickly, she untied the safety rope around her waist, giving herself more slack, then retied it. More shards punctured the structure, this time dangerously close. The crow's nest groaned and finally began to give way when a cannonball from the Crazy Horse struck the Stormfang's armored shell, sending a tremor through the entire ship. The sudden shock broke the crow's nest apart, sending Sophie tumbling into open air.

Her rifle slipped from her grasp and plummeted downward. *Please don't fall in the water*, she thought as gravity yanked her body downward. The safety rope around her waist caught with a harsh jolt, saving her from a deadly plunge. She swung hard, colliding with the mast just above the sail, her breath escaping in a painful gasp.

Ice shards streaked toward her again. Gretta wasn't giving her a moment's respite. Sophie gritted her teeth and pulled out her pistol. Without wasting time, she fired three regular bullets at the brown-clad mage. Gretta's ice construct of herself absorbed the shots and shattered, but the shockwave bullet that followed caught her off guard, slamming her to the deck. Sophie's final two fire bullets struck the wood near her, setting small patches of the deck ablaze.

With Gretta momentarily down, Sophie knew she needed to reposition **fast**. Her current spot was too exposed. She hopped off the sail beam, using the safety rope to swing down toward the mast's ladder. As soon as her boots hit the rungs, she untied the rope and let it fall away, her fingers working quickly despite the tremors in her limbs.

She descended the ladder with practiced urgency, the sounds of cannon fire and rifle shots filling the air around her. One down, she thought grimly. *Now let's see if I can survive the rest of this battle.*

[----- ⚓ -----]

Down on the main deck of the Stormfang, chaos reigned. The crew exchanged volleys of rifle fire with the pirates on the Crazy Horse, bullets tearing into both ships. Occasional blasts of magic struck the Stormfang, shaking the deck as arcane energy burned and cracked the wood. Sparks' armor shell, however, proved its worth, deflecting cannonballs that would have otherwise devastated the ship.

A bolt of lightning suddenly slammed into the deck, blasting Harmon and Bobby off their feet. Smitty reacted swiftly, conjuring a waterspout that trapped Harmon in a column of swirling water, preventing him from being flung overboard. At that exact moment, Eclipse Lepele, surrounded by a flash of red energy, moved so fast it appeared to Annabelle as though he had teleported. He caught Bobby by the arm just before the man could fall through the hold's access door.

"We'll have none of that," Lepele said firmly, hauling Bobby back onto the deck. The red aura around him faded as he stabilized both of them. Bullets rained down on the Stormfang in relentless waves, forcing the crew to take cover.

Before anyone could react further, a chilling blast of ice magic surged across the deck. It enveloped the mast and froze Phelps, encasing his stone-armored form in a massive block of ice. His scream was abruptly silenced as he was frozen solid.

"What the hell is that?!" Popper shouted, his voice panicked. "Who can do magic like that?"

"The brown girl that killed the Copper's village!" Annabelle yelled back, recognizing the deadly power at work. "She's on the Crazy Horse!" Ducking behind the stairs leading to the bridge, she frantically reloaded her rifle. The situation was becoming overwhelming, and Annabelle couldn't deny the truth anymore. "This here's a setup!" she muttered under her breath.

"How are ye on bullets?" Captain Kidd shouted, his voice cutting through the chaos.

The crew's responses echoed back, grim and unified: "We're runnin' low!"

"Runner!" Kidd called out, glancing around for Gimble.

"He ain't back from the cannons yet," Annabelle answered, shaking her head.

A rifle suddenly clattered onto the bridge deck, bouncing to a stop near Captain Kidd. He and Lepele both looked up to see the crow's nest in flames, riddled with ice shards.

"Griffin!" Lepele called up as he spotted Sophie balancing precariously on the crossbeam of the sails.

315

"Belle!" Kidd ordered urgently. "Go see what's keepin' Gimble, and get us some more bullets!"

"Aye, Cap'n!" Annabelle replied. She quickly secured her rifle in a deck holder and sprinted toward the stairs, weaving around debris and dodging incoming fire.

Sophie climbed down the mast ladder as fast as she could, finally dropping onto the deck.

"Nice of you to join us, Griffin!" Lepele called, half-smiling as he reloaded his own rifle.

"I got yer rifle up here!" Kidd yelled, signaling to her from behind the helm.

Sophie made her way across the deck, her boots thudding against the wood as cannon fire from the Crazy Horse rattled the Stormfang. Without warning, a glowing portal suddenly appeared in her path. Her eyes widened in alarm as a bomb dropped out of the swirling vortex and clattered onto the deck.

Reacting instinctively, Sophie kicked the bomb away. At the exact moment, a cannonball struck the Stormfang's armored hull, sending a tremor through the ship. The vibration disrupted her kick, causing the bomb to veer only a short distance away. It rolled just off the starboard side before detonating in a deafening explosion. The shockwave sent splinters of wood flying and rocked the ship violently.

Chapter 22

Inside the armory, tension hung thick in the air. Everyone stared at the door that Regina had encased in a large silver crystal. Nearly all the crew members, save for Brother Marcus, Regina, Lisa, and the ship's doctor, Mr. Gary, pointed their weapons at the barrier. Regina clutched her wand tightly, a faint glow pulsing along its length as she kept her mana primed and ready.

"Why isn't she knocking on the crystal?" Regina asked, her eyes narrowing.

"Do ye hear that?" Ethan called to the room, leaning against the wall, his ears straining.

A hush fell over the room. Faint sounds echoed beyond the walls, knocking, scraping, wood creaking and breaking. Everyone tensed, their breaths held. Suddenly, with a deafening crash, a monstrous figure broke through the left wall. It was made entirely of metal, its hands ending in deadly axe blades. The creature widened the opening with a bite from its jagged, gaping maw, tearing a large chunk of wood from the wall like it was prey. Behind it, two more metal beasts emerged: the wildcat-shaped monster from earlier and a reptilian-shaped creature reminiscent of a dinosaur, their eyes glowing ominously with blue mana.

"Fall back!" Marcus shouted, helping Gary move the wounded Gimble away from the breach as fast as possible.

The rest of the crew opened fire on the intruders, but the bullets ricocheted off the metal bodies, sparking uselessly.

Another crash echoed from the right side of the room. A fourth monster, this one with rotating sawblades for hands, carved through the wall. It was followed by yet another dinosaur-like construct, both advancing menacingly toward Lisa, Regina, and the crew near them.

"We're trapped!" Ethan yelled, firing another ineffective shot. He glanced nervously at the monsters closing in on both sides.

Jeffie stepped in front of Lisa, his knees trembling but his resolve unwavering. He still wore the soup pot on his head like a makeshift helmet. In one hand, he held a cutlass; in the other, the sword's scabbard. "Stay back, ma'am!" he said, his accent making it sound like *mom*. His voice wavered, but his stance was firm.

With a brutal swing, the axe-handed monster struck Jeffie's helmet, sending him sprawling to the floor, unconscious. Regina gasped as the creature advanced on Lisa, its blue mana-infused eyes shining coldly. Without hesitation, Regina ran forward and raised her arms, summoning Galahad. The spirit manifested instantly, his shield intercepting the axe monster's next blow with a resounding Tinny-zap sound. The beast pushed against the barrier with terrifying force. Galahad stood firm against the pressure, manifesting a shield between Regina and the monster.

"I can't hold him much longer!" Regina cried, her voice strained.

Lisa stood frozen, paralyzed by fear. The memory of Brother Albert's death resurfaced in her mind, the helplessness, the blood, the overwhelming terror. Tears welled in her eyes. All she could see was his bloody smile reassuring her everything would be okay.

With a savage roar, Leopard Gimble charged into the axe monster, tackling it and driving it back into the wall. The impact sent the mechanical creature crashing to the floor. But before Gimble could recover, the dinosaur monster pounced on him, its claws raking into his chest as it pinned him down. Gimble screeched in pain, blood staining his fur.

"Get off him!" Ethan shouted. He grabbed a rifle from the wall and smashed the butt of it against the dinosaur's head, knocking it off Gimble. Before he could celebrate his success, the half-gator monster lunged forward and clamped its jaws around Ethan's arm, wrenching the rifle away. It swung Ethan into the wall like a rag doll, sending him crumpling to the floor.

"Goddess," Lisa sobbed, paralyzed by the horrifying sight. "Goddess, please help us..."

But no divine aid came. Instead, a calm, disembodied voice Erisol spoke in her mind: "Unity is not here. She can't be. *There is only you, Avatar.*"

Lisa's eyes widened as she processed the words. Ethan was being tossed around *just like Brother Albert had been*. Not this time.

"**NO!**" she screamed, summoning her courage. A blue spell circle materialized in front of her, glowing with her arcane fury. The ocean itself answered her call, water surging through a nearby porthole. She directed the torrent into the half-gator monster, knocking it off Ethan and pinning it to the floor with crushing force. It still clung to Ethan's arm, but at least it couldn't thrash him anymore.

"Hold it down, Green Girlie!" Sparks called out. "We've got it now!"

The crew rallied. With axes, cutlasses, and brute strength, they attacked the pinned monster, hacking at its metal limbs until the blue mana faded from its body. The pieces clattered lifelessly to the floor.

"We need help over here!" Marcus shouted from across the room. He held a makeshift spear, his stance defensive but desperate, as the sawblade monster bore down on him.

Lisa turned, weaving another spell circle. She summoned a column of water and blasted the sawblade monster, slamming it into the far wall. Regina, inspired by the tactic, conjured her own water spell. Blue runes flared to life around her, commanding "column," "flood," "cut," and "swirl." She directed the water into the axe monster, filling its interior and spinning it like a violent whirlpool. The force tore through its internal pieces, severing vital connections.

With a final surge of mana, Regina released the spell. Water and metal parts crashed to the floor as the axe monster well to pieces.

The remaining metal creatures collapsed simultaneously, their glowing eyes fading as the blue mana holding them together dissipated. A heavy silence followed, broken only by labored breathing.

Suddenly, a mighty thud echoed from the crystal-covered door, as if a torrent of water had struck it.

[----- ⚓ -----]

Annabelle reached the crew and utility deck, frowning at the broken entry door hanging off its hinges. She shoved it aside and stepped in, calling out, "The Cap'n ain't gonna like you scallywags destroyin' his ship!" But her words faltered when she spotted …her … the blue-haired hussy from West's. The one who killed Brother Albert.

The sight of Isabella reignited Annabelle's fury. This blue hussy had no business aboard Annabelle's ship. Without hesitation, Annabelle unhooked her anchor from her belt and shouted, "Oi, blue hussy! What ye doin' on me ship?!"

Isabella, still facing away from Annabelle, answered in a cold, emotionless tone. "The Stormfang must be destroyed, and the crew must die." Blue mana particles shimmered faintly as her magic flowed around her, flying away like a swarm of blue fireflies.

"Ye don't say," Annabelle muttered deviously, the corners of her mouth curling in a grin. She raised her hand and cast a wave spell with extra power, sending a forceful surge of water crashing into Isabella. The wave hurled the blue-haired woman forward, slamming her head against the large silver crystal Regina must have used to block the armory entrance. Isabella crumpled to the ground momentarily, her magic flickering out.

"Now get off me ship 'fore ye get some more o' that, *hussy!*" Annabelle taunted, her voice dripping with venom.

Isabella rose slowly, her expression eerily blank. In a flat, mechanical voice, she asked, "What is a hussy?"

Annabelle blinked, momentarily caught off guard. "Are ye serious?" she muttered under her breath, but quickly shook off her confusion. She cast another wave spell, but this time, the water seemed to part harmlessly around Isabella, barely slowing her down as she advanced with steady determination.

"Oi, come on!" Annabelle cursed, gripping her anchor tightly. She sidestepped Isabella's first attempt to grab her with a metal hand and countered with a swift three-hit combo. Her anchor slammed into Isabella's face and chest, but it was like hitting solid steel. Isabella didn't even flinch.

Without warning, Isabella retaliated with a powerful backhanded strike. The blow sent Annabelle sprawling across the deck, pain exploding in her side as she hit the floor hard.

"The orange avatar must die," Isabella intoned, her metal limbs emanating an ominous hum.

[----- ✿ -----]

Meanwhile, Regina picked her way through the wreckage left behind by Isabella's metal minions. The machine shop and storage compartments on the starboard side were in ruins, along with most of the crew quarters. As she approached the scene, she spotted Annabelle on the ground with Isabella looming over her like a specter of death.

Regina's mind raced. Direct attacks wouldn't work on Isabella, she had learned that much from their last encounter. But maybe she didn't need to stop Isabella, only

319

disorient her. Drawing on her training with Eclipse Lepele and Sophie, Regina arranged her mana into Maelstrom mastery and cast Morning Mist. A dense fog quickly filled the corridors, shrouding everything in a thick, obscuring haze.

[----- ⚓ -----]

Annabelle groaned, pulling herself off the floor. "Damn... that blue hussy hits like a damn cannon." She wiped a trickle of blood from her lip and grabbed her anchor again. The fog rolled in around her, cloaking the hallway in a ghostly mist. *Me girlie Regina!* Annabelle realized, a grin forming despite the pain.

Through the fog, Annabelle saw faint glimmers of blue light, Isabella's eye, metal forearm, and leg shining like beacons in the haze. The woman seemed to be feeling her way forward, her movements slow and methodical.

Perfect! Annabelle said to herself. She swung her anchor, hurling it through the mist. The metal hook struck Isabella in the head with a solid clang.

"...Ouch," Isabella exclaimed in her cold, detached tone.

Annabelle snorted. "Looks like ye can feel somethin', huh?" She yanked the anchor back, then hurled it again, this time hitting Isabella square in the torso. The blue-haired woman staggered slightly but continued advancing.

Not waiting for retaliation, Annabelle moved swiftly through the fog, positioning herself against the hallway wall. She had to keep moving.

[----- ✿ -----]

Regina crouched at the edge of the hallway, conjuring three smaller hexagonal crystals that fit snugly in her hand. Watching Annabelle's strikes gave her an idea. Silently, she threw one of the crystals, aiming for Isabella's back. It struck true and drew Isabella's attention.

Isabella turned, her glowing eye scanning the mist. She walked toward the sound of the impact, unaware of the illusion Regina had created to stand in her place.

From the safety of her position, Regina whispered through her projections, "Annabelle, I have an idea to get her off the ship."

Her voice echoed through the fog as if it came from multiple directions. Annabelle spotted Regina's real form near the wall and gave her a nod, flashing a toothy grin.

"Right then, let's show her how the Fang bites," Annabelle whispered, tightening her grip on the anchor. The two girls prepared to launch their coordinated attack, their combined ingenuity and grit ready to drive the intruder from their midst.

[----- ⊞ -----]

The main deck of the Stormfang descended into chaos after the bomb exploded the bomb off the starboard side. The Accursed Raider seized the opportunity to close in alongside the Stormfang, throwing a pair of ropes with hooked metal spikes over the hull. The hooks dug deep into the wood, anchoring the Raider firmly to the Stormfang.

A group of men dressed in black, their faces obscured by rags tied around their heads, began running across the gap using the rope bridge. Only their piercing eyes remained visible in the gloom, glinting with menace as they prepared to board.

"On yer feet, girlie," Popper said as he hauled Sophie upright. Smitty raised his hands, summoning a towering wall of water between the Stormfang and the Crazy Horse. "There's still work to be done!"

Sophie shook off the fog in her mind, still reeling from the bomb's shockwave. "Where's my rifle?" she asked, her voice sharper now.

"Here, missy!" Captain Kidd called from behind the helm, tossing the rifle toward her. "Nearly took me head off when ye dropped it! Keep yer hands on it will ye!"

Sophie caught the rifle with a quick nod. "Will do, Captain."

Before she could set her sights on a target, Gretta waved her hands, casting a freezing spell that solidified Smitty's sea wall into brittle ice. The structure shattered and tumbled into the sea just as another volley of cannonballs from the Crazy Horse slammed into the Stormfang's armor shell. This time, the impact produced a strange, undulating sound, as if the metal walls were vibrating like a discordant musical note.

Seeing the incoming cannon fire, Sophie shouted, "DOWN!" Instinctively, she and most of the crew dropped flat to the deck. The sudden move caught the boarding attackers off guard.

In that exact moment, Gretta unleashed a barrage of ice shards that tore into the advancing raiders. Some were killed instantly, while others were thrown overboard by the force of the attack. Bobby, however, was too slow to react. Three cylindrical ice stakes impaled him, two in the arm and one in the leg. He screamed in agony as blood seeped from the icy wounds.

"Harmon, get Bobby outta there!" Smitty barked.

Harmon grabbed Bobby and dragged him away from the anchor points where the Raider's men were flooding onto the deck. The attackers were now regrouping near the ropes, ready to engage in close combat.

Sophie scanned the scene with an unfamiliar clarity. The Crazy Horse wasn't sending a boarding party; they were sticking to cannon and magic attacks from a distance. The Raider, however, had moved in to deliver its assault crew. *If we can neutralize Crazy Horse's firepower, we might have a chance to escape*, she reasoned.

With a plan forming in her mind, Sophie addressed Smitty and Popper, who were closest to her. "Keep my back safe! I'll try to deal with that other ship."

"Get to it, missy," Smitty responded, his voice strained from maintaining a protective shield. "But make it quick. The shield won't hold much longer."

"Got it." Sophie rolled to her feet, raised her rifle, and aimed at her target: *Gretta*.

The woman who had stolen so much from Sophie was standing near the mast of the Crazy Horse, her eyes scanning the deck for another opportunity to unleash her ice magic. Sophie fired a regular bullet, striking the mast just above Gretta's head. The crack of the shot drew Gretta's attention. She turned her gaze to Sophie, locking eyes with her in a glare of pure fury.

Sophie didn't flinch. She immediately fired again, this time, a fire rune bullet. Gretta conjured an ice wall in an instant; the bullet exploded on impact, sending shards of fire-heated ice scattering across the deck. Sophie didn't stop. She fired round after round at the mast and deck of the Crazy Horse, each bullet meant to disrupt their movements and damage the ship itself.

The Crazy Horse retaliated with another barrage of cannon fire. The cannonballs tore through the air, smashing into the Stormfang's portside shield with devastating force. The impact was different this time. Instead of deflecting the shots, the shield buckled, sending shockwaves through the ship's frame. The Stormfang lurched violently to port, causing the starboard side to rise sharply.

"The port shield is gone!" Captain Kidd roared over the chaos. "Hold on to somethin'!"

The crew scrambled for support as the ship tilted dangerously, the fight intensifying with each passing second. Sophie clutched the mast's ladder as the deck swayed beneath her, steeling herself for the next phase of the battle. There was no turning back now. They either fought their way out or sank to the bottom trying.

The attackers from the Raider were thrown into disarray as the Stormfang lurched violently. Some raiders were flung overboard, splashing into the sea below. The ship rolled sharply to starboard, sending another wave of attackers flying into the water. Popper crashed into the ship's side, managing to drive a dagger into the wooden hull to keep himself from following them.

Lepele, gripping tightly to the rigging, shouted over the chaos, "Griffin! Do something about that damn ship!"

"I'm trying!" Sophie called back, holding on for dear life to both the rigging and her rifle as the ship rolled beneath her.

"Oi, well stop trying and get it done! The ocean is hungry, girlie!" Captain Kidd bellowed with a grin. As the Stormfang rocked fiercely from side to side, he yelled, "Detach the shields!"

"Always the easy jobs with ye, Captain," Popper muttered as he dangled from his dagger embedded in the hull.

"If it's so easy, then hop to it!" Smitty shot back, holding onto a rope tied to the mast.

Lepele looked around, bracing himself against the mast. "How do you detach them?" he shouted.

"There's a red handle on each of the arms that releases the joining nut!" Bobby called out through gritted teeth, his voice strained from pain as he clung to the railing near the stairs to the bridge. He let out a scream as the motion of the ship jarred his wounds.

Lepele spotted the red handle on the forward part of the starboard side. As the Stormfang tipped back to starboard, he tightened his grip on the mast. When the ship rolled into port, he took a leap of faith, aiming for the handle. He landed short but scrambled forward, grabbing hold of the flapping rope just as the ship rocked again.

He seized the handle and gave it a hard pull. It didn't budge.

"By the ancestors, what now?!" Lepele growled, straining against the stubborn mechanism.

At the aft section of the deck, Smitty reached the second handle and yanked on it with all his strength. It refused to give. "By the sea! Cap'n, the release is stuck!" he yelled in frustration.

The Stormfang rolled back hard to starboard, forcing Lepele and Smitty to dangle precariously from the release ropes. The movement gave Popper and Harmon a chance to reach the handles on the starboard side, but when they pulled, they encountered the same problem.

"Dammit, Sparks!" Harmon roared, pulling with all his might.

After several agonizing moments, the portside handles finally gave way under the weight of Lepele and Smitty. The port shield tore free, crashing against the side of the Stormfang with a thunderous impact, splintering parts of the hull before plunging into the sea. The Crazy Horse seized the moment, unleashing another volley of cannonballs. This time, the shots struck the Stormfang's unprotected belly, ripping through the lower deck and inflicting significant damage.

"Griffin!" Lepele bellowed, still clinging to the release rope. "*I gave you an order, Sentinel!*"

"I can't get a shot with the ship bouncing around like this!" Sophie shouted back, gripping the rigging for balance.

"And here I thought you goddess girls could do anything," Kidd taunted, his voice filled with sharp humor as he braced himself against the helm.

Sophie narrowed her eyes. *The same trick may work twice, she thought*, steadying herself. She waited for the next roll of the ship, her mind racing for an opportunity.

The ship rocked hard to port again as the detached shield slammed into the hull. The force of the impact sent Popper and Harmon swinging on the release ropes. Their combined weight finally triggered the starboard release mechanism, and the second shield fell free with a loud crash. It collided with the Stormfang's hull, causing more damage before plunging into the ocean. The ship rolled sharply to starboard, tossing everyone on deck as they scrambled to hold on.

The Stormfang steadied itself, rocking gently side to side as Sophie seized the moment. She quickly loaded her rifle: three void bullets followed by four fire bullets. *Mana reserves be damned!* she thought, determination hardening her resolve. Without even glancing at the bridge of the Crazy Horse, Sophie leaned over the Stormfang's rail, aiming for the cannon deck of the enemy vessel.

She pulled the trigger.

The first void bullet hit, and a small black sphere of energy formed on impact, disintegrating a section of the Crazy Horse's hull. The second and third shots followed in rapid succession, tearing through wood, iron, and cannon mounts. But the exertion was punishing. Sophie gasped as she felt her mana draining far more rapidly than she anticipated. Her vision swam, and she gritted her teeth, feeling the heavy weight of depletion. She wasn't quite at mana zero, but she felt dangerously close.

Breathe, Sophie. Focus.

With shaking hands, she fired the fire bullets next. Each shot sent a jolt of agony through her mana pathways, draining what little energy she had left. The first two fire bullets fizzled out, snuffed by the remaining moisture inside the Crazy Horse's structure. But the third and fourth hit something dry enough to ignite, and flames began to spread, until a twisting jet of water surged through the gaps in the hull, extinguishing them.

"Dammit! I was so close!" Sophie screamed, frustration mounting as she slumped to the deck. She opened the rifle's stock to reload but found herself paralyzed by indecision, her thoughts clouded by anger and exhaustion.

"The true warrior fights fiercely," came a voice in her mind…Titus, her ever-irreverent spirit animal bonded from the goddess of War. "But their mind remains as still as a peaceful pond. Only in a tranquil mind can a true warrior lead their armies to victory."

Sophie blinked. *Titus? Since when are you a poet?* Yet, his words pierced through the mental storm raging within her. Slowly, her chaotic thoughts calmed, like turbulent waters settling into a quiet stream. She could think again.

What worked? The void bullets. Yes…

She reached into her jacket, pulling out seven more void bullets. Her gut twisted with dread at the thought of the mana toll, but this was their best, no, their only chance.

The Stormfang's cannons roared, blasting into both the Crazy Horse and the Accursed Raider. Both enemy ships returned fire, further damaging the Fang's hull. Sophie sighted through her rifle, focusing on the ragged gaps her previous shots had torn into the Crazy Horse's hull. The damage was extensive, but not yet fatal. If she could weaken the structure in just the right places, the ship would start taking on water.

She targeted the lowest section of the hull above the waterline and fired the first void bullet. The impact tore another gaping void into the ship, but the mana cost was staggering. Sophie felt as though she were lifting a massive weight. Before she could dwell on the pain, she fired again. The next shot landed just above the first, joining the two spheres of disintegration. It felt like lifting two weights at once, her arm trembled under the strain.

"Five more... I can do this," she whispered to herself.

She cocked the handle and took another shot. This time, pain bloomed in her chest like burning thorns, and her vision blurred. Her head throbbed as though a hammer pounded inside her skull. Gritting her teeth, Sophie forced herself to keep going, cocking the rifle and pulling the trigger once more. Her mana reserves screamed in protest. Her whole body trembled as another shot left the barrel.

Two more... you can't stop now...

Sophie's fingers felt numb as she chambered the next round. Her vision swam, the hull of the Crazy Horse now just a distorted blur. She blinked rapidly, trying to steady her focus, but it was no use. Still, she pulled the trigger. Agonizing lightning coursed through her arm and chest as the last shot emptied her mana reserves. Tears streamed from her eyes as she collapsed against the railing.

For a moment, all was still. Then, the Stormfang's cannons fired once more, their shots slamming into the weakened Crazy Horse. The already damaged hull buckled under the impact, and an ear-splitting explosion tore through the enemy ship. Flames and debris erupted as the Crazy Horse began to list and take on water.

"Griffin!" Lepele's voice rang out in alarm.

Sophie barely heard him. Her body refused to move. Exhausted, she slumped to the deck, her rifle clattering beside her. She had done all she could. The rest is in her crew's hands now.

[-----✝-----]

The armory was a scene of exhaustion and damage control as the crew worked to treat their wounded and clean up the wreckage left by the mechanical monsters. Brother Marcus carefully wrapped a broken splint around Ethan's arm, using a piece of shattered wood to stabilize it. His voice was blunt and to the point.

"I'm sure it's broken," Marcus said, tightening the bandage.

Ethan winced through the pain but managed a smirk. "Aye, I'll take yer word for it, mate."

Nearby, Lisa wrestled the dented pot helmet off Jeffie's head, revealing a nasty bruise that had formed underneath. She placed her hands gently on his head, her Earthbloom sense sweeping through him. Despite the severity of the impact, he appeared to be alright, just knocked out cold. Not taking any chances, Lisa weaved a red healing circle. Red runes glowed as she focused on repairing the minor damage to his brain and reducing the swelling in his head.

"Green missy, over here!" Gary's urgent voice broke through her concentration. "I need your help with Gimble NOW! He's dyin'!"

Lisa's heart sank. She hurried to where Mr. Gimble lay on the floor, now back in his human form. His chest was covered in blood-soaked bandages. Gary, crouched over him, listened to his chest with grim concentration.

"I don't hear a heartbeat," Gary shouted, panic tightening his voice. "Now, missy! Get to work!"

Lisa knelt beside them, closing her eyes and listening with her Earthbloom senses. She searched desperately for any sign of life in Gimble, but found nothing. She tried again, willing herself to sense even a flicker of life, but there was only emptiness. Tears welled in her eyes as the crushing truth hit her. Gimble was gone.

"I… I am so sorry," she whispered, voice trembling. "He's passed to the next life."

Gary's eyes widened in disbelief. "No… ye have a goddess' power! Ye can bring him back, can't ye?"

Lisa shook her head, tears now streaming freely down her face. "I cannot… I cannot bring someone back to life," she said softly.

Gary's shoulders slumped as he absorbed her words. Slowly, he reached out to close Gimble's lifeless eyes. "Then what good are ye, anyway..." he muttered bitterly, though regret flickered in his eyes almost immediately. He sighed heavily and composed himself. "Who else needs help?"

Jeffie stirred nearby, holding his head groggily. Gary moved over to him, his manner turning more businesslike.

Lisa stayed where she was, grief pinning her in place. Gimble had been one of the most cheerful and dependable crew members, always quick with a joke or a helping hand. And she had failed him. The sense of helplessness crushed her spirit. Perhaps her father had been right, *maybe she didn't belong out here. Maybe she could only be helpful at home.*

"Miss Lisa," Marcus called gently, his voice breaking through her spiral of despair. He knew her well enough to see how much she was struggling. She needed a task, something to focus on. "Can you come look at Ethan's arm? Maybe your Earthbloom magic can help with his injuries."

Lisa sniffled, wiping her tears away as best she could. "Yes, I will be right there." she said quietly, steeling herself.

Nearby, Sparks nudged a pile of dormant metal parts with his boot. "What should we do with all this here scrap?" he asked aloud, looking at the remnants of the mechanical monsters.

"What, ye want to wake it up or somethin'?" Gary shot back with a sharp edge in his voice as he checked on Jeffie.

"Nay," Sparks replied calmly. "I want to give it to the sea, make sure that if it wakes up, it does it deep beneath the waves."

Lisa knelt beside Ethan, her Earthbloom senses already scanning his broken arm. "Your arm is fractured in three places," she informed him gently. "There is also a lot of muscle and tissue damage. I will heal the fractures now, but I will need more time to fix the rest later."

"Do what ye can, missy," Ethan groaned, bracing himself for the healing process.

325

Marcus stood aside to give her room and walked over to where Flint and Sparks were gathering the metal debris. "I like your plan, Sparks. Mind if I help?"

"Be my guest," Sparks replied. "We're tossin' this junk out the porthole over there."

Marcus and Flint began hauling the twisted, jagged remains of the monsters toward the porthole. The ship rocked as the Stormfang fired another volley of cannonballs, briefly shaking the deck beneath them.

As Lisa worked on Ethan's arm, his grunts and cries of pain echoed around the armory. Sparks and Marcus continued tossing out pieces of the mechanical monsters. Marcus couldn't help but stare at the debris in disbelief. It was hard to imagine that these inert scraps had formed the terrifying creatures that had almost killed them all. He shook his head and kept working.

[-----✿-----]

In the hallway, Annabelle and Regina coordinated their attacks under the cover of fog. They continued to move and launch strikes at Isabella. Regina hurled crystal magic disks she had conjured, while Annabelle threw her anchor, scoring some hits and missing others. Regina used her "Hide and Seek" projections to confuse Isabella, projecting her voice from various points in the mist.

"Annabelle, you go now," Regina's voice echoed from one of her projections. She hurled two crystal disks into what she hoped was Isabella's back, watching as blue mana particles flared, briefly illuminating the fog.

Isabella spun around, her metal arm lashing out in a wide backhand, but it connected with nothing but mist. Regina crept silently through the fog until she was behind Annabelle and gave her a nod, signaling for the next attack.

Grinning, Annabelle swung her anchor, listening to the chain jingle as it built momentum. With a powerful throw, she sent the anchor hurtling toward Isabella.

Just before the anchor could strike, the chain glowed with Isabella's blue mana, suddenly yanking Annabelle forward.

"Oi, what gives?!" Annabelle protested, struggling to pull back against the force.

Without a word, Isabella used her magic to wrap the chain around Annabelle and pulled her in. With terrifying strength, she slammed Annabelle to the deck, knocking the wind out of her and dispersing much of the fog.

"The orange avatar must die," Isabella said flatly, as though reciting an order.

Annabelle gasped, trying to catch her breath as Isabella's metal hand pressed down on her midsection. She kicked furiously, aiming for Isabella's back and head, but it was like kicking solid stone.

Regina's mind raced as she searched for a way to *help*. *Illusions won't work*, Isabella had a firm grip on Annabelle and wouldn't be fooled. Without sunlight, fluid, or anything to blind her, Regina was running out of options. Then, her eyes fell on Isabella's braided ponytail.

Creeping through the mist, Regina snuck up behind Isabella, using one of her projections to distract her. Once in position, she grabbed the blue ponytail and yanked with all her might. Isabella's head jerked back in surprise, forcing her to release Annabelle but keeping her grip on the anchor chain through her mechanamagic.

Regina strained, pulling with everything she had. Isabella sprawled backward, her normal hand clawing at Regina.

"Let me go," Isabella commanded, her voice as cold and mechanical as ever.

Regina noticed that Isabella's metal hand had to remain extended and focused to maintain control over Annabelle. Seizing the opportunity, Regina quickly cast "Envoûtement des Cercles Éternels," briefly trapping Isabella in a series of glowing magical rings. Regina used the moment to retreat further into the fog, switching her mana to crystalmancy and envisioning the training gloves she wore during sparring sessions with Sophie and Eclipse Lepele.

Meanwhile, Annabelle struggled against the chain binding her. She clenched her jaw in frustration; *This hussy is using me own anchor belt to tie her up, embarrassing me in front of Regina no less.*

'Not happening,' Annabelle thought furiously. She tapped into the storm inside her, channeling her embarrassment and rage into raw maelstrom energy. With a burst of orange seawater, she expelled Isabella's blue mana from the chain, breaking the enchantment and freeing herself, though she hit the deck hard in the process.

Isabella recoiled, pulling back her metal hand as if struck by a painful backlash. She shook it quickly, as though trying to clear an ache. Just then, one of Regina's projections appeared in front of her, and Isabella instinctively swung with a wide, spinning punch. The blow shattered the illusion, leaving her momentarily off-balance.

"Now!" Regina whispered to herself.

She stepped out of the mist and landed a swift three-hit combo: a straight left, a right jab, and a powerful left haymaker to Isabella's face. The crystal-coated strikes connected with satisfying force, until Isabella caught Regina's hand with her unforgiving metal grip.

The pressure shattered the crystal glove, making Regina scream in pain. Galahad manifested immediately, his shield forming around her wrist to protect her from further damage.

"The purple avatar punches much harder than you," Isabella stated coldly. She twisted Regina's arm slightly, as if testing the shield. "The silver avatar Fournier must be either killed or captured."

Before Isabella could tighten her grip further, Annabelle sprang into action. Drawing her cutlass, she charged and slashed Isabella across the back.

"Oi, hussy! The fight's over here!" Annabelle roared.

The force of the strike made Isabella stumble forward, releasing Regina's hand. She let out a detached "Ahhh" of pain but didn't collapse. Regina cradled her wrist, her face pale and trembling from the near-crushing grip.

Annabelle stood her ground, cutlass ready, her storm-charged eyes glaring daggers at the blue-haired intruder.

The Stormfang suddenly rocked violently to the port side, slamming Annabelle, Regina, and Isabella into the wall with bone-jarring force. It felt as though the ship itself was punishing them for their continued battle. Before they could recover, the ship tilted violently to the starboard side, throwing them into the opposite wall with equal brutality.

Annabelle, coughing from the impact, instinctively yanked the chain on her anchor belt, pulling the anchor into her grasp. Digging it deep into the wall, she clung to it, knowing from her instincts that the ship wasn't done punishing them. As the vessel began to tilt again, Annabelle wrapped the chain tightly around her arm, bracing herself.

327

Galahad manifested around Regina, using his mana-generated shield to protect her from further harm. Regina found herself falling but was caught by the shield's protection, her body gently held before she managed to hook her arm through the jagged remains of the door to the machine shop.

On the other side of the room, Isabella steadied herself with unnatural grace. As the ship tilted portside down again, she drove her metal hand through the ship's wall, anchoring herself with mechanical precision. Her icy blue gaze focused intently on the two girls across from her.

"Oi! Ye gonna pay for that damage, hussy?" Annabelle taunted, hanging from her anchor with her legs braced against the wall.

Isabella's head tilted in confusion. "What is a hussy?"

Annabelle blinked. "You! You're the hussy!" she snapped, bewildered that this woman didn't understand such a basic insult.

Isabella's brow furrowed slightly, her head tilting from side to side like she was trying to understand the unfamiliar term. Before anyone could react further, the ship rocked sharply to starboard again. Regina and Annabelle were flung to the floor as Isabella released her hold on the wall and landed smoothly on the now diagonal deck, crouched like a predator ready to pounce.

The port shield smashed against the ship's hull with a resounding, resonating clang. The reverberation shook the entire structure, followed by the deep groan of cannon fire tearing into the Stormfang's belly. Annabelle's stomach twisted. She knew what that sound meant.

The Fang is in trouble now... She's gonna start takin' on water, and we're in the middle of nowhere. No one's comin' to save us. Annabelle thought grimly. Her gaze hardened as she turned to Regina. "We gotta wrap this up! Ye gotta come up with' somethin', girlie!"

The ship rolled again, pulling the detached port shield down and righting itself violently. With the morning mist completely dispersed, the three combatants could now see each other clearly. Annabelle and Regina exchanged a glance, silently preparing themselves for the final round. Isabella's focus remained locked on Annabelle, identifying her as the larger threat. Annabelle taunted her by giving a wink and a predatory grin.

When the ship finally stabilized, Isabella struck. Blue mana surged from her metal arm as she reached out to take control of Annabelle's anchor belt. Anticipating the move, Annabelle unclipped the belt and dashed toward her cutlass, sliding across the floor using a burst of seawater thanks to her Maelstrom Mastery under her hands. She snatched the cutlass and rose, spinning into a wide arc that sliced across the back of Isabella's leg, forcing a detached "Ahhhh" from the woman.

[----- ✿ -----]

Meanwhile, Regina ran into Ethan's machine shop, searching frantically for a grease pencil or chalk, anything that might allow her to draw a portal ritual. She knew from her previous encounter with Hema that she'd need more than brute force to win a fight like this.

[----- ⚓ -----]

328

Isabella, regaining her balance, hurled Annabelle's anchor belt back at her with a burst of blue magic. Annabelle dodged, leaping off the wall and using her momentum to drive her knee into Isabella's torso. "Damn you, hussy! Fall already!" Annabelle shouted in frustration as she brought both elbows down on Isabella's head.

Isabella's expression remained eerily calm as she reached up and grabbed Annabelle by the throat with her metal hand. Annabelle gasped, struggling as Isabella's grip tightened like a steel vice. Desperately, she drove her cutlass into Isabella's side, but the mechana-witch released her neck and otherwise barely reacted beyond a slow trickle of blood.

"The orange avatar must die," Isabella stated coldly, pulling the cutlass free and tossing it aside.

Annabelle was slammed to the deck again, choking and disoriented. She glanced around desperately for a weapon but saw only debris scattered across the floor. She considered reaching for her necklace, but hesitated, she promised the captain, not to let them out. Before she could think further, Isabella used her magic to send the anchor belt flying at her again. Annabelle grabbed the chain and yanked with all her strength, growling, "Gimme me belt, hussy!"

As Isabella pulled back with her magic, Annabelle allowed herself to be dragged forward just enough to execute a double-footed riptide kick, channeling maelstrom power to slam into Isabella's chest. The force finally drove the woman back several steps. Isabella stumbled, her concentration on the chain breaking as she released her control over it.

Annabelle hit the deck next to her cutlass and scrambled to her feet, her stormy orange eyes blazing with determination. For the first time, she saw a flicker of uncertainty cross Isabella's face.

[----- ✿ -----]

Regina tore through the wreckage in the machine shop, searching desperately for something to draw with. Broken machinery, shattered desks, and scattered tools littered the floor. She flung open a destroyed storage desk, finding nothing but wood scraps, tool inserts, and a repair kit. Her heart raced as she heard a loud crash from the hallway, followed by Annabelle swearing and the detached, mechanical voice of Isabella uttering a cold "Owww." Another crash and the clang of metal on metal echoed after it.

Come on, Regina. Think. There has to be something here! she urged herself in frustration.

[----- ⚓ -----]

In the hallway, Annabelle was battling both exhaustion and the overwhelming force of her opponent. She staggered, holding her cutlass defensively as Isabella advanced. Annabelle's anchor belt lay uselessly on the floor behind her, a reminder of how the blue-haired woman had twisted her magic to control it. Still, she smirked despite her injuries, taunting Isabella.

"Me cutlass... too scary for ye, eh?" Annabelle asked, catching her breath between pained gulps of air.

"No," Isabella replied calmly. "It is too dense for my magic to manipulate." The stab wound on her midsection oozed blood, but she didn't even flinch. She seemed unaffected by pain, her goddess-gifted resilience making her an unrelenting force. Once more, Isabella repeated her chilling command: "The orange avatar must die."

Isabella lunged with a punch from her metal hand, but Annabelle danced back with a quick dodge. She countered with a rising slash of her cutlass aimed at Isabella's neck. The blade clanged against the metal arm with no effect. Isabella retaliated with a kick to Annabelle's midsection, sending her stumbling back. Annabelle barely had time to react before Isabella's next punch struck her square in the nose, drawing blood. Staggering, Annabelle pulled away just in time to avoid a follow-up uppercut that whistled past her face.

[----- ✿ -----]

Meanwhile, Regina's frustration boiled over. There was nothing to draw with, and time was running out. Her eyes locked on the repair kit, and inspiration struck. She grabbed a tin of grease from the kit, dipping her fingers into the sticky substance. *This will have to do!* she thought, glancing around for a clean surface. The debris-covered floor was useless. Annabelle didn't have much time left, and Regina knew she couldn't afford to waste a second cleaning up. Her gaze shifted to the flat wall near the door...perfect.

[----- ⚓ -----]

Isabella's dispassionate voice echoed through the hall. "You are very resilient," she observed, then said, "The orange avatar must die," stepping closer to Annabelle, who was still recovering from the blow to her nose. Blood dripped from Annabelle's nostrils as she knelt on the floor, panting hard.

"Ye... gotta find somethin' else to say," Annabelle huffed between breaths. "That... is gettin' old."

Forcing herself to her feet, Annabelle clenched her fists. Her cutlass was out of reach, and her battered body couldn't handle much more. Her anchor belt was too much of a liability. She had no choice but to rely on her fists. But before she could strike, a shimmering window-like portal suddenly materialized behind Isabella. The portal displayed the deck of another ship, where figures were frantically running and firing weapons.

Regina! Annabelle thought, recognizing the magic at play. She understood immediately, her job now is to force Isabella through that portal.

Isabella threw another punch, but Annabelle ducked under it, sidestepping to let Isabella stumble forward. Without hesitation, Annabelle summoned a powerful wave of maelstrom energy, slamming it into Isabella's back and knocking her off balance. Summoning all her remaining strength, Annabelle unleashed a second wave in front of Isabella, crashing into her like a battering ram and propelling her straight through the portal.

"Close the window!" Annabelle shouted at the top of her lungs.

[----- ✿ -----]

In the machine shop, Regina tapped the center of the grease-drawn ritual circle, her hand glowing with mana. The portal shimmered and vanished instantly. She wiped her hand on her coveralls and hurried back to the hallway.

"Annabelle!" Regina called, her voice filled with worry as she saw her friend sprawled out on the floor, surrounded by wreckage. Annabelle was breathing heavily through her mouth, her face bruised and battered. Blood stained her clothes, and her usually fierce eyes were clouded with exhaustion.

"Hey, Regina," Annabelle greeted softly, her voice light and calm despite her condition. She gave a weak grin. "Ye can do the same healin' thing as Lisa, right? 'Cause... I could really use some of that 'bout now."

Regina knelt beside her, carefully placing a hand on her shoulder. "You'll be okay, Annabelle," she reassured her. "Let me take care of you."

Chapter 23

Sophie's void bullets had left the Crazy Horse crippled, the sea greedily swallowing the wounded ship despite Gretta's desperate attempts to seal the gaping holes with ice. The damage was too severe, and no amount of freezing magic could stop the ocean from claiming its prize. That left the Stormfang facing off against the lone Accursed Raider, whose crew showed no intention of relenting. The raiders swarmed across a makeshift rope bridge connecting their ship to the Stormfang, armed and merciless, ready to fight to the death.

On the deck, Eclipse Lepele fought like a whirlwind. His "Intensity" magic imbued each strike with explosive force and a red glow, every slash broke through defenses, every kick sent raiders flying over the rail and into the sea. Sophie watched from the top of the stairs leading to the bridge, her head pounding from mana exhaustion. Despite the pain, she kept firing her pistol, sticking to regular bullets since she had no mana left to fuel her Alrunia rounds. Her priority was protecting the wounded, Bobby and Popper, while providing support to Captain Kidd, who held his position behind the helm.

"Heads up, Griffin!" Lepele shouted as he cut down an attacker near the main mast.

Sophie turned her focus to the rope bridge and froze. A large, stocky man was charging across it with a barrel strapped to his back, its wick burning ominously.

That's a bomb!

Sophie's heart skipped a beat. Fighting through her splitting headache, she raised her pistol, steadied her shaking hands, and fired three shots. The first two missed, but the third hit the man square in the neck. He stumbled, his balance lost, and tumbled off the rope bridge into the dark waters below.

Hearing rapid footsteps on the stairwell, Sophie spun around just in time to see an attacker in black rushing her with a sword. She didn't hesitate, she fired a shot into the intruder's chest, sending the lifeless body tumbling to the deck. Turning back to survey the fight, she saw Smitty near the mast, wielding his Maelstrom mastery like a weapon. With fluid precision, he conjured a whip of seawater, striking a pair of attackers and hurling them skyward before sending them crashing into the sea with a second strike. Another raider tried to flank Harmon, but Smitty lashed out with his second water whip, smashing the enemy to the deck.

A second bomber stepped onto the rope bridge. Sophie retook aim, her vision swimming. Her first shot went wide. The second missed entirely. She tried to fire a third, but her pistol clicked…*empty*. With a frustrated growl, she ejected the spent cartridges and quickly loaded two more bullets from her jacket. As she fumbled to snap the cylinder shut, Captain Kidd fired his rifle, hitting the bomber with two well-placed shots and sending him careening into the sea.

"Another one down," Kidd muttered. "Stay sharp Girlie!"

The fighting paused as the attackers on the rope bridge and deck suddenly parted, stepping aside to allow a new figure to cross. The atmosphere shifted as an ominous presence swept across the Stormfang. A woman emerged, walking calmly across the bridge. She wore a tan outfit reminiscent of a beekeeper's suit, though the material was completely opaque. The only visible features were her glowing red eyes, gleaming with malevolent intent through her mask. Each and every raiding pirate on the deck immediately ceased their attacks and knelt before her.

"Where is Annabelle Salazar?" the woman demanded, her voice cold and commanding.

Smitty, ever defiant, raised his voice from his position near the mast. "Annabelle ye say, never heard of her." he taunted.

The woman, Mage, tilted her head in irritation. "You don't say," she muttered, summoning a shadowy blade into her hand. Without further ceremony, she issued her command: "Leave none of them alive."

With that, she dropped to the floor like she stepped through a trapdoor.

The raiders roared as they resumed their attack, surging forward with renewed ferocity. Lepele, Smitty, and Harmon fought back with everything they had, while Sophie and Captain Kidd provided cover fire from the bridge. Sophie fired quickly at anyone daring to ascend the access stairs, taking down attackers so fast she barely had time to reload. She silently cursed her lack of man to use fire or shockwave bullets, those would have made things much easier.

Mage reappeared without warning behind Smitty. Before he could react, she placed her hand on his back.

"Curse of Shadows." she called, releasing a pulse of dark magic directly into his body.

Smitty screamed, collapsing to his knees as black, shadowy tendrils spread across his back. He coughed violently, expelling dark mist from his mouth as if it were choking him from the inside.

"NO, Smitty!" Kidd shouted, his voice cracking with panic. He opened fire wildly, desperately searching for Mage amidst the chaos.

The raiders pressed their advantage, driving towards the bridge. Sophie found herself in a relentless rhythm, fire, reload, fire, barely able to keep up. She fired at anyone who came near the stairs. Her head throbbed mercilessly. *I need mana bullets...* she lamented. Just one shockwave shot could give us breathing room... But there was no time for regrets. The song of battle was still playing, and it is far from the final stanza.

Harmon struggles to pull Smitty to his feet. Smitty is still violently coughing up thick, shadowy mist as if his body is rejecting a poison. Lepele slashes his way through the raiders, clearing a path with fierce precision while Harmon follows close behind. He pulls and fires one of the flintlock pistols into the face of a raider who tries to block their retreat.

"We have to make a stand on the bridge!" Lepele shouts, deflecting an incoming blade and kicking his opponent off the deck.

"Aye, mate," Harmon replies, his voice strained as he fires a shot that drops another attacker.

Suddenly, Mage rises from a shadow in front of them, her red eyes glowing malevolently through her veiled mask. She brandishes her shadow-forged sword and taunts, "Where do you think you're going?"

Lepele doesn't falter. Keeping his eyes locked on Mage, he calmly says to Harmon, "When I give the word... pull a Gimble."

Harmon hesitates for a moment, his hand trembling as he holds up Smitty's shadow material leaking from his mouth like he was some kind of macabre ashtray. "Aye," he replies, not entirely sure what Lepele has in mind.

With swift precision, Lepele angles his short sword to catch the sunlight, reflecting a blinding beam directly into Mage's masked face. She shrieks and recoils, momentarily disoriented.

"NOW!" Lepele shouts and delivers a powerful intensity-fueled kick to Mage's chest, knocking her flat onto the deck.

Harmon doesn't waste the opportunity. He drags Smitty to Lepele's left and unleashes his remaining bullets to clear the path. Sophie, stationed at the top of the access stairs, fires two well-placed shots, keeping the raiders at bay long enough for Harmon to haul Smitty onto the bridge. The first mate collapses next to Bobby, still convulsing and hacking up tendrils of Shadow.

"Get him stable!" Kidd orders from behind the helm, quickly reloading his rifle.

Before Lepele can ascend the stairs, Mage rises from a shadow behind him, slashing with her dark blade. He barely evades the strike, stumbling forward before twisting to face her.

"You picked the wrong fight today, *shadow witch*." Lepele growls, his eyes narrowing. He ignites his red Intensity magic and charges her, shoulder-first, catching her off guard. The impact drives her backward, but he doesn't stop there—he unleashes a flurry of rapid attacks, each strike imbued with glowing red magical force. Mage blocks and deflects as best she can, but she's forced to retreat, clutching a fresh wound on her abdomen where Lepele's blade found its mark.

"How...?" she gasps, her voice laced with disbelief. She presses a hand to her torn suit, trying to shield herself from the sunlight.

"Like I said...you picked the wrong one," Lepele replies coldly. "Eclipse Antonio Lepele, of Aurorium Kutora Mura."

Before he can finish her off, a blade swings at him from the side. He deflects it instinctively but finds himself surrounded by raiders. Mage slips into the shadows, disappearing amidst her supporters.

On the bridge, Sophie and Harmon work tirelessly to hold the access stairs. Sophie's pistol barks out shots as raiders attempt to rush them, while Harmon reloads as fast as his shaking hands allow. Captain Kidd, meanwhile, targets attackers on the deck below, covering Lepele as best he can.

"The other copper's trapped," Kidd says, slamming fresh rounds into his rifle.

Sophie yells out, "We've gotta help him!"

"Working on it," Kidd replies, taking a moment to make a high-pitched bird call. He then fires several precise shots into the crowd surrounding Lepele, clearing a path for him to escape.

Lepele doesn't hesitate. He sprints toward the bridge, cutting down a few stragglers along the way. Mage appears before him again, rising from the deck like a spectre. Before she can attack, a crack echoes across the ship, a bullet from Kidd's rifle tears into her side, causing her to stumble. Lepele pushes past her, his focus on the access stairs.

Mage glares up at Kidd, her red eyes seething with hatred. She sinks into the shadows once more, vanishing from sight. Lepele reaches the bridge and raises his hands to signal he's not an enemy.

"Don't shoot!" he yells before rushing up the stairs. **"Captain Kidd!!"** He screams a warning while pointing his short sword at Captain Kidd.

Kidd turns at the sound of his name, but just as he does, something catches his eye, a tan, gloved hand reaching for him. Mage materializes from a shadow near the helm and lays her hand on him.

"Curse of Shadows," she intones, unleashing dark energy into him.

Kidd screams in agony, dropping his rifle as the shadow magic courses through his body. Lepele lunges at her, but Mage vanishes again, retreating into the floor before he can reach her.

She reappears near the rope bridge leading to the attacking ship. With an air of triumph, she daintily takes a seat and begins to laugh, her ominous voice echoing across the deck through every shadow.

[----- ⚓ -----]

Annabelle stumbles slightly, her teeth rattling in her skull despite the healing she received from Regina. "She needs more practice with that spell," she mutters, shaking her head. Still, she's grateful, after that brutal fight with the blue-haired "hussy," her whole body felt like it had been put through a wringer. She grabs a bag of rifle bullets from the armory, noting the grim scene inside. Gimble's lifeless body lies covered by a tarp from the armory, and the rest of the crew looks battered and worn, with stab wounds and bruises marking nearly everyone. The armor room, it seemed, had been both a shelter and a deathtrap.

She heads for the bridge, her footsteps steady due to the healing she received from Regina's Earthbloom healing. As she reaches the main deck, she hears a chilling, familiar laugh echo through the air. Her stomach ties itself in knots. She knows that laugh... It's that damn Shadow wench! Her eyes scan the scene, raiders grouped around the access stairs to the bridge, taking potshots at the bridge where Sophie and Harmon are ducking from the shots while returning shots of their own.

Annabelle doesn't hesitate. She draws her fancy pistol from Verdantia and opens fire, the crack of each shot catching the attackers off guard. They scatter from the access stairs, retreating toward the masts. Annabelle sprints up to join Sophie and Harmon, their weapons clutched in readiness.

"No need to fear! Annabelle is ..." she starts, but her words falter when she spots Kidd and Smitty. Both men are on the deck behind the helm, writhing and coughing up thick, shadowy mist. Her heart sinks. And then she sees her. The red-eyed witch responsible for it all...*Mage*, wearing a light brown ... outfit that keeps the sun from burning her body. She sits smugly on the main deck, near the rope bridge, her laugh echoing from every shadow as if this were all a hilarious game.

Rage ignited in Annabelle like a storm at sea.

She clenched her fists. "Oh, it's her... that shadow-wielding **HEFFER!**" she roared in fury.

335

Then—a voice. Deep. Otherworldly. Familiar, it rang in her mind, encouraging her. *"Ye canna allow this, Bella. Grant us freedom... and we'll deliver the punishment these fools deserve."*

It struck something primal within her. Burning. Angry. Deadly.

Annabelle's hand snapped to her necklace. "Aye," she snarled, her voice full of venom, her anger sharpening into focus.

She fed mana into the necklace, not with strain, but ease. The artifact drank deep, but now her pool ran deeper.

Praise Chaos!

The Goddess had blessed her with power to spare. What once drained her now felt like nothing more than a gulp.

The world held its breath.

A frigid wind swept across the deck. Mist coiled up from the floorboards, curling around her boots. Somewhere within the fog, the ship's bell began to toll...slow, heavy, funereal.

Sophie felt her blood run cold. Whatever Annabelle was doing...something. Whatever she was going to do, it was powerful.

Please, ancestors, she begged silently. *Let this turn the tide.*

The mist thickened. The bell tolled again.

And then...they came.

Thirteen figures emerged from the fog, silent and spectral, taking formation behind their captain. Bone and rot, seaweed and gold teeth, dressed in the ragged remains of long-dead buccaneers. Rusted cutlasses. Jagged pikes. Chains. Hooks. Even anchors dragged behind them like war trophies.

At her right stood one taller than the rest. He said nothing, only nodded once.

The Corsair. Her First Mate.

Annabelle turned to the invaders who dared sully her deck. Her eyes...black, bottomless voids...flashed with green fire as she raised her arm.

"DEFEND ME SHIP AND KILL... 'EM ALL!"

"Belle, no!" Kidd rasped from the deck, still choking on the shadow rot devouring his lungs.

But Annabelle didn't flinch. She gripped the necklace tighter. The green glow pulsed brighter.

And then, the silence was shattered.

With a deafening scream, The Corsairs descended upon the raiders like a nightmare unchained.

Corsetti lunged from the mist and drove his rusted blade through a man's chest, the steel scraping bone with a screech. Behind him, Ada blitzed past, caught a raider mid-swing, and snapped his neck with one skeletal hand. She tossed the corpse aside like a doll, then speared the next through the throat as he fell.

Winky locks onto Eclipse Lepele and runs towards him with death on his mind.

"Oi Scallywag!" Annabelle calls out, stopping the Corsair *dead* in his tracks, "All these raiders on me deck and ye go after the *one* copper I *like*?" She turns to look at him and says, "Get yer tail back to what I told ye!"

Winky hangs his head in shame and says, "Sorry, Cap'n," through his connection to her through her necklace. Before pointing to a raider dressed in black and asking, "Can I take him?"

"Aye," Annabelle says back, her voice full of disapproval like an irritated parent, "the ones in black, Winky, only the ones in black!"

"Aye, Cap'n," Winky replies before throwing his cutlass into the raider's chest and leaping on top of him, knocking him down and then pulls his cutlass with a triumphant laugh before slashing another raider.

"Hey, pirate girl!" Lepele calls to Annabelle from the bridge, "What the hell was that?!?"

"Aye, sorry, copper," Annabelle says with a fun yet murderous grin. "They don't get out much, and ye know old habits die hard."

The undead Corsairs tear into the raiders with ruthless, almost joyful brutality.

To Sophie's horror, they didn't just kill…they relished it.

One Corsair barreled straight into a knot of defenders, heedless of their blades. Steel rang against bone and rotten flesh, but the creature didn't slow. When it reached them, it drove its cutlass into one raider's gut, lifted him like a rag doll, and hurled him into the others, toppling the group in a heap.

Then, with a shriek that sounded more like laughter than rage, it leapt onto the pile, hacking and stabbing with wild, gleeful abandon.

The living fought back with desperate fury, but their weapons were useless. Swords bit into ribs, tore through limbs, but the dead did not falter.

One raider lunged from behind, ramming a spear through a Corsair's torso. For a moment, he thought it had worked.

Until the skeleton turned.

It reached down, pulled the spear free with a sickening crack, and snapped it in half across its knee, a bone-rattling sound that echoed like laughter. Then it turned on the man.

With a single slash, it carved off the raider's mask.

What lay beneath, something, ignited the Corsair's rage. It kicked the man to the deck and fell upon him, hacking and stabbing long after his body stopped moving.

When it was done, the creature threw back its head and howled at the morning sky…not in victory, but in fury.

"Aye, Marlo," Annabelle called from the stairs, her voice full of encouragement. "Make 'em feel yer fury."

Sophie shivered.

Annabelle had never been the kindest girl, especially not to her, but this... this is different.

She wasn't giving orders anymore.

She was enjoying it.

Watching her undead crew rip the enemy to pieces, Annabelle didn't look like a commander.

She looked like a queen at her blood-drenched coronation.

Annabelle began to sing.

Her voice was low and steady, like she was back on deck, tightening ropes, trimming sails, working the lines as if nothing were wrong at all.

Oh ho ho and a bottle full of rum…

Oh ho ho, and the work is never done…

Sophie froze. Horror prickled across her skin.

The Corsairs were making a sound, not humming, exactly, but something close. A low, guttural resonance rattled from their skeletal throats, like wind groaning through

337

hollow bones. It rose and fell in time with Annabelle's shanty, not random noise, but rhythm. A chant. A corrupted echo.

As if the dead were singing with her.

All while mercilessly carving through the enemy.

Sophie clutched the edge of the rail. Her lips moved without thought, a reflex buried deep in memory.

"Ancestors, please protect me from the evil that I see…"

She whispered it again. And again.

The dead kept singing and kept killing.

The Corsair named Ruby dragged a raider across the deck by his ankles, his screams echoing like a dying gull's cry. Something about the sound seemed to offend her.

She stopped, turned, and began stabbing him, again and again, with her decayed cutlass. Each strike was more frenzied than the last. She didn't stop when the screaming did. She gave him one final thrust, as if to make sure he stayed silent forever.

"Fall back! FALL BACK!" A raider shrieked from the chaos, but it was already too late.

The Corsairs gave no quarter.

If anything, they hunted harder once the prey tried to run.

The moment the formation broke, the dead surged like a riptide of cutlasses, pikes, hooks, and anchors. Raiders who turned to flee were cut down from behind, cleaved mid-step, impaled without warning, devoured by steel and fury.

There was no mercy. No hesitation.

No code of honor among the dead.

Only the unrelenting pursuit of death.

The voice of The Corsair, her First Mate, echoed in Annabelle's mind. Deep. Hollow. It sounded familiar, like she had listened to it before.

"What about the laughing one, Captain?"

Annabelle's lips curled into a cruel grin. She slowly raised her hand and pointed across the deck.

Mage.

Her red eyes narrowed in recognition.

"Do yer worst," Annabelle said, her voice dark with satisfaction. "She's earned it."

Three Corsairs turned their burning sockets toward Mage. Their jaws clicked in eerie unison, like teeth grinding in anticipation. They began to advance through the mist…slow, steady, inevitable.

Mage rose to her feet, spear forming in her hand with a flick of her wrist. "You think you can challenge the darkness?" she growled.

The Corsairs hissed and charged, their movements wild and ragged. Mage parried the first strike with precision and drove her spear through a ribcage. She fell into the shadows around her and appeared behind Ada.

She places her hand on Ada's back and casts "Curse of Shadows!"

No reaction. No magic. No effect.

Annabelle's laughter rang from the access stairs, mocking and gleeful. "Hold still, darling! They just want to play!"

Mage's jaw tightened. Her stance shifted, defensive now. The Corsairs pressed in, relentless.

And then the raid descends into panic.

From across the deck, raiders began to scream.

"Retreat! RETREAT!"

Their lines broke. Fear overtook discipline. One by one, they turned and fled toward the rope bridge, chased by the sound of undead footsteps and blood-drenched steel.

"Captain, they're retreating!" Biscuits called out, eager but unsure what to do next.

Annabelle's smile widened, wicked and triumphant.

"Then what're ye waitin' for?" she growled. "Ye know where they're goin'."

"Aye, Captain!" Biscuits howled with a chuckle.

The Corsairs surged forward with savage purpose, their rotted boots pounding the deck as they gave chase. Anyone they came across was cut down without mercy.

Blood-curdling screams erupted across the water, from the deck of the Accursed Raider, as Annabelle's undead crew spilled aboard like a plague of brutality.

Meanwhile, Sophie rushed to where Kidd and Smitty lay, hoping to find something to ease their suffering. Shadows poured from Kidd's mouth with each ragged breath, his body writhing under the weight of the curse.

She glanced back toward the chaos, watching Mage dart through the mist, her form flickering as she vanished and reappeared across the deck.

Sophie frowned. "Why doesn't she just... teleport away?"

"Shadow walk." Lepele corrected, supporting Smitty's slumping weight.

His eyes stayed on Mage.

"That magic's from Umbrathorn. I've got Shadows and Sentinels who use it. During the day, it's much weaker."

On the deck, Annabelle's patience snapped. "Hold still, ye cursed heifer! Stop runnin'!"

Her undead crew swung wildly at Mage, missing again and again as the shadow-wielder vanished and reappeared like smoke in the wind.

"*WHAT ARE YE SCALLYWAGS DOIN' OUT THERE?!*" Annabelle barked through their mental link.

"Sorry, Captain! She keeps slippin' away!" Hollow-Leg Pete answered sheepishly.

Lepele scanned the battlefield. Bodies everywhere. Blood. Shadow. Fire. And Mage, still moving, but slower. Her suit was torn in places. Thin lines of sunlight crisscrossed the deck like glowing blades.

"Pirate girl!" he shouted. "She can't shadow walk if someone's holding her!"

Annabelle froze. A wicked grin spread across her face, her blackened eyes flashing.

"Aye," she said softly. "Thanks for the advice, mate."

Ada struck like a guillotine.

She tackled Mage from behind, slamming her into the deck. The others pounced, tearing at her suit, exposing pale flesh to the burning sunlight.

Mage shrieked, her skin burned where the sun burned away her shadows. Her magic flickered and failed. Shadows peeled off her body like smoke retreating from flame.

Pinned beneath a ring of undead, she screamed, and kept crying out in pain not from the brutal cutting but the sunlight burning her skin.

Suddenly, an explosion rocked the Accursed Raider, followed by two more in rapid succession. Fire tore through the ship's midsection, ripping up the deck and hurling debris into the sea like cannon shot.

Annabelle blinked, then felt it. The familiar, cold pull as two of her Corsairs returned to rest within the necklace.

"Sorry about that, Captain," came Corsetti's voice, echoing faintly in her mind. "Me body got blown up when I lit their fuel barrels."

"Aye, same here," Winky added. "Did what we could, though."

Annabelle sighed, but smiled.

"*'Tis no problem, boyos. Ye did good*" she said gently. "*Now rest... 'til I needs ye again.*"

Captain Kidd gasped, choking on shadows that poured from his mouth like smoke. His trembling hand reached out, grabbing the sleeve of Sophie's jacket.

His eyes, clouded with darkness, locked onto hers.

He looked at her. Then at Annabelle. Then back again. Silently pleading: *Ye gotta stop her... before she loses control of herself.*

Sophie nodded and turned, steeling herself.

Annabelle stood shrouded in mist, flanked by two of her Corsairs. The deck groaned beneath them, water rushing in below.

"Uh, Anna?" Sophie called gently as she approached. "I think it's time to stop."

Annabelle turned slowly. Her eyes were pitch black—bottomless, unreadable. A grin stretched across her face like she was winning at a card game.

"Sorry, Copper. Can't hear ye right now. Bit busy."

"Annabelle," Sophie said, firmer now. "The ship's sinking. We need to go. Now."

The Corsair's voice drifted through Annabelle's mind, deep and fog-wrapped. "She's right, Bella. I can feel yer ship sinkin' into the sea..."

Annabelle's jaw tensed. Her fingers curled tightly around her necklace.

Then she sighed, like a child told to put down a favorite toy, and muttered, "Fine."

Her voice sharpened through the bond, "Alright, ye lot! Get back to the Stormfang. Cut the rope bridge. And make sure that Mage wench ends up in the drink."

She paused, then added, almost lazily, "Oh... and stab her a few more times. For good measure."

"Aye, Captain!" came the gleeful reply.

The Corsairs marched across the rope bridge. In seconds, it was severed, planks and rope crashing into the sea.

Mage didn't scream as they tossed her overboard, but the splash when she hit the water closed the verse with a powerful short stanza.

[----- ⚓ -----]

After the Stormfang is freed from the Accursed Raider, Annabelle commands her corsairs to sweep the ship for any remaining stowaways before returning to their eternal slumber in her necklace. Their spectral figures dissolve into the rising mist, leaving only silence in their wake.

Annabelle surveys the aftermath. The ship is battered and taking on water, groaning under the weight of its wounds. The casualties and damage reports quickly filter in. Four crewmembers escaped unharmed, but three have minor injuries, cuts and bruises from flying debris or being thrown around during the fight. Two others have significant injuries that will need immediate treatment, and two…Gimble and Phelps…have passed beyond the veil.

Captain Kidd and Smitty are both gravely afflicted by what Lepele calls the "curse of shadows." He grimly informs the crew that without intervention, the curse will slowly consume them from the inside out. Sophie stands nearby, still recovering from mana depletion. Her exhaustion is etched across her face.

Among the passengers, Brother Marcus and Lisa are bruised but otherwise stable. Regina is visibly shaken but unharmed, a testament to the guardian spirit, Galahad. Lepele, though battered and bloodied from his fight with Mage and the boarding party, insists he's fit to continue.

The weight of responsibility settles heavily on Annabelle's shoulders. With both the captain and first mate incapacitated, command of the Stormfang falls to her. She presses her lips into a tight line and grips the railing, staring at the broken ship around her. The deck is littered with shattered wood, blood stains, and discarded weapons. Cannon fire from the Crazy Horse and Raider has left holes in the hull, and the ship is already taking on water.

"Acting Captain Salazar," Lepele says, stepping beside her, his voice level but weary.

"Aye," Annabelle replies quietly, her mind racing. She may have laughed in the face of danger before, but now, everyone's lives on board depend on her following decisions. She doesn't know exactly what to do yet, but one thing is sure…they don't have much time.

Chapter 24

Journal Entry May 4th, 1910

After a hard-fought battle, the Avatars and I find ourselves aboard the heavily damaged Stormfang in the middle of the sea near the mid-point between Verdantia and Magitekopolis, where no suitable ports or islands are close enough to warrant changing course. With Captain Lowe and Mr. Smith incapacitated, Annabelle Salazar becomes the ranking officer aboard the ship, responsible for prioritizing the crew's actions and making decisions.

The battle left us with severe casualties and the loss of the ship's runner, Mr. Gimble. His bravery and sacrifice will not be forgotten. Phelps, another valued crew member, also fell in the skirmish, a stark reminder of the high stakes we face. The ship itself took significant damage, with both the port and starboard shields rendered inoperable and sections of the hull breached by cannon fire. We are taking on water, and repairs must be made quickly to prevent further deterioration.

The combat skills of our enemies, particularly Isabella and the enigmatic Mage, were formidable. Isabella, with her mechanical enhancements and cold, detached manner, proved to be a relentless adversary. Her single-minded focus on eliminating Annabelle and me raises questions about the true extent of her programming and the forces behind her. Mage's shadow manipulation and her brutal efficiency in battle have left both Captain Lowe and Mr. Smith cursed, their conditions worsening by the hour.

Regina displayed remarkable bravery and resourcefulness, using her abilities to create barriers and heal the wounded, though she struggles with the emotional toll of our losses. Lisa, too, has shown great fortitude, her healing magic providing much-needed relief to our injured comrades. Sophie, despite severe mana depletion, fought valiantly from the crow's nest, her sharpshooting pivotal in damaging the enemy ships.

Annabelle's use of her necromancy was both awe-inspiring and terrifying. Summoning her undead crew turned the tide in our favor, yet it was clear she was inexperienced with such magic. The blacked-out eyes and the sheer ferocity of her summoned wraiths instilled fear even among our own ranks. There is a tragic weight to the souls bound to her necklace, a reminder of the fine line she treads between power and peril.

With the attacking ships either sunk or heavily damaged, we have repelled our attackers, but at significant cost. Supplies are running low, and the morale of the crew is frayed. We must find a way to navigate to safety, repair the Stormfang, and tend to our wounded. The avatars and I will need to work closely with Annabelle, guiding her decisions and supporting her leadership during this critical time.

[----- ⚓ -----]

"So, why don't we just use the pumps?" Annabelle asked Sparks as the two sat in the galley's seating area.

"The pumps are underwater, Cap'n," Sparks explained, leaning forward with a serious expression. "We can't fire them up like this. Plus, the hull's been breached pretty badly, water'll just rush right back in. We've gotta patch it first."

"Great," Annabelle muttered, crossing her arms. "How long's that gonna take?"

"Dunno," Sparks admitted, shaking his head. "I can't tell how extensive the damage is with all that water down there."

"Oh, for the love of the sea..." Annabelle sighed, then fixed Sparks with a determined look. "I need a solution, Sparks. Anything ye got."

"I'll come up with somethin', Cap'n. Just gimme some time." Sparks promised, his mind already racing through options.

"Don't take too long. Tis a long swim to port," Annabelle replied, running a hand through her hair and lowering her head into her hands, hoping for a moment of silence.

"Cap'n?" a voice interrupted her thoughts. It was Gary, the ship's doctor.

Annabelle groaned internally before raising her head to meet his gaze. Gary was haggard, his clothes stained with blood—not his own, thankfully.

"Aye, Doc. What's up?" she asked.

"I need one of yer sisters," Gary began, his voice strained. "Bobby's in bad shape. He'll die if his wounds aren't healed soon."

Annabelle raised an eyebrow. "Okay, and?" she prompted. "Just tell Lisa you need her help. Regina's busy with Copper Lepele."

"She say *she busy cookin'*," Gary grumbled. "But this ain't somethin' that can wait."

Annabelle frowned. "What about the Cap'n and Smitty? Any chance of them beatin' that curse on their own?"

Gary shook his head wearily. "Both of 'em are down hard. Coughing up shadows. I moved 'em to the observation deck, Copper Lepele said extra sunlight might hold the curse off for a while."

Annabelle checked her pocket watch. "Almost sundown," she muttered.

Gary sighed heavily, standing up. "Guess I'd better see how Copper and your motor-mouth sister are faring."

Annabelle bit her tongue, suppressing the urge to snap at him. They needed the doctor, after all.

"About the green missy?" Gary asked, hesitating.

"Aye, I'll handle it," Annabelle replied, waving him off.

Gary nodded and left, leaving her momentarily alone in the seating area. Before she could fully relax, Marcus appeared, his arm in a blood-spotted sling.

"Miss Annabelle," he began, stepping forward cautiously.

"Nope. Nope," Annabelle interrupted, standing up quickly. The weight of command bore down on her like an anchor.

"But I just wanted to..."

"Nope. I'm busy, Brother Marcus. This'll have to wait," she cut him off, making her way toward the kitchen entrance. "Find me later."

"Of course," Marcus called after her as she hurried off. He couldn't help but think how hard it must be for someone as naturally chaotic as Annabelle to keep things in order.

Annabelle strode to the galley kitchen entrance and pushed the door open without knocking. The ship belonged to her for the moment, at least until Captain Kidd returned. Inside, Jeffie was chopping vegetables, while Lisa sliced meat, probably prepping a stew.

"Welcome, Cap'n!" Jeffie greeted her cheerfully. "To what do we owe yer company?"

"Gots business," Annabelle replied curtly. She gave him a hard stare, silently telling him to leave.

Jeffie got the message. "I need some celery from cold storage," he said, placing his knife in a table holster to secure it. He grabbed a box from a wall shelf and slipped out of the kitchen, giving Annabelle the space she clearly demanded.

The moment he was gone, Annabelle rounded on Lisa. "Doc Gary says ye don't wanna heal no one." she said bluntly, her patience already worn thin.

Lisa sighed and turned toward her avatar sister. "It is not that," she replied evenly. "We must do the meal service. Everyone needs to eat. Not everyone needs healing."

"Princess, no one can eat if they're dead," Annabelle shot back, narrowing her eyes.

"Gary's the ship's doctor. I just want to work in the kitchen, okay?" Lisa said, her tone sharpening as she turned her focus back to the task at hand.

Annabelle pressed a hand to her face in frustration. "What is wrong with ye now?"

Lisa glanced over her shoulder. "Look, Anna, I have got work to do. Can you just leave?"

Annabelle's temper flared. She stomped toward Lisa, standing toe-to-toe and glaring up into her forest-green eyes. "Listen to me, princess," she growled through clenched teeth. "Yer gonna go to the crew deck and heal everyone ye can. Then, you can cook to your heart's content. Got it?"

Lisa met Annabelle's fiery stare with defiance. "Or what? What are you going to do?"

Annabelle's fists twitched at her sides. She had sworn not to hit Lisa again, even gave her word as a privateer, no less. It had seemed like an easy promise to keep... until now. She clenched her jaw, resisting the urge, and instead grabbed Lisa's wrist.

"Anna, stop it!" Lisa protested, yanking back but not freeing herself from Annabelle's grip.

"Cap'n," Annabelle corrected, dragging her toward the door. "If yer gonna talk to me, you call me Cap'n or Captain Salazar."

"Stop it, Captain!" Lisa snapped, pulling harder, though her struggle was no match for Annabelle's strength. The shorter girl hauled her through the galley and into the seating area without slowing down.

"Dammit, Anna! I am going to fall!" Lisa shouted as they reached the stairs.

"Then hurry up," Annabelle retorted, charging down the steps without pause. "I don't have all day," she added, using her *proper voice to mock* Lisa's refined tone.

Lisa stumbled along, fuming, as Annabelle dragged her down to the crew berthing and utility decks. Annabelle finally stopped in front of the converted hospital area.

The injured lay in makeshift beds, with those in the worst condition, like Bobby and Ethan, resting on the lower bunks. Those with minor wounds were perched on the top.

"Wait... why are we here?" Lisa protested. "I need to get back to the kitchen!"

"Not happening," Annabelle said firmly. "Yer a healer. These folks need healing."

"I cannot..." Lisa whispered, shrinking into herself. The memories of finding Gimble dead and losing Brother Albert resurfaced like dark shadows in her mind. Her voice trembled. "What if I fail again? I keep messing up... It is better if I just work in the kitchen."

Annabelle's tone softened slightly, though she kept her commanding air. "Sure thing, missy. Just come with me," she said, brushing off Lisa's excuse. She led her into the room filled with injured crew. Lisa's eyes fell on Bobby and Ethan's pale, suffering faces. Reality hit hard.

"Oi, Cap'n!" the men called out in unison, their voices laced with biting pirate humor. "Welcome to the butcher's block!"

"Aye, thanks, boyos," Annabelle replied, smirking. "Miss Lisa here has somethin' to tell you. I've got other business to tend to, lots going on."

The crew sent her off with playful jeers. "Knock 'em dead, Cap'n!"

Lisa stood frozen, the weight of their eyes on her. Tears threatened to spill as she fought to find her voice. The sight of the battered crew, men clinging to their strength through humor, cut deep.

"What's up, Green Ma'am?" Bobby rasped, his voice light despite his injuries. He lay on the lower bunk, bandaged and pale, yet managed a crooked smile. "What'cha cookin'? Somethin' good, I hope. Could be me last meal, ye know."

His words shattered the shell Lisa had built around herself. Here was a man teetering between life and death, more concerned about a comforting meal than his wounds. Her tears began to flow uncontrollably. She tried to sniff them away, wiping at her face, but they kept coming.

"Excuse me for a moment," she whispered, her voice breaking.

"See, Bobby, ye went and made 'er cry," Popper teased from the top bunk. "She's too sad to cook now!"

Lisa fled the room, stepping into the damaged corridor. Annabelle was leaning against the wall, waiting for her.

"Well?" Annabelle asked, raising a brow.

Lisa responded with an obscene gesture hand gesture, then sighed in defeat. "Tell Jeffie he will have to handle kitchen duty by himself."

Annabelle grinned, shifting into a mock version of Lisa's proper voice. "Oh, what are you going to do, me dear sister?"

"I have healing work to do," Lisa answered, pulling a handkerchief from her purse to dry her eyes. Her expression hardened as she added, "Now do something about the ship sinking. I do not want to waste my time saving these men just for all of us to drown any way."

Annabelle scowled. "We're workin' on it, princess."

Lisa shot her an obscene gesture, this time with a smile.

"Oi, princess, yer not supposed to flip off the Cap'n, ye know," Annabelle teased.

Lisa shrugged, her smile widening, and headed back into the makeshift infirmary. The men turned to her expectantly.

"Alright, gentlemen," she began. "I have two things to tell you. First, I will not have time to cook today, so please be nice to Jeffie." She paused to smile warmly before continuing, "Second, I have been told that Earthbloom healing can hurt, a lot, especially when the injuries are bad. But I'll do my best to make it bearable. Bobby, shall we get started?"

"Aye," Bobby replied, his features brightening at the thought of relief. "What do ye need me to do?"

"Just hold on," Lisa said gently, focusing her Earthbloom senses on him. She surveyed his wounds carefully, preparing to create the spell circle that would begin the healing process.

[-----✿-----]

Eclipse Lepele and Regina began clearing Captain Kidd's operations room, removing furniture to make space for the ritual circles. They relocated anything portable, the journals, tools, and smaller maps, to the "Mermaid" room. Annabelle, acting as Captain, took the ship's coin chest and Kidd's ledger, the book he used to manage payments and income, to her own quarters on the stateroom deck.

Lepele straightened from where he'd been crouched near Kidd's large meeting table, holding a sheet of paper with a detailed ritual diagram. He handed it to Regina. "You said you're a good ritualist, right?" he asked, his tone carrying a hint of challenge.

Regina accepted the paper and examined the design. It was intricate, a fusion of five interlocked circles. The outermost was a containment circle, basic but crucial, tying the others together. Within it, a slightly smaller circle connected three internal ritual arrays arranged in a triangular pattern.

The first inner circle on the upper left is centered around a sunlight rune, designed to generate pure sunlight energy. The second, on the upper right, targets the body's arcane nexus, focusing on the flow and storage of mana. The third circle, positioned at the base of the triangle, is a balancing element, resembling a detailed yin-yang symbol. At the heart of the entire structure is a protection rune shaped like a fusion of a five-pointed star and a shield. Scattered throughout the design were more minor healing runes, steady but straightforward, to prevent the ritual from causing harm to the subject by keeping their body stabilized during the process.

Regina furrowed her brow as she absorbed the mechanics of the circle. "I think I can do it," she said, though uncertainty crept into her voice. "But... what is it?"

"It's a level-three cleansing circle, specifically for shadow walkers," Lepele explained. "I'll go over the details with you when we have more time. For now, you need to draw two of these, one under the Captain's bed and another where this table is."

He raps his knuckles against the table for emphasis. "While you handle that, Griffin and I will move the table and bring up a replacement bed from the crew berthing."

"Okay," Regina nodded, pulling a can of grease from her maintenance bag and cracking it open.

"Come on, Griffin. Help me with the table," Lepele ordered. Sophie silently took hold of the opposite end. Together, they released it from the floor's locking mechanism and lifted it free.

The two maneuvered the bulky table out of the operations room, passing behind the helm where Harmon wrestled with the wheel. The ship groaned beneath them, taking on more water and making steering a nightmare. Harmon gritted his teeth but gave them a brief nod as they passed.

Lepele and Sophie carefully descended the access stairs, now twisted with grim memories. Earlier that day, Annabelle had summoned her undead corsairs and turned them loose on the raiders, staining the decks with blood. They continued past the observation deck door, pausing only when they had to wrestle the table around a staircase that was just a little too narrow.

"Eclipse," Sophie finally spoke as they maneuvered the table onto the stateroom deck. "How do you know so much about that Shadow witch Mage?"

Lepele grunted, pushing the table forward. "I don't know *her*; just her magic," he clarified. "When you become an Eclipse, you have to understand the abilities of the Shadows and Sentinels under your command. I've got eight shadow walkers in my patrol."

They reached the storage room at the end of the hallway and laid the table down.

"That ritual I gave Regina," Lepele continued, inspecting the table's underside for any mechanism to fold it up, "is for cleansing shadow walkers who've overused their magic."

"Overused?" Sophie echoed, tilting her head as she removed one of the table legs. "Don't they just run out of mana?"

"Yes and no," Lepele said, loosening another leg. "Shadow walker magic has a corrupting effect. The more powerful the spells, the worse it gets. If they push too far, the corruption manifests, like that red glow in their eyes. Apex Garde is a shadow walker, and he says they can't allow themselves to become tier-three mages. At that point, they'd lose themselves entirely to the corruption."

"That magic system sounds awful," Sophie muttered, setting the detached leg aside.

"Magic always has its drawbacks," Lepele said with a sigh. "Look at your punch-and-kick magic. Overuse it, and you'll shatter your own bones."

Sophie pondered Lepele's words, recalling her mother's advice: *Don't use your Kiroku-Mbili spells to open a fight. Use them to finish it.* Lost in thought, she detached the last table leg from the top.

They carried the disassembled table to the "Seaweed Room" on the port side, storing the legs inside a wardrobe and laying the tabletop flat on the floor. Task complete, they headed back to the stairs leading to the crew decks.

"How many do you have in your patrol?" Sophie asked, breaking the silence as they climbed.

"Twelve Shadows and... seven Sentinels," Lepele replied, his voice faltering slightly.

"Sorry. I didn't think about..." Sophie trailed off, offering a quiet apology. He told her earlier that when his ship went down, the Sentinel he was traveling on was attacked, and he died in the attack.

Lepele shook his head. "No, it's fine," he said, his tone steady but distant.

They reached the crew and utility deck, a scene of wreckage and chaos from Annabelle and Regina's earlier battle with Isabella. The walls bore deep gashes, and debris was scattered everywhere. A sudden scream pierced the air, drawing their attention. Bobby cried out in pain as Lisa worked on his leg, her spell circle glowing in mid-air. She focused intensely on healing the shattered bones, her expression unflinching as the ritual circle around them pulsed with steady energy.

Lepele and Sophie exchanged a glance but didn't interrupt. They left Lisa to her work and crossed the hall to the sleeping quarters. Inside, they found a usable bed frame, a lower bunk whose top half had been smashed to pieces, leaving jagged remnants of its supports. Together, they lifted the frame and started back up the stairs.

The ship lurched suddenly, tilting forward and down. Both of them stumbled as water surged somewhere deep below deck, groaning through the ship's structure.

Sophie tightened her grip on the frame and tried to suppress a rising sense of panic. *Even if we save Kidd and Smitty... how are they supposed to fix this? We're sinking. We're going to drown out here...*

"Hey." Lepele's voice snapped her out of her thoughts. He was watching her, his gaze steady. "They have their job, and we have ours."

"But..." Sophie hesitated. "We're going to sink. How can you be so calm about this?"

Lepele took a slow breath and spoke with a calm certainty. "We might sink. That's true. But I'm talking to a girl who's met one of the twelve goddesses of the pantheon, and who had a conversation with her mother after she died." He shrugged lightly, giving her a small smile. "If anyone can get us through this, it's you four. Now, can you grab your end?"

Sophie blinked, the weight of his words settling over her like a warm reassurance. She nodded, tightening her grip on the bed frame. Together, they resumed their climb, step by step, carrying hope with them despite the storm threatening to swallow the ship whole.

[----- ⚓ -----]

Annabelle worked the crank of the improvised air pump in the hold, her muscles straining with each pull. Sparks had rigged up a diving system, weighted boots and a shoulder-mounted helmet, to explore the flooded hold. He'd warned her, repeatedly, that if she stopped cranking, he'd run out of air and die down there. They'd lost enough sailors already, so she kept going, pushing the heavy handle up and down like rowing with one oar.

She glanced around the hold, now nearly submerged. It looked like a lake had taken residence inside the Stormfang, and all hope of limping into port with just a flooded hold had vanished after the ship's last lurch forward. *We're not gonna make it,* she thought grimly, sweat beading on her brow.

"Acting Captain Salazar," came a voice from the stairwell door. Annabelle sighed. She didn't need to turn around to recognize it, Doc Gary. Probably here to dump more bad news on her. She'd been happier a moment ago, just mindlessly working the crank.

"Yes, Doc Gary?" Annabelle answered without looking at him. "Ye'll have to come around if ye wanna talk. I can't stop this crank unless we're okay with losin' Sparks."

Doc Gary circled around until he was in her line of sight. His face was somber, which was never a good sign. "I took another look at the Captain and Smitty."

"And?" Annabelle asked, still cranking steadily.

"I don't have a spell to cleanse them of that curse the shadow woman put on them," he admitted.

Annabelle's grip tightened. "How's that possible? Don't you have that cure-all magic or somethin'?"

Gary shook his head. "I can cure most afflictions, but curses are a different matter. The one on Kidd and Smitty is powerful, grinding up their insides, slow but deadly. The best hope we've got is the Copper's ritual. Maybe it'll wash the curse away."

"Hopefully," Annabelle echoed tersely. She didn't want to dwell on the idea of losing both Smitty and Kidd. "How's Lisa doin' with the healing?"

"Last I saw, she was nearly done with Bobby and will move on to Ethan next," Gary replied, offering at least one bit of good news.

Annabelle sighed and kept cranking. "Come on, Sparks, ye makin' any progress down there?" she muttered under her breath. Her arms burned with the effort, the repetitive motion growing more exhausting by the second. She turned to Gary, flashing a persuasive smile. "Hey, Doc, you wanna take over? It's a great workout."

Gary scratched the back of his neck awkwardly. "Ah... I've got things to fix in the infirmary. You know, just in case more bad stuff happens." He hurried off before Annabelle could press him further.

"Yer loss!" she called after him, trying to con him one last time. "This is premium exercise!"

He was gone in a flash, leaving her alone with the relentless pump. Another fifteen minutes crawled by before Sparks finally surfaced, climbing the ladder from the flooded hold in his waterlogged, makeshift diving gear. Annabelle exhaled in relief, letting go of the crank and shaking out her sore arms.

"Sparks!" she greeted him enthusiastically. "Tell me about me ship," she said, her voice slipping into her best commanding captain tone.

"It ain't good, Cap'n," Sparks began, pulling off his diving helmet. "The hull took a hell of a beating in that fight. The outer hull held up enough to keep us from completely sinking, but the inner hull's got multiple gashes and punch-outs."

Annabelle frowned. "So, how do we fix it?"

Sparks hesitated before giving a grim shake of his head. "I don't know if we can, Cap'n."

Annabelle's jaw tightened. "Sparks," she said firmly, "there ain't nothin' ye can't fix. Just tell me what ye needs."

Sparks sighed and glanced down at the flooded hold. "We've got us two problems," he explained, raising one finger. "First, we gotta drain the water from the hold." He raised a second finger. "Then we've gotta patch every hole in the inner hull to keep more water from rushin' in. Honestly, Cap'n, this ship needs a dry dock for repairs."

Annabelle sat down on a nearby crate, the weight of their predicament pressing down on her. Silence hung in the air as the hopelessness of the situation threatened to swallow her whole.

"Look at ye, givin' up without even tryin'," came an unfamiliar voice behind her. "I knew ye wasn't ready."

Annabelle whipped around to see Simba, the Goddess's pet monkey, crouched on the deck, idly playing with the water pooled around his feet. His orange eyes gleamed with malicious taunts.

"What are ye doin' here, monkey?" Annabelle growled, glaring at Simba. "I didn't give ye permission to come aboard me ship."

"I'm here because Mommy Chaos told me to keep an eye on ye," Simba replied, mocking her pirate accent with exaggerated flair.

Annabelle scowled. "Look, monkey, I'm busy. Why don't ye go play at the bottom of the sea or somethin'?"

"Ye know, I told Mommy Chaos ye weren't ready to be her avatar," Simba continued smugly. "Such a simple problem, and ye can't even solve it." He snickered, still imitating her speech.

"Simple problem?" Annabelle's temper flared. "Bah, beat it, monkey." She turned back to Sparks, who stood quietly waiting. "Sorry about that, mate."

"No problem," Sparks said with a shrug. "Regina talks to herself all the time. She once told me she was chattin' with someone called *Tiktik*. Thought it was just an imaginary friend." He paused, giving her a curious glance. "Didn't know ye had one too."

"I can promise ye, mate, he ain't me friend," Annabelle muttered darkly.

Behind her, Simba snickered. "I could make better friends than ye, girlie," he teased.

Annabelle clenched her jaw but ignored him. She had more pressing matters to deal with. "Anyways," she said, refocusing on Sparks, "back to fixin' the ship. What's the plan?"

"I just don't see how we can manage it, Cap'n," Sparks replied, shaking his head. "In a perfect world, we'd put the ship in dry dock to get her properly repaired."

"Dry dock? Sparks, ye sound like a shore-lover," Annabelle teased, trying to keep the mood light. "What's so great about dry dock anyway?"

Sparks gestured with his hands as he explained. "Dry dock's got cranes, Cap'n. Big ones. They lift the ship outta the sea, drain the water, and keep her stable while repairs get done to the hull, inside and out. After that, they lower her back into the water, good as new."

Simba snorted with laughter. "I bet ye won't figure it out, 'Anna,'" he mocked from behind her.

Annabelle ground her teeth in frustration but didn't give Simba the satisfaction of a response. Instead, she spoke aloud, her mind starting to churn with ideas. "So, all we need is a way to lift the ship outta the water long enough to drain it and patch the damage."

"Er... aye, Cap'n, but without a crane, I don't see how..." Sparks began before Annabelle cut him off with a wave of her hand.

"Mate, ye let me worry about the how," she said confidently. "Do ye have everything ye need to patch up the inner hull?"

"I think so, but I'd have to check to be sure." Sparks replied, scratching his chin.

"Good. Go check, then meet me on the bridge," Annabelle ordered.

"Aye, Cap'n," Sparks said with a salute, before hauling his underwater helmet and heading out of the hold.

[-----✿-----]

On the bridge, Sophie and Lepele carefully carried Smitty on a stretcher up from the observation deck. He was unconscious, the shadow curse slowly killing him from within. Wisps of dark, shadowy substance escaped his mouth and nose with each

350

labored breath. Once inside Captain Kidd's operations room, they laid him on the salvaged bed they'd secured with rope.

Annabelle stood at the doorway, her gaze heavy and full of sorrow. Captain Kidd, the closest thing she had to a father, lay on his own bed, shadow material flowing freely from his mouth and nose. Her heart ached as she shifted her eyes to Smitty, the ship's first mate and her Maelstrom Mastery teacher. Both men were suffering because of her. If not for the ambush that targeted her, they wouldn't be dying. Guilt pressed down on her like the weight of the sea.

A pair of warm, gentle hands wrapped around her own. Annabelle didn't need to look to know it was Regina comforting her.

"It'll be okay, Annabelle," Regina promised softly.

Annabelle squeezed Regina's hands and offered her a small smile. "I know. Thanks, girlie."

Once Sophie moved the stretcher out of the way, Lepele knelt beside the ritual circles they had prepared earlier. He touched the circles with his hand, activating them. Columns of light flared to life, particles of mana spiraling upward as the cleansing power enveloped both Captain Kidd and Smitty. The ritual began burning away the shadow mana inside their bodies, hopefully purging the curse entirely.

Regina arranged her mana into Earthbloom form and listened to her *sense*, surveying the two men. She saw the shadowy curse being stripped away in the ritual's light, but the damage it had already done was severe. Their organs were ravaged, ground down by the curse. Without this ritual, both men would have been dead by the morning.

For fifteen long minutes, the cleansing ritual continued, the light gradually fading as the circle's power completed its work. Smoke rose from the greasy lines of the ritual design as they broke down, leaving a faint residue on the floor. Regina quickly checked both men with her *sense* again and gasped. Though the curse itself had been purged, something was wrong. Small dark embers of shadow magic were reigniting inside their bodies, like smoldering coals ready to flare up again.

"Oh no…" she said absently. Without hesitation, she raised her hand and drew a red spell circle in the air. Runes for "Mend," "Heal," "Soothe," and "Strengthen" shimmered into existence. Standing over Captain Kidd, she targeted his organs with her healing magic and began the painstaking work of restoring his body.

Just then, Lisa made it up to the bridge fresh from her work the infirmary. "I'm here, Anna. What did you…" She stopped abruptly, her eyes widening as she took in the scene. Instinctively, she listened to her own *sense*, surveying the damage. What she saw confirmed what she feared: the men's insides looked as though they'd been through a meat grinder. The remnants of shadow magic were still present, slowly growing in strength. The cleansing ritual had weakened the curse, but the damage it had caused was immense. Worse still, with the curse gone, their bodies were beginning to fail.

Lisa didn't waste time. Without a word, she walked over to Smitty's bedside, weaving a red spell circle with six complex runes hovering in the air. Dodging the ropes securing the bed frame, she scanned his body carefully, assessing the extent of the internal damage. She focused her magic on stabilizing and repairing his shredded organs.

The two avatar sisters worked in quiet synchronization, the glow of their spell circles illuminating the room as they fought to keep Captain Kidd and Smitty alive.

Five minutes into the healing, both Captain Kidd and Smitty began to scream, the deep Earthbloom magic causing intense pain as it repaired their mangled insides. Healing beyond surface-level injuries was excruciating, but the fact that they were reacting at all meant progress.

"Well, at least that problem's fixed," Annabelle muttered, her eyes lifting with a glimmer of hope. She watched the color slowly returning to their faces. Soon, Kidd and Smitty would recover, and she could hand over command. Relief began to creep in, until Lisa crushed her hopes.

"It is not solved," Lisa said, finishing the healing on Smitty's heart and moving to his lungs. "The curse is still there. It is gaining strength even now."

"Oh no…" Lepele murmured, his brow furrowing in frustration. "I'd hoped the level-three cleansing would destroy it entirely, but it looks like it only forced the curse to retreat."

Annabelle's hope faltered. "But… they're gonna get better, right?"

"No," Lepele said gravely. "we'll have to keep cleansing and healing them until we reach a proper ethereal healer, someone who can completely burn the curse out."

Annabelle frowned. "Why not just keep cleansin' 'em? Then we wouldn't have to keep patchin' 'em up."

Lepele shook his head. "We can't. The ritual puts a huge strain on their arcane nexus. We have to wait at least six hours before doing it again. Otherwise, it'll do serious damage to their mana core, and repeated cleansings too soon would kill them outright."

Lisa glanced up from her work. "And during those six hours, their bodies will break down. Healing them will feel like being put through a meat grinder, then getting stitched back together over and over." She hesitated before continuing quietly, "Maybe we should consider just letting them go, like Gimble and…"

"**NO!**" Annabelle roared, her voice like thunder. "We willna be doin' any of that! Ye just keep doin' yer flower healing!"

"I am just saying…" Lisa tried again gently, "this is going to be torture for them, Anna. That might be crueler than…"

"Than what? Letting that wench's curse grind them up from the inside out?" Annabelle snapped, her fury flaring. She glared at Kidd, the thought of losing him cutting deep into her chest. Memories of their trials since the lifeboat incident swirled through her mind, each one fueling her anger and determination.

Lisa felt Annabelle's raw emotion like a tidal wave. She sighed and relented. "You are right, Anna. Forget I said anything."

Annabelle took a deep breath, steadying herself. "Come on, everyone," she said, her voice softer now. "Let's give Regina and Lisa room to work." She bit her tongue before calling Lisa *Princess*. The girlie is working hard to save Smitty, she didn't deserve Annabelle's ire.

Annabelle, Sophie, and Lepele left the operations room and made their way to the galley's seating area. Annabelle sat heavily at the table closest to the wall, burying her head in her hands. The weight of the entire ship rested on her shoulders, and for once, she had no quip or retort. Silence clung to her like a storm cloud.

Sophie watched her with quiet concern. Annabelle loved to talk, when she wasn't, things were dire. Respecting her space, Sophie turned her attention to the schematic Regina had used to draw the ritual circles. She traced the intricate lines with her eyes, trying to make sense of the symbols and runes.

"Do you know how to read that?" Lepele asked, breaking the silence.

"I can see it's a combination ritual," Sophie said, though her uncertainty crept into her voice.

"Here, let me show you," Lepele offered, holding out his hand.

Sophie passed him the schematic, and the two sat beside Annabelle. Lepele laid the diagram flat on the table and began explaining, tracing his finger around the largest circle.

"This is the containment circle," he said. "It keeps the ritual's effects confined within its boundaries." He moved his finger to the inner circle that intersected three smaller circles. "This is the joining circle. See how it touches the other three? It blends their effects together."

He pointed to the first of the smaller circles. "This one has a sunlight rune. By itself, this circle would just emit a blast of sunlight." He moved to the next. "This is a targeting circle, it focuses the spell on the subject's arcane nexus: the parts of the body that generate and channel mana." Finally, he traced the last of the three. "This is the blending circle. It combines the effects of the sunlight and targeting circles. In short, the ritual directs sunlight energy at the subject's arcane nexus to cleanse it. The rest of the sigils provide healing and stabilization, preventing the ritual from killing the subject."

Sophie stared at the schematic, absorbing every word. *Regina knew all this without any explanation...* she thought, her mind racing. *How much does that girl really know?*

Annabelle lifted her head from her hands and glanced at the schematic Lepele was explaining. Sparks' words echoed in her mind, *cranes that could lift the ship out of the water.* A spark of an idea flickered. "Let me see that," she said, tugging the paper from Lepele and Sophie.

She spread it out on her own table, deep in thought. *What kind of Maelstrom spell could I use to lift the ship and hold it up long enough for the water to drain? A waterspout... or multiple waterspouts?* Annabelle clenched her jaw in frustration. *If only Smitty were here, he'd have just the right spell for this.* She cursed under her breath.

A sudden burst of mocking laughter echoed through the room. Annabelle tensed and didn't have to look to know who it was.

"If only ye'd done like Mommy Chaos told ye and learned yer magic," Simba taunted, his voice grating as he imitated her patois. "I knew ye couldna do it! Yer the worst avatar, Captain Salad-jar!" He cackled and rolled on a nearby table, clutching his belly. "Ye'll probably end up killin' the other avatars too!"

"Stupid monkey," Annabelle muttered under her breath, trying to block him out.

Marcus and Sparks entered the galley, approaching Lepele and Sophie. Sparks carried a weary but determined look, while Marcus's arm remained in a sling. They sat at a table near Lepele, and Annabelle gave them a distracted wave, still turning the idea over in her mind. Simba's laughter buzzed in the background like an annoying insect she could not swat.

"Hello, Miss Annabelle," Marcus greeted warmly.

Annabelle acknowledged him with another wave, but her thoughts were racing, and she didn't say anything. Time felt like it was slipping away, every minute bringing the Stormfang closer to a parking slip at the bottom of the sea. She needs a solution, and she needs it fast.

A few moments later, Lisa and Regina arrived, entering the seating area mid-conversation.

"But why do you use so many runes?" Regina asked, curious about Lisa's Earthbloom magic. Regina had found she could cast Earthbloom spells efficiently with just four runes. Yet Lisa often used six, sometimes seven. To Regina, it seemed like an unnecessary effort.

"Because more runes let you fine-tune your spells," Lisa explained. "If you use too few, it's like chopping vegetables with a spoon. You can do it, but the results will not be quite right."

Lisa rubbed her hands absently, recalling the sting of punishment from her training days. "My Earthbloom teacher used to smack my hands with a wooden spoon if she caught me casting with fewer than five runes."

Regina's eyes widened in shock. "She sounds like a terrible teacher." she said, cringing at the thought of being hit for a mistake.

"She was... dedicated to her standards." Lisa replied cautiously, defending her former teacher without outright lying.

Annabelle glanced up briefly, listening to their exchange while still puzzling over the idea of using a Maelstrom spell. As the others talked, Simba's mocking words continued to needle at the edges of her mind. She clenched her fists. *I'll show him. I'll show all of them.*

The seed began to take root in her thoughts.

Lisa and Regina sat near the group as Acting Captain Salazar stood, seizing the room's attention.

"Listen up, everyone! I gots me a plan," Annabelle announced, her voice full of confidence. "The way I sees it, we need to get the ship fixed now."

"Wow, real genius insight," Sophie quipped, her tone dripping with sarcasm.

Annabelle ignored the comment, brushing off Sophie's negativity. She didn't have the time or patience for it right now. "So here's how it's gonna work. Everyone here's gonna have themselves a job. Lisa, ye'll use yer magic to push the water out of the hold through the deck access."

"Okay," Lisa said, though her brow furrowed in thought. "But more water just come back rushing back in?"

Annabelle waved her hand dismissively. "I'll get to that," she said, brushing aside another potential roadblock. "Regina, Lepele, and everyone else who can move will help Sparks patch up the inner hull once the water's gone."

"Wait." Sophie crossed her arms. "What are you gonna be doing?"

Annabelle grinned, leaning forward. "Glad ye asked, Copper. I'm gonna lift the ship up into the air and hold it there while ye all work on the repairs."

A wave of protests broke out instantly. Everyone began demanding how exactly she intended to do that, except for Sparks, who remained quiet and respectful. Annabelle appreciated that. He wasn't here to drown her in negativity like the others.

"Don't ye worry about that!" Annabelle said confidently, holding up a hand to silence them. "Don't ye trust ole Cap'n Salazar?" she added, mimicking one of Captain Kidd's favorite sayings to persuade the crew.

"Nope," Sophie deadpanned without hesitation.

"You are not that good at magic," Lisa pointed out bluntly.

"I think you can do it," Regina said softly, trying to support her friend, though a shadow of doubt lingered in her mind. She'd never seen Annabelle pull off anything remotely close to this scale before.

Marcus and Sparks remained silent. Sparks, ever the team player, didn't add to the negativity. Marcus, on the other hand, felt it wasn't his place to openly question Annabelle's orders as her guide.

Simba's mocking laughter rang out, grating against Annabelle's nerves like nails on a chalkboard. "Ye've done it again, Cap'n Salad-jar!" he taunted, rolling on the table and clutching his sides in hysterics.

Annabelle tensed, her jaw tightening. She wasn't about to let a damn monkey or anyone else derail her plan. "Listen," she said, her voice firm. "I know ye have yer doubts, but trust me…I will get it done."

The room fell into an uneasy silence, the lack of protests momentarily boosting Annabelle's confidence. She took it as confirmation that her leadership was shining through.

Sophie blinked in disbelief. *Does she seriously believe she's some kind of super Mage now?*

Lisa stared, equally stunned. *Annabelle believes she can control water well enough to lift the entire ship. Without wrecking it?*

Regina smiled faintly, watching Annabelle's enthusiasm. She was happy to see her friend so energized, even if deep down, she couldn't shake her worries.

Finally, Sophie snapped out of her thoughts and said, "You're gonna mess this up."

Annabelle flinched, just as Simba's cackling grew louder. The monkey pointed at her and howled with glee. Annabelle had had enough.

"Ye have yer orders," she barked, cutting off any further argument. "Now get to it!"

Before Sophie could fire back, she felt a nudge under the table. Lepele tapped her with his foot and shot her a look that said *That's enough*. Begrudgingly, she kept quiet, though her expression made it clear she wasn't convinced.

The crew slowly rose to carry out their tasks. Annabelle stayed rooted in place for a moment, her pride wounded but her resolve unshaken. One way or another, she is going to **make this work**.

Seeing that he'd most likely be needed for the upcoming tasks, Marcus turned to Lisa and Regina. "Can one of you ladies heal my arm?"

"I'll do it," Regina volunteered. She arranges her mana into Earthbloom and listened to her *sense*, scanning Marcus' arm to assess the damage. The wounds were deep, inflicted by swords, knives, and bayonets during the chaotic fight when the ship had rolled.

With a focused gesture, Regina traced a red spell circle in the air. Runes for "Mend," "Heal," "Connect," and "Soothe" glowed within the circle. Red mana particles streamed from the spell to Marcus' arm, gradually mending the torn tissue.

Marcus tensed as the healing magic surged through him. It felt like a wave of hot water coursing through his arm, comforting and scalding all at once. He winced, teeth clenched, as the magic oscillated between soothing warmth and sharp, burning intensity. The sensation ebbed and flowed until finally, the pain began to recede and the wounds knitted closed.

"When I heal folks, they don't wince like that from surface wounds," Lisa remarked with a sweet but pointed tone, raising an eyebrow at Regina's technique. "You should use more runes."

Marcus flexed his arm experimentally and nodded in thanks. The pain was gone, though the warmth of the healing magic still lingered faintly beneath his skin.

"Much appreciated, Miss Regina," he said with a small smile, breaking the tension between the two avatars.

Lisa huffed softly but chose not to press the issue further. There were more important things to focus on now.

Chapter 25

The next thirty minutes were a blur of frantic activity. Crew members capable of movement rushed to assist Sparks, setting up repairs for the gaping holes in the ship's inner hull. Lisa and Marcus worked tirelessly, securing the injured crew with ropes and promising to return to heal them once the immediate crisis was under control. Amid the Chaos, Marcus found a moment to send a desperate message to Sister Ingrid, detailing the dire state of the Stormfang.

Annabelle stood in the center of the mayhem, her mind racing. Every second of hesitation brought them closer to disaster as the ship continued to sink into the sea. She considered using waterspouts to lift the boat, but the logistics proved overwhelming. How could she stabilize the vessel without it crashing back into the water? The solution remained maddeningly out of reach. Meanwhile, Simba's incessant taunting gnawed at her nerves.

"Ole Cap'n Salad-Jar can't even move some water," Simba jeered, his singsong voice grating in her ears.

Annabelle clenched her jaw, forcing herself to ignore him. She gripped her amulet and reached out to Corsair, the first mate of her loyal undead crew. *He knows Maelstrom magic. He could help.* "Corsair, ye do the Maelstrom mastery, right?" she asked through their connection, her voice tight with urgency.

The reply came slowly, as though Corsair was waking from a deep sleep. "Aye, Cap'n. I am skilled in magic of the Maelstrom."

Annabelle's hope flared. "I needs to lift me ship and hold it in the air for a long time. Do ye have a spell for that?"

Corsair paused before responding. "I can think of a spell that might work... but ye'd need to be at least a tier-two mage to cast it, and a whole lot of mana."

"Cap'n Salad-Jar, look at where ye are," Simba crooned, still mocking her. "Avatar ye ain't up ta par!"

"Stupid monkey." Annabelle muttered under her breath, her frustration bubbling over. Everything…the survival of her crew, the fate of the Stormfang, everyone's lives depending on her.

"He is a stupid little simian," Corsair agreed dryly, his voice a small but comforting presence.

"Thank ye kindly, Corsair," Annabelle said, exhaling sharply. "Now, tell me more about this spell."

"It'd be easier to show ye, Bella," Corsair explained, his tone gentle but insistent. He reached out across their spectral connection, offering a gesture akin to a handshake that would deepen their explanation.

Annabelle hesitated. The sensation was strange, unfamiliar. "What's this?" she asked, unsure of what Corsair was doing. Before she could fully process his answer, Simba's mocking voice cut through her thoughts like a knife.

"Cap'n Salad Jar, how scared ye are," Simba laughed, louder now. "Oh, Cap'n Salad Jar!"

Her teeth clenched as rage surged within her. *Fine! Whatever the Corsair was doing couldn't be as bad as listening to stupid Simba a moment longer.* Annabelle reached out fully, accepting Corsair's *hand*. The world around her shifted, and she suddenly stood in a strange, ethereal space, no walls, no floor, only a vast and misty void.

Corsair appeared before her, his presence both solid and surreal. He stood tall, his features calm and courteous despite the desperate circumstances. He bowed low and took her hand, pressing a respectful kiss to her knuckles. His tired yet confident demeanor provided a brief and much-needed reprieve from the storm of doubt and anxiety.

"Cap'n Bella, tis an honor," Corsair greeted warmly.

Annabelle felt her tension ease for just a moment. "Thank ye, Corsair, but time's not on our side. Me ship's goin' under, I need that spell now," she said, her urgency slicing through the brief calm.

Corsair straightened, his eyes gleaming with understanding. "Aye, Cap'n. Let's get to it, then."

"The waterspout spell leads to an advanced spell called Torrent, which creates a powerful whirlpool," Corsair explained, conjuring a swirling vortex of water in the spectral space.

Annabelle frowned. "That doesn't really help, Corsair. I don't wanna sink the Fang, ye know," she muttered, frustration seeping into her voice. *Her mind raced, desperately searching for an alternative. Time was slipping away, and the lives of her crew hung in the balance.*

"Please bear with me, Cap'n Bella," Corsair continued calmly. "The Torrent is a tier-two spell, and it branches into two tier-three spells." He raised his hand, summoning two conjured images: a vast, churning whirlpool and a towering column of water. "The first is called the Abyssal Maelstrom, and the second is Mountain's Surge. I believe Mountain's Surge would serve ye best. But..." His expression became serious. "It may be beyond yer skill, Cap'n. It requires a massive amount of mana, precise channeling, and shaping."

Annabelle straightened, her jaw tightening in defiance. "Then I'll just practice here, and when I'm back on the Fang, I'll be ready," she said, her determination crystallizing. She couldn't allow failure, not with her crew depending on her.

"Nay, Cap'n," Corsair said, shaking his head. "That will not work. This place is spectral, only yer spirit is here. Yer body remains on the Fang, and it won't react to what ye do here until ye return."

Annabelle clenched her fists. "Such negativity, Corsair. I thought ye were on me side," she retorted, her voice sharp. Doubt had no place here; she needed every ounce of belief she could muster.

Corsair raised a brow but smiled softly. "Apologies, Cap'n Bella. I am on yer side ... always. Would ye like me to demonstrate the Mountain's Surge?"

"Aye." Annabelle said, forcing a smile to match his. "Show me what I need to do."

Corsair nodded and stepped back, preparing to demonstrate the powerful spell that is their only hope.

[----- ⚓ -----]

Acting Captain Salazar stood on the deck, her heart pounding as she glanced down at the hold. The water level had risen so high she could see it from above. A tightness gripped her chest, fear clawing at her insides. *I could get everyone killed.* Simba's unrelenting taunts echoed in her mind, only worsening the anxiety.

"We ready down here?" Sparks shouted from the hold, his voice echoing up to the deck.

"Arr!" Annabelle called back, trying her best to sound confident. She glanced over at Marcus, who stood beside Lisa. His expression was reassuring as he gave her a thumbs-up, gripping a retaining rope for stability.

"Everyone's tied down, Captain Salazar," Marcus confirmed.

Annabelle's eyes shifted to Lisa, whose worried face betrayed her doubt.

The memory of Annabelle's overconfident stunt on Order Island, where she had nearly drowned herself and the other avatars, clearly hadn't faded. "Please do not drown us," Lisa said reflexively, her voice tight with concern.

Simba erupted in laughter, the sound stabbing Annabelle's nerves. She sneered at Lisa, irritated by the negativity.

I don't need this right now. Ignoring them both, Annabelle clapped her hands together and began channeling her mana. She summoned every ounce of energy within her, shaping it with fierce intent. Reaching out to the sea, she commanded it to obey. A large circle of water began forming around the ship, responding to her will. Her braids and locs whipped wildly around her as the raw power surged through her body, vibrating the air like an electric storm.

Lisa's eyes widened in shock. The sheer amount of mana Annabelle was controlling was overwhelming. She could feel it, mana particles flowing like a waves crashing into her from Annabelle's very being. Her hair whipped chaotically in the mana storm, and her bandana flew off, lost to the winds. *How is she doing this?* Lisa wondered, awe replacing her fear.

At last, blessed silence. Simba finally stopped laughing.

"Ow," the monkey cried from behind Annabelle. "I'm Sorry, Mommy Chaos!" His voice was unusually sheepish. "Yes, Mommy, I will..." He leapt onto Annabelle's shoulder and sat quietly. "The Goddess Chaos is indeed generous," he explained, his tone suddenly reverent.

Annabelle felt an immense surge of mana rush through her, flooding her senses. An understanding of mana shaping, deep and instinctual, blossomed within her mind and. For the first time, the intricacies of advanced spell casting clicked into place as easy as her favorite shanty.

"Her gifts are the most valuable in all the sea," Simba added, speaking with a rare sincerity.

Annabelle opened her eyes, her hands unfolding slowly to her sides. With gritted teeth, she willed the sea to obey. The water responded, forming a pair of massive columns of water with an empty void of air between them, and then they surged upward, wrapping around the bow and stern of the Stormfang. Slowly but surely, the ship rose high into the air as Annabelle raised her hands above her head, her entire body trembling under the strain.

The hull tilted as water poured out, cascading down the central void between the water column. Bit by bit, the hold began to drain.

"As long as you believe, the Goddess' gifts will never fade," Simba said, his voice surprisingly encouraging.

"Aye," Annabelle managed to respond through gritted teeth. She smirked despite the pressure weighing down on her. The monkey had finally come around to her side. "I'll hold me ship 'ere. Now ye get to fixin' her!" she ordered as loud as she could, her voice strained but resolute.

"Right," Lisa replied, springing into action. She leaned over the edge of the deck and saw how much water still remained in the hold. Drawing a deep breath, she conjured a large blue spell circle, seven intricate runes glowing within it. She stretched out her hand, commanding the water to rise. The liquid obeyed, flowing up through the deck access and arcing away from the ship, careful not to interfere with Annabelle's towering water columns.

Lisa's hands trembled slightly. She couldn't risk her mana clashing with Annabelle's. *No mistakes.*

"What can I do to help?" Marcus asked, stepping forward. He was no longer worried about having to hold onto Lisa or Annabelle—the ship was remarkably steady in the air.

"Find Sparks and the others," Lisa told him, keeping her focus on the rising water. "Help them with the hull repairs. We will handle things up here."

Marcus nodded and jogged off, his confidence growing. Acting Captain Salazar was holding the ship steady like a veteran Maelstrom mage. *The crew had a chance...if they all worked together.*

[-----✿-----]

Meanwhile, down in the hold, the repair crew had divided into two teams. One group consisted of Sparks, Regina, and Bobby, now back on his feet. The other included Sophie, Eclipse Lepele, and Popper.

The water level in the hold was dropping rapidly, aided by both Lisa's spell and the water pouring out through the gaping holes in the inner and outer hull. The ship, suspended high in the air by Annabelle's magic, groaned slightly as it adjusted to the strain. Each team stayed busy, preparing for the repairs. Sparks worked a handheld torch to keep a cauldron of tar warm, while Sophie used a fire rune embedded in a wooden piece to heat another cauldron on their side.

Regina leaned over the railing and assessed the hold's water level. After a moment, she called out, "Should be done in a couple more minutes!"

Lepele gave her a thumbs-up, confirming he heard her. In his other hand, he held a tar brush, ready to start the repairs. Regina, also holding a brush, adjusted the tool purse Sparks had given her, which was loaded with hammers and extra nails.

Sophie took a deep breath, steadying herself. *How long can Annabelle hold the ship up like this?* Even with Lisa helping, there was no telling.

The rune-powered fire beneath her tar cauldron flickered and faded. She reached into her vest for another Alrunia fire rune but hesitated. Her mana reserves were still low, and she could feel the dull throb of exhaustion threatening to resurface. *Not yet*, she thought, slipping the rune back into her pocket.

Lepele glanced over the edge and shouted, "Let's go!" He hurried down the ladder into the drained section of the hold. Sophie secured the lid on the tar pot and attached a rope to its handle. Carefully, she lowered it down to Lepele, who caught it with ease. Once he had the pot in place, Sophie tossed the rope over and climbed down to join him.

Above them, Popper maneuvered a large wooden plank into position. He lowered it on a rope with several hooks attached to the corners. After Lepele detached the plank, Popper pulled the rope back up, secured a second plank, and began lowering it down to the repair team.

On the opposite side of the hold, Regina was already at work. She brushed thick layers of tar around the edges of a large hole in the inner hull, applying it exactly as Sparks had instructed, *Nice and thick*. The tar clung heavily to the wood, sticky and glossy under the flickering torchlight.

"Good, thick coat, just like that," Sparks told her approvingly as he stepped forward with a rectangular plank of wood, nails clenched between his teeth. The two of them positioned the plank over the hole. It was immediately clear that the hole was both longer and broader than the plank. They rotated the wood vertically, covering the top half of the gap. Once it was aligned, Sparks pressed it into the tar. He handed Regina nails one by one, and she hammered them in with steady precision.

Meanwhile, Sophie and Lepele encountered a similar problem on their side. The hole was too large to cover with one plank lengthwise, so they fastened it horizontally instead, using thick coats of tar to secure the plank before nailing it down.

"Hey, hey!" Popper called down cheerfully as he lowered another plank.

"Right on time," Sophie yelled back as she caught it. She wiped sweat from her brow and got back to work, knowing time was critical. The team moved in synchronization, each step precise and methodical. Every moment mattered if they wanted to avoid a trip to the bottom of the sea.

With two nails driven into the plank securing it to the bulkhead, Lepele steadied it while Sophie caught the next thick plank of wood Popper lowered from above. She detached the hooks and called up, "Ready!" Popper pulled the rope back up for the next plank as Sophie and Lepele quickly moved to position the new one. Sophie held it steady while Lepele nailed it into place.

On the opposite side of the hold, Sparks and Regina worked at a similar pace. Sparks pressed a plank against the next section of the inner hull while Regina hammered in nails with focused intensity. Sparks, still clutching spare nails between his teeth, released the board once it was secure and moved to fetch another. Regina continued driving in nails with fierce determination. Though she hurried, she made sure every nail was positioned perfectly. Glancing around at the walls of the hold, she realized the enormity of their task, they had so many more gaps to patch, and time was slipping through their fingers.

Once all the nails were in, Regina grabbed her tar brush and began coating the plank in a thick, sticky layer of black tar. She ensured the entire surface was sealed before moving to the next section.

On the other side, Sophie and Lepele operated like a well-rehearsed team, working quickly and in near silence. Lepele held the next plank in position while Sophie drove in the retaining nails. The rhythmic pounding of the hammer echoed through the hold as water continued to slosh around their feet in shallow puddles.

With the board secure, Lepele caught the next plank from Popper, while Sophie finished driving in the last nails. She stowed the hammer in the tool bag Regina had given her. It reminded her of her momma's purse; large, bulky, and full of valuable tools. Pulling the brush from the tar bucket, she coated the freshly installed plank in a smooth, dark layer of tar.

"Speed it up, Griffin," Lepele ordered, glancing at the number of gaps still left to patch.

"Right," Sophie answered without complaint. She grabbed the tar bucket and tool bag, moving quickly about two king's steps to the next damaged section. Dropping the bucket with a thud, she slung the tool bag over her shoulder and immediately pulled out her brush. Dipping it in the tar, she spread the viscous liquid around the edges of the new opening.

At Lepele's prompt, she stepped aside as he placed the next rectangular plank over the damage. They worked like clockwork, Sophie returned the brush to the bucket, grabbed her hammer, and swiftly began driving nails into the plank. Lepele nodded in approval as he prepared to retrieve the next board.

"Good work, Griffin. Keep it up," Lepele encouraged her before heading to the ladder to bring down more supplies.

On the other side, Regina and Sparks were making steady progress. Sparks returned from the ladder with the fourth rectangular plank and held it up beside the previous one. "Hope we made enough," he remarked, holding it in place for Regina.

As she hammered in the nails, Regina's mind began to wander. *What if we didn't make enough planks?* The thought gnawed at her. *They could try to cut more, but how long would Annabelle's spell last? Is there time?* She hesitated for a moment, her eyes darting around the hold. There could be something else they could use to patch the holes.

"Regina, girl, we gotta hurry up. The Cap'n's countin' on us," Sparks reminded her gently, bringing her focus back to the task at hand.

"Right," she said with a nod, shaking off her worries and returning to the hammering.

The repairs continued at a relentless pace, each team driven by the unspoken knowledge that the fate of the Stormfang rested on their shoulders.

[-----⚙-----]

On the main deck, Lisa watched Annabelle, who stood like a force of nature, holding the ship aloft with her pirate magic. Mana surged from Annabelle's body like a geyser, forming a whirlwind that whipped her messy hair in every direction. To anyone else, it might have looked effortless, as if Annabelle were posing for a portrait. But Lisa's Earthbloom sense told a different story. The raw power radiating from Annabelle was staggering—blinding, like staring directly into the sun. *Is this a gift from her goddess?* Lisa wondered. *Could I achieve something similar with Unity's capabilities?*

Concern flickered across her face. "Anna, are you okay?" she asked cautiously.

"Aye, prin…Lisa," Annabelle replied, catching herself mid-sentence. "But I gotta concentrate ta keep this up," she added, her voice surprisingly calm, like she was relaxing on a back porch with a glass of sweet tea.

Lisa nodded, reassured for the moment. She stepped away, noticing that the water in the hold was finally gone. With no one else on deck, she decided to check on Captain Kidd and Mr. Smitty. She made her way to the operations room and quietly opened the door.

Inside, the two men lay tied down to their beds, unconscious. Wisps of shadow magic drifted like smoke from their mouths, remnants of the curse grinding away at them from the inside. Lisa frowned, her mind racing. Is this because of that cleansing ritual? Did it somehow strengthen their bodies against the curse, or just slow it down?

Listening to her *sense*, Lisa examined their condition more closely. The dark patches of shadow magic within them were still growing, but much more slowly than before. *At least we bought some time.* Still, the sight filled her with unease. There was nothing she could do for them now, and lingering here would not help.

Lisa quietly closed the door and headed toward the hold. If they needed more hands for repairs, she'd offer whatever help she could.

[-----✠-----]

Marcus and Harmon arrive in the hold as Team Regina and Team Sophie worked on repairing the inner hull. Without wasting any time, they jumped in to assist Marcus joining Regina's team while Harmon joined Sophie's. Both men grabbed rectangular planks from the rope hooks, allowing Popper and Blaze to pull up the ropes and load the next set of planks.

"Harmon," Sophie called out as he carried a plank nearly the size of his arm span. "How's the wife and kids?" she asked, throwing out the common deckhand joke.

"Ah, ye know," Harmon replied with a grin, balancing the heavy wood in his hands. "They only love me when I send coin." He chuckled and positioned the plank against the damaged hull as Lepele stepped aside to fetch the next one.

"Better keep up, Griffin," Lepele said, issuing a friendly challenge.

"Yes, sir," Sophie replied as she pounded nails into the plank with swift, forceful strikes.

"Oi, ye're hittin' those nails like they wronged ye," Harmon teased.

"Just practicing for when I get me a husband." Sophie shot back with a playful smirk between hammer blows.

"Goddess bless that poor man," Harmon laughed.

When the retaining nails were secured, Sophie handed him her tool bag and hammer. "Here, finish the rest of the nails while I paint the tar."

"Aye, missy." Harmon said with a mock salute, accepting the hammer.

Nearby, Marcus watched as Regina hammered nails into a wide plank that Sparks was holding steady. Unsure what to do, Marcus awkwardly positioned another plank on the floor and glanced around for a hammer.

"Oi, Mr. Marcus!" Sparks called over. "The tar's over there." He gestured toward a cauldron sitting in a puddle of water. "Ye gotta paint the hole with tar before placing the plank, sir."

"Oh... okay," Marcus replied, shifting the wide plank and glancing around awkwardly as it partially blocked his vision.

Once Regina finished hammering the retaining nails, Sparks grabbed the tar bucket and headed toward Marcus. "Make way, Mr. Marcus, I'll handle the tar."

After another fifteen minutes, both teams completed the last of the repairs under Sparks' direction. They used every bit of tar from the cauldrons to coat the wide planks, sealing them securely to keep water from flooding back into the hold.

As the teams regrouped, Regina noticed they were standing in what used to be Lisa's infamous mountain of luggage. Only a single solitary trunk remained. Frowning, she scanned the hold. "Wait... where did all of Lisa's suitcases go?" she asked aloud.

"Huh?" Sophie replied, pausing mid-stroke as she applied more tar. She turned and blinked in realization, ninety-nine percent of Lisa's luggage was gone. Slowly, a grin spread across her face. "Oh no. Her things must've been swept away when the hold flooded," she said, laughing.

"Lisa's not gonna like that," Regina giggled, covering her mouth to stifle her laughter.

"Not going to like what?" Lisa's voice cut through the hold as she approached the group.

Sophie pointed to the solitary trunk and smirked. "Your luggage got away," she said, trying to contain her laughter.

Regina turned away, biting her lip to keep from laughing out loud.

Lisa's eyes locked onto the lone trunk, lying there like the last survivor of a massacre. Her stomach dropped. All her prized possessions... gone? Still in disbelief, she glanced around at the puddles of seawater, tar buckets, and scraps of wood. "Where did it all go?" she asked, her voice laced with growing anxiety. "Did you hide it or something? Where are my things?"

Sophie struggled to hold back her laughter but managed to answer. "Lisa, girl, the hold was flooded. Your stuff must've been swept into the sea." She half-smiled, trying to soften the blow. "I'm sorry."

Lisa stared at the empty space where her luggage mountain had once been, her mind racing to process the loss. Regina and Sophie exchanged glances, both silently battling their urge to burst out laughing.

Lisa's jaw tightened as she thought about everything lost to the sea, beautiful dresses, beauty supplies, and the comfy night clothes her mother's staff had packed for her. All of it... gone forever. She took a deep breath, fighting to stay composed. "No, I'm not going to cry," she said quietly, struggling to maintain her dignity.

"That's the spirit, girl," Sophie said with an encouraging smile.

"Hey, Griffin!" Lepele's voice echoed from across the hold. "Are you out of tar?"

Realizing she had been standing around too long and had drawn attention, Sophie quickly called back, "No, Eclipse!"

"Then get back to work and stop foolin' around with your friends," Lepele ordered.

Sophie rolled her eyes and returned to her task. Once her bucket of tar was empty and the final repairs were completed, the teams began clearing out. Everyone except Regina and Sparks climbed the ladders to the walkways overlooking the hold, heading toward the main deck and bridge.

Sparks cupped his hands and called up to the bridge. "Oi, Cap'n! Ye can let us down now!"

After a brief pause, Annabelle's voice echoed in response. "Aye! Hold on to something!"

The crew braced themselves, unsure of what was coming next.

[----- ⚓ -----]

On the bridge, Annabelle struggled to maintain the Mountain's Surge spell. Exhaustion weighed on her, the strain of channeling so much mana burning into her fingertips like needles. Slowly, she began lowering her arms to ease the ship's descent, but the pain worsened. It felt as though the gift the goddess had bestowed upon her was slipping away. The knowledge of mana shaping that had come so naturally moments ago now faded, leaving her grasp tenuous at best. Her control faltered.

"Hey, what is this now?" she protested, glancing at Simba. "I ain't done!"

"The goddess won't do everything for ye," Simba replied matter-of-factly, his tone offering no sympathy.

Fear gripped Annabelle's heart. They were still high above the sea, and without the goddess's support, lowering the ship safely seemed impossible. "Come on, Simba! We were just starting to get along."

"I don't like you," Simba said bluntly. "Mommy Chaos told me to help you, that's all."

Annabelle cursed under her breath. The pain spread up to her elbows, her reserves draining fast. She could no longer sustain the spell. Knowing she had no choice, she shouted down to the crew, "Ye better hold on ta somethin', 'cause we're goin' down fast!"

The Mountain's Surge collapsed, the mana surge finally abandoning her completely. The Stormfang plunged into a free fall, gravity pulling it toward the sea with terrifying speed. Annabelle's mind raced. *I can't let it smash into splinters!*

Summoning the last dregs of her energy, she reached out to the water below. A series of waterspouts burst upward, spinning violently beneath the ship. Annabelle gritted her teeth, guiding the spouts to slow the fall. The ship shuddered as the waterspouts caught its massive weight, straining to hold it aloft. But she could feel the magic slipping from her control, this wouldn't last.

As the spouts vanished, Annabelle cast a final desperate spell. She summoned the most significant wave she could, forcing it to surge under the Stormfang's hull. The ship slammed into the wave, water crashing over the deck as it was shoved forward. The impact was brutal, but it cushioned the fall enough to keep the ship in one piece.

The Stormfang rocked violently on the waves, tossed like a plaything by the chaotic sea. Annabelle collapsed to her knees, gasping for air. The sea, as always, was a harsh and unpredictable lover.

But they were still afloat, and that is all that matters.

[----- ✿ -----]

Down in the hold, the crash hit hard, throwing everyone around like rag dolls. They had all braced themselves, knowing that if Annabelle warned about rough waves, it meant *serious danger*. Everyone held on tight, but no one had told the hastily repaired planks. The force of the impact was too much. The bond of nails and tar cracked under pressure as water from the smuggler's compartments forced its way through. Small fountains of seawater began streaming through the patches they had worked so hard to secure.

"No, no, no!" Sparks cried out, distressed. "What're we gonna do now?!"

"It almost held," Regina said, trying to inject a bit of hope into the situation. Maybe, just maybe, Sparks would find some comfort in that.

"Almost don't count, missy," Sparks replied bitterly. "We threw everything we had into this fix, and it didn't work." He slumped into the water gathering on the floor, defeated. "We got nothin'."

Regina's heart sank at the sight of her mentor crushed under the weight of failure. She couldn't bear to see him like this. "Come on, Mr. Sparks," she said gently but firmly. "There's got to be a way to fix it, right?"

Sparks shook his head, his expression filled with defeat. "Yeah... if we could fly." He sighed deeply and met her eyes, full of regret. "I'm so sorry, Regina. I know ye wanted to save yer peoples."

Her people. Sparks meant her family, her father, Jules, and her little brother Mattie. She'd been ready to save them from their fate with that murder woman, Hema. But now... now, she couldn't let it end here. *I can't let it end here*; she told herself firmly.

Determined, Regina leaned in and kissed Sparks on the cheek. His eyes widened in surprise. "Don't ye worry, Mr. Sparks," she said with a bright, resolute smile. "I'm gonna fix it. Ye just sit tight, okay?"

Sparks stared at her, stunned by the sudden confidence radiating from her. For a moment, he was speechless.

Regina turned and approached one of the leaking planks. She pressed her hand against it, and for a second, the flow of water stopped, until the sea pushed back, invading the hold once more. *What can I do to keep the water from pushing in?* she wondered frantically. Capture magic wouldn't work. Child's play doesn't have anything that can help this. If only she'd mastered construct magic...

The idea hit her like a tidal wave. Constructs! I **can** create things ... crystals.

She pulled out her wand, touched it to the inner hull beside the repair, and focused her mana. She carefully arranged it, shaping it into a dense, solid crystal using her newly learned Crystalmancy. Slowly, a shimmering silver crystal began to encase the damaged section. Regina took her time, ensuring the crystal grew thick and sturdy, fully sealing the area around the patch. It took several long minutes of intense concentration, but when she finally stepped back, the water had stopped. The solid crystal held firm, protecting the patchwork repair.

"There," Regina said softly, catching her breath. "All fixed up."

Sparks lifted his head from where he'd been slumped, blinking at the sight of the crystal barrier. He stood slowly, his wrinkled face transforming into a grin, yellowed teeth on full display. Without warning, he let out a joyful laugh and scooped Regina into a firm hug, lifting her feet clear off the floor.

Regina giggled, surprised but delighted by his sudden emotional turnaround.

Realizing he might have overstepped, Sparks quickly set her down. "Sorry, Regina," he said, scratching the back of his head. He turned his attention to the crystal repair and asked, "Won't this just disappear?"

"Yes," Regina admitted with a nod. "But I poured a lot of mana into it and made it really solid. It should last for hours. I'll have to come back and repair it before it fades, but we've got some time."

Sparks's grin widened. "Well then, Miss Regina," he said with renewed enthusiasm, "let's get to fixin' up the ship!"

They wasted no time. Over the next twenty minutes, Regina poured more of her mana into covering each tar-plank repair with silver crystals. The process drained her mana reserves, leaving her with a growing headache, but the effort was worth it. By the time they were done, the ship had stopped leaking.

Sparks beamed with pride and happiness, and Regina felt a surge of relief. For now, the Stormfang is holding firm.

[-----✝-----]

Everyone made their way from the hold to the main deck. Lisa took the opportunity to remove the remaining seawater from the hold, guiding it over the side with her magic. Harmon, Popper, Blaze, and Flint got to work clearing and organizing the deck. Meanwhile, Sparks took the helm, driven by a sudden sense of urgency. He corrected the course Annabelle had plotted earlier and adjusted the compass, determined to keep the ship on track.

Below deck, the four avatars and Brother Marcus gathered in the galley's seating area. Annabelle collapsed into a chair, feeling utterly drained. The gift from Chaos had come at a steep price, her body ached, and her mana reserves were nearly depleted. Across from her, Regina sat with her head in her hands, struggling against the dull throb of a mana drain headache creeping behind her ears. Sophie joined them, tired but not nearly as affected as the others. Lisa, sullen and quiet, sank into a chair across from Sophie, the weight of her losses heavy on her shoulders. Nearly everything she owned had been swept away by the sea, leaving her with only a few dresses in her wardrobe. It felt like some cruel payment to the ocean.

Marcus observed the avatars, his charges weary and worn from the day's trials. He couldn't do much to ease their burdens, but he could do something small. He moved behind the serving counter and called out to Jeffie, who was hard at work preparing dinner service.

"Mr. Jeffie, could you put on a pot of ember-root tea?" Marcus asked.

"I can give ye a kettle," Jeffie called back. "Gotta get dinner going."

"That will work," Marcus replied, making his way to the kitchen entrance.

Jeffie left a metal kettle on the counter for him. Marcus grabbed it, placed it on the stove, and used a diminutive steel striker and flint attached to a ring on the wall to ignite a fire. As the kettle heated, he went to the galley storage room to collect a few dried ember-root leaves.

A short while later, Marcus returned with a tray of four steaming mugs of tea. The avatars sat silently, weighed down by the day's events, until Marcus approached.

"Ladies, I have tea for you," he announced with a smile.

The avatars perked up, grateful for a warm drink. He handed out the mugs, feeling satisfied that he could offer some comfort. They each took a sip, expecting the soothing touch of their goddess's tea—until the taste hit them.

"Ugh! Foot tea!" Regina exclaimed, gagging. "Brother Marcus, this is a mean joke!"

"What is this nasty tea?!" Annabelle added, recoiling. "Oi, where's the goddess tea, bloke?!"

"Why... why does this taste so horrible?" Sophie asked, staring at her mug in disbelief.

"I like it," Lisa said calmly, taking another sip of her ember-root tea.

Sophie gave her a suspicious look, wondering if she was just saying it to make Marcus feel better.

"How could you possibly like this foot tea?" Regina asked, narrowing her eyes. Then, after a pause, she added, "Wait... do you like feet?"

Annabelle burst into a loud belly laugh, pointing at Lisa. "Aye! That's it...Lisa likes feet!"

Lisa rolled her eyes, maintaining her composure. "For your information," she began with dignity, "drinking ember-root tea is an excellent way to boost your body's mana production and combat the effects of mana overuse." She turned to Marcus and said, "Thank you for making this for us, Brother Marcus. You are a wonderful guide and servant."

"Good servants don't make nasty tea!" Annabelle retorted, grinning. "Ye wanna be a good servant? Go make us some goddess tea instead!"

Marcus remained calm. "I must insist that you ladies finish your ember-root tea before indulging in any goddess tea. I've noticed signs of mana drain in all of you, and I'm concerned for your wellbeing."

Annabelle, Sophie, and Regina shot him skeptical looks, clearly unimpressed. Lisa, however, nodded and gave him a small smile. "Thank you for your concern, Brother Marcus," she said gently, before taking another sip of her tea.

[----- ⚓ -----]

Annabelle woke up hunched over the table, her body still aching from the strain of casting that tier-three spell to lift the ship. She groaned softly, wiping her face with her hands, and stood slowly. *Why'd they just leave me here to sleep?* she wondered, her joints stiff as she stretched. Curious about what was going on, she made her way out of the galley and climbed the stairs to the bridge.

When she reached the top, she saw Sparks at the helm, steering the ship with a steady hand. Popper, Flint, and Bobby worked the deck and adjusted the sails under the moonlit sky. The door to Captain Kidd's operations room stood open, and inside, Annabelle spotted Lepele crouched beside the captain's bed. He appeared to be sliding a wooden door under it, placing it next to another one already there.

"What's givin', Copper?" Annabelle asked, stepping closer to get a better look.

Lepele straightened, brushing off his hands. "I made a pair of shadow cleansing ritual circles on these doors," he explained. "This way, we don't have to move the beds to draw new circles each time."

"Aye, that's a smart idea," Annabelle said approvingly. She glanced over at Captain Kidd and Smitty, both moaning in pain, coughing up thick, shadowy material onto their sheets. Her concern deepened. "Looks like it's time to get it goin'."

Lepele shook his head. "Gotta wait for the Nozaki girl," he replied. "If I cleanse them now, they'll need immediate healing, or the damage from the curse will kill them." He gave her a serious look. "I already sent a runner for her, but she hasn't shown up yet."

Annabelle sighed. Lisa probably needs a nudge. She turned to leave for the stateroom deck but was stopped by Sparks.

"Actin' Cap'n," Sparks called, stepping away from the helm. "Can ye take the wheel for a bit?"

Annabelle blinked, hesitation creeping in. "Why?" She did her best to sound confident, though the thought of steering the ship still made her nervous. *What if I mess up the course?*

"I need to wake Regina. She said her crystals would need repairs in just over an hour," Sparks explained, fishing his pocket watch out and tucking it away again. "Don't worry, I marked the compass. Just keep us on that heading, and we'll make it to Magitekopolis. Harmon'll be up soon to take over."

Annabelle eyed him curiously. "What's gotten into ye, Sparks? Ye usually don't bother with the ship runnin' stuff. Thought ye hated it."

"I do," Sparks admitted, holding out a hand to the wheel. His expression hardened, something Annabelle wasn't used to seeing from him. "But listen, if we don't make it to port as fast as we can, we're gonna sink."

Annabelle's heart sank. She gripped the helm, feeling its weight as the wheel pushed back against her hands, more resistant than she remembered. "Sparks," she said softly, watching the man she'd known for years.

"Listen, Cap'n," Sparks continued, his tone grave. "I'm gonna act as yer first mate, make sure everyone's workin' and the ship gets to port so Kidd and Smitty can be saved." He wiped a hand through his hair. "But I'll need ye to back me up... and listen to me advice."

"Of course," Annabelle assured him.

He gave her a look so serious it sent a chill through her. "No, I mean really listen. Not like how ye listen to Smitty or Kidd. Ye have to take me seriously."

Annabelle nodded, meeting his gaze. "I will," she said firmly. "I promise."

"Good." Sparks exhaled and glanced up at the night sky. "First thing, ye gotta get some sleep. Once ye're off the helm, go lie down. I'll do the same after I help Regina with her repairs."

"Arr," Annabelle responded quietly. She hesitated, then asked, "What brought this on, really, Sparks?"

He hesitated, his face tightening. Finally, he answered, "Yer little sister."

Annabelle's eyes widened slightly. Sparks looked down at the deck, his voice thick with emotion. "I... I can't let 'er down," he admitted. He took a deep breath, then looked up, his blue eyes burning with fierce resolve. "And I won't let 'er die out here in these mean seas."

Annabelle studied his face, etched with determination and fear for Regina's safety, and felt a renewed sense of responsibility settle over her. Sparks wasn't someone who spoke like this lightly. He was counting on her, and for the first time in a while, she truly felt the weight of her role as captain.

"Thank ye, Sparks," she said quietly, gripping the helm a little tighter.

"Let's get it done," Sparks replied with a nod, before heading below deck to wake Regina.

"Aye, first mate," Annabelle said with a grin. "She's a special one." She paused for a moment, then added playfully, "We can let the copper die, right?"

Sparks shot her a pointed look, the intensity of his gaze saying all that needed to be said. *A captain doesn't talk about her crew like that.* Disappointment simmered in his expression, making Annabelle instantly regret the joke.

"Six in the mornin', Captain," he replied curtly, waving as he descended the stairs to the lower decks.

Annabelle sighed and turned her attention back to the helm, guiding the ship along the course Sparks had set. She smiled to herself. *Gots me a first mate now*, she thought, feeling a rare sense of accomplishment. My first real step as a captain.

For the next ten minutes, Annabelle concentrated on keeping the ship steady, the wheel occasionally resisting under her grip. As she adjusted the course again, she felt that familiar presence of another avatar approaching. Without looking, she called over her shoulder, "Evenin', Lisa."

"Good evening, Anna," Lisa replied, yawning, her green hair hanging messily over her shoulders.

Lepele stepped out of the operations room and spotted her. "Good evening, Miss Nozaki," he greeted with a tired nod.

Lisa waved in acknowledgment. "Shall we begin?" Lepele asked, his exhaustion evident in his voice.

"Yes," Lisa answered, brushing her hair from her face. "I am very sleepy and want to go back to bed."

Without further delay, Lepele activated the two cleansing circles. Bright columns of light flared up from beneath the beds, flooding the room like the sudden arrival of dawn. Neither Annabelle nor Lisa dared to look directly at the ritual, shielding their eyes from the blinding glow. As the light faded, Lisa used her Earthbloom sense to examine the captain and Smitty.

She frowned as she assessed the damage. Captain Kidd's condition was dire, his organs ravaged by the curse to the brink of death. Mr. Smitty wasn't far behind, but the captain required immediate healing if he had any chance of surviving the night.

Standing over Kidd, Lisa gracefully traced a red spell circle in the air with her finger. Five glowing runes appeared around the circle, pulsing softly as she infused them with mana. Healing magic flowed from the circle in streams of red particles, pouring into the captain's chewed-up body. His wounds began to mend, though the damage was so severe that he gasped and screamed from the pain. Lisa gritted her teeth and pushed her magic harder, racing to repair his organs before the curse could claim him.

With the captain stabilized, she quickly moved to Smitty's bed and repeated the process. Her magic flared once more, her hands moving with precision despite her growing exhaustion.

Annabelle glanced over her shoulder now and then, catching brief glimpses of the red glow illuminating the room. Seeing Lisa hard at work brought her a measure of relief. *She's got them sorted*, Annabelle thought, turning her attention back to the compass. She cursed softly under her breath upon noticing she'd drifted off course again. With a quick turn of the wheel, she corrected it.

After completing the healing, Lisa walked out of the operations room, her face pale and weary. She approached Annabelle and said, "They need to eat something. Their bodies have been through a lot, and the curse will start weakening them again soon if they do not get some food they wont be able to tough it out."

Annabelle glanced at her, then at the wheel. "I'm kinda stuck steer'n the ship right now. Can ye do it?" She flashed her most charming, pleading smile despite the late hour.

Lisa sighed but relented. "Fine, I will make it," she said, rubbing her temples. "But you are feeding them after. I need to get some sleep."

"You're the best sister ever, Lisa," Annabelle said gratefully, trying to lighten her mood.

"Tell that to Evelyn," Lisa replied with a dismissive wave as she headed down the stairs to prepare food for the captain and Smitty.

Chapter 26

Journal Entry May 5th, 1910:

The Stormfang remains afloat due to the incredible efforts and abilities of the avatars. Annabelle Salazar performed an amazing tier three maelstrom mastery spell, lifting the ship into the air and allowing the water filling the hold to drain. This allowed the crew to effect repairs on the inner hull. Mr. Sparks informed me that Stormfang's less-than-legal activities may have inadvertently saved our lives. The hidden smuggler's compartments created a double hull, with most of the damage affecting the outer hull, while the inner hull sustained more manageable damage.

Despite Mr. Sparks' reputation as an unparalleled engineer, his initial repairs to the inner hull failed once the ship was lowered back into the water. Fortunately, Regina Fournier's crystalmancy was the key to reinforcing and completing the repairs, keeping the boat afloat.

A significant concern remains the affliction of Captain Kidd and First Mate Smitty with a "Curse of Shadows." We currently have no means to remove this curse. Eclipse Lepele's extensive knowledge of shadow magic, derived from his experience as an Aurorium Eclipse with shadow magic subordinates, provided us with the tools to keep the men alive temporarily. The rituals produce gruesome results, but they are buying us time until we can find someone capable of removing the curse.

[-----✠-----]

Sophie and Eclipse Lepele carried a set of marked doors to the bridge, prepped for the cleansing ritual. Earlier, Lepele had drilled Sophie on drawing ritual circles until her hands ached and the pattern imprinted itself in her mind.

As they worked, Lisa arrived, rubbing her eyes and yawning. Her exhaustion was evident in the slump of her shoulders.

"Good afternoon, Miss Nozaki," Lepele greeted her with a nod. "Rough day?"

Lisa yawned again, stretching. "Feels like I have been sleeping forever and still cannot shake it off," she admitted, rolling her neck. "time to till the soil." She said using a common refrain from Verdantia.

"Right away." Lepele activated the ritual beneath Captain Kidd's bed with a steady pulse of his mana.

Sophie crouched and placed her hand on the circle. A surge of pain struck her palm, and she jerked back, hissing in pain. "Ow! What the…? This is like mana backlash!"

"Anytime now, Griffin," Lepele prompted her, arching an eyebrow.

"I... I can't." Sophie stared at the circle, baffled.

"Move." Lepele strode across the room to Smitty's bed as she stepped aside. His touch on the circle beneath Kidd's bed sent bright, cleansing light streaming through the room. Smoke-like shadows poured from Smitty's mouth and nose, twisting in the light's path.

Sophie felt her chest tighten, her silence born of frustration and inadequacy. Lepele easily managed what had stumped her.

The ritual intensified, a column of white light spiraling around Smitty's bed. Lepele rejoined Sophie and Lisa, his presence steady as they watched Harmon steer the ship. Their shadows danced across the walls under the intense glow of the ritual magic.

"So," Lepele began, turning to Sophie, "you've never done ritual work before?"

"I thought it would be simple," Sophie confessed, frowning. "Like rune magic. But I got hit with mana backlash the moment I tried to activate it."

Lisa blinked at her, confusion dulling her features. "You cannot? I thought rituals were... universal?"

Sophie bristled, glaring at Lisa, who now looked half-asleep. Something is definitely wrong with her. *Why's she so drained?*

"It might be your rune magic affinity," Lepele suggested, his tone thoughtful. "We'll need to figure it out." He touched Lisa's shoulder gently. "Your turn, Miss Nozaki."

Startled awake, Lisa hurried to Kidd's side, summoning a red spell circle. The runes around it glowed fiercely as mana flowed into Kidd's body. His pained gasps echoed through the room.

"So," Lepele continued as though Kidd's cries weren't ringing in their ears, "what do you know about activating rituals?"

"You draw a shape, usually a circle, and channel mana into it," Sophie explained, watching Lisa work. "That activates the ritual."

"That's a... rudimentary way to describe it," Lepele replied dryly, crossing his arms. "A ritual circle is a set of instructions. Think of the ritual you used to bond with your badge."

Sophie nodded, recalling the ceremony from her promotion to Sentinel years ago

"The instructions in that circle were more than symbolic," Lepele elaborated. "They dictated how you and your badge would connect, granting you command over its functions. You need to ask yourself, how did the ritual affect you?"

Sophie's thoughts drifted to her badge ritual. She could still picture the circle etched into the floor, her badge placed at its center. She had stood inside that circle, anticipation prickling her skin. The answer seemed straightforward, position, but Lepele was not the type to accept easy answers. There had to be something deeper involved.

Her brow furrowed as she remembered the circle beginning to glow. The light had surged outward, washing over her and the badge alike. That light... it was mana.

Eclipse Porcello had activated the ritual with his mana, which travelled along the circle, connecting her to her badge. It was the caster's mana, no, wait. Maybe not.

"Mana," she ventured aloud. "The caster's mana is what links everything together."

Lepele nodded approvingly but corrected her, "That's a solid guess. But not quite. The caster's mana is transformed into ritual energy. The shape then uses that energy to carry out its instructions. Once all the energy is expended, the ritual completes, and the medium, whatever was used to draw the shape, breaks down into ether and vanishes."

"Oh, I see." Sophie nodded slowly as the explanation clicked. "But then why did I get backlash when I tried to activate the cleansing ritual?"

"My guess is you used your rune affinity instead of neutral mana," Lepele speculated thoughtfully.

Meanwhile, Lisa finished healing Captain Kidd and moved to Smitty's side. As her magic flared to life, Smitty let out a tortured scream, his body writhing on the bed.

"That has to be hard on her," Sophie remarked quietly, keeping her voice low enough that Lisa wouldn't overhear.

"It's not the only thing troubling her," Lepele responded cryptically, a shadow of concern passing over his face. Then, he shifted the conversation. "Have you been taught proper mana infusion?"

"Of course," Sophie replied, the question rubbing her pride the wrong way. "It's part of basic mana training with the den mother." She crossed her arms, her tone defensive.

Lepele fell silent, letting Smitty's pained cries echo through the room. Finally, he broke the quiet. "Your rune magic... it's your secondary discipline, correct?"

"Yes," Sophie confirmed, her voice softening as she explained, "Momma wanted me to learn Kiraku Mbilli, and dad was always too busy with missions to teach me his magic."

Lepele's brow rose in mild surprise. "How busy could he have been that he didn't even teach magic to his own Sentinel daughter?"

"He was always on missions," Sophie said with a sigh. "When I asked why he was gone all the time, that's what she'd tell me *'Everyone wants the Seeker.'*."

"The Seeker," Lepele echoed, his expression shifting as recognition dawned. "Oscar Griffin." He looked at Sophie, as if seeing her in a new light. "Of course. Your father was Oscar *The Seeker* Griffin."

"You knew my father?" Sophie asked, her curiosity sharpening.

"Only by reputation," Lepele replied. "He was one of the Seekers from Islewind. So that means your mother..." He paused, sifting through his thoughts. "Your mother was Arisa Songhe from the Pack?"

"You met my momma?" Sophie's eyes widened slightly.

"Nope," Lepele said with a shake of his head. "Your parents have some big reputations in the clan. I still remember the morning we got the news about your father's death. A few years back now." His voice softened with nostalgia.

"Yeah... that was a really rough time for Momma," Sophie replied, her expression clouding. "She tried to put on a strong face for me and Ben, but I'd hear her crying in her room at night."

Lisa finished her healing work on Smitty, who finally slipped into a peaceful sleep, free from the deadly curse. She scanned the two men one last time with her

Earthbloom sense before stepping back, satisfied. Wiping the sweat from her brow, she said, "They need to eat something."

"I'll take care of that," Lepele offered. He turned to Sophie with a casual shrug. "You should grab some tea with your... sister."

Sophie arched an eyebrow at him. "I think she can handle herself," she said, though his bemused *what did I say?* look made her relent. "Come on, let's get some tea."

The two made their way to the galley. Lisa sat down while Sophie went to fetch tea. To her surprise, Marcus was stationed behind the counter, keeping the crew away from Mr. Jeffie while he worked in the kitchen. Thankfully, Marcus already had emberroot tea brewing, knowing both Lisa and Regina were draining a lot of mana to keep the ship steady and its crew alive.

Sophie returned with two steaming cups, only to find Lisa slumped over the table, fast asleep. Her forest-green hair fanned out across the tabletop, resembling a blanket of fine, silky grass. Sophie tapped the table with her foot, jolting Lisa awake.

Lisa sat up abruptly, gathering her hair and pushing it out of her face. "Oh, sorry. I must have nodded off," she mumbled.

"Don't worry about it," Sophie reassured her as she slid one of the cups closer. "Why are you so tired, though?"

Lisa stifled a yawn. "I am not sure. No matter how much sleep I get, it is like... I never get enough." She took a careful sip of the tea, her shoulders sagging with weariness.

They sat in companionable silence for a few moments, both sipping the bitter drink. Eventually, Sophie broke the quiet. "How much mana does it take for your healing spells?" she asked, taking another sip of her own tea.

Lisa considered the question. "It depends on the injury," she said thoughtfully. "With the Captain and Mr. Smith, it is a lot. Their wounds are deep, and the curse doesn't help. It takes quite a bit of mana to repair all the damage." She paused, tapping her fingers on the table. "You know, now that I think about it, Mr. Smith is usually in better shape than the captain after the cleansing ritual. I wonder why that is."

"Maybe it's because he's fatter than the captain," Sophie quipped, cracking a grin.

Lisa burst out laughing, and Sophie couldn't help but join in. For a moment, the tension eased, their laughter filling the room.

As the laughter died down, Sophie took another sip of her now lukewarm tea. She grimaced. "I still have no idea how you can things like that." she said, shaking her head.

[-----✠-----]

Journal Entry May 6th, 1910 (Day 2)

The operations aboard the Stormfang remain intensely focused on reaching port in Magitekopolis. Mr. Sparks has proven to be a competent first mate, efficiently organizing the ship's schedule and managing regular operations. This allows Miss Salazar to concentrate on keeping the boat afloat.

Miss Fournier's crystalmancy repairs of the ship's inner hull and Miss Nozaki's Earthbloom healing of the captain and first mate have been effective but costly. Both avatars are severely drained from using their deep mana reserves, leaving them utterly exhausted. This constant, costly expenditure of mana has raised concerns about the long-term effects on their health and abilities.

Based on his calculations, Mr. Sparks estimates that we should arrive in Magitekopolis in six more days. I am deeply concerned that Miss Nozaki and Miss Fournier may be permanently damaging themselves by continuously pushing their limits. Eclipse Lepele has expanded Miss Griffin's training to include ritual magic, a task she finds daunting.

[-----✿-----]

In the hold of the ship, Regina concentrated as she used her wand to cast a repair spell on her crystal constructs. Though strong, the constructs degraded over time, and if she didn't keep them intact, the sea would burst in, dragging the ship and its crew into a watery grave. With a weary sigh, she repaired the final construct, buying the crew another precious few hours of safety at the cost of nearly all her mana.

"Done." she announced, lowering her wand near the ladder leading out of the hold. She yawned and stretched, her arms trembling slightly from exhaustion. "What's next, Mr. Sparks?" she asked with a grin, trying to stay upbeat.

Sparks scratched the back of his head. "Well, I'm off to check the engines, see if we can get to Magitekopolis any faster." He smiled warmly but quickly added, "But ye? Ye should head to the galley, get a meal and some emberroot tea. You've earned it."

Regina frowned. "I don't want to go to the galley. Why can't I help with the engines?" She wiped sweat from her brow, her weariness seeping into her voice.

"Because, Regina, you need food and rest," Sparks explained gently, his tone calm but firm.

"I'm fine," she insisted. "no more *foot tea*!" Her voice trembled slightly, frustration and hurt bubbling to the surface. "Why don't you want me to work with you anymore?"

"Gina..." Sparks sighed, stepping closer. "I wish I could spend all day working with ye, but yer exhausted. If ye don't rest, you won't have the strength to fix those crystals when we need you to again."

Her eyes stung as tears threatened to spill. "But why?" she asked, saddened because she missed working with Sparks. "All I do is eat, sleep, and fix the crystals. Over and over. I'm so tired of that gross tea!"

"Ye need to drink it," Sparks said with a touch of exasperation. "It'll help ye recover."

"It tastes like feet!" she shot back.

Sparks raised an eyebrow. "And how would ye know what feet taste like?"

Regina froze, stumped by the question, and stared at him in silence. Sparks chuckled softly but quickly sobered.

"Come on, Gina. Let's get ye something good from Jeffie," he said, placing a hand on her shoulder.

Before his hand could rest, Galahad manifested in a sudden flash of mana, his protective presence startling Sparks. The spirit's intervention drained a bit of Regina's already depleted mana reserves, a fact not lost on Sparks, whose face turned grim.

Regina stood her ground, her defiance written in every tense muscle, her headache pounding in protest of her stubbornness. Sparks exhaled deeply.

"Okay, okay," he relented. "We'll work together. But ye got to promise me, ye won't use any more magic."

"Arr," Regina replied cheerfully, clearly satisfied.

"Nope, not good enough," Sparks countered, crossing his arms like a stern taskmaster. "say the words, little silver missy."

Regina scowled but reluctantly lifted her wand as if taking an oath. "I promise I won't use any magic," she declared with a giddy smile, happy to work with Sparks again.

"Good." Sparks nodded. "I'm trusting ye here."

They walked to the engine room on the port side of the hold. Sparks pulled a wrench from his tool bag and worked the bolt holding the door shut. With a creak, the door opened, revealing the rectangular engine case still full of water. Sparks muttered a curse under his breath and shook his head.

Regina immediately arranged her mana into Earthbloom and then began forming a blue Earthbloom spell circle, spinning her finger in the air.

"Regina..." Sparks' disapproving voice cut through her concentration.

She stopped, glanced at him, and then began whistling as though she hadn't done anything wrong.

"Regina," he repeated, his tone like that of a scolding parent. "Ye promised missy."

"I wasn't gonna use magic," she said, feigning innocence. "Honest!"

"Uh-huh," Sparks replied, unconvinced. He grabbed a small bucket from the maintenance room and began slowly draining the engine compartment.

"I'll check the other engine," Regina said, turning on her heel and marching to the starboard side of the hold. She pulled a wrench from her tool purse, because yes, it is definitely a purse, and loosened the retaining nut on the door. This engine compartment was completely dry and in good working order.

"Mr. Sparks!" she called across the hold. "This one looks good to go!"

"That's a relief!" Sparks called out. "But this engine's rusted solid. We're gonna have to pull it," he explained.

Regina sighed and closed the starboard engine compartment door, securing the nut. She made her way back to the port side, where Sparks was already preparing the hook and chain assembly. Together, they hoisted the engine from its casing. As the machine hung suspended, Regina inspected the mechanism closely. It was a complex fusion of smaller parts, likely the handiwork of Sparks himself.

Transporting the waterlogged engine to his workshop proved challenging without working cranes or magic. Fortunately, Sparks wasn't above flexing his authority as first mate. He called in some powder-mag crew members, who grudgingly hauled the heavy propulsion system into the workshop via the ceiling-mounted hook-and-chain system.

Once inside, Sparks and Regina set to work disassembling the engine. As she suspected, Sparks had built this machine, its parts came apart too neatly for anyone else's design. Each section released easily after removing a single bolt, the interlocking pieces separating with an efficiency that impressed her. However, each time a piece was pulled free, a surge of seawater gushed out, drenching the workbench and soaking nearby tools and rags in greasy water.

When the engine was fully broken down into six sections, Sparks and Regina each took a minor component to inspect. The rhythmic tinkering of tools filled the room as they worked.

Regina yawned loudly, stretching her arms high above her head. She cast a glance over her shoulder to see if Sparks had noticed. He hadn't or so she thought.

"Regina," Sparks said without looking up, his tone firm. "Ye need to eat and drink a cup of emberroot tea. Yer fading."

"I'm not hungry," she protested, pouting. "And I told you, I don't want any of that nasty foot tea."

Sparks set down the mechanism he was working on, his hands falling still. He stood silently for a moment, and Regina braced herself for a scolding. Her father, Jules, would have yelled at her by now, usually over nothing. But Sparks just paused, searching for the right approach. Finally, he spoke with quiet authority.

"Regina," he repeated.

"Fine," she grumbled. She placed a strange coil-like part into an empty drawer under the table and added the rest of her pieces beside it. "But I'm coming right back after I eat," she warned, pointing a finger at him.

"Fine," Sparks agreed. "And remember, no food or drink in here, missy."

"Fine," Regina shot back, crossing her arms and narrowing her eyes.

"That's fine," Sparks teased, meeting her glare with a smirk.

"I know that's fine," she retorted, heading for the door. "I'll see you later."

She made her way to the galley and grabbed a bowl of potato soup. Marcus handed her a mug of emberroot tea with a knowing grin, not allowing her to leave without it. Regina quickly wolfed down the soup, forcing herself to take bitter sips of the dreaded tea between bites.

When she finished, she placed her dishes in the wash basin and hurried back to Sparks' workshop, determined to keep her promise to return quickly.

"Told ya I'd be back," Regina announced with a defiant grin as she strode into the workshop.

"That's fine," Sparks replied, barely glancing up from his work. "Did ye eat all yer food?"

"Yep," she said confidently.

"And drink all yer tea?"

"Every foot-tasting drop," she grumbled, making a face.

"Good. Now shut yer trap and get back to work," he said, his focus still on the engine part in his hands.

"Arr," she replied playfully. She sat at the worktable, pulled out her component, and grabbed a tool to scrape away the grit and grime left by the sea.

They worked in focused silence for a while, the rhythmic clinks and taps of their tools echoing softly through the workshop. After thirty minutes, Sparks noticed an unusual quiet behind him. He turned and saw Regina slumped over the bench, fast asleep, her cheek resting on her arm. The day's exhaustion had finally caught up with her.

He chuckled softly and shook his head. Quietly, he placed his own part into a drawer under his table and walked over to her. Carefully, he lifted her into his arms. Regina stirred slightly but didn't wake, instead leaning into him instinctively.

"I'm just resting my eyes," she mumbled drowsily. "I'll get it fixed in a little bit..."

Sparks smiled and carried her out of the workshop, making his way to her stateroom. Once there, he gently lowered her into her hammock and pulled the blanket over her. She snuggled into it, pulling the cover close.

"Good night, Dad," she murmured softly in her sleep, her voice barely audible.

Sparks froze for a moment, his expression softening into a tender smile. He quietly stepped out of the room, closing the door gently behind him. She needed her rest, after all.

[-----✝-----]

Journal Entry: May 7th, 1910 (Day 3)

The ship soldiers on toward the nearest port, carried by the unwavering efforts of Regina Fournier. Her conjured crystals continue to hold against the relentless pressure of the sea. However, the journey remains torturous for both Captain Lowe and First Mate Smith, whose bodies are relentlessly ravaged by the Mage's Curse of Shadows.

Eclipse Lepele and Lisa Nozaki have devised a treatment regimen to combat the curse. It involves a cleansing ritual to reduce the curse's influence, followed by Earthbloom magic to repair the damage inflicted. Yet this cycle of destruction and healing is grueling for the pair of afflicted men, their bodies caught in a painful loop of breaking and mending.

Miss Nozaki is paying a steep price as well. The strain of expending vast amounts of mana has left her suffering from mana depletion, much like Miss Fournier. Both young women, Avatars of Change and Unity, continue to push themselves to their limits, risking not only their well-being but possibly their very lives to see us through this perilous voyage.

I must confess, it is difficult to witness such sacrifice. Their courage and resilience inspire awe, but I fear for the cost they may yet have to pay.

[-----⊕-----]

Sophie and Eclipse Lepele spent the morning sparring in the exercise room, the ship's hold still too waterlogged for use. Lepele's skill was overwhelming, each session ended with Sophie hitting the mat, time after time. His attacks were basic, his counters effortless, yet devastating. Every fall became a lesson, his quiet teaching refining her hand-to-hand techniques bit by bit.

Frustrated after landing flat again, Sophie glared up at him. "Okay, I'm gonna do it this time," she vowed, pushing herself off the mat.

"Sure you will. I have faith," Lepele teased, offering a smirk as he pulled her to her feet.

Sophie reset her stance, determined. After a quick nod from him, she lunged with a sharp jab, then sidestepped and followed up with a hook punch. Lepele shifted back, opening up space. Seeing her chance, Sophie surged forward with a straight punch. He blocked it, countering with a punch of his own. She twisted her torso to dodge and swung wide for a clean hit, but his knee shot up, stopping her fist cold.

Quickly retreating, Sophie barely had time to reset as Lepele advanced, his dreaded hair trailing like a shadow behind him. She ducked under his next punch and tried to pivot away, only to be caught off guard by a cross punch to her nose. The force sent her crashing to the mat once more.

"So, why did that happen?" Lepele asked, standing over her with his gloved hands relaxed at his sides.

"Because you blocked my last attack," Sophie replied, irritation creeping into her voice.

"Wrong again." He shook his head and leaned forward, locking eyes with her. "You're not practicing defense. When your attack fails, you're left wide open, scrambling to survive. That's the kind of mistake that'll get you killed in the field." He tapped her arm and straightened. "That's enough for today. We need to get the doors ready."

They removed their gloves and placed them in the box mounted on the wall before heading to the armory utility deck, where the marked doors were stored. Working with methodical precision, they laid the doors flat and drew ritual circles using grease salvaged from the ruined machine shop. Once the preparation was complete, they carefully carried the doors to the captain's operations room, placing them beneath Kidd and Smitty's beds.

A few minutes later, Lepele sent Sophie to check on Lisa while he finished the setup. In Lisa's stateroom, Sophie found her friend deep in slumber, tangled in her hammock. Gently shaking the hammock, Sophie whispered, "Hey, girl. Time for the ritual."

Lisa stirred and blinked at her. "Already?" she mumbled in a groggy voice. "Ugh... I just need to get dressed."

Watching her usually vibrant, green-haired friend struggle to stay awake tugged at Sophie's heart. Lisa seemed so worn down. Sophie's frown deepened, but she remained silent.

"I am okay. Do not worry so much," Lisa reassured her, noticing the concern in Sophie's violet eyes. "I promise." She stood and stretched before giving Sophie a small, tired smile. "I will meet you up there."

"Okay," Sophie replied softly, letting the lie slide without comment.

She left the room, her mind churning. The frown refused to leave her face. *I must do something to help her*, she thought as she walked to the operations room.

A short while later, Lisa emerged, more composed but still yawning and stretching frequently. Together, they joined Lepele on the main deck. At Lisa's nod, he began the cleansing ritual. The intense light of the circle flared around Kidd and Smitty's beds. Lisa clapped her hands against her cheeks to stay alert, trying to shake off the exhaustion weighing her down.

Once the ritual ended, Lisa stepped forward, her Earthbloom sense sweeping over the two cursed men. As expected, Captain Kidd was in far worse shape than Smitty. Sighing quietly, Lisa set to work, beginning her healing with Kidd. His agonized screams echoed across the room as the red particles from her spell circle surged into his body, knitting his wounds back together piece by painful piece.

Sophie watched as Lisa moved from Captain Kidd's bedside. He lay there drenched in sweat, perhaps worse, and barely conscious. Once, he had been a charismatic man, his good looks and sharp wit his tools for navigating life. Now, he was reduced to clinging to survival, his breath ragged but steady for the moment. With his lungs freshly healed by Lisa's magic, he would savor the brief reprieve before the curse inevitably spread through him again. Sophie's heart ached at the sight, the weight of his suffering pressing down on her.

Her attention shifted to Smitty's tortured moans and cries. Lisa was hard at work again, pouring her remaining strength into healing him. Smitty was a stark contrast to Kidd, always quiet and thoughtful, constantly calculating his next word or next move. But now, his sole focus was survival, his mind fully engaged in enduring the agony. It was a testament to his resilience. Sophie admired that about the entire privateer crew; they faced death with defiance, fighting to live until the very end. If the sea ever swallowed them, she was sure they would give it indigestion on the way down.

Lisa finally stepped back, wiping sweat from her brow. "And... we are done," she sighed, massaging her temples as a headache crept in from excessive mana use. As she walked toward the door, both Kidd and Smitty weakly raised a thumbs-up in gratitude from their beds.

Annabelle appeared at the top of the stairs, balancing a tray with two bowls of oatmeal. "'scuse me, copper," she said as she brushed past Sophie, heading into the operations room to feed the men. Lepele followed close behind to assist her.

Sophie and Lisa made their way to the galley for breakfast. They found seats against the wall, and Marcus soon arrived with two bowls of oatmeal, topped with apple slices and a thin sprinkle of cinnamon. He also set down two cups of emberroot tea. Sophie smiled and thanked him for his attentiveness.

After Marcus returned to the serving counter, Sophie turned to Lisa and gently touched her arm. It was both cold and clammy with sweat. "How are you holding up?"

Lisa took a sip of her tea before responding. "I am... okay. Just very sleepy," she admitted. "Healing the Captain and Mr. Smith takes so much out of me." She ate a spoonful of her oatmeal, pausing in thought. "It is strange, though. The curse does not seem to affect Mr. Smith as badly as it does the Captain. I wonder why that is."

"Yeah, *that is weird*," Sophie agreed, taking a cautious sip of the tea. She grimaced and shook her head. "Ugh. I still don't understand how you drink this stuff."

Lisa smiled teasingly. "I like the taste of emberroot tea. Something must be wrong with you." she joked.

Regina plopped down beside them, her silver hair sticking to her temples. "Hello, lasses," she greeted in an exaggerated pirate accent. "How goes the day?"

"It's good," Sophie replied with a smile. "How are you holding up?"

"Arr," Regina continued in her faux patois, "the ship needs so much of me magic that I canna do most anythin' but sleep in me bunk."

Lisa groaned in exasperation, her patience worn thin. "You have only been on this ship for a month! By the harvest, stop talking like that!" she snapped.

Regina blinked, momentarily surprised, then burst out laughing. Sophie chuckled too, the tension in the air easing as the three friends shared the moment.

"Fine," Regina relented, too tired to argue with Lisa. She turned to Sophie and added in her faux pirate accent, "Tough one we got here."

Sophie giggled. "Nah, she's fine. She just has her ways."

Lisa huffed in mock indignation, turning her nose up with a sharp "Hmph."

The three continued their breakfast, trading playful jabs and teasing remarks. Eventually, Lisa and Regina excused themselves to get more sleep, leaving Sophie to face another round of ritual training under Eclipse Lepele.

In the training area, Lepele had drawn a ritual circle on a tattered sheet of paper and nailed it to the wall. His instructions were straightforward: the ritual would reveal a secret password once she figured out what she was doing wrong.

Sophie struggled for hours. Every time she tried to infuse the circle with mana through her pointer and middle fingers, the ritual rejected her attempt with an unpleasant sting, her hand throbbing from backlash. Frustration mounted with each failure. She glared at the circle as if it had personally offended her. How could this simple shape on a piece of paper outmatch me? Infusing runes was second nature to her, easy and instinctive. But this ritual continued to resist her, mocking her with every failed attempt.

Between her bouts of failure, her mind wandered to her conversation with Lisa. Why wasn't Smitty as severely affected by the curse as Captain Kidd? Smitty was a mage, while the Captain wasn't. Was the curse somehow targeting non-mages more severely?

"How's it coming?" Lepele's voice broke her thoughts. He approached from behind, a knowing smirk tugging at his lips. "Figured out the secret yet?"

"No, sir," Sophie admitted sheepishly. "But I do have another question."

"After you try again," Lepele replied, gesturing to the paper.

Sighing, Sophie cleared her mind, pressed her fingers to the ritual, and attempted to channel her mana. The circle rejected her once more, sending a sharp, stinging pain up her hand. She winced and cried out, "Ow! Dammit!"

"You'll get there, Griffin," Lepele reassured her with a calm nod. "Remember, don't channel your mana through your affinity. Now, what's your question?"

Shaking her hand to ease the pain, Sophie explained, "Lisa said the shadow curse doesn't seem to hurt Smitty as much as the Captain. I was thinking... could it be because Smitty's a mage?"

Lepele placed a hand on his chin, thoughtfully considering her theory. After a moment, he nodded. "You might be onto something. Grab your inspection glasses and meet me in the Captain's operations room." He paused, his eyes twinkling with mischief. "After you try one more time."

Sophie barely hid her scowl as she reluctantly gave the ritual another attempt. "Ow! Dammit!" she yelped as the backlash struck again.

Lepele stifled a grin. "See you on the bridge," he said, turning to leave.

Sophie grumbled under her breath, rubbing her sore hand as she made her way to her stateroom. She retrieved her inspection glasses from her bag and headed to the bridge. There, Lepele stood next to Annabelle, who was calmly steering the ship from the helm.

Sophie opened the door to the captain's operations room and slipped the glasses on. Her vision shifted, the glasses reveal the details hidden to the naked eye. Shadows leaked from the bodies of both Kidd and Smitty, but the shadows radiating from the captain glowed with a stronger, dark-blue light. When she focused on Smitty, something caught her attention—normal mana particles were drifting from his hands, glowing softly with white light.

"Why?" she whispered to herself, her investigative instincts taking over. "Why channel mana if you're cursed?"

She watched closely as the mana particles flowed toward the shadow curse. The cursed particles seemed to absorb the mana, causing them to dim and then vanish entirely. Her mind raced, piecing together the puzzle.

"That's it!" she quietly exclaimed, as the idea solidified in her mind.

Sophie quietly closed the door to the operations room, careful not to disturb the two cursed men any further. She stepped onto the bridge and found Lepele leaning against the railing, faintly glowing with red mana.

"I get it now," Sophie said, her voice steady with realization. "Smitty's less affected by the curse because he's channeling mana. The curse is somehow using their mana as a fuel source."

Lepele straightened immediately, the spark of an idea flashing across his face. "Of course!" he exclaimed, excitement lighting up his expression. "It's a curse," he added, as if the simple statement explained everything.

Sophie blinked in confusion. "I don't get it," she admitted.

Annabelle glanced over from the helm. "Aye, copper, ye ain't making a lick of sense."

Lepele sighed, pinching the bridge of his nose. "By the ancestors, what are they teaching you girls these days?" He took a deep breath and launched into an explanation. "There are two types of magical actions: spells and curses. With a spell, a mage uses their own mana to sustain the effect from start to finish. But a curse... that's different. A mage uses only a small amount of mana to trigger a change in the world or in a person. The curse then draws on the target's own mana to sustain and spread itself."

"So... Mage's 'Curse of Shadows' is feeding on the men's mana?" Sophie asked, piecing it together.

"Exactly. That's why it's ravaging Captain Kidd worse than Smitty," Lepele confirmed. "What we need is a ritual."

"A ritual for what?" Annabelle asked, narrowing her eyes. "Yer not makin' sense again, copper."

Lepele shot her an exasperated look. "We also need to have a talk about what you keep calling me." He cleared his throat and continued, "If we can create a ritual to drain their mana, the curse won't have as much fuel to do damage. That way, Miss Nozaki won't have to exhaust herself with constant healing."

He turned to Annabelle. "Pirate girl, do you have a ritualist on your crew?"

"Oi! Privateer, copper!" Annabelle snapped. "I ain't no skull."

Lepele smirked. "Yeah, well, my name ain't copper, so you're pirate girl to me," he teased. "Now, ritualist, do you have one or not?"

Annabelle grumbled under her breath and shifted the wheel slightly to keep the ship on course. "Don't think so," she replied after a moment.

"Come on, Griffin, we have to check," Lepele said, already heading off.

"Right," Sophie said, feeling a renewed sense of purpose. *Finally, there was something she could do,* something that might ease Lisa's burden.

The two split up to search the ship. Lepele headed to the crew deck while Sophie descended to the cannon deck. Entering the powder magazine, she found a group of men locked in an intense card game. She cleared her throat and announced, "Are any of you gents a ritualist?"

Blaze, Ethan, Flint, and Gary all paused, exchanging looks before shrugging in unison.

"Sorry, missy," Blaze spoke up, shaking his head. "No ritualist here. So, if ye could beat it, that'd be great."

The other men chuckled softly, returning to their game, but Sophie wasn't deterred. She nodded and moved on, determined to keep searching.

Sophie left the powder mag without wasting another second on Blaze and his card game. She headed to the stateroom deck, convinced she knew just the person who could help. Reaching Regina's door, she knocked. When no response came, Sophie opened the door to find the silver-haired girl fast asleep in her hammock.

"Regina!" Sophie called at full volume. Not even a flinch. Regina really could sleep through a gunfight.

Sophie walked over and shook the hammock. "Wake up, Regina."

Regina bolted upright, eyes wide. "What? What is it? Are we under attack?"

"No, girl," Sophie said, shaking her head. "I need your help with a ritual."

"A ritual?" Regina groaned in disbelief. "Can't you just have the Eclipse do it? He knows rituals." She flopped back into her hammock with a huff.

"He sent me," Sophie fibbed, keeping her tone serious.

"Ugh, can't this wait? I'm really tired," Regina mumbled, her eyes already closing again.

Knowing Regina would fall back asleep if she didn't intervene, Sophie gave the hammock another shake. "This could help save the captain," she urged earnestly.

Regina let out a long sigh. "Okay, okay" she relented, sitting up and rubbing her eyes. "But I need to get ready." She glanced at Sophie and added, "Can you grab me a cup of coffee from the galley?"

"Okay," Sophie agreed, narrowing her eyes. "But you are getting up, right? You won't go back to sleep?"

"Yes, I'm getting up," Regina said, sounding exasperated.

Sophie nodded and left, heading up to the galley. Brother Marcus was working the serving counter. He handed Sophie a cup of coffee with a matching saucer. Sophie admired how snugly the saucer fit over the cup's opening despite clearly belonging to a different set, a testament to the crew's resourcefulness.

Returning to Regina's room, Sophie opened the door slowly, just in case. She needn't have bothered, Regina was fast asleep again. Sophie strode over and shouted, "HEY! WAKE UP!"

Regina shot upright, blinking in confusion. "What! What's going on?"

"I thought you were getting up," Sophie said flatly, raising an eyebrow.

"I was?" Regina muttered, spotting the coffee in Sophie's hand. Her eyes lit up as she reached for it. "Oh, coffee," she murmured, snatching the cup and leaving Sophie holding the saucer. Without hesitation, Regina downed the coffee in one long gulp, finishing with a satisfied sigh. "Ahhh."

"Damn, girl. That coffee was hot. How'd you do that?" Sophie asked, incredulous of what she just saw.

"It wasn't that hot," Regina said with a shrug. She hopped out of the hammock, clad only in her underwear. "I've had hotter coffee, burned my mouth once, actually. This was good, though. Oh! Let's go get more!" She headed toward the door.

"Girl, you're in your underwear!" Sophie exclaimed, stopping her in her tracks.

Regina looked down at herself, then back at Sophie. "Oh. Yeah. I should probably get dressed."

She threw on a pair of coveralls gifted by Mr. Sparks and tied her hair into two buns, securing them with pencils from her pocket. Together, they returned to the galley, where Regina marched straight to the counter and placed her empty cup down with a bright smile.

"Good morning, Brother Marcus! I'd like another cup of coffee, please."

Marcus studied her for a moment, noting her wide eyes and forced energy. He could see the dark circles under her eyes, a clear sign she was running on little to no sleep. Checking his watch, he saw that it was just before three o'clock. With a sigh, he suggested, "Miss Fournier, it looks like you've already had some coffee. How about a cup of emberroot tea instead?"

"Foot tea?!" Regina protested loudly. "*No way.* I want coffee."

"Okay," Marcus relented with a sly smile. He took the cup, washed it, and returned it filled, not with coffee, but with emberroot tea. "As requested," he said, setting the cup down.

Regina took a sip, only to immediately spit it out in disgust. "Marcus! I said no foot tea!"

"My mistake, Miss Fournier," Marcus said smoothly. "Unfortunately, Miss Griffin had the last of the coffee. I'll need to brew a fresh pot. In the meantime, why don't you finish your emberroot tea? I'll bring you coffee when it's ready."

Regina narrowed her eyes. "I've had enough foot tea, Brother Marcus," she said firmly, rejecting his ploy.

Marcus chuckled under his breath as she glared at the offending drink. Sophie watched the exchange with amusement, shaking her head at Regina's dramatic disdain for emberroot tea.

"So, what are you and Miss Griffin working on?" Marcus asked, shifting the conversation.

Regina shrugged. "She needs my help crafting a ritual circle."

"What kind of ritual circle?" Marcus pressed, keeping his tone casual.

"Something to do with the captain," Regina replied, taking another reluctant sip of her foot tea.

"Well, when you find out, let me know," Marcus suggested with a friendly smile.

"Okay," Regina said as she walked back to the table where Sophie was waiting. She sat down and asked, "What do you need the ritual to do?"

"We want to drain mana from Captain Kidd and Smitty," Sophie explained.

Regina nearly choked on her tea. "Drain their mana? Why? If they hit zero mana while cursed, they'll die."

"Uh... well," Sophie hesitated. "We think the curse is using their mana to spread through their bodies."

At that moment, Eclipse Lepele entered the galley, scanning the room. Sophie waved him over. "The Eclipse can explain it better," she said to Regina.

Lepele took a seat beside Regina, across from Sophie. He glanced between the two of them. "Regina, you're up? I didn't expect to see you awake."

"Yeah. Sophie said you needed my help with a ritual," Regina replied, lowering her teacup halfway to the table.

"Did she now?" Lepele turned to Sophie, raising an eyebrow. "And what else did she tell you?" His tone was light but probing, and Sophie recognized the tactic from her training: *friendly questioning to coax information.*

"She said you want to drain mana from the captain and Smitty because the curse is using their mana to fuel itself," Regina said, resting her arms on the table. "But if you drain too much, they'll die. I mean, maybe it's better than letting the curse kill them, but that's still a rough way to go." She paused to take another sip of tea and added, "I suppose you could use a draining ritual to siphon their mana... but what are you planning to do with it once it's out? Are you going to use it to power a healing ritual? Or maybe speed up the ship?" She eyed Lepele curiously.

Lepele stared at her for a moment, his face expressionless, his mind clearly turning over her words.

Sophie giggled. "Yeah, she does that sometimes," she said, referring to Regina's habit of letting her thoughts spill out in rapid bursts.

Lepele shook his head slightly and responded, "I don't plan on draining all their mana. I'm thinking we reduce it to 'mana low.' That should deprive the curse of enough fuel to slow it down and hopefully keep it from doing so much damage."

"Which would mean Lisa wouldn't have to heal them as much," Sophie added, nodding in understanding.

Regina tilted her head thoughtfully. "Okay... but what are you going to do with the mana you collect?" she asked, sipping her tea and grimacing at the taste.

"I hadn't thought about that," Lepele admitted, leaning back in his chair to consider the possibilities. "Maybe we could use the mana to fuel a healing ritual?" he pondered aloud.

"I don't know any healing rituals," Regina said, shaking her head. "Those are really complicated. Do you know any? My mom's friend Miss Fleurette probably does, but I can't exactly ask her right now. I should remember to get a few next time I see her." She paused thoughtfully. "Maybe we could create a wind ritual to fill the sails and push the ship faster to port. Do you know any wind rituals?"

"I do not," Lepele replied. "Do you know of any rituals that can restore someone's mana?"

Regina frowned in thought. "Not exactly," she admitted. Her mind worked through her knowledge of how the body processed energy. "But Earthbloom healing transforms mana into vital energy, helping the body repair itself. Maybe we could use that as a template and craft a ritual to inject mana directly into the liver."

Lepele raised an eyebrow. "Why the liver?"

"That's where the body stores mana," Regina explained, recalling information from the journal they had read at the Black Sun facility in Verdantia.

Lepele seemed impressed and took a moment to process her suggestion. "Can you create a ritual shape to handle all that?"

"I think so," Regina said with a nod. "But I'll need a notebook to sketch out the details of each circle." She finished her tea and added with a playful smile, "And maybe a cup of coffee."

Lepele gave her a skeptical look. "Aren't you a bit young for coffee? I'll get you some water and something tasty to eat instead." He turned to Sophie. "Griffin, can I talk to you for a moment?"

The two of them got up and walked toward the serving counter. Once out of earshot, Lepele grabbed Sophie's arm firmly. "I didn't tell you to wake her up. She needs her rest!" he said, his voice stern.

"I'm sorry, Eclipse," Sophie said, her voice low. "I didn't think..."

"Exactly. You didn't think and you need to start." He released her arm and continued, "Go find a notebook or something to write in, and this time, make sure not to wake Nozaki."

"Yes, Eclipse," Sophie replied, swallowing her embarrassment.

With a dismissive gesture, Lepele motioned toward the door, and Sophie hurried off to complete her task.

She eventually found an almost-empty notebook in the powder mag. Not wanting to disturb the ongoing card game, she quietly checked that no one would miss the book before heading back to the galley. When she returned, Regina was seated with Lepele, deep in discussion. Sophie handed the notebook to Regina.

"Will this work?" Sophie asked.

Regina opened the book, flipping through the first few pages. They contained inventory records from the powder mag, lists of cloth, gunpowder, string, and sewing needles, along with notes on how many cloth packages were prepared for cannon use. However, most of the pages beyond the fourth were blank.

"Yeah, this'll do," Regina said with a satisfied nod. She pulled a pencil from her hair and began sketching ritual designs on the empty pages. After four failed attempts, she frowned and reviewed her latest work carefully, just as Mr. Beasley from school had taught her. She sighed, realizing the design wouldn't be effective.

Taking a break, she sipped another cup of emberroot tea to ward off an oncoming headache. On her sixth attempt, she finally produced a circle that looked both functional and efficient. She slid the notebook across the table to Sophie.

"That should do it," Regina announced confidently.

Sophie studied the ritual circle Regina had drawn. It consisted of a large central circle with intricate writing along its edge and four smaller circles inside, each filled with runes and sigils. While she could follow the structure, the exact function of the circle eluded her. Still, she didn't want to admit that. "Looks good," she said, offering a reassuring smile. Remembering the instructions Lepele had given her for the cleansing rituals, she asked, "How big does the circle need to be?"

Regina finished her tea and explained, "Any smaller than fifty centimeters, and it won't work. With the room's dimensions in mind, you're probably looking at a meter to a meter and a half in diameter."

"I can handle that... I think," Sophie replied, mentally calculating the effort it would take to craft such a large and complex circle. It was going to take time.

Regina stretched and yawned. "I'm going to grab a nap before I have to repair my crystals again," she said, standing up. She paused and looked at Sophie. "Unless you need help drawing the circle?"

"No, get your sleep." Sophie insisted with a grin. "I've got this."

Regina nodded and left, and Sophie walked her back to her room to make sure she settled in. Afterward, Sophie began roaming the ship in search of something large enough to draw the ritual circle on. She eventually found herself in the hold, where she spotted Lisa's lone surviving suitcase. Chuckling at the thought of using it, she kept searching until her eyes landed on a thick training mat hanging from the wall.

Spreading her arms, Sophie quickly measured the width of the mat. It was more than large enough for the circle. Satisfied, she pulled out the notebook with Regina's design and got to work.

It took Sophie an hour to carefully draw Regina's ritual circle on the training mat hanging near one of Regina's crystals. The crystal was starting to crack under the relentless pressure of seawater crashing against the inner hull of the ship.

"There you are," Lepele called from behind as he climbed down the ladder into the hold. "Getting an early start?" he asked, referring to the cleansing ritual circles they had been drawing on the doors.

"Oh no," Sophie corrected. "I was working on the ritual circle Regina designed for me."

"How's that coming along?" Lepele asked.

"I just finished," Sophie replied, wiping her hands on her pants.

Lepele stepped in front of the mat, examining the symbols, runes, and sigils. "Can I see your reference?"

Sophie handed him the notebook, opened to the page with Regina's final design. Lepele studied the notebook, glanced back at the mat, and nodded. "Yeah, that looks about right."

"Do you know what this circle does?" Sophie asked, curious.

Lepele scratched his head. "I can tell it creates a field to collect mana, but beyond that, I'd need your friend to explain the finer details." He handed the notebook back to her. "Let's get started on the cleansing rituals."

Together, they drew two ritual circles on the doors, with Lepele complimenting Sophie on her improved technique. Once they finished, they carried the four doors up to the bridge to wait for Lisa. Lepele then sent Sophie back to retrieve the training mat circle. Instead of struggling to carry the heavy mat up the stairs, Sophie tied a pull rope to it, making sure not to disturb the carefully drawn design. She hauled it up and returned to the bridge.

When she arrived, she saw the operations room glowing brightly from the active cleansing rituals. Lisa stood beside Harmon, who was steering the ship from the helm.

"How are you holding up?" Sophie asked as she approached.

Lisa yawned, covering her mouth with one hand. "I am okay. My mother says hello," she replied casually.

"You talked to your mom?" Sophie asked, raising an eyebrow.

"My dad made me promise to send him updates every day to let him know I am alive and what I am doing," Lisa explained.

Sophie's eyes widened. "What did you tell him about the pirate attack?"

Lisa smiled mischievously. "Oh, I, uh... forgot to mention that."

The two giggled at Lisa's omission. Sophie noticed the dark circles under her friend's eyes.

"Are you sure you're okay? You look exhausted," Sophie said gently.

Lisa sighed. "I am tired. But I cannot let the captain and Mr. Smith die."

As if on cue, the bright light from the cleansing rituals began to dim, fading like curtains being drawn over a window. Lepele turned toward Lisa and announced, "You're up."

Lisa nodded at Sophie. "If you will excuse me, I have some healing to do." She made her way into the operations room, ready to begin her routine.

Sophie and Lepele unhooked the training mat and carried it to the bridge. From the operations room, the anguished cries and moans of the cursed men echoed as

Lisa worked to heal their internal organs and repair the damage inflicted by the curse of shadows.

When the session ended, both Smitty and the captain managed weak smiles and gave Lisa a thumbs-up in gratitude. Lisa stepped out, visibly drained from the intense Earthbloom healing spell.

"I'll be back later for more tender loving care," she joked darkly as she left.

The men chuckled softly despite their pain, waving goodbye as Lisa made her way toward the kitchen for a much-needed cup of emberroot tea.

Sophie and Lepele entered the operations room and hung the training mat with the ritual circle on the wall, using the hooks usually reserved for the captain's maps. Lepele placed his hand on the circle. "Here goes nothing," he said, activating the ritual.

Sophie felt a faint tug on her mana as the circle began to glow dimly. She slipped on her inspection glasses and watched as mana particles flowed from Captain Kidd, Smitty, Lepele, and even herself into the ritual. Through the enhanced vision of her glasses, the circle glowed much brighter as it absorbed the mana.

Satisfied, Lepele and Sophie exited the room just as Annabelle and Sparks arrived with food and water for the Captain and Smitty, ensuring the two men got nourishment before the curse resumed its relentless assault on their bodies.

"When will we know if the ritual's working?" Sophie asked as she and Lepele descended the stairs from the bridge to the deck.

"When Miss Nozaki heals them again, she'll be able to tell if the curse is doing less damage to their bodies." Lepele explained.

They reached the galley entrance and spotted Regina and Lisa at one of the tables, eating their dinner. Sophie gave them a small wave, deciding she wasn't hungry, and continued on her way to the training room.

Once inside, Sophie approached the ritual circle that Lepele had nailed to the wall. After working with Regina's circle earlier, she felt more confident. Now she could bring this one to life.

She pressed her two fingers to the circle and began channeling her mana, expecting success. Instead, pain shot through her hand as the circle rejected her mana with a surge of backlash.

"Ow! Dammit." Sophie hissed, pulling her hand away and shaking it.

Chapter 27

Journal Entry: May 8th, 1910 (Day 4)

Without the engines' assistance, the Stormfang crawls steadily toward the ports of Magitekopolis. When not fulfilling his duties as first mate, Mr. Sparks devotes himself to engine repairs, sometimes with the assistance of Miss Fournier. Their combined efforts reflect a determined fight to restore the ship's mechanical power and hasten our journey.

The burden on both Miss Fournier and Miss Nozaki has eased somewhat, thanks to Miss Griffin's investigative insight. The draining circle ritual they devised has proven effective in reducing the curse of shadows' impact. According to Eclipse Lepele, the curse relies on its victims' mana to propagate. With less mana available, the curse inflicts less damage, making the cleansing ritual more effective and easing the healing workload on Miss Nozaki.

Miss Fournier also benefits from the draining circle, as she can siphon small amounts of the collected mana to sustain her crystalmancy. However, the mana she draws is not sufficient to fully counteract her own mana depletion. While this temporary reprieve has helped, both avatars remain at risk of overexertion. They continue to push themselves to their limits, striving to keep the Stormfang afloat and its crew alive in these perilous conditions.

[----S-----]

Sparks worked tirelessly to keep the Stormfang and its crew moving forward during this grueling *Dead Man's Sprint* to Magitekopolis. They were still three days from port, and he prayed that no new problems would arise. One more issue, just one, could spell disaster, sinking the ship and sending everyone, including the four so-called avatar sisters, to the depths of the sea.

His days had become a taxing routine, broken into six-hour blocks. Each cycle began with waking Regina to repair her crystal barriers that held back the sea. This was always followed by their usual debate: whether she should eat a meal, drink emberroot tea, and then go back to sleep. With Sophie's help, Sparks had discovered that the draining circle ritual could provide Regina with just enough mana to slightly ease her crystal work, though not enough to fully offset her mana depletion or stave off the headaches.

After dealing with Regina, Sparks oversaw the deck crew. With the utility deck damaged beyond use, he rotated crew members between deck and runner duties to keep everyone working. Nobody got to slack off, except Dr. Gary and Ethan, who were focused on medical tasks. The crew grumbled, but they did their jobs; they wanted their coin, after all. Sparks received daily updates from Acting Captain Annabelle Salazar, who also reported on any complaints from the crew. Sparks had to admit she was handling the weight of command well, perhaps one day, she'd live up to her father's legendary reputation. He did what he could to ease her burden.

Today's assignments were set: Blaze as runner, Flint and Popper on deck and sails, Harmon steering the ship, Jeffie in the kitchen, and Brother Marcus handling the serving counter. Eclipse Lepele and Sophie filled in wherever needed but primarily focused on maintaining the life-saving rituals for Captain Kidd and Smitty. Sparks dreamed of a day when these endless complaints and crises would finally end.

When he could steal time away from his duties, Sparks poured his energy into repairing the engines. He hoped to get them running soon so the Stormfang could reach port before Lady Luck turned her back on them. As he passed the training gym, he heard Sophie inside, swearing in frustration as she struggled with her ritual training. He chuckled to himself. *Seriously, who gets backlash from rituals?*

In his workshop, Sparks focused on the final obstacle: the rusted, clogged cylinder block. It was jammed with debris, including dead fish and sediment, preventing the pistons from moving. Sparks began by removing the rotating wheel from the belt. Fortunately, the belt was undamaged. He carefully placed each piece into a drawer to keep the work area tidy. Next, he attached a wrench to the bolt securing the mechanism and attempted to turn it. The bolt refused to budge, likely due to being either rusted solid or blocked by obstructions.

Grunting with effort, Sparks pulled on the wrench with all his might, straining until his muscles burned, but the bolt remained stubbornly in place. He growled in frustration, then took a deep breath to clear his head. "Maybe pushing will work," he muttered to himself.

He repositioned the wrench, braced himself, and pushed with all his strength, screaming through clenched teeth. Still nothing. The engine sat on the table, unmoved, like a defiant child refusing to listen.

Sparks paused, shaking his aching hands. He wasn't about to let the machine win. Determined, he fastened a heavy strap across the top of the cylinder block, securing it tightly to the bench. He made sure the wrench was firmly attached to the rotation bolt. This time, he wasn't holding back. He took a step back to gather momentum, inhaling deeply and focusing all his frustration, everything from the endless repairs to dealing with a crew afflicted by "Itchy Diaper Syndrome" (his term for those who whined about having to work).

With a sharp exhale, Sparks charged forward, slamming his full weight into the wrench. His hand collided with it in a single, explosive motion, channeling all his kinetic energy through the tool and into the bolt.

The bolt finally moved, a few centimeters, but it moved.

"By the sea," Sparks breathed with a triumphant grin. "You're gonna move if it kills me."

The three pistons sank just an inch into the block before stopping cold. Sparks threw all his weight behind the wrench, but it didn't budge beyond that first little bit. His frustration flared, a few centimeters wasn't going to be the last word today. He gritted his teeth and pulled with all his strength. The wrench suddenly slipped off the bolt, and his knuckles slammed into the housing. The sharp metal tore into his skin, leaving bloody scrapes. He grits his teeth in pain, staring at the fresh wounds on his gnarled hands.

Disrespect. From the ship's crew, from the avatars, from the acting Captain, he could tolerate all of that. But not from a damn piece of machinery.

"Dammit, you will respect me," Sparks growled under his breath. He raised the wrench and smashed it against the housing again and again, each blow ringing through the workshop. The machine had to work. *It had to because... she couldn't take much more.*

He stopped, lowering the wrench as his stomach twisted with despair. Regina. His silver-haired "assistant," the motor-mouthed girl who was giving every last ounce of herself to keep the Stormfang afloat. Sparks could see it in her eyes, hear it in her voice, she is fading away. She had less and less to give each day. The reaper would be coming for her soon if things didn't change, and Sparks couldn't bear the thought of a world without her endless chatter about magical tools and solutions to ease every minor inconvenience.

Tears welled in his eyes and streamed down his face. Everyone always said, *Sparks can fix anything. There's nothing he can't fix.* But not this time. Not when it mattered most. He sank to the floor, his hands shaking. The truth hit him like a blow: *he wasn't a genius mechanic, just a lucky old fool who is running out of time ... and luck.*

A knock on the door interrupted his spiral of despair. "Mr. Sparks?" Sophie's voice called from the other side. Is everything alright in here? I heard some loud banging."

He quickly wiped his tears with a rag from his pocket. "Yeah, girlie, just working on the engine," he replied, steadying his voice.

The door opened, and Sophie stepped inside. She found Sparks sitting on the floor, his eyes still red. "Can I sit?" she asked gently.

Without thinking, Sparks waved her over, inviting her to sit across from him.

Sophie crossed her legs and lowered herself onto the dirty floor. "How are you holding up, Mr. Sparks? Is 'Sparks' even your real name?" she asked absentmindedly.

He chuckled softly. "Of course not. It's me sea name," he explained, leaving his real name unspoken. "What brings ye to me workshop?"

"Honestly? I'm just a bit lonely," Sophie admitted with a shrug.

Sparks raised an eyebrow. "Lonely? You've got that other copper on board with ye. How could ye be lonely?"

"The Eclipse is my superior," Sophie replied. "We don't really have a connection outside of the clan. Normally, I'd train with Regina or eat with Lisa, but now they're just..." She trailed off, the weight of her unspoken fears pressing down on her.

"Slipping away," Sparks finished for her, his voice softer now. He knew the feeling all too well. "What about Belle?" he asked, thinking of Annabelle.

Sophie gave him a look, her violet eyes silently asking, *Are you serious?*

The two shared a laugh. Sparks shook his head and smiled. "She's a lot sometimes, sure. But she loves you other girls. You two bicker like cantankerous old cats, but I can tell you love her too."

"Bite your tongue," Sophie said with a grin.

They laughed again, the tension easing as the shared moment grounded them. Sparks stood, the weight of his anguish lifting. He extended a hand to Sophie. "Well, we gots ourselves work to do."

Sophie took his hand and stood. "Back to the sawmill," she agreed with a small smile.

[-----S-----]

Sparks had finished repairing and reassembling the engine. Now came the hard part, getting it down to the hold and installed. He made his way to the powder mag and was greeted by an annoying sight: Ethan, Gary, and *Blaze* sitting around a table playing crew. Blaze, in particular, was supposed to be today's runner.

"I need you mates to help me move the engine," Sparks announced in his usual tone as he stepped into the room.

"In a minute," Blaze replied dismissively, not bothering to look up from his cards.

"Blaze, ain't ye supposed to be the runner today?" Sparks asked, the offence already simmering in his chest as he moved closer to the table.

"Nah, I didn't sign up for that, mate," Blaze said casually, laying a card down without pausing. "Ye will have to get yerself another sod."

Sparks crossed his arms, his voice turning firm. "Look, the card game can wait. Let's get this engine down to the hold and installed."

Blaze smirked, still not looking at him. "Look, *First Mate*," he said, drawing out the title in a mocking tone. "We're in the middle of a game, so why don't you just beat it?"

Sparks paused, taking a deep breath to make sure he was ready *for what had to be done*. Without warning, he slammed Blaze's head down onto the table, sending coins and cards scattering across the floor. Sparks gripped Blaze's greasy hair and yanked his head back, forcing him to meet his eyes.

"Blaze," Sparks growled, his voice low and deadly, "I told ye to be the runner today. So why are ye down here playin' crew?"

Blaze instinctively raised his hand to cast his fire-snap spell, but froze when he felt cold steel press against his neck. Sparks had drawn his knife. The fear in Blaze's eyes was unmistakable.

"Go ahead, do it cannon cocker." Sparks taunted, his voice chilling and somber.

The room fell silent except for the distant creaks of the ship rocking with the sea. Blaze's hand slowly dropped as he realized just how serious Sparks was.

"No? Are ye sure, Blaze?" Sparks prodded, his knife still resting lightly on the man's neck.

"Everything okay in here?" Annabelle's voice broke the tense silence from the doorway. Her tone carried both curiosity and caution, unsure how the situation had escalated or where it might lead.

"Everything's fine, Actin' Cap'n," Sparks replied without breaking eye contact with Blaze. "Ain't it, Blaze?"

Blaze didn't speak but gave a stiff nod of agreement.

"See, Cap'n? Just a happy crew talkin' bidness," Sparks said, his words cold as ice.

Annabelle eyed the scene warily but didn't press further. "We got ship's bidness to talk about, First Mate. Wrap things up here and meet me on the observation deck."

"I'll be right there, Cap'n," Sparks said, his gaze still fixed on Blaze, making sure the man understood that Annabelle wouldn't be coming to save him.

After Annabelle left, Sparks leaned in closer, his voice dropping to a dangerous whisper. "Listen here, cannon cocker. When I tell ye to do somethin', ye do it. Got that?"

Blaze nodded quickly, careful not to cut himself on the knife.

"The next time I catch ye mouthin' off..." Sparks paused to let the threat linger. "Trust me, mate, ye don't want there to be a next time. We clear?"

"Aye, First Mate," Blaze replied, his earlier defiance replaced by caution.

Sparks finally removed the knife and stepped back, his demeanor shifting to a mock friendliness. "Good. Now, I need ye all to move that engine from my workshop down to the hold."

"Right away," Gary said quickly, clearly eager to de-escalate the situation.

"Very good," Sparks said with a false smile. He walked to the doorway and glanced back at the trio. "No more crew today, boys. Ye got work to do."

The three men exchanged glances before responding with a collective "Arr," acknowledging the Order.

Satisfied, Sparks headed for the observation deck to meet Annabelle.

[-----✝-----]

Journal Entry May 9th (Day 5)

The Stormfang presses onward across the sea, bound for the port of Magitekopolis. Mr. Sparks has managed to repair the engines, but he discovered that the battery is completely inoperable due to flooding, rendering it useless. Although the engine could run on fuel, the supply was exhausted during Captain Lowe's attempt to escape from the trio of pirate ships, making Sparks' efforts seem futile.

The arduous journey is taking its toll on everyone aboard. Avatars Fournier and Nozaki are pushing themselves to their limits, depleting their mana reserves to dangerous levels. If this continues much longer, I fear for their lives. The emotional cost of watching their fellow avatars deteriorate is also weighing heavily on Avatars Salazar and Griffin.

Annabelle Salazar, now acting as Captain, channels her frustration into her work, ensuring the crew remains busy, fed, and the ship stays afloat. Her leadership during this crisis is commendable, reflecting her growing potential to be a ship's Captain. Sophie Griffin, on the other hand, is immersing herself in her training and the tasks assigned by Eclipse Lepele. This focus helps her avoid the painful memories of the Granmark massacre. The thought of facing her clan in Magitekopolis, whom she hasn't reported to since that day, adds another layer of emotional strain for Sophie.

[-----✝-----]

"The ship should arrive at Gearhaven on the morning of May 11th," Marcus wrote in his scrapbook, using his ritual pen to send the message to Sister Ingrid. The ink pen ritual spell was something he had learned from his mentor, Brother Albert. He paused for a moment, thinking of Albert. If he could see me now, what would he say?

A few seconds later, the pen began moving on its own, scrawling Ingrid's response across the page:

"The Order will have assistance ready at Gearhaven port Number Six. We have notified the Aurorium Clan, and they will be prepared to receive Sophie Griffin and the assumed Eclipse Lepele from Umbrathorn."

The pen briefly paused before lifting itself upright to deliver another message.

"When you arrive, all passengers from your ship will be taken to the nearby Good King Lucas Hospital to address their injuries, conditions, and curses. The Order will cover all associated costs."

Marcus exhaled in relief and wrote beneath the response, "I understand. Thank you, Sister."

The pen stirred one last time, etching a final message:

"Take care of the avatars and yourself."

With that, the pen rested on the page, signifying that the ritual spell had ended. Marcus gently closed the scrapbook and tucked the pen away, mentally preparing for the challenges still ahead.

Marcus stood behind the serving counter in the galley, preparing a fresh pot of emberroot tea for the crew, especially for Miss Regina and Miss Lisa. The rest of the crew loitered around the room after breakfast, lacking anywhere else to go. Mr. Sparks had recently cracked down on the games of crew, confiscating every deck of cards aboard the ship.

Regina entered the galley, her silver hair slightly disheveled from her morning crystal repairs. She walked up to the counter and grinned. "Breakfast and a cup of coffee, mate!" she ordered in her ever improving pirate patois.

"You're in luck, Miss Fournier," Marcus said smoothly, adopting the tone of a waiter. "The cook's made pancakes, eggs, and sausages."

"Yum!" Regina replied, abandoning her act for a moment. Marcus smirked, knowing the patois would return soon enough.

He turned to the serving table behind him and grabbed a plate. He added a generous stack of pancakes, a pair of boiled eggs still in their shells, and three sausages—he knew Regina loved sausages. He poured a hot drink into a mug and set both the plate and mug on the counter in front of her.

Regina glanced into the mug, immediately spotting the telltale yellow tint. "Oi, Brother Marcus! This is foot tea! I ordered coffee!" she reminded him.

"My mistake," Marcus said smoothly. He thought on his feet. "I must apologize, Miss Regina. I'll brew a fresh pot and bring you a cup."

"Aye, see that ye do." Regina replied, slipping back into her pirate patois. She pointed two fingers from her eyes toward Marcus in a mock warning before heading to her table.

As she started eating, Sophie and Lisa entered the seating area. Lisa dragged herself to the table beside Regina, her head resting in her hands. The signs of her depleted mana reserves were evident in her exhaustion. Meanwhile, Sophie went to the counter to collect plates for both herself, and Lisa. Marcus followed with mugs of emberroot tea for them both. Sophie wasn't under the same physical strain as the others, but she drank the bitter tea out of solidarity.

Ever the observer, Marcus watched the trio closely as he served their tea. His focus lingered on Lisa, the avatar of Unity. "And here's your tea, ladies," he said with a smile, his eyes quietly assessing her.

Lisa had always been reserved and thoughtful, her mind constantly churning. Even when silent, she was engaged in deep thought. But now... Something is missing. Her green eyes were dull, her expression vacant. There were no signs of inner contemplation. Instead, she moved mechanically, cutting her pancakes and eating them as if on autopilot.

Marcus recognized the signs. The constant mana depletion was draining her. She was still in there, but much of her mental energy was now consumed just to maintain basic tasks. Her body was likely diverting every bit of energy it could spare to replenish her mana.

The relentless cycle of cleansing and healing was physically grinding down Captain Kidd and Mr. "Smitty" Smith. Marcus knew the ordeal would leave both men with lasting mental scars. But the slow, steady attrition on Lisa seemed worse. Each session drained her a little more, chipping away at the vibrant girl she used to be.

Breaking his train of thought, Lisa stopped cutting her pancakes and gave Marcus a faint smile. "Can I have a cup of orange juice?" she asked softly.

"Of course, Miss Lisa," Marcus replied with a nod. He headed toward the cold storage, determined to get her what she needed.

[----- ⚓ -----]

"It's like he thinks he's the boss of everyone," Blaze grumbled, sitting across from Annabelle on the observation deck. He rubbed the bandage on his neck, glaring as if Sparks himself were in the room.

Annabelle leaned back in her chair, the deck unofficially serving as her operations room since Captain Kidd and Smitty were occupying the actual one. She sat near the back of the deck by the entry doors, her posture casual but her eyes sharp. "Blaze," she said sternly, "he is the boss of everyone." She paused for a moment, letting that sink in before adding with a playful smirk, "'cept me, of course."

Blaze rolled his eyes. "So what? We're just supposed to go along with every stupid idea he comes up with?" He waved his hands dramatically. "Like, we pulled that damn engine up and down the ship only to find out the battery was bad. Total waste of me time!"

Annabelle was beginning to understand why Captain Kidd had his *mean streaks*. Sometimes, you had to show authoritarian leadership to keep scallywags like Blaze from feeling comfortable enough to gripe about every minor inconvenience. She leaned forward slightly, fixing him with a serious look. "Blaze, we're running from the reaper. If there's an idea that might help us win that race, then yes, ye will do whatever it takes to bring that idea into port."

Blaze scoffed but said nothing. From the corner of her eye, Annabelle caught movement, Simba, Chaos' spirit animal, hopping between tables behind Blaze. His presence is always such a pain.

"Uh-oh," Simba teased in her mind.

Blaze wasn't done pushing. "So, if Sparks told us to strip down to our knickers and run around the deck 'cause it might get us there faster, we'd do that too?" he challenged, poking holes in her logic.

Annabelle's smile disappeared. "You're getting paid, right?" she asked coolly, her tone sharp enough to cut.

"Theatrically," Blaze shot back, his voice laced with mockery.

"Oh, he's sayin' yer a thief", Simba taunted, his voice chuckling in her mind.

Annabelle felt her anger rising but forced herself to take a calming breath. She wouldn't give Blaze the satisfaction of rattling her. "If ye want yer cut, and if ye want to eat, then do what yer told," she said calmly, running her hands through her hair. "Otherwise, go it alone and let's see how ye fare."

Blaze's eyes narrowed, and he pursed his lips in defiance. "Ye'd keep me cut from the haul?" he asked, his voice low and dangerous.

Annabelle leaned back, letting the balance of power shift fully to her. "Ye get paid to work this ship," she said. "If ye won't work, don't expect coin."

"The Cap'n, *the real captain,* would pay what he owes," Blaze countered, pushing the insult further. "Maybe I'll just take me share."

Simba chimed in again. "Captain Salad Jar's about to have a mutiny on her hands. Haven't even been Cap'n for a week." he teased, the spirit clearly enjoying the tension.

Annabelle slammed her fist on the table with a loud bang, silencing both Blaze and Simba. Blaze flinched, his bravado momentarily shattered as he stared at her with wide eyes.

"Ye haven't had enough of yer mouth getting yer neck in trouble yet?" Annabelle said, her voice cold. Her icy stare locked on him. "Ye wanna make some coin, Blaze? Then be smarter. Think before ye start something ye can't finish."

The words hung in the air between them like a challenge. Blaze sat quietly, his expression a mixture of fear and simmering anger. For now, he didn't dare push her any further.

Annabelle leaned forward, resting her nose on her folded hands. She exhaled slowly, letting some of the tension drain from her body. "I'll talk to Sparks about letting ye play crew," she offered Blaze as a gesture of goodwill. "But he's the first mate. If ye want yer coin, ye do yer duty. That's the deal."

Blaze hesitated, then gave her a curt nod. "Good day... *Cap'n.*" he said before standing and walking off toward the galley seating area.

Simba leapt onto a nearby table and smirked at her. "Ohhh, I guess yer the mean kind of captain after all, huh, Captain Salad Jar?" he teased, hopping from one tabletop to another.

Without a word, Annabelle conjured a column of seawater beneath the spirit monkey, intending to launch him skyward. However, the water twisted unnaturally and veered off course, splashing diagonally across the room and drenching her instead.

The moment Simba landed, he burst into laughter, rolling on the table. "Better luck next time! Girlie." he cackled.

Soaked and thoroughly humiliated, Annabelle sighed in frustration, dropping her head into her hands. Her dreadlocks fell like curtains around her face. "Ye are the worst monkey," she muttered. "Why don't ye go play in the sea?"

"Ye first, girlie." Simba shot back with a grin.

Annabelle groaned but didn't bother to argue further.

Moments later, Marcus walked through the double doors and approached her table. He stopped and asked politely, "May I sit, Acting Captain?"

"What do ye want, Brother Marcus?" Annabelle mumbled, her voice muffled by her hands.

Taking that as permission, Marcus sat down across from her. His tone turned serious. "Miss Annabelle, we need to talk about Miss Lisa."

Annabelle tensed but kept her face buried in her hands. "What about Lisa?"

Marcus straightened, gathering his thoughts. "You need to tell her to stop healing the captain and Mr. Smith," he said carefully.

"WHAT?!" Annabelle's head snapped up, her eyes blazing with fury. "Are ye out of yer damn mind?!?"

Marcus held up his hands in surrender. "Please, hear me out, Miss Salazar."

"No, I will not hear ye out!" she barked. "Yer the worst servant of all time, ye know that?" Her voice was thick with accusation.

"Miss Salazar, please," Marcus urged, his tone steady. "Just listen to me."

Annabelle clenched her jaw but finally waved her hand dismissively. "Fine. Speak," she ordered, not even looking at him.

Marcus remained calm, his resolve unwavering. "Miss Nozaki has impressive mana reserves, but she's draining herself constantly to heal the captain and Mr. Smith. It's chipping away at her," he explained. "She's showing signs of something we call *mana depletion*. If she keeps pushing herself like this, it could kill her. if she was a regular mage she would be dead already."

Annabelle's eyes blazed even brighter with anger. "If she stops healing the Cap'n and Smitty, they'll die fer sure!" she retorted. "How is that better?!"

The air between them grew tense, the weight of both their arguments hanging heavily on Annabelle's shoulders. Marcus didn't back down, knowing the stakes for all of them were dangerously high.

"If she dies before we reach Magitekopolis, the Captain and Mr. Smith will die anyway," Marcus said, adding weight to his argument. "And the world will lose the influence of the Goddess Unity. How could that be a good thing?"

Annabelle paused, her jaw tightening. "Ye are me servant. How could ye even suggest this?"

"I serve all four of you," Marcus said. "And right now, I'm acting on Miss Lisa's behalf. Would you truly sacrifice her life to save the captain and Mr. Smith?"

"Yes," Annabelle answered immediately, refusing to let herself imagine a world without Kidd in it.

"You don't mean that," Marcus countered. "You can't tell me you'd be happy to grind Lisa up and toss her into the sea like some broken machine."

"The sea is hard, Brother Marcus," Annabelle said coldly, as if that alone explained everything.

"Is it the sea?" Marcus challenged. "Or is it you? Had Brother Albert and I misjudged you that much?"

"We all make mistakes," Annabelle retorted, her voice full of careless indifference.

Marcus stared at her, stunned by the callousness in her tone. Slowly, he leaned back in his chair, realizing he had miscalculated. Perhaps there was no reasoning with her right now. With a sigh, he stood and said, "Very well. Good day, Acting Captain." He turned toward the door, already deciding to speak to Lisa directly.

Before he could leave, the door opened, and Lisa stepped onto the deck. Her green hair was tied loosely into a bun, and her posture showed the exhaustion weighing heavily on her. Marcus hesitated, sure she had overheard everything.

"Miss Lisa," he said cautiously. "I'm concerned about your…"

Lisa raised her hand, stopping him mid-sentence. "I heard," she said quietly. Her voice lacked anger, though weariness softened every word.

"See?" Annabelle chimed in from her seat, her voice mocking. "Told ye he's a bad servant."

Marcus tried again. "Miss Nozaki, I fear you will…"

Lisa raised her hand again, silencing him.

Annabelle stood and approached Marcus, ready to tell him off, but stopped short when she got a proper look at Lisa. The bags under her eyes were darker than ever, her face thinner. Lisa looked like someone who had been stranded on a desert island for weeks. Annabelle's smug facade crumbled as concern set in.

Simba hopped to the table beside Annabelle, his voice uncharacteristically gentle. "Ye can't do this to her."

Annabelle froze, her mind flashing back to that night on the lifeboat, just her and Kidd, long before he became a captain. She remembered saying that tearful goodbye to the crew of the Espada Sovereign and the overwhelming pain of accepting that loss. Tears welled in her eyes and spilled down her cheeks as the memories took hold.

Without thinking, she pushed past Marcus and faced Lisa. "Lisa," she began, her voice cracking as the pain of impending loss swelled in her throat. She struggled to find the words, tears streaming freely down her face. Finally, she forced them out. "Ye have to stop healing the Cap'n."

Annabelle wiped at her face, still choking on emotion. "Yer too important, girlie," she whispered, her voice raw and broken. Deep down, she knew it was a truth she had tried to deny, she had failed, and now it was costing her Kidd. All she could do was cry.

"No," Lisa replied softly.

Annabelle stopped, her tears slowing as she looked up at Lisa in disbelief. "What'd ye say?"

"I am not going to let the captain or Mr. Smith die," Lisa said softly but firmly, meeting Annabelle's tear-streaked gaze. She could feel Annabelle's deep grief through their shared connection to the goddesses.

"Please, Miss Lisa," Marcus urged, his voice gentle. "You have to think of yourself. I like the Captain too, but I can't let you give your life to keep him alive."

Lisa turned to Marcus, her exhaustion weighing heavily on her body. She felt the toll of mana depletion, the way her body ached with each step. For a moment, she considered what Marcus was saying, letting Captain Kidd and Mr. Smith die to save herself. But the familiar twist in her gut told her all she needed to know. *The goddess disapproves of that idea.*

Closing her eyes, she took a slow, steadying breath. "I cannot do that." Lisa explained quietly.

Annabelle gritted her teeth and wiped away her tears. Forcing herself to speak through the pain in her throat, she said, "I'm ordering ye to stop healing them. If I have to tie ye up, I…" The words broke as fresh tears spilled down her face. She couldn't finish.

"I refuse," Lisa said simply, her tone resolute.

"Miss Lisa…" Marcus tried again but stopped at her stern glance.

"Marcus, please stop," she said gently but firmly.

"If ye keep this up, yer gonna die, Princess," Annabelle warned, her voice raw and desperate.

"Then get the ship to port faster," Lisa replied, her voice steady. "But I am not letting anyone else die on this ship."

Without warning, Annabelle pulled Lisa into a fierce hug, tears soaking into her dress. "I swear it," Annabelle whispered. "I swear I'll get ye to port, Princess."

Lisa winced and pinched Annabelle hard under her arm. "Ow! Princess!" Annabelle yelped, pulling back. "What gives?"

"I told you to stop calling me Princess," Lisa said, a tired smile tugging at her lips.

Annabelle blinked at her, momentarily stunned, before breaking into a soft chuckle. Lisa turned to Marcus and asked, "Brother Marcus, would you escort me to my room?"

Marcus wiped away a tear of his own and gave her a warm smile. "It would be my pleasure," he said, offering his arm.

Lisa hooked her arm through his, and the two walked together through the double doors, leaving Annabelle standing alone on the deck. shee rubbed her arm absently, still wondering where Lisa had learned to pinch that hard.

"Hey," Simba called, hopping onto a table behind her. "What're ye standing around fer, ye gots work to do, Missy."

Annabelle shot him a glare and flicked her fingers, conjuring a splash of seawater toward him. The water, however, twisted out of control and splashed back in her face.

Simba burst out laughing. "Nice try, Salad Jar."

Annabelle wiped the water from her face, refusing to let defeat or despair creep into her heart. She squared her shoulders and marched purposefully off the observation deck, climbing the stairwell to the bridge. When she reached the helm, she found Sparks steering the ship.

"First Mate," she called out, her tone authoritative, "ye're gonna get those engines workin'."

Sparks blinked at her in confusion. "Cap'n, I already told ye the battery's dead. Ain't nothin' more I can do."

Annabelle stepped closer, folding her arms across her chest. "Ye're me First Mate, right?"

"Aye, Cap'n," Sparks replied cautiously.

Annabelle narrowed her eyes and leaned in slightly. "What kind of First Mate doesn't obey the captain's orders? Yer job is to lead by example."

"Cap'n, there just ain't no way," Sparks insisted.

"Did I ask ye if there was a way?" she shot back. "Or did I order ye to get the engines workin'?"

Sparks hesitated. "But Cap'n, tis impossible."

Annabelle raised an eyebrow, letting the silence stretch. "Maybe I should make Blaze the First Mate," she said casually. "Bet he'd find a way."

Sparks opened his mouth to protest, but the words caught in his throat. He paused, a spark of inspiration igniting in his mind. His gaze shifted forward, scanning the horizon, then back to the helm. He repeated the motion twice more, the gears in his head turning. Slowly, an idea began to take shape.

Finally, Sparks straightened and nodded. "Cap'n, take the helm. I gots work to do."

Annabelle grabbed the wheel without hesitation. Sparks hurried down the stairs but paused halfway and ran back up, ruffling Annabelle's dreadlocks as he passed.

"Thanks, Cap'n," he said with a grin before dashing off, energized by his new plan.

Annabelle smirked, gripping the helm tightly. We'll get there. *We have to.*

[-----✛-----]

Journal Entry May 10th, 1910 (Day 6)

With renewed inspiration, Mr. Sparks has created a temporary solution to get the engines running again; with Regina Fournier's help, he made an apparatus that channels the energy released from detonating the gunpowder "pillows" that are used to charge the cannons. The good news is that the ship is now moving faster. Since the engine speed remains constant, if the ship needs to speed up for any reason, it would have to do so with the sails.

I am hopeful that this repair will get us to port soon enough to save Captain Lowe and Mr. Smith, without sacrificing Lisa Nozaki.

[----- ⚓ -----]

"Aye, that ain't good," Sparks said, lowering his spyglass. He stood beside Annabelle on the bridge as she guided the ship, following the mark he had set on the compass. Behind them, Lisa was in the middle of healing Captain Kidd and Smitty after their latest cleansing session.

"What is it?" Annabelle asked, glancing ahead at the dark clouds gathering on the horizon. The ominous mass churned like a great beast blocking their path.

"There's a storm dead ahead," Sparks replied, slipping the spyglass into his pocket. "Big one. If we run into it, it'll be trouble. We'll have to divert, go around it. Could cost us a day or more."

"A whole day?" Annabelle repeated, disbelief lacing her voice. She looked over her shoulder at Lisa, who was still working her Earthbloom healing on the captain and Smitty. Time was not on their side. She shook her head and set her jaw. "Nothin' doin'. We're goin' straight through it."

Sparks frowned, concern deepening the lines on his face. "Cap'n, that's not just any storm. The ship's already banged up real bad. If we go through that, it could easily send us straight to the bottom of the sea."

"Uh oh," Simba's voice chimed in, mockingly. "Captain Salad Jar's about to lose her precious ship."

Annabelle clenched her teeth but forced herself to ignore the taunting monkey. Instead, she turned to Sparks and flashed her signature grin. "Trust a lass, Sparks. We're gonna make it through."

Sparks stared at her for a long moment, his blue eyes searching her face. Then, with a resigned sigh, he shook his head and said, "Aye, Cap'n." He turned and descended the stairs, shouting down to the crew, "OI! We're cuttin' straight through the storm, boyos! Get the ship ready!"

On deck, the crew immediately sprang into action, their movements quick and methodical despite the anxiety settling over them like the calm before a violent gale. Annabelle tightened her grip on the wheel, her gaze fixed on the approaching storm. She could feel the tension in the air, thick and heavy, as if the sea itself had every intention of swallowing the Stormfang whole.

But Actin' Captain Annabelle Salazar isn't about to let that happen.

401

[----- ⚓ -----]

After Acting Captain Salazar gave the Order, and repeatedly assured the crew she wasn't joking, they got to work preparing the Stormfang to face the storm head-on. True to her name, the Stormfang would do her best to bite through whatever fury the sea hurled at her. Despite the ship's battered and fragile condition, Annabelle clung to the hope that they'd emerge on the other side still afloat.

Annabelle ordered everyone without a specific role to secure themselves below decks, warning them that the ride through the storm would be rough.

In the galley, Marcus and Jeffie prepared meals for the crew, using the last of their bread and most of the remaining meat to make sandwiches. Each sandwich was wrapped in serving paper and placed into a numbered sack. Marcus noticed there were twenty sacks in total, but neither seven nor thirteen was included. Curious, he asked Jeffie about the missing numbers.

"Ah, ye see," Jeffie explained with a shrug, "Everyone wants number seven, and no one wants number thirteen. Superstitious lot, the crew. So I made 'em twenty-one and twenty-two instead."

Once the sandwiches were packed, they added pieces of fruit to each sack. Supplies were running low, leaving the crew with a random selection, some got apples, others oranges, and a few received pears. Jeffie shook his head as he handed Marcus the final sack.

"They're gonna fight over the fruit," he said with resignation. "Bet ye a week's wages."

Annabelle gave out final assignments, sending Regina to the hold to keep an eye on the crystal constructs she had created to seal the ship's inner hull. Knowing the crystals might crack under the storm's pressure, Annabelle also assigned Sophie to assist her, with Bobby accompanying them to keep the pair out of trouble.

She ordered Lisa and Eclipse Lepele to secure themselves in the captain's operations room, predicting that Kidd and Smitty would need another cleansing and healing cycle before they cleared the storm.

Sparks, however, took control of the helm, overriding Annabelle's intention to steer the ship herself. "Ye ain't got the experience for this, Cap'n," he said firmly. "And ye've got a habit of doing dangerous things at the worst moments. Let me handle it."

Grumbling but reluctantly agreeing, Annabelle tied herself to the taffrail alongside him. Meanwhile, Popper and Harmon fastened harnesses around their bodies and anchored themselves to the masts. The harnesses wouldn't guarantee survival if the storm hit hard enough, but at least they'd have a better chance of not being swept overboard by the gale-force winds and lashing waves.

Before the storm overtook them, Sparks made a final attempt to convince Annabelle to take cover in the operations room with Lisa.

"Look, Cap'n, ye don't need to be out here," he argued. "It's yer order that brought this storm to us, might as well keep yerself safe while I guide us through it."

Annabelle narrowed her eyes and shook her head. "Ain't no way, Sparks. I'm the acting Cap'n. This is me ship, and I'm gonna see her through this."

Sparks sighed but gave up the argument, turning his attention to the dark, roiling clouds looming ever closer.

As the Stormfang surged into the edge of the storm, Annabelle raised her voice above the howling winds, calling out to her crew:

"Oi! Listen up! I'm ordering every one of ye to live through this!"

A chorus of defiant, unified voices roared back at her from the deck. "ARR, Cap'n!"

With everyone braced for battle against nature's fury, the Stormfang plunged into the storm, her crew steeled for the fight of their lives.

The storm overtook the Stormfang with merciless speed. The sea raged and crashed against the ship's battered hull, furious waves hammering her like fists. Gale-force winds tore across the deck, slamming into Acting Captain Salazar and First Mate Sparks. Annabelle clung tightly to the railing around the bridge, her dreadlocks whipping across her face and shoulders like stinging ropes. Sparks gripped the railing with both hands, steadying himself as he barked orders to the deck crew below.

"Keep the sails steady, boys!" Sparks roared through the deafening winds. His voice barely carried, but the crew worked with military precision, adjusting the rigging as the ship was tossed by the storm's relentless assault. Sparks focused on steering the ship forward, determined to push through the chaos.

Annabelle, still gripping the railing, felt the raw power of the storm coursing through the air and sea. It was terrifying, yet …. Exhilarating, like her own Goddess of Chaos, the storm is a primal force beyond her control. The dread that seeped into her bones awakened the Corsair spirit inside her, his voice crackling to life through their connection.

"Bella, what are ye doin'?" he warned urgently. "Yer ship's in no shape to survive a storm like this!"

"Corsair," Annabelle ordered through gritted teeth, "I be yer captain, and I order ye to be more positive, and support me this very moment!" Deep down, she silently prayed he had a way to help her use her Maelstrom mastery to guide the ship through the storm.

"Aye, Cap'n." The Corsair sighed, his tone resigned but supportive, "Open yerself up to the surging power of the storm…let it flow through ye. But do it right this time."

Annabelle thought about Regina and Lisa's Earthbloom sense and closed her eyes, trying to connect with the storm through her Maelstrom mastery. She reached outward, extending her mana to meet the storm's fury.

"Nay, Bella, not like that!" the Corsair scolded. "Keep yer mana inside ye and just listen fer the storm's power instead."

She withdrew her mana and focused inward, letting the storm's presence wash over her senses. It was chaotic yet rhythmic, a living force pulsing with power. Slowly, a deep understanding of the Maelstrom's nature stirred within her.

"Aye, that's it," the Corsair encouraged, his voice softer now. "Now show the storm ye mean no harm. Dance with it. Let it know yer its friend."

Annabelle took a deep breath and released her grip on the railing. Moving with deliberate grace, she let her body flow like the wind, guiding her mana to influence the storm's path. She danced across the deck as though leading a partner, her arms weaving through the air. Slowly, the winds that had battered the ship began to shift. A protective shell of wind formed around the Stormfang, deflecting the storm's wrath away from the deck. The howling winds faded to a steady breeze.

The bow and stern of the ship still faced the storm's full force, but the deck was no longer under siege. Rain fell in gentler sheets, and the crew's frantic pace eased as they realized they could breathe again.

At the helm, Sparks stared at the sudden change with disbelief. He turned to Annabelle, watching her move as if conducting the storm itself. "Belle... is that ye makin' this happen?"

"Aye," Annabelle confirmed, a cocksure smile spreading across her face as she guided the wind and rain in a careful dance around her ship.

Sparks shook his head in awe. "Well, Cap'n, if I may ask, please keep that up until we pass through this storm."

Annabelle arched an eyebrow and grinned mischievously while dancing. "Go on. Say it," she teased.

Sparks rolled his eyes but obliged. "Aye, Cap'n. I never shoulda doubted ye. Ye are truly amazin'."

"Thanks, first mate," Annabelle said with a wink, moving with renewed confidence. She continued to coax the storm's fury around the ship, her body swaying in harmony with the elements as she protected her crew from nature's wrath.

For the first time in hours, hope surged through the Stormfang.

[----- ✿ -----]

"Just one more to go," Sparks said, his voice gentle as he carried Regina on his back. She was completely drained from maintaining the crystal repairs and keeping the ship afloat through the storm.

"Yay... almost done," Regina mumbled sleepily, resting her head against his shoulder. A wide yawn escaped her, and she barely kept her eyes open.

Sparks approached the final silver crystal, which was riddled with cracks. "Alright, Regina. This is the last one," he coaxed, shaking her gently to keep her awake.

Regina let out a small groan but lifted her head and touched her wand to the damaged crystal. The tip of her wand glowed faintly as she activated the repair spell. Sparks stood still, watching as the crystal slowly began to mend. He could tell it was taking longer than usual. Each time she'd repaired a crystal during their perilous journey to Magitekopolis, the process had stretched out, her mana reserves clearly running low.

Regina gritted her teeth, her exhaustion showing in every motion. She let out a soft grunt of effort, willing the spell to complete. Finally, the crystal reformed into a solid, unbroken structure.

"All done," she sighed, letting her head slump back onto Sparks' shoulder.

"Good job, girlie," Sparks said with a smile. "Now, how 'bout we head to the galley for breakfast?"

"Coffee. No more foot tea," Regina demanded, her voice muffled against his back.

"Regina..." Sparks said in a lightly scolding tone, the kind a father might use on his mischievous daughter.

"Fine... coffee first, then foot tea," she relented with a tired sigh. Even though her words were compliant, there was a playful edge in her voice; she'd come to respect her as a mentor.

Sparks chuckled and carried her off toward the galley, both of them eager for a well-earned meal.

"When we arrive at port, one of the deckhands will ring the bell," Annabelle explained, pointing to the large brass bell mounted at the bow. "That'll signal the blokes workin' the pier that we're in distress. After that, we'll have to follow the flag boy's directions to wherever they want us to dock."

"We need to make sure they pull the ship from the water as quickly as possible," Marcus reminded the group. "Miss Fournier's crystal constructs will likely break down once she's away from the ship."

"Good point." Lepele agreed. He turned to Sophie. "Griffin, when they start ringing the bell, activate your badge's in distress call."

"Right." Sophie acknowledged with a nod, already planning her next steps.

"Port six should be ready for us," Marcus continued. "We'll be arriving a bit earlier than expected, though."

Annabelle hesitated, her gaze turning toward the captain's operations room. "And what about... the Cap'n and Smitty?"

"The hospital knows about the shadow curse," Marcus reassured her. "Apparently, there's already a plan in place. The Order has taken care of all the logistics. All we must do is reach port."

Before anyone could say more, a loud thud echoed from the operations room behind them. They turned to see Lisa lying on the floor, struggling to rise. Without hesitation, everyone except Annabelle rushed to her side.

"Lisa, girl, are you okay?" Sophie asked, reaching her first.

Lisa shook her head slightly, her breathing heavy. "Yes... I just fell down is all." She steadied herself and glanced toward Mr. Smith. Listening to her Earthbloom sense, she took in his condition and frowned. "I must finish healing him."

"Miss Lisa, you must rest," Marcus said from behind Sophie, his voice filled with concern. "We're almost at port. You've done enough…"

Lisa cut him off with a sharp, determined look. "I will be fine. Just help me up." Her tone left no room for argument. "I am almost done."

Sophie helped Lisa to her feet. Lisa inhaled deeply and raised her hand, conjuring a red spell circle. It was smaller and less intricate than usual, bearing only five runes instead of the typical six. Exhaustion weighed heavily on her mind, making it difficult to concentrate. The circle flickered, unstable, but she gritted her teeth and pushed through, channeling her remaining mana. *I will not fail, not again*, she swore to herself.

The healing process dragged on painfully. Lisa's focus wavered, her head pounding as she fought to keep the spell intact. Red mana particles flowed into Mr. Smith's body, slowly mending his internal injuries. His painful moans and screams went unnoticed by her until the spell finally ended, leaving her nearly empty of energy. She swayed on her feet, her body trembling from the effort.

For the first time, a deep worry crept into Lisa's mind. She had never felt this drained before, not even when she'd healed Brother Albert that terrible night behind the tavern. She barely registered Sophie's steadying hand on her arm.

"Come on," Sophie said gently. "Let's get you to the galley for some foot tea."

Lisa nodded weakly, leaning lightly on Sophie's arm as they made their way out of the operations room. Despite her fatigue, she maintained her grace, walking with as much poise as she could manage. Sophie guided her to the galley seating area and helped her into a chair.

"Emberroot tea," Lisa requested softly, her voice barely above a whisper. "Please. No more of that -awful foot tea talk."

Sophie chuckled and gave her arm a reassuring squeeze. "Just take it easy."

As Lisa closed her eyes and leaned back in the chair, she felt the weight of exhaustion settle over her like a heavy blanket. But for now, she was safe and so was the crew. They are nearly there, nearly finished

Chapter 28

Journal Entry: May 11th, 1910

The Stormfang has defied both nature and fate, its survival a testament to the grit of its crew and the brilliance of those who guide it. Hours now separate us from Magitekopolis, though the ship groans with every wave, each creak a reminder of how close we sail to a watery grave.

Miss Salazar's Maelstrom Mastery, an awe-inspiring communion with the very storm that sought to drown us, became our salvation. She did not merely withstand the tempest; she bent it to her will, transforming our demise into a harrowing waltz with nature's fury. The toll on her spirit is undeniable, yet her sacrifice has granted us this vital chance at survival.

Regina Fournier and Lisa Nozaki are locked in their own battles against exhaustion. Regina's masterful use of crystalmancy, a true gift from the goddess of Change, maintains the integrity of the hull's crystal structures. Lisa's relentless healing efforts, despite dangerous mana depletion, have kept Captain Kidd and Mr. Smitty alive, defying the curse that clings to their sinew.

Now, as dawn breaks, the spires of Magitekopolis emerge from the horizon like silent sentinels. Relief and dread mingle in the salty air. Will the city's healers save our wounded, or has this voyage claimed too much from all of us already?

The harbor draws near, its safety tantalizingly close yet agonizingly distant. The Stormfang teeters on the edge of breaking, her battered heart in sync with ours. This day will decide whether we are survivors or the following names whispered in maritime tragedy.

[----- ⚓ -----]

The flag of Magitekopolis fluttered in the dawn light like a beacon of salvation, its presence lifting the spirits of everyone aboard the Stormfang. For a crew battered by relentless storms and curses, the sight offered a brief reprieve from their war of attrition with both nature and fate.

Magitekopolis stretched before them, a stark contrast to Verdantia's verdant landscapes. Where Verdantia's rustic charm lay hidden among a sea of green, Magitekopolis sprawled like a metallic forest. Its skyline was dominated by towering structures, with Gearhaven's intricate ceiling of mechanical wonders glistening under the sunrise. Below, the city's lower tiers remained cloaked in the last shadows of night.

For Marcus, this was his first visit to the Kingdom. His past duties with the Scribes of Saint Lorraine had taken him across the Umbrathorn Empire, recording events and absorbing foreign cultures. Later, as a member of the Colleges of Sages, his travels brought him to Stoneridge, Opulentia, and Islewind to study natural phenomena and expand the boundaries of knowledge. Of all the cities he had encountered, Magitekopolis most resembled Opulentia, though Gearhaven's towering structures seemed almost otherworldly in their scale. Now, however, he had little time to marvel. The avatars were teetering on the brink of death, and Marcus would not allow them to fall, not while he still drew breath.

The ship crossed a buoy marking the harbor boundary. Annabelle's voice rang out across the deck.

"Ring the bell!"

Blaze immediately abandoned his runner duties and sprinted to the ship's bell. Unhooking the ball and releasing the pin that kept it secure, he pulled hard on the rope, sending a booming chime echoing across the port. It was a cry for help, a signal to all who could hear: the Stormfang has arrived, and she is in dire need.

Without hesitation, Sophie touched the badge pinned to her chest and commanded, "Distress." The badge responded instantly, emitting a pulse meant to alert the Aurorium clan of her presence and plea for assistance.

Annabelle stepped forward, her eyes locking on Sparks as he manned the wheel. "Move aside, First Mate. This here's the Captain's job," she declared, her voice firm with authority.

Sparks raised an eyebrow, glancing between her and the helm. "Cap'n, steering into port's harder than it looks. I can handle it."

Annabelle's gaze sharpened, her tone unyielding. "Are ye doubtin' me, First Mate?"

"Nay, Cap'n," Sparks replied with a sigh of resignation. He held the wheel steady as Annabelle approached.

She took hold of the helm, her hands settling confidently on the spokes as Sparks stepped back. A surge of pride welled within her as the crew's eyes shifted toward her, their trust reflected in their tired but hopeful faces. Guiding the Stormfang through the narrowing channels, she searched for a place to dock.

"Watch the flagman over there," Sparks called, pointing to a figure waving signal flags in frantic arcs. "He's tryin' to get your attention."

Annabelle spotted him and squinted. "Aye, I sees him," she muttered, feigning nonchalance to mask her initial oversight. "He's a bit short for a flagman, don't ye think?"

Sparks shook his head and smirked, refraining from comment as he turned to bark orders. "Trim the sails! Get that gangplank ready!"

The crew sprang into action, moving with renewed purpose. The Stormfang was finally within reach of safety, though the weight of their ordeal still pressed heavily on their shoulders. The next moments would determine whether they had truly escaped death's grasp or merely postponed it.

Following the directions of the comically short flagman, Annabelle guided the Stormfang toward an unfamiliar slip. A group of dockworkers and two large cranes stood ready at the edge, their presence a promising sign of assistance. Annabelle narrowed her eyes. Not only was the flagman too short in her estimation, but his signals didn't seem quite right. She adjusted the wheel according to his instructions, muttering to herself about his technique.

Sparks' voice buzzed somewhere behind her, but she had no time for his criticism. Just as she tried to correct course, the Stormfang scraped hard against the pier with a bone-jarring lurch.

"Bloody hell!" Sparks leapt forward, grabbing the wheel and yanking it sharply to port, steering the ship away from further damage. The Stormfang groaned in protest but obeyed, its hull sparing the pier from further destruction. Sparks glared at Annabelle, his tone a mixture of frustration and disbelief. "Cap'n, please don't destroy my ship."

"Oi! The flagman is too short!" Annabelle shot back, crossing her arms defensively.

"He ain't," Sparks countered flatly. "Ye just weren't followin' his signals."

Before Annabelle could fire off a retort, Sophie's voice rang out from the deck below.

"Hey! Where'd you learn how to drive a ship?"

"Oi, quiet, you!" Sparks barked, waving her off. "Just get that gangplank built!" Turning back to Annabelle, he shook his head. "Now, Cap'n, either follow the flagman or let me steer."

"Aye, First Mate," Annabelle muttered, her tone sheepish. She straightened up and craned her neck to see the flagman better, resolutely ignoring Simba's chuckling from the deck. This time, she followed the signals to the letter, guiding the Stormfang into position between the towering cranes.

"Drop anchor!" Sparks ordered. The crew moved swiftly, dropping anchor to hold the ship steady.

With precision that demonstrated years of practice, the mecha-mages activated their cranes, their magic winding thick ropes through the machinery's mechanical arms. The ropes were attached to heavy straps, which slithered beneath the Stormfang's hull like giant serpents. Large teeth on the straps dug into the wood, gripping the ship securely. Slowly, the cranes lifted the vessel from the water, halting when the hull was mainly suspended. The mages' control ensured the ship remained steady, as if cradled by massive iron hands.

The pier crew worked quickly, securing the gangplank. With Sparks' nod of approval, the crew lowered and tied it to the deck. Dockworkers on the pier looped ropes through islets fixed to the wooden columns, stabilizing the connection between ship and shore like a physician bracing a patient.

"Bring out your sick and wounded!" the pier master bellowed up at the Stormfang.

"Aye!" Sparks shouted back.

Sophie and Lepele hurried to the bridge, ready to retrieve Captain Kidd and Smitty from the infirmary, as previously planned. But Annabelle stepped in front of them, holding out a hand to stop them.

"Nay," she said firmly. "These two are crew. We got 'em. Ye go get Lisa and Regina."

Lepele hesitated, then nodded. "Aye, Cap'n," he replied, tapping Sophie's arm to prompt her. Together, they headed below decks to find the silver and green Avatars, their footsteps echoing softly as they vanished into the shadows of the ship.

Sophie found it strange that Lepele had followed Annabelle's orders without question. Usually, he would push back or outright ignore her authority. But this time was different, and she couldn't help but wonder why.

"Oi! Ye lazy bones, come and get the Cap'n and First Mate on the double!" Annabelle called out, her voice cutting through the morning air.

The crew responded in unison with a hearty, "Aye, Cap'n!" before moving into action.

Marcus stepped forward from behind Annabelle and asked, "Miss Annabelle, what can I do to assist?"

She blinked, as though momentarily surprised to see him, then regained her composure. "Oh, aye. Brother Marcus, proceed down the gangplank and get everything straightened out," she instructed.

"As you wish, Acting Captain Salazar," Marcus replied, offering a polite nod before heading down the stairs from the bridge. He made his way across the deck, clearing a path to the gangplank.

Meanwhile, the crew carefully lifted Captain Kidd and Smitty onto stretchers retrieved from the ship's hold. The stretchers were damp and uncomfortable, but neither man complained. Both were too preoccupied with vomiting shadow material as the curse continued to worsen.

"Ye can lead the way, Cap'n," Sparks offered, stepping up beside Annabelle. "I'll settle things up here."

"Nay, First Mate," Annabelle replied with a firm shake of her head. "I'm the Acting Cap'n. I'll be the last to step off this ship. Ye lead the men down, Mr. Sparks."

Sparks studied her for a moment, then gave a respectful nod. "Aye, Cap'n." He turned to the rest of the crew gathered near the bridge. "Follow me, men!" he shouted, his voice ringing with authority. With that, he strode confidently across the deck and onto the gangplank, leading the way off the Stormfang.

Annabelle stood tall, watching as her crew moved to execute their duties. For all the death-defying feats they accomplished, they had finally found their way to safety.

[----- ⊕ -----]

On the stateroom deck, Sophie and Lepele arrived at the quarters of their fellow avatars. Sophie stopped outside Regina's door and placed a hand on it.

"I'll get Regina," she suggested. "She likes to sleep in her underwear... and that could make things... awkward."

Lepele nodded knowingly. "Good point, torchbearer. I'll handle Nozaki." He turned and headed toward Lisa's stateroom.

Sophie entered Regina's room and called out loudly, "All right, girl, time to get off this ship!" To her surprise, there was no response. Sure, Regina could sleep like the dead, but something felt off.

She strode to the hammock and gave it a firm shake. "Regina, wake up."

A groggy voice mumbled, "Huh? Is it time to repair the crystals again?"

"No, girl. We're leaving. Now get up." Sophie ordered, her concern deepening.

"Okay..." Regina whispered faintly. "Just wake me when it's time to fix the crystals." Her voice was barely audible, almost dreamlike.

Sophie's heart raced. She grabbed Regina by the shoulders, pulling her into a sitting position. "No, Regina! Get up!"

410

"I'm up," Regina assured, her eyes still closed. "Let's go fix the crystals…"

Panic gripped Sophie. She slapped Regina across the face. "WAKE UP!"

Startled, Regina jolted awake. Still disoriented and sensing an attack, her survival instincts kicked in. Mana surged through her body as she formed a crystalline gauntlet around her fist and swung, a move straight out of her combat training with Lepele.

The crystal-encased punch connected hard with Sophie's nose. "OW! Dammit girl!" Sophie yelled, clutching her face. "It's me! Wake the hell up!"

Regina blinked, finally registering Sophie in front of her. "Sophie? Why'd you hit me?" she asked, rubbing her burning cheek.

Sophie, holding her nose in pain, grumbled, "We're at Magitekopolis. We gotta go."

"Oh." Regina blinked again, her foggy mind slowly clearing. "Why didn't you just say that?"

Sophie glared at her, then noticed the silver avatar's state of undress. "Come on, girl. You gotta get dressed." She opened the wardrobe and asked, "White dress, blue dress, yellow dress, or green dress?"

When no response came, Sophie turned and saw Regina lying back in her hammock, fast asleep again. Sophie sighed heavily. "Yellow dress it is."

She wrestled Regina into the dress, managing to put her glasses in the pocket before hoisting the half-conscious girl onto her back like a piggyback ride. She makes it to the hallway, and at the same time, Lepele emerges from Lisa's room with the green avatar draped over his back, modestly wrapped in a bed sheet. The two of them exchanged a worried glance, silently agreeing on the urgency of getting medical help.

They began the slow ascent up the stairs. Sophie, for the first time, felt relieved that Regina was the smallest of the avatars. Carrying Lisa or even Annabelle would have made this climb hellish. *Maybe Regina was due for a growth spurt soon*, she thought wryly.

When they reached the main deck, Sophie spotted Annabelle overseeing the evacuation. The orange-haired avatar's expression shifted immediately to one of deep concern as her eyes locked on the unconscious forms of Regina and Lisa.

Annabelle froze, her stomach lurching. She raised a hand to her mouth in dread. *No… they couldn't be…*

"They are fine. Just exhausted," Lepele reassured her, his voice calm as they passed the bridge.

Annabelle exhaled shakily and wiped her face, forcing her composure to return. "Aye. Thanks, mate," she called back, though her eyes lingered on her 'sisters' with quiet worry.

Sophie led the way down the steeply angled gangplank, carefully gripping the side ropes to steady herself. Lepele followed close behind, both mindful of their precious burdens. The descent was slow, with each step taken deliberately to avoid slipping. When they finally reached the pier, a mage dressed in white approached. Using the same mecha-magic that the blue-haired witch Isabella, he maneuvered two beds in front of them.

"Lay them down here," the mage instructed.

Sophie and Lepele complied, gently placing Regina and Lisa on the beds. The mage's hands glowed faintly as he guided the beds into the backs of two white carriages, each prepared to rush the patients to the hospital.

"Sentinel Griffin!"

Sophie turned at the sound of her name. Through the commotion of the crew evacuating the ship, medical teams tending to the wounded, and pier workers stabilizing the Stormfang, she spotted a man calling to her. His Aurorium Shadow badge gleamed on his chest as he raised a hand, signaling her to approach.

Sophie made her way toward him, weaving through the crowd, with Lepele close on her heels. The Shadow, dressed simply in denim pants and a collared shirt, waited patiently. His badge rested on his left breast pocket, exactly where it should be.

"Good morning," Sophie greeted him as she reached him. "Sentinel Griffin," she added, extending her hand.

The Shadow touched his badge, and Sophie felt her own badge deactivate the distress signal. He then took her hand and introduced himself. "Shadow Mercado."

Mercado glanced at Lepele and said, "If you'll excuse us, sir. We have clan business."

"Of course," Lepele replied smoothly. "Eclipse Antonio Lepele of the Aurorium Kutora Mora." He offered his hand for a shake.

"Eclipse, you say?" Mercado's eyes narrowed slightly. "Where is your badge?"

"It was lost when the ship I was aboard was destroyed during a pirate attack," Lepele explained. "I can authenticate myself once we reach Aurorium Magitekopolis."

"That won't be necessary just yet. My orders are to escort Sentinel Griffin to the hospital for further instructions. If you are who you claim to be, we'll verify your identity there."

"Very well," Lepele said with a nod.

Mercado turned back to Sophie. "Sentinel, your pistol." he ordered, extending his hand.

Sophie hesitated, her unease bubbling to the surface. "I'd rather keep it, Shadow."

"You forget yourself, Sentinel. That was not a request." Mercado replied firmly, his tone cold.

Reluctantly, Sophie drew her pistol, keeping it pointed at the ground, and handed it over. Mercado touched his badge, and a shimmering pocket of space appeared. He placed the pistol inside before it vanished.

"Now, if you two will follow me," he ordered, turning on his heel and walking toward a nearby carriage.

Mercado opened the door to the passenger compartment, revealing a stark, utilitarian interior. Unlike the comfortable carriages Sophie had ridden in Verdantia, this one was designed to transport prisoners. Hard wooden seats lined the walls, and metal islets for securing handcuffs were mounted along the benches.

Sophie stepped inside and took a seat, her discomfort growing as she glanced around the barren compartment. Lepele paused outside, speaking to Mercado.

"If it's all the same to you, I'd prefer to ride in the second seat," Lepele requested politely. "I've been cooped up on that ship for weeks. I'd like to enjoy the open air."

"With all due respect, *Eclipse,* I don't know you, and you're not wearing a badge," Mercado replied with thinly veiled disdain. "You can ride in the cattle car, or you can walk."

"As you say, Shadow," Lepele responded with a composed expression. He climbed into the carriage and sat across from Sophie, his movements calm despite the insult.

The carriage door shut behind them with a heavy clang. Neither spoke, but a silent understanding passed between them: *their situation had just grown more precarious*.

[-----✟-----]

Marcus descended the gangplank, making his way to the pier supervisor at the far end of the bustling dock. The man, dressed in a worn but well-kept uniform, was directing the organized chaos of evacuation and repairs. Marcus introduced himself politely.

"Ah, I've been expecting you," the supervisor replied. "Your colleagues will meet you at the hospital."

Marcus nodded and stepped aside to observe the ongoing operations. The crew was carefully bringing Captain Kidd and Mr. Smitty down the gangplank, moving slowly to prevent any mishaps with their fragile cargo. Once they reached solid ground, medical workers coordinated with a mecha-mage who used his magic to guide the two stretchers into waiting carriages.

The carriages intrigued Marcus. Lacking horses, they instead emitted a faint, familiar blueish-green glow. They drove off smoothly, powered by the same mana-leeching technology as the boats Magitekopolis had gifted to the Order.

"Those are mana-leeching carriages," the supervisor explained when Marcus asked. "The crown's testing them further before selling to the public or other kingdoms."

Marcus gave a thoughtful nod and continued to watch. Shortly after, Sophie and Lepele arrived with Regina and Lisa, both avatars still unconscious. The medical staff promptly took charge, loading the girls into standard carriages. Apparently, there were only so many mana-leeching models available.

Marcus's attention shifted again as another Aurorium clan member approached Sophie and Lepele, summoning them away. From their tense body language and brief exchange, Marcus surmised that Lepele had been right, the clan was likely displeased with Sophie's decision to return to Brother Albert instead of seeking protection from the Aurorium after the Granmark massacre. Marcus silently resolved to do what he could to help her mend ties with the clan.

The Stormfang's crew soon followed, descending the gangplank and gathering at a safe distance on the pier. Sparks called out to them, rallying them with a calm but firm presence. A few anxious crew members fired questions at him.

"What are we gonna do now, Sparks?"

"Are we still gonna get paid?"

"What about me tings?"

"Listen, boys, we're gonna figure this out," Sparks assured them. "Look, Belle's comin'. She'll explain everything."

Annabelle, the last to leave the Stormfang, hopped off the gangplank, struggling with a large ledger book and a heavy chest. Seeing her burden, Marcus stepped forward.

"Let me take the chest for you, Miss Salazar," he offered.

"Nay, mate," Annabelle replied with a slight smile. "I'll hold the coin. Ye take the book." She handed him the ledger.

"Of course, Miss Salazar," Marcus said, taking the book and falling into step beside her.

They approached the crew, who were gathered around Sparks and growing increasingly restless. Annabelle heard their nervous chatter and complaints but chose not to entertain them. Instead, she raised her voice.

"Oi! Quiet!"

The sharp command silenced the words of discontent. Annabelle took a deep breath, giving herself a moment of control before continuing.

"Right, so we all know the ship ain't in the best of shape," she began firmly.

Behind her, the mecha-mages activated the cranes, lifting the Stormfang entirely out of the water. A torrent of seawater trapped between the inner and outer hulls came crashing down onto the pier below, missing the crew but splashing into the bay with a loud roar.

Moments later, a massive section of the outer hull broke free and plunged into the water with a resounding splash, narrowly missing the pier. The sight drew a few whispers and sharp intakes of breath from the crew. Annabelle glanced back briefly but kept her composure.

The worst might be over, but it was clear the Stormfang had barely survived.

Annabelle stared at the Stormfang, her stomach sinking. Captain Kidd was going to have a fit when he saw the state of his beloved ship. Turning back to the crew, she found their faces painted with disbelief and weariness, their morale plummeting with every creak and groan from the crippled vessel.

"Believe it or not," she said quickly, forcing a smile, "that's just cosmetic damage. A bit of wood and some paint, and she'll be back on the sea, making coin in no time."

Before the words had time to settle, a series of explosions tore through the Stormfang. The ship shuddered violently as its engines were blasted from the hull, one flew clear over the pier, crashing into the water, while the other was hurled near a line of moored ships, obliterating a marker buoy.

A stunned silence followed... until Simba broke into raucous laughter. He rolled on the pier deck, tears streaming down his face.

"Oi, Cap'n Salad Jar!" he hollered between guffaws. "Yer ship just blew up!"

Annabelle shut her eyes, taking a slow, steadying breath. She didn't even have the heart to look at the wreckage. But when she opened her eyes again, Sparks' devastated expression hit her harder than the blast itself. The Stormfang meant the world to him. Accepting the reality of their situation, Annabelle made a choice.

"Obviously," she announced, forcing herself to meet the crew's eyes, "the ship's gonna need more than a bit of work."

Sparks scoffed bitterly, his gaze still fixed on the mangled ship.

"So here's the deal," Annabelle continued, her voice steady but resolute. "If ye want yer cut and a chance to find another ship, I'll pay you out here and now." She paused, taking a breath and summoning all the charm she could muster. "But if ye stay on, I'll put ye up and feed ye until we're ready to sail again."

"Oi, put us up where?" Blaze shot back immediately, his arms crossed. *Annabelle could always count on Blaze to be a scallywag full of negativity.*

"I'm sure Brother Marcus can set ye all up with living arrangements," she replied, glancing toward him for backup.

Marcus hesitated, buying time to think. He was aware that their accommodations differed from those available on Order Island. But he nodded confidently. "Yes, Miss Salazar—sorry, Acting Captain Salazar. I'm sure the Aurorium Clan would be happy to assist with accommodations for everyone."

"Live with the Coppers?" Bobby exclaimed in horror. "Nope, I'll take me coin."

The rest of the crew quickly echoed his sentiment, grumbling and nodding in agreement. Annabelle's heart sank further as the crew's decision became clear. They were leaving. All of them, except Sparks. He remained silent, standing by her side like he always did.

Admitting defeat, Annabelle sighed. "Oi, gimme some space. I'll pay ye," she said quietly.

With Marcus's help, she began working through Captain Kidd's ledger. She showed him how to log payments while she distributed the coins. When she started, the ship's chest had been almost complete. By the time she handed the last man, Gary, his one hundred and fifty-five coins, the chest was nearly empty. Only a glimmer of coin remained at the bottom, the red lining starkly visible through the few remaining pieces.

Annabelle stood there, staring at the depleted chest, her fingers brushing over its rim. Just like that, she is another failed paper captain. Her crew was gone, and the ship's funds barely stretched to cover a good room and one fine meal, indeed, nothing more.

She watched the men walk away, their laughter and farewells fading into the distance. Her shoulders slumped as the weight of her failure pressed down on her. This was Captain Kidd's ship, his dream, and she had failed. Tears welled in her eyes, blurring her vision as a deep sense of helplessness clawed at her.

"Don't worry about it, Belle." Sparks' voice came from behind her, calm and steady. "It's just a rough patch."

Annabelle turned around and saw Sparks smiling at her, the first genuine smile she'd seen from him since he'd stepped up as her first mate. Somehow, despite everything, that smile warmed her enough to hold herself together a little longer.

"Come, Miss Salazar," Marcus suggested, gesturing toward a nearby lot where a collection of for-hire carriages stood waiting, some horse-drawn, others powered by mana-leeching engines. "Let's go check on everyone at the hospital."

Annabelle hesitated, glancing back at the Stormfang. It was in pieces; half-flooded, half on fire. The poor girl would never float again, not in this state. Her voice was hollow when she finally spoke. "What about the Fang?"

Marcus followed her gaze, concern softening his features. "You two stay here. I'll speak to the pier manager," he said gently, handing the ledger book to Sparks. With a reassuring nod, he jogged over to the pier supervisor, who stood at a podium, scribbling in a large book.

The pier was almost empty now, save for workers securing ropes to the wrecked ship, their mecha-magic animating the cranes above. Marcus adjusted his clothes and approached the man.

"Excuse me, sir," Marcus began, clearing his throat to catch the supervisor's attention.

"Yes? How can I help you?" the man replied, his accent carrying a rising intonation at the end of his sentence. He barely glanced up from his work.

"I was wondering—what's the plan for repairing the ship?" Marcus asked.

The supervisor finally looked up, raising an eyebrow. "Repair?" he repeated, incredulous. He gestured toward the Stormfang, now little more than a shattered carcass. "Did you just see the ship explode? It might be in your best interest to scrap this poor thing for the wood." His tone left no doubt about his opinion of the Stormfang's future.

Marcus exhaled slowly, the exhaustion of the past few weeks weighing heavily on him. "And if we want to proceed with repairs?"

The supervisor's expression softened slightly. "My company was paid to lift the ship and provide an estimate for repairs," he explained, jotting another note in his book. "We'll send that estimate to your colleagues at the hospital. From there, the decision will be yours."

Marcus nodded, biting back his frustration. "Thank you, sir. I'll be in touch."

With that, he turned back toward Sparks and Annabelle, the enormity of their situation pressing down like a lead weight.

[-----✝-----]

Marcus, Annabelle, and Sparks arrived at the hospital's main entrance in a carriage. Annabelle stepped out first, clutching the ship's chest, while Sparks followed with the Stormfang's ledger. Marcus, ever the loyal servant, paid the ten-coin fee to the driver, who tipped his hat and drove off. The trio paused to take in the sight before them, a grand entrance made of brick and glass, flanked by two tall spires that framed the awning over the double doors.

"Well, shall we?" Marcus prompted, gesturing toward the entrance.

They stepped inside and found themselves in a large waiting area filled with rows of chairs arranged to maximize space. Although half the seats were occupied, many rows remained empty, creating an eerie quiet despite the occasional coughs and murmurs from patients and visitors.

At the far end of the room, a desk marked with a large metal sign reading *Reception* stood under the glow of lamps. Marcus headed for the desk while Annabelle and Sparks lingered near the seating area, quietly observing their surroundings.

"Excuse me, madam," Marcus said as he reached the desk, offering a polite nod. "My name is Brother Marcus Igbinedion. I was informed that members of the Order of Saint Lorraine are expecting me."

The receptionist, a woman with brown hair cut in neat bangs, flipped through the papers on her desk without looking up. "You're looking for the Order delegation, right?" she asked in a flat, businesslike tone.

"Yes, I believe so," Marcus confirmed.

After finding the document she sought, the woman finally looked at him through round glasses perched on her nose. She glanced back at the paper and said, "Okay, I'll let them know you're here. Please have a seat in the waiting area."

"Thank you," Marcus replied. He turned and scanned the room for Annabelle and Sparks, spotting them near the entrance doors; deep in conversation with Eclipse Lepele. Surprised, Marcus made his way over to the group.

"Well, hello, Eclipse Lepele," Marcus greeted as he joined them. "It's unexpected to find you here. I assumed you would be with the Aurorium by now."

"I'm waiting for them," Lepele explained simply.

Marcus nodded, then asked, "How is Miss Griffin faring? I noticed... tension earlier when you were both taken away."

Lepele crossed his arms and exhaled. "She's in custody, most likely in a holding cell," he said, his voice tinged with resignation.

Annabelle burst into sudden laughter. "What?!?" She turned to Marcus with a mischievous grin. "I've gotta see this." Her laughter slowed only when Sparks gave her foot a light tap with his boot.

Lepele shook his head. "From what I gathered, the clan has listed Sentinel Griffin as a deserter. For us, that's a serious matter," he explained gravely.

Marcus frowned, the weight of the revelation settling over him. "Oh, this is bad," he said thoughtfully. "I hope there's something I can do to help her situation."

Lepele gave a noncommittal shrug. "We'll see," he replied, his tone offering little hope.

The group fell into a contemplative silence, each of them pondering the challenges that lay ahead.

"Brother Marcus, I want to see the copper," Annabelle began, only to be interrupted by Lepele clearing his throat. She rolled her eyes and corrected herself. "Sorry, the purple copper in her jail cell," she lied with an exaggerated grin. "Ye know, I just want to lend her a bit a moral support."

Marcus raised an eyebrow but kept his response neutral. "That's very kind of you to think of Miss Sophie's wellbeing."

"So, as soon as ye can get me in to see her," Annabelle continued, giving him a playful smile. "Be a good servant about it."

Lepele chuckled dryly. "Can he check to make sure everyone's still alive first, pirate girl? Or do you not care about your Captain and First Mate anymore?"

Annabelle's smile vanished, and she crossed her arms. In her proper voice, she replied, "Eclipse Lepele raises an excellent point. Mister Brother Marcus, please check on my fellow avatars and crew. Then, as a secondary priority, arrange for me to visit... young *Miss purple copper*."

"Of course, Miss Salazar," Marcus answered with a polite nod.

"Hello, Brother Marcus," a familiar voice called from behind. He turned to see Sister Alameda approaching. She smiled warmly and added, "And Miss Salazar, how are you today?"

"Aye, Sister Al," Annabelle greeted her, a hint of surprise in her tone. "How have ye been?"

"Oh, I've been well," Alameda replied cheerfully. "I've missed spending time with you avatars, though."

"Yer such a good servant," Annabelle said with a grin, clearly enjoying herself.

"Sister, how are you here?" Marcus asked. "Sister Ingrid explained that only one of us could be away from Order Island at a time."

"Oi! You see us talking, *Brother Marcus*?" Annabelle cut in, waving a hand at him theatrically. "This is why yer a bad servant!"

Alameda chuckled softly. "I'll handle this, Miss Salazar. Please, allow me to take Brother Marcus away for a few words. I'll do my best to straighten him out."

"Aye see that ye do," Annabelle said, imitating a spoiled aristocrat, complete with a haughty tilt of her head.

Alameda gently tugged Marcus's arm, leading him toward the double swinging doors that separated the reception area from the hospital's main hall.

"She really likes you," Alameda teased once they were out of earshot.

417

"She has definitely warmed up to me," Marcus quipped with a grin. Then, his expression turned serious. "What can you tell me about the situation?"

They walked into a small room about the size of a broom closet, where a man in a gray vest, matching trousers, and a bow tie awaited them.

"Third floor, please," Alameda requested.

"Very good, ma'am," the man replied. He raised his hand, and a door slid shut. With a subtle motion of his hand toward the wall, the room began to rise.

Marcus blinked in surprise. "A lift? Disguised as a broom closet?"

"They call it a mecha-lift," Alameda explained.

"We could use a few of these on Order Island," Marcus observed.

"We could," she agreed, "but they require a mecha-mage to operate."

She turned the conversation back to their earlier topic. "Sister Ingrid and I are meeting with Apex Garde and a team from the Aurorium Clan to address the curse affecting the pirate captain and his first mate."

"Privateer," Marcus corrected gently. "They take offense to being called pirates. They call regular pirates *Skulls*."

"Thank you for the clarification, Brother," Alameda acknowledged. "Fortunately, Apex Garde is also here to handle the Griffin situation."

"Why is that fortunate?" Marcus asked, curiosity sharpening his tone.

"Apex Garde leads Aurorium Kutora Mora and is a tier-two shadow caster," Sister Alameda explained as they ascended. "His team is highly skilled in tier-three spells and curses. They started working as soon as Miss Annabelle's shipmates arrived."

"And the ladies, Nozaki and Fournier, how are they doing?" Marcus inquired.

"The doctors are examining them now. We'll be updated as soon as there's news," she replied.

The lift came to a stop with a loud, metallic click. The operator raised his hand, and the door slid open with a faint hum.

"Third floor," he announced.

Sister Alameda gave him a polite nod. "Thank you." She and Marcus exited the lift, heading down a long hallway. At the end of the corridor, she opened a large wooden door, leading them into a spacious conference room.

Inside, Sister Ingrid sat at a circular table across from a man with light-brown skin and long black hair streaked with grey. His hair was tied into a neat bun atop his head. He wore the Aurorium service "B" uniform, a black jacket with silver trim over a white shirt and black tie. His Apex badge gleamed on his chest, a white crystal like "A" against a dark background, speckled with metallic flecks resembling stars.

"Ah, speak of the guide," Sister Ingrid said, standing to greet them. "Apex Garde, may I introduce Brother Marcus Igbinedion, the guide to the avatars."

Apex Garde rose from his seat and extended his hand. "Apex Garde, Keeper of Aurorium Kutora Mora."

"It's a pleasure, Apex," Marcus replied, shaking his hand firmly.

Garde gestured to a seat beside Sister Ingrid, inviting Marcus to join them. Marcus sat down, taking out his journal as Sister Alameda quietly closed the door behind them.

"Welcome, Brother Marcus," Sister Ingrid said softly, her expression warm. "You've had quite the adventure."

"Thank you, Sister," Marcus responded with a faint smile.

Apex Garde leaned forward slightly, resting his hands on the table. "Brother Marcus, what can you tell me about Sentinel Griffin?" he asked.

"Miss Sophie embodies the esteem and values of the Aurorium Clan. I can confidently say we wouldn't have made it this far without her," Marcus answered, hoping to favorably sway the Apex. "Eclipse Lepele mentioned she's ready to take the Shadow exam this year."

Garde's eyebrows lifted with interest. "Who did you say?"

"Eclipse Antonio Lepele," Marcus clarified. "Miss Sophie rescued him from captivity a few weeks ago. I believe he's from your village."

Garde's eyes sharpened with recognition. "Where is this *Eclipse Lepele* now?"

"He's in the hospital's main waiting area on the ground floor. I was just speaking with him," Marcus explained.

Without a word, Garde glanced over his shoulder. A young woman dressed in a similar Aurorium uniform, her badge marking her rank as Shadow, stood silently. With a respectful bow, she excused herself and left the room to carry out the unspoken command.

"Did I do something wrong?" Marcus asked, concern creeping into his voice.

"We believed Eclipse Lepele to be deceased," Apex Garde explained. "He was presumed lost during a mission. Shadow Hayashi will confirm his identity downstairs. Now, back to Sentinel Griffin." He redirected the conversation smoothly.

Marcus straightened. "Of course. Miss Sophie's investigative skills were essential to uncovering the group we've identified as *The Order of the Black Sun*. I'm certain Miss Annabelle wouldn't be with us today without her. Miss Sophie balanced everything within our little group in ways I hadn't fully appreciated until now."

"How is it that the Order had possession of Sentinel Griffin and didn't return her until now?" Garde questioned his tone firm.

"I think it's best to start at the beginning," Marcus replied. He recounted the events that had led to this point, beginning with Brother Albert gathering the Avatars and Sophie's discovery of the massacre at Granmark, where she found her mother dead. He described the time spent on Order Island, the events at the Luminous, and the mission in Verdantia, incorporating the information he knew. Finally, he explained the harrowing voyage from Verdantia to Magitekopolis.

"I will not lie and say we did not know where to take Miss Sophie," Marcus admitted, meeting Garde's gaze. "But I do believe it was the goddess' will for her to remain with us."

Apex Garde leaned back, contemplating the account. "It seems our little torchbearer has had quite the adventure."

At that moment, Shadow Hayashi returned with Eclipse Lepele in tow. "Apex, I've confirmed it, this is indeed Eclipse Lepele."

"By the Ancestors..." Garde breathed in awe, rising from his chair. He barely noticed that Lepele was out of uniform and without a badge. Moving quickly, he shook Lepele's hand warmly. "Lightbringer, I thought we had lost you."

"To be honest, Apex, I thought you lost me too," Lepele said with a grin.

The two men shared a brief laugh before Garde composed himself. He turned to face the table where Marcus sat beside Sister Ingrid, with Sister Alameda observing quietly from a chair near the wall.

"I appreciate your honesty, Brother Marcus," Garde said. "You've given me a great deal to think about."

"I only want what's best for Miss Sophie, in her service to both the goddess and your clan," Marcus replied earnestly.

"You've got a good man there, Sister Ingrid," Garde remarked, nodding to her before addressing the room. "If you'll excuse me, I have matters to discuss with my Eclipse."

The Aurorium members departed, leaving Marcus alone with Sisters Ingrid and Alameda.

"It's always good to see you, Brother Marcus," Sister Ingrid said, her tone warm. "Have you had breakfast? We have much to discuss."

"I haven't," Marcus admitted, "but I'd like to make sure Miss Salazar and Mr. Sparks are taken care of first."

"Don't worry about that," Ingrid assured him with a smile. "Sister Alameda can handle it. Besides, Miss Annabelle likes her more than you anyway."

Marcus chuckled softly with a nod.

Autor Bio

Jackson Owens has been creating stories since childhood, driven by a love of imaginative worlds and compelling characters. His goal is simple: to craft tales worthy of sharing shelf space with the books that inspired him. When he isn't writing, Jackson works in information technology and enjoys playing guitar, experimenting with 3D printing, and dreaming up new adventures.

www.ingramcontent.com/pod-product-compliance
Lightning Source LLC
Chambersburg PA
CBHW011343010726
47493CB00011B/2934